O is for Outlaw

Sue Grafton has become one of the most popular female writers, both in the UK and in the US. Born in Kentucky in 1940, she began her career as a TV scriptwriter before Kinsey Millhone and the 'alphabet' series took off. She plans to take Kinsey all the way through the alphabet to Z. Sue lives and writes in Montecito, California and Louisville, Kentucky.

Also by Sue Grafton

Sue Grafton

O is for Outlaw

&

P is for Peril

PAN BOOKS

O is for Outlaw 1999 by Henry Holt, New York.
First published in Great Britain 1999 by Macmillan.
First published in paperback 2000 by Pan Books.
P is for Peril first published 2001 by G.P. Putnam's Sons, Inc., New York.
First published in Great Britain 2001 by Macmillan.
First published in paperback 2002 by Pan Books.

This omnibus first published 2008 by Pan Books
an imprint of Pan Macmillan Ltd
Pan Macmillan, 20 New Wharf Road, London N1 9RR
Basingstoke and Oxford
Associated companies throughout the world
www.panmacmillan.com

ISBN 978-0-330-45786-6

1 3 5 7 9 8 6 4 2

A CIP catalogue record for this book is available from
the British Library.

Printed and bound in Great Britain by
Mackays of Chatham plc, Chatham, Kent

O is for
Outlaw

FOR MY GRANDDAUGHTER, KINSEY,
with a heart full of love

The author wishes to acknowledge the invaluable assistance of the following people: Steven Humphrey; Detective Peggy Moseley, Los Angeles Police Department; Captain Ed Aasted and Sergeant Brian Abbott, Santa Barbara Police Department; Pat Zuberer, Library Clerk, Barbara Alexander and Betsey Daniels, Librarians, Ronetta Coates, student, Louisville Male High School; Beverly Herrlinger, Curriculum Coordinator, Jefferson County High School Admissions Office; Ray Connors; Kathy Humphrey, Communications Director, California State Senate; Marshall Morgan, M.D., Medical Director, Emergency Room, UCLA Medical Center; H. Ric Harnsberger, M.D., Professor of ENT/Neuroradiology and Director, Neuroradiology Section, University of Utah Medical Center; Barry and Bernice Ewing, Eagle Sportschairs; Lee Stone; Harriet Miller, Mayor, City of Santa Barbara; Danny Nash, Jefferson County Clerk's Office, Louisville, Kentucky; Erik Raney, Deputy, Santa Barbara County Sheriff's Department; Kevin Rudan, Resident Agent, Secret Service; Don and Marilyn Gevirtz; Julianna Flynn; Ralph Hickey; Lucy Thomas and Nadine Greenup, Librarians, Reeves Medical Center, Cottage Hospital;

Denise Huff, R.N., Cottage Hospital Emergency; Gail Abarbanel, Director, Rape Treatment Center, Santa Monica/UCLA Medical Center; Jay Schmidt; Jamie Clark; and Mary Lawrence Young.

To the reader,

Just a brief note to clarify the time frame for these "alphabet" novels. For those of you confused about what appear to be errors in my calculation of ages and dates, please be aware that "A" Is for Alibi takes place in May of 1982, "B" Is for Burglar in June of 1982, "C" Is for Corpse in August of 1982, and so forth. Since the books are sequential, Ms. Millhone is caught up in a time warp and is currently living and working in the year 1986, without access to cell phones, the Internet, or other high-tech equipment used by modern-day private investigators. She relies instead on persistence, imagination, and ingenuity: the stock-in-trade of the traditional gumshoe throughout hard-boiled history. As her biographer, I generally avoid mention of topical issues and date-related events. You'll find few, if any, references to current movies, fads, fashions, or politics. This book is an exception in that events connect back to the Vietnam War, which ended in 1971, fifteen years before the incidents described herein. Given narrative requirements, I populate historical actions with fictional characters and project wholly invented persons into academic institutions and political arenas, in which their "real-life" counterparts will doubtless dispute their presence. In my view, the delight of fiction is its enhancement of the facts and its embellishment of reality. Aside from that—as my father used to say—"I know it's true because I made it up myself."

Respectfully submitted,
Sue Grafton

ONE

The Latin term *pro bono*, as most attorneys will attest, roughly translated means *for boneheads* and applies to work done without charge. Not that I practice law, but I am usually smart enough to avoid having to donate my services. In this case, my client was in a coma, which made billing a trick. Of course, you might look at the situation from another point of view. Once in a while a piece of old business surfaces, some item on life's agenda you thought you'd dealt with years ago. Suddenly, it's there again at the top of the page, competing for your attention despite the fact that you're completely unprepared for it.

First there was a phone call from a stranger; then a letter showed up fourteen years after it was sent. That's how I learned I'd made a serious error in judgment and ended up risking my life in my attempt to correct for it.

I'd just finished a big job, and I was not only exhausted but my bank account was fat and I wasn't in the mood to take on additional work. I'd pictured a bit of time off, maybe a trip someplace cheap, where I could lounge in the sun and read the latest Elmore

1

Leonard novel while sipping on a rum drink with a paper umbrella stuck in a piece of fruit. This is about the range and complexity of my fantasies these days.

The call came at 8 A.M. Monday, May 19, while I was off at the gym. I'd started lifting weights again: Monday, Wednesday, and Friday mornings after my 6 A.M. run. I'm not sure where the motivation came from after a two-year layoff, but it was probably related to thoughts of mortality, primarily my own. In the spring, I'd sustained damage to my right hand when a fellow dislocated two fingers trying to persuade me to his point of view. I'd been hurt once before when a bullet nicked my right arm, and my impulse in both instances had been to hit the weight machines. Lest you imagine I'm a masochist or accident-prone, I should state that I make a living as a private investigator. Truth be told, the average P.I. seldom carries a gun, isn't often pursued, and rarely sustains an injury more substantial than a paper cut. My own professional life tends to be as dull as anyone else's. I simply report the exceptions in the interest of spiritual enlightenment. Processing events helps me keep my head on straight.

Those of you acquainted with my personal data can skip this paragraph. For the uninitiated, I'm female, thirty-six years old, twice divorced, and living in Santa Teresa, California, which is ninety-five miles north of Los Angeles. Currently, I occupy one small office in the larger suite of offices of Kingman and Ives, attorneys at law. Lonnie Kingman is my attorney when the occasion arises, so my association with his firm seemed to make sense when I was looking for space. I'd been rendered a migrant after I was unceremoniously shit-canned from the last job I had: investigating arson and wrongful death claims for California Fidelity Insurance. I've been with Lonnie now for over two years, but I'm not above harboring a petty desire for revenge on CFI.

During the months I'd been lifting weights, my muscle tone had improved and my strength had increased. That particular morning, I'd worked my way through the customary body parts: two sets, fifteen reps each, of leg extensions, leg curls, ab crunches, lower back, lat rows, the chest press and pec deck, along with the shoulder press, and various exercises for the biceps and triceps. Thus pumped up and euphoric, I let myself into my apartment with the usual glance at my answering machine. The message light was blinking. I dropped my gym bag on the floor, tossed my keys on the desk, and pressed the PLAY button, reaching for a pen and a pad of paper in case I needed to take notes. Before I leave the office each day, I have Lonnie's service shunt calls over to my apartment. That way, in a pinch, I can lie abed all day, dealing with the public without putting on my clothes.

The voice was male, somewhat gravelly, and the message sounded like this: "Miss Millhone, this is Teddy Rich. I'm calling from Olvidado about something might innerest you. This is eight A.M. Monday. Hope it's not too early. Gimme a call when you can. Thanks." He recited a telephone number in the 805 area code, and I dutifully jotted it down. It was only 8:23 so I hadn't missed him by much. Olvidado is a town of 157,000, thirty miles south of Santa Teresa on Highway 101. Always one to be interested in

3

something that might "innerest" me, I dialed the number he'd left. The ringing went on so long I thought his machine would kick in, but the line was finally picked up by Mr. Rich, whose distinctive voice I recognized.

"Hi, Mr. Rich. This is Kinsey Millhone up in Santa Teresa. I'm returning your call."

"Hey, Miss Millhone. Nice to hear from you. How are you today?"

"Fine. How are you?"

"I'm fine. Thanks for asking, and thanks for being so prompt. I appreciate that."

"Sure, no problem. What can I do for you?"

"Well, I'm hoping this is something I can do for you," he said. "I'm a storage space scavenger. Are you familiar with the term?"

"I'm afraid not." I pulled the chair out and sat down, realizing Ted Rich was going to take his sweet time about this. I'd already pegged him as a salesman or a huckster, someone thoroughly enamored of whatever minor charms he possessed. I didn't want what he was selling, but I decided I might as well hear him out. This business of storage space scavenging was a new one on me, and I gave him points for novelty.

He said, "I won't bore you with details. Basically, I bid on the contents of self-storage lockers when the monthly payment's in arrears."

"I didn't know they did that on delinquent accounts. Sounds reasonable, I suppose." I took the towel from my gym bag and ruffed it across my head. My hair was still damp from the workout and I was getting chillier by the minute, longing to hit the shower before my muscles stiffened up.

"Oh, sure. Storage unit's been abandoned by its owner for more'n sixty days, the contents go up for auction. How else can the company recoup its losses? Guys like me show up and blind-bid on the contents, paying anywheres from two hundred to fifteen hundred bucks, hoping for a hit."

"As in what?" I reached down, untied my Sauconys, and slipped them off my feet. My gym socks smelled atrocious, and I'd only worn them a week.

"Well, most times you get junk, but once in a while you get lucky and come across something good. Tools, furniture—stuff you can convert to hard cash. I'm sure you're pro'bly curious what this has to do with you."

"It crossed my mind," I said mildly, anticipating his pitch. For mere pennies a day, you too can acquire abandoned bric-a-brac with which to clutter up your premises.

"Yeah, right. Anyways, this past Saturday, I bid on a couple storage bins. Neither of 'em netted much, but in the process I picked up a bunch of cardboard boxes. I was sorting through the contents and came across your name on some personal documents. I'm wondering what it's worth to you to get 'em back."

"What kind of documents?"

"Lemme see here. Hold on. Frankly, I didn't expect to hear so soon or I'd have had 'em on the desk in front of me." I could hear him rattling papers in the background. "Okay now. We got a pink-bead baby bracelet and there's quite a collection of school-type memorabilia: drawings, class pictures, report cards from Woodrow Wilson Elementary. This ringin' any bells with you?"

"*My* name's on these papers?"

"Kinsey Millhone, right? Millhone with two *l*'s. Here's a history report entitled 'San Juan Capistrano Mission,' with a model of the mission made of egg cartons. Mrs. Rosen's class, fourth grade. She gave you a D plus. 'Report is not bad, but project is poorly presented,' she says. I had a teacher like her once. What a bitch," he said idly. "Oh, and here's something else. Diploma says you graduated Santa Teresa High School on June tenth, 1967? How'm I doin' so far?"

"Not bad."

"Well, there you go," he said.

"Not that it matters, but how'd you track me down?"

"Piece of cake. All I did was call Directory Assistance. The name Millhone's unusual, so I figure it's like the old saying goes: Apples don't fall far from the tree and so forth. I proceeded on the assumption you were somewheres close. You could've got married and changed your name, of course. I took a flier on that score. Anyways, the point is, how d'you feel about gettin' these things back?"

"I don't understand how the stuff ended up in Olvidado. I've never rented storage space down there."

I could hear him begin to hedge. "I never said Olvidado. Did I say that? I go to these auctions all over the state. Lookit, I don't mean to sound crass, but if you're willing to pony up a few bucks, we can maybe make arrangements for you to get this box back."

I hesitated, annoyed by the clumsiness of his maneuvering. I remembered my struggle in Mrs. Rosen's class, how crushed I'd been with the grade after I'd worked so hard. The fact was, I had so little in the way of personal keepsakes that any addition would be treasured. I didn't want to pay much, but neither was I willing to relinquish the items sight unseen.

I said, "The papers can't be worth much since I wasn't aware they were missing." Already, I didn't like him and I hadn't even met him yet.

"Hey, I'm not here to argue. I don't intend to hose you or nothin' like that. You want to talk value, we talk value. Up to you," he said.

"Why don't I think about it and call you back?"

"Well, that's just it. If we could find time to get together, you could take a look at these items and then come to a decision. How else you going to know if it's worth anything to you? It'd mean a drive down here, but I'm assuming you got wheels."

"I could do that, I suppose."

"Excellent," he said. "So what's your schedule like today?"

"Today?"

"No time like the present is my attitude."

"What's the big hurry?"

"No hurry in particular except I got appointments set up for the rest of the week. I make money turnin' stuff over, and my garage is already packed. You have time today or not?"

"I could probably manage it."

"Good, then let's meet as soon as possible and see if we can work somethin' out. There's a coffee shop down the street from me. I'm on my way over now

7

and I'll be there for about an hour. Let's say nine-thirty. You don't show? I gotta make a run to the dump anyways so it's no skin off my nose."

"What'd you have in mind?"

"Moneywise? Let's say thirty bucks. How's that sound?"

"Exorbitant," I said. I asked him for directions. What a hairball.

I showered and flung on the usual blue jeans and T-shirt, then gassed up my VW and headed south on 101. The drive to Olvidado took twenty-five minutes. Following Ted Rich's instructions, I took the Olvidado Avenue exit and turned right at the bottom of the off-ramp. Half a block from the freeway, there was a large shopping mall. The surrounding land, originally given over to agricultural use, was gradually being converted to a crop of new and used cars. Lines of snapping plastic flags defined tent shapes above the asphalt lot where rows of vehicles glinted in the mild May sun. I could see a shark-shaped mini-blimp tethered and hovering thirty feet in the air. The significance escaped me, but what do I know about these things?

Across from the mall, the business establishments seemed to be equally divided among fast-food joints, liquor stores, and instant-copy shops that offered passport photos. There was even a facility devoted to walk-in legal services; litigate while you wait. BANKRUPTCY $99. DIVORCE $99. DIVORCE W/KIDS $99 + FILING FEE. *Se habla español.* The coffee shop he'd specified appeared to be the only mom-and-pop operation in the area.

I parked my car in the lot and pushed into the place, scanning the few patrons for someone who fit his description. He'd indicated he was six foot two and movie-star handsome, but then he'd snorted with laughter, which led me to believe otherwise. He'd said he'd watch the door for my arrival. I spotted a guy, who raised a hand in greeting and beckoned me to his booth. His face was a big ruddy square, his sunburn extending into the V of his open-collared denim work shirt. He wore his dark hair combed straight back, and I could see the indentation at his temples where he'd removed the baseball cap now sitting on the table next to him. He had a wide nose, drooping upper lids, and bags under his eyes. I could see the scattering of whiskers he'd missed during his morning shave. His shoulders were beefy and his forearms looked thick where he had his sleeves rolled up. He'd removed a dark brown windbreaker, which now lay neatly folded over the back of the booth.

"Mr. Rich? Kinsey Millhone. How are you?" We shook hands across the table, and I could tell he was sizing me up with the same attention to detail I'd just lavished on him.

"Make it Teddy. Not bad. I appreciate your coming." He glanced at his watch as I slid in across from him. "Unfortunately I only got maybe fifteen, twenty minutes before I have to take off. I apologize for the squeeze, but right after we spoke, I hadda call from some guy down in Thousand Oaks needs an estimate on his roof."

9

"You're a roofer?"

"By trade." He reached in his pants pocket. "Lemme pass you my card in case you need somethin' done." He took out a slim Naugahyde case and removed a stack of business cards. "My speciality is new roofs and repairs."

"What else is there?"

"Hey, I can do anything you need. Hot mops, tear-offs, torch-downs, all types of shake, composition, slate, clay tile, you name it. Corrective and preventative is my area of expertise. I could give you a deal . . . let's say ten percent off if you call this month. What kind of house you in?"

"Rented."

"So maybe you got a landlord needs some roof work done. Go ahead and keep that. Take as many as you want." He offered me a handful of cards, fanned out face down like he was about to do a magic trick.

I took one and examined it. The card bore his name, telephone number, and a post office box. His company was called OVERHEAD ROOFING, the letters forming a wide inverted V like the ridgeline of a roof. His company motto was *We do all types of roofing*.

"Catchy," I remarked.

He'd been watching for my reaction, his expression serious. "I just had those made. Came up with the name myself. Used to be TED'S ROOFS. You know, simple, basic, something of a personal touch. I could have said 'Rich Roofs,' but that might have gave the wrong impression. I was in business ten years, but then the drought came along and the market dried up—"

"So to speak," I put in.

He smiled, showing a small gap between his two front lower teeth. "Hey, that's good. I like your sense of humor. You'll appreciate this one. Couple years without rain and people start to take a roof for granite. Get it? Granite . . . like the rock?"

I said, "That's funny."

"Anyways, I've had a hell of a time. I hadda shut down altogether and file bankruptcy. My wife up and left me, the dog died, and then my truck got side-swiped. I was screwed big time. Now we got some bad weather coming in, I figured I'd start fresh. Overhead Roofing is a kind of play on words."

"Really," I said. "What about the storage-space business? Where did that come from?"

"I figured I hadda do something when the roofing trade fell in. 'As it were,'" he added, with a wink at me. "I decided to try salvage. I had some cash tucked away the wife and the creditors didn't know about, so I used that to get started. Takes five or six thousand if you want to do it right. I got hosed once or twice, but otherwise I been doing pretty good, even if I do say so myself." He caught the waitress's attention and held his coffee cup in the air with a glance back at me. "Can I buy you a cup of coffee?"

"That sounds good. How long have you been at it?"

"About a year," he said. "We're called 'pickers' or storage-room gamblers, sometimes resellers, treasure hunters. How it works is I check the papers for auction listings. I also subscribe to a couple newsletters. You never know what you'll find. Couple of weeks ago, I paid two-fifty and found a painting worth more than fifteen hundred bucks. I was jazzed."

"I can imagine."

"Of course, there's rules to the practice, like anything else in life. You can't touch the rooms' contents, can't go inside before the bidding starts, and there's no refunds. You pay six hundred dollars and all you come up with is a stack of old magazines, then it's too bad for you. Such is life and all that."

"Can you make a living at it?"

He shifted in his seat. "Not so's you'd notice. This is strictly a hobby in between roofing engagements. Nice thing about it is it doesn't look good on paper so the wife can't hit me up for alimony. She was the one who walked out, so up hers is what I say."

The waitress appeared at the table with a coffee pot in hand, refilling his cup and pouring one for me. Teddy and the waitress exchanged pleasantries. I took the moment to add milk to my coffee and then tore the corner off a pack of sugar, which I don't ordinarily take. Anything to fill time till they finished their conversation. Frankly, I thought he had the hots for her.

Once she departed, Teddy turned his attention to me. I could see the box on the seat beside him. He noticed my glance. "I can see you're curious. Wanna peek?"

I said, "Sure."

I made a move toward the box and Teddy put a hand out, saying, "Gimme five bucks first." Then he laughed. "You shoulda seen the look on your face. Come on. I'm teasing. Help yourself." He hefted the box and passed it across the table. It was maybe three feet square, awkward but not heavy, the cardboard powdery with dust. The top had been sealed, but I could see where the packing tape had been cut and the flaps folded back together. I set the box on the seat beside me and pulled the flaps apart. The contents seemed hastily thrown together with no particular thought paid to the organization. It was rather like the last of the cartons packed in the moving process: stuff you don't dare throw out but don't really know what else to do with. A box like this could probably sit un-opened in your basement for the next ten years, and nothing would ever stimulate a search for even one of the items. On the other hand, if you felt the need to inventory the contents, you'd still feel too attached to the items to toss the assortment in the trash. The next time you moved, you'd end up adding the box to the other boxes on the van, gradually accumulating suf-ficient junk to fill a . . . well, a storage bin.

I could tell at a glance these were articles I wanted. In addition to the grade school souvenirs, I spotted a high school diploma, my yearbook, some textbooks, and, more important, file after file of mimeographed pages from my classes at the police academy. Thirty bucks was nothing for this treasury of remembrances.

Teddy was watching my face, trying to gauge the dollar signs in my reaction. I found myself avoiding eye contact lest he sense the extent of my interest. Stalling, I said, "Whose storage space was it? I don't believe you mentioned that."

"Guy named John Russell. He a friend of yours?"

"I wouldn't call him a friend, but I know him," I said. "Actually, that's an in-joke, like an alias. 'John Russell' is a character in an Elmore Leonard novel called *Hombre*."

"Well, I tried to get ahold of him, but I didn't have much luck. Way too many Russells in this part of the state. Couple of dozen Jonathans, fifteen or twenty Johns, but none were him because I checked it out."

"You put some time in."

"You bet. Took me couple hours before I gave it up and said nuts. I tried this whole area: Perdido, LA County, Orange, San Bernardino, Santa Teresa County, as far up as San Luis. There's no sign of the guy, so I figure he's dead or moved out of state."

I took a sip of my coffee, avoiding comment. The addition of milk and sugar made the coffee taste like a piece of hard candy.

Teddy tilted his head at me with an air of bemusement. "So you're a private detective? I notice you're listed as Millhone Investigations."

"That's right. I was a cop for two years, which is how I knew John."

"The guy's a cop?"

"Not now, but he was in those days."

"I wouldn't have guessed that . . . I mean, judging from the crap he had jammed in that space. I'da said some kind of bum. That's the impression I got."

"Some people would agree."

"But you're not one of 'em, I take it."

I shrugged, saying nothing.

Teddy studied me shrewdly. "Who's this guy to you?"

"What makes you ask?"

"Come on. What's his real name? Maybe I can track him down for you, like a missing persons case."

"Why bother? We haven't spoken in years, so he's nothing to me."

"But now you got me curious. Why the alias?"

"He was a vice cop in the late sixties and early seventies. Big dope busts back then. John worked undercover, so he was always paranoid about his real name."

"Sounds like a nut."

"Maybe so," I said. "What else was in the bin?"

He waved a hand dismissively. "Most of it was useless. Lawnmower, broken-down vacuum cleaner. There was a big box of kitchen stuff: wooden rolling pin, big wooden salad bowl, must have been three feet across the top, set of crockery bowls—what do you call it? That Fiesta Ware shit. I picked up a fair chunk of change for that. Ski equipment, tennis racquets, none of it in prime condition. There was an old bicycle, motorcycle engine, wheel cover, and some car parts. I figure Russell was a pack rat, couldn't let go of stuff. I sold most of it at the local swap meet; this was yesterday."

I felt my heart sink. The big wooden bowl had belonged to my Aunt Gin. I didn't care about the Fiesta Ware, though that was hers as well. I was wishing I'd had the option to buy the wooden rolling pin. Aunt Gin had used it to make sticky buns—one of her few domestic skills—rolling out the dough before she sprinkled on the cinnamon and sugar. I had to let that one go; no point in longing for what had already been disposed of. Odd to think an item would suddenly have such appeal when I hadn't thought of it in years.

15

He nodded at the box. "Thirty bucks and it's yours."

"Twenty bucks. It's barely worth that. It's all junk."

"Twenty-five. Come on. For the trip down memory lane. Things like that you're never going to see again. Sentimental journey and so forth. Might as well snap it up while you have the chance."

I removed a twenty from my handbag and laid it on the table. "Nobody else is going to pay you a dime."

Teddy shrugged. "So I toss it. Who cares? Twenty-five and that's firm."

"Teddy, a dump run would cost you fifteen, so this puts you five bucks ahead."

He stared at the money, flicked a look to my face, and then took the bill with an exaggerated sigh of disgust with himself. "Lucky I like you or I'd be pissed as hell." He folded the twenty lengthwise and tucked it in his pocket. "You never answered my question."

"Which one?"

"Who's this guy to you?"

"No one in particular. A friend once upon a time . . . not that it's any of your business."

"Oh, I see. I get it. Now, he's 'a friend.' Inneresting development. You musta been close to the guy if he ended up with your things."

"What makes you say that?"

He tapped his temple. "I got a logical mind. Analytical, right? I bet I could be a peeper just like you."

"Gee, Teddy, sure. I don't see why not. The truth is I stored some boxes at John's while I was in the middle of a move. My stuff must have gotten mixed up with his when he left Santa Teresa. By the way, which storage company?"

His expression turned crafty. "What makes you ask?" he said, in a slightly mocking tone.

"Because I'm wondering if he's still in the area somewhere."

Teddy shook his head, way ahead of me. "No go. Forget it. You'd be wasting your time. I mean, look at it this way. If the guy used a phony name, he prob'ly also faked his phone number and his home address. Why contact the company? They won't tell you nothin'."

"I'll bet I could get the information. That's what I do for a living these days."

"You and Dick Tracy."

"All I'm asking is the name."

Teddy smiled. "How much's it worth?"

"How much is it *worth*?"

"Yeah, let's do a little business. Twenty bucks."

"Don't be silly. I'm not going to *pay* you. That's ridiculous."

"So make me an offer. I'm a reasonable guy."

"Bullshit."

"All I'm saying is you scratch my back and I'll scratch yours."

"There can't be that many storage companies in the area."

"Fifteen hundred and eleven, if you take in the neighboring counties. For ten bucks, I'll tell you which little town it's in."

"No way."

17

"Come on. How else you going to find out?"

"I'm sure I can think of something."

"Wanna bet? Five says you can't."

I glanced at my watch and slid out of the seat. "I wish I could chat, Teddy, but you have that appointment and I have to get to work."

"Whyn't you call me if you change your mind? We could find him together. We could form us a partnership. I bet you could use a guy with my connections."

"No doubt."

I picked up the cardboard box, made a few more polite mouth noises, and returned to my car. I placed the box in the passenger seat and then slid in on the driver's side. I locked both doors instinctively and blew out a big breath. My heart was thumping, and I could feel the damp of perspiration in the small of my back. "John Russell" was the alias for a former Santa Teresa vice detective named Mickey Magruder, my first ex-husband. What the hell was going on?

TWO

I slouched down in my car, scanning the parking lot from my position at half mast. I could see a white pickup parked at the rear of the lot, the truck bed filled with the sort of buckets and tarps I pictured essential to a roofing magnate. An oversized toolbox rested near the back of the cab, and an aluminum extension ladder seemed to be mounted on the far side with its two metal antislip shoes protruding about a foot. I adjusted the rearview mirror, watching until Ted Rich came out of the coffee shop wearing his baseball cap and brown windbreaker. He had his hands in his pants pockets and he whistled to himself as he walked to the pickup and fished out his keys. When I heard the truck rumble to life, I took a moment to lean sideways out of his line of sight. As soon as he passed, I sat up again, watching as he turned left and entered the line of traffic heading toward the southbound freeway on-ramp.

I waited till he was gone, then got out of the VW and trotted to the public phone booth near the entrance to the parking lot. I placed his business card on the narrow metal shelf provided, hauled up the phone book, and checked under the listings for United States

Government. I found the number I was looking for and dug some loose change from the bottom of my shoulder bag. I inserted coins in the slot and dialed the number for the local post office branch printed on Rich's business card. The phone rang twice and a recorded message was activated, subjecting me to the usual reassurances. All the lines were busy at the moment, but my call would be answered in the order it was received. According to the recording, the post office really appreciated my patience, which shows you just how little they know about yours truly.

When a live female clerk finally came on the line, I gave her the box number for Overhead Roofing, possibly known as Ted's Roofs. Within minutes, she'd checked the rental agreement for his post office box and had given me the corresponding street address. I said thanks and depressed the plunger. I put another coin in the slot and punched in the phone number listed on the business card. As I suspected, no one answered, though Rich's machine did pick up promptly. I was happy to hear that Ted Rich was Olvidado's Number 1 certified master installer of fire-free roofing materials. The message also indicated that May was weather-proofing month, which I hadn't realized. More important, Teddy wasn't home and neither, apparently, was anyone else.

I returned to the car, fished an Olvidado city map from the glove compartment, and found the street listed on the ledger. By tracing the number and the letter coordinates, I pinpointed the location, not far from where I sat. Oh, happiness. I turned the key in the ignition, put the car in reverse, and in less than five minutes I was idling in front of Teddy's house, whence he operated his roofing business.

I found a parking spot six doors down and then sat in the car while my good angel and my bad angel jousted for possession of my soul. My good angel reminded me I'd vowed to reform. She recited the occasions when my usual vile behavior had brought me *naught but grief and pain*, as she put it. Which was all well and good, but as my bad angel asserted, this was really the only chance I was going to have to get the information I wanted. If Rich had "shared" the name of the storage company, I wouldn't have to do this, so it was really all his fault. He was currently on his way to Thousand Oaks to give an estimate on some guy's roof. The round-trip drive would take approximately thirty minutes, with another thirty minutes thrown in for schmoozing, which is how men do business. The two of us had parted company at ten. It was now ten-fifteen, so (with luck) he wouldn't be back for another forty-five minutes.

I removed my key picks from my shoulder bag, which I'd left on the backseat under the pile of assorted clothes I keep there. Often in the course of surveillance work, I use camouflage garments, like a quick-change artist, to vary my appearance. Now I pulled out a pair of navy coveralls that looked suitably professional. The patch on the sleeve, which I'd had stitched to my specifications, read SANTA TERESA CITY SERVICES and suggested I was employed by the public works department. I figured from a distance the Olvidado citizens would never know the difference. Wriggling around in the driver's seat, I pulled the coveralls over my usual

21

jeans and T-shirt. I tugged up the front zipper and tucked my key picks in one pocket. I reached for the matching clipboard with its stack of generic paperwork, then locked the car behind me and walked as far as Ted Rich's gravel drive. There were no vehicles parked anywhere near the house.

I climbed the front steps and rang the doorbell. I waited, leafing through the papers on the clipboard, making an official-looking note with the pen attached by a chain. I rang again, but there was no reply. *Quelle surprise*. I moved to the front window, shading my eyes as I peered through the glass. Aside from the fact that there was no sign of the occupant, the place had the look of a man accustomed to living by himself, an aura epitomized by the presence of a Harley-Davidson motorcycle in the middle of the dining room.

Casually, I glanced around. There was no one on the sidewalk and no hint of neighbors watching from across the way. Nonetheless, I frowned, making a big display of my puzzlement. I checked my watch to show that I, at least, was on time for our imaginary appointment. I trotted down the front steps and headed back along the driveway to the rear of the house. The backyard was fenced, and the shrubbery had grown up tall enough to touch the utility wires strung along the property line. The yard was deserted. Both sectional doors of the two-car garage were closed and showed hefty padlocks.

I climbed the back porch steps and then checked to see if any neighbors were busy dialing 9-1-1. Once assured of my privacy, I peeped in the kitchen window. The lights were off in the rooms within view. I tried the door handle. Locked. I stared at the Schlage, wondering how long it would take before it yielded to my key picks. Glancing down at knee height, I noticed that the bottom half of the door panel boasted a sizable homemade pet entrance. Well, what have we here? I reached down, gave the flap a push, and found myself staring at a section of kitchen linoleum. I thought back to Ted Rich's reference to his divorce and the death of his beloved pooch. The opening to the doggie door appeared to be large enough to accommodate me.

I set the clipboard on the porch rail and got down on my hands and knees. At 5 feet 6 inches and 118 pounds, I had only minor difficulties in my quest for admittance. Arms above my head, my body tilted to the diagonal, I began to ease myself through the opening. Once I'd succeeded in squeezing my head and shoulders through the door, I paused for a quick appraisal to assure myself there was no one else in residence. My one-sided view was restricted to the chrome-and-Formica dinette set, littered with dirty dishes, and the big plastic clock on the wall above. I inched forward, rotating my body so I could see the rest of the room. Now that I was halfway through the doggie door, it dawned on me that maybe I should have asked Rich if he'd acquired a new mutt. To my left, at eye level, I could see a two-quart water bowl and a large plastic dish filled with dry dog food. Nearby, a rawhide bone sported teeth marks that appeared to have been inflicted by a creature with a surly disposition.

Half a second later, the object of my speculation appeared on the scene. He'd probably been alerted by the noise and came skidding around the corner to see what was up. I'm not dog oriented by nature and I hardly know one breed from the next, with the exception of Chihuahuas, cocker spaniels, and other obvious types. This dog was big, maybe eighty pounds of lean weight on a heavily boned frame. What the hell was he doing while I was ringing the bell? The least he could have done was barked properly to warn me off. The dog was a medium brown with a big face, thick head, and a short, sleek coat. He was heavy through the chest and he had a dick the size of a hairy six-inch Gloria Cubana. A ruff of coarse hair was standing up along his spine, as though from permanent outrage. He stopped in his tracks and stood there, his expression a perfect blend of confusion and incredulity. I could almost see the question mark forming above his head. Apparently, in his experience, few human beings had tried to slither through his private entrance. I ceased struggling, to allow him time to assess the situation. I must not have represented any immediate threat because he neither lunged nor barked nor bit me cruelly about the head and shoulders. On the contrary, he seemed to feel that something was required of him in the way of polite behavior, though I could tell he was having trouble deciding what would be appropriate. He made a whining sound, dropped to his belly, and crept across the floor to me. I stayed where I was. For a while, we lay face-to-face while I suffered his meaty breath and he thought about life. Me and dogs always seem to end up in relationships like this.

"Hi, how're you," I said finally, in what I hoped was a pleasant tone (from the dog's perspective).

He put his head down on his paws and shot me a worried look.

I said, "Listen, I hope you don't mind if I slide on in, because any minute your neighbor's going to look out the window and catch sight of my hineybumper hanging out the doggie door. If you have any objections, speak now or forever hold your peace."

I waited, but the dog never even bared his gums. Using my elbows for leverage, I completed ingress, saying, "Nice dog," "What a good pooch," and similar kiss-ass phrases. His tail began to thump with hope. Maybe I was the little friend his dad had promised would come and play with him.

Once inside the kitchen, I began to rise to my feet. This, in the dog's mind, converted me into a beast that might require savaging. He leapt up, head down, ears back, beginning an experimental growl, his entire chest wall vibrating like a swarm of bees on the move. I sank down to my original submissive position. "Good boy," I murmured, humbly lowering my gaze.

I waited while the dog tested the parameters of his responsibility. The growling faded in due course. I tried again. Lifting on to my hands and knees seemed acceptable, but the minute I attempted to stand, the growling started up again. Make no mistake about it, this dog meant business.

"You're very strict," I said.

I waited a few moments and tried yet again. This time the effort netted me a furious bark. "Okay, okay." The big guy was beginning to get on my nerves. In theory, I was close enough to the doggie door to effect an escape, but I was fearful of going head first, thus exposing my rear end. I was also worried about going out feet first lest the dog attack my upper body while I was wedged in the opening. Meanwhile, the kitchen clock was ticking like a time bomb, forcing a decision. The curtain or the box? I could visualize Ted Rich barreling down the highway in my direction. I had to do *something*. Still on my hands and knees, I crawled forward a step. The dog watched with vigilance but made no menacing gesture. Slowly, I headed across the kitchen floor toward the front of the house. The dog tagged along beside me, his toenails clicking on the grimy linoleum, his full attention focused on my plodding journey. Already, I realized I hadn't really thought this thing through, but I'd been so intent on my ends, I hadn't fully formulated the means.

Babylike, in my romper, I traversed the dining room, bypassed the motorcycle, and entered the living room. This room was carpeted but otherwise contained little in the way of interest. I crawled down the hallway with the dog keeping pace, his head hanging down till his gaze was level with mine. I suppose I should state right here that what I was doing isn't routine behavior for a private eye. My conduct was more typical of someone intent on petty theft, too mulish and impetuous to use legitimate means (provided she could think of any). In the law enforcement sector, my actions would be classified as trespass, burglary, and (given the key picks in my pocket) possession of burglary tools—California Penal Code sections 602, 459, and 466 respectively. I hadn't stolen anything (yet) and the item I was after was purely intellectual, but it was nonetheless illegal to squirm through a doggie door and start crawling down a hall. Caught in the act, I'd be subject to arrest and conviction, perhaps forfeiting my license and my livelihood. Well, dang. All this for a man I'd left after less than nine months of marriage.

The house wasn't large: a bath and two bedrooms, plus the living room, dining room, kitchen, and laundry room. I must say the world is very boring at an altitude of eighteen inches. All I could see were chair legs, carpet snags, and endless stretches of dusty baseboard. No wonder house pets, when left alone, take to peeing on the rugs and gnawing on the furniture. I passed a door on the left that led back into the kitchen, with the laundry room to one side. When I reached the next door on the left, I crawled in and surveyed the premises, mentally wagging my tail. Unmade double bed, night table, chest of drawers, doggie bed, and dirty clothes on the floor. I did a U-turn and crawled into the room across the hall. Rich was using this one as a combination den and home office. Along the wall to my right, he had a row of banged-up file cabinets and a scarred oak desk. He also had a Barcalounger and a television set. The dog climbed on the recliner with a guilty look, watching to see if I was going to swat his hairy butt. I smiled my encouragement. As far as I was concerned, the dog could do anything he wanted.

I made my way over to the desk. "I'm getting up to take a peek, so don't get your knickers in a twist, okay?" By now, the dog was bored, and he yawned so hard I heard a little squeak at the back of his throat. Carefully, I eased into a kneeling position and searched the surface of the desk. There on a stack of papers lay the answer to my prayers: a sheaf of documents, among

27

them the receipt for Rich's payment to the San Felipe Self-Storage Company, dated Saturday, May 17. I tucked the paper in my mouth, sank down on all fours, and crawled to the door. Since the dog had lost interest, I was able to make quick work of the corridor in front of me. Crawling rapidly, I rounded the corner and thumped across the kitchen floor. When I reached the back door, I grabbed the knob and pulled myself to my feet. Exploits like this aren't as easy as they used to be. The knees of my coveralls were covered with dust, and I brushed off some woofies with a frown of disgust. I took the receipt out of my mouth, folded it, and stuck it in the pocket of my coveralls.

When I glanced through the back door to make sure the coast was clear, I spotted my clipboard still sitting on the porch rail where I'd left it. I was just chiding myself for not tucking it someplace less conspicuous when I heard the sound of gravel popping and the front of Rich's pickup appeared in my field of vision. He pulled to a stop, cranked on the handbrake, and opened the truck door. By the time he got out, I'd taken six giant steps backward, practically levitating as I fled through the kitchen to the laundry room, where I slid behind the open door. Rich had slammed his door and was apparently now making his way to the back porch. I heard him clump up the back steps. There was a pause wherein he seemed to make some remark to himself. He'd probably found my clipboard and was puzzling at its import.

The dog had heard him, of course, and was up like a shot, hurtling for the back door as fast as he could. My heart was thumping so loud it sounded like a

28

clothes dryer spinning a pair of wet tennis shoes. I could see my left breast vibrating against the front of my coveralls. I couldn't swear to this, but I think I may have wee-weed ever so slightly in my underpants. Also, I noticed the cuff of my pant leg was now protruding through the crack in the door. I'd barely managed to conceal myself when Rich clattered in the back door and tossed the clipboard on the counter. He and the dog exchanged a ritual greeting. On the part of the dog, much joyous barking and leaps; on Rich's part, a series of exhortations and commands, none of which seemed to have any particular effect. The dog had forgotten my intrusion, sidetracked by the merriment of having his master home.

I heard Rich move through the living room and proceed down the hall, where he entered his office and flipped on the television set. Meanwhile, the dog must have been tickled by a tiny whisper of recollection because he set off in search of me, his nose close to the floor. Hide and seek—what fun—and guess who was It? He rousted me in no time, spying my coveralls. Just to show how smart he was, he actually seemed to press one eye to the crack before he gave my pant leg a tug. He shook his head back and forth, growling with enthusiasm while he yanked on my cuff. Without even thinking, I poked my head around the door and raised a finger to my lips. He barked with enthusiasm, thus releasing me, and then he pranced back and forth hoping I would play. I have to say, it was pathetic to see an eighty-pound mutt having so much fun at my expense. Rich, unaware of the cause, bellowed orders to the pooch, who stood there torn between obedience to his master and the thrill of discovery. Rich called him again, and he bounded away with a series of exuberant yelps. Back in the den, Rich told him to sit and, apparently, he sat. I heard him bark once to alert his master there was game afoot.

I didn't dare delay. Moving with a silence I hoped was absolute, I slipped to the back door and opened it a crack. I was on the brink of escape when I remembered my clipboard, which was resting on the counter where Rich had tossed it. I paused long enough to grab it and then I eased out the back door and closed it carefully behind me. I crept down the porch steps and veered left along the drive, tapping the clipboard casually against my thigh. My impulse was to bolt as soon as I reached the street, but I forced myself to walk, not wanting to call attention to my exodus. There's nothing so conspicuous as someone in civilian clothes running down the street as though pursued by beasts.

THREE

The drive back to Santa Teresa was uneventful, though I was so juiced up on adrenaline I had to make a conscious effort not to speed. I seemed to see cops everywhere: two at an intersection directing traffic where a stoplight was on the fritz; one lurking near the on-ramp, concealed by a clump of bushes; another parked on the berm behind a motorist, who waited in resignation for the ticket to come. Having escaped from the danger zone, I was not only being meticulous about obeying the law but struggling to regain a sense of normalcy, whatever *that* is. The risk I'd taken at Teddy's house had fractured my perception. I'd become, at the same time, disassociated from reality and more keenly connected to it so that "real life" now seemed flat and strangely lusterless. Cops, rock stars, soldiers, and career criminals all experience the same shift, the plunge from soaring indomitability to unconquerable lassitude, which is why they tend to hang out with others of their ilk. Who else can understand the high? You get amped, wired, blasted out of your tiny mind on situational stimulants. Afterward, you have to talk yourself down, reliving your experience until the

31

charge is off and events collapse back to their ordinary size. I was still awash with the rush, my vision shimmering. The Pacific pulsated on my left. The sea air felt as brittle as a sheet of glass. Like flint on stone, the late morning sun struck the waves in a series of sparks until I half expected the entire ocean to burst into flames. I turned on the radio, tuning the station to one with booming music. I rolled down the car windows and let the wind buffet my hair.

As soon as I got home, I set the cardboard box on the desk, pulled the storage company receipt from my pocket, and tossed the coveralls in the wash. I never should have broken into Teddy's house that way. What was I thinking? I was nuts, temporarily deranged, but the man had irritated me beyond reason. All I'd wanted was a piece of information, which I now possessed. Of course, I had no idea what to do with it. The last thing I needed was to reconnect with my ex.

We'd parted on bad terms, and I'd made a point of abolishing my memories of him. Mentally, I'd excised all reference to the relationship, so that now I scarcely allowed myself to remember his name. Friends were aware that I'd been married at the age of twenty-one, but they knew nothing of who he was and had no clue about the split. I'd put the man in a box and dropped him to the bottom of my emotional ocean, where he'd languished ever since. Oddly enough, while my second husband, Daniel, had betrayed me, gravely injuring my pride, he hadn't violated my sense of honor as Mickey Magruder had. While I may be careless about the penal code, I'm never casual about the law. Mickey had crossed the line, and he'd tried dragging me along with him. I'd moved on short notice, willing to abandon most of my belongings when I walked out the door.

The overload of chemicals began to drain from my system, letting anxiety in. I went into my kitchenette and tranquilized myself with the ritual of a sandwich, smoothing Jif Extra Crunchy peanut butter on two slices of hearty seven-grain bread. I arranged six bread-and-butter pickles like big green polka dots on the thick layer of caramel-colored goo. I cut the finished sandwich on the diagonal and laid it on a paper napkin while I licked the knife clean. One virtue of being single is not having to explain the peculiarities of one's appetites in moments of stress. I popped open a can of Diet Coke and ate at the kitchen counter, perched on a stool with a copy of *Time* magazine, which I read back to middle. Nothing in the front ever seems to interest me.

When I finished, I crumpled the paper napkin, tossed it in the trash, and returned to my desk. I was ready to go through the box of memorabilia, though I half dreaded what I would find. So much of the past is encapsulated in the odds and ends. Most of us discard more information about ourselves than we ever care to preserve. Our recollection of the past is not simply distorted by our faulty perception of events remembered but skewed by those forgotten. The memory is like orbiting twin stars, one visible, one dark, the trajectory of what's evident forever affected by the gravity of what's concealed.

I sat down in my swivel chair and tilted back on its axis. I propped my feet on my desk, the box open on the floor beside me. A hasty visual survey suggested

that the minute I'd walked out, Mickey'd packed everything of mine he could lay his hands on. I pictured him
carting the box through the apartment, snatching up
my belongings, tossing them together in a heap. I could
see dried-out toiletries, a belt, junk mail and old magazines rubber-banded in a bundle, five paperback novels,
and a couple of pairs of shoes. Any other clothes I'd
left were long gone. He'd probably shoved those in a
trash bag and called the Salvation Army, taking satisfaction in the idea that many much-loved articles
would end up on a sale table for a buck or two. He
must have drawn the line at memorabilia. Some of it
was here, at any rate, spared from the purge.

I reached in and fumbled among the contents, letting
my fingers make the selection among the unfamiliar
clusters, a grab bag of the misplaced, the bygone, and
the abandoned. The first item I retrieved was a packet
of old report cards, bound together with thin white
satin ribbon. These, my Aunt Gin had saved for reasons that escaped me. She wasn't sentimental by
nature, and the quality of my academic performance
was hardly worth preserving. I was a quite average
student showing no particular affinity for reading,
writing, or arithmetic. I could spell like a champ and I
was good at memory games. I liked geography and
music and the smell of LePage's paste on black and
orange construction paper. Most other aspects of
school were terrifying. I hated reciting *anything* in front
of classmates, or being called on perversely when my
hand wasn't even raised. The other kids seemed to
enjoy the process, while I quaked in my shoes. I threw
up almost daily, and when I wasn't sick at school I

would try to manufacture some excuse to stay home or go to work with Aunt Gin. Faced with aggression on the part of my classmates, I quickly learned that my most effective defense was to bite the shit out of my opponent. There was nothing quite as satisfying as the sight of my teeth marks in the tender flesh of someone's arm. There are probably individuals today who still bear the wrathful half moon of dental scars.

I sorted through the report cards, all of which were similar and shared a depressingly common theme. Scanning the written comments, I could see that my teachers were given to much hand wringing and dire warnings about my ultimate fate. Though cursed with "potential," I was apparently a child with little to recommend her. According to their notes, I daydreamed, wandered the classroom at will, failed to finish lessons, seldom volunteered an answer, and usually got it wrong when I did.

"Kinsey's bright enough, but she seems absentminded and she has a tendency to focus only on subjects of interest to her. Her copious curiosity is offset by an inclination to mind everybody else's business. . . ."

"Kinsey seems to have difficulty telling the truth. She should be evaluated by the school psychologist to determine . . ."

"Kinsey shows excellent comprehension and mastery of topics that appeal to her, but lacks discipline. . . ."

"Doesn't seem to enjoy team sports. Doesn't cooperate with others on class projects. . . ."

"Able to work well on her own."

"Undisciplined. Unruly."

"Timid. Easily upset when reprimanded."

"Given to sudden disappearances when things don't go her way. Leaves classroom without permission."

I studied my young self as though reading about a stranger. My parents had been killed in a car wreck on Memorial Day weekend. I'd turned five on May 5 that year, and they died at the end of that month. In September, I started school, armed with a lunch box, my tablet paper, a fat, red Big Bear pencil, and a lot of gritty determination. From my current vantage point, I can see the pain and confusion I hadn't dared experience back then. Though physically undersized and fearful from day one, I was autonomous, defiant, and as hard as a nut. There was much I admired about the child I had been: the ability to adapt, the resilience, the refusal to conform. These were qualities I still harbored, though perhaps to my detriment. Society values cooperation over independence, obedience over individuality, and niceness above all else.

The next packet contained photos from that same period. In class pictures, I was usually half a head shorter than anyone else in my class. My countenance was dark, my expression solemn and wistful, as if I longed to be gone, which of course I did. While others in the class stared directly at the camera, my attention was inevitably diverted by something taking place on the sidelines. In one photograph, my face was a blur because I'd turned my head to look at someone in the row behind me. Even then, life must have seemed more interesting slightly off-center. What I found unsettling was the fact I hadn't changed much in the years between.

I probably should have been out somewhere looking for new clients instead of allowing myself to be distracted by the past. What could have happened that would result in Mickey's belongings being sold at public auction? Not that it was any of my business, but then again, that's exactly what gave the question its appeal.

I went back to the cardboard box and pulled out an old tape recorder as big as a hardback book. I'd forgotten that old thing, accustomed by now to machines the size of a deck of cards. I could see a tape cassette inside. I pushed the PLAY button. No go. The batteries were probably already dead the day Mickey tossed it in the box with everything else. I opened my desk drawer and took out a fresh pack of C batteries, shoving four, end to end, into the back of the machine. I pushed PLAY again. This time the spindles began to turn and I heard my own voice, some rambling account of the case I was working on at the time. This was like historical data sealed in a cornerstone, meant to be discovered later after everyone was gone.

I turned it off and set the tape machine aside. I reached into the box again. Tucked down along the side, I found ammo for the 9mm Smith & Wesson Mickey'd given me for a wedding present. There was no sign of the gun, but I could remember how thrilled I'd been with the gift. The finish on the barrel had been S & W blue, and the stock was checked walnut with S & W monograms. We'd met in November and married the following August. By then, he'd been a cop for almost sixteen years, while I'd joined the department in May, a mere three months before. I took the gift of a firearm as an indication that he saw me as a colleague, a status he accorded few women in those days. Now I could see there were larger implications. I mean, what kind of guy gives his young bride a semiautomatic on their wedding night? Impulsively, I pulled open my bottom drawer, searching for the old address book where I'd tucked the only forwarding information I'd ever had for him. The phone number had probably been relinquished and reassigned half a dozen times, the address just as long out of date.

I was interrupted by a knock. I hauled my feet off the desk and crossed to the door, peering through the porthole to find my landlord standing on the porch. Henry was wearing long pants for a change, and his expression was distracted as he stared out across the yard. He'd turned eighty-six on Valentine's Day: tall and lean, a man who never actually seemed to age. He and his siblings, who were respectively eighty-eight, eighty-nine, ninety-five, and ninety-six, came from such vigorous genetic stock that I'm inclined to believe they'll never actually "pass." Henry's handsome in the manner of a fine antique, handcrafted and well constructed, exhibiting a polish that suggests close to nine decades of loving use. Henry has always been loyal, outspoken, kind, and generous. He's protective of me in ways that feel strange but are welcome, nonetheless.

I opened the door. "Hi, Henry. What are you up to? I haven't seen you for days."

"Thank goodness you're home. I have a dental

appointment in"—he paused to glance at his watch—
"approximately sixteen and three-quarter minutes,
and both my cars are out of commission. My Chevy's
still in the shop after that paint can fell on it, and now
I discover the station wagon's dead. Can you give me
a lift? Better yet, if you lend me your car, I can save
you the trip. This is going to take awhile and I hate
to tie you up." Henry's five-window butter-yellow
1932 Chevy coupe had suffered some minor damage
when several paint cans shuddered off the garage shelf
during a cluster of baby earthquakes late in March.
Henry's meticulous about the car, keeping it in pristine condition. His second vehicle, the station wagon,
he used whenever his Michigan based sibs came to
town.

"I'll give you a ride. I don't mind a bit," I said. "Let
me grab my keys." I left the door ajar while I snagged
my handbag from the counter and fished out the keys
from the outer compartment. I picked up my jacket
while I was at it and then pulled the door shut behind
me and locked it.

We rounded the corner of the building and passed
through the gate. I opened the passenger side door and
moved around the front of the car. He leaned across
the seat and unlocked the door on my side. I slid under
the wheel, fired up the ignition, and we were under
way.

"Great. This is great. I really appreciate this," Henry
said, his tone completely false.

I glanced over at him, making note of the tension
that had tightened his face. "What are you having
done?"

39

"A crown 'ack 'ere," he said, talking with his finger stuck at the back of his mouth.

"At least it's not a root canal."

"I'd have to kill myself first. I was hoping you'd be gone so I could cancel the appointment."

"No such luck," I said.

Henry and I share an apprehension about dentists that borders on the comical. While we're both dutiful about checkups, we agonize over any work that actually has to be done. Both of us are subject to dry mouth, squirmy stomachs, clammy hands, and lots of whining. I reached over and felt his fingers, which were icy and faintly damp.

Henry frowned to himself. "I don't see why he has to do this. The filling's fine, really not a problem. It doesn't even hurt. It's a little sensitive to heat, and I've had to give up anything with ice—"

"The filling's old?"

"Well, 1942—but there's nothing *wrong* with it."

"Talk about make-work."

"My point exactly. In those days, dentists knew how to fill a tooth. Now a filling has a limited shelf life, like a carton of milk. It's planned obsolescence. You're lucky if it lasts you long enough to pay the bill." He stuck his finger in his mouth again, turning his face in my direction. "See this? Only fifteen years old and the guy's already talking about replacing it."

"You're kidding! What a scam!"

"Remember when they put fluoride in the city water and everybody thought it was a communist plot? Dentists spread that rumor."

"Of course they did," I said, chiming in on cue.

"They saw the handwriting on the wall. No more cavities, no more business." We went through the same duet every time either one of us had to have something done.

"Now they've cooked up that surgery where they cut half your gums away. If they can't talk you into that, they claim you need braces."

"What a *crock*," I said.

"I don't know why I can't have my teeth pulled and get it over with," he said, his mood becoming morose.

I made the usual skeptical response. "I wouldn't go that far, Henry. You have beautiful teeth."

"I'd rather keep 'em in a glass. I can't stand the drilling. The noise drives me crazy. And the scraping when they scale? I nearly rip the arms off the chair. Sounds like a shovel on a sidewalk, a pickax on concrete—"

"All right! Cut it out. You're making my hands sweat."

By the time I pulled into the parking lot, we'd worked ourselves into such a state of indignation, I was surprised he was willing to keep the appointment. I sat in the dentist's waiting room after Henry's name was called. Except for the receptionist, I had the place to myself, which I thought was faintly worrisome. How come the dentist only had one patient? I pictured Medicaid fraud: phantom clients, double-billing, charges for work that would never be done. Just a typical day in the life of Dr. Dentifrice, federal con artist and cheater with a large sadistic streak. I did give the guy points for having recent issues of all the best magazines.

From the other room, over the burbling of the fish tank, which is meant to mask the shrieks, I could hear the sounds of a high-speed drill piercing through tooth enamel straight to the pulsing nerve below. My fingers began to stick to the pages of *People* magazine, leaving a series of moist, round prints. Once in a while, I caught Henry's muffled protest, a sound suggestive of flinching and lots of blood gushing out. Just the thought of his suffering made me hyperventilate. I finally got so light-headed I had to step outside, where I sat on the mini-porch with my head between my knees.

Henry eventually emerged, looking stricken and relieved, feeling at his numbed lip to see if he was drooling on himself. To distract him on the ride home, I filled him in on the cardboard box, the circumstances under which it originated, Mickey's paranoia, the John Russell alias, and my own B & E adventure at Ted Rich's place. He liked the part about the dog, having urged me repeatedly to get one of my own. We had the usual brief argument about me and household pets.

Then he said, "So, tell me about your ex. You said he was a cop, but what's the rest of it?"

"Don't ask."

"But what do you think it means, his being delinquent with his storage fees?"

"How do I know? I haven't talked to him in years."

"Don't be like that, Kinsey. I hate it when you're stingy with information. I want the story on him."

"It's too complicated to get into. Maybe I'll tell you later, when I've figured it out."

"Are you going to follow up?"

"No."

"Maybe he got lazy about paying his bills," he said, trying to draw me in.

"I doubt it. He was always good about that stuff."

"People change."

"No, they don't. Not in my experience."

"Nor in mine, now you mention it."

The two of us were silent for a block, and then Henry spoke up. "Suppose he's in trouble?"

"Serves him right if he is."

"You wouldn't help?"

"What for?"

"Well, it wouldn't hurt to check."

"I'm not going to *do* that."

"Why not? All it'd take is a couple of calls. What's it going to cost?"

"How do you know what it'd cost? You don't even know the man."

"I'm just saying, you're not busy . . . at least, as far as I've heard. . . ."

"Did I ask for advice?"

"I thought you did," he said. "I'm nearly certain you were fishing for encouragement."

"I was *not*."

"I see."

"Well, I wasn't. I have absolutely no interest in the man."

"Sorry. My mistake."

"You're the only person in my life who gets away with this shit."

*

43

When I got back to my desk, the first thing my eye fell on was my address book lying open to the M's. I flipped the book shut and shoved it in a drawer, which I closed with a bang.

FOUR

I sat down in my swivel chair and gave the carton a shove with my foot. I was tempted to chuck the damn thing, salvage the personal papers and dump the rest in the trash. However, having paid the twenty bucks, I couldn't bring myself to do it. It wasn't so much that I was cheap, though that was certainly a factor. The truth is, I was curious. I reasoned that just because I looked through the box didn't make me responsible for anything else. It certainly wouldn't *obligate* me to try to locate my ex. Sorting through the items would in no way compel me to take action on his behalf. If Mickey'd fallen on hard times, if he was in a jam of some kind, then so be it. *C'est la vie* and so what? It had nothing to do with me.

I pulled the wastebasket closer to the box, pushed the flaps back, and peered in. In the time I'd been gone, the elves and fairies still hadn't managed to tidy up the mess. I started tossing out loose toiletries: a flattened tube of toothpaste and a shampoo bottle with a thin layer of sludge pooled along its length. Something had leaked out and oozed down through the box, welding articles together like an insidious glue. I threw out a hodgepodge of over-the-counter medications, an ancient diaphragm, a safety razor, and a toothbrush with bristles splayed out in all directions. It looked like I'd used it to clean the bathroom grout.

From under the toiletries, I excavated a bundle of junk mail. When I picked up the stack, the rubber band disintegrated, and I plunked the bulk of it in the wastebasket. A few stray envelopes surfaced, and I pulled those from among the discarded magazines and dog-eared catalogs—bullshit from the look of them: a bank statement for an account I'd closed many years before, a department store circular, and a notice from Publisher's Clearing House telling me I'd been short-listed for a million bucks. The third envelope I picked up was a credit card bill that I *sincerely* hoped I paid. What a disgrace that would be, a blot on my credit rating. Maybe that's why American Express wasn't sending me any preapproved cards these days. And here I'd been feeling so superior. Mickey's payments might be delinquent, but not mine, she said.

I turned the bill over to open it. Stuck to the back was another envelope, this one a letter that must have arrived in the same post. I pulled the second envelope free, tearing the paper in the process. The envelope itself bore no return address, and I didn't recognize the writing. The script was tight and angular, letters slanting heavily to the left, as if on the verge of collapsing. The postmark read SANTA TERESA, APRIL 2, 1972. I'd left Mickey the day before, April Fool's Day, as it turned out. I removed the single sheet of lined paper, which was covered with the same inky cursive, as flattened as bent grass.

Kinsey,

Mickey made me promise not to do this, but I think you should know. He was with me that night, sure, he pushed the guy, but it was no big deal. I know because I saw it and so did a lot of other people whoer on his side. Benny was fine when he took off. Him and Mickey couldn't have connect after because we went back to my place and he was their till midnight. I told him I'd testify, but he says no because of Eric and his situation. He's completly innocent and desperetly needs your help. What difference does it make where he was as long as he didn't do it? If you love him, you should take his part insted of being such a bitch. Being a cop is his whole life, please don't take that away from him. Otherwise I hope you find a way to live with yourself because your runing everything for him.

D.

I read the note twice, my mind blank except for a clinical and bemused response to all the misspellings and run-on sentences. I'm a snob about grammar and I have trouble taking anyone seriously who gets "there" possessives confused with "there" demonstratives. I didn't "rune" Mickey's life. It hadn't been up to me to save him from anything. He'd asked me to lie for him and I'd flatly refused. Failing that, he'd probably concocted this cover story with "D"—whoever she was. From the sound of it, she knew me, but I couldn't for the life of me remember her. D. That could be Dee. Dee Dee. Donna. Dawn. Diane. Doreen. . . .

Oh, shit. Of course.

There was a bartender named Dixie who worked in a place out in Colgate where Mickey and some of his cop buddies hung out after work. It wasn't uncommon for the guys to band together to do their after-hours drinking. In the early seventies, there were frequent watch parties at the end of a shift, revelries that sometimes went on until the wee hours of the morning. Both public and private drunkenness are considered violations of police discipline, as are extramarital affairs, failure to pay debts, and other scurrilous behavior. Such violations are punishable by the department, because a police officer is considered "on duty" at all times as a matter of public image and because tolerating such conduct might lead to similar infractions while the officer is formally at work. When complaints came in about the shift parties, the officers moved the drink fests from the city to the county, effectively removing them from departmental scrutiny. The Honky-Tonk, where Dixie worked, became their favorite haunt.

At the time I met Dixie, she must have been in her mid-twenties, older than I was by four or five years. Mickey and I had been married for six weeks. I was still a rookie, working traffic, while he'd been promoted to detective, assigned first to vice and then to burglary and theft under Lieutenant Dolan, who later moved on to homicide. Dixie was the one who organized the celebration for any transfer or promotion, and we all understood it was just one more excuse to party. I remembered sitting at the bar chatting with her while Mickey sucked back draft beers, playing pool with his cronies or trading war stories with the veterans coming back from Vietnam. At eighteen, he'd served a fourteen-month combat tour in Korea, and he was always interested in the contrast between the Korean War and the action in Vietnam.

Dixie's husband, Eric Hightower, had been wounded in Laos in April 1971, returning to the world with both legs missing. In his absence, she'd put herself through bartending school and she'd worked at the Tonk since the day Eric shipped out. After he came home, he'd sit there in his wheelchair, his behavior moody or manic, depending on his medications and his alcohol levels. Dixie kept him sedated on a steady regimen of Bloody Marys, which seemed to pacify his rage. To me, she seemed like a busy mother, forced to bring her kid to work with her. The rest of us were polite, but Eric certainly didn't do much to endear himself. At twenty-six, he was a bitter old man.

I used to watch in fascination while she assembled Mai Tais, gin and tonics, Manhattans, martinis, and revolting concoctions like pink squirrels and crème de menthe frappés. She talked incessantly, hardly looking at what she did, eyeballing the pour, spritzing soda or water from the bar hose. Sometimes she constructed four and five drinks at the same time without missing a beat. Her laugh was husky and low-pitched. She exchanged endless ribald comments with the guys, all of whom she knew by name and circumstance. I was impressed with her bawdy self-assurance. I also pitied her her husband, with his sour disposition and his obvious limitations, which I assumed extended into sex. Even so, it never occurred to me that she would screw around on him, especially with *my* husband. I must have been brain-dead not to notice—unless, of course, she was inventing this stuff to provide Mickey with the alibi that I'd declined to supply.

Dixie was my height, rail thin, with a long narrow face and an untidy tangle of auburn hair halfway down her back. Her brows were plucked, a wispy pair of arches that fanned out like wings from the bridge of her nose. Her eyes were darkly charcoaled, and she wore a fringe of fake lashes that made her eyes jump from her face. She was usually braless under her T-shirt, and she wore miniskirts so short she could hardly sit down. Sometimes she veered off in the opposite direction, donning long granny dresses or India-print tunics over wide-legged pantlets.

I read her note again, but sure enough, the content was the same. She and Mickey had been having an affair. That seemed to be the subtext of her communication, though I found it hard to believe. He'd never given any indication he was even *interested* in her, or maybe he had and I'd been too dumb to pick up on it. How could she have stood there and chatted with me if the two of them were making it behind my back? On the other hand, the idea was not entirely inconsistent with Mickey's history.

Before we'd connected, he'd been involved in numerous affairs, but he was, after all, single and savvy enough to avoid emotional entanglements. In the late sixties, early seventies, sex was casual, recreational, indiscriminate, and uncommitted. Women had been liberated by the advent of the birth control pill, and dope had erased any further prohibitions. This was the era of love-ins, psychedelics, dropouts, war protests, body paint, assassinations, LSD, and rumors of kids so stoned their eyeballs got fried because they stared at the sun too long.

It was also the era in which law enforcement began to change. In 1964, the Supreme Court had ruled, in the matter of Escobedo *v.* Illinois, that the refusal by the police to honor Escobedo's request to consult his lawyer during the course of an interrogation constituted a violation of the Sixth Amendment. Two years later, 1966, in Miranda *v.* Arizona, the Supreme Court came down again on the side of the plaintiff, citing a breach of Sixth Amendment rights. From that point on, the climate in law enforcement underwent a shift, and the image of Dirty Harry was replaced by at least the appearance of restraint.

Mickey chafed at the limitations set by policy and, on a broader level, at legal restrictions he felt interfered with his effectiveness. He was an old-fashioned cop. He identified with the crime victim. In his mind, theirs were the only claims that counted. Let the perpetrator fend for himself. He hated having to protect the guilty, and he had no patience for the so-called rights of those arrested. I sometimes suspected he'd formed his attitudes from the reams of pulp fiction he'd read growing up. Please understand that none of this was evident to me when we first met. I was not only infatuated with his attitude but wide-eyed with admiration at what I mistook for worldliness. I suspect in Mickey's view certain rules and regulations simply didn't apply to him. He operated outside the standards most other cops finally came to accept. Mickey was accustomed to getting his way, experienced in what he called "certain time-honored methods for persuading a suspect to

51

make himself agreeable in the matter of inculpatory statements." Mickey usually said this in a tone that made everybody laugh.

Mickey was revered by his fellow officers and, until that March, his departmental run-ins were focused on a series of minor infractions. He was late with his reports and occasionally insubordinate, though he seemed to have an instinct for how far he could push. He'd been the subject of two citizens' complaints: once for offensive language and once for excessive use of force. In both incidents the department investigated and found in his favor. Still, it didn't look good. His was an odd mix of the offbeat and the conventional. In his personal life, he was scrupulously honest—about his taxes, his bills, his personal debts. He was loyal to his friends and discreet with regard to others. He also honored his commitments, except (apparently) to me. He would never violate a confidence, never rat out a pal or a fellow officer. Among men, he was esteemed. With women, he was regarded with an admiration bordering on hero worship. I know because I did this myself, elevating his nonconformity to something praiseworthy instead of faintly dangerous.

Looking back on it, I can see that I didn't want to know the truth about him. I had graduated from the police academy in April of 1971 and was hired by the Santa Teresa Police Department as soon as I turned twenty-one in May. I'd met Mickey the previous November, and I was dazzled by the image he projected: seasoned, gruff, cynical, wise. Within months we fell in love, and by August we were married—all of this before either of us understood what the other was about. Once committed, I was determined to see him as the man I wanted him to be. I needed to believe. I saw him as an idol, so I accepted his version of events even when common sense suggested he was slanting the facts.

In the fall of 1971, after Mickey was reassigned to burglary and theft, he developed what was euphemistically referred to as a "personality conflict" with Con Dolan, who headed crimes against property. Lieutenant Dolan was an autocrat and a stickler for regulations, which caused the two of them to clash time and time again. Their differences put an end to Mickey's hopes for advancement.

Six months later, in the spring of 1972, Mickey resigned from the department to avoid yet another tangle with Internal Affairs. He was, at that time, under investigation for voluntary manslaughter after he'd been involved in a bar dispute. His altercation with a transient named Benny Quintero resulted in the man's death. This was March 17, St. Patrick's Day, and Mickey was off duty, drinking at the Honky-Tonk with a bunch of buddies, who supported his account. He claimed the man was drunk and abusive and exhibited threatening behavior. Mickey removed him bodily to the parking lot, where the two engaged in a brief shoving match. To hear Mickey tell it, he'd pushed the guy around some, but only in response to the drunk's attack. Witnesses swore he hadn't landed any blows. Benny Quintero left the scene, and that was the last anyone reported seeing him until his body was discovered the next day, beaten and bloody, dumped by the side of Highway 154. Internal Affairs launched an investigation, and Mickey's attorney, Mark Bethel, advised him to keep his mouth shut. Since Mickey was the prime suspect, facing the possibility of criminal charges, Bethel was doing what he could to cover his backside. IA can coerce testimony but is forbidden to share findings with the DA's office. There could be serious consequences all the same. Given the overarching need for honest officers, the department was determined to pursue the matter. Mickey resigned in order to avoid questioning. If he hadn't left when he did, he'd have been fired anyway for his refusal to respond.

The day Mickey turned in his badge, his weapon, and his radio, his fellow officers were incensed. Department regulations prohibited his superiors from making any public statement, and Mickey downplayed his departure, which made him look all the more heroic in the eyes of his comrades. The impression he gave was that, despite their treatment of him, his loyalty to the department overrode his right to defend himself against accusations completely contrived and unfair. So convincing was he that I believed him myself right up to the moment when he asked me to lie for him. A criminal investigation was initiated, which is where I came in. Apparently, there were four hours unaccounted for in Mickey's alibi for that night. He refused to say where he'd been or what he'd done between the time he left the Honky-Tonk and the time he arrived home. He was suspected of following the guy and finishing the job elsewhere, but Mickey denied the whole thing. He asked me to cover for him, and that's when I walked.

I left him April 1 and filed for divorce on the tenth

of that month. Some weeks later, the findings from the coroner's exam revealed that Quintero, a Vietnam veteran, had suffered a service-related head injury. In combat, he'd been hit by sniper fire, and a stainless-steel plate now served where a portion of his skull had been blown away. The official cause of death was a slow hemorrhage in the depths of his brain. Any minor blow could have generated the fatal seepage. In addition, the toxicology report showed a blood alcohol level of .15 with traces of amphetamine, marijuana, and cocaine. There was no actual evidence that Mickey had encountered Benny after their initial scuffle in the parking lot. The DA declined to file charges, so Mickey was off the hook. By then, of course, the damage had been done. He'd been separated from the city and he was, soon afterward, permanently separated from me. In the intervening years, my disenchantment had begun to fade. While I didn't want to see him, I didn't wish him ill. The last I'd heard he was doing personal security, a once-dedicated cop demoted to working night shift in an imitation cop's uniform.

I read the letter again, wondering what I would have done if I'd received it back then. I felt a ripple of anxiety coursing through my frame. If this was true, I had indeed contributed to his ruin.

I opened the drawer and took out my address book, which opened as if by magic to the page where he was listed. I picked up the handset and punched in the number. The line rang twice, and then I was greeted with a big two-tone whistling and the usual canned message telling me the number in the 213 area code was no longer in service. If I felt I'd reached the recording in error, I could recheck the number and then dial it again. Just to be certain, I redialed the number and heard the same message. I hung up, trying to decide if there were any other possibilities I should pursue.

FIVE

I hadn't visited the house on Chapel Street for a good fifteen years. I parked out in front and let myself into the yard through a small wrought-iron gate. The house was white frame, a homely story-and-a-half, with an angular bay window and a narrow side porch. Two second-story windows seemed to perch on the bay, and a simple wood filigree embellished the peaked roof. Built in 1875, the house was plain, lacking sufficient charm and period detail to warrant protection by the local historical preservationists. Out front, a stream of one-way traffic was a constant reminder of downtown Santa Teresa, only two blocks away. In another few years, the property would probably be sold and the house would finish its days as a secondhand furniture store or a little mom-and-pop business. Eventually, the building would be razed and the lot would be offered up as prime commercial real estate. I suppose not every vintage single-family dwelling can be spared the wrecker's ball, but a day will soon come when the history of the common folk will be entirely erased. The mansions of the wealthy will remain where they stand, the more ponderous among them converted for use by museums, art academies, and charitable foundations. A middle-class home like this would scarcely survive to the turn of another century. For the moment, it was safe. The front yard was well tended and the exterior paint looked fresh. I knew from past occasions the backyard was spacious, complete with a hand-laid brick patio, a built-in barbecue pit, and an orchard of fruit trees.

I pressed the front doorbell. A shrill note echoed harshly through the house. Peter Shackelford, "Shack," and his wife, Bundy, had been close friends of Mickey's long before we met. Theirs was a second marriage for both—Shack was divorced, Bundy widowed. Shack had adopted Bundy's four kids and raised them as his own. In those days, the couple entertained often and easily: pizza, potluck suppers, and backyard barbecues, paper plates, plastic ware, and bring-your-own-bottle, with everyone pitching in on cleanup. There were usually babies in diapers, toddlers taking off on cross-lawn forays. The older kids played Frisbee or raced around the yard like a bunch of hooligans. With all the parents on the scene, discipline was casual and democratic. Anyone close to the miscreant was authorized to act. In those days, I wasn't quite so self-congratulatory about my childless state, and I would occasionally keep an eye on the little ones while their parents cut loose.

Mickey and Shack had joined the Santa Teresa Police Department at just about the same time and had worked in close proximity. They were never partners, per se, but the two of them, along with a third cop named Roy "Lit" Littenberg, were known as the Three

Musketeers. Lit and Shack were part of the crowd at the Honky-Tonk the year Mickey went down. I was hoping one or the other would know his whereabouts and his current status. I also needed confirmation of the letter's contents. I'd been convinced Mickey was guilty of the beating that resulted in Benny's death. I wasn't sure what I'd do if it turned out he'd had a legitimate alibi for that night. The idea made my stomach roil with anxiety.

Shack answered the door half a minute later, though it took him another ten seconds to figure out who I was. The delay gave me a chance to register the changes in him. In the period when I'd known him, he must have been in his late thirties. He was now in his early fifties and a good twenty-five pounds heavier. Gravity had tugged at all the planes in his face, now defined by a series of downward-turning lines: dense brows over drooping eyelids, sagging cheeks, a bushy mustache and heavy mouth curving down toward his double chin. His thick salt-and-pepper hair was clipped close to his head as though he were still subject to departmental regulations. He was wearing shorts, flip-flops, and a loose white T-shirt, the sagging neckline revealing a froth of white chest hair. Like Mickey, Shack had lifted weights three days a week, and there was still the suggestion of power in the way he carried himself.

"Hello, Shack. How are you?" I said, when I could see that my identity had been noted. I didn't bother to smile. This was not a social visit, and I guessed his feelings for me were neither friendly nor warm.

His tone when he spoke was surprisingly mild. "I always figured you'd show up."

"Here I am," I said. "Mind if I come in?"

"Why not?"

He stepped aside, allowing me to enter the front hall ahead of him. Given the echoes of the past, the quiet seemed unnatural. "Might as well follow me out back. I don't spend a lot of time in this part of the house." Shack closed the door and moved down the hall toward the kitchen.

Even the most cursory glance showed half the furniture was gone. In the living room, I spotted a coffee table, miscellaneous side tables, and a straight-back wooden chair. The silver-dollar-sized circles of matted carpeting indicated where the couch and easy chairs had once been. The built-in bookcases, flanking the fireplace, were now bereft of books. In their place, twenty-five to thirty framed photographs showed a myriad of smiling faces: babies, children, and adults. Most were studio portraits, but there were several enlargements of snapshots from family gatherings.

"Are you moving?"

He shook his head. "Bundy died six months ago," he said. "Most of the furniture was hers anyway. I let the kids take what they wanted. There's plenty left for my purposes."

"Is that them in the photographs?"

"Them and their kids. We got thirteen grandchildren among the four of them."

"Congratulations."

"Thanks. The youngest, Jessie . . . you remember her?"

"Dark curly hair?"

"That's her. The wild one in the bunch. She hasn't

married to date, but she adopted two Vietnamese children."

"What's she do for a living?"

"Attorney in New York. She does corporate law."

"Do any of the others live close?"

"Scott's down in Sherman Oaks. They're spread out all over, but they visit when they can. Every six–eight months, I fire up the Harley and do a big round trip. Good kids, all of them. Bun did a hell of a job. I'm a sorry substitute, but I do what I can."

"What are you up to these days? I heard you left the department."

"A year ago this May. I don't do much of anything, to tell you the truth."

"You still lifting weights?"

"Can't. I got hurt. Had an accident on duty. Some drunk ran a red light and broadsided my patrol car. Killed him outright and knocked me all to hell and gone. I got a fractured fifth vertebra so I ended up taking an industrial retirement. A worker's comp claim."

"Too bad."

"No point complaining about things you can't change. The money pays the bills and gives me time to myself. What about you? I hear you're a P.I."

"I've been doing that for years."

He led me through the kitchen to the glassed-in porch that ran along the rear of the house. He seemed to live the way I did, confined to one area like a pet left alone while its owners are off at work. The kitchen was completely tidy. I could see a single plate, a cereal bowl, a spoon, and a coffee mug in the dish rack. He

61

probably used the same few utensils, carefully washing up between meals. Why put anything away when you're only going to take it out and use it again? There was something homely about the presence of the dishes in the rack. From the look of it, he lived almost exclusively in the kitchen and enclosed porch. A futon, doubling as a couch, was set up at one end, blankets neatly folded with the pillows stacked on top. There was a TV on the floor. The rest of the porch was taken up with woodworking equipment: a lathe, a drill press, a router, a couple of C clamps, a vise, a wood chisel, a table saw, and an assortment of planes. He was in the process of refinishing two pieces. A chest of drawers had been stripped, pending further attention. A wooden kitchen chair had been laid on its back, its legs sticking out as stiffly as a dead possum's. Shack must sleep every night with the heady scent of turpentine, glue, tung oil, and wood shavings. He caught my look and said, "Virtue of being single. You can do anything you want."

I said, "Amen to that."

Once upon a time, Bundy had sewn the café curtains, hanging them on rods across the middle of the row of windows. The green and white checked cotton, probably permanent press, still looked fresh: crisp, carefully laundered, with little clip-on curtain rings. I found my eyes filling inexplicably with tears and had to feign attention to the backyard, which I could see through the glass. Many of the trees remained, as bent as old spines, curving toward the ground from a once-proud height. A saddle of purple morning glories was cinched to the fence, the chicken wire now swaybacked from the weight of the vines. The barbecue grill top had turned red-brown with rust, replaced by a portable kettle grill parked closer to the back steps.

Shack leaned against the wall with his arms folded across his chest. "So what's the reason for the call?"

"I'm looking for Mickey. The only number I have is a disconnect."

"You have business with him?"

"I may. I'm not sure. Do I need your approval before I telephone the man?"

Shack seemed amused. Bundy had always given him a hard time. Maybe he missed the rough and tumble of conversation. Live alone long enough and you forget what it's like. His smile faded slightly. "No offense, kiddo, but why not leave him alone?"

"I want to know he's okay. I don't intend to bother him. When's the last time you spoke?"

"I don't remember."

"I see. Do you have any idea what's going on with him?"

"I'm sure he's fine. Mickey's a big boy. He doesn't need anyone hovering."

"Fair enough," I said, "but I'd like the reassurance. That's all this is. Do you have his current phone or address?"

Shack shook his head and his mouth pulled down. "Nope. He initiates contact when it suits. In between calls, I make a point of leaving him alone. That's the deal we made."

"What about Lit?"

"Roy Littenberg died. The Big C took him out in less than six weeks. This was three years ago."

"I'm sorry to hear that. I liked him."

"Me too. I see his boy now and then: Tim. You'll never guess what he does."

"I give up."

"He bought the Honky-Tonk. Him and Bundy's boy, Scottie, pal around together whenever Scottie's in town."

I said, "Really. I don't remember meeting either one. I think both were off in Vietnam when Mickey and I were hanging out here." In Santa Teresa, all paths were destined to cross and recross eventually. Now the next generation was being folded into the mix. "Can you think of anyone else who might know what Mickey's up to?"

Shack studied me. "What's my motive in this?"

"You could be helping him."

"And what's yours?"

"I want the answer to some questions I should have asked back then."

"About Benny?"

"That's right."

His smile was shrewd. He cupped a hand to his ear. "Do I hear guilt?"

"If you like."

"A little late, don't you think?"

"Probably. I'm not sure. The point is, I don't need your permission. Now, will you help me or not?"

He thought about it briefly. "What about the lawyer who represented him?"

"Bethel? I can try. I should have thought of him. That's a good idea."

"I'm full of good ideas."

"You think Mickey was innocent?"

"Of course. I was there and I saw. The guy was fine when he left."

"Shack, he had a *plate* in his head."

"Mickey didn't hit him. He never landed a blow."

"How do you know he didn't go after him again? The two might have gotten into it somewhere else. Mickey wasn't exactly famous for his self-control. That was one of my complaints."

Shack wagged his head. The gesture turned into a neck roll, complete with cracking sound. "Sorry about that. I'm going to see the chiropractor later on account of this effing neck of mine. Yeah, it's possible. Why not? Maybe there was more to it than Mickey let on. I'm telling you what I saw, and it was no big deal."

"Fair enough."

"Incidentally—not that it's any of my business—but you should've stood by him. That's the least you could do. This isn't just me. A lot of the guys resented what you did."

"Well, I resented Mickey's asking me to lie for him. He wanted me to tell the DA he was in at nine o'clock that night instead of midnight or one A.M., whatever the hell time it was when he finally rolled in."

"Oh, that's right," he said snidely. "You never tell lies yourself."

"Not about murder. Absolutely not," I snapped.

"Bullshit. You really think Magruder beat a guy to death?"

"How do I know? That's what I'm trying to find

out. Mickey was off course. He was intent on the Might and the Right of the law, and he didn't give a damn what he had to do to get the job done."

"Yeah, and you ask my opinion there should have been more like him. Besides, what I hear, you're not exactly one to be casting stones."

"I'll grant you that one. That's why I'm not in uniform today. But my butt wasn't on the line back then, *his* was. If Mickey had an alibi, he should have said so up front instead of asking me to lie."

Shack's expression shifted and he broke off eye contact.

I said, "Come on, Shack. You know perfectly well where he was. Why don't you fill me in and we can put an end to this?"

"Is that why you're here?"

"In the main," I said.

"I can tell you this much: He wasn't on Highway 154 hassling a vet. He wasn't anywhere within miles."

"That's good. I believe you. Now could we try this? Mickey had a girlfriend. You remember Dixie Hightower? According to her, they were together that night 'getting it on,' to use the time-honored phrase."

"So he was sticking it to Dixie. Whoopee-do. So what? Everybody screwed around in those days."

"I didn't."

"Maybe not when you were married, but you were the same as everyone else . . . only maybe not as open or as honest."

I bypassed the judgment and went back to the subject under discussion. "Someone could have warned me."

66

"We assumed you knew. Neither of 'em went to any great lengths to cover up. Think of all the times you left the Honky-Tonk before him. What'd you think he was doing, going to night school? He was nailing her. Big deal. She was a bimbo tended bar. She wasn't any threat to you."

I swallowed my outrage, dismissing it as unproductive. I needed information, not an argument. Betrayal is betrayal, no matter when the truth of it sinks in. Whether Dixie was a threat to that marriage was beside the point. Even fourteen years later, I felt humiliated and incensed. I closed my eyes, detaching myself emotionally as though at the scene of a homicide. "Do you know for a fact he was with her that night?"

"Let's put it this way. I saw 'em leave the Tonk together. She was in her car. He was behind her in his. Nights her hubby was home, they checked into that dinky little motel out on Airport Road."

"Wonderful. How considerate of them. They were there that night?"

"Probably. I couldn't say for sure, but I'd be willing to bet."

"Why didn't *you* speak up for him?"

"I would have, for sure. I'd've gone to the wall, but I never had the chance. Mickey turned in his badge and that was the end of it. If you can't reach him, you can always ask her."

"Dixie?"

"Sure. She's around."

"Where?"

"You're the detective. Try the telephone book. She's still married to whosie-face . . . cripple guy. . . ."

"His name was Eric."

"That's right. Him and Dixie made a fortune and bought a mansion. Sixteen thousand square feet, something like that. Big."

"You're kidding."

"I'm not. It's the honest-to-God truth. They're living in Montebello on a regular estate."

"How'd he do that? The last I saw he was a hopeless drunk."

"He got into AA and straightened up his act. Once he sobered up, he figured out a way to build designer wheelchairs. Custom jobs with all the bells and whistles, depending on the disability. Now he's added sports chairs and prostheses. He has a plant in Taiwan, too, making parts for other companies. Donates a ton of stuff to children's hospitals across the country."

"Good for him. I'm glad to hear that. What about her? What's she doing with herself?"

"She's living the life of Riley, turned into Mrs. Gotrocks. Country club membership and everything. You look 'em up, tell 'em I said hi."

"Maybe I'll do that."

After I left Shack's, I went into the office, where I opened the mail. There was nothing of interest and no pressing business. Most of my other cases were in limbo, pending callbacks or responses to written inquiries of various sorts. I tidied my desk and washed the coffeepot. I dusted the leaves on the fake ficus. I had no reason to stay, but I couldn't go home yet. I was restless, brooding about Mickey in a series of thought loops that went around and around. Had I erred? Had I acted in haste, jumping to conclusions because it suited me? By the time Quintero died, I was disenchanted with Mickey anyway. I wanted out of the marriage, so his involvement in Quintero's death provided the perfect excuse. But maybe that's all it was. Could he have resigned from the department to spare my pride and, at the same time, to avoid exposing Dixie? If Mickey was innocent, if I'd known where he was that night, the case might have gone differently and he might still be a cop. I didn't want to believe it, but I couldn't escape the thought.

I lay down on the carpet and flung an arm across my eyes. Was there really any point in obsessing about this? It was over and done with. Fourteen years had gone by. Whatever the truth, Mickey'd elected to resign. That was a fact. I'd left him, and our lives were irreparably changed. Why pursue the matter when there wasn't any way to alter what had happened?

What was at stake was my integrity, whatever sense of honor I possessed. I know my limitations. I know the occasional lapses I'm capable of, but a transgression of this magnitude was impossible to ignore. Mickey had lost what he'd loved best, and maybe that was simply his inevitable fate. Then again, if I'd been an unwitting accomplice to his downfall, I needed to own up to it and get square with him.

SIX

Forbes Run was a meandering lane-and-a-half, a ribbon of pavement that snaked back and forth as it angled upward into the foothills. Massive branches of live oak hung out over the road. There were no houses visible, as far as I could see, but a series of markers suggested that large properties branched off at intervals. I watched the numbers progress, the signs leapfrogging from one side of the road to the other, alternating even and odd: 317, 320, 323, 326. The Hightowers' estate, at 329, was surrounded by a low fieldstone wall, accessible through wooden gates that opened electronically as soon as I pressed the button. Either the Hightowers were expecting someone or they didn't much care who appeared at their door.

The driveway extended perhaps a quarter of a mile and conjured up visions of a proper English manor house at the far end, a three-story Tudor with a steeply pitched slate roof. What I spotted, at long last, was nothing of the kind. The house was contemporary: long and low, hugging the ground, with an oversized roofline rising to a center peak. I could see four wide fieldstone chimneys, clusters of fan palms, and colossal black boulders the size of my car that must have erupted from Vesuvius and been transported to the grounds for effect. To the right, I could see a line of four garage doors.

I parked in the large circular parking area in front and made my way up the wide, sloping concrete walk. A woman, perhaps thirty, in tennis shoes, jeans, and a white T-shirt, was already standing in the open doorway, awaiting my arrival. This definitely wasn't Dixie, and I wondered for a fleeting moment if I'd come to the wrong house.

"Ms. Yablonsky?" she said.

"Actually, I'm not. I'm looking for Eric and Dixie Hightower. Am I in the right place?"

"Sorry. Of course. I thought you were someone else. We've been interviewing for staff positions, and the woman's half an hour late. Is Mrs. Hightower expecting you?" The woman herself remained nameless and without title: parlor maid, factotum, personal assistant. I guess she felt she was under no obligation to introduce herself.

"I'm an old friend," I said. I took out a business card and handed it to her.

She read the face of it, frowning. "A private detective? What's this about?"

"I'm hoping they can put me in touch with a mutual acquaintance. A guy named Mickey Magruder. My ex-husband."

"Oh. Why don't you come in and I'll tell Mrs. Hightower you're here."

"Is Eric home?"

71

"Mr. Hightower's out of town, but he should be home soon."

I stepped into the foyer, waiting uneasily while she disappeared from sight. I'm sometimes puzzled by wealth, which seems to have a set of rules of its own. Was I free to amble about or should I wait where I was? There was an angular stone bench positioned against one wall. The woman hadn't suggested I sit and I was loath to presume. Suppose it turned out to be a sculpture that collapsed under my weight? I did a one-eighty turn so I could scrutinize the place like a burglar-in-training, a little game I play. I noted entrances and exits, wondering about the possibility of a wall safe. If I were bugging the place, where would I tuck the surveillance equipment?

The floors were polished limestone, as pale as beach sand. I could see ancient marine creatures pressed into the surface, a tiny fossil museum at my feet. A wide corridor stretched off to the right. The ceiling was twelve feet high with floor-to-ceiling windows on one side. The facing walls were painted a snowy white and hung with a series of bright abstracts, oil paintings six feet tall, probably expensive and done by someone dead.

Before me, a pair of double doors stood open and I could see into the living room, easily thirty feet long. Again, the walls on the far side were floor-to-ceiling glass, this time with a panoramic view of pines, live oaks, giant ferns, eucalyptus, and the mountains beyond. I listened and, hearing nothing, tiptoed into the room to have a better look. The wood-beamed

72

ceiling slanted upward to near-cathedral height. On the left, there was a marble-faced fireplace with a hearth twenty-six feet long. On the other end of the room, glass-enclosed shelves showcased a variety of art objects. To the left, I could see a built-in wet bar. The furniture was simple: large armless black leather couches and chairs, chrome-and-glass tables, a grand piano, recessed lighting.

I heard footsteps tap-tap-tapping down the hallway in my direction. I'd just managed to giant-step my way across the foyer to my original position when Dixie came into view. She wore skintight blue jeans, boots with spike heels, and a buff-colored blazer over a snowy white silk tank top. Her jewelry was Bakelite, two chunky bracelets that clattered on her narrow wrist. Now forty years old, she was still extremely thin: small hips, flat stomach, scarcely any butt to speak of. The shoulder pads in her jacket made it look like she was wearing protective gear. Her hair was pulled back away from her face, an oh-so-chic mess in a shade that suggested copious chemical assistance, a red somewhere between claret and burnt ocher. Gone were the false lashes and all the heavy black eyeliner. Curiously, the absence of makeup made her eyes seem much larger and her features more delicate. Her skin was sallow and there were dark circles under her eyes, lines in her forehead, cords showing in her neck. Hard to believe she hadn't yet availed herself of a little surgical refreshment. Even so, she looked glamorous. There was something brisk and brittle in the way she carried herself. She seemed to know who I was, using my name with an artificial warmth as she held out her hand. "Kinsey. How nice. What an incredible surprise. Stephie said you were here. It's been years."

"Hello, Dixie. You look great. I wasn't sure you'd remember me."

"How could I forget?" she said. "I'm sorry you missed Eric." Her gaze took me in without so much as a flicker of interest. Like her, I wore jeans, though mine were cut without style, the kind worn to wash cars or clean hair clots from the bathroom standpipe. In the years since I'd seen her, she'd risen in social stature, acquiring an almost indescribable air of elegance. No need to wear diamonds when plastic would do. Her jacket was wrinkled in the manner of expensive fabrics . . . linens and silks . . . you know how it is with that shit.

She glanced at her watch, which she wore on the inner aspect of her wrist. The watch was forties vintage, stingy-sized crystal surrounded by little bitty diamonds on a band of black cording. I'd seen nicer versions at the swap meet, which just goes to show what I know about these things. Hers was probably rare, recognizable on sight by those who shopped in the tony places she did. "Would you like a drink?" she asked. "It's nearly cocktail time."

My watch said 4:10. I said, "Sure, why not?" I almost made a joke about crème de menthe frappés, but a black guy in a white jacket had materialized, a silver tray in hand. A bartender of her own? This was getting good.

She said, "What would you like?"

"Chardonnay sounds fine."

"We'll be out on the patio," she remarked, without directly addressing her faithful attendant. My, my, my. Another cipher accounted for in the nameless servant class. I noticed Dixie didn't need to specify what she'd be drinking.

I followed her through the stone-floored dining room. The table was a rhomboid of cherry, with sufficient chairs assembled for a party of twelve. Something odd was at work, and it took me a moment to figure out what it was. There were no steps, no changes in elevation, no area rugs, and no signs of wall-to-wall carpet within view. I thought of Eric in his wheelchair, wondering if the floors were left bare for his benefit.

It struck me as peculiar that Dixie hadn't yet questioned the reason for my unannounced arrival at her door. Maybe she'd been waiting for me all these years, rehearsing responses to numerous imaginary conversations. She'd always known she'd been screwing around with Mickey, whereas I'd just found out, which put me at a disadvantage. I don't often go up against other women in verbal combat. Such clashes are strange, but not without a certain prurient attraction. I thought of all the male-fantasy movies where women fight like alley cats, pulling at each other's hair while they roll around on the floor. I'd never had much occasion, but maybe that would change. I could feel myself getting in touch with my "inner" mean streak.

Dixie opened a sliding glass door and we passed out onto a spacious screened-in patio. The floor here was smooth stone, and the area was rimmed with a series of twenty-foot trees in enormous terracotta pots. The branches were filled with goldfinches, all twittering as they hopped from limb to limb. There was a grouping of upholstered patio furniture nearby, in addition to a glass-topped table and four thickly cushioned chairs. Everything looked spotless. I wondered where the little birdies dropped their tiny green and white turds.

"This is actually a combination greenhouse and aviary. These are specimen plants, proteas and bromeliads. South American," she said.

I murmured "gorgeous" for lack of anything better. I thought a bromeliad was a remedy for acid indigestion. She gestured toward the conversational grouping of chairs. From somewhere, I could already smell dinner in the making. The scent of sautéed garlic and onion, like a sumptuous perfume, floated in the air. Maybe one of those no-name indentured servants would appear with a tray of eats, little tidbits of something I could fall on and snarf down without using my hands.

As soon as we sat down, the man reappeared with drinks on his tray. He gave us each a tiny cloth napkin in case we urped something up. Dixie's beverage of choice was a martini straight up in a forties-style glass. Four green olives were lined up on a toothpick like beads on an abacus. We each took a sip of our respective libations. My Chardonnay was delicate, with a long, slow, vanilla finish, probably nothing from a screw-top bottle at the neighborhood Stop 'n' Shop. I watched her hold the gin on her tongue like a communion ritual. She set the glass down with a faint tap and reached into her blazer pocket to extract a pack of cigarettes and a small gold lighter. She lit the cigarette, inhaling with a reverence that suggested smoking was another sacrament. When she caught me observing her, she opened her mouth to emit a thick tongue of smoke that she then sucked up her nose. "You don't smoke these days?"

I shook my head. "I quit."

"Good for you. I'll never give it up myself. All this talk about health is fairly tedious. You probably exercise, too." She cocked her head in reflection, striking a bemused pose. "Let's see. What's in fashion at the moment? You lift weights," she said, and pointed a finger in my direction.

"I jog five days a week, too. Don't forget that," I said, and pointed back at her.

She took another sip of her drink. "Stephie tells me you're looking for Mickey. Has he disappeared?"

"Not as far as I know, but I'd like to get in touch with him. The only number I have turns out to be a disconnect. Have you heard from him lately?"

"Not for years," she said. A smile formed on her lips, and she checked her fingernails. "That's a curious question. I can't believe you'd ask me. I'm sure there are other folks much more likely to know."

"Such as?"

"Shack, for one. And who's the other cop? Lit something. They were always thick as thieves."

"I just talked to Shack, which is how I got to you. Roy Littenberg died. I didn't realize you and Eric were still in town."

She studied me for a moment through her cigarette smoke. Miss Dixie wasn't dumb, and I could see her analyze the situation. "Where's all this coming from?"

"All what?"

"You have something else in mind."

I reached down for my shoulder bag and removed the letter from the outside pocket. "Got your letter," I said.

"My letter," she repeated blankly, her gaze fixed on the envelope.

"The one you sent me in 1972," I said. "Mickey tossed it in a box with some other mail that must have come the same day. He failed to deliver it, so I never read the letter until today." For once, I seemed to have captured her full attention.

"You're not serious."

"I am." I held up the letter like a paddle in a silent auction: My bid. "I had no idea you were balling my beloved husband. You want to talk about that?"

She laughed and then caught herself. Her teeth were now as perfect as white horseshoes hinged together at the rear of her mouth. "Sorry. I'm sorry. I hope you won't take offense, but you're such a boob when it comes to men."

"Thanks. You know how I value your opinion."

"Nothing to be ashamed of. Most women don't have the first clue about men."

"And you do?"

"Of course." Dixie studied me over the ribbon of cigarette smoke, taking my measure with her eyes. She paused and leaned forward to tap off a cylinder of ash into a cut-glass dish on the coffee table in front of her.

"What's your theory, Miss Dixie, if I may be so bold as to inquare?" I said, affecting a Southern accent.

"Take advantage of *them* before they take advantage of you," she said, her smile as thin as glass.

78

"Nice. Romantic. I better write that down." I pretended to make a note on the palm of my hand.

"Well, it's not *nice* but it's practical. In case you haven't noticed, most men don't give a shit about romance. They want to get in your panties and let it go at that. What else can I say?"

"That about covers it," I said. "May I ask, why him? There were dozens of cops at the Honky-Tonk back then."

She hesitated, apparently considering what posture to affect. "He was very good," she said, with a trace of a smile.

"I didn't ask for an evaluation. I'd like to know what went on."

"Why the attitude? You seem so . . . belligerent. In the end, you'd have left him anyway, so what do you care?"

"Indulge me," I said. "For the sake of argument."

She lifted one thin shoulder in a delicate shrug. "He and I were an item long before the two of you met. He broke it off for a while and then he came back. Why attach anything to it? We were not in love by any stretch. I might have *admired* him, but I can't say I liked him much. He had a rough kind of charm, but then again, you know that. I wouldn't even call it an affair in any true sense of the word. More like sexual addiction, a mutual service we performed. Or I should say, that's what it was for me. I don't know about him. It's a question of pathology. He probably couldn't help himself any more than I."

"Oh, please. Don't give me that horseshit about

sexual addiction. What crap," I said. "Did it ever occur to you that wedding vows mean something?"

"Yours didn't seem to mean much. Until death do us part? At least I'm still married, which is more than you can say. Or am I wrong about that? Rude of me. You might have married someone else and had a whole passel of kids. I would have asked before now, but I didn't see a ring."

"Were you with him the night Benny Quintero died?"

Her smiled faded. "Yes." Flat. No hesitation, no emotion, and no elaboration.

"Why didn't he tell me?"

"Did you really want to know?"

"It would have helped. I'm not sure what I'd have done, but it might have made a difference."

"I doubt that. You were such a cocky little thing. Really, quite obnoxious. You knew it all back then. Mickey wanted you spared."

"And why is that?"

"He was crazy about you. I'm surprised you'd have to ask."

"Given the fact he was screwing you," I said.

"You knew his history the day you married him. Did you seriously imagine he'd be monogamous?"

"Why'd you take it on yourself to tattle when Mickey asked you not to?"

"I was afraid he'd get a raw deal—which he did, as it turns out."

"Did Eric know about Mickey?"

There was the tiniest flicker of hesitation. "We've come to an accommodation—"

"I'm not talking about now. Did he know back then?"

She took a long, deliberate drag on her cigarette while she formed her reply. "Life was difficult for Eric. He had a hard time adjusting after he got back."

"In other words, no."

"There was no emotional content between Mickey and me. Why inflict unnecessary pain?"

"How about so your respective spouses knew the truth about you? As long as there's no love—as long as it's simply sexual servicing, as you claim—why couldn't you tell us?"

She was silent, giving me a wide-eyed stare.

"The question isn't hypothetical. I really want to know," I said. "Why not be honest with us if your relationship meant so little?" I waited. "Okay, I'll help. You want the answer? Try this. Because we'd have kicked your respective butts and put an end to it. I don't know about Eric, but I have no tolerance for infidelity."

"Perhaps there are things about loyalty you never grasped," she said.

I closed my eyes briefly. I wanted to lift her front chair legs and flip her backward, just for the satisfaction of hearing her head thud against the stone floor. Instead, I silently recited what I remembered of the penal code: *An assault is an unlawful attempt, coupled with a present ability, to commit a violent injury on the person of another. . . . A battery is any willful and unlawful use of force or violence upon the person of another.*

I smiled. "You think it was okay to make fools of

us? To gratify your whims at our expense? If you think *that's* loyalty, you're *really* fucked."

"You don't have to be crude."

Someone spoke from the far side of the patio. "Excuse me. Dixie?"

Both of us looked over. Stephie stood in the doorway.

For once, Dixie seemed embarrassed, and the color rose in her cheeks. "Yes, Stephie. What is it?"

"Ms. Yablonsky's here. Did you want to talk to her now or should I reschedule?"

Dixie exhaled with impatience, stubbing out her cigarette. "Have her wait in my office. I'll be there in a minute."

"Sure. No problem." Stephie closed the sliding glass door, watching for a moment before she moved away.

"This has gone far enough," Dixie said to me. "I can see you enjoy getting up on your high horse. You always liked claiming the moral high ground—"

"I do. That's correct. It's mine to claim in this case."

"When you've finished your drink, you can let yourself out."

"Thanks. This was fun. You haven't changed at all."

"Nor have you," she said.

SEVEN

I was halfway down the driveway, heading toward the road, when I saw a vehicle coming my way. It was a custom van of a sort I hadn't seen before, sleek, black, and boxy, with Eric Hightower at the wheel. I'm not sure I would have recognized him if I hadn't been half expecting to see him anyway. I slowed the VW to a crawl and gave a tap to the horn as I rolled down my window. He drew alongside me and pulled to a stop, rolling his window down in response. Underneath the tank top he wore, his bulging shoulders and biceps looked smooth and tanned. In the old Honky-Tonk days, his gaze was perpetually glassy and his skin had the pallor of a man who'd made a science of mixing his medications with alcohol, LSD, and grass. Then, his beard had been sparse and he'd worn his straight black hair loose across his shoulders or pulled back in a ponytail and tied with a rag.

The man who studied me quizzically from the driver's side of the van had been restored to good health. His head was now shaved, his skull as neat as a newborn's. Gone were the beard and the bleary-eyed stare. I'd seen pictures of Eric in uniform before he left for Vietnam: young and handsome, twenty-one years old, largely untouched by life. After two tours of duty, he'd come back to the world looking gaunt and abused, ill-humored and withdrawn. He'd seemed to have a lot on his mind, but nothing he was capable of explaining to the rest of us. And none of us dared ask. One look at his face was sufficient to convince us that what he'd seen was hellish and wouldn't bear close scrutiny. In retrospect, I suspect he imagined us judgmental and disapproving when in truth we were frightened of what we saw in his eyes. Better to look away than suffer that torment.

"Can I help you?" he asked.

"Hi, Eric. Kinsey Millhone. We hung around together years ago at the Tonk out in Colgate."

I watched his features clear and then brighten when he figured out who I was. "Hey. Of course. No fooling. How're you doing?" He leaned his left arm out the window and we touched fingertips briefly, as close to a handshake as we could manage from separate vehicles. His dark eyes were clear. In his drinking days, he'd been scrawny, but the process of aging had added the requisite fifteen pounds. Success sat well on him. He seemed substantial and self-possessed.

I said, "You look great. What happened to your hair?"

He glanced at himself in his rearview mirror, running a hand across his smooth-shaven skull. "You like it? It feels weird. I did that a month ago and can't quite decide."

"I do. It's better than the ponytail."

"Well, ain't that the truth. What brings you here?"

"I'm looking for my ex-husband and thought you might have a line on him." The possibility seemed far-fetched and I wondered if he'd press me on the subject, but he let it pass.

"Magruder? I haven't seen him in years."

"That's what Dixie said. I talked to Mickey's buddy, Shack, a little while ago and your names came up. You remember Pete Shackelford?"

"Vaguely."

"He thought you might know, but I guess not, huh?"

Eric said, "Sorry I can't help. What's the deal?"

"I'm not really sure. It looks like I have a debt to settle with him and I'd like to clear it."

"I can ask around, if you want. I still see some of those guys at the gym. One of them might know."

"Thanks, but I can probably manage on my own. I'll call his lawyer, and if that fails I've got some other little ways. I know how his mind works. Mickey's devious."

Eric's gaze held mine, and I felt an unspoken communication scuttle between us like the shadow of a cloud passing overhead. His mood seemed to shift and he let the sweep of his arm encompass the tree-strewn property surrounding us on all sides. "So what do you think? Nine point nine acres and it's paid off—all mine. Well, half mine, given California's community property laws."

"It's beautiful. You've done well."

"Thanks. I had help."

"Dixie or AA?"

"I'd have to say both."

85

A plumber's truck appeared in the driveway, pulling up behind Eric's van. He glanced back and waved to let the driver know he was aware of him and wouldn't take all day. He turned back to me. "Why don't you turn the car around and come back to the house? We can all have dinner together and spend time catching up."

"I'd love to, but I'd better not. Dixie's got interviews and I have some things to take care of myself. Maybe another time. I'll give you a call and we can set something up." I put my car in gear.

"Great. Do that. You promise?"

"Scout's honor."

The driver of the truck behind him gave an impatient beep on his horn. Eric glanced back at him and waved again. "Anyway, nice to see you. Behave yourself."

"You too."

He rolled his window up, and I could see him accelerate with the help of a device on his steering wheel. It was the only reminder I'd had that he was a double amputee. He tapped his horn as he departed and I continued down the driveway, the two of us moving in opposite directions.

I headed into town, pondering the nature of the divine comedy. Two of my pet beliefs had been reversed in the past few hours. Given the brevity of my marriage to Mickey, I'd always assumed he'd been faithful. That notion turned out to be false so it was stricken from the record, along with any lingering confidence I felt. I'd also suspected—well, let's be honest about this—I'd been *convinced* Mickey'd played a part in Benny Quintero's death. It turned out he hadn't, so we could strike that one, too. Guilty of infidelity, innocent of manslaughter. Someone with talent could convert that to lyrics for a country-western tune. In some ways Dixie'd nailed it. Did I really want to know about this shit? I guess I didn't have a choice. The question was what to do with it?

The minute I hit the office, I hauled out the telephone book and leafed through the yellow pages to the section listing attorneys. I ran a finger down the column until I found Mark Bethel's name in a little box of its own. The ad read CRIMINAL DEFENSE and, under that heading, specified the following: Drugs, Molest, Weapons, White Collar, DUI, Theft/Fraud, Assault, Spousal Abuse, and Sex Crimes, which I thought just about covered it—except for murder, of course. Mark Bethel had been Mickey's attorney when he resigned from the department, a move Mickey'd made on Mark's advice. I'd never been crazy about Mark, and after Mickey's unceremonious departure there was little reason for our paths to cross. On the odd occasion when I ran into him around town, we tended to be cordial, feigning a warmth neither of us felt. We were bound by old business, one of those uneasy alliances that survived more on form than content. Despite my lukewarm attitude, I had to admit he was an excellent attorney, though in the past few years he'd set his practice aside in his bid for public office—one Republican among many hoping for a shot at Alan Cranston's Senate seat in the coming November elections. In the past ten

87

years, his political ambitions had begun to emerge. He'd allied himself with the local party machine, ingratiating himself with Republicans by working tirelessly on Deukmejian's 1982 gubernatorial campaign. He'd opened his Montebello home for countless glitzy fundraisers. He'd run for and won a place on the county board of supervisors; then he'd run for state assembly. Logically, his next step should have been a try for Congress, but he'd skipped that and entered the primary for a U.S. Senate seat. He must have felt his political profile was sufficient to net him the kind of votes he'd need to outstrip Ed Zschau. Fat chance, in my opinion, but then what did I know? I hate politicians; they lie more flagrantly than I do and with a lot less imagination. It helped that Bethel was married to a woman who had a fortune of her own.

I'd heard through the grapevine Laddie Bethel was bankrolling the major portion of his campaign. She'd made a name for herself locally as a fund-raiser of some persuasion for numerous charitable organizations. Whatever worthy cause she adopted, she certainly wasn't shy about sending me donation requests with a return envelope enclosed. Inevitably, there was a series of amounts to be circled: $2,500, $1,000, $500, $250. If the charitable event was an evening affair—"black tie optional" (in case your green one was at the cleaners)—I'd also be offered the opportunity to buy a "table" for my cronies at a thousand dollars a plate. Little did she know I was, by nature, so cheap that I'd sit there and pick the stamp off the prestamped envelope. In the meantime, Mark maintained an office and a secretary with his old law firm.

I dialed Mark Bethel's office, and his secretary answered, followed by an immediate "May I put you on hold?"

By the time I said sure, she was already gone. I was treated to a jazz rendition of "Scarborough Fair."

Mark's secretary clicked back on the line. "Thanks for holding. This is Judy. May I help you?"

"Yes, hi, Judy. This is Kinsey Millhone. I'm an old friend of Mark's. I think I met you at the Bethels' Christmas party a couple of years back. Is he there by any chance?"

"Oh, hi, Kinsey. I remember you," she said. "No, he's off at a committee meeting, probably gone for the day. You want him to call in the morning, or is there something I can do?"

"Maybe," I said. "I'm trying to get in touch with my ex-husband. Mickey Magruder was a client of his."

"Oh, I know Mickey," she said, and right away I wondered if she *knew* him in the biblical sense.

"Do you know if Mark has a current address and phone number?"

"Hold on and I'll check. I know we have something, because he called here a couple months ago and I spoke to him myself." I could hear pages rattling as she leafed through her book.

"Ah, here we go." She recited an address on Sepulveda, but the house number differed from the one I had. The digits were the same but the order was changed, which was typical of Mickey. In his semiparanoid state, he'd give the correct information but with the numbers transposed so you couldn't pin him down. He thought your address was your own damn business and phones were meant for *your* convenience, not anyone else's. If other people couldn't call him, what did he care? I don't know how he managed to receive his mail or have pizza delivered. Those were not issues he found interesting when his privacy was at stake. Judy chimed back in, and the phone number she recited was a match for the one I had in my book.

I said, "You can scratch that one out. I tried it a while ago, and it's a disconnect. I thought maybe Mickey moved or had the number changed."

I could hear her hesitate. "I probably shouldn't say this. Mark hates when I discuss a client, so please don't tell him I said this—"

"Of course not."

"When Mickey called—this would have been mid-March—he did ask to borrow money. I mean, he didn't ask *me*. This is just what I heard later, after Mark talked to him. Mark said Mickey'd had to sell his car because he couldn't afford the upkeep and insurance, let alone the gas. He's got financial problems even Mark couldn't bail him out of."

"That doesn't sound good. Did Mark lend him any money?"

"I'm not really sure. He might have. Mickey was always one of Mark's favorites."

"Could you check your message carbons and see if Mickey left a number where Mark could reach him?"

"I'll check if you like, but I remember asking at the time, and he said Mark would know."

"So Mark might have another number?"

"It's possible, I guess. I can ask and have him call you."

"I'd appreciate that. He can buzz me tomorrow and we'll take it from there." I left her my number and we clicked off.

My evening was unremarkable—dinner with Henry at Rosie's Tavern half a block away—after which I curled up with a book and read until I fell asleep, probably ten whole minutes later.

I turned off the alarm moments before it was set to ring. I brushed my teeth, pulled on my sweats, and went out for a three-mile jog. The bike path along the beach was cloaked in the usual spring fog, the sky a uniform gray, the ocean blended at the horizon as though a scrim of translucent plastic had been stretched taut between the two. The air temperature was perfect, faintly chill, faintly damp. I was feeling light and strong, and I ran with a rare sense of happiness.

Home again, I showered, dressed, and ate breakfast, then hopped in my car and hit the road for San Felipe with the receipt from the storage company tucked in my pocket. I'd dressed up to some extent, which in my case doesn't amount to much. I only own one dress: black, collarless, with long sleeves and a tucked bodice (which is a fancy word for front). This entirely synthetic garment, guaranteed wrinkle-free (but probably flammable), is as versatile as anything I've owned. In it, I can accept invitations to all but the snootiest of cocktail parties, pose as a mourner at any funeral, make court appearances, conduct surveillance, hustle clients, interview hostile witnesses, traffic with known felons, or pass myself off as a gainfully employed

91

person instead of a freelance busybody accustomed to blue jeans, turtlenecks, and tennis shoes.

Before I departed, I'd taken a few minutes to complete a generic claim form that I'd dummied up from my days of working at California Fidelity Insurance. As I headed south on 101, I practiced the prissy, bureaucratic attitude I affect when I'm masquerading as someone else. Being a private investigator is made up of equal parts ingenuity, determination, and persistence, with a sizable dose of acting skills thrown in.

The drive to San Felipe took forty-five minutes. The scenery en route consisted largely of citrus and avocado groves, stretches of farmland, and occasional roadside markets selling—what else?—oranges, lemons, and avocados. I spotted the storage company from half a mile away. It was just off the main road, countless rows of two-story buildings, occupying two square blocks. The architectural style suggested a newly constructed California prison, complete with floodlights and tall chain-link fences.

I turned in at the gate. The buildings were identical: cinder block and blank doors, with wide freight elevators and a loading ramp at each end. The units were marked alphabetically and numerically in a system I couldn't quite decipher. The doors in each section appeared to be color-coded, but maybe that was simply an architectural flourish. It couldn't be much fun designing a facility that looked like cracker boxes arranged end to end. I passed a number of broad alleyways. Arrows directed me to the main office, where I parked and got out.

I pushed through the glass door to a serviceable

space, maybe twenty feet by twenty with a counter running across the center. The area on the far side of the counter was taken up by rental-quality file cabinets and a plain wooden desk. This was not a multilayered company with the administration assuming any lofty position. The sole individual on duty apparently functioned as receptionist, secretary, and plant manager, sitting at a typewriter with a pencil in his mouth while he hunt-and-pecked his way through a memorandum of some sort. I guessed he was in his late seventies, round-faced and balding, with a pair of reading glasses worn low on his nose. I could see his belly bulging out like an infant monkey clinging closely to its mother's chest. "Be with you in just a second," he said, typing on.

"Take your time."

"How do you spell 'mischeevious'?"

"M-i-s-c-h-i-e-v-o-u-s."

"You sure? Doesn't look right."

"Pretty sure," I said.

When he'd finished, he stood up, separated the carbons, and tucked both the original and the copies in matching blue folders. He came over to the counter, hitching up his pants. "Didn't mean to keep you waiting, but I was on a tear," he said. "When business is slow, I write stories for my great-grandson. Kid's barely two and reads like a champ. Loves his pappaw's little booklets written just for him. This one's about a worm name of Wiggles and his escapades. Lot of fun for me, and you should see Dickie's little face light up. I figure one day I'll get 'em published and have 'em done up proper. I have a lady friend offered to do the illustrations, but somebody told me that's a bad idea. I guess these New York types like to hire their own artists."

"News to me," I said.

His cheeks tinted faintly and his tone of voice became shy. "I don't suppose you know an agent might take a look at this."

"I don't, but if I hear of one, I'll let you know."

"That'd be good. Meantime, what can I do for you?"

I showed him my California Fidelity Insurance identification, which bore an old photograph of me and the company seal of approval.

His gaze shifted from the photo to my face. "You oughta get you a new photo. This doesn't do you justice. You're a lot better looking."

"You really think so? Thanks. By the way, I'm Kinsey Millhone. And you're . . . ?"

"George Wedding."

"Nice to meet you."

"I hope you're not selling policies. I'd hate to disappoint, but I'm insured to the hilt."

"I'm not selling anything, but I could use some help." I hesitated. I had a story all ready. I intended to show him a homeowner's claim listing several items lost to flooding when some water pipes broke. Of course, this was all completely false, but I was hoping he'd react with sufficient moral indignation to set the record straight. What I wanted was the address and phone number Mickey'd used when he'd rented the space. I could then compare the information to facts already in my possession and thus (perhaps) figure out where the hell Mickey was. In my mind, on the way down, I'd spun the story out to a convincing degree, but now that I was here I couldn't bring myself to tell it. This is the truth about lying: You're putting one over on some poor gullible dunce, which makes him appear stupid for not spotting the deception. Lying contains the same hostile elements as a practical joke in that the "victim" ends up looking foolish in his own eyes and laughable in everyone else's. I'm willing to lie to pompous bureaucrats, when thwarted by knaves, or when all else fails, but I was having trouble lying to a man who wrote worm adventure stories for his great-grandson. George was patiently waiting for me to go on. I folded the bogus claim in half until the bottom of the page rested a couple of inches from the top and the only lines showing were those containing the name, address, and telephone number of "John Russell."

"You want to know the truth?"

"That'd be nice," he said blandly.

"Ah. Well, the truth is I was fired by CFI about three years ago. I'm actually a private investigator, looking for a man I was once married to." I pointed to John Russell's name. "That's not his real name, but I suspect the address may be roughly correct. My ex scrambles numbers as a way of protecting himself."

"Is this police business? Because my records are confidential, unless you have a court order. If you think this fellow was using his storage unit for illegal purposes . . . manufacturing drugs, for instance . . . you might talk me into it. Otherwise, no deal."

I could almost have sworn George was inviting me to fib, given that he'd laid out the conditions under which he might be persuaded to open his files to me. However, having started with the truth, I thought I might as well stick to my guns. "You're making this tough. I wish I could tell you otherwise, but this isn't related to any criminal activity—at least, as far as I know. Uhm . . . wow . . . this is hard. I'm not used to this," I said. "He and I parted enemies and it's just come to my attention I misjudged him badly. I can't live with my conscience until I square things with him. I know it sounds corny, but it's true."

"What'd you do?" George asked.

"It's not what I did. It's what I didn't do," I said. "He was implicated in a murder—well, not a murder, really, manslaughter is more like it. The point is I didn't wait to hear his side of it. I just assumed he was guilty and walked out on him. I feel bad about that. I promised 'for better or for worse' and gave him 'worse.' "

"So now what?"

"So now I'm trying to track him down so I can apologize. Maybe I can make amends . . . if it's not too late."

George's face was a study in caution. "I'm not entirely clear what you want from me."

I passed him the form, tilting my head to read the header along with him. I pointed to the relevant lines. "I think this is partly right. I've got two versions of this address. If yours matches this one or if you have another variation yet, I can probably determine which is correct."

He studied the name and address. "I remember this fellow. Went delinquent on his payments. We emptied his unit and auctioned everything off."

"That's what worries me. I think he's in trouble. Do you think you can help?"

I could see him vacillate. I left the clipboard up on the counter, angled in his direction. I could see his gaze retracing the lines of print. He moved to a file cabinet, scanned the labels on the drawer fronts, and opened the third one down. He pulled out a fat binder and laid it across the open drawer. He wet his thumb and began to leaf through. He found the relevant page, popped open the rings, removed a sheet of paper, and copied it, handing me the information without another word.

EIGHT

I returned to the office, where I spent the rest of the day paying bills, returning phone calls, and taking care of correspondence. There was no message from Mark Bethel. I'd try him again if I didn't hear from him soon. I locked my office at four-thirty, shoving my Los Angeles street map in the outer pouch of my bag. I left my car for the time being and walked over to the public library, where I checked the crisscross for the area encompassed by the three differing Sepulveda street numbers Mickey'd listed as his home address. It was impossible to determine the best candidate from looking at a map. I was going to have to make a run down there. It was time to satisfy myself as to his current situation, maybe even time for the two of us to talk. I had a big whack of money in my savings account. I was willing to offer my help if Mickey wasn't too proud to accept. I walked back to the office, where I picked up my car and made the short drive home. I didn't even have the details and I was already sick about the part I'd played in his slide from grace.

I arrived at my apartment to find two gentlemen standing on my doorstep. I knew in a flash they were plainclothes detectives: neatly dressed, clean-shaven, their expressions bland and attentive, the perfect law enforcement presence on this May afternoon. I felt a spritz of electricity coursing through my frame. My hands were left tingling and the skin on my back suddenly felt luminous, like a neon sign flashing GUILT—GUILT—GUILT. My first thought was Teddy Rich had reported an intruder, that an officer had been dispatched, that he'd called for a tech who'd subsequently dusted for prints. Mine would have shown up on the inner and outer aspects of the pet door, on the edge of the desk, on the back doorknob, in other places so numerous I could hardly recall. I'd been a cop for two years and a P.I. since then. (I'd also been arrested once, but I don't want to talk about that now, thanks.)

The point is, my prints were in the system, and the computer was going to put me inside Teddy Rich's house. The cops would ask what I was doing there and what could I say? Was there an innocent explanation? I couldn't think of one to save me. The dog, of course, would pick me out of a police lineup, tugging at my pant leg, joyously barking, jumping, and slobbering on my shoes as they cuffed me and took me away. I could try to plea-bargain right up front or wait until sentencing and throw myself on the mercy of the court.

I hesitated on the walkway, my house keys in hand. Surely, the cops had more pressing cases to pursue these days. Why would they even bother with a crime scene tech? The notion was absurd. These fellows might not be cops at all. Maybe Teddy figured out what I'd done and had sent these two goons to crush my elbows, my knees, and other relevant joints. Somewhat chirpily, I said, "Hi. Are you looking for me?"

The two of them seemed to be approximately the same age: late thirties, trim, fit, one dark, the other fair. The blond carried a briefcase in his left hand like he was doing door-to-door sales. He spoke first. "Miss Millhone?" He wore a red plaid shirt under a tweed sport coat, his Adam's apple compressed by the knot in his solid red tie. His slacks were dark cotton, wrinkled across the crotch from sitting in the car too long.

"That's right."

He held out his right hand. "My name's Felix Claas. This is my partner, John Aldo. We're detectives with the Los Angeles Police Department. Could we talk to you?"

Aldo held out two business cards and a wallet he flipped open to expose his badge. Detective Aldo was a big guy with a muscular body, probably six-three, 240 pounds. He wore his dark hair slightly shaggy, and his dark eyes receded under wide dark eyebrows that came together at the bridge of his nose. His slacks were polyester, and he had a sport coat neatly folded and laid across one arm. His short-sleeved cotton shirt exposed a matting of silky hair on his forearms. He looked like a man who preferred wearing sweats. I'd heard his first name as "John," but I noticed on his business card the spelling was the Italian, Gian, and I made the mental correction. In the flush of apprehension, I'd already forgotten the first detective's name. I glanced down at the cards again. Felix Claas was the blond, Gian Aldo, the darker one.

Claas spoke up again, smiling pleasantly. His blond hair looked wet, parted on the side and combed straight back behind his ears. His eyebrows and lashes were an almost invisible pale gold, so that his blue eyes seemed stark. His lips were full and unusually pink. He had a cleft in his chin. "Great town you have here. The minute we crossed the county line, I could feel my blood pressure drop about fifteen points."

"Thanks. We're lucky. It's like this all year long. We get a marine layer sometimes in the summer months, but it burns off by noon so it's hard to complain." Maybe this pertained to an old case of mine.

Detective Aldo eased into the conversation. "We had a chat with Lieutenant Robb. I hope we haven't caught you at a bad time."

"Not at all. This is fine. You're friends of his?"

"Well, no, ma'am, we aren't. We've talked to him by phone, but we only met today. Seems like a nice guy."

"He's great. I've known Jonah for years," I said. "What's this about?"

"A case we've been working on. We'd like to talk to you inside, if you don't object."

Detective Claas chimed in, "This shouldn't take long. Fifteen–twenty minutes. We'll be as quick as we can."

"Sure. Come on in." I turned and unlocked the front door, talking over my shoulder. "When'd you get up here?"

"About an hour ago. We tried calling your office, but they told us you'd left. We must have just missed you."

"I had some errands to run," I said, wondering why I felt I owed them an explanation. I stepped across the threshold and they followed me in. In the past few years, a number of investigations had taken me to Los Angeles. One of the cases I'd handled for California Fidelity had exposed me to a bunch of bad-asses. This was probably related. The criminal element form a special subset, the same names surfacing over and over again. It's always interesting to find out what the cruds are up to.

I took a mental photograph of my apartment, idly aware of how it must appear to strangers. Small, immaculate, as compact as a ship's interior complete with cubbyholes and built-ins. Kitchenette to the right; desk and seating arrangement to the left. Royal-blue shag carpet, a small spiral staircase leading to a loft above. I set my shoulder bag on one of the stools at the kitchen counter and moved the six steps into the living room.

The two detectives waited in the doorway deferentially.

"Have a seat," I said.

Aldo said, "Thanks. Nice place. You live alone?"

"As a matter of fact, I do."

"Lucky you. My girlfriend's a slob. There's no way I can keep my place looking this clean."

Claas sat down on the small sofa tucked into the bay window, setting his briefcase on the floor beside him. While Claas and Aldo seemed equally chatty, Claas was more reserved, nearly prim in his verbal manner, while Aldo seemed relaxed. Detective Aldo took one of the two matching director's chairs, which left me with the other. I sat down, feeling subtly maneuvered, though I wasn't sure why. Aldo slouched in the chair with his legs spread, his hands hanging between his knees. The canvas on the director's chair sagged and creaked beneath his shifting weight. His thighs were enormous, and his posture seemed both indolent and intimidating. Claas flicked him a look and he altered his posture, sitting up straight.

Claas turned his attention back to me. "We understand you were married to a former vice detective named Magruder."

I was completely taken aback. "Mickey? That's right. Is this about him?" I felt a tingle of fear. Connections tumbled together in a pattern I couldn't quite discern. Whatever was going on, it had to be associated with his current financial straits. Maybe he'd robbed a bank, scammed someone, or pulled a disappearing act. Maybe there was a warrant outstanding, and these guys had been assigned the job of tracking him down. I covered my discomfort with a laugh. "What's he up to?"

Claas's expression remained remote. "Unfortunately, Mr. Magruder was the victim of a shooting. He survived . . . he's alive, but he's not doing well. Yesterday we finally got a line on him. At the time of the assault, he didn't have identification in his possession, so he was listed as a John Doe until we ran his prints."

"He was *shot*?" I could feel myself move the needle back to the beginning of the cut. Had I heard him correctly?

"Yes, ma'am."

"He's all right, though, isn't he?"

Claas's tone ranged somewhere between neutrality and regret. "Tell you the truth, it's not looking so good. Doctors say he's stable, but he's on life support. He's never regained consciousness, and the longer this goes on, the less likely he is to make a full recovery."

Or any at all was what I heard. I could feel myself blink. Mickey dying or dead? The detective was still talking, but I felt I was suffering a temporary hearing loss. I held a hand up. "Hang on. I'm sorry, but I can't seem to comprehend."

"There's no hurry. Take your time," Aldo said.

I took a couple of deep breaths. "This is weird. Where is he?"

"UCLA. He's currently in ICU, but he may be transferred to County, depending on his condition."

"He always had good insurance coverage, if it's a question of funds." The notion of Mickey at County didn't sit well with me. I was taking deep breaths, risking hyperventilation in my attempt to compose myself. "Can I see him?"

There was a momentary pause, and then Claas said, "Not just yet, but we can probably work something out." He seemed singularly unenthusiastic, and I didn't press the point.

Aldo watched me with concern. "Are you okay?"

"I'm fine. I'm just surprised," I said. "I don't know what I thought you were doing here, but it wasn't this. I can't believe anything bad could ever happen to him. He was always a brawler, but he seemed invincible . . . at least to me. What happened?"

"That's what we're trying to piece together," Claas

said. "He'd been shot twice, once in the head and once in the chest. A patrolman spotted him lying on the sidewalk little after three A.M. The weapon, a semiautomatic, was found in the gutter about ten feet away. This was a commercial district, a lot of bars in the area, so it's possible Mr. Magruder got into a dispute. We have a couple of guys out now canvassing the neighborhood. So far no witnesses. For now, we're working backward, trying to get a line on his activities prior to the shooting."

"When *was* this?"

"Early morning hours of May fourteenth. Wednesday of last week."

Claas said, "Do you mind if we ask you a couple of questions?"

"Not at all. Please do."

I expected one of them to take out a notebook, but none emerged. I glanced at the briefcase and wondered if I was being recorded. Meanwhile, Claas was talking on. "We're in the process of eliminating some possibilities. This is mostly filling in the blanks, if you can help us out."

"Sure, I'll try. I'm not sure how, but fire away," I said. Inwardly, I flinched at my choice of words.

Claas cleared his throat. His voice was lighter, reedier. "When you last spoke to your ex-husband, did he mention any problems? Threats, disputes, anything like that?"

I leaned forward, relieved. "I haven't spoken to Mickey in fourteen years."

Something flickered between them, one of those

105

wordless conversations married couples learn to conduct with their eyes. Detective Aldo took over. "You're the owner of a nine-millimeter Smith and Wesson?"

"I was at one time." I was on the verge of saying more but decided to rein myself in until I figured out where they were going. The empty box that had originally housed the gun was still sitting in the carton beside my desk, less than six feet away.

Claas said, "Can you tell us when you purchased it?"

"I didn't. Mickey bought that gun and gave it to me as a wedding gift. That was August of 1971."

"Strange wedding present," Aldo remarked.

"He's a strange guy," I said.

"Where's the gun at this time?"

"Beats me. I haven't laid eyes on it for years. I assumed Mickey took it with him when he moved to L.A."

"So you haven't seen the gun since approximately . . ."

I looked from Claas to Aldo as the obvious implications began to sink in. I'd been slow on the uptake. "Wait a minute. *That* was the gun used?"

"Let's put it this way: Yours was the gun that was found at the scene. We're still waiting for ballistics."

"You can't think I had anything to do with it."

"Your name popped up in the computer as the registered owner. We're looking for a starting point, and this made sense. If Mr. Magruder carried the gun, it's possible someone took it away from him and shot him with it."

"That puts *me* in the clear," I said facetiously. I felt

like biting my tongue. Sarcasm is the wrong tack to take with cops. Better to play humble and cooperative.

A silence settled between the two. They'd seemed friendly and confiding, but I knew from experience there'd be a sizable gap between the version they'd given me and the one they'd withheld. Aldo took a stick of gum from his coat pocket and tore it in half. He tucked half in his pocket and slipped the paper wrapper and the foil from the other half. He slid the chewing gum into his mouth. He seemed disinterested for the moment, but I knew they'd spend the return trip comparing notes, matching their reactions and intuitions against the information I'd given them.

Claas shifted on the couch. "Can you tell us when you last spoke to Mr. Magruder?"

"It's Mickey. Please use his first name. This is hard enough as it is. He left Santa Teresa in 1972. I don't remember talking to him after we divorced."

"Can you tell us what contact you've had since then?"

"You just asked that. I've had none."

Claas's gaze fixed on mine, rather pointedly, I thought. "You haven't spoken to him in the past few months," he said—not a question, but a statement infused with skepticism.

"No. Absolutely not. I haven't talked to him."

While Detective Claas tried to hold my attention, I could see that Aldo was making a discreet visual tour of the living room. His gaze moved from item to item, methodically assessing everything within range. Desk, files, box, answering machine, bookshelves. I could almost hear him thinking to himself: *Which of these objects doesn't belong?* I saw his focus shift back to the cardboard box. So far, I hadn't said a word about the delinquent payments on Mickey's storage bin. On the face of it, I couldn't see how withholding the information represented any criminal behavior on my part. What justice was I obstructing? Who was I aiding and abetting? I didn't shoot my ex. I wasn't in custody and wasn't under oath. If it seemed advisable, I could always contact the detectives later when I "remembered" something relevant. All this went through my mind in the split second while I was busy covering my butt. If the two picked up on my uneasiness, neither said a word. Not that I expected them to gasp and exchange significant looks.

Detective Claas cleared his throat again. "What about him? Has he been in touch with you?"

I confess a little irritability was creeping into my response. "That's the same thing, isn't it, whether I talk to him or he talks to me? We divorced years ago. We don't have any reason to stay in touch. If he called, I'd hang up. I don't want to talk to him."

Aldo's tone was light, nearly bantering. "What are you so mad about? The poor guy's down for the count."

I felt myself flush. "Sorry. That's just how it is. We're not one of those couples that turned all lovey-dovey once the papers were signed. I have nothing against him, but I've never been interested in being his best friend . . . nor he mine, I might add."

"Same with my ex," he said. "Still, sometimes there's a piece of business—you know, a stock certificate or news of an old pal. You might forward the mail, even if you hate their guts. It's not unusual for one ex to drop the other a note if something relevant comes up."

"Mickey doesn't write notes."

Claas shifted in his seat. "What's he do then, call?"

I could feel myself grow still. Why was he so determined to pursue the point? "Look. For the fourth or fifth time now, Mickey and I don't talk. Honest. Cross my heart. Scout's honor and all that. We're not enemies. We're not antagonistic. We just don't have that kind of relationship."

"Really. How would you characterize it? Friendly? Distant? Cordial?"

"What *is* this?" I said. "What's the relevance? I mean, come on, guys. You can't be serious. Why would I shoot my ex-husband with my own gun and leave it at the scene? I'd have to be nuts."

Aldo smiled to himself. "People get rattled. You never know what they'll do. We're just looking for information. Anything you can give us, we'd appreciate."

"Tell me your theory," I said.

"We don't have a theory," Claas said. "We're hoping to eliminate some angles. You could save us a lot of time if you'd cooperate."

"I'm *doing* that. This is what cooperation looks like, in case you're not accustomed to it. You're barking up the wrong tree. I don't even know where Mickey lives these days."

The two detectives stared at me.

"I'm telling you the truth."

Detective Claas asked the next question without

109

reference to his notes. "Can you tell us where you were on March twenty-seventh?"

My mind went blank. "I haven't the faintest idea. Where were you?" I said. I could tell my hands were going to start shaking. My fingers were cold, and without even thinking about it, I crossed my arms and tucked my hands against my sides. I knew I looked stubborn and defensive, but I was suddenly unnerved.

"Do you have an appointment book you might check?"

"You know what? I think we should stop this conversation right now. If you're here because you think I was somehow involved in a shooting, you'll have to talk to my attorney because I'm done with this bullshit."

Detective Aldo seemed surprised. "Hey, come on. There's no call for that. We're not accusing you of anything. This is an exchange of information."

"What was exchanged? I tell you things, but what do you tell me? Or did I miss that part?"

Aldo smiled, undismayed by my prickliness. "We told you he was injured and you told us you never talked to him. See? We tell you and then you tell us. It's like a dialogue. We're trading."

"Why did you ask where I was March twenty-seventh? What's that about?"

Claas spoke up. "We checked his telephone bills. There was a call to this number that lasted thirty minutes. We assumed the two of you talked. Unless someone else lives here, which you've denied."

"Show me," I said. I held out my hand.

He leaned down and reached into the partially

opened briefcase, sliding out a sheaf of phone bills, which he passed to me without comment. On top of the stack was Mickey's bill for April, itemizing his March service. I glanced at the header, noting that the phone number on the account was the same one I had. At that point, his February bill was already in arrears. The past-due notice warned that if his payment wasn't received within ten days, his service would be terminated. I let my eye drift down the column of toll calls and long-distance charges for March. Only two calls had been made, both to Santa Teresa. The first was March 13, made to Mark Bethel's office. I'd heard about that from Judy. The second was to my number. Sure enough, that call was made on March 27 at 1:27 P.M. and lasted, as specified, for a full thirty minutes.

NINE

I'm not sure how I got through the remainder of the conversation. Eventually the detectives left, with phony thanks on their part for all the help I'd given them, and phony assurances on mine that I'd contact them directly if I had anything more to contribute to their investigation. As soon as the door closed, I scurried into the bathroom, where I stepped into the empty bathtub and discreetly spied on them through the window. I kept just out of sight while Detectives Claas and Aldo, chatting in low tones, got into what looked like a county-issued car and drove away. I'd have given anything to know what they were saying—assuming the discussion was about Mickey or me. Maybe they were talking sports, which I don't give a rat's ass about.

As soon as they were gone, I returned to my desk and flipped back through my desk calendar to the page for March 27. That Thursday was entirely empty, as were the days on either side: No appointments, no meetings, no notation of events, professional or social. Typically, I'd have spent the day at the office, doing God knows what. I was hoping my desk calendar would jump-start my recollection. For the moment, I was stumped. All I knew was I hadn't talked to Mickey on March 27 or any other day in recent years. Had someone broken into my apartment? That was a creepy prospect, but what other explanation was there? Mickey could have dialed my number and spoken to someone else. It was also possible someone other than Mickey made the call from his place, establishing a connection that didn't actually exist. Who would go to such lengths? A person or persons who intended to shoot my ex-husband and have the finger point at me.

It rained during the night, one of those rare tropical storms that sometimes blow in from Hawaii without warning. I woke at 2:36 A.M. to the sound of heavy raindrops drumming on my skylight. The air gusting through the open window smelled of ocean brine and gardenias. May in California tends to be cool and dry. During the summer months following, vegetation languishes without moisture, a process of dehydration that renders the chaparral as fragile as ancient parchment. The rolling hills turn gold while the roadsides glow hazy yellow with the clouds of wild mustard growing along the berm. By August, the temperatures climb into the 80s and the relative humidity drops. Winds tear down the mountains and squeeze through canyons. Between the sundowners, Santa Anas, and the desiccated landscape, the stage is set for the arsonist's match. Rains might offer temporary relief, delaying the inevitable by a week or two. The irony is that rain does little more than encourage growth, which in turn provides nature with additional combustible fuel.

113

By the time I woke again at 5:59, the storm had passed. I pulled on my sweats and went out for my run, returning to the apartment only long enough to toss a canvas duffel in the car and head over to the gym. I lifted weights for an hour, working my way through my usual routine. Though I'd only been back at the process for two months, I was seeing results, shoulders and biceps taking form again.

I was home at nine. I showered, ate breakfast, tossed some items in my fanny pack, grabbed my shoulder bag, left a note on Henry's door, and hit the road for L.A. Traffic was fast-moving, southbound cars barreling down the 101. At this time of day, the road was heavily populated with commercial vehicles: pickups and panel trucks, semis and moving vans, empty school buses, and trailers hauling new cars to the showrooms in Westlake and Thousand Oaks. As I crested the hill and eased down into the San Fernando Valley, I could see the gauzy veil of the smog that had already begun to accumulate. The San Gabriel Mountains, often obscured from view, were at least visible today. Every time I passed this way, new construction was under way. What looked like entire villages would appear on the crest of a hill, or a neighborhood of identical condominiums would emerge from behind a stand of trees. Billboards announced the availability of new communities previously unheard of.

Overhead, two bright yellow aircraft circled, one following the other in an aerial surveillance focused on those of us down below. The berm was littered with trash, and at one point I passed one of those perplexing curls of tire tread that defy explanation. Once I reached

Sherman Oaks, I turned right on the San Diego Freeway. The foliage along the berm was whipped by the perpetual wind of passing vehicles. Several towering office buildings obstructed the view, like sightseers on a parade route with no consideration for others. I took the off-ramp at Sunset and drove east until the UCLA campus began to appear on my right. I turned right onto Hilgard, right again on Le Conte, and right onto Tiverton, where I paid for a parking voucher. There were no parking spots available in the aboveground lot. I began my descent into the underground levels, circling down and down until I finally found a spot on C-1. I locked my car and took the elevator up. The extensive grass and concrete plaza served both the Jules Stein Eye Clinic and the UCLA Hospital and Medical Center. I crossed to the main entrance and entered the lobby, with its polished granite walls and two-tone gray carpet with a smoky pink stripe along the edge. The reception area on the right was filled with people awaiting word of friends and family members currently undergoing surgery. Two teenage girls in shorts and T-shirts were playing cards on the floor. There were babies in infant seats and a toddler in a stroller, flushed and sweating in sleep. Others were reading newspapers or chatting quietly while a steady foot traffic of visitors crossed and recrossed the lounge. The lobby chairs and adjoining planters were boxy gray modules. On the left, the gift shop was faced in a curious hue somewhere between mauve and orchid. A large glass case contained sample floral arrangements in case you arrived to see someone without a posy in hand.

Dead ahead, above the information desk, the word

INFORMATION was writ large. I waited my turn and then asked a Mrs. Lewis, the patient information volunteer, for Mickey Magruder's room. She was probably in her seventies, her eyelids crepey as a turtle's. Age had cut knife pleats in the fragile skin on her cheeks, and her lips were pulled together in a pucker, like a drawstring purse. She did a quick check of her files and began to shake her head with regret. "I don't show anybody by that name. When was he admitted, dear?"

"On the fourteenth. I guess he could be registered as Michael. That's how the name reads on his birth certificate."

She made a note of the name and consulted another source. Her knuckles were knotted with arthritis, but her cursive was delicate. "Well, I don't know what to tell you. Is it possible he's been discharged?"

"I doubt it. I heard he was in a coma in ICU."

"You know, he might have been taken to the Santa Monica facility on Sixteenth Street. Shall I put in a call to them?"

"I'd appreciate that. I drove all the way down from Santa Teresa, and I'd hate to go home without finding him."

I watched her idly as she dialed and spoke to someone on the other end. Within moments, she hung up, apparently without success. "They have no record of him there. You might try Saint John's Hospital or Cedars-Sinai."

"I'm almost certain he was brought here. I talked to police detectives yesterday, and that's what they said.

He was admitted early Wednesday morning of last week. He'd been shot twice, so he must have been brought in through Emergency."

"I'm afraid that doesn't help. All I'm given is the patient's name, room number, and medical status. I don't have information about admissions."

"Suppose he was transferred? Wouldn't you receive notice?"

"Ordinarily," she said.

"Look, is there anyone else I could talk to about this?"

"I can't think who, unless you'd want to speak to someone in administration."

"Can't you check with Intensive Care? Maybe if you describe his injuries, they'll know where he is."

"Well," she said hesitantly, "there *is* a trauma social worker. She'd certainly have been alerted if the patient were the victim of a violent crime. Would you like me to call her?"

"Perfect. Please do. I'd appreciate your help."

By now, other people were lining up behind me, anxious for information and restless at the delay. Mrs. Lewis seemed reluctant, but she did pick up the phone again and make an in-house call. After the first couple of sentences, her voice dropped out of hearing range and she angled her face slightly so I couldn't read her lips. When she replaced the receiver, she wouldn't quite look at me. "If you'd care to wait, they said they'd send someone."

"Is something wrong?"

"Not that I know, dear. At the moment, the social

worker's out of her office . . . probably on the floor somewhere. The ICU charge nurse is going to try paging her and get back to me."

"Then you're telling me he's here?"

The man behind me said, "Hey, come on, lady. Give us a break."

Mrs. Lewis seemed flustered. "I didn't say that. All I know is the social worker might help if you want to wait and talk to her. If you could just have a seat. . . ."

"Thanks. You won't forget?"

The man said, "Hell, I'll tell you myself."

I was too distracted to engage in a barking fest, so I let that one pass. I made my way over to an empty chair. Driving down to L.A., I hadn't pictured things turning out this way. I'd fancied a moment by Mickey's bed, some feeling of redemption, the chance to make amends. Now his latent paranoia was rubbing off on me. Had something happened to him? Had Detectives Claas and Aldo been holding out? It was always possible he'd been admitted under an assumed name. Crime victims, like celebrities, are often afforded the added measure of protection. If that were the case, I wasn't sure how I was going to sweet-talk my way into his alias. All I knew was I wouldn't budge until I got a lead on him.

Someone had left behind a tattered issue of *Sunset Magazine*. I began to leaf through, desperate for a diversion from my anxiety about him. I needed to get "centered." I needed serenity, a moment of calm, while I figured out whose butt I was going to kick and how hard. I settled on an article about building a brick patio, complete with layouts. Every ten or fifteen seconds I looked up, checking the clock, watching visitors, patients, and hospital personnel entering the lobby, emerging from the cafeteria, passing through the seeing-eye doors. It was important to dig out the area to a depth of six inches, adding back a layer of gravel and then a layer of sand before beginning to lay brick. I chose the herringbone pattern for my imaginary outdoor living space. Thirty minutes went by. I finished all the articles on horticulture and went on to check out the low-fat recipes utilizing phyllo and fresh fruit. I didn't want to eat anything that had to be kept under a moist towel before I baked it.

Someone sat down in the chair next to mine. I glanced over to find Gian Aldo, and he was pissed. The woman at the desk had clearly ratted me out. Aldo said, "I figured it was you. What the hell's going on? I get a call saying some woman's over here making a stink, trying to get Mickey's room number from a poor unsuspecting volunteer."

I felt the color rise in my cheeks. "I didn't 'make a stink.' I never even raised my voice. I came to see how he was. What's the big deal?"

"We asked to be notified if anyone came in asking for Magruder's room."

"How was I supposed to know? I'm concerned, worried sick. Is that against the law?"

"Depends on your purpose. You could've been the shooter . . . or hadn't you thought about that?"

"Of course I thought about that, but I didn't shoot the man," I said. "I was anxious about him and thought I'd feel better if I could see him."

Aldo's dark brows knit together and I could tell he

was struggling to moderate his attitude. "You should have given us warning. We could have met you on arrival and saved you the time and aggravation."

"Your overriding purpose in life."

"Look, I was in the middle of a meeting when the call came through. I didn't have to rush right out. I could have let you sit and stew. It would have served you right." He stared off across the lobby. "Actually, my overriding purpose is protecting Magruder. I'm sure you can appreciate the risk, since we don't have the faintest idea who plugged him."

"I get that." I could see the situation from his perspective. This was an active investigation, and I'd gummed up the works by ignoring protocol. Since Mickey was my ex and since mine was the gun that was found at the scene, my sudden appearance at the hospital didn't look that good. "I'm sorry. I get antsy for information and tend to cut to the chase. I should have called you. The fault was mine."

"Let's don't worry about that now." He glanced at his watch. "I have to get back to work, but if you want, I can take you up to ICU for a couple minutes first."

"I can't have time alone with him?"

"That's correct," he said. "For one thing, he's still unconscious. For another, it's my responsibility to keep him safe. I answer to the department, no ifs, ands, or buts. I don't mean to sound harsh, but that's the way it is."

"Let's get on with it then," I said, suppressing the surge of rebelliousness. Clearly, I'd have to yield to him in everything. This man was officially the keeper of the gate. Seeing Mickey was more important than bucking authority or winning arguments.

I got up when he did and followed him through the lobby, feeling like a dog trained to heel. We took a right down the corridor, saying nothing to each other. He pressed for the elevator. While we waited, he pulled out a package of gum and offered me a piece. I declined. He removed a stick for himself, tore it in half, peeled off the paper, and popped the gum in his mouth. The elevator doors slid open. I entered behind him, and we turned and faced front while we ascended. For once I didn't bother to memorize the route. There was no point in scheming to find Mickey on my own. If I pulled any shenanigans, Detective Aldo was going to nail my ass to the wall.

We entered the 7-E Intensive Care Unit, where the detective was apparently known by sight. While he had a brief conversation with the nurses at the desk, I had a chance to get my bearings. The atmosphere was curious: the lights slightly dimmed, the noise level reduced by the teal-and-gray patterned carpeting. I guessed at ten or twelve beds, each in a cubicle within visual range of the nurses' station. The beds were separated by lightweight green-and-white curtains, most of which were drawn shut. These were the patients who teetered on the edge, tethered to life by the slimmest of lines. Blood and bile, urine, spinal fluid, all the rivers in the body were being mapped and charted while the soul journeyed on. Sometimes, between breaths, a patient slipped away, easing into the greater stream from which all of us emerge and to which all must return.

Aldo rejoined me and steered me around the desk to the bed where Mickey lay. I didn't recognize the man, though a quick glance at Aldo assured me this was him. He wasn't breathing on his own. There was a wide band of tape across the lower portion of his face. His mouth was open, attached to a ventilator by a translucent blue tube about the same diameter as a vacuum cleaner hose. The top half of the bed was elevated as if he were on permanent display. He lay close to one side, almost touching the side rails, which had been raised to contain him like the sides of a crib. He wore a watch cap of gauze. The bullet wound had left him with two blackened eyes, puffy and bruised as though he'd been in a fistfight. His complexion was gray. There was a tube in the back of one hand, delivering solutions from numerous bags hanging on an IV pole. I could count the drips one by one, a Chinese water torture designed to save life. A second tube snaked out from under the covers and into a gallon jug of urine accumulating under the bed. What hair I could see looked sparse and oily. His skin had a fine sheen of moisture. Years of sun damage were now surfacing like an image on film bathed in developing fluid. I could see soft down on the edges of his ears. His eyes weren't fully closed. Through the narrow slits I could watch him track an unseen movie or perhaps lines of print. Where was his mind while his body lay so still? I disconnected my emotions by focusing on equipment that surrounded his bed: a cart, a sink, a stainless-steel trash can with a pop-up lid, a rolling chair, a glove dispenser, and a paper towel rack—utilitarian articles that hardly spoke of death.

The presence of Detective Aldo lent a strange air of unreality to our reunion. Mickey's chest rose and fell in a regular rhythm, a bellows effect forcing his lungs to inflate. Under his hospital gown, I could see a tube top of white gauze bandages. When I'd met him, he was thirty-six. He was now almost fifty-three, the same age as Robert Dietz. For the first time I wondered if my involvement with Dietz had been an unwitting attempt to mend the breach with Mickey. Were my internal processes that obvious?

I stared at Mickey's face, watching him breathe, glancing at the blood pressure cuff that was attached to one arm. At intervals, the cuff would inflate and deflate itself, with a whining and a wheeze. The digital readout would then appear on the monitor above his head. His blood pressure seemed stable at 125 over 80, his pulse 74. It's embarrassing to remember love once the feeling's died, all the passion and romanticism, the sentimentality and sexual excess. Later, you have to wonder what the hell you were thinking of. Mickey had seemed solid and safe, someone whose expertise I admired, whose opinions I valued, whose confidence I envied. I'd idealized him without even realizing what I was doing, which was taking my projection as the stone-cold truth. I didn't understand that I sought in him the qualities I lacked or hadn't yet developed. I'd have denied to the last breath that I was looking for a father figure, but of course I was.

I became conscious of Gian Aldo, who stared at

Mickey with a silence similar to mine. What could either of us say beyond the trite and the obvious? I finally spoke up. "I should let you get back to work. I appreciate this."

"Any time," he said.

He walked me down through the hospital and across the plaza. I punched the elevator button and he waited with me dutifully. "I'm fine," I said, meaning he could leave.

"I don't mind," he said, meaning not-on-your-sweet-life.

When the elevator arrived, I got in and turned, giving him a little wave as the doors slid shut. I found my car, unlocked it, turned the key in the ignition, and put the gears in reverse. By the time I made the three circles upward to ground level, he was waiting in his car by the exit, his engine idling. I pulled out of the lot onto Tiverton, and when I reached Le Conte I turned left. Detective Aldo did likewise, keeping pace with me as I headed toward the freeway. He was still asserting his control, as I was keenly aware. I could understand his desire to see me off, though I felt like the villain in a Western movie being escorted out of town. I kept track of his car in my rearview mirror—not that he made any effort to disguise his intent. West on Sunset, north on the 405, driving toward the 101, we formed a two-car motorcade at sixty miles an hour. I began to wonder if he was going to follow me all the way home.

I watched the cross streets go by: Balboa, White Oak, Reseda . . . did the man have no faith? What'd he think I was going to do, circle back to UCLA? At Tampa, I saw him lean forward and pick up his radio mike, apparently responding to a call. The subject must have been urgent because he suddenly veered off, crossing two lanes of traffic before he headed down the exit ramp. I kept my acceleration constant, my gaze fixed on the mirror to see if he'd reappear. Detective Aldo was a sneak, and I wouldn't put it past him to try a little misdirection. Winnetka, DeSoto, Topanga Canyon passed. It looked like he was gone. For once my angels were in agreement. One said, Nobody's perfect, and the other said, Amen.

I took the next off-ramp.

TEN

Mickey had been shrewd in listing an address on Sepulveda. According to the *Thomas Guide*, there are endless variations. Sepulveda Boulevard seems to spring forth in the north end of the San Fernando Valley. The street then traces a line south, often hugging the San Diego Freeway, all the way to Long Beach. The North and South Sepulveda designations seem to jump back and forth, claiming ever-shifting sections of the street as it winds from township to township. There are East and West Sepulveda Boulevards, a Sepulveda Lane, Sepulveda Place, Sepulveda Street, Sepulveda Eastway, East Sepulveda Fire Road, Sepulveda Westway. By juggling the numbers, Mickey could just about ensure that no one was ever going to pinpoint his exact location. As it happened, I'd collected three variations of the same four digits: 2805, 2085, and 2580.

I placed the addresses in numerical order, beginning with 2085, moving on to 2580, and then to 2805. I reasoned that even if finances had forced him to sell his car, he still had to get around. He might use a bike or public transportation traveling to and from his place of employment—unless, of course, he'd also lost his job.

He probably did his shopping close to home, frequenting the local restaurants when he felt too lazy to prepare a meal, which (if the past was any indication) was most of the time. The detectives had mentioned the shooting had occurred in a commercial district with lots of bars close by. Already in my mind, a mental picture was forming. Mickey'd never owned a house, so I was looking for a rental, and nothing lavish, if I knew him.

I cruised the endless blocks of Sepulveda I'd selected. While this wasn't L.A. at its worst, the route was hardly scenic. There were billboards everywhere. Countless telephone poles intersected the skyline, dense strands of wire stretching in all directions. I passed gas stations, a print and copy shop, three animal hospitals, a 7-Eleven, a discount tire establishment. I watched the numbers climb, from a car wash to a sign company, from a construction site to a quick lube to an auto body shop. In this area, if you weren't in the market for lumber or fast food, you could always buy discount leather or stock up at the Party Smarty for your entertaining needs.

It wasn't until I reached the 2800 block in Culver City that I sensed this was Mickey's turf. The H-shaped three-story apartment building at 2805 had a rough plaster exterior, painted drab gray, with sagging galleries and aluminum sliding glass doors that looked like they'd be difficult to open. Stains, shaped like stalactites, streaked the stucco along the roofline. Weeds grew up through cracks in the concrete. A dry gully ran along the south side, choked with boulders and refuse. The wire fence marking the property line now

127

leaned against the side of the apartment complex in a tangle of dead shrubs.

I drove past, scanning the nearest intersection, where I saw an electronics shop, a photo lab, a paint store, a mini-mart, a pool hall, a twenty-four-hour coffee shop, two bars, and a Chinese restaurant, Mickey's favorite. I spotted a driveway, and at the first break in traffic I did a turn-around, coming up on the right side of the street in front of 2805. I found a parking place two doors away, turned off the engine, and sat in my car, checking out the ambience, if the concept isn't too grand. The building itself was similar to one Mickey occupied when the two of us first met. I'd been appalled then, as I was now, by his indifference to his environment. The sign out front specified *studios and 1 & 2 bedroom apartments* NOW RENTING, as if this were late-breaking news.

The landscaping consisted of a cluster of banana palms with dark green battered leaves that looked like they'd been slashed by a machete. Traffic in the area was heavy, and I found myself watching the cars passing in both directions, wondering if Detective Aldo was going to drive by and catch me at the scene. The very thought made me squirm. It wasn't as though he'd forbidden me to make an appearance, but he wouldn't be happy if he figured it out.

I started the car and pulled away from the curb. I drove down half a block and turned right at the first corner and then right again, into the alley that ran behind the row of buildings and dead-ended at the gully. Someone had compressed the buckling wire fence so that one could cross the boundary and ease down into the ditch. I pulled in beside the garbage bins and made another U-turn, so that I now faced the alley entrance. I took a minute to grab my fanny pack from the backseat and transfer my key picks, a penlight, my mini-tool kit, and a pair of rubber gloves. I clipped the fanny pack around my waist, locked the car, and got out.

I padded down the walkway between Mickey's building and the apartment complex next door. At night this area would be dark, since the exterior light fixtures were either dangling or missing altogether. A line of gray-painted water meters was planted along the side, real shin-bangers. By straining only slightly— which is to say, jumping up and down like a Zulu—I was able to peek in the windows through the wrought-iron burglar bars. Most of what I saw were bedrooms barely large enough for a king-sized bed. The occupants seemed to use the windowsills to display an assortment of homely items: cracker boxes, framed snapshots, mayonnaise jars filled to capacity with foil-wrapped condoms. In one unit, someone was nurturing a handsome marijuana plant.

Mickey's apartment building didn't have a lobby, but an alcove in the front stairwell housed a series of metal mailboxes with names neatly embossed on short lengths of red, blue, and yellow plastic. Even Mickey couldn't buck post office regulations. By counting boxes, I knew there were twenty apartments distributed on three floors, but I had no way to guess how many flats were the one- and two-bedroom units and how many were studios. His was unit 2-H. The manager was on the ground floor in 1-A to my immediate right.

The name on the mailbox read HATFIELD, B & C. I decided to postpone contact until after I'd reconnoitered Mickey's place.

I went up the front stairs to the second floor, following the progression of front doors and picture windows that graced each flat. There were no burglar bars up here. Mickey's was the corner unit at the rear of the building on the right-hand side. There was a neat yellow X of crime-scene tape across his door. An official caution had been affixed advising of the countless hideous repercussions if crime-scene sanctity was breached. The gallery continued around the corner and ran along the back of the building, so that Mickey's rear windows overlooked the alleyway below and the gully to the right. A second set of stairs had been tacked on back here, probably to bring the building into compliance with fire department codes. Mickey probably considered this a mixed blessing. While the privacy offered a potential intruder unimpeded access to his windows, it also gave Mickey an easy means of egress. When I peered over the railing, I could see my VW below like a faithful steed, so close I could have leapt down and galloped off at a moment's notice.

All Mickey's sliding glass windows were secured. Knowing him, he'd tucked heavy wooden dowels into the inside track so the windows would only slide back a scant six inches. The lock on his front door, however, seemed to be identical to those on the neighboring apartments. The manager must have discouraged swapping out the standard model for something more effective. I studied my surroundings. The alley was deserted and I saw no signs of any other tenant. I slipped on my rubber gloves and went to work with my pick. A friend in Houston had recently sent me a keen toy: a battery-operated pick that, once mastered, worked with gratifying efficiency. It had taken me awhile to get the hang of it, but I'd practiced on Henry's door until I had the technique down pat.

The door yielded to my efforts in less than fifteen seconds, the pick making no more noise than an electric toothbrush. I tucked the pick back in my fanny pack, loosened one end of the yellow tape, and stepped over the doorsill, turning only long enough to resecure the tape through the gap before I closed the door behind me. I checked my watch, allowing myself thirty minutes for the search. I figured if a neighbor had observed me breaking in, it would take the L.A. cops at least that long to respond to the call.

The interior was dim. Mickey's curtains were drawn, and sunlight was further blocked by the six-story building across the alley. Mickey still smoked. Stale fumes hung in the air, having permeated the carpet, the drapes, and all the heavy upholstered furniture. I checked the cigarette butts that had been left in the ashtrays, along with an array of wooden kitchen matches. All were the same Camel filters he'd been smoking for years, and none bore the telltale red rim suggesting female companionship. An Elmore Leonard paperback had been left on the arm of the sofa, open at the midpoint. Mickey had introduced me to Elmore Leonard and Len Deighton. In turn, I'd told him about Dick Francis, though I'd never known if he read the British author with the same pleasure I did. The walls were done in a temporary-looking pine paneling that was nearly sticky with the residue of cigarette tars. The living room and dining room formed an L. The furniture was clumsy—big overstuffed pieces of the sort you'd buy at a flea market or pick off the sidewalk, like an alley fairy, on collection day. There was a shredder against one wall, but the bin had been emptied. In Mickey's view of the world, no scrap of paper, no receipt, and no piece of correspondence should go into the trash without being scissored into tiny pieces. He probably dumped the bin at frequent intervals, using more than one trash can, so that a thief breaking in wouldn't have the means to reassemble vital documents. No doubt about it, the man was nuts.

I moved into the dining area, past four mismatched chairs and a plain wooden table that was littered with mail. I paused, picking through the stack that was piled at one end. I was careful not to sort the envelopes, though my natural inclination was to separate the bills from the junk. I spotted a number of bank statements, but there were no personal letters, no catalogs, and no credit card bills. I had little interest in his utility bills. What did I care how much electricity he used? I longed for a phone bill, but there were none to be found. The cops had lifted those. I picked up the handful of bank statements and slipped them down the front of my jeans into my underpants, where they formed a crackling paper girdle. I'd look at them later when I was home again. None of the other bills seemed useful so I left them where they were. Best to keep the federal mail-tampering convictions to a minimum.

Off the dining area, I entered a galley-style kitchen so small I could reach the far wall in two steps. Stove, apartment-sized refrigerator, sink, microwave oven. The only kitchen window was small and looked out onto the alley. On the counter, he kept a round glass fishbowl into which he tossed his extra packets of matches at the end of the night, a road map of his journey from bar to bar. The upper cabinets revealed a modest collection of Melamine plates and coffee mugs, plus the basic staples: dry cereal, powdered milk, sugar, a few condiments, paper napkins, and two sealed bottles of Early Times bourbon. The cupboards below were packed back to front with canned goods: soups, beans, Spam, tuna packed in oil, tamales, Spaghetti-O's, applesauce, evaporated milk. In the storage space under the kitchen sink, I found an empty bourbon bottle in the trash. Tucked in among the pipes, I counted ten five-gallon containers of bottled water. This was Mickey's survival stock in case a war broke out or L.A. was invaded by extraterrestrials. The refrigerator was filled with things that smelled bad. Mickey had tossed in half-eaten items without the proper wrapping, which resulted in dark chunks of hardening Cheddar cheese, a greening potato covered with wartlike sprouts, and half an air-dried tomato drawing in on itself.

I retraced my steps. To the left of the living room was the door to the bedroom, with a closet and under-sized bath beyond. The chest of drawers was filled with the usual jockey shorts and T-shirts, socks, handker-chiefs. The bed-table drawer contained some interest-ing items: a woman's diaphragm and a small spray bottle of cologne with a partial price label on the bottom. The cologne had apparently been purchased from a Robinson's Department Store, since I could still make out a portion of the identifying tag. I removed the top and took a whiff. Heavy on the lily of the valley that I remembered from the early days of our romance. Mickey's mother must have worn something similar. I remembered how he'd lay his lips in the hollow of my throat when I was wearing it myself. I put the cologne bottle down. There was a tissue paper packet about the size of a stick of gum. I unfolded the paper and picked up a thin gold chain threaded through the clasp of a small gold heart locket with an ever-so-tiny rose enameled in the center. Not to sound cynical, but Mickey'd given me one just like this about a week into our affair. Some men do that, find a gimmick or shtick that works once—the gift of a single red rose—and recycle the same gesture with every woman who comes along.

In a cleaning bag, he'd hung two dark blue uniforms with patches on the sleeves. I slid a hand up under the bag and checked one of the light blue patches. *Pacific Coast Security* was stitched in gold around the rim. Also hanging in the closet were a couple of sport coats, six dress shirts, four pairs of blue jeans, two pairs of chinos, a pair of dark pants, and a black leather jacket I knew very well indeed. This was the jacket Mickey wore the first time we went out, the jacket he was wearing when he kissed me the first time. I was still living with Aunt Gin, so there was no way we could go inside to misbehave. Mickey backed me up against the trailer door, the leather in his jacket making a characteristic creaking sound. The kiss went on so long we both sank down along the frame. I was Eva Marie

Saint with Marlon Brando—*On the Waterfront*—which is still one of the best screen kisses in recorded history. Not like love scenes nowadays where you watch the guy stick his tongue down the girl's throat, trying to activate her gag reflex. Mickey and I might've made love right there on the doorstep except we'd have been visible to everybody in the trailer park, which we knew was bad form, making us vulnerable to arrest.

I shook my head and closed the closet door while a sexual shiver ran down my frame. I tried the door next to it, which seemed to be an exit onto the rear gallery. The lock here was new. There was no key in the deadbolt, but it probably wasn't far. Mickey wouldn't make it easy for someone breaking into the apartment, but he'd want the key handy in case of fire or earthquake. I pivoted, letting my gaze move across the area, remembering his tricks. I knelt and felt my way along the edge of the carpeting. When I reached the corner, I gave the loosened carpet a tug. I lifted that section and plucked the key from its hiding place. I unlocked the back door and left it temporarily ajar.

I went back to the bedroom door and stood there, looking out at the living room. The cops had doubtless cruised through here once, sealing the apartment afterward, pending a more thorough investigation. I tried to see the place as they had, and then I looked at it again from personal experience. With Mickey, the question wasn't so much what was visible as what wasn't. This was a man who lived in a constant state of readiness and, as far as I could tell, his fears had only accelerated in the past fourteen years. In the absence of global conflict, he lived in anticipation of civil insurrection: unruly hordes who would overrun the building, breaking into every unit, clamoring for food, water, and other valuables like toilet paper. So where were his weapons? How did he intend to defend himself?

I tried the kitchen first, tapping along the baseboards for the sound of hollow spaces. I'd seen him install other "safes"—compartments with false fronts where you could tuck cash, guns, and ammunition. I started with the kitchen sink. I took out all the gallon water containers, exposing the "floor" and rear wall of stained plywood. I shone the penlight from top to bottom, side to side. I could see four screw heads, one set in each corner, darkened to match the panel. I unbuckled my fanny pack, opened my mini-tool kit, took out a battery-operated drill, and set about removing screws. A person could develop carpal tunnel syndrome doing this the old-fashioned way. Once the screws were out, the partition yielded to gentle pressure, exposing a space that was six to eight inches deep. Four handguns were mounted in a rack on the rear wall, along with boxes of ammunition. I replaced the panel with care and continued my search. I considered this a fact-finding mission. Like the LAPD detectives, my prime purpose was determining just why Mickey'd been shot. I didn't want to remove anything of his unless I had to. Better to leave the items undisturbed where possible.

At the end of thirty minutes, I'd uncovered three small recesses hollowed out behind the switch plates in the living room. Each contained a packet of identification papers: birth certificate, driver's license, social security card, credit cards, and currency. Emmett Van-over. Delbert Amburgey. Clyde Byler. None were names I recognized, and I assumed he'd invented them or borrowed them from deceased persons whose vitals he'd gleaned from public records. In every bogus document, Mickey's photo had been inserted. I left everything where it was and moved on. I'd also discovered that the back of the couch could be removed to reveal a space large enough to hide in. The paneling, while cheap, turned out to be securely fastened to the walls, but I did find tight rolls of crisp twenty-dollar bills tucked into either end of the big metal curtain rods in the living and dining rooms. A quick count suggested close to twelve hundred dollars.

In the bathroom, I removed a length of PVC, two inches in diameter, that had been set into the wall adjacent to the water lines. The pipe contained a handful of gold coins. Again, I left the stash where it was and carefully realigned the pipe in its original site. The only place I bombed out was one of his favorites, that being down the bathtub drain. He liked to drill a hole in the rubber stopper and run a chain up through the plug. He'd attach the relevant item to the chain, which he then left dangling down the drain with all the slimy hair and soap scum. This was usually where he kept his safe deposit key. I took a minute to lean over the rim of the tub. The rubber stopper was attached by a chain to the overflow outlet, but when I flashed the light into the drain itself, there was nothing hanging down the hole. Well, shoot. I consoled myself with the fact that I'd otherwise done well. Mickey probably had other secret repositories—maybe new ones I hadn't even thought about—but this was the best I could do in the time allotted. For now, it was time to clear the premises.

I let myself out the back door, using Mickey's key to lock the door behind me. I slipped the key in my pocket, stripped off my rubber gloves, and zipped them into my pack. I went downstairs and knocked at the manager's front door. I'd assumed that B & C Hatfield were a married couple, but the occupants turned out to be sisters. The woman who opened the door had to be in her eighties. "Yes?"

She was heavy through the middle, with a generously weighted bosom. She wore a sleeveless cotton sundress with most of the color washed away. The fabric reminded me of old quilts, a flour-sacking floral print in tones of pale blue and pink. Her breasts were pillowy, powdered with talcum, like two domes of bread dough proofing in a bowl. Her upper arms were soft, and I could see her stockings were rolled down below her knees. She wore slippers with a half-moon cut out of one to accommodate a bunion.

I said, "Mrs. Hatfield?"

"I'm Cordia," she said cautiously. "May I help you?"

"I hope so. I'd like to talk to you about Mickey Magruder, the tenant in Two-H."

She fixed me with a pair of watery blue eyes. "He was shot last week."

"I'm aware of that. I just came from the hospital, where I was visiting him."

"Are you the police detective?"

"I'm an old friend."

She stared at me, her blue eyes penetrating.

"Well, actually, I'm his ex-wife," I amended, in response to her gaze.

"I saw you park in the alley while I was sweeping out the laundry room."

I said, "Ah."

"Was everything in order?"

"Where?"

"Two-H. Mr. Magruder's place. You were up there quite a while. Thirty-two minutes by my watch."

"Fine. No problem. Of course, I didn't go in."

"No?"

"There was crime scene tape across the door," I said.

"Place was posted, too. Big police warning about the penalties."

"I saw that."

She waited. I would have continued, but my mind was blank. My thought process had shorted out, catching me in the space between truth and lies. I felt like an actor who'd forgotten her lines. I couldn't for the life of me think what to say next.

"Are you interested in renting?" she prompted.

"Renting?"

"Apartment Two-H. I assume that's why you went up."

"Oh. Oh, sure. Good plan. I like the area."

"You do. Well, perhaps we could let you know if the unit becomes available. Would you care to come in and complete an application? You seem discombobulated. Perhaps a drink of water?"

"I'd appreciate that."

139

I entered the apartment, stepping directly into the kitchen. I felt like I'd slipped into another world. Chicken was stewing on the back of the stove. A second woman, roughly the same age, sat at a round oak table with a deck of cards. To my right, I could see a formal dining room: mahogany table and chairs, with a matching hutch stacked with dishes. Clearly, the floor plan was entirely different from Mickey's. The temperature on the thermostat must have been set at eighty, and the TV on the kitchen counter was blaring stock market quotes at top volume. Neither Cordia nor her sister seemed to be watching the screen. "I'll get you the application," she said. "This is my sister, Belmira."

"On second thought, why don't I take the application home with me? I can fill it out and send it back. It'll be simpler that way."

"Suit yourself. Have a seat."

I pulled out a chair and sat down across from Belmira, who was shuffling a tarot deck. Cordia went to the kitchen sink and let the faucet water run cold before she filled a glass. She handed me the water and then crossed to a kitchen drawer, where she extracted an application. She returned to her seat, handed me the paper, and picked up a length of multicolored knitting, six inches wide and at least fifteen inches long.

I took my time with the water. I made a study of the application, trying to compose myself. What was wrong with me? My career as a liar was being seriously undermined. Meanwhile, neither sister questioned my lingering presence.

Cordia said, "Belmira claims she's a witch, though

you couldn't prove it by me." She peered toward the dining room. "Dorothy's around here someplace. Where'd she go, Bel? I haven't seen her for an hour."

"She's in the bathroom," Bel said, and turned to me. "I didn't catch your name, dear."

"Oh, sorry. I'm Kinsey. Nice meeting you."

"Nice to meet you, too." Her hair was sparse, a flyaway white with lots of pink scalp showing through. Under her dark print housedress, her shoulders were narrow and bony, her wrists as flat and thin as the handles on two soup ladles. "How're you today?" she asked shyly, as she pulled the tarot deck together. Four of her teeth were gold.

"I'm fine. What about yourself?"

"I'm real good." She plucked a card from the deck and held it up, showing me the face. "The Page of Swords. That's you."

Cordia said, "Bel."

"Well, it's true. This is the second time I pulled it. I shuffled the deck and drew this as soon as she stepped in, and then I drew it again."

"Well, draw something else. She's not interested."

I said, "Tell me about your names. Those are new to me."

Bel said, "Mother made ours up. There were six of us girls and she named us in alphabetical order: Amelia, Belmira, Cordia, Dorothy, Edith, and Faye. Cordi and I are the last two left."

"What about Dorothy?"

"She'll be along soon. She loves company."

Cordia said, "Bel will start telling your fortune any minute now. I'm warning you, once she gets on it, it's hard to get her off. Just ignore her. That's what I do. You don't have to worry about hurting her feelings."

"Yes, she does," Bel said feebly.

"Are you good at telling fortunes?"

Cordia cut in. "Not especially, but even a blind hog comes across an acorn now and then." She had taken up her knitting, which she held to the light, her head tilted slightly as the needles tucked in and out. The narrow piece of knitting trailed halfway down her front. "I'm making a knee wrap, in case you're wondering."

My Aunt Gin taught me to knit when I was six years old, probably to distract me in the early evening hours. She claimed it was a skill that fostered patience and eye–hand coordination. Now, as I watched, I could see that Cordia had dropped a few stitches about six rows back. The loops, like tiny sailors washed overboard, were receding in the wake of the knitting as each new row was added. I was about to mention it when a large white cat appeared in the doorway. She had a flat Persian face. She stopped when she saw me and stared in apparent wonderment. I'd seen a cat like that once before: long-haired, pure white, one green eye and one blue.

Bel smiled at the sight of her. "Here she is."

"That's Dorothy," Cordia said. "We call her Dort for short. Do you believe in reincarnation?"

"I've never sorted that one through."

"We hadn't either till this kitty came along. Dorothy always swore she'd be in touch with us from the Other Side. Told us for years, she'd find a way to come back.

Then, lo and behold, the neighbor's cat had a litter the very day she passed on. This was the only female, and she looks just like Dort. The white hair, the one blue eye, the one green. Same personality, same behavior. Sociable, pushy, independent."

Bel chimed in. "The cat even passes wind the way Dorothy did. Silent but deadly. Sometimes we have to get up and leave the room."

I pointed to the knitting. "It looks like you dropped some stitches." I leaned forward and touched a finger to the errant loops. "If you have a crochet hook, I can coax them up the line for you."

"Would you? I'd like that. Your eyes are bound to be better than mine." Cordia bent over and reached into her knitting bag. "Let's see what I've got here. Will this do?" She offered me a J hook.

"That's perfect." While I began the slow task of working the dropped stitches up through the rows, the cat picked her way across the floor and jumped up in my lap. I jerked the knitting up and said, "Whoa!" Dorothy must have weighed twenty pounds. She turned her backside to me and stuck her tail in the air like a pump handle, exhibiting her little spigot while she marched in place.

"She never does that. I don't know what's got into her. She must like you," Belmira said, turning up cards as she spoke.

"I'm thrilled."

"Well, would you look at this? The Ten of Wands, reversed." Bel was laying out a reading. She placed the Ten of Wands with the other cards on the table in some mysterious configuration. The card she'd assigned me, the Page of Swords, had now been covered by the Moon.

I freed one hand and cranked Dorothy's tail down, securing it with my right arm as I pointed to the cards. "What's that one mean?" I thought the Moon might be good, but the sisters exchanged a look that made me think otherwise.

Cordia said, "I told you she'd do this."

"The Moon stands for hidden enemies, dear. Danger, darkness, and terror. Not too good."

"No kidding."

She pointed to a card. "The Ten of Wands, reversed, represents obstacles, difficulties, and intrigues. And this one, the Hanged Man, represents the best you can hope for."

"She doesn't want to hear that, Bel."

"I do. I can handle it."

"This card crowns you."

"What's that? I'm afraid to ask," I said.

"Oh, the Hanged Man is good. He represents wisdom, trials, sacrifice, intuition, divination, prophecy. This is what you want, but it isn't yours at present."

"She's trying to help with my knitting. You might at least leave her be until she finishes."

"I can do both," I said. Though, truthfully, Dorothy's presence was making the task difficult. The cat had rotated in my lap and now seemed intent on smelling my breath. She extended her nose daintily. I paused and breathed through my mouth for her. "What's that card?" I asked, while she butted my chin with her head.

"The Knight of Swords, which is placed at your feet. This is your own, what you have to work with. Skill, bravery, capacity, enmity, wrath, war, destruction."

"The wrath part sounds good."

"Not overall," Bel corrected. "Overall, you're screwed. You see this one? This card stands for pain, affliction, tears, sadness, desolation."

"Well, dang."

"Exactly. I'd say you're up poop creek without a roll of TP." Belmira turned up another card.

Dorothy climbed up on my chest, purring. She put her face in mine and we stared at each other. I glanced back at the tarot deck. Even I, believing none of this, could see the trouble I was in. Aside from the Hanged Man, there was a fellow burdened with heavy sticks, yet another fellow face down on the ground with ten swords protruding from his back. The card for Judgment didn't seem to bode well either, and then there was the Nine of Wands, which showed a cranky-looking man clinging to a staff, eight staves in a line behind him. That card was followed by a heart pierced with three swords, rain and clouds above.

By then, I'd succeeded in rescuing the lost stitches, and I reached around Dorothy to return the knitting to Cordia. I thought it was time to get down to business, so I asked Cordia what she could tell me about Mickey.

"I can't say I know all that much about him. He was extremely private. He worked as a bank guard until he lost his job in February. I used to see him going out in his uniform. He looked handsome, I must say."

"What happened?"

145

"About what?"

"How'd he lose his job?"

"He drank. You must have known that if you were married to him. Nine in the morning, he reeked of alcohol. I don't think he *drank* at that hour. This was left from the night before, fumes pouring through his skin. He never staggered, and I never once heard him slur his words. He wasn't loud or mean. He was always a gentleman, but he was losing ground."

"I'm sorry to hear that. I knew he drank, but it's hard to believe he reached a point where drinking interfered with his work. He was a cop in the old days when I was married to him."

"Is that right," she said.

"Was there anything else you could tell me about him?"

"He was quiet, no parties. Paid his rent on time until the last few months. No visitors except for the nasty fellow with all the chains."

I turned my attention from Dorothy. "Chains?"

"One of those motorcycle types: studs and black leather. He had a cowboy mentality, swaggered when he walked. Made so much noise it sounded like he was wearing spurs."

"What was that about?"

"I have no idea. Dort didn't like him. He was very rude. He knocked her sideways with his foot when she tried to smell his boot."

Bel said, "Oh, dear. This card represents the King of Cops . . . reversed again. That's not good."

I looked over with interest. "The King of Cops?"

"I didn't say cops, dear. I said Cups. The King of

Cups stands for a dishonest, double-dealing man: rogu-ery, vice, scandal, you name it."

Belatedly, I felt a flutter of uneasiness. "Speaking of which, what made you think I was a cop when I came to the door?"

Cordia looked up. "Because an officer called this morning and said a detective would be stopping by at two this afternoon. We thought it must be you since you were up there so long."

I felt my heart give a little hiccup, and I checked my watch. Nearly two o'clock now. "Gee, I better hit the road and let the two of you get back to work," I said. "Um, I wonder if you could do me a little favor. . . ."

Bel turned up the next card and said, "Don't worry about it, dear. We won't mention you were here."

"I'd appreciate that."

"I'll take you out the other door," Cordia said. "So you can reach the alley without being seen. The detec-tives park in the front . . . at least, they did before."

"Why don't I leave you a number? That way you can get in touch with me if anything comes up," I said. I jotted down my number on the back of my business card. In return, Cordia wrote their number on the edge of the rental application. Neither questioned my request. With a tarot like mine, they must have assumed I was going to need all the help I could get.

ELEVEN

On the way home, I stopped off at McDonald's and bought myself a QP with cheese, an order of fries, and a medium Coke. Once I'd picked Dorothy's hair off my lip, I steered with one hand while I munched with the other, all the time moaning with pleasure. It's pitiful to have a life in which junk food is awarded the same high status as sex. Then again, I tend to get a lot more of the one than I do of the other. I was back in Santa Teresa by four-fifteen. The only message on my machine was from Mark Bethel, who'd finally returned my Monday-afternoon call at eleven-thirty Wednesday morning.

I dialed his number, taking a moment to unzip my jeans and remove Mickey's mail from my underpants. Naturally, Mark was out, so I ended up talking to Judy. "You almost caught him. He left fifteen minutes ago."

"Shoot. Well, I'm sorry I missed him. I just got back from Los Angeles. I have news about Mickey and I may need his help. I'm in for the afternoon. If he has a chance to call, I'd love to talk to him."

"I'm afraid he's gone for the day, Kinsey, but if you

148

like you can catch him at seven tonight at the Lam-para," she said, naming a downtown theater.

"Doing what?" I asked, though I had a fair idea. Mark Bethel was one of fourteen Republican candi dates who'd be battling it out in the primary coming up on June 3, a scant twelve days off. I'd heard four of them had been invited to debate the issues at an event being sponsored by the League for Fair Government.

"This is a public debate: Robert Naylor, Mike Anto-novich, Bobbi Fiedler, and Mark, talking about elec-tion issues."

"Sounds hot," I said, thinking, Who's kidding who? The California Secretary of State, March Fong Eu, was predicting the lowest voter turnout in forty six years. Of the candidates Judy'd mentioned, only Mike Anto-novich, the conservative L.A. County supervisor, had even a slim chance at winning. Naylor was an assem-blyman from Menlo Park, the only Northern Califor-nian in the race until Ed Zschau had stepped in. Zschau was the front-runner. Rumor had it that the *San Diego Union*, the *San Francisco Chronicle*, the *San Francisco Examiner*, and the *Contra Costa Times* were all com-ing out in support of him. Meanwhile, Bobbi Fiedler, a San Fernando Valley congresswoman and a seasoned politician, had had the rug pulled out from under her when a grand jury indicted her for allegedly bribing another candidate into leaving the race. The charges turned out to be groundless and had been dismissed, but her supporters had lost enthusiasm and she was having trouble recovering her momentum. As for Mark, this was his second fling at a statewide election, and he was busy pouring Laddie's money into TV spots in which he touted himself for running such a clean campaign. Like anyone gave a shit. The notion of sitting through some droning political debate was enough to put me in a coma of my own.

Meanwhile, Judy was saying, "Mark's been preparing for days, mostly on Prop Fifty-one. That's the Deep Pockets Initiative."

"Right."

"Also Props Forty-two and Forty-eight. He feels pretty strongly about those."

I said, "Hey, who wouldn't?" I pushed some papers around my desk, uncovering the sample ballot under the local paper and a pile of mail. Proposition 48 would put a lid on ex-officials' pensions. Yawn, snore. Prop 42 would authorize the state to issue $850 million in bonds to continue the Cal-Vet farm and home loan program. "I didn't know Mark was a veteran," I said, making conversation.

"Oh, sure, he enlisted in the army right after his college graduation. I'll send you a copy of his CV."

"You don't have to do that," I said.

"It's no trouble. I have a bunch of 'em going out in the mail. You know, he won a Purple Heart."

"Really, I had no idea."

While Judy nattered on, I found the comic section and read *Rex Morgan, M.D.*, which was at least as interesting. Judy interrupted herself, saying, "Shoot. There goes my other phone. I better catch that in case it's him."

"No problem."

As soon as I hung up, I propped my feet up on my desk and turned my attention to the mail I'd snitched.

I picked up my letter opener and slit the envelopes. The bank statements showed regular paycheck deposits until late February, then nothing until late March, when he began to make small deposits at biweekly intervals. Unemployment benefits? I couldn't remember how that worked. There was probably a waiting period during which claims were processed and approved. In any event, the money he was depositing wasn't sufficient to cover his monthly expenses, and he was having to supplement the total out of his savings account. The current balance there was roughly $1,500. I'd found cash hidden on the premises, but no sign of his passbook. It would be nice to have that. I was surprised I hadn't come across it in my initial search. The monthly statements would have to do.

By comparing the activity in his savings and checking accounts, I could see the money jump from one to the other and then slide on out the door. Canceled checks indicated that he'd continued to pay as many bills as he could. His rent was $850 a month, which had last been paid March 1, according to the canceled check. Through the last half of February and the first three weeks of March, there were three checks made out to cash totaling $1,800. That seemed odd, given his financial difficulties, which were serious enough without pissing away his cash. The police probably had the April statement, so there was no way for me to tell if he'd paid rent on the first or not. My guess was that sometime in here he'd let his storage fees become delinquent.

By April, he was already in arrears on his telephone bill, and his service must have been cut before he had a chance to catch up. The cash he'd hidden probably represented a last resort, monies he was reluctant to spend unless his situation became desperate. Maybe his intent was to disappear, once all his other funds were depleted.

On the twenty-fifth of March, there was a one-time deposit of $900. I decided that was probably from the sale of his car. A couple of days later, on the twenty-seventh, there was a modest deposit of $200, which allowed him to pay his gas and electric bills. I did note that the $200 appeared the very day the call was made from his apartment to my machine. Someone paid him to use the phone? That would be weird. At any rate, he probably figured he could stall eviction for another month or two, at which point—what? He'd take his cash and phony documents and leave the state? Something about this gnawed at me. Mickey was a fanatic about savings. It was his contention that everyone should have a good six months' worth of income in the bank . . . or under the mattress, whichever seemed safer. He was such a nut on the subject, I'd made it a practice myself since then. He had to have another savings account somewhere. Had he put the money in a CD or a pension fund at his job? I wasn't even sure why he'd been fired. Was he drunk on duty? I sat and thought about that and then called directory assistance in Los Angeles and got the number for Pacific Coast Security in Culver City. I figured I had sufficient information to fake my way through. I knew his date of birth and his current address. His social security number would have been an asset, but all I remembered of it was the last four digits: 1776. Mickey always made a point about the numbers being the same as the year the Declaration of Independence was signed.

I dialed the number for Pacific Coast Security and listened to the phone ring, trying to figure out what I was going to say, surely not the truth in this case. When the call was picked up, I asked for Personnel. The woman who answered sounded like she was already halfway home for the day. It was close to five by now and she was probably in the process of clearing her desk. "This is Personnel. Mrs. Bird," she said.

"Oh, hi. This is Mrs. Weston in the billing department at UCLA Medical Center. We're calling with regard to a patient who's been admitted to ICU. We understand he's employed by Pacific Coast Security, and we're wondering if you can verify his insurance coverage."

"Certainly," she said. "The employee's name?"

"Last name Magruder. That's M-A-G-R-U-D-E-R. First name, Mickey. You may have him listed as Michael. Middle initial B. Home address 2805 Sepulveda Boulevard; date of birth, sixteen September 1933. Admitted through emergency on May fourteenth. We don't have a complete social security number, but we'd love to pick that up from you."

I could hear the woman breathing in my ear. "We heard about that. The poor man. Unfortunately, like I told the detectives, Mr. Magruder no longer works for us. He was terminated as of February twenty-eighth."

"Terminated as in fired?"

"That's right."

153

"Well, for heaven's sake. What for?"

She paused. "I'm not at liberty to discuss that, but it had to do with d-r-i-n-k-i-n-g."

"That's too bad. What about his medical insurance? Is there any possibility his coverage was extended?"

"Not according to our records."

"Well, that's odd. He had an insurance card in his wallet when he was brought in, and we were under the impression his coverage was current. Is he employed by any other company in the area?"

"I doubt it. We haven't been asked for references."

"What about Unemployment. Has he applied for benefits? Because he may qualify for medical under SDI." Yeah, right, SDI. Like we were all so casual about State Disability Insurance we didn't even need to spell it out.

"I really can't answer that. You'd have to check with them."

"What about money in his pension fund? Did he have automatic debits to his savings out of each paycheck?"

"I don't see where that's relevant," she said. She was beginning to sound uneasy, probably wondering if this was a ruse of some kind.

"You would if you saw the way his bill was mounting up," I said tartly.

"I'm afraid I can't discuss it. Especially with the police involved. They made a big point of that. We're not supposed to talk to anyone about anything when it comes to him."

"Same here. We've been asked to notify Detective Aldo if anyone even asks for his room."

"Really? They didn't say anything like that to us. Maybe because he hadn't worked here for so long."

"Consider yourself lucky. We're on red alert. Did you know Mr. Magruder personally?"

"Sure. The company's not all that big."

"You must feel terrible."

"I do. He's a real sweet guy. I can't imagine why anyone would want to do that to him."

"Awful," I said. "What about his social security number? We have the last four digits . . . 1776 . . . but the emergency room clerk couldn't understand what he was saying so she missed the first portion. All I need are the first five digits for our records. The director's a real stickler."

She seemed startled. "He was conscious?"

"Oh. Well, I don't know, now you mention it. He must have been, at least briefly. How else would we have this much?" I sensed her debate. "It's in his best interests," I added piously.

"Just a minute." I heard her clicking her computer keys, and after a moment she read off the first five digits.

I made a note. "Thanks. You're a doll. I appreciate that."

There was a pause, and then her curiosity got the better of her. "How's he doing?"

"I'm sorry, but I'm not allowed to divulge that information. You'd have to ask the medical staff. I'm sure you can appreciate the confidentiality of these matters, especially here at UCLA."

"Of course. Absolutely. Well, I hope he's okay. Tell him Ingrid said hi."

"I'll pass the word."

Once she'd hung up, I opened my desk drawer and took out a fresh pack of lined index cards. Time for clerical work. I began jotting down notes, writing as fast as I could, one item per card, piling them up as I went. I had a lot of catching up to do, days of accumulated questions. I knew some of the answers, but most of the lines I was forced to leave blank. I used to imagine I could hold it all in my head, but memory has a way of pruning and deleting, eliminating anything that doesn't seem relevant at the moment. Later, it's the odd unrelated detail that sometimes makes the puzzle parts rearrange themselves like magic. The very act of taking pen to paper somehow gooses the brain into making the leap. It doesn't always happen in the moment, but without the concrete notation, the data disappear.

I checked my watch. It was 6:05 and I was so cockeyed with weariness my clothes had begun to hurt. I turned the ringer off the phone, went up the spiral stairs, stripped, kicked my shoes off, wrapped myself in a quilt, and slept.

I woke at 9:15 P.M., though it felt like midnight. I sat up in bed, yawning, and tried to get my bearings. I felt weighted with weariness. I pushed the covers aside and went over to the railing. Below, on my desk, I could see the light on my answering machine blinking merrily. Shit. If not for that, I'd have crawled back in bed and slept through till morning.

I pulled a robe on and picked my way down the stairs barefoot. I pressed PLAY and listened to a message from Cordia Hatfield, the manager of Mickey's building. "Kinsey, I wonder if you could give us a call when you come in. There's something we think you should be aware of."

She'd called at 8:45, so I felt it was probably safe to return the call. I dialed the number, and Cordia picked up before I'd even heard the phone ring once. "Hello?"

"Cordia, is that you? This is Kinsey Millhone up in Santa Teresa. The phone didn't even ring."

"Well, it did down here. Listen, dear, the reason I called is that detective stopped by shortly after you left. He spent quite a bit of time up Two-H, and when he finished he came right here. He seemed perturbed, and he asked if anyone had gone in. We played dumb. He was quite insistent, but neither of us breathed a word."

"Ah. Was this the tall dark guy, Detective Aldo?"

"That's the one. We're old. What do we know, with all our brain cells gone? We didn't *lie* to him exactly, but I'm afraid we did skirt the truth a bit. I told him I was perfectly capable of taking in rent checks and calling the plumber if a toilet backed up, but I don't go skulking around, spying on the tenants. What they do is their business. Then I showed him my foot and told him, 'With this bunion, I'm lucky to get around. I can't be tromping up and down.' He changed the subject after that."

"What set him off?"

"He said something was missing, though he wouldn't say what. He had a boxload of items with him and told me he'd removed the crime tape. 'For all the good it did,' is how he put it. He was sour on the subject, I can tell you that."

"Thanks for the warning."

"You're entirely welcome. Main reason I called is you're free to enter the apartment, but it won't be long. The owners are pressing to get Mr. Magruder out of there. I guess the detective notified the management company, so they know he's in a coma. They snapped right to it, taking advantage of his condition. Shame on them. Anyway, if you're interested in *renting*, you should take a look."

"I may do that. I'd like that. When would be good?"

"The sooner the better. You're only two hours away."

"You're talking about *tonight*?"

"I think you'd be smart. The owners have already served him with a three-day pay or quit, so technically the sheriff could have a new lock on the door by tomorrow morning."

"Can't we do something to prevent that?"

"Not as far as I know."

"What if I pay what he owes, plus the next month's rent? Wouldn't that cancel the action?"

"I doubt it. Once a tenant starts paying late or doesn't pay at all, the owners would just as soon clear the place out and get someone else in."

I thought about the drive, rolling my eyes with dismay. "I wish I'd known this when I was down there earlier."

"If you're coming, you best hurry. It's entirely up to you, of course."

"Cordia, it's already close to nine-thirty. If I come down tonight, I'd still have to pack and get gas, which means I probably won't arrive before midnight." I didn't mention I was close to naked.

"That's not late for us. Bel and I only need four hours' sleep, so we're up till all hours. The advantage in coming now is you'd have all the time you want and not a soul to disturb you."

"Mickey's neighbors won't notice if his lights are on?"

"Nobody pays attention. Most of these folk work so they're usually in bed by ten. And if it gets too late, you can always spend the night with us. We have the only three-bedroom unit in the building. The guest room is really Dort's, but I'm sure she wouldn't mind the company. We had quite a little chat about you after you left."

I let go of my resistance and took a deep breath. "All right. I'll do it. See you in a bit."

I changed into my jeans, turtleneck, and tennis shoes, which were light and silent, good for late-night work. At least I'd been inside Mickey's place and knew what to expect. I still had the key I'd removed from his back door, but I intended to take my pick in case the need arose. Since I had no intention of driving home in the wee hours of the morning, I got out my duffel and threw in the oversized T-shirt I wear as a nightie. I routinely carry a toothbrush, toothpaste, and fresh underwear in the bottom of my shoulder bag. The remainder of the space in the duffel I filled with tools:

rubber gloves, my battery-operated pick, drill and drill bits, screwdriver, lightbulbs, pliers, needle-nose pliers, magnifying glass, and dental mirror, along with two flashlights, one standard and one on a long stem that could be angled for viewing those hard-to-reach places Mickey loved so much. I suspected I'd uncovered the majority of his hiding places, but I didn't want to take the chance, especially since this represented my last opportunity to snoop. I also took a second canvas duffel bag, folded and placed inside the first. I now planned to confiscate Mickey's contraband and hold it at my place until he could let me know what he wanted done with it.

I stopped at a service station to have my gas tank filled. While the guy cleaned the windshield and checked the oil, I popped into the "refreshment center" and bought myself a big nasty sandwich—cheese and mystery meat—and a large Styrofoam container of coffee that smelled only faintly scorched. I bought a separate carton of milk, poured out some of the black liquid, and refilled the cup to the brim with milk, then added two paper packets of sugar just to make sure my brain would be properly abuzz.

I was on my way by ten past ten, the VW windows rolled down, the engine whining with the effort of maintaining a constant 60 mph. I ate as I drove and somehow avoided spilling coffee down my front. There were a surprising number of cars on the road, interspersed with semis and RVs, all of us traveling at breakneck speeds. The sense of urgency was multiplied by the darkness that encompassed us, headlights and taillights forming ever-shifting patterns. In the stretch between Santa Teresa and Olvidado, the moon sat above the water like an alabaster globe resting on a pyramid of light. Along the shoreline, the waves were like loosely churning pearls tumbling through the surf. The ancient scent of seaweed drifted in the night air like a mist. Seaside communities appeared and disappeared as the miles accumulated. Hillsides, visible in the distance by day, were reduced to pinpoints of light that wound along the slopes.

I crested the Camarillo grade and coasted down the far side into the westernmost perimeter of the San Fernando Valley. There were no stars in sight. The Los Angeles light pollution gave the night sky a ghostly illumination, like an aurora borealis underlaid by smog. I cut south on the 405 as far as National, took the off-ramp and headed east. At Sepulveda, I hung a left and slowed, finally spotting Mickey's building in the unfamiliar night landscape. I parked out on the street, taking my shoulder bag and duffel. I locked the car behind me and prayed that the chassis, the wheels, and the engine wouldn't be dismantled and gone by morning.

The lights were on in the Hatfields' kitchen. I tapped at the door, and Cordia let me in. Bel was sleeping upright in her chair, so Cordia and I had a whispered conversation while she showed me the guest room with its adjoining bath. Dorothy followed like a puppy-cat, making sure she was in the center of any ongoing discussion. I had to pause more than once to rub behind her ears. I tossed my shoulder bag on the bed. Dorothy promptly claimed ownership, using all twenty pounds to squish and flatten the contents. The last I saw, she had settled like a chicken on a nestful of eggs.

TWELVE

I went up the front stairs and along the gallery, lighting my way with the larger of my flashlights. The two apartments I passed were shrouded in darkness, the sliding glass windows open into what I was guessing were bedrooms. I continued around the corner, where I let myself into Mickey's back door, using the key I'd lifted. I debated about leaving the door locked or unlocked and decided to leave it locked. Ordinarily, I'd have opted to leave the door ajar in case I had to make a hasty exit, but I was feeling anxious and didn't like the possibility of someone coming in on me unheard. I moved through the apartment to the living room. The only light was a thin shaft coming in from the gallery between drapery panels in the dining L. I shone the flashlight beam like a sword, cutting through the shadows. Since I'd been here earlier, the fingerprint technician had been busy with his brushes, leaving powder residue on countless surfaces. I made a quick foray through the dining area and kitchen, then back through the bedroom and bathroom to make sure I was alone.

I returned to the living room and secured the openings between the drapes. I pulled on my rubber gloves. Despite the fact the cops had come and gone, I didn't want to leave evidence that I'd been in the place. I like to think I'd learned something from my little trip through Ted Rich's doggie door. I turned on the overhead light, pausing to swap Mickey's 60-watt bulb for one of the 200-watt bulbs I'd brought with me. Even a cursory glance showed Detective Aldo had been there. Kitchen cabinets stood open. All the mail was missing, and the fishbowl full of matches had been upended on the dining-room table. I pictured the police sorting through the collection for clues, carefully making notes about the bars and restaurants Mickey'd frequented. In truth, only about half the matchbooks would be from places he'd been. The rest were packets other people had acquired for him while traveling, a practice left over from his youth, when he'd assembled hundreds of such covers and mounted them in albums. Who knows why kids like to do shit like that?

I got down to work, methodically emptying the miniature safes he'd created behind the electrical plates. The three sets of phony IDs, the credit cards, and the currency went into my duffel. I spent a long time in his kitchen, sorting through containers with a fine-tooth comb, checking in and behind and under drawers. Once again, I removed the five-gallon water bottles from under the sink and unscrewed the back panel. This time I lifted out the handguns from the rack he'd built and put them in my duffel with the IDs.

I went into the bedroom and took the chenille bedspread and sheets off his bed. Tacky little thing that I am, I paused to check for evidence of recent sexual excess but found none. I pulled off the mattress and checked it carefully, looking for evidence that he'd opened a seam and restitched it. Good theory; no deal. I lay on my back and hunched my way under the bed, where I peeled back the gauzy material that covered the bottom of his box spring. I shone the flashlight across the underside, but no dice. I put the mattress back in place and then remade the bed. This was worse than hotel work, which I'd also done in my day.

I crawled the entire perimeter of wall-to-wall carpeting, pulling up section after section without finding much except a centipede that scared the hell out of me. I tried the bed-table drawer. The diaphragm was gone, as were the bottle of cologne and the tissue paper packet with the enameled heart and gold chain. Well, well, well. His latest inamorata must have heard about the shooting. She was certainly quick to erase the signs of their relationship. She must've had a key of her own, letting herself in sometime between my initial visit and this one. Could she be someone in the building? That was a notion worth exploring.

I spent a good thirty minutes in the bathroom, where I lifted the lid to the toilet tank and used my dental mirror and the angled flashlight to check for items concealed behind it. Nothing. I took all the toiletries out of the medicine cabinet and lifted the entire cabinet off the wall brackets to see if he'd hollowed out a space in the wall behind it. Nope. I checked inside the shower rod, checked the cheap-looking vanity for false fronts or concealed panels. I unscrewed the heater vent and tapped along the baseboards listening for hollow spots. I removed the PVC under the bathroom sink. The gold coins were still there. I loaded those in my duffel and replaced the length of pipe. No telling what the next tenant would make of it if the fake plumbing were discovered at some future date. In the hollow core of the toilet paper roll I found a hundred-dollar bill.

I went through his closet, checking his pockets, looking behind the hanging row of clothes for the possibility of a false wall at the rear. Nothing. The numerous zippered pockets in the black leather jacket were all empty. At the back of the closet, I found his answering machine, which he'd probably unplugged once his phone service was "disconnected or no longer in service." I opened the lid, but the cops had apparently taken the tape. I found one additional stash behind the closet switch plate. In a narrow slot that ran back along a stud, Mickey'd tucked a sealed number ten envelope. I put it in my duffel for later scrutiny.

I had one other cache to unload that I'd saved until last. I went back into the living room and turned off the overhead light. I moved from window to window, looking out at the dark. It was two-thirty in the morning and, for the most part, windows in neighboring buildings were black. Occasionally I would see a light on, but the drapes would be drawn and no one was peeking through the slit. I picked up no movement in the immediate vicinity. Traffic noises had all but died.

I unhooked the two sets of drapes and lifted down the rods. I removed the finials, flashed a light down into the hollow core, and removed the cash. I replaced the rods and rehung the drapes, moving with a sudden sense of anxiety. I lifted my head. Had I heard something?

Maybe the removal of the crime tape was done to tempt me, and Detective Aldo was outside waiting. He'd be thrilled to catch me with the duffel load of burglar tools, the handguns, and the phony documents. I kept the overhead light off, restricting myself to the use of my penlight as I went through the apartment, quickly gathering my tools, checking to see that I'd left no personal traces. The whole time I had the feeling I'd overlooked something obvious, but I knew I'd be pushing my luck to go back and try to figure it out. I was so focused on escape that I came close to missing the crunch of cinders and the putter of a motorcycle as it glided to a stop in the alleyway below.

Belatedly, I realized I'd picked up the muted roar as the motorcycle passed along the street out in front. The rider must have cut the switch at the entrance to the alley, coasting the rest of the way. I went over to the rear window and opened the drapes a crack. From that angle, I couldn't see much, but I was relatively certain someone was moving along the alley. I closed my eyes and listened. Within thirty seconds, I could hear the chink of boots on the stair treads, accompanied by a jingle as each step was mounted. The guy was coming up the back way. Possibly a tenant or a neighbor. I turned off my flashlight and followed the sounds of the guy's progress as he rounded the gallery along the back of the building and came up to Mickey's front door. I had hoped to hear him pass. Instead, I heard a tap and a hoarse whispering. "Hey, Mr. Magruder. Open up. It's me."

I passed through Mickey's bedroom and headed for

the rear door, fumbling in my jeans pocket for the key. My hand was steady, but every other part of me was shaking so hard I couldn't hit the keyhole. I was afraid to use my flashlight because the guy had now moved to Mickey's bedroom window, where the tapping became sharper, a harsh clicking as though he might be rapping on the glass with a ring. "Open the fuck up and get your ass out here." He had moved the few steps to the front door, where he began to knock again. This time, the pounding was of the fee-fi-fo-fum variety and seemed to shake the intervening walls.

The next-door neighbor, whose bedroom must have been contiguous with Mickey's, yelled out his window, "Shaddup, you prick! We're tryin' to sleep in here."

The guy at the door said something even worse than the F word, which I won't repeat. I could hear him jingle his way toward the neighbor's bedroom window, where I pictured him bashing through the glass with his fist. Sure enough, I heard the impact of his blow and the subsequent tinkling of glass, followed by a startled yelp from the tenant. I took advantage of this tender Hallmark moment to shine a quick light on the keyhole. I turned the key in the lock and was almost out the door when I stopped in my tracks. I'd never get into this apartment again. By morning the sheriff's deputy would arrive and the locks would be changed. While I could probably pick my way in, I didn't want to take the risk. Now that all the stashes had been cleaned out, there was only one thing of value. I set down the two duffels and returned to Mickey's closet, where I lifted the leather jacket from its hanger and

167

shrugged myself into it, then grabbed the two duffels and eased out the back door, barely pausing long enough to lock it.

I was halfway down the back stairs when a face appeared above me. Over the wrought-iron railing, I saw shaggy corn-yellow hair, a long bony face, narrow shoulders, and a sunken chest in a blue denim jacket with the sleeves cut out. I slung one duffel over my shoulder, hugged the other to my body, and began to bound down the stairs, taking them two at a time while the guy in the jacket strode toward the landing. I reached the bottom of the stairs at the same moment he started down. I could hear every step he took because of the jingling of his boots, which must have been decorated with chains. I ran on tiptoe, keeping wide on the outside, conscious to avoid knocking into the water meters near the building.

The manager's apartment was fully dark by now, but Cordia, as promised, had left the back door unlocked. I turned the knob and opened the door to let myself in. My entrance was delayed briefly when the duffel over my shoulder got hung up on the door frame. I jerked it free and flung both duffels into the room. I was just turning to close the door when Dorothy streaked out through the narrow opening. She must have come running to see what I was up to and then couldn't resist making a bid for freedom. Once out, she stopped, astonished to find herself alone in the chilly dark at that hour. I heard a thumping noise and a resounding curse. The guy must have caught a foot on a water meter and gone down sprawling. I could hear him cussing as he recovered his gait and came limping down on us in a towering rage. If he caught up with Dorothy, he was going to wring her neck and fling her over the fence, thus forcing her return to this life in some other form. I grabbed her by the tail and dragged her backward while she struggled to gain purchase on the concrete with her outstretched claws. I hauled her, squawking, into the dark of the kitchen, closed the door, and bolted it in one motion.

I sank down on the floor, clutching her against me while my heart kept on banging and my breath came in gasps. I heard the jingling footsteps approach and come to a halt outside the Hatfields' door. The guy kicked the door hard enough to hurt himself. He must have had a flashlight with him, because a beam was soon being played across the far wall, briefly raking the kitchen table. The wand of light streaked back and forth. At one point, I could tell he'd angled up on tiptoe, trying to shine the light down into the darkened area where I was crouched. Meanwhile, Dorothy strained against my embrace and finally manage to wiggle free. I lunged, but she eluded me. She gave me a cranky look and then made a point of sashaying toward the dining room so that her path took her directly through his beam of light. There was a long, labored silence. I thought he'd break the door down, but he must have thought better of it. Finally, I heard the scritch and jingle of his boots as they receded along the walkway.

I slumped against the door, waiting to hear his motorcycle start up and go screaming away in the night. There was no such reassuring sound. I finally staggered to my feet, retrieved the two duffels, and crept through the dining room toward the guest room. The nightlight in the hallway illuminated my way. The two other bedroom doors were closed, Cordia and Belmira having slept through the uproar in the enveloping silence of poor hearing. Once in the guest room, I kicked my shoes off and lay down on the bed, still wearing Mickey's jacket. Dorothy was already on the bed. The pillow turned out to be hers so I wasn't allowed the full use of it, just a few paltry inches around the edges. The still-indignant cat now felt compelled to wash from head to toe, comforting herself after the insult of having her tail pulled so rudely. The bedroom curtains were closed, but I found myself staring at them, fearful a fist would come smashing through the glass. Dorothy's steady licking took on a restful quality. The warmth of my body activated Mickey's personal scent from the lining of the jacket. Cigarette smoke and Aqua Velva. I stopped shivering and eventually fell asleep with Dorothy's feet resting neatly in my hair.

I woke to the smell of coffee. I was still wearing Mickey's jacket, but someone had placed a heavy afghan across my legs. I put a hand above my head, feeling across the pillow, but Dorothy was gone. The door was open a crack. Sunlight made the curtains glow. I looked at my watch and saw that it was close to eight. I put my feet over the side of the bed and ran a hand through my hair, yawning. I was getting too old to horse around at all hours of the night. I went into the bathroom and brushed my teeth, then showered and dressed again. In the end, I looked much as I had when I'd arrived.

Belmira was sitting at the kitchen table, watching a talk show, when I finally made my appearance. She was a tiny thing, quite thin, so short her feet barely touched the floor. Today, she wore a white bib apron over a red-and-white print housedress. She was shelling peas, the colander in her lap, a paper bag sitting next to her with the rim folded back. Dorothy was on the counter licking butter from the butter dish.

Bel smiled at me shyly. "Coffee's over there," she said. "The sheriff's deputy just arrived with the locksmith, so Cordia went upstairs to let them in. Did you sleep well?"

"I didn't get enough of it, but what I had was fine." I crossed to the coffeepot, an old-fashioned percolator sitting on the stove. There was a mug on the counter, along with a carton of milk. I poured a cup of coffee and added milk.

"Would you like to have an egg? We have cereal, too. Cordi made some oatmeal with raisins. That's what we have. Brown sugar's in the canister if you want to help yourself."

"I think I better go on up and see if I can catch Mickey's neighbors before they go off to work. I can always have breakfast once the deputy's gone." At the door, I looked back. "Did she say anything about a motorcycle parked in the alley?"

Belmira shook her head.

I took my coffee mug with me and headed for the stairs. I could see the sheriff's patrol car parked at the curb, not far from my VW, which as far as I could tell was still intact. The day was sunny and cool, the air already fragrant with the morning's accumulation of exhaust fumes. I passed along the second-floor gallery. A few neighbors had gathered to watch the locksmith at work. Maybe, for them, this was a cautionary tale about paying the rent on time. Most seemed dressed for work except for one woman in her robe and slippers, who'd also brought her morning coffee with her. Like rubberneckers passing a highway accident, they looked on, both repelled and attracted by the sight of someone else's misfortune. This was all faintly reminiscent of the fires that burned across the Santa Teresa foothills back in 1964. During the long smoky evenings, people had gathered on the street in clusters, sipping beer and chatting while the flames danced across the distant mountains. The presence of catastrophe seemed to break down the usual social barriers until the atmosphere was nearly festive.

Cordia Hatfield was keeping a careful eye on the situation, standing in the open doorway with a white sweater thrown over her shoulders. Her oversized blue-and-white checked housedress was worn ankle-length, and she sported the same pair of slippers with her bunion peeking out. She turned as I approached. "I see you found the coffee. How'd you sleep last night?"

"Dorothy was stingy with the pillow, but aside from that I did great."

"She was never one to share. Even when she came back, she insisted on having her old room. We were going to keep it closed up for guests, but she refused to use the litter box until she got her way."

Mickey's immediate neighbor, who appeared to be

somewhere in his forties, emerged from his apartment, pulling on a tweed sport coat over a royal-blue Superman T-shirt. His shiny brown hair extended to his waist. He wore large metal-framed glasses with yellow lenses. A mustache and a closely trimmed beard bracketed a full complement of white teeth. His jeans were ripped and faded, and his cowboy boots had three-inch platform soles. Behind him, I could see the broken bedroom window, patched together now with cardboard and a jagged bolt of silver duct tape. He said, "Hey, Ms. Hatfield. How are you today?"

She said, "Morning. Just dandy. What happened to your window? That'll have to be repaired."

"Sorry about that. I'll take care of it. I called a glass company on Olympic, and they said they'd be out to take a look. Has Mickey been evicted?"

"I'm afraid so," she said.

The deputy clearly wasn't needed, so he returned to his car and went about his business. The locksmith beckoned to Cordia. She excused herself, and the two of them moved inside to have a consultation. The next-door neighbor had paused to watch the proceedings and he now greeted a couple who came out of the third apartment on that side. Both were dressed for work. The woman murmured something to her husband and the two continued toward the stairs. Mickey's neighbor nodded politely in my direction, acknowledging my presence.

I murmured, "Hi, how're you?"

"Good, thanks. What kind of crap is this? This dude's in a coma and they're changing the locks on him?"

"I guess the owners are pretty hard-nosed."

"They'd have to be," he said. "So how's Mickey doing? You a friend of his?"

"You could say that, I guess. We used to be married."

"No shit. When was this?"

"Early seventies. It didn't last long. I'm Kinsey, by the way. And you're . . ."

"Ware Beason," he said. "Everybody calls me Wary." He was still working to absorb the information about my marital connection to Mickey. "An ex-wife? How cool. Mickey never said a word."

"We haven't kept in touch. What about you? Have you known him long?"

"He's lived in that apartment close to fifteen years. I've been here six. Now and then I run into him at Lionel's Pub and we have a few beers. He feeds my fish if we have a gig someplace."

"You're a professional musician?"

Wary shrugged self-consciously. "I play keyboard in a combo. Mostly weekends here locally, though I sometimes play out of town as well. I also wait tables at a health food café down on National. I take it you heard about what happened?"

"I did, but it was purely by accident. I didn't even know he was in trouble until earlier this week. I'm from Santa Teresa. I tried calling from up there, but his phone was disconnected. I didn't think too much of it until a couple of detectives showed up and said he'd been shot. I was horrified."

"Yeah, me too. I guess it took 'em awhile to figure

out who he was. They showed up at my door about seven A.M. Monday. Big dark-haired guy?"

"Right. He's the one I talked to. I thought I better head on down in case there was something I could do."

"So how's he feeling? Have you seen him?"

"He's still in a coma so it's hard to say. I went over there yesterday and he didn't look too good."

"Damn. That's a shame. I should probably go myself, but I've been putting it off."

"Don't even bother unless you notify the cops. You can only visit with their permission, and then they keep someone with you in case you try to pull the plug."

"Jeez. Poor guy. I can't believe it."

"Me neither," I said. "By the way, what was that bunch of hollering last night? Did you hear it? It sounded like somebody went berserk and started banging on the walls."

"Hey, no shit. That was me he was yelling at. And look what he did, bashed his fist through the glass. I thought he'd dive in after me, but he took off."

"What was he so mad about?"

"Who knows? He's some pal of Mickey's; at least, he acts that way. Mickey never seemed that glad to see him."

"How often did he show up?"

"Every couple of weeks. They must've had some kind of deal going, but I can't think what."

"How long has that gone on?"

"Maybe two–three months. I should probably put it this way: I never saw him before then."

"You know his name?"

Wary shook his head. "Nope. Mickey never introduced us. He seemed embarrassed to be seen with him, and who wouldn't be?"

"No shit."

"Guy's a scuzball, a real sleaze. Every time I see that show about America's Most Wanted, I start lookin' for his face."

"Literally? You think he's wanted by the cops?"

"If he's not, he will be. What a creep."

"That's odd. Mickey always hated lowlifes. He used to be a vice detective. We worked for the same department up in Santa Teresa."

"You're a cop too?"

"I was. Now I work as a P.I."

"A private investigator?"

"That's right."

"Oh, I get it. You're looking into this."

"Not officially, no, but I *am* curious."

"Hey, I'm with you. Anything I can do to help, you just say."

"Thanks. What about the scuzball? Couldn't he be the one who shot Mickey? He sounds like a nut to me."

"Nah, I doubt it. If he did, he wouldn't come around pounding on the door, thinking Mickey'd be there. Guy who shot Mickey must have figured he was dead." Wary glanced at his watch. "I better get a move on. How long you going to be here?"

"I'm not sure. Another hour, I'd guess."

"Can I buy you breakfast? That's where I'm heading. There's a place around the corner. Wouldn't take more'n thirty minutes if you have to get back."

I did a quick debate. I hated to leave the premises, but there really wasn't anything more to do. Wary might prove to be useful. More important, I was starving. I said "sure" and then took a brief time-out to let Cordia know where I was going.

Wary and I headed down the front stairs, chatting as we went. Idly, he said, "If you want, after breakfast, I'll show you where he was shot. It's just a couple blocks away."

THIRTEEN

I'll skip the breakfast conversation. There's nothing so boring as listening to other people get acquainted. We chatted. We traded brief, heavily edited autobiographical sketches, stories about Mickey, theories about the motive for the shooting. In the meantime, I discovered that I liked Wary Beason, though I promptly erased all his personal data. As crass as it sounds, I didn't seriously think I'd ever see him again. Like the passenger sitting next to you on a cross-country plane ride, it's possible to connect with someone, even when the encounter has no meaning and no ultimate consequence.

I did appreciate his showing me the spot where Mickey was gunned down, a nondescript section of sidewalk in front of a coin and jewelry shop. The sign in the window advertised rare coins, rare stamps, pocket watches, antiques, and coin supplies. "We also make low-rate loans," the sign said. At 3 A.M. I didn't think Mickey'd been there to negotiate a loan.

Wary remained silent while I stood for a minute, looking out at the surrounding businesses. There was a pool hall across the street. I assumed the detectives had checked it out. Also the bar called McNalley's, half a block down.

"You mentioned you used to drink with Mickey at Lionel's. Is the pub close by?"

"Back in that direction," Wary said, gesturing.

"Any chance Mickey could have been there earlier that night?"

"No way. Mickey'd been eighty-sixed from Lionel's until he paid his tab." Wary took off his glasses and cleaned the yellow lenses on the hem of his T-shirt. He held his frames to the light so he could check for streaks, and then he put his glasses on again and waited to see what I would ask next.

"Where was he, then? You have a guess?"

"Well, he wasn't at McNalley's, because that's where I was. I know the cops checked the bars all up and down the street. They didn't learn a thing . . . or so they said."

"He was out doing something, and he was doing it on foot."

"Not necessarily. I mean, just because he'd sold his car doesn't mean he hoofed it. Somebody could've picked him up and taken him somewhere. Out for drinks or dinner. Could have been anyplace."

"Back up a minute. Do you happen to remember when he sold his car?"

"Couple of months back."

"You're talking about the end of March?"

"That sounds right. Anyway, the point is, nobody even saw him leave the building that night."

"So what's your theory?"

"Well, let's just say for the sake of argument he was

179

in someone else's car. They go out for dinner or drinks and end up closing the place down. Two in the morning, they drive back to Culver City. He—"

"Or she," I inserted, promptly.

Wary smiled. "Right. . . . The shooter could have dropped Mickey at the corner and then driven down a block like he's on his way home. Shooter parks, waits in the dark while Mickey walks the intervening block. Minute he comes abreast, the shooter steps out and— *boom!*—plugs him twice. Shooter tosses the gun and takes off before anybody figures out what's up."

"You really think it happened like that?"

Wary shrugged. "It could have, that's all I'm saying. The cops canvassed all the bars and pool halls within a ten-block radius. Mickey hadn't been in any of 'em, but they know he'd been drinking *somewhere* because he had a blood alcohol of point one-four."

"How'd you hear that?"

"The detective, the dark one, mentioned it in passing."

"Really. That's interesting. What'd they make of it, did anybody say?"

"No, and I didn't think to ask. Mickey always had a buzz on. He was probably pushing point oh-eight any given day of the week."

"He was legally drunk?"

"Legally plastered is a better way to put it. For a while, he straightened up. He went on the wagon, but it didn't last long. February he went on a bender, and I guess that's when he got himself fired from his job. He tried to straighten up again, after that, but without much success. He'd go a couple days and then fall right back. I give him credit. He did try. He just wasn't strong enough to do it by himself."

I was suddenly feeling restless and needed to move. I started walking again and Wary followed, catching up with me. I said, "What about the woman he was seeing?"

He gave me an odd look, equal parts surprise and embarrassment. "How'd you know about her?"

I tapped my temple. "A little birdie told me. You know who she was?"

"Nope. Never met her. Mickey made sure."

"How come?"

"Maybe he thought I'd try to hustle her myself."

"Did you actually see her?"

"In passing. Not to recognize later. She always came up the back stairs and let herself in that way."

"She had her own key?"

"She must have. Mickey never left his doors unlocked. Some days she showed up before he got home from work."

"What about her car? Did you ever see a vehicle parked out back?"

"Never looked. I figured it was his business. Why should I butt in?"

"How often was she there?"

"I'd say every two to three weeks. Not to be gross about it, but the walls in the building are not exactly soundproof. I have to say Mickey's alcohol intake never seemed to hamper him in the performance of his duties."

"How do you know it was him? Isn't there a chance he lent his apartment to someone else? Maybe he had a friend who needed a place to misbehave."

"Oh, no. It was him. I'd take an oath on that. He's been involved with this woman for at least a year."

"How do you know there was only one? He might have had a string of women."

"Well, it's possible, I guess."

"Any chance she lived in the building?" I asked.

"In *our* building? I doubt it. Mickey would've felt hemmed in by anybody living that close. He liked his freedom. He didn't like anybody checking up on him. Like sometimes—say, he was gone for the weekend—I might ask him, you know, How's the weekend, where'd you end up? Simple shit like that. Mickey wouldn't answer questions. If you pressed, he changed the subject."

"What about since the shooting? Do you think the woman's been there?"

"I really couldn't say for sure. I go to work at four and don't get home till after midnight. She could have gone in while I was off. Actually, come to think of it, I thought I heard her yesterday. Again last night, too, before that biker geek showed up. What an asshole. Glass company says it'll cost me a hundred bucks to get that fixed."

"Wary, that was me you heard last night. I went in and pulled his personal belongings before they had a chance to change the locks. I suspected his girlfriend'd been there, because a couple of personal articles I'd seen suddenly came up missing."

We'd reached the building by then. It was time to hit the road. I thanked him for his help. I made a note of his phone number and then gave him my business card with my home number jotted on the back. We parted company at the stairs.

I watched Wary go up, and then I went back to the Hatfields' to collect the two duffels. They invited me for lunch, but I'd just finished breakfast and I was anxious to get back. We said our good-byes. I thanked them profusely, including Dort in my expressions of appreciation. I didn't dare be rude in case they were right about her incarnation.

Their door closed behind me, and I was just heading for my car when I chanced to glance over at the line of mailboxes under the stairs. Mickey's was crammed with mail. I stared, transfixed. Apparently, the cops had neglected to put a hold on the mail coming in. I wondered how many civil and criminal codes I'd violated so far. Surely, one more transgression wouldn't add that much to my sentence. I felt along the bottom of my shoulder bag, extracted my key picks, and went to work on the lock. This one was so easy it would have yielded to a hairpin, which I don't happen to carry. I pulled out the wad of mail and perused it in haste. The bulk of it consisted of an oversized pulp weekly devoted to survivalist lore: ads for mercenaries, articles about pending gun legislation, government cover-ups, and citizens' rights. I put the magazine back in the box so the contents would appear untouched. The remaining two envelopes I shoved in my shoulder bag for later consideration. I'll tell you right now, they

183

turned out to be nothing, which disappointed me greatly. I hate risking jail time on behalf of third-class mail.

When I arrived in Santa Teresa at 1:35, I snagged the morning paper from the doorstep and let myself in. I tossed the paper on the counter, set the duffels on the floor, and crossed to my desk. There were several messages waiting on my answering machine. I played them, taking notes, aware that it was probably time to get down to paid employment. In the interest of earning a living, I drove over to the office and devoted the rest of the afternoon to servicing the clients with business pending. In any given month, I might juggle some fifteen to twenty cases, not all of them pressing. Despite the fact I had money in the bank, I couldn't afford to neglect matters already in the works. I'd just spent the past three days chasing down Mickey's situation. Now it was time to get my professional affairs in order. I had calls to return and receipts to tally and enter on the books. There were numerous invoices to be typed and submitted, along with the accompanying reports to write while my notes were still fresh. I also had a few stern letters to compose, trying to collect from slow-pays (all attorneys, please note), plus bills of my own to pay.

I was checking my calendar for the days ahead when I remembered the phone call made from Mickey's number to mine on March 27. I'd never checked my office schedule to see where I was that day. As with my day planner at home, that Thursday was blank. March

26 and 28 were both blank too, so I couldn't use either as a springboard for recollection.

At five-thirty, I locked up and drove back to my apartment through the Santa Teresa equivalent of rush-hour traffic, which meant it took me fifteen minutes to get home instead of the usual ten. The sun had finally burned through a lingering marine layer, and the heat in the vehicle was making me sleepy. I could tell I'd have to atone for my late-night activities. I parked down the street from my apartment and pushed through the gate. My place felt cozy, and I was relieved to be home. The emotional roller coaster of the past few days had generated an odd mood—weariness masquerading as depression. Whatever the source, I was feeling raw. I set my shoulder bag on a bar stool and went around the end of the counter into the kitchen-ette. I hadn't eaten since breakfast. I opened the refrigerator and stared at the empty shelves. When I thought about Mickey's cupboards, I realized my food supplies didn't look much better than his. Absurd that we'd married when we were simultaneously too much alike and much too different.

Soon after the wedding, I began to realize he was out of control . . . at least from the perspective of someone with my basically fearful nature. I wasn't comfortable with what I perceived as his dissipation and his self-indulgence. My Aunt Gin had taught me to be moderate—in my personal habits if not in my choice of cusswords. At first, Mickey's hedonism had been appealing. I remembered experiencing a nearly giddy relief at his gluttony, his love of intoxication, his insatiable appetite for sex. What he offered was a tacit

185

permission to explore my lustiness, unawakened until then. I related to his disdain for authority and I was fascinated by his disregard for the system, even while he was employed in a job dedicated to upholding law and order. I, too, had tended to operate outside accepted social boundaries. In grade school and, later, junior and senior high schools, I was often tardy or truant, drawn to the lowlife students, in part because they represented my own defiance and belligerence. Unfortunately, by the age of twenty, when I met Mickey, I was already on my way back from the outer fringes of bad behavior. While Mickey was beginning to embrace his inner demons, I was already in the process of retreating from mine.

Now—fifteen years later—it's impossible to describe how alive I was for that short period.

For dinner, I made myself an olive-pimento-cheese sandwich, using that divine Kraft concoction that comes in a jar. I cut the bread neatly into four fingers with the crusts intact and used a section of paper toweling as both napkin and plate. With this wholesome entrée, I sipped a glass of Chardonnay and felt thoroughly comforted. Afterward, I wadded up my dinnerware and tossed it in the trash. Having supped and done the dishes, I placed the two duffels on the counter and unloaded my tools and the booty I'd lifted from Mickey's the night before. I laid the items on the counter, hoping the sight of them would spark a new interpretation.

There was a knock at my door. I grabbed the newspaper and opened it, spreading it over the items as if I'd been reading with interest, catching up on events. I crossed to the door and peeked through the porthole to find my landlord standing on the porchlet with a plate of homemade brownies covered in plastic wrap. Henry's a retired commercial baker who now occupies his time catering tea parties for elderly widows in the neighborhood. He also supplies Rosie's restaurant with a steady line of baked goods: sandwich breads, dinner rolls, pies, and cakes. I confess I was not entirely happy to see him. While I adore him, I'm not always candid with him about my nocturnal labors.

I opened the door. We made happy noises at each other while Henry stepped in. I tried to steer him toward the sofa, hoping to divert his attention, but before I could even protest, he leaned over and closed the newspaper to make room for the plate. There sat the four handguns, the packets of phony documents, credit cards, and cash. To all appearances, I'd turned to robbing banks for a living.

He set the plate on the counter. "What's all this?"

I put a hand on his arm. "Don't ask. The less you know, the better. You'll have to trust me on this."

He looked at me quizzically, an expression in his eyes I hadn't seen before: trust and mistrust, curiosity, alarm. "But I want to know."

I had only a split second to decide what to say. "This is Mickey's. I lifted the stuff because a sheriff's deputy was scheduled to change the locks on his doors."

"Why?"

"He's being evicted. I had one chance to search, and I had to take advantage."

"But what *is* all this?"

187

"I have no idea. Look, I know how his mind works. Mickey's paranoid. He tends to hide anything of value. I went through his apartment systematically, and this is what I found. I couldn't leave it there."

"The guns are stolen?"

"I doubt it. Mickey always had guns. In all likelihood, they're legal."

"But you don't know that for sure. Mickey didn't authorize you to do this. Couldn't you end up in trouble?"

"Well, yeah, but I can't worry about that *now*. I didn't know what else to do. They were locking him out. This stuff was hidden in the walls, behind panels, in phony bathroom pipes. Meanwhile, he's in the hospital, completely out of it."

"What happens to his possessions? Doesn't he have furniture?"

"Tons. I'll probably offer to have things moved into storage until we see how he fares."

"Have you spoken to the doctors yet?"

"They're not going to talk to me. The cops put the lid on that possibility. Anyway, I made a big point of saying we've been out of touch for years. I can't come along afterward and ask for daily updates like I'm so distraught. They'd never believe me."

"But you said you weren't going to get involved in this."

"I know. I'm not. Well, I am a little bit. At the moment, I don't even know what's going on."

"Then leave it alone."

"It's too late for that. Besides, you're the one who said I ought to check it out."

"But you never listen."

"Well, I did this time."

"Will you listen if I tell you to butt out?"

"Of course. Once I know what it's about."

"Kinsey, this is clearly police business. You can't keep quiet about this stuff. You ought to call those detectives—"

"Nope. Don't want to. I'm not going to do that. I don't like those guys."

"At least they can be objective."

"So can I."

"Oh, really?"

"Yes, *really*. Henry, don't do this."

"What am I doing?"

"You're disapproving of my behavior. It tears me up."

"As well it should."

I clamped my mouth shut. I was feeling stubborn and resistant. I was already in the thick of it and couldn't bail out. "I'll think about it some."

"You better do more than that. Kinsey, I'm concerned about you. I know you're upset, but this really isn't like you."

"You know what? It *is* like me. This is exactly who I am: a liar and a thief. You want to know something else? I don't feel bad about it. I'm completely unrepentant. More than that. I like it. It makes me feel alive."

A shadow crossed his face and something familiar seemed to scurry into hiding. He was silent for a moment and then said mildly, "Well. In that case, I'm sure you don't need any lectures from me."

He was gone before I could reply. The door closed

quietly behind him. The plate of brownies remained. I could tell they were still warm because the air was filled with the scent of chocolate and the plastic wrap was foggy with condensation. I stood where I was. I felt nothing. My mind was blank except for the one assertion. I had to do this. I did. Something inside me had shifted. I could sense the muscles in my face set with obstinacy. There was no way I'd let go, no way I'd back away from this . . . whatever it was.

I sat down at the counter, propping my feet on the rung of the kitchen stool. I folded the newspaper neatly. I picked up the envelope and opened the seal. Inside were two passbooks for Mickey's savings accounts, six cash-register receipts, a Delta ticket envelope, and a folded sheet of paper. I examined the passbooks first. The first had once held a total of $15,000, but the account had been closed and the money withdrawn in January of 1981. The second savings account was opened that same January with a deposit of $5,000. This was apparently the money he'd been living on of late. I noticed that a series of $600 cash withdrawals corresponded to deposits in his checking account with the following discrepancy: Mickey would pull $600 and deposit $200, apparently keeping $400 in pocket change—"walking around" money, as he used to refer to it. I had to guess this was petty cash, used to pay his bar bills, his dinners out, items from the market. The six cash-register receipts were dated January 17, January 31, February 7, February 21, March 7, and March 21. The ink was faded, but the name of the establishment wasn't that hard to read: the Honky-Tonk. I was assuming he'd sold his car sometime in the third week in March because he'd deposited $900 in his checking account. The loss of his transportation might explain the sudden cessation of visits after so many regular Friday-night appearances. Why drive all the way to Santa Teresa to have a drink when there were bars in his neighborhood? I set the question aside since there was no way to answer it. Before examining the last item, I pulled out my index cards and made some notes. There's always the temptation to let this part slide, but I had to capture the data while everything was fresh in my mind.

Once I'd jotted down what I remembered, adding the cash count, credit card numbers, passbook numbers, and dates of receipts, I gave myself permission to proceed, opening the Delta ticket envelope, which really interested me. The flight coupons had been used. I removed the itinerary and the passenger receipt. Mickey had flown to Louisville, Kentucky, by way of Cincinnati on Thursday, May 8, returning late in the day on Monday, May 12. This impromptu five-day excursion had cost him more than $800 in plane fares alone.

I reached for the remaining item, a folded piece of paper, and read the brief statement, which was dated January 15, 1981. This was a simple letter agreement between Mickey Magruder and Tim Littenberg, signed by the latter, in which he acknowledged receipt of the sum of $10,000, a no-interest loan with a five-year balloon payment due and payable five months ago— January 15, 1986.

I packed up the guns and other items, hid them in a safe place, and grabbed my jacket and handbag.

FOURTEEN

The main drag in Colgate is four lanes wide, lined with an assortment of businesses ranging from carpet stores to barbershops, with a gas station on every other corner and an automobile dealership on the blocks between. Colgate—sprawling, eclectic, and unpretentious—provides housing for those who work in Santa Teresa but can't afford to live there. The population count of the two communities is roughly the same, but their dispositions are different, like siblings whose personalities reflect their relative positions in the family matrix. Santa Teresa is the older of the two, stylish and staid. Colgate is the more playful, less insistent on conformity, more likely to tolerate differences among its residents. Few of its shops stay open after 6 P.M. Bars, pool halls, drive-in theaters, and bowling alleys form the exception.

The parking lot at the Honky-Tonk looked much as it had fourteen years before. Cars had changed. Whereas in the seventies the patrons were driving Mustangs and VW vans painted in psychedelic shades, streetlights now gleamed on Porsches, BMWs, and TransAms. Crossing the lot, I experienced the same curious excitement I'd felt when I was single and hunting. Given my current state of enlightenment, I wouldn't dream of circulating through the bar scene—barhopping, we called it—but I did in those days. In the sixties and seventies, that's what you did for recreation. That's how you met guys. That's how you got laid. What Women's Liberation "liberated" was our attitude toward sex. Where we once used sex for barter, now we gave it away. I marvel at the prostitutes we must have put out of business, doling out sexual "favors" in the name of personal freedom. What were we thinking? All we ended up with were bar bums afflicted with pubic vermin.

The Honky-Tonk had expanded, incorporating space formerly occupied by the adjacent furniture store that used to advertise liquidation sales every six to eight months. There was a line at the door, where one of the bouncers was checking IDs by running them through a scanner. Each patron, once cleared, was stamped HT on the back of the right hand, the HT of the Honky-Tonk apparently serving as clearance to drink. That way the waiters and bartenders didn't have to card each cherubic patron ordering rum and Coke—the drinker's equivalent of the training bra.

Now sporting my ink brand, I walked through a fog of cigarette smoke, trying to get a feel for the age and financial status of the crowd inside. There was a large infusion of college students, fresh-faced, uninhibited, their naïveté and bad judgment not yet having come home to roost. The rest were chronic singles, the same aging bachelors and divorcées who'd been eyeballing each other since I'd first buzzed through.

SUE GRAFTON

There was still sawdust on the floor. Between the dark-painted wainscoting and the pressed-tin ceiling, the walls were hung with old black-and-white photographs showing Colgate as it had been sixty years before: bucolic, unspoiled, rolling hills stretching out as far as the eye could see. The images were illuminated by gaudy beer signs, red and green neon tinting the vanished grasslands and sunsets.

There were also countless photographs of local celebrities and regulars, pictures taken on St. Patrick's Day, New Year's Eve, and other occasions when the Tonk closed its doors to the public and hosted private parties. I spotted two 8-by-11 photos of Mickey, Pete Shackelford, and Roy Littenberg. The first showed them in police uniform, standing at parade rest: solemn-faced, stiff-backed, serious about law and order. In the second, they were seasoned, men who'd become cynics, guys with old eyes who now smiled over cigarettes and highballs, arms flung casually across one another's shoulders. Roy Littenberg was the oldest by a good ten years. Of the three, he was now dead and Mickey was barely clinging to life. I wondered if there was a way to conjure them up out of memories and smoke—three cops, like ghosts, visible as long as I didn't turn and try to look at them directly.

Two long narrow rooms ran side by side, lined with wooden booths. Each had its own sound system, waves of music pounding against the senses as I moved from room to room. The first held the bar and the second a dance floor, surrounded by tables. The third room, since added, was sufficient to accommodate six pool tables, all of them occupied. The guys played Foosball

194

and darts. The "girls" trooped in and out of the ladies' room, touching up their eye makeup, hiking up their pantyhose. I followed them in, taking advantage of an empty stall to avail myself of the facilities. I could hear two women in the adjoining stall, one barfing up her dinner while the other offered encouraging comments. "That's fine. Don't force it. You're doing great. It'll come." If I'd even heard of it in my day, I'd have assumed Bulimia was the capital of some newly formed Baltic state.

When I left the stall, there were four women in line and another three in front of the mirrors. I waited for an empty place at a sink, washing my hands while I checked my reflection. The fluorescent lighting gave my otherwise unblemished skin a sickly appearance, emphasizing the bags under my eyes. My hair looked like thatch. I wore no lipstick, but that was probably just as well, as the addition would have played up the yellow cast in my aging complexion. I was wearing Mickey's black leather jacket as a talisman, the same old blue jeans, and a black turtleneck, though I'd traded my usual tennis shoes for my usual boots. Mostly, I was dawdling, avoiding the moment when I'd have to perch on a bar stool and buy myself a drink. The two young women emerged from their stall, both of them thin as snakes. The barfer pulled out a prepasted toothbrush and began to scrub. In five years the stomach acid would eat through her tooth enamel, if she didn't drop dead first.

I emerged from the ladies' room, passing the dance floor on my left. I ventured over to the bar, where I bought myself a draft beer. In the absence of available bar stools, I drank the beer standing by myself, trying to look like I was keeping an appointment. Now and then I'd glance at my watch, like I was somewhat annoyed because I didn't have all night. I'm sure many people nearby were completely fooled by this. A few guys assessed me from a distance, not because I was "hot" but because I represented fresh meat, waiting to be graded and stamped.

I deleted my ego from the situation and tried to scrutinize the place from Mickey's point of view. What had possessed him to lend Tim Littenberg the money? Mickey wasn't one to take risks like that. He kept his assets liquid even if he earned very little in the way of interest. He was probably happiest making deposits to the Curtain Rod Savings and Loan. Tim Littenberg— or his dad—must have made a hell of a pitch. Nostalgia might have played a part. Lit and his wife were never good with money. They'd lived from paycheck to paycheck, overdrawn, in debt, their credit cards maxed out. If Tim had needed a stake, they probably didn't have the cash to lend. Whatever the motivation, Mickey'd apparently made the deal. The note had been signed and payment had come due. I'd seen no evidence the loan had been repaid. Curious. Mickey certainly needed the money, and the Honky-Tonk was clearly doing good business.

Near the wall, a bar stool became vacant and I eased into the spot. My eyes strayed back to the mounted photographs and I studied the one hanging next to me. The Three Musketeers again. In this one, Mickey, Shack, and Lit were sitting at the bar, glasses aloft, offering a toast to someone off to their left. Dixie was visible in the background, her eyes fastened on Mickey—a look both hungry and possessive. Why hadn't I seen that at the time? What kind of dunce was I? I squinted at the picture, taking in the faces, one by one. Lit had always been the best-looking of the three. He was tall, narrow through the shoulders, long arms and legs, beautiful long fingers. I'm a sucker for good teeth and his were even and white, except for one cuspid that sat slightly askew, giving his smile a boyish appeal. His chin was pronounced, his bony jaw wide at the apex. His Adam's apple danced when he spoke. The last time I'd seen him was maybe four years ago and then just in passing. His hair was thinning by then. He'd been in his early sixties, and from what Shack had said he was already in the midst of a struggle for his life.

I rotated slightly on the bar stool and scanned the area, hoping to see Tim. I'd never met Lit's son. Back when I was married to Mickey and hanging out with his parents, he was already grown and gone. He'd joined the army in 1970, and for the period in question he was off in Vietnam. In those days, a lot of STPD cops were ex-army, very gung-ho about the military, supportive of our presence in Southeast Asia. The public by then had lost patience with the war, but not in that circle. I'd seen pictures of Tim that his parents passed around. He always looked grubby and content, a cigarette between his lips, his helmet pushed back, his rifle resting against his knees. Lit would read portions of his letters in which he described his exploits. To me, he sounded reckless and defiant, a bit too enthusiastic, a twenty-year-old kid who spent his days stoned, who loved to kill "gooks" and brag about it later to his friends back home. He'd been brought up on charges after a particularly nasty incident involving two dead Vietnamese babies. Lit stopped saying much after that, and by the time of Tim's dishonorable discharge he'd fallen silent on the subject of his son. Maybe the Honky-Tonk was Lit's hope for Tim's rehabilitation.

Almost at once, my gaze settled on a guy I would have sworn was him. He was somewhere in his mid-thirties, close to my age, and bore at least a superficial resemblance to Roy Littenberg. He had the same lean face, the distinctive jaw and jutting chin. He wore a dark purple shirt and plain mauve tie under a dark sport coat, jeans, desert boots. I'd caught him in conversation with a waitress—probably a dressing down, since she seemed upset. She had straight black hair, very glossy in the light, cut at an angle, with a line of blunt-cut bangs across the front. She wore black eyeliner and very red lipstick. I pegged her in her thirties, though close up she might have been older. She nodded, her face stony, and moved away, heading in my direction. She gave her order to the bartender, fussing with her order pad to cover her agitation. Hands shaking, she lit a cigarette, took a long drag, and then blew the smoke out in a thin jet. She left the cigarette in an ashtray on the bar.

I swiveled slightly and spoke to her. "Hi. I'm looking for Tim Littenberg. Is he on the premises?"

She looked at me, her gaze dropping to my jacket and then quizzically to my face again. She hiked a thumb in his direction. "Purple shirt," she said.

Tim had turned to greet a fellow in a tweedy sport coat, and I saw him signal the bartender to comp the guy to a drink. The two shook hands and Tim patted his back in a friendly gesture that probably didn't have much depth. Roy Littenberg had been fair-haired. His son's coloring was dark. His mouth was pouty and his eyes were darker than his father's, deep-set, smudged with shadow. His smile, when it showed, never touched his eyes. His attention flicked restlessly from room to room. He must constantly estimate the status of his customers, gauging their ages, their levels of inebriation, screening each burst of laughter and every boisterous interchange for the possibility of violence. Every hour the Honky-Tonk was open, the crowd became looser and less inhibited, louder, more aggressive as the alcohol went down.

I watched him approach the bar, coming within a few feet of me. Nearby, the waitress turned abruptly with her tray to avoid contact with him. His gaze touched her and then drifted, caught mine, veered off, and then returned. This time his eyes held.

I smiled. "Hi. Are you Tim?"

"That's right."

I held a hand out. "I'm Kinsey. I knew your father years ago. I was sorry to hear he died."

We shook hands. Tim's smile was brief, maybe pained, though it was impossible to tell. He was lean like his father, but where Lit's countenance was open and sunny, his son's was guarded. "Can I buy you a drink?"

"Thanks, I'm fine for now. The place really jumps. Is it always like this?"

He said, "Thursdays are good. Revving up for the weekend. This your first time in?" He was managing to conduct our conversation without being fully engaged. His face was slightly averted, his focus elsewhere: polite, but not passionate about the need to socialize.

"I was in years ago. That's how I knew your father. He was a great guy." This didn't seem to elicit any particular response. "Are you the manager?"

"The owner."

"Really. Oh, sorry. No offense," I said. "I could see you keeping a close eye out."

He shrugged.

I said, "You must know Mickey Magruder."

"Yeah, I know Mickey."

"I heard he'd bought a part interest in the place, so I was hoping to run into him. He's another cop from the old days. He and your dad were pals."

Tim seemed distracted. "Three Musketeers, right? I haven't seen him for weeks. Would you excuse me?"

I said, "Sure." I watched him cross the room to the dance floor, where he intervened in an exchange between a woman and her date. The guy was stumbling against her and she was struggling to keep him upright. Other couples on the dance floor were giving them a wide berth. The woman finally gave him a shove, both annoyed and embarrassed by his drunkenness. By the time Tim reached them, one of his bouncers had appeared and he began to walk the fellow toward the door, using the kind of elbow grip employed by street cops and mothers with small children acting up in department stores. The woman detoured to a table and snatched up her jacket and her handbag, prepared to follow. Tim intercepted her. A brief discussion ensued. I hoped he was persuading her to take a taxi home.

Moments later, he reappeared beside me, saying, "Sorry about that."

"I hope he's not getting in a car."

"The bouncer took his keys," he said. "We'll let him chill out in back and then see he gets home in one piece. He tends to hassle people when he's like that. Bad for business."

"I'll bet."

His smile was directed somewhere to my left. He gave my arm a pat. "I better go check on him. Hope to see you again."

"You can count on it," I said.

There was only a momentary hitch in his otherwise smooth delivery. "Good deal. Anything you want, you can let Charlie know." He caught the bartender's eye and pointed at me. The bartender nodded and, with that, Tim was gone.

I waited about a minute and then set my half-filled beer glass on the bar and made my way to the pay phones at the rear exit, near the office. I wanted to make sure I knew how to find him in his off-hours. I could have hung around until the place closed and followed him home, but I thought I'd try something more direct. I hauled out the phone book and looked up his address and phone number under *Littenberg, Tim and Melissa.*

I leaned to my left and looked down the shadowy corridor, where I could see three blank doors in addition to the one leading to the office. One of the busboys came in from outside, a draft of cold air following him in. I straightened up, put a coin in the slot, and dialed, listening to a recorded female voice that apprised me of the time to the minute and the second. I said *uh-huh, uh-huh*, like I was oh-so-interested. I watched until the busboy disappeared around the corner, moving into the bar.

The area was quiet. I replaced the handset and proceeded along the corridor, opening one door at a time. The first door exposed a mop closet: brooms, gallon containers of disinfectants, kitchen linens stacked on the shelves. The second door turned out to be the employees' lounge, lined with metal lockers and two sinks, an assortment of dumpy sofas, and a lot of ashtrays, most of which were full. No sign of the drunk; I wondered where he'd gone. The third door was locked. I leaned my head against the door, listening, but there was no sound.

Tim's office was just opposite. I crossed the corridor in two steps and gripped the doorknob with care. I turned it slowly to the right and pushed the door open the faintest crack. Tim was at his desk, his back to me, talking on the telephone. I couldn't hear his conversation. I sincerely hoped he wasn't busy putting out a contract on me. I eased the door shut and peeled my hand away from the knob to avoid any rattles and clicks. Time to get out. I really didn't want anyone to find me back here. I returned to the main corridor, where I checked in both directions. There was no evidence of an alarm system: No passive infrared beams, no numbered key pad by the rear exit. Interesting.

I drove home with an eye plastered to my rearview mirror. There was no reason in the world to think Tim's call had anything to do with me. He *had* made a beeline to the office after I'd mentioned Mickey's name, but that was the stuff of B-movies. Why would he rub me out? I hadn't done anything. I hadn't said a word about the ten grand he owed. I was saving that for next time. Actually, he could have paid it back, for all I knew.

It was only 10 P.M.: Lots of traffic on the freeway and none of it seemed sinister. Tim didn't know me from Adam, so he couldn't know where I lived or what kind of car I drove. Besides, Santa Teresa doesn't have any mobsters . . . at least as far as I know.

When I reached my neighborhood, I cruised the block, looking for a parking place that wasn't shrouded in darkness. I spotted only one unfamiliar car, a dark-toned Jaguar sitting at the curb across the street from my apartment. I pulled up around the corner onto Bay and waited to make sure no one had followed me. Then I locked up and walked the half block back. I was feeling foolish, but I still preferred to listen to my intuition. I knew the gate hinge would squeak, so I avoided it and approached by traversing the neighbor's yard along the wooden fence. Maybe I was being dumb, but I couldn't help myself.

When I reached the far side of Henry's garage, I lifted my head above the fence and looked. I'd left the back light on, but now my porchlet was in shadow. Henry's lights were out as well. A mist seemed to hover in the grass like smoke. I waited without moving, letting my eyes adjust to the dark. As in most cases,

even the darkest night isn't without its ambient illumination. The moon was caught in the branches of a tree.
Splashes of light spilled down in an irregular pattern. I
listened until the crickets began to chirp again.

I divided Henry's backyard into segments and
scanned them one by one. Nothing to my immediate
left. Nothing near his back step. Nothing near the tree.
The garage cast a triangle of blackness onto the patio
so that not all his lawn furniture was visible. Still, I
could have sworn I saw a form: the head and shoulders
of someone sitting in one of his Adirondack chairs. It
could have been Henry, but I didn't think so. I sank
down below the fence. I reversed myself, easing back
through the neighbor's yard to the street beyond. The
leather boots I wore weren't designed for tiptoeing on
wet grass, and I slipped as I crept along, hoping not to
fall on my ass.

Once I gained the street, I had to wipe some doggie
doo off my shoe heel, lest the odor alone make a target
of me. I fumbled in the bottom of my bag until I found
my penlight. I shielded the narrow beam with the palm
of my hand and swept the Jaguar. All four doors were
locked. I half expected the vanity plate to read HITZ R
US. Instead, it said DIXIE. Well, that was interesting. I
approached the backyard this time from the neighbor's
property to the left of Henry's, first navigating up their
driveway, then making a wide circle across Henry's
yard along the rear flower beds. From this vantage
point, I could see the silhouette of her tangled hair. She
must have been dying to smoke. As I watched, her
desire for a cigarette overrode her caution. I heard the
flick of a lighter. She cupped a hand to her face and

applied the flame to the end of a cigarette and inhaled with a nearly audible sigh of relief. No weapon, at any rate, unless she could wield one with her feet.

By then, I was close to the back of the Adirondack. "Gee, Dixie. Never light up. Now all the snipers in the neighborhood can get a bead on you."

She gasped, nearly levitating from her seat as she whipped her head around. She grabbed the arm of her chair and her handbag tumbled from her lap. I saw the cigarette fly off in the dark, the ember making a most satisfactory arc before it was snuffed in the wet grass. She was lucky she hadn't sucked it down her throat and choked to death. "Shit. Oh, shit! You scared the crap out of me," she hissed.

"What the hell are you doing here?"

She had a hand to her chest, trying to still her wildly banging heart. She bent at the waist, hyperventilating. I was singularly unimpressed with the possibility of heart failure. If her heart seized, she died. I was not going to do CPR on her. She was wearing what looked like a flight suit, a one-piece design with a zipper up the front. The oversized, baggy look was offset by the fact that she had the sleeves rolled midway up her arm, thus demonstrating how petite she was. She stooped to pick up her shoulder bag, which was battered leather, shaped like a mail carrier's pouch.

She tucked it under one arm. She put a hand to her forehead and then to her cheek. "I need to talk to you," she said, still sounding shaken.

"Had you thought about calling first?"

"I didn't think you'd agree to see me."

"So you wait in the dark? Are you *nuts*?"

"I'm sorry. I didn't mean to scare you. The old gentleman in the house was up when I arrived an hour ago. I could see him in the kitchen when I came around the corner, so I unscrewed the porch bulb. I didn't want him to notice and wonder what I was doing."

"What *are* you doing? I'm still not entirely clear."

"Could we go inside? I promise I won't stay long. I didn't bring a jacket and I'm freezing."

I felt a flash of annoyance. "Oh, come on," I said.

I set off across the yard. When I reached the porch, I gave the bulb a twist and saw the light come on. She followed me meekly. I took out my house keys and unlocked the door.

I took a moment to slip my shoes off. "Wipe your feet," I said crossly before I entered the living room.

"Sorry. Of course."

I pulled out a kitchen stool for her and then went around the kitchen counter and retrieved a brandy bottle from the liquor cabinet. I took out two jelly glasses and twisted the cork, pouring us both two fingers. I tipped my head back and flung the brandy to the back of my throat. I swallowed liquid fire, my mouth coming open, invisible flames shooting out. Damn, that was nasty, but it brought relief. I shuddered involuntarily the way I do when swilling NyQuil. I was calmer by the time I looked up at her. She'd chugalugged as I had, but she seemed better able to take the brandy in stride.

"Thanks. That's great. I hope you don't mind if I have a cigarette," she said, reaching into her bag as if with my consent.

"You can smoke outside. I don't want you smoking in here."

"Oh. Sorry," she said, and put the pack away.

"And quit apologizing," I said. She'd come here for something. Time to get on with it. I said, "Speak," like she was a dog about to demonstrate a trick.

Dixie closed her eyes. "What Mickey and I did was inexcusable. You have every right to be angry. I was obnoxious on Monday when you came to the house. I apologize for that, but I was disconcerted. I always assumed you'd received my letter and elected to do nothing. I guess I enjoyed blaming you for being disloyal. It was hard to give that up." She opened her eyes then and looked at me.

"Go on."

"That's it."

"No, it's not. What else? If that's all you wanted, you could have written me a note."

She hesitated. "I know you crossed paths with Eric on your way down the drive. I appreciated your keeping quiet on the subject of me and Mickey. You could have caused me a lot of trouble."

"*You* made the trouble. I didn't have anything to do with it."

"I'm aware of that. I know. But I've never been sure if Eric knew about what happened."

"He never mentioned it?"

"Nothing."

"Consider yourself lucky. I'd leave it at that, if I were you."

"Believe me, I will."

I felt myself subdivide, one part fully present, the other part watching from a distance. What she'd said so far was true, but there was bound to be more. Lacking my native talent in the liar-liar-pants-on-fire department, she couldn't help but color slightly, a bright coin of pink appearing on each cheek.

I said, "But what? You want assurances I'll keep my mouth shut from here on out?"

"I know I can't ask."

"That's correct. On the other hand, I don't know what purpose it would serve. Believe it or not, just because you 'done me wrong' doesn't mean I'd turn around and do likewise. Is there anything else?"

Dixie shook her head. "I should probably go." She picked up her handbag and began to search for her keys. "I know he invited you to dinner. Eric's always been fond of you. . . ."

I thought, *He has?*

"He's anxious to have you over, and I hope you'll agree. He might think it odd if you refused the invitation."

"Would you give it a rest. I haven't seen either one of you in fourteen years, so why would it seem odd?"

"Just think about it. Please? He said he'd probably call you early in the week."

"All right. I'll consider it, but no guarantees. It seems awkward to me."

"It doesn't have to be." She stood and held out a hand to me. "Thank you."

I shook hands with her, though I wondered in the moment if we'd made some unspoken pact. She moved to the door, turning back, her hand on the knob.

"How'd you do in the search for Mickey? Any luck?" she asked.

"The day after I talked to you, a couple of LAPD detectives showed up on my doorstep. He was shot last week."

"He's dead?"

"He's alive but in bad shape. He may not survive."

"That's awful. That's terrible. What happened?"

"Who knows? That's why they drove up here to talk to me."

"Have they made an arrest?"

"Not yet. All I know about it is what they told me so far. He was found on the street a couple of blocks from his apartment. This was Wednesday of last week. He's been in a coma ever since."

"I'm . . . I don't know what to say."

"There's nothing required."

"Will you let me know what you hear?"

"Why would I do that?"

In a fragile voice, she said, *"Please?"*

I didn't bother to reply. Then she was gone, leaving me staring at the door. I resented her thinking she had equal grieving rights. More than that, I wondered what she was really up to.

FIFTEEN

Friday morning, I woke up at 5:58, feeling logy and out of sorts. Every bone in my body was begging for more sleep, but I pushed aside the covers and reached for my sweats. I brushed my teeth and ran a comb through my hair, which was sticking out in all directions as though electrified. I paused near the gate and did an obligatory stretch. I started with a fast walk and then broke into a trot when I reached the beachfront park that runs along Cabana Boulevard.

The morning sky was dense with cloud cover, the air hazy. Without the full range of sunlight, all the warm reds and yellows had been leached from the landscape, leaving a muted palette of cool tones: blues, grays, taupe, dun, smoky green. The breeze blowing off the beach smelled of wharf pilings and seaweed. In the course of my run, I could feel the interior fog begin to lift. Intense exercise is the only legal high I know . . . except for love, of course. Whatever your inner state, all you have to do is run, walk, ride a bike, ski, lift weights, and suddenly your optimism's back and life seems good again.

Once recovered from my run, I drove over to the

gym, which is seldom crowded at that hour, the pre-work fanatics having already come and gone. The gym itself is spartan, painted gunmetal gray, with industrial carpeting the same color as the asphalt in the parking lot outside. There are huge plate-glass mirrors on the walls. The air smells of rubber and sweaty armpits. The prime patrons are men in various stages of physical fitness. The women who show up tend to fall into two categories: the extremely lean fitness fiends, who trash themselves daily, and the softer women who arrive after any food-dominated holiday. The latter never last, but good for them anyway. Better to make *some* effort than do nothing for life. I fell somewhere between.

I started with leg extensions and leg curls, muscles burning as I worked. Abs, lower back, on to the pec deck and chest press, then on to shoulders and arms. Early in a workout, the sheer number of body parts multiplied by sets times the number of repetitions is daunting, but the process is curiously engrossing . . . pain being what it is. Suddenly I found myself laboring at the last two machines, alternating biceps and triceps. Then I was out the door again, sweaty and exhilarated. Sometimes I nearly wrench my arm from its socket patting myself on the back.

Home again, I turned on the automatic coffeepot, made the bed, showered, dressed, and ate a bowl of cereal with skim milk. Then I sat with my coffee and read the local paper. Usually, as the day wears on, my flirtation with good health is overrun by my tendency to self-abuse, especially when it comes to junk food. Fat grams are my downfall, anything with salt, additives, cholesterol, nitrates. Breaded and deep-fried or sautéed in butter, smothered in cheese, slathered with mayonnaise, dripping with meat juices—what foodstuff couldn't be improved by proper preparation? By the time I finished reading the paper, I was nearly dizzy with hunger and had to suck down more coffee to dampen my appetite. After that, all it took was a big gob of crunchy peanut butter I licked from the spoon while I settled at my desk. I'd decided to skip the office as I'd dutifully caught up with paperwork the day before.

I placed Detective Aldo's business card on the desk in front of me and put a call through to Mark Bethel. I'd actually given up hope of ever speaking to him in person. Sure enough, he'd popped down to Los Angeles for a campaign appearance. I told Judy about Mickey and she went through the usual litany, expressing concern, shock, and dismay at life's uncertainties.

"Can Mark do anything to help?" she asked.

"That's why I called. Would you ask him if he'd talk to Detective Aldo and find out what's going on? They're not going to tell me, but they might talk to him since he's Mickey's attorney—or at least he was."

"I'm sure he'd do that. Do you have a number?"

I recited the number and gave her Detective Felix Claas's name as well. I also gave her Mickey's address in Culver City.

She said, "I'm making a note. He should be calling when he's finished. Maybe he can touch base with Detective Aldo while he's still in Los Angeles."

"Thanks. That'd be great."

"Is that it?"

"Just one more thing. Can you ask Mark what's going to happen to Mickey's bills? I'm sure they're piling up, and I hate to see his credit get any worse than it is."

"Got it. I'll ask. He'll think of something, I'm sure. I'll have him call you when he gets in."

"No need for that unless he has a question. Just let him know what we talked about and he can take it from there."

I sat at my desk, wondering what to do next. Once more, I hauled out the assorted items I'd lifted from Mickey's and studied them one by one. Phone bill, the Delta Airlines ticket envelope, receipts from the Honky-Tonk, savings passbooks, phony documents. Emmett Vanover . . . Delbert Amburgey . . . Clyde Byler, all with trumped-up personal data and a photo of Mickey's face plastered in the relevant spots. I went back to the plane ticket, which was issued in the name Magruder. The flight coupons were missing—I assumed, used for the trip—but the passenger receipt and itinerary were still in the ticket envelope. This was an expensive round trip for a guy with no job. What was the relevance, if any? The trip to Louisville might have been personal. Hard to know about that, since we hadn't talked in years. I laid the ticket on the desk beside the other items, lining them up in various configurations as though a story could be fabricated from the proper sequence of events.

When I was a kid, my Aunt Gin kept me supplied with activity books. The paper was always cheap, the games and puzzles designed to shut me up temporarily so she could read for an hour without my interrupting. I'd lie on the trailer floor with my big pencil and a box of crayons. Sometimes the instructions would entail the finding and circling of particular words in a gridwork of letters, sometimes a search for specific objects in a convoluted jungle picture. My favorite was dot-to-dot, in which you constructed a picture by connecting consecutively numbered points on the page. Tongue peeking out of the corner of my mouth, I'd laboriously trace the line from number to number until a picture emerged. I got so good at it, I could stare at the spaces between numbers and see the picture without ever setting pencil to paper. This didn't require much in the way of brains as the outline was usually simple: a teddy bear or a wagon or a baby duck, all dumb. Nonetheless, I can still remember the rush of joy when recognition dawned. Little did I know that at the age of five I was already in training for my later professional life.

What I was looking at here was simply a more sophisticated version of dot-to-dot. If I could understand the order in which the items were related, I could probably get some notion of what was going on in Mickey's life. For now, what I was missing were the links between events. What was he up to in the months before the shooting? The cops had to be pursuing many of these same questions, but it was possible I was in possession of information they lacked . . . having stolen it. In the rudimentary conscience I seemed to be developing, I knew I could always opt for the Good Citizen's Award by "sharing" with Detective Aldo. In the main, I don't hold back where cops are concerned. On the other hand, if I dug a little deeper, I might figure it out for myself, recapturing the thrill of discovery. There's nothing like the moment when everything finally falls into place. So why give that up when, with just a tiny bit more effort, I could have it all? (These are the sorts of rationalizations Ms. Millhone engages in when failing to do her civic duty.)

I hauled up my handbag and began to sift through the contents, coming up with Wary's phone number on the back of a business card. Maybe Mickey had said something to him about the trip. I picked up the phone and dialed Los Angeles. It was only ten-fifteen. Maybe I could catch him before he went off to breakfast. I had a vision of Wary's wire-rimmed glasses and his waist-length brown hair. Two rings. Three. When he finally answered, I could tell from his voice he'd been deeply asleep.

"Hey, Wary. How're you? Did I wake you?"

"No, no," he said valiantly. "Who's this?"

"Kinsey in Santa Teresa." Silence. "Mickey's ex."

"Oh, yeah, yeah. Got it. Sorry I didn't recognize your voice. How're you?"

"Fine. And you?"

"Doing great. What's up?" I could hear him lock his jaw in the effort to suppress a yawn.

"I have a quick question. Did Mickey say anything about the trip he made to Louisville, Kentucky?"

"What trip?"

"This was week before last. He departed May eighth and returned on the twelfth."

"Oh, that. I knew he was gone, but he never said where. Why'd he go?"

"How do I know? I was hoping *you'd* tell *me*. Given his finances, I'm having trouble understanding why he took off for five days. The plane ticket cost a fortune, and he probably had to add meals and a motel on top of that."

"Can't help you there. All I know is he went some-place, but he never said why. I didn't even know he left the state. Dude didn't like to fly. I'm surprised he'd get on a plane going anywhere."

"Did he talk to anyone else, someone in the building he might have mentioned it to?"

"Could have. I doubt it. It's not like he had buddies he confided in. Say, you know what might help? I just thought of this. Once his phone was disconnected, he used to pop in and borrow mine. Kind of pay-as-you-go, but he was always careful to keep square. I can find the numbers, if you want."

I closed my eyes, saying small prayers. "Wary, I'd be indebted to you for life."

"Hey, cool. I'm going to put the phone down and go look on my desk."

I heard a clunk and I was guessing the handset was now resting on his bed table while he padded around, probably bare-assed naked. A full minute passed, and then he picked up the phone again. "You still there?"

"Indeed."

"I got the statement right here. They bill on the fifteenth, so this was in yesterday's mail. I haven't even opened it yet. I know some calls he made were out-of-state because he left me ten bucks and said he'd pay the difference later when the bill came in."

"Really. Did you ever hear what was said?"

"Nope. I made it a point to leave the room. I figured it was private. You know him. He never explained anything, especially when it came to his work. He was stingy with exposition in the best of circumstances."

"What makes you think this was work?"

"His attitude, I guess. Cop mode, I'd call it. You could see it in his body, the way he carried himself. Even half in the bag, he knew his stuff." I could hear him shuffling papers. Distracted, he said, "I'm still looking. Have you heard anything?"

"About Mickey? Not lately. I guess I could call Aldo, but I'm afraid to ask."

"Here we go. Okay. Oh. There was just one. This's the seventh of May. Lookit here. You're right. He called Louisville." He read the number off to me. "Actually, he made two to the same number. The first was quick, less than a minute. The longer one—ten minutes—was shortly afterward."

I was frowning at the phone. "It must have been important to him if he flew out the next day."

"A man of action," he said. "Listen, I gotta get off the phone and go take a leak, but I'll be happy to call you back if I think of anything else."

"Thanks, Wary."

Once I hung up, I sat and stared at the phone, trying to "get centered," as we say in California. Ten-twenty here . . . that would make it one-twenty in Kentucky. I had no clue who he'd called, so I couldn't think of a ruse. I'd have to make it up as I went along. I dialed the number.

"Louisville Male High School. This is Terry speaking. May I help you?"

Male High School? Terry sounded like a student, probably working in the office. I was so nonplused I couldn't think of anything to say. "Oops. Wrong number." I put the handset back. Belatedly, my heart thumped. What was this about?

217

I took a couple of deep breaths and dialed again.

"Louisville Male High School. This is Terry speaking. May I help you?"

"Uh, yes. I wonder if I might speak to the assistant principal?"

"Mrs. Magliato? One minute." Terry put me on hold, and ten seconds later the line was picked up.

"Mrs. Magliato. May I help you?"

"I hope so. My name is Mrs. Hurst from the General Telephone offices in Culver City, California. A call was placed to this number from Culver City on May seventh, and the charges are currently in dispute. The call was billed to last-name Magruder, first name Mickey or Michael. Mr. Magruder indicates that he never made such a call, and we've been asked to identify the party called. Can you be of some assistance? We'd appreciate your help."

"What was that name again?"

I spelled it out.

She said, "Doesn't sound familiar. Hold on and I'll ask if anybody else remembers talking to him."

She put me on hold. I listened to a local radio station, but the sound was pitched too low for me to hear what was being said. She came back on the line. "No, I'm sorry. None of us talked to anyone by that name."

"What about the principal? Any possibility he might have taken the call himself?"

"For starters, it's a she and I already asked. The name doesn't ring a bell."

I thought about the names on the phony documents and pulled them closer. "Uh, what about the names Emmett Vanover, Delbert Amburgey, and Clyde

Byler?" I repeated them before she asked, which seemed to piss her off.

"I know I didn't speak to any one of them. I'd remember the names."

"Could you ask the office staff?"

She sighed. "Just a moment," she said. She put a palm across the receiver and I could hear her relay the question. Muffled conversation ensued and then she removed her hand. "Nobody spoke to any of them either."

"No one from Culver City?"

"No-oo." She sang the word on two notes.

"Ah. Well, thanks anyway. I appreciate your time." I hung up the phone and thought about it for a minute. Who did Mickey talk to for ten minutes? It certainly wasn't her, I thought. I got up from the desk and went back to the kitchen, where I took out a butter knife and the jar of extra-crunchy Jif. I took a tablespoon of peanut butter on the blade and spread it on the roof of my mouth, working it with my tongue until my palate was coated with a thin layer of goo. "Hello, this is Mrs. Kennison," I said aloud, in a voice that sounded utterly unlike me.

I returned to the phone and dialed the number again. When Terry answered, I asked the name of the school librarian.

"You mean Ms. Calloway?" she said.

"Oh, that's right. I'd forgotten. Could you transfer me?"

Terry was happy to oblige, and ten seconds later I was going through the same routine, only this time with a variation. "Mrs. Calloway, this is Mrs. Kennison with

219

the district attorney's office in Culver City, California. A call was placed to this number from Culver City on May seventh, billed to last-name Magruder, first name Mickey or Michael—"

"Yes, I spoke to him," she said, before I could finish my tale.

"Ah. Oh, you did. Well, that's wonderful."

"I don't know if I'd call it *wonderful*, but it was pleasant. He seemed like a nice man: articulate, polite."

"Can you remember the nature of the query?"

"It was only two weeks ago. I may be close to retirement, but I'm not suffering from senile dementia— not yet, at any rate."

"Could you fill me in?"

"I could if I understood what this had to do with the district attorney's office. It sounds fishy as all get out. What'd you say your name was? Because I'm making a note of it, and I intend to check."

I hate it when people think. Why don't they just mind their own business and respond to my questions? "Mrs. Kennison."

"And the reason for the call?"

"I'm sorry, but I'm not at liberty to say. This is a legal matter, and there's a gag order in effect."

"I see," she said, as if she didn't.

"Can you tell me what Mr. Magruder wanted?"

"Why don't you ask him?"

"Mr. Magruder's been shot. He's in a coma at the moment. That's as much as I can tell you without being cited for contempt of court."

That seemed to work. She said, "He was trying to track down a former Male High School student."

"Can you give me the name?"

"What's your first name again?"

"Kathryn. Kennison. If you like, I can give you my number here and you can call me back."

"Well, that's silly. You could be anyone," she snapped. "Let's just get this over with. What is it you want?"

"Any information you can give me."

"The boy's name was Duncan Oaks, a 1961 graduate. His was an outstanding class. We still talk about that group of students."

"I take it you were the school librarian back then?"

"I was. I've been here since 1946."

"Did you know Duncan Oaks personally?"

"Everybody knew Duncan. He worked as my assistant in his sophomore and junior years. By the time he was a senior, he was the yearbook photographer, prom king, voted most likely to succeed—"

"He sounds terrific."

"He was."

"And where is he now?"

"He became a journalist and photographer for one of the local papers, the *Louisville Tribune*, long since out of business, I'm sorry to say. He died on assignment in Vietnam. The *Trib* got swallowed up by one of those syndicates a year later, 1966. Now whoever you are and whatever you're up to, I think I've said enough."

I thanked her and hung up, still completely unenlightened. I sat and made notes, using the cap of the pen to scrape the peanut butter from the roof of my mouth. Was this an heir search? Had Mickey taken on a case to supplement his income? He certainly had the background to do P.I. work, but what was he doing and who'd hired him to do it?

I heard a tap at my door and leaned over far enough to see Henry peering through the porthole. I felt a guilty pang about the night before. Henry and I seldom had occasion to disagree. In this case, he was right. I had no business withholding information that might be relevant to the police. *Really*, I was going to reform, I was almost sure. When I opened the door, he handed me a stack of envelopes. "Brought you your mail."

"Henry, I'm sorry. Don't be mad at me," I said. I tossed the mail on the desk and gave him a hug while he patted me on the back.

"My fault," he said.

"No, it's not. It's mine. You're entirely right. I was being obstinate."

"No matter. You know I worry about you. What's wrong with your voice? Are you catching cold?"

"I just ate something and it's stuck in my teeth. I'll call Detective Aldo today and tell him what I've found."

"I'd feel better if you did," he said. "Did I interrupt? We can do this another time if you're hard at work."

"Do what another time?"

"You said you'd give me a lift. The fellow from the body shop called to say the Chevy's ready."

"Sorry. Of course. It's taken long enough. Let me get my jacket and my keys."

On the way over to the body shop, I brought Henry up to date, though I was uncomfortably aware that even now I wasn't being completely candid with him. I wasn't lying outright, but I omitted portions of the story. "Which reminds me," I said. "Did I tell you about that call to my place?"

"What call?"

"I didn't think I'd mentioned it. I don't know what to make of it." I laid out the business about the thirty-minute call from Mickey's place to mine in late March. "I swear I never talked to him, but I can tell the detectives didn't believe me."

"What was the date?"

"March twenty-seventh, early afternoon, one-thirty. I saw the bill myself."

"You were with me," he said promptly.

"I was?"

"Of course. That was the day after the quakes that dumped the cans on my car. I'd called the insurance company and you followed me over to the shop. The claims adjuster met us there at one-fifteen."

"That was *that* day? How do you remember these things?"

"I have the estimate," he said and pulled it from his pocket. "The date's right here."

The incident returned in a flash. In the early morning hours of March 27 there'd been a series of temblers, a swarm of quakes as noisy as a herd of horses thundering across the room. I'd woken from a sound sleep with my entire bed shaking. The brightly lighted numbers on my digital alarm showed 2:06. Clothes hangers were tinkling, and all the glass in the windows rattled like someone rapping to get in. I'd been up like a shot, pulling on my sweats and my running shoes. Within seconds that quake passed, only to be followed by another. I could hear glass crashing in the sink. The walls had begun to creak from the strain of the rocking motion. Somewhere across the city, a transformer exploded and I was blanketed in darkness.

I'd grabbed my shoulder bag and fumbled down the spiral stairs while I groped in the depths for my penlight. I'd found it and flicked it on. The wash from the beam was pale, but it lighted my way. In the distance, I could hear sirens begin to wail. The trembling ceased. I'd taken advantage of the moment to snag my denim jacket and let myself out the door. Henry was already making his way across the patio. He carried a flashlight the size of a boom box, which he shone in my face. We spent the next hour huddled together in the backyard, fearful of returning indoors until we knew we were safe. The next morning, he'd discovered the damage to his five-window coupe.

I'd followed him to the body shop and an hour later I'd driven him home. When I'd returned to my apartment, my message light was blinking. I'd hit the REPLAY button, but there was only a hissing that extended until the tape ran out. I was mildly annoyed. I assumed it was pranksters and let it go at that. Henry was standing right there and heard the same thing I did; he suggested a malfunction when the power had been restored. I'd rewound the tape to erase the hiss and had thought no more about it. Until now.

SIXTEEN

As soon as I got home, I put a call through to Detective Aldo, eager to assert my innocence on this one small point. The minute he picked up the phone and identified himself, I launched right in. "Hi, Detective Aldo. This is Kinsey Millhone, up in Santa Teresa." Little Miss Cheery making friends with the police.

I was just embarking on my explanation of the March phone call when he cut me short. "I've been trying to get in touch with you for days," he said tersely. "This is to put you on notice. I know for a fact you violated crime-scene tape and entered that apartment. I can't prove it for now, but if I find one shred of evidence, we'll charge you with willful destruction or concealment of evidence and resisting a peace officer in the discharge of his duties, punishable by a fine not exceeding one thousand dollars, or by imprisonment in a county jail not exceeding one year, or by both. You got that straight?"

I'd opened my mouth to defend myself when he slammed down the phone. I depressed the plunger on my end and replaced the handset, my mouth as dry as sand. I felt such a hot flash of guilt and embarrassment,

I thought I'd been catapulted into early menopause. I put a hand against my flaming cheek, wondering how he knew it was me. Actually, I wasn't the only one guilty of illegal entry. Mickey's phantom girlfriend had entered the premises at some point between my two visits, making off with her diaphragm, her necklace, and her spray cologne. Unfortunately, aside from the fact that I didn't know who she was, I couldn't accuse her without accusing myself as well.

I spent the rest of the day slinking around with my mental tail between my legs. I hadn't been so thoroughly rebuked since I was eight and Aunt Gin caught me smoking an experimental Viceroy cigarette. In this case, I was so heavily invested in Mickey's concerns, I couldn't afford to have my access to his life curtailed. I'd hoped clearing myself with Aldo in the matter of the phone call would net me information about the current status of his investigation. Instead, it was clear that his trust was so seriously eroded he'd never tell me a thing.

I used the early evening hours to pick my way through a plate of Rosie's stuffed beef rolls. She was pushing *vese porkolt*, which (translated from Hungarian) turned out to be heart and kidney stew. Remorseful as I felt, I was prepared to eat my own innards, but my stomach rebelled at the notion of vital piggie organs simmered with caraway seeds. I spent the hours after supper tending to my desk at home, atoning for my sins with lots of busywork. When all else fails, cleaning house is the perfect antidote to most of life's ills.

I waited until close to midnight to return to the Honky-Tonk. I wore the same outfit I'd worn the night before since it was previously smoked on and required laundering anyway. I'd have to hang Mickey's leather jacket on the line for days. This was now Friday night and, if memory still served me, the place would be packed with feverish weekend celebrants. Driving by, I could see the parking lot was jammed. I cruised the surrounding blocks and finally squeezed into a space just as a Ford convertible was pulling out. I walked the block and a half through the darkened Colgate neighborhood. This was an area that had once been devoted solely to single-family homes. Now a full third had been converted to small businesses: an upholsterer, an auto repair shop, and a beauty salon. There were no sidewalks along the street so I kept to the middle of the road and then cut through the small employee parking lot at the rear exit.

I circled the building to the entrance, where the line of people awaiting admittance seemed to be singles and couples in roughly equal numbers. I gave the bouncer my driver's license and watched him run it through his scanning device. I paid the five-dollar cover charge and received the inked benediction on the back of my right hand.

As I moved through the front room, I was forced to run the gauntlet of chain smokers standing four deep at the bar—shifty-eyed guys trying to look a lot hipper than they actually were. The music coming from the other room was live that night. I couldn't see the band, but the melody (or its equivalent) pounded, the beat distorted through the speakers to a tribal throb. The lyrics were indecipherable but probably consisted of sophomoric sentiments laid out in awkward rhyming

227

couplets. The band sounded local, playing all their own tunes, if this one was any indication. I've picked up similar performances on local cable channels, shows that air at 3 A.M. as a special torture to the occasional insomniac like me.

I was already wishing I'd stayed at home. I'd have turned and fled if not for the fact that Mickey'd been here himself six consecutive Fridays. I couldn't imagine what he'd been doing. Maybe counting drinks, calculating Tim's profits, and thus computing his gross. Maybe Tim had cried poor, claiming he wasn't making sufficient money to repay the loan. If Tim's bartender happened to have his hand in the till, this could well be true. Bartenders have their little methods, and an experienced investigator, sitting at the bar, can simultaneously chat with other patrons and do an eyeball audit. If the bartender was skimming, it would have been in Mickey's best interests to spot the practice and blow the whistle on him. It was equally possible Mickey's presence was generated by another motive— a woman, for instance, or the need to escape his financial woes in L.A. Then, too, a heavy drinker doesn't really need an excuse to hit a bar anywhere.

I did the usual visual survey. All the tables were full, the booths bulging with customers packed four to a bench. The portion of the dance floor I could see from where I stood was so dense with moving bodies there was scarcely any room to spare. There was no sign of Tim, but I did see the black-haired waitress, inching through the mob in front of me. She held her tray aloft, balancing empty glasses above the reach of jostling patrons. She wore a black leather vest over nothing at all, her arms long and bare, the V of the garment exposing as much as it concealed. The dyed black of her hair was a harsh contrast to the milky pallor of her skin. A dark slash of lipstick made her mouth look grim. She leaned toward the bartender, calling her order over the generalized din.

There's a phenomenon I've noticed when I'm driving on the highway. If you turn and look at other drivers, they'll turn and look at you. Maybe the instinct is a holdover from more primitive days when being the object of scrutiny might mean you were in peril of being killed and consumed. Here, it happened again. Soon after I spotted her, she turned instinctively and caught my gaze. Her eyes dropped to Mickey's leather jacket. I shifted my attention, but not before I saw her expression undergo a change.

Thereafter, I was careful to avoid her, and I focused instead on what was going on nearby. I kept picking up an intermittent whiff of marijuana, though I couldn't trace the source. I started watching people's hands, since dopers seldom hold a joint the way they'd hold an ordinary cigarette. The average smoker tucks a cigarette in the V formed between the index and middle fingers, bringing the cigarette to the lips with the palm of the hand open. A doper with a joint makes an O-ring with the thumb and index finger, the doobie at the center, the three remaining fingers fanned out so the palm forms a shelter around the burning joint. Whether the intent is to shield the dope from the wind or from public view, I've never been able to determine. My own dope-smoking days are long since past, but the ceremonial aspects seem consistent to this day. I've seen a doper ask for a joint by simply forming that O and pressing it to his lips, a gesture that signals, Shall we smoke a little cannabis, my dear?

I began to circle the bar, moving casually from table to table until I spotted the fellow with a joint between his lips. He was sitting alone in a booth on the far side of the room, close to the corridor that led to the telephones and rest rooms. He was in his mid-thirties, vaguely familiar with his long, lean face. He was a type I'd found appealing when I was twenty: silent, brooding, and slightly dangerous. His eyes were light and close-set. He sported a mustache and goatee, both contributing to the look of borderline scruffiness. He wore a loose khaki-colored jacket and a black watch cap. A fringe of light hair extended well below his collar. He carried himself with a certain worldliness, something in the hunch of his shoulders and the mild knowing smile that flitted across his face.

Tim Littenberg emerged from the back corridor and paused in the doorway while he adjusted his cuffs. The two of them, the joint smoker and the bar owner, ignored each other with a casualness that seemed phony from my perspective. Their behavior reminded me of those occasions when illicit lovers run across each other in a social setting. Under the watchful eyes of their respective spouses, they'll make a point of avoiding contact, thus trumpeting their innocence, or so they think. The only problem is the aura of heightened awareness that underlies the act. Anyone who knows either can detect the charade. Between the man in the booth and Tim Littenberg there was an unmistakable air of self-consciousness. Both seemed to be watching the black-haired waitress, who seemed equally conscious of them.

Within minutes, she'd circled and arrived at the booth. Tim moved away without looking at her. The guy with the joint leaned forward on his elbows. He reached out and put a hand on her hip. He motioned for her to sit. She slid into the bench across from him with her tray between them as though the empty glasses might remind him she had other things to do. He took her free hand and began to talk earnestly. I couldn't see her face, but from where I stood she didn't seem relaxed or receptive to his message.

"You know that guy?" a voice said into my right ear.

I turned to find Tim leaning close to me, his voice amazingly intimate in the midst of loud music and high-pitched voices. I said, "Who?"

"The man you're watching, sitting in the booth over there."

"He seems familiar," I said. "Mostly, I was trying to remember where the rest rooms are."

"I see."

I stole a look at his face and then looked off in the other direction, deflecting the intensity with which he'd fixed his attentions on me. He said, "Remember Mickey's friend Shack?"

"Sure. We talked earlier this week."

"That's his son, Scottie. The waitress is his girl-friend, Thea. In case you're wondering," he added, with a hint of irony.

231

"You're kidding. That's Scott? No wonder he looked familiar. I've seen pictures of him. I take it you're still friends?"

"Of course. I've known Scottie for years. I don't like dope in my bar, but I don't want to make a fuss so I tend to ignore him when he's got a joint."

"Ah."

"I'm surprised you're back. Are you looking for someone in particular, or will I do?"

"I was hoping to find Mickey. I told you that last night."

"That's right. So you did. Can I buy you a drink?"

"Maybe when I finish this. I'm really fine for now."

He reached over and removed the beer glass from my hand and helped himself to a sip. "This is warm. Let me get you a fresh one in an icy mug." He caught the bartender's eye and lifted the glass, indicating a replacement. Tim was wearing a dark navy suit with a dress shirt that was oxblood red. His tie bore a pattern of diagonal wishbones, navy and red on a field of light blue. The musky bite of his aftershave filled the air between us. His pupils were pinpricks and his skin had a sheen. Tonight, instead of seeming restless and distracted, his demeanor was slow, every gesture deliberate as if he were slogging his way through mud. Well, well, well. What was he on? I felt a faint ridge of fear prickling up along my spine, like a cat in the presence of aliens.

I watched a frosty mug of beer being passed in my direction, hand over hand, like a bucket brigade. Tim placed the mug in my hand, at the same time resting his free hand against the middle of my back. He was standing too close, but in the press of the crowd it was hard to complain. I longed to back away, but there wasn't room. I said, "Thanks."

Again, he bent low and put his mouth close to my ear. "What's the story with Mick? This is twice you've been in."

"He lent me his jacket. I was hoping to return it."

"You and he have something going?"

"That's none of your business."

Tim laughed and his gaze glided off, easing toward Thea, who was just rising from the booth. Scott Shackelford was staring down at the table, pinching out the joint, which was barely visible between his fingers. Thea picked up her tray and began to push toward the bar, studiously avoiding the sight of Tim. Maybe she was still pissed off for what he'd said to her last night. I didn't want the beer, but I didn't see a place to set it down.

I said, "I'll be right back."

Tim touched my arm. "Where're you going?"

"To take a whiz. Is that okay?"

Again, he laughed, but it was not the sound of merriment.

I pushed my way through the crowd, praying he'd lose interest during the time I was gone. The first flat surface I saw, I put the beer glass down and walked on.

The rest room was undergoing one of those temporary lulls where I was the only person present. I crossed to the window and opened it a crack. A wedge of cold air slanted in, and I could see the smoke drift out. The quiet was like a tonic. I could feel myself resist the notion of ever leaving the room. If the window had been lower, I'd have crawled on out. I went into a stall and peed just for something to do.

I was standing at the sink, soaping my hands, when the door opened behind me and Thea walked in. She crossed to the adjacent sink and began washing her hands, her manner businesslike. I didn't think her arrival was an accident, especially when she could have used the employees' lounge around the corner. She caught my reflection in the mirror and gave me a pallid smile as if she'd just that moment noticed I was standing there. She said "Hi" and I responded in kind, letting her define the communication since she'd initiated it.

I pulled out a sheet of paper towel and dried my hands. She followed suit. A silence ensued and then she spoke up again. "I hear you're looking for Mickey."

I focused my attention, hoping she couldn't guess how very curious I was. "I'd like to talk to him. Have you seen him tonight?"

"I haven't seen him for weeks."

"Really? That seems odd. Somebody told me he was usually here on Fridays."

"Uh-uh. Not lately. No telling where he's at. He could be out of town."

"I doubt it. Not that he told me."

She took a lipstick from her pocket and twisted the color into view, sliding it across her lips. I read an article once in some glamour magazine—probably waiting for the dentist and hoping to distract myself—in which the author analyzed the ways women wear down a tube of lipstick. A flat surface meant one thing, slanted meant something else. I couldn't recall the theory, but I noticed hers was flat, the lipstick itself coming perilously close to the metal.

She screwed the lipstick down and popped the top back on while she rubbed her lips together to even out the color. She corrected a slight mishap at the corner of her mouth, then studied her reflection. She tucked her coal-black hair behind her ears. Idly, she pursued the subject without any help on my part. "So what's your interest?" She used her tongue to remove a smudge of lipstick from her two front teeth.

"He's a friend."

She studied me with interest. "Is that why you have his jacket?"

"He's a *good* friend," I said, and then glanced down at myself. "You recognize this?"

"It sure looks like his. I spotted it when you were in here the other night."

"Last night," I said, as if she didn't know.

"Really. Did he give you that?"

"It's on loan. That's why I'm looking for him, to give it back," I said. "I tried calling, but his phone's been disconnected."

She'd taken out a mascara wand, leaning close to the mirror while she brushed through her lashes, leaving little dots of black. As long as she was wangling for information, I thought I'd wangle some myself.

I said, "What about you? Are you a friend of his?"

She shrugged. "I wait on him when he's in and we shoot the breeze."

"So nothing personal."

"I have a boyfriend."

"Was that him?"

"Who?"

"The guy in the watch cap, sitting at the booth out there?"

She stopped what she was doing. "As a matter of fact, yes. What makes you ask?"

"I was thinking to cop a joint when I saw you sit down. Is he local?"

She shook her head. "L.A." There was a pause and then she said, "How long have you dated Mickey?"

"It's kind of hard to keep track."

"Then this is recent," she said, turning the question into a statement to offset the inquisition.

I started fluffing at my hair the way she'd been fluffing hers. I leaned close to the mirror and checked some imaginary eye makeup, running the flat of one knuckle along the lower edge of one eye. She was still waiting for an answer. I looked at her blankly. "Sorry. Did you ask me something?"

She took a pack of unfiltered Camels from her jeans and extracted a cigarette. She applied a flame to the tip, using a wooden match she had scratched on the bottom of her shoe. "I didn't know he was dating."

"Who, Mickey? Oh, please. He's always on the make. That's half his charm." I could picture the ashtray in his apartment, the numerous unfiltered Camel cigarette butts, along with the array of kitchen matches that looked just like hers. "He's so secretive. Jeez. You never know what he's up to or who he's doing these days."

She said, "I didn't know that about him." She

turned to face me, leaning her backside against the sink with her weight on one hip.

I was warming to the subject, lies tumbling out with a tidy little mix of truth. "Take my word for it. Mickey doesn't give you a straight answer about anything. He's impossible that way."

"Doesn't that bother you?" she asked.

"Nah. I used to be jealous, but what's the point? Monogamy's not his thing. I figure what the hell? He's still a stud in his way. Take it or leave it. He's always got someone waiting in the wings."

"You live in L.A.?"

"I'm mostly here. Anytime I'm down, though, I stop by his place."

The information I was doling out seemed to make her restless. She said, "I have to get back to work. If you see him, tell him Thea said 'hi.'" She dropped the cigarette on the floor and stepped on it. "Let me know if you find him. He owes me money."

"You and me both, kid," I said.

Thea left the room. I confess I smirked when she banged the door shut. I caught sight of myself in the mirror. "You are such a little shit," I said.

I leaned on the sink for a minute, trying to piece together what I'd learned from her. Thea couldn't know about the shooting or she wouldn't have been forced to try to weasel information out of me. She must have hoped he was out of town, which would go a long way toward explaining why he hadn't been in touch with her. It wasn't difficult to picture her in a snit of some kind. There's no one as irrational as a woman on the make. She might seize the opportunity to screw around on her steady boyfriend, but woe betide the man who screwed around on *her*. Given the fact that Mickey's phone was out, she must have driven down to his apartment to collect her personal belongings. She certainly hadn't warmed to the idea that he and I were an item. I wondered how Scottie Shackelford would feel if he found out she was boffing Mick. Or maybe he knew. In which case, I wondered if he'd taken steps to put a stop to it.

SEVENTEEN

I came out of the ladies' room and paused inside the doorway to the bar, glancing to my left. Scott Shackelford was no longer sitting in the booth. I spotted him at the bar, chatting with the bartender, Charlie. The crowd was beginning to thin out. The band had long ago packed up and departed. It was nearly one-forty-five and the guys looking to get laid were forced to zero in on the few single women who remained. The busboys were loading dirty glassware into plastic bins. Thea was now standing at the bar with Scott, using a calculator to add up her tips. I zipped up the front of Mickey's jacket. As I made my way to the front door, I became aware that she was watching me.

The chilly air was a relief after the smoky confinement of the bar. I could smell pine needles and loam. Colgate's main street was deserted, all the neighboring businesses long since shut down for the night. I cut through the parking lot on the way to my car, hands in my jeans pockets, the strap of my handbag hooked over my right shoulder. Streetlights splashed the pavement with pale circles of illumination, emphasizing the darkness beyond their reach. Somewhere behind me, I heard the basso profundo rumble of a motorcycle. I looked over my shoulder in time to see a guy on a bike turning into the alley to the rear of the bar. I stared, walking backward, wondering if my eyes were deceiving me. I'd only caught a glimpse of him, but I could have sworn this was the same guy who'd shown up at Mickey's Wednesday night in L.A. As I watched, he cut the engine and, still astride, began to roll his bike toward the trash bins. A wan light shining down from the rear exit shone on his corn-yellow hair and glinted against the chrome of the bike. He lifted the bike backward onto the center stand, locked the bike, dismounted, and rounded the building, walking toward the main entrance with a jingling sound, his jacket flapping open. The body type was the same: tall, thin, with wide bony shoulders and a sunken-looking chest.

I dog-trotted after him, slowing as I reached the corner to avoid running into him. He'd apparently already entered the bar by the time I got there. The bouncer saw me and glanced at his watch with theatrical emphasis. He was in his forties, balding, big-bellied, wearing a sport coat that fit tightly through the shoulders and arms. I showed him the stamp on the back of my hand, demonstrating the fact I'd already been cleared for admittance. "I forgot something," I said. "Mind if I go back in real quick?"

"Sorry, lady. We're closed."

"It's only ten of two. There's still a ton of people inside. Five minutes. I swear."

"Last call was one-thirty. No can do."

"I don't want a *drink*. This is for something I left. It'll only take two minutes and I'll be right out again.

Please, please, please?" I put my knees together and clasped my hands like a little child at prayer.

I saw him repress a smile, and he motioned me in with an indulgent rolling of his eyes. It's perplexing to realize how far you can get with men by pulling girlish shit. I paused, looking back at him as if my question had just occurred to me. "Oh, by the way . . . the fellow who just went in?"

He stared at me flatly, unwilling to yield anything more than he had.

I held a hand above my head. "About this tall? Denim jacket and spurs. He arrived on a motorcycle less than a minute ago."

"What about him?"

"Can you tell me his name? I met him a couple of nights ago and now I've forgotten. I'm too embarrassed to ask so I was hoping you'd know."

"He's a pal of the owner's. He's a two-bit punk. You got no business hanging out with a little shit like him."

"What about Tim? What's their relationship?"

He looked at his watch again, his tone shifting to exasperation. "Are you going to go in? Because technically we're closed. I'm not supposed to admit anyone after last call."

"I'm going. I'm going. I'll be out in a second. Sorry to be such a pest."

"Duffy something," he murmured. "Nice girl like you ought to be ashamed."

"I promise I am. You have no idea."

Once inside, I dropped the Gidget act and studied the faces within range of me. The overhead lights had

241

come on and the busboys were now stacking chairs on the tabletops. The bartender was closing out the register and the party hearties seemed to be getting the hint. Thea and Scott were sitting in a booth. Both had cigarettes and fresh drinks: one for the road, to get their alcohol levels up. I crossed the front room, hoping to avoid calling attention to myself. Good luck with that. Three single guys gave me the toe-to-head body check, glancing away without interest, which I thought was rude.

I headed for the back corridor, operating on the assumption that Duffy Something was in Tim's office since I didn't see him anywhere else. I passed the ladies' room and the pay phones and turned right into the short hallway. The door to the employees' lounge stood open, and a couple of waitresses were sitting on the couch smoking while they changed their shoes. Both looked up at me, one pausing long enough to remove the cigarette from her lips. "You need help?" Smoke wafted out of her mouth like an SOS.

"I'm looking for Tim."

"Across the hall."

"Thanks." I backed away, wondering what to do next. I couldn't simply knock on his door. I had no reason to interrupt, and I didn't want the biker to get a look at me. I glanced at the door and then back at the two. "Isn't somebody in there with him?"

"No one important."

"I hate to interrupt."

"My, ain't we dainty? Bang on the door and walk in. It's no big deal."

"It's not that important. I'd rather not."

"Oh, shit. Gimme your name and I'll tell him you're here."

"Never mind. That's okay. I can catch him later." I backed up in haste, then scooted around the corner and out the back exit. I walked forward a few steps and then turned and stared. Where the front of the building was only one story tall, the rear portion was two. I could see lights on upstairs. A shift in the shadows suggested movement, but I couldn't be sure. What was going on up there? No way to know unless I created the opportunity to pick my way in.

Meanwhile, I'd have given a lot to know what the biker was saying to Tim. From the location of Tim's office, I knew any exterior windows would have to be around the far corner to my left. I stood there, debating the wisdom of trying to eavesdrop. That corner of the building was shrouded in darkness, and it looked like I'd have to squeeze into the space between the Honky-Tonk and the building next to it. This was a feat that not only promised a bout of claustrophobia but the onslaught of hordes of domestic short-haired spiders the size of my hand. With my luck, the windowsills would be too high for peeking and the conversation too muffled for revelations of note. It was the thought of the spiders that actually clinched the vote.

I opted instead for a close-on inspection of the motor-cycle. I fished out my penlight and flashed the beam across the bike. The make was a Triumph. The license plate was missing, but by law the registration should have been available on the bike somewhere. I ran a hand across the seat, hoping it would lift to reveal a storage compartment. I was in the process of the search when the rear door banged open and the two waitresses walked out. I shoved the penlight in my pocket and turned my attention toward the street, like I was waiting for someone. They moved off to my right, deep in conversation, crossing my line of vision without exhibiting any curiosity about what I was doing. As soon as they were gone, I turned off the penlight and slipped it in my bag.

Out in the street, the last of the bar patrons were straggling to their cars. I could hear doors slamming, car engines coughing to life. I abandoned the search and decided to return to my car. I jogged the two blocks, my shoulder bag banging against my hip. When I reached the VW, I unlocked the door and slid under the wheel. I stuck my key in the ignition, fired up the engine, and snapped on my headlights. I made an illegal U-turn and drove back to the Tonk.

Once in view of the place, I doused my headlights and pulled over to the right. I parked the car in the shadow of a juniper bush. I slouched down on my spine, keeping an eye on the rear exit over the rim of my sideview mirror. The biker showed up about ten minutes later. He mounted his bike, backed off his center stand, and dropped his weight down with a quick stomp that jolted his engine to life. He cranked the throttle with one hand, revving the bike until it roared in protest. He kept one foot on the ground while he pivoted his bike, the backside swinging wildly as he took off. I watched him slide through the stop sign and hang a left onto Main. By the time I could follow, he was easily five blocks ahead. Within minutes, I'd lost sight of him.

I cruised on for a while, wondering if he'd turned off on a side street close by. This was an area that consisted largely of single-family residences. The stretches of roadway between subdivisions and shopping malls were lined with citrus orchards. The Colgate Community Hospital appeared on my right. I turned left toward the freeway but saw no sign of the biker's taillight. If he'd already turned on the 101, he'd be halfway to town and I didn't have a prayer of catching up with him. I pulled over to the curb and shut off the ignition. I cranked down the driver's side window and tilted my head, listening for the distant racketing of the motorcycle in the still night air. Nothing at first and then . . . faintly . . . I picked up the rat-a-tat-tat, at a much reduced speed. The source of the sound was impossible to pinpoint, but he couldn't be far. Assuming it was him.

I started the VW and pulled out again. The road here was four lanes wide, and the only visible side street went off to the left. There was a nursery on the corner. The sign read BERNARD HIMES NURSERY & TREE FARM: *Shade Trees, Roses, Fruit Trees, Ornamental Shrubs.* The street curved along beside the tree farm and around to the right again. As nearly as I remembered, there was no other exit, and anyone driving back there would be forced to return. The Santa Teresa Humane Society had its facility toward the far corners of the cul-de-sac, as did the County Animal Control. The other businesses were commercial enterprises: a construction firm, warehouses, a heavy-equipment yard.

I turned left, driving slowly, checking both sides of

245

the street for signs of the biker. Passing the nursery on my right, I thought I saw a flicker of light, in a strobe effect, appearing through the thicket of specimen trees. I squinted, unsure, but the darkness now appeared unbroken and there was no sound. I drove on, following the street to its dead end, a matter of perhaps half a mile. Most of the properties I passed were either entirely dark or minimally lighted for burglar-repellent purposes. Twice, I caught sight of private security vehicles parked to one side. I imagined uniformed guards keeping watch, possibly with the help of attack-trained dogs. I returned to the main road without any clear-cut evidence the biker had come this way. It was now after two. I took the southbound on-ramp to the 101. Traffic was sparse, and I returned to my apartment without seeing him again.

Mercifully, the next morning was a Saturday and I owed myself nothing in the way of exercise. I pulled the pillows over my head, shutting out sound and light. I lay bundled under my quilt in an artificial dark, feeling like a small furry beast. At nine, I finally crawled out of my burrow. I brushed my teeth, showered, and shampooed the previous night's smoke from my hair. Then I wound down the spiral stairs and put on a pot of coffee before I fetched the morning paper.

Once I'd finished breakfast, I put a call through to Jonah Robb at home. I'd first encountered Jonah four years before when he was working missing persons for the Santa Teresa Police Department. I was checking on the whereabouts of a woman who later turned up dead. Jonah was separated from his wife, struggling to come to terms with their strange bond, which had started in junior high school and gone downhill from there. In the course of their years together, they'd separated so many times I think he'd lost count. Camilla worked him like a yo-yo. First, she'd kick him out; then she'd take him back or leave him for long periods, during which he wouldn't see his two daughters for months on end. It was in the midst of one of their extended separations that he and I became involved in a relationship. At some point I finally understood that he'd never be free of her. I broke off intimate contact and we reverted to friends.

He'd since been promoted to lieutenant and was now working homicide. We remained buddies of a sort, though I hadn't set eyes on him for months. The last time I'd run into him was at a homicide scene, where he confessed Camilla was pregnant—by someone else, of course.

"What's up?" he said, once I'd identified myself.

I gave him a rundown on the situation. The LAPD detectives had filled him in on the shooting, so he knew that much. I gave him a truncated version of my dealings with them and then filled in additional details: the money Tim owed Mickey, the biker appearing at his Culver City apartment and again at the Honky-Tonk.

Jonah said, "Did you get the license plate?"

"There wasn't one. I'm guessing the bike's stolen, but I can't be sure. I can't swear he's connected to the shooting, but it seems too coincidental he'd show up in both places, especially since he's said to be a friend of

Tim's. Can you ask Traffic to keep an eye out? I'd love to know who he is and how he's mixed up in this."

"I'll see what I can do and call you back," he said. "What's the story on the gun that was left at the scene? Was that really yours?"

"Afraid so," I said. "That was a wedding gift from Mickey, who purchased it in his name. Later, we switched the registration. It's a sweet little Smith and Wesson I haven't seen since the spring of '72, which is when I left. Maybe Mickey had it on him and the shooter took it away."

"How's he doing?"

"I haven't heard. I'll try calling in a bit, but the truth is, I don't want to ask for fear the news won't be good."

"I don't blame you. Scary shit. Is there anything else?"

"What's the word on the Honky-Tonk? What's going on out there?"

"Nothing that I've heard. As in what?"

"I don't know. It could be dope," I said. "I've been in there twice, and it feels *off* to me. I guess, at the back of my mind, I'm wondering if Mickey picked up on it too. I'm assuming he came up at first to bug Tim about the money owed. But why the return trips?"

"I'll ask around. It's possible the vice guys know something that I don't. What about yourself? How are you these days?"

"Doing great, considering I'm suspected of trying to kill my ex. Speaking of which, how's Camilla?"

"She's big. Baby's due July fourth, and according to the amnio it's a boy. We're excited about that."

"She's living with you?"

"Temporarily."

"Ah."

"Well, yeah. Her turd of a boyfriend abandoned her as soon as he found out she was pregnant. She's got nobody else."

"The poor thing," I said, in a tone of voice that went over his head.

"Anyway, it gives me a chance to spend time with the girls."

"That it does," I said. "Well, it's your life. Good luck."

"I'm going to need it," he said dryly, but he sounded pretty cheerful for a guy whose nuts were being slammed in a car door.

After he hung up, I dialed UCLA and asked for ICU. I identified myself to the woman who answered and asked about Mickey. She put me on hold. When she came back on, an eternity later, I realized I'd stopped breathing.

"He's about the same."

I said, "Thanks," and hung up quickly before she changed her mind.

I spent the bulk of the day in a fit of cleaning, armed with sponges and rags, a bucket of soapy water, a dustcloth, and a vacuum cleaner, plus newspapers and vinegar water for the windows I could reach. The phone rang at four. I paused in my labors, tempted to let the answering machine pick up. Of course, curiosity got the better of me.

"Hey, Kinsey. Eric Hightower here. I hope I didn't catch you at a bad time."

"This is fine, Eric. How are you?"

"Doing good," he said. "Listen, Dixie and I are putting together a little gathering: cocktails and hors d'oeuvres. This is strictly impromptu, just a couple dozen folk, but we wanted you to come. Any time between five and seven."

I took advantage of the moment to open my mail, including the manila envelope Bethel's secretary had sent. Inside was his curriculum vitae. I tossed it in the wastebasket, then took it out again and stuck it in the bottom drawer. "You're talking about tonight?"

"Sure. We've got some friends in from Palm Springs so we're geared up anyway. Can you make it?"

"I'm not sure. Let me take a look at my calendar and call you right back."

"Bullshit. Don't do that. You're stalling while you think of an excuse. It's four now. You can hop in the shower and be ready in half an hour. I'll send the car at four-forty-five."

"No, no. Don't do that. I'll use my own."

"Great. We'll see you then."

"I'll do what I can, but I make no promises."

"If we don't see you by six, I'm coming after you myself."

As soon as he hung up, I let out a wail, picturing the house, the servants, and all their la-di-da friends. I'd rather have a root canal than go to these things. Why hadn't I just lied and told him I was tied up? Well, it was too late now. I put the cleaning gear away and trudged up the spiral stairs. I opened my closet door and stared at my dress. I admit to a neurotic sense of pride in only owning that one garment, except for times like this. I took the dress from the closet and held it up to the light. It didn't look too bad. And then a worse thought struck. What if *they* were all decked out in designer jeans? What if I was the only one who showed up in a dress made of a wrinkle-free synthetic fabric that scientific tests would later prove was carcinogenic? I'd end up looking like a social geek, which is what I am.

EIGHTEEN

I drove into the parking area at the Hightowers' estate shortly after 6 P.M. The house was ablaze, though it wouldn't be dark for another hour yet. The evening was cool, 62 degrees, according to the report on my car radio. I parked my 1974 VW between a low-slung red Jaguar and a boxy chrome-trimmed black Rolls, where it sat looking faintly plaintive, a baby humpback whale swimming gamely among a school of sharks. In a final moment of cunning, I'd solved my fashion dilemma with the following: black flats, black tights, a very short black skirt, and a long-sleeved black T-shirt. I'd even applied a touch of makeup: powder, lip gloss, and a smudgy line of black along my lashes.

A middle-aged white maid in a black uniform answered the door chimes and ushered me into the foyer, where she offered to take my bag. I declined, preferring to retain it on the off chance I'd spy the perfect opportunity to flee the premises. I could hear a smattering of conversation, interspersed with the kind of laughter that suggests lengthy and unrestrained access to booze. The maid murmured a discreet directive and began to cross the living room in her especially silent maid's shoes. I followed her through the dining room and out into the screened atrium, where some fifteen to twenty people were already standing about with their drinks and cocktail napkins. A serving wench was circulating with a tray of hors d'oeuvres: teeny-weeny one-bite lamb chops with paper panties on the ends.

As is typical of California parties, there was a percentage of people dressed far better than I and a percentage dressed like bums. The very rich seem particularly practiced at the latter, wearing baggy chinos, shapeless cotton shirts, and deck shoes with no socks. The not-so-very-rich have to work a little harder, adding an abundance of gold jewelry that might or might not be fake. I tucked my bag against the wall behind a nearby chair and then stood where I was, hoping to get my bearings before the panic set in. I didn't know a soul and I was already flirting with the urge to escape. If I didn't see Eric or Dixie in the next twenty seconds, I'd ease right on out.

A black waiter in a white jacket appeared at my shoulder and asked if I'd like a drink. He was tall and freckle-faced, somewhere in his forties, his tone refined, his expression remote. His name tag said STEWART. I wondered what he thought of the Montebello social set and sincerely hoped he wouldn't take me for one of them. On second thought, there probably wasn't too much danger of that.

"Could I have Chardonnay?"

"Certainly. We're pouring Kistler, Sonoma-Cutrer, and a Beringer Private Reserve."

"Surprise me," I said, and then I tilted my head. "Don't I know you from somewhere?"

"Rosie's. Most Sundays."

I pointed in recognition. "Third booth back. You're usually reading a book."

"That's right. I work two jobs at the moment, and Sunday's the only day I have to myself. I got three kids in college and a fourth going off next year. By 1991, I'll be a free man again."

"What's the other job?"

"Telephone sales. I have a friend owns the company, and he lets me fill in when it suits my scheduling. His turnover's fast anyway, and I'm good at the spiel. I'll be back in a moment. Don't you go away."

"I'll be here."

Halfway across the room I caught sight of Mark Bethel in conversation with Eric, hunkered beside Eric's wheelchair. Eric had his back to me; Mark was just to the left of him and facing my way. Mark's face was long and his hairline was receding, which gave him a high-domed head with a wide expanse of brow. He wore glasses with tortoise-shell rims, behind which his eyes were a luminous gray. While technically not good-looking, the television cameras were amazingly kind to him. He'd removed his suit coat and, as I watched, I saw him loosen his tie and roll up the sleeves of his crisp white dress shirt. The gesture suggested that despite his buttoned-down appearance he was ready to go to work for his constituents. It was the sort of soft-focus image that would probably show up later in one of his commercials. The thrust of his campaign was shamelessly orchestrated: babies and old folk and the

American flag waving over patriotic music. His opponents were portrayed in grainy black-and-white, overlaid with tabloid-type headlines decrying their perfidy. Mentally, I slapped myself around some for being such a cynic. Mark's wife, Laddie, and his son, Malcolm, were standing a few feet away, chatting with another couple.

Laddie was the exemplary political mate: mild, compassionate, so subtle in her affect that most people never guessed the power she held. Her eyes were a cool hazel, her dark hair streaked blond, probably to disguise any early hints of gray. Her nose was slightly too prominent, which saved her from perfection and thus endeared her to some extent. Never compelled to work, she'd devoted her time to a number of worthy causes—the symphony, the humane society, the arts council, and numerous charities. As hers was one of the few familiar faces present, I considered crossing the room and engaging her in conversation. I knew she'd at least *pretend* to be attentive, even if she couldn't quite remember who I was.

Malcolm, in another five years, was going to be a knockout. Even now, he was graced with a certain boy beauty: dark-haired and dark-eyed, with a succulent mouth and slouching, lazy posture. I'm a sucker for the type, though I tend to be careful about guys that good-looking as they often turn out to be treacherous. He seemed to have an awareness of the ladies, who were, likewise, more than casually aware of him. He wore desert boots, faded jeans, a pale blue dress shirt, and a navy blazer. He seemed poised, at ease, accustomed to attending parties given by his parents' snooty friends. He looked like a stockbroker in the making, maybe a commodities analyst. He'd end up on financial-channel talk shows, discussing shortfalls, emerging markets, and aggressive growth. Once off the air, the female anchor, ever bullish, would pursue him over drinks and then fuck his baby brains out, strictly no-load with no penalty for early withdrawal.

"Excuse me, dear."

I turned. The woman to my right handed me her empty glass, which I took without thinking. While she was clearly speaking in my direction, she managed to address me without direct eye contact. She was a gaunt and gorgeous fifty with a long flawless face and blown-about red hair. She wore a long-sleeved black silk body suit and blue jeans so tight I was surprised she could draw breath. With her flat tummy, tiny waist, and minuscule hips, my guess was she'd had sufficient liposuction to create an entire separate human being. "I need a refill. Gin and tonic. Make it Bombay Sapphire and no ice this round, please."

"Bombay Sapphire. No ice."

She leaned closer. "Darling, where's the nearest loo? I'm about to pee my pants."

"The loo? Let's see." I pointed toward the sliding glass doors that opened into the dining room. "Through those glass doors. Angle left. The first door on your right."

"Thanks ever so."

I set her empty glass in a potted palm, watching as she tottered away on her four-inch heels. She did as directed, passing through the glass doors to the dining room. She angled left to the first door, tilted her head, tapped lightly, turned the knob, and went in. Turned out to be a linen closet, so she walked right out again, looking mildly embarrassed and thoroughly confused. She spotted another door and corrected for her error with a quick look-around to see if anyone had noticed. She knocked and went in, then did an about-face, emerging from a closet filled with stereo equipment. Well, darn. I guess I know as much about the loo as I do about high-priced gins.

I eased my way through the crowd, intercepting Stewart, who was returning with my wine. The next time I saw the woman, she avoided me altogether, but she'd probably drop a hint to Dixie about having me removed. In the meantime, a young woman appeared with another tray of hors d'oeuvres, this time halved new potatoes the size of fifty-cent pieces, topped with a dollop of sour cream and an anthill of black caviar. Within minutes, everybody's breath was going to smell like fish.

Eric's conversation with Mark had come to an end. Across the room, I caught Mark's attention and he moved in my direction, pausing to shake a few hands en route. By the time he finally reached me, his public expression had been replaced by a look of genuine concern. "Kinsey. Terrific. I thought that was you. I've been trying to reach you," he said. "When'd you get here?"

"A few minutes ago. I figured we'd connect."

"Well, we don't have long. Laddie committed us to another party and we're just about to leave. Judy passed along the news about Mickey. What a terrible thing. How's he doing?"

"Not well."

Mark shook his head. "What a shitty world we live in. It's not like he didn't have enough problems."

"Judy said you talked to him in March."

"That's right. He asked me for help, in a round-about way. You know how he is. By the way, I did talk to Detective Claas while I was down in L.A., though I didn't learn much. They're being very tight-lipped."

"I'll say. They certainly don't appreciate my presence on the scene."

"So I hear."

I could just imagine the earful he picked up from the LAPD. I said, "At this point, what worries me are Mickey's medical bills. As far as I can tell, he lost all his coverage when he was fired from his job."

"I'm sure that's not an issue. His bills can be paid from funds from Victims of Major Crimes, through the DA's office. It's probably been set in motion, but I'll be happy to check. By the way, I stopped off at Mickey's on my way back from L.A. I thought I should meet his landlady in case a question came up."

"Oh, great. Because the other thing I'm concerned about is his eviction. The sheriff's already been there and changed the locks."

"I gathered as much," he said. "Frankly, I'm surprised to see you take an interest. I was under the impression you hadn't spoken to him for years."

"I haven't, but it looks like I owe him one."

"How so?"

"You know I blamed him for Benny Quintero's

death. Now I find out Mickey was with Dixie that night."

"I heard that story too, but I was never sure how much credit to attach."

"You're telling me they lied?"

"Who's to say? I've made it my practice not to speculate. Mickey didn't confide and I didn't press him for information. Fortunately, we never had to defend the point one way or the other."

I saw him glance in Laddie's direction, gauging their departure, which was imminent. Laddie had found Dixie and she was proffering regrets. Hugs, air kisses, and niceties were exchanged.

Mark said, "I better catch up. Give me a couple of days. I'll let you know about his bills. Glad we had a chance to chat." He gave my shoulder a squeeze and then joined Laddie and Malcolm, who were waiting in the dining room. Dixie followed them out, apparently intending to see them as far as the door.

Meanwhile, Eric had wheeled around and his face seemed to brighten at the sight of me. He pointed to a corner chair and then pushed himself in that direction. I nodded and followed, admiring his physique. His knit shirt fit snugly, emphasizing his shoulders and chest, along with his muscular arms. He looked like an ad for a fitness supplement. When he pivoted his chair, I could see the point where his thighs ended, six inches above the knees. He held a hand out to me. I leaned down and bussed his cheek before I took a seat. His after-shave was citrus and his skin was like satin. He said, "I didn't think you'd come."

"I probably won't stay long. I don't know a soul here except for Mark and his crew. The kid's attractive."

"And bright. Pity about his father. He's a waste of time."

"I thought you liked Mark."

"I do and I don't. He's phony as all get out, but aside from that he's great."

"That's a hell of an endorsement. What'd he do to you?"

Eric gestured dismissively. "Nothing. Forget it. He asked me to do a film clip for his ad campaign. Primary's only ten days off, and there's nothing like a cripple to pick up a few last-minute votes."

"Ooh, you're a cynic. You sound worse than I do. Did it ever occur to you he might see you as a shining example of success and achievement, overcoming the odds and similar sentiments?"

"No. It occurred to me he wants me on his team in hopes other Vietnam vets will follow suit. Prop Forty-two is his pet project. The truth is, he needs a banner issue because he's floundering. Laddie's not going to like it if he's trounced at the polls."

"What difference does it make? I didn't think he had a chance anyway."

"It's one thing to lose and another thing to lose *badly*. He doesn't want to look like a has-been right out of the gate."

"Easy come, easy go. They'll survive, I'm sure."

"Possibly."

"Possibly? I like that. What's that supposed to mean?"

I saw his gaze shift and glanced up in time to see Dixie return. "Things aren't always as they appear."

"The Bethels are unhappy?"

"I didn't say that."

"Incompatible?"

"I didn't say that, either."

"Then what? Come on. I won't repeat it. You've got me curious."

"Mark has places to go. He can't do that divorced. He needs Laddie's money to make it work."

"What about her? What's her stake in it?"

"She's more ambitious than he is. She dreams about the White House."

"You're not serious."

"I am. She grew up in the era of Jackie O and Camelot. While other girls played with Barbies, she was making a list of which rooms to redo."

"I had no idea."

"Hey, Mark wants it too. Don't get me wrong, but he'd probably be content with the Senate while she's longing for a place in all the history books. He won't make it this round—the competition's too fierce—but in four years, who knows? As long as he can rally support, he's probably got a shot at it one day. Meanwhile, if he starts looking like a loser, she might bump him and move on."

"And that's enough to keep their marriage afloat?"

"To a point. In the absence of passion, rampant ambition will suffice. Besides, divorce is a luxury."

"Oh, come on. Couples get divorced every day."

"Those are the people with nothing at stake. They can afford to set personal happiness above all else."

"As opposed to what?"

"The status quo. Besides, who wants to start over at our stage in life? Are you eager to fling yourself into a new relationship?"

"No."

Eric smiled. "My sentiments exactly. I mean, think of all the stories you'd have to retell, the personal revelations, the boring family history. Then you'd have to weather all the hurt feelings and the fear and the stupid misunderstandings while you get to know the other person and they get to know you. Even if you take the risk and pour yourself heart and soul into someone new, the odds are your new love's a clone of the one you just dumped."

I said, "This is making me ill."

"It's really no big deal. You put up with things. You look the other way, and sometimes you have no choice but to bite your tongue. If both parties are committed—whatever their reasons—it can work."

"And what if both aren't committed?"

"Then you have a problem and you have to deal with it."

NINETEEN

I'm going to skip a bunch of stuff here because, really, who cares? We ate. We drank, and then we ate some more. I didn't spill, fart, fall down, or otherwise disgrace myself. I talked to the couple from Palm Springs, who turned out to be nice, as were most of the other folk. I listened with feigned interest to a lengthy discussion about vintage Jaguars and antique Rolls-Royces and another in which the participants told where they were when the last big local earthquake struck. Some of the answers were: the south of France, Barbados, the Galápagos Islands. I confessed I was in town, scrubbing out my toilet bowl, when a bunch of water slopped up and splashed my face. That got a big laugh. What a kidder, that girl. I felt I was just getting the hang of how to talk to the rich when the following occurred.

Stewart crossed the atrium with a bottle of Chardonnay and offered to fill my glass. I declined . . . I'd had plenty . . . but Dixie leaned toward him so he could refill hers. The collar of her silk shirt gaped briefly in the process, and I caught a glimpse of the necklace she wore in the hollow of her throat.

Threaded on a gold chain was a tiny gold heart with a
pink rose enameled in the center. I felt my smile falter.
Fortunately, Dixie was looking elsewhere and didn't
notice the change in my expression. I could feel my
cheeks heat. The necklace was a duplicate of the one
I'd seen in Mickey's bed-table drawer.

Now it was possible—remotely possible—he'd given
her the necklace fourteen years before, in honor of the
affair they were having back then. I set my glass on the
table next to me and got to my feet. No one seemed to
pay attention as I walked across the room. I passed
through the doors into the dining room, where I spotted the same maid who'd answered the door.

I said, "Excuse me. Where's the nearest bathroom?"
I couldn't, for the life of me, refer to it as the "loo."

"Turn right at the foyer. It's the second door on the
right."

"I think someone's in there. Dixie said to use hers."

"Master bedroom's at the end of the hallway to the
left of the foyer."

"Thanks," I said. As I passed the chair where I'd
secured my handbag, I leaned down and picked it up. I
moved through the living room and out into the foyer,
where I turned left. I walked quickly, keeping my
weight on my toes so the tap of my heels wouldn't
advertise my passage. The double doors to the master
bedroom stood open to reveal a room twice the size of
my apartment. The pale limestone floors were the same
throughout. All the colors here were muted: linens like
gossamer, wall coverings of pale silk. There were two
bathrooms, his 'n' hers, one on either side of the room.
Eric's was nearer, fitted with an enormous roll-in

shower and a wall-mounted bar to one side of the toilet. I turned on my heel and headed into the second.

Dixie's dressing table was a fifteen-foot slab of marble that stretched along one wall. There was a second wall of closets, a glass shower enclosure, a massive tub with jacuzzi, and a separate dressing room with an additional U of hanging space. I closed the bathroom door behind me and started going through her belongings. This impulse to snoop was getting out of control. I just couldn't seem to keep my nose out of other people's business. The more obstacles the merrier. I found the cologne bottle in a cluster of ten others on a silver tray. On the bottom was the same partially torn label I'd seen at Mickey's. I sniffed at the spray. The scent was unmistakably the same.

I returned to the bedroom, where I crossed to the bed. I opened the top drawer in the first of the two matching bed tables. There sat the diaphragm case. I could hardly believe she was screwing him again . . . or was it *still*? No wonder she'd been nervous, prowling my backyard, angling for information about his current state. She must have wondered at his silence, wondered where he'd been the night she retrieved her personal items. Did she know he'd been shot? Hell, she might have done it herself if she'd found out about Thea. Maybe she was only quizzing me to determine what, if anything, I knew. I thought back to my conversation with Thea at the Honky-Tonk. Now I wondered if *she'd* seen the diaphragm *et al.*, assuming it was mine while I'd assumed it belonged to her.

I closed the drawer and retraced my steps, emerging from the master suite just as Eric appeared, wheeling himself in my direction. I said, "Great bathroom. The maid sent me down here because the other was in use."

"I wondered where you went. I thought you left."

"I was just powdering my nose," I said, and then glanced at my watch. "Actually, I do have to go, now you mention it. I agreed to meet someone at eight, and it's almost that now."

"You have a date?"

"You don't have to sound so surprised."

He smiled. "Sorry. I didn't mean to pry."

"Could you give Dixie my thanks? I know it's rude not to do it personally, but I thought I'd slip out without making a fuss. Sometimes one person leaves and it starts an exodus."

"Sure thing."

"I appreciate the invitation. This was fun."

"We'll have to try it again. What's your schedule like next week?"

"My schedule?"

"I thought we'd have lunch, just the two of us," he said.

"Ah. I don't remember offhand. I'll check when I hit the office and call you on Monday."

"I'll be waiting."

Inwardly, I found myself backing away. Ordinarily, I don't imagine men are coming on to me, but his tone was flirtatious, which didn't sit well with me. I became especially chirpy as I made my retreat. Eric seemed amused by my discomfiture.

*

I was letting myself into my apartment some fifteen minutes later when I heard the last of a message being left on my machine. Jonah. I dropped my bag on the floor and snatched at the phone, but by then he'd hung up. I pressed the PLAY button and heard the rerun of his brief communication.

"Kinsey. Jonah here. It looks like we found your boy. Give me a call, and I'll fill you in on the nitty-gritty details. Not a very nice guy, but you probably know that already. I'm at home."

I looked up his home number and dialed with impatience, listening to ring after ring. "Come on, come on. . . ."

"Hello?"

Oh, shit. Camilla.

I said, "Could I speak to Lieutenant Robb? I'm returning his call."

"And who's this?"

"Kinsey Millhone."

Dead silence.

Then she said, "He's busy at the moment. Is this something I can help you with?"

"Not really. He has some information for me. Could I speak to him, please?"

"Just a minute," she said, not entirely happy about the situation. I heard a clunk as she placed the handset on the tabletop, then the tapping of her heels as she walked away. After that, I was treated to all the quaint, domestic sounds of the Robbs' Saturday night as they hung around the house. I could hear the television set in a distant room. Closer to the phone, one of his girls, probably Courtney, the older one, played chopsticks on an out-of-tune piano, never quite finishing her portion of the musical duet. I listened to countless repetitions of the first fifteen to twenty notes. The other daughter, whose name I forget, would chime in at the wrong spot, which caused the first girl to protest and start over again. The second child kept saying, "Stop it!" which the first girl declined to do. In the meantime, I could hear Camilla's comments to Jonah, who apparently hadn't been told there was a call for him. I could hear the sound of water running, the clattering of plates. I knew she was doing it deliberately, forcing me to eavesdrop on the small homely drama being played out for my benefit.

I whistled into the mouthpiece. I said "HELLO!" about six times, to no avail. I knew if I hung up, all I'd get was a busy signal when I tried calling back. *Clump, clump, clump.* I heard advancing footsteps on the hardwood floor. I yelled "HEY!" *Clump, clump, clump.* The footsteps receded. Another round of chopsticks was played. Shrieks from the girls. Chitchat between husband and wife. Camilla's seductive laughter as she teased Jonah about something. Once more I cursed myself for never learning how to do the piercing whistle you make when you put two fingers between your teeth. I'd pay six hundred dollars if someone could teach me that. Think of the taxis you could summon, the waiters you could signal across a crowded room. *Clump, clump, clump.* Someone approached the phone, and I heard Jonah remark with annoyance, "Hey, who left this off? I'm expecting a call."

I yelled "JONAH!" but not quickly enough to prevent his replacing the handset in the cradle. I redialed the number, but the line was busy. Camilla'd probably picked up another phone in haste, just to make certain I couldn't get through. I waited a minute and tried again. Still busy. On my fourth attempt, I heard the phone ring, only to have Camilla pick up again. This time she didn't even bother to say hello. I heard her breathe in my ear.

I said, "Camilla, if you don't put Jonah on the phone, I'm going to get in my car and drive over there right this minute."

She sang out, "Jonah? For you."

Four seconds later he said, "Hello?"

"Hi, Jonah. It's Kinsey. I just got home and picked up your message. What's going on?"

"Listen, you're going to love this. Bobbi Deems pulled your biker over last night when she saw he had a taillight out. Kid's name is Carlin Duffy, and it turns out he's driving with an expired Kentucky driver's license and expired registration. Bobbi cited him for both and impounded the bike."

"Where in Kentucky?"

"Louisville, she said. You want him, he'll be in court in thirty days."

"What about before then? Does he have a local address?"

"More or less. He claims he's living in a maintenance shed at that nursery off the 101 at the Peterson exit. Apparently, he works there part-time in exchange for rent, a claim the owner confirms. Meanwhile, Bobbi

269

ran a background check on this crud, who's got a criminal history as long as your arm: arrests and convictions going back to 1980."

"For what?"

"Mostly nickel-and-dime stuff. He never killed anyone."

"I'm so relieved," I said.

"Let's see what we got here: wanton endangerment, criminal recklessness, theft, receiving stolen property, criminal mischief, trying to flee a halfway house where he was serving a ninety-day sentence for giving a false name to a police officer. The guy's not too bright, but he's consistent."

"Any outstanding warrants?"

"Nada. For the moment, he's clean."

"Too bad. It'd have been nice to have him picked up so I could talk to him."

"You'll definitely want to do that. Here's the best part. You ready? You want to know who his brother is? You'll never guess."

"I give up."

"Benny Quintero."

I could feel myself squint. "You're kidding me."

"It's true."

"How'd you figure that one out?"

"I didn't. Bobbi did. Apparently, Benny's name was listed as the owner on the bike registration, so Bobbi put Duffy through his paces. She'd forgotten the story, but she remembered Benny's name. Duffy claims they're half brothers. His mom was originally married to Benny's dad, who died in World War Two. Ten years later, she moved to Kentucky, where she married

Duffy's dad. He was born the next year, fifteen-year age gap between the two boys. Carlin was thirteen when Benny came out to California and got himself killed."

"Is that why he's here?"

"You'd have to ask him. I'm thinking it's a good bet, unless you happen to believe in coincidence."

"I don't."

"Nor do I."

"So where is he now?"

"Well, he can't be far off if he's hoofing it."

"He could have stolen a car."

"Always possible, I guess, though outside his area of expertise. Anyway, if you decide to go looking for him, take someone along. I don't like the idea of your seeing him alone."

"You want to go?"

"Sure, I'd love it. Wait a second." He put a hand across the mouthpiece. Camilla must have been hovering nearby, listening to every word, because she squelched the idea before he even had the chance to ask. He removed his hand from the mouthpiece, addressing me again. "I'm tied up tonight, but how's Monday. Does that work?"

"Sounds ducky."

"You'll call me?"

"Of course."

"I'll see you then," he said.

As soon as he clicked off, I grabbed my handbag and walked out the door. I wasn't going to wait until Monday. How ridiculous. Duffy could be long gone; I couldn't take the risk. I stopped for gas on the way out. The nursery was maybe ten minutes away, but the needle on my gas gauge was now pointing at E, and I wasn't sure how much driving I'd have to do catching up with him.

It was twenty of nine when I finally pulled into the parking lot at the nursery. The sign out front indicated the place was open until 9 P.M. on weekends. The property must have occupied some ten to fifteen acres, the land sandwiched between the highway on one side and the side street into which I'd turned. The gardening center was immediately in front of me, a low white glass-and-frame building that accommodated numerous bedding, landscape, and house plants, seeds, gardening books, bulbs, herbs, pottery, and gifts, for "that special someone with a talent for growing."

To the right, behind the chain-link enclosure, I could see an array of fountains and statuary for sale, ceramic, plastic, and redwood planters, along with big plastic bags of fertilizers, mulches, garden chemicals, and soil amendments. To the left, I could see a series of greenhouses, like opaque glass barracks, and, beyond them, row after row of trees, a shaggy forest of shadows stretching back toward the freeway.

Now that the sun was fully down, the lingering light had shifted to a charred black, permeated by the smell of sod. The area along the side street was well lighted, but the far reaches of the nursery were shrouded in darkness. I scrounged around in the backseat and found a medium-weight denim jacket that I hoped would offer warmth against the chill night air. I locked the car and went into the gardening center with its harsh fluorescent lights shining down on banks of seed packs and gaudy indoor blooms.

The girl at the counter wore a forest-green smock with the name *Himes* embroidered across the pocket. As I closed the door, she gave the air a surreptitious fanning. She was in her teens, with dry blond hair and heavy pancake makeup over bumpy cheeks and chin. The air smelled of a recently extinguished clove cigarette.

"Hi. I'm looking for Carlin. Is he here?"

"Who?"

"Carlin Duffy, the guy with the bike who's living in the shed."

"Oh, Duffy. He's not here. The cops took his bike and locked it in the impound lot. He said it's going to cost a bundle to get it out."

"Bummer."

"He was really pissed. What a bunch of pigs."

"The worst. You two are friends?"

She shrugged. "My mom doesn't like him. He's a bum, she says, but I don't see why it's his fault if he's new in town."

"How long's he been here?"

"Maybe five or six months. He came like right before Christmas, sometime right around in there. Mr. Himes caught this other guy, Marcel? Do you know him?"

"Uh-uh."

"Marcel stole a bunch of these plants and sold 'em on the street? Mr. Himes fired his sorry butt as soon as he found out."

"And Duffy got his job shortly afterward?"

"Well, yeah. Mr. Himes had no idea Marcel was cheating him until Duffy bought a dieffenbachia off him and brought it in," she said. "I mean, Duffy's smart. He figured it's a scam right off. He only paid Marcel I guess a buck or two and there's our tag . . . like for $12.99 . . . pasted on the side."

"What about Marcel? I bet he swore up and down he didn't do it, right?"

"Right. What a dork. He acted all crushed and upset, like he's completely innocent. Oh, sure. He said he'd sue, but I don't see how he could."

"His word against Duffy's, and who's going to believe *him*. Is Marcel black, perchance?"

She nodded. "You know how they are," she said, rolling her eyes. For the first time, she assessed me. "How do you know Duffy?"

"Through his brother, Ben."

"Duffy has a brother? Well, that's weird," she said. "He told me his family's dead and gone."

"His brother's been dead for years."

"Oh. Too bad."

"What time will he be back?"

"Probably not until ten."

"Well, shoot," I said.

"Did he say he'd meet you here?"

"Nah. I saw him at the Tonk last night and then lost track of him."

"He's probably there tonight," she said helpfully. "You want to use the phone? You could have him paged. He's pals with the owner. I think his name is Tim."

"Really? I know Tim," I said. "Maybe I'll pop over there, since it isn't far. Meantime, if he comes in? Tell him I was here. I'd like to speak to him."

"About what?"

"About *what*?" I repeated.

"In case he asks," she said.

"It's sort of a surprise."

TWENTY

I cruised through the parking lot across from the Honky-Tonk and miraculously found a space about six slots down. It was not quite nine, and the Saturday-night boozers were just beginning to roll in. The Tonk wouldn't start jumping until ten o'clock when the band arrived. I crossed the street, pausing while a red-and-white panel truck idled near the garbage bins. No sign of the driver, but the logo on the side read PLAS-STOCK. I could see that second-floor lights were on in the building. Shifting shadows suggested someone moving around up there.

I continued on across the street, approaching the bar from the rear. Idly, I tried the back door, but it was locked. I guess it would be hard to insist on a cover charge out front if wily patrons could go around the back and get in for free. I moved to the front entrance. The bouncer remembered me from the night before so he waved off my ID and stamped the back of my hand. This was the third night in a row I'd checked into the place, and I was feeling like a regular. During the period when Mickey and I were married, we were here four nights out of seven, which didn't seem odd at the time. He hung out with other cops, and that's what they did after work in those days. I was with Mickey so I did what he did as a matter of course. The Honky-Tonk was family, providing a social context for those of us without any other close ties. Looking back, I realize what an enormous waste of time it was, but maybe that was our way of avoiding each other, bypassing the real work of marriage, which is intimacy. I'm still lousy at being close, having so little practice in the past umpteen years.

I found a stool at the bar and ordered a beer. I sat with my back to the mirrored wall of glittering liquor bottles, one elbow on the bar, a foot swinging in time to whatever anonymous music played. I spotted Thea at just about the same time she spotted me. She held my gaze for a moment, her features drawn and tense. Gone was the leather vest that had exposed her long bare arms. In its place she wore a white turtleneck and tight jeans. Her belt was silver, the buckle shaped like a lock with a heart-shaped keyhole in the center. Preoccupied, she took an order from a table of four and then crossed to the bar, where she chatted with Charlie briefly before she moved toward me.

"Hello, Thea," I said. Close up, I realized she was pissed as hell. "Are you mad about something?"

"You can bet your sweet ass. Why didn't you tell me about Mickey? You *knew* he'd been shot and you never said a word."

"How'd you hear?"

"Scottie's father told us. You talked to me at least twice so you could have *mentioned* it."

"Thea, I wasn't going to walk in here cold and make

that announcement. I didn't even know you were friends until you asked about his jacket. By then, I figured there was something more going on."

She shot an uneasy glance at a table near the poolroom door where Scottie was sitting, facing two men who had their backs to us. He'd apparently been watching us across the room. As if on cue, he excused himself to his companions and got out of his chair, then ambled in our direction with a beer bottle in his hand. I couldn't help but notice the change in his appearance. His mustache was neatly trimmed, and he'd shaved his goatee. He was also better dressed— nothing fancy, but attractive—cowboy boots, jeans, and a blue denim work shirt with the sleeves buttoned at the wrist. I thought he'd cut his hair, but as he drew near I could see he'd simply pulled it back and secured it in a rubber band.

Thea murmured, "Please don't say anything. He'd kill me if he knew."

"What time are you off? Can we meet and talk then?"

"Where?"

"What about that twenty-four-hour coffee shop over by the freeway?"

"Two A.M., but I can't promise—"

By then, Scottie'd reached us and we abandoned the exchange. His smile was pleasant, his tone mild. "Hi. How are you? I understand you're a friend of my dad's. I'm Scott Shackelford." He held out his right hand and we shook. I saw no indication that he was stoned or drunk.

"Nice meeting you," I said. "Tim told me who

you were, but I didn't have the chance to introduce myself."

He put his left arm around Thea's neck in a companionable half nelson, holding the beer bottle just in front of her. The gesture was both casual and possessive. "I see you know Thea. How're you doin', babe," he said. He kissed her affectionately on the cheek.

Thea's eyes were on me as she murmured something noncommittal. She was clearly not all that crazy about the choke hold.

He turned back to me, his tone now tinged with concern. "We heard about Mickey. That's a hell of a thing. How's he doing?"

"He's fair. I called down there this afternoon, and the nurse said he's the same."

Scott shook his head. "I feel bad for the guy. I didn't know him well, but he used to come in here—what? Every couple of weeks?"

"About that," Thea said, woodenly.

"Anyway, it's been months."

"I heard he sold his car, so maybe he couldn't drive up as often," I said. I was trying to think up a graceful excuse to extract myself. I'd only come here to find Duffy, and he was nowhere to be seen.

Scottie went on. "By the way, Tim said if you came in, he wants to talk to you."

"About what?"

"Beats me."

"Where is he?"

He looked around the room lazily, his mouth pulling down. "I'm not sure. I saw him a little while ago. Probably in his office if he's not out here somewhere."

"I'll try to catch him later. Right now—"

"Say, you know what? That's my dad and his friend at the table over there. Why don't you stop by and say hi?" He was pointing toward the two men he'd been sitting with.

I looked at my watch. "Oh, gee. I wish I had time, but I have to meet someone."

"Don't be like that. He'd like to buy you a drink. If anyone asks, Thea or Charlie can tell 'em where you're at, right, Thea?"

"I have to get back to work," she said. She eased out from under his arm and returned to the bar, where her order was waiting. She took the tray and moved off without looking back at us.

Scottie followed her with his eyes. "What's bugging her?"

"I have no idea. Look, I was just on my way to the ladies' room. I'll join you in a minute, but I really can't stay long."

"See you shortly," he said.

Scottie moved off toward the table. In retrospect, I decided he'd probably cleaned up his appearance in deference to his father. Pete Shackelford had always been a stickler about personal tidiness. I cut left toward the rest rooms. As soon as I was out of his line of sight, I headed down the corridor toward the rear exit. I had no intention of having a drink with Shack. He knew way too much about me and, as far as I could tell, he was already prepared to rat me out.

As I passed the short corridor where Tim's office was located, I stopped in my tracks. There was now a tarp flung across boxes stacked against the wall. Curious, I had a quick peek: ten sealed cartons with the Plas-Stock logo stamped on the sides. Clearly, this was a shipment unloaded from the panel truck currently idling outside. I dropped the corner into place. All four doors off that corridor were closed, but I could see a thin slit of light coming from under the third door on the left. That door was locked last I checked, and I couldn't help but wonder if it was locked again. I glanced around casually. I was alone in the hall and it wouldn't take but two seconds to see if it was secure. I eased to the left and placed my hand on the knob, taking care not to rattle it as I turned it in my hand. Ah. Unlocked. I wondered what was in there that required such security.

I pushed the door back, stuck my head in the opening. The floor area was only large enough to accommodate a set of stairs leading up and a padlocked door on the left, possibly a closet. I could see a dim light shining from the top of the narrow stairway. I stepped inside, closed the corridor door quietly behind me, and began to climb. It wasn't my intention to be sneaky, but I noticed I was walking on the outer edges of the treads, where there was less likelihood of creaking.

At the top of the stairs there was a landing about six feet square with a ladder affixed to one wall, probably leading to the roof. The only door off the landing was ajar, light flooding out from the space beyond. I pushed the door back. The room was huge, stretching off into the shadows, easily extending the length and breadth of the four large rooms below. The floor was linoleum, trampled in places where sooty footprints had permanently altered the color. I could see numerous electrical outlets along the walls and five or six large clean patches. The space was dense with the kind of dry heat that suggests poor insulation. The walls were unfinished plywood. There was a plain wooden table, two dozen folding chairs, a big garbage can jammed with scraps. I'd imagined cases of wine and beer stacked along the walls, but there was nothing. What had I pictured? Drugs, illegal aliens, child pornography, prostitution? At the very least, broken and outdated restaurant equipment, the old jukebox, the remains of New Year's Eve and St. Paddy's decorations from celebrations long past. This was boring.

I cruised the room, taking care to stay on the balls of my shoes. I didn't want anyone downstairs wondering who was clumping around up here. Still nothing of interest. I left the lights as I'd found them and crept back down the stairs. Again, I placed my hand carefully around the doorknob and turned it in silence. The hallway appeared empty. I exited the door, using my palm to blunt the click of its closing.

"Can I help you?"

Tim was standing in the shadows to the left of the door.

I shrieked. I flung up my hands and my shoulder bag flew out of my grasp, contents tumbling out as it hit the floor. "*Shit!*"

Tim laughed. "Sorry. I thought you saw me. What were you doing?" He was casually dressed: jeans and a V-neck knit pullover.

"Nothing. I opened that door by mistake," I said. I

dropped to my knees, trying to gather up items that seemed to be strewn everywhere. "Scottie said you wanted to see me. I was looking for your office. This door was unlocked. I tried the knob and it was open so I just went on in. I figured you might be upstairs, so I called out a big *yoo-hoo*."

"Really. I didn't hear you."

He hunkered, setting my handbag upright. He began to toss the contents back in, while I watched in fascination. Fortunately, I wasn't carrying a gun and he didn't seem to register the presence of my key picks. He was saying, "I don't know how you women do this. Look at all this stuff. What's this?"

"Travel toothbrush. I'm a bit of a fanatic."

He smiled. "And this?" He held up a plastic case.

"Tampons."

As he picked up my wallet, it flipped open to my driver's license, which he glanced at idly. The photostat of my P.I. license was in the window opposite, but if he noticed he gave no indication. He tossed the wallet into the handbag. Shack had probably already blown my cover anyway.

"Here, let me do that," I said, happy to be in motion lest he see my hands were shaking. Once we'd retrieved everything, I rose to my feet. "Thanks."

"You want to see what's up there? Here, come on. I'll show you."

"No, really. That's fine. I actually peeked at the space a few minutes ago. I was hoping you still had the old jukebox."

"Unfortunately, no. I sold that shortly after we bought the place. Great space up there, isn't it? We're thinking about expanding. We were using it for storage until it occurred to me there were better uses for that much square footage. Now all I have to do is get past fire department regulations—among other things."

"You'd do what, add tables?"

"Second bar and a dance floor. First, we have to argue with the city of Colgate and the county planning commission. Anyway, that's not what I wanted to talk to you about. You want to step into my office? We don't have to stand around out here talking in the dark."

"This is fine. I told Scottie I'd stop by his table and have a drink with his dad."

"We heard about Mickey."

"Word travels fast."

"Not as fast as you'd think. Shack tells us you were a cop once upon a time. . . ."

"So what?"

Tim went right on. "We're assuming you're conducting an investigation of your own."

Thank you, Pete Fucking Shackelford, I thought. I tried to think how to frame my reply.

Meanwhile, Tim was saying, "We have a pal in L.A. who might be of help."

"Really. And who's that?"

"Musician named Wary Beason. Mickey's neighbor in Culver City."

Pointerlike, I could feel my ears prick up. "How do you know him?"

"Through his jazz combo. He's played here a couple times. He's very talented."

"Small world."

"Not really. Mickey told him we booked bands, so Wary got in touch and auditioned. We liked his sound."

"I'm surprised Wary didn't call you and tell you about the shooting."

"Yeah, we were too. We've been trying to reach him, but so far no luck. We thought you'd want to talk to him if you went to L.A."

"Maybe I'll do that. Mind if I ask you about a couple of things while I have you?"

"Sure. No problem."

"What's Plas-Stock?"

Tim smiled. "Plastic cutlery, plates, glassware, that kind of thing. We're doing a big buffet for the Memorial Day weekend. We'll comp you to it if you're interested. Anything else?"

"Did you ever pay Mickey the ten grand you owed him?"

His smile lost its luster. "How'd you hear about that?"

"I came across a reference to it in his papers. According to the note, payment was due in full on January fifteenth."

"That's right, but things were tight right about then so he gave me an extension. I pay him off in July."

"If he lives," I said. "Is that what he was doing when he came up here, negotiating the agreement?"

"Mickey's a drinker."

"I'm puzzled why he'd give you an extension when he's having financial problems of his own."

Tim seemed surprised. "Mickey has money problems? That's news to me. Last time I saw him, he didn't

285

act like a guy with worries. You think the shooting had something to do with business?"

"I'm really not sure. I was curious why he was spending so much time up here."

Tim crossed his arms, leaning against the wall. "Don't quote me on this, especially not to Scottie, but if you want my opinion Mickey was hot to get in Thea's pants."

"What about her? Was she interested in him?"

"Let's put it this way: Not if she's smart. Scottie's not the kind of guy you mess with." I saw him lift his eyes to someone in the passage behind me. "You looking for me?"

"Charlie needs your approval on an invoice. The guy wants a check before he heads back to L.A."

"Be right there."

I glanced back. One of the other waitresses had already turned on her heel and disappeared.

Tim patted my arm. "I better take care of this. Whatever you want, it's on the house."

"Thanks."

I followed two steps behind Tim, entering the bar with another quick visual search for Duffy. Still no sign of him. Shack, at Scottie's table, caught sight of me and waved. I guessed there wasn't going to be a way to get out of this. Shack must have enjoyed the opportunity to burn me. Scottie turned to see who his dad was waving at, and then he motioned me over. I felt like a mule, stubbornly resisting even while I was being propelled in that direction.

Shack was sitting on the far side of the table, and he

rose to his feet, saying, "Well, would you look who's here? We were just talking about you."

"I don't doubt that a bit."

"Sit down, sit down. Grab a seat."

The other fellow at the table rose and sank in his seat respectfully, the physical equivalent of a gent tipping his hat to a lady.

I said, "I really can't stay long."

"Sure you can," Shack said. He reached over and grabbed a chair from a nearby table, pulling it up next to him. I sat down, resigned. Shack's gaze rested on his son, his satisfaction and pride giving a lift to his normally heavy features. He was wearing a plaid wool shirt, unbuttoned to accommodate his thick neck. His companion appeared to be in his fifties, gray hair cut close, weathered complexion suggesting years of sun exposure. Like Shack, he was heavyset, bulky through the shoulders, his belly protruding as if he were six months pregnant.

Shack hooked a thumb at him and said, "This is Del. Kinsey Millhone."

"Hello."

Del nodded and then half rose again and shook my hand across the table. "Del Amburgey. Nice to meet you," he said.

We went through that "how're-you-tonight" shit while I squirmed inwardly, trying to think of something bland to say. "Are you here for a visit, or are you local?"

"I live up in Lompoc, so it's a little bit of both. I come down here now and then to see what you big-city folks are up to."

"Not much."

Shack said, "Well, that's not entirely true. This little gal was a cop back when I was in uniform. Now she's a P.I. . . ."

"What's a P.I.?" Del asked.

"A private investigator," Shack said.

I thought I was going deaf. He talked on. I watched his mouth move, but the sound was gone. I didn't look at Scott, but I was acutely aware that he was taking in the information with something close to alarm. His expression didn't seem to change, but his face shut down. Out of the corner of my eye, I could see his hands resting on the table, still relaxed, his fingers loose on the beer bottle, which he tilted to his lips. Aside from the casualness of the gesture, his body was completely still. I tuned in to Shack's commentary, wondering if there were any way to contain the damage he was doing.

". . . just about the time Magruder left the department. What was that, '71?"

"The spring of '72," I said. He knew exactly when it was. We locked eyes briefly, and I could tell blowing my cover allowed him to enjoy a moment of revenge. Whatever I was up to, he would leave me fully exposed. Better take control, I thought, get a jump on the little shit. "That was when Mickey and I split up. I lost touch with him after that."

"Until recently," Shack amended.

I looked at Shack without comment.

He went blithely on. "I guess those two LAPD detectives drove up here and talked to you. They came around my place yesterday. They seemed to think you might've had a hand in it, but I told 'em I didn't see how. You showed up at my door Monday. I didn't think you'd call attention to yourself if you'd shot him the week before. You're not that dumb."

"That was a ruse and you fell for it," I said. I was smiling, but my tone of voice was snide.

"What brings you out to Colgate?"

"Mickey lent Tim ten grand. A no-interest loan with a five-year balloon. I was curious if the money was repaid when it came due." Scottie began to tap one foot, which caused his knee to jump. He crossed his legs, trying to cover his agitation.

"When was that?" Shack asked, still enough of a cop to pursue the obvious.

"January fifteenth. Just about the time Mickey started coming in," I said. "You didn't know about the loan?"

"You ready for a drink? I'm heading to the bar," Scottie said. He was on his feet, his eyes pinned on me.

"Nothing for me, thanks."

"What about you, Dad? Del?"

"I'll go another round. My turn to buy," he said. He leaned forward, hauling his wallet from his right rear pocket.

Scottie waved him off. "I'll take care of it. What's your pleasure? Another of the same?"

"That'd be great."

"Make that two," Shack said.

Once Scottie left, Shack changed the subject, engaging me in chitchat so banal I thought I'd scream. I

289

endured about three minutes of his asinine conversation and then took advantage of Scott's absence to slide out of my seat.

"You leaving us?" Shack said.

"I have to meet someone. It's been nice seeing you."

"Don't rush off," he said.

I made no reply. Del and I exchanged nods. I shouldered my bag and turned, scanning the crowd as I made my escape. Still no sign of Duffy, which was just as well. I didn't want Tim or Scottie to see me talking to him.

TWENTY-ONE

The outside air was chilly. It was not even ten o'clock, and the main street of Colgate was streaming with traffic, car stereos thumping. The occupants seemed to number four and five to a car, windows rolled down, everyone looking for action of some undisclosed kind. I could hear a chorus of honks, and coming up on my right I saw a long pink stretch limo bearing a bride and groom. They were standing on the backseat, their upper torsos extending through the sliding moon-roof window. With one hand, the bride clung to her veil, which whipped out behind her like a trail of smoke. With her other hand, she held her bouquet aloft, her arm straight up in a posture that mimicked the Statue of Liberty. The groom appeared to be smaller, maybe eighteen years old, in a lavender tuxedo with a white ruffled shirt, purple bow tie, and cummerbund. His hair was cut close, his ears redtipped with cold. Numerous cars tagged along behind the limo, all honking, most decorated with paper flowers, streamers, and clattering tin cans. Their destination seemed to be the Mexican restaurant down the block from the Tonk. Other drivers and pedestrians

291

were honking and hooting happily in response to this moving pageant.

I found my car and got in, pulling into the line of traffic behind the last of the procession. Of necessity I drove slowly, forced to a crawl as car after car turned left into the restaurant parking lot, waiting for breaks in the traffic. Glancing over to my right, I spotted Carlin Duffy walking with his head down, his hands in his jacket pockets. I'd only seen the man twice, but his height and his yellow hair were unmistakable. Had he been at the Tonk and I'd missed seeing him? He appeared to be heading toward the nursery, a distance of perhaps a mile and a half. Like a gift, the man turned, extending his right hand, his thumb uppermost.

I pulled over, leaning across the seat to unlock the passenger door. He already seemed puzzled that anyone, let alone a woman, would give him a ride at that hour. I said, "I can take you as far as the 101 at Peterson. Will that do?"

"That'd be good."

Spurs jingling, he slid into the passenger seat and slammed the door. He looked back over his shoulder with a snort of derision. "You see them beaners? What a bunch of Pacos. Groom looks like he's thirteen. Probably knocked her up. He shoulda kept his pecker in his pocket."

"Nice talk," I said.

He looked at me with interest. At close range, his features seemed too pinched for good looks: narrow-set light eyes and a long thin nose. He had one goofy incisor that seemed to stick straight out. The rest of his teeth were a snaggle of overlapping edges, some rimmed with gold. The yellow in his hair was the result of peroxide, the roots already turning dark. He smelled funky, like wood smoke and dirty gym socks. He said, "I seen you before."

"Probably at the Honky-Tonk. I was just there."

"Me too. Took a bunch of money off some niggers playin' pool. What's your name?"

"I'm Kinsey. And you're Carlin Duffy. I've been looking for you."

He flashed a look in my direction and then stared out the windshield, his face shutting down. "Why's that?"

"You know Mickey Magruder."

He seemed to assess me and then looked out the side window, his tone dropping into a range somewhere between sullen and defensive. "I didn't have nothing to do with that business in L.A."

"I know. I thought we'd figure out what happened, just the two of us. Your friends call you Carlin?"

"It's Duffy. I'm not a fruit," he said. He looked at me slyly. "You're a lady cop, ain't you?"

"I used to be. Now I'm a private eye, working for myself."

"What d'you want with me?"

"I'd like to hear about Mickey. How'd the two of you connect?"

"Why should I tell you?"

"Why shouldn't you?"

"I don't know nothin'."

"Maybe you know more than you think."

He considered that, and I could almost see him shift gears. Duffy was the sort who didn't give anything

293

away without getting something in return. "You married?"

"Divorced."

"Tell you what. Let's pick us up a six-pack and go back to your place. We can talk all you want."

"If you're on parole, an alcohol violation's the last thing you need."

Duffy looked at me askance. "Who's on parole? I done my bit and I'm free as a bird."

"Then let's go to your place. I have a roommate and I'm not allowed to bring in guests at this hour."

"I don't have a place."

"Sure you do. You're living in the maintenance shed at Bernie Himes's nursery."

He kicked at the floorboard, running an agitated hand through his hair. "Goddang! Now, how'd you know that?"

I tapped my temple. "I also know you're Benny Quintero's brother. Want to talk about him?"

I had by then passed the entrance to the nursery, heading across the freeway toward the mountains.

"Where you goin'?"

"To the liquor store," I said. I pulled into a convenience mart in a former gas station. I took a twenty from my shoulder bag and said, "It's my treat. Get anything you want."

He looked at the bill and then took it, getting out of the car with barely suppressed agitation. I watched him through the window as he went into the place and began to cruise down the aisles. There was nothing I could do if he cruised right out the side door and took off on foot. He probably decided there wasn't much point. All I had to do was drive over to the nursery and wait for him there.

The clerk at the counter kept a careful eye on Duffy, waiting for him to shoplift or maybe pull a gun and demand the contents of the cash drawer. Duffy removed two six-packs of bottled beer from the glass-fronted cooler on the rear wall and then paused on one aisle long enough to pick up a large bag of chips and a couple of other items. Once at the counter, he paid with my twenty and tucked the change in his pants pocket.

When he got back in the car, his mood seemed improved. "You ever try licorice and beer? I got us some Good and Plentys and a whole bunch of other shit."

"I can hardly wait," I said. "By the way, what's the accent, Kentucky?"

"Yes, ma'am."

"I'll bet it's Louisville, right?"

"How'd you know?"

"I have an instinct for these things."

"I guess so."

Having established my wizardry, I drove back over the freeway, turned right onto the side street, and pulled into the lot for the nursery. I parked in front of the gardening center, which was closed at this hour and bathed in a cold fluorescent glow. I locked my car, hefted my bag to my shoulder, and followed Carlin Duffy as he made his way down the mulch-covered path. This was like walking into a deep and well-organized woods, wide avenues cutting through crated and evenly spaced trees of every conceivable kind.

Most were unrecognizable in the dark, but some of the shapes were distinctive. I could identify palms and willows, junipers, live oaks, and pines. Most of the other trees I didn't know by name, rows of shaggy silhouettes that rustled in the wind.

Duffy seemed indifferent to his surroundings. He trudged from one darkened lane to the next, shoulders hunched against the night air, me tagging along about ten steps behind. He paused when we reached the shed and fumbled in his pocket for his keys. The exterior was board-and-batten, painted dark green. The roofline was flat, with only one window in view. He snapped open the padlock and stepped inside. I waited until he'd turned on a light and then followed him in. The shed was approximately sixty feet by eighty, divided into four small rooms used to house the two forklifts, a mini-tractor, and a crane that must have been pulled into service for the planting of young trees. Anything more substantial would have required larger equipment, probably rented for the occasion.

The interior walls were uninsulated, the floor dirt and cinder crunching under our feet. One of the rooms had been hung with tarps and army surplus blankets, draped from the ceiling to form a tentlike substructure. Inside, I could see a canvas-and-wood cot with a rolled-up sleeping bag stashed at one end. We moved into the shelter, where illumination was provided by a bare hanging 60-watt bulb. There was also a space heater, a two-burner hot plate, and a mini-refrigerator about the size of a twelve-pack of beer. Duffy's clothes were hung on a series of nails pounded into the side wall: jeans, a bomber jacket, a wool shirt, black leather pants, a black leather vest, and two sweatshirts. Being fastidious by nature, I had to ponder the absence of visible clean underwear and a means of bathing and brushing his teeth. This might not be the sort of fellow one would want to have a lengthy chat with in a small unventilated space.

I said, "Cozy."

"It'll do. You can set on the cot and I'll take this here."

"Thanks."

He placed the brown paper bag on an orange crate and removed the six-packs. He liberated two bottles and put the balance in his mini-refrigerator, leaving several on top. He reached in his pocket, took out a bottle opener, and flipped the caps from two beers. He set his bottle aside long enough to open the bag of chips and a can of bean dip, which he held out to me. I grabbed a handful of chips and put them in my lap, holding on to the can so I could help myself to dip.

"You want a paper plate for that?"

"This is fine," I said.

Having cleared the orange crate, he used it as a stool on which he perched. He opened his box of candy-coated licorice and tossed two in his mouth, sipping beer through his teeth with a little moan of delight. Before long, his teeth and his tongue were going to be blacker than soot. He leaned over and turned on the small electric space heater. Almost immediately, the coils glowed red and the metal began to tick. The narrow band of superheated air made the rest of the room seem that much colder by contrast. I confess, there was something appealing about this room within a room. It reminded me of "houses" I made as a kid, using blankets draped over tabletops and chairs.

"How'd you find me?" he asked.

"That was easy. You got pulled over and cited for a defective taillight. When they ran your name through the system, there you were in all your glory. You've spent a lot of time in jail."

"Well, now, see? That's such bullshit. Okay, so maybe sometimes I do something bad, but it's nothing *terrible*."

"You never killed anyone."

"That's right. I never robbed nobody. Never used a gun . . . except the once. I never done drugs, I never messed with women didn't want to mess with me, and I never laid a hand on any kids. Plus I never done a single day of federal time. It's all city and county, mostly ninety-day horseshit. Criminal recklessness. What the fuck does that mean?"

"I don't know, Duffy. You tell me."

"Accidental discharge of a firearm," he said contemptuously. The crime was apparently so bogus, I was surprised he'd mention it. "It's New Year's Eve . . . this is a couple years now. I'm in this motel in E-town, having me a fine old time. I'm horsin' around, just like everyone else. I pop off a round, and the next thing you know, bullet goes through the ceiling and hits this lady in the ass. Why's that my fault?"

"How could it be?" I echoed, with equal indignance.

"Besides, jail's not so bad. Clean, warm. You got your volleyball, indoor tawlits, and your color television set. Food stinks, but medical care don't cost you a cent. I don't know what to do with myself half the time anyway. This pressure builds up and I blow. Jail's kind of like a time-out till I get my head on straight."

- I said, "How old are you?"

"Twenty-seven. Why?"

"You're getting kind of old to be sent to your room."

"Probably so, I guess. I intend to straighten up my act, now I'm out here. Meantime, it's fun breakin' rules. Makes you feel free."

"I can relate to that," I said. "You ever hold a real job?"

He seemed mildly insulted that I'd question his employment history. "I'm a heavy equipment operator. Went to school down in Tennessee and got certified. Scaffolds, cranes, forklifts, dozers, you name it. Graders, backhoes, hydraulic shovels, boom lifts, anything Caterpillar or John Deere ever made. Ought to see me. I set up there in the cab and go to town." He spent a moment shifting gears with his mouth, using his beer bottle as a lever while he operated an imaginary loader.

"Tell me about your brother."

He set the empty bottle at his feet, leaning forward, elbows on his knees, his face animated. "Benny was the best. He looked after me better than my dad and momma. We done everything together, except when he went off to war. I was only six years old then. I remember when he come home. He'd been in the hospital and then rehab, on account of his head. After that, Momma said, he changed. She said he's moody and temperamental, kind of slow off the mark. Didn't matter to me; 1971, he bought the Triumph: three-cylinder engine, twin-style clutch. Wasn't new at the

time, but it was hot. Nobody hardly fooled with Har-
ley-Davidsons back then. None of them Jap bikes,
neither. It was all BSA and Triumph." He motioned
for me to hand him the chips and the can of bean dip.

"What brought him to California?"

"I don't know for sure. I think it had to do with his
benefits, something about the VA fuckin' with his
paperwork."

"But why not in Kentucky? They have VA offices."

Duffy cocked his head, crunching on potato chips
while he wiped his lips with the back of his hand. "He
knew someone out here he said could cut through the
red tape. Hey, I got us some nuts. Reach me that bag."

I pushed the brown bag in his direction. He pulled
out a can of peanuts and pulled the ring. He poured
some into his palm and some into mine. I said, "Someone in the VA?"

"He never said who it was, or, if he did, I don't
remember. I's just a kid back then."

"How long was Benny here before he died?"

"Maybe a couple weeks. My momma flew out,
brought his body back for burial, and had his bike
shipped home. I still go to see him every chance I get.
They got this whole section of Cave Hill Cemetery just
for veterans."

"How much was she told about the circumstances
of his death?"

"Some cop punched him out. They scuffled at the
Honky-Tonk and Benny wound up dead."

"That must have been hard."

"You got that right. That's when I started havin'

problems with the law," he said. "I did Juvie till I was finally old enough to be tried as an adult."

"When did you get out here?"

"Five–six months back. My dad died September. He had emphysema, smokin' three packs a day. Even at the end, he'd risk blowing hisself up, puffing on butts while he's hooked up to oxygen. Momma died a month later. I guess her heart give out on her while she was out rakin' leaves. I'd been over to the Shelby County jail on a DUI. Now that was bullshit for sure. I blew— what, point oh two over the limit? BFD is what I say. Anyway, once I finished out my time, I hitched my way home and here's the whole house is mine, plus furniture, motorcycle, and a bunch of other junk. Took me a long time to get the bike fixed up."

"Must have felt strange."

"Yeah, it did. I wandered around the place doing anything I felt like, though it wasn't any fun. I got lonesome. You spend time in jail, you get used to havin' other people near."

"And then what?"

"Well, Momma always kept Benny's room just like it was. Clothes on the floor, bed messed up the way he left it the day he come out here. I went through the place, just a cleanin' and sortin' and throwin' stuff out. Partly I was curious and partly I just needed me a little somethin' to do. I come across Benny's lockbox."

"What kind of lockbox?"

"Gray metal, about so-by-so." With his hands, he indicated a box maybe twelve inches by six. "It was under his bed, tucked up in the box springs."

"You still have it?"

"Naw. Mr. Magruder took it, so he probably hid it someplace."

"What was in the box?"

"Let's see. This press pass, belonged to a fellow named Duncan Oaks. Also, Oaks's dog tags and this black-and-white snapshot of Benny and some guy we figured had to be Oaks."

Duncan Oaks again. I wondered if Mickey'd put the items in a safe deposit box. Mentally, I made a note. Next time I was down there, I'd have to try again if I could pick my way in. So far, I hadn't come across a safe deposit key, but maybe another search would yield results. "Tell me about your relationship with Mickey."

"Mr. Magruder's a good dude. I like him. He's a tough old bird. Once he knocked me on my ass so bad I won't never forget. Popped me smack in the jaw. I still got a tooth loose on account of it." He wiggled an incisor to demonstrate his point.

"Why'd you come out to California, to track him down?"

"Yes, ma'am."

"How'd you find him? He moved to Culver City fourteen years back. He's cagey about his phone number and his home address."

"Hell, don't I know? I got that from Tim, guy owns the Tonk. I tried the bar first because that's where the fight between him and my brother took place. I figured someone might remember him and tell me where he was."

"What was your intention?"

"To kill his ass, what else? I heard he's the one who punched Benny's lights out. After we talked, I begun to see things his way."

"Which was what?"

"He figured he was framed, and I'd agree with him."

"How so?"

"He had him an alibi. He was bonin' this married lady and didn't want to pull her into it, so he kept his mouth shut. I talked to this cop said he saw the whole thing. Mostly, insults and pushing. The two never even struck a blow. I guess somebody come along later and beat the crap out of Benny. What kilt him was havin' that metal plate in his head. Blood seeped into his brain, and it swelled up like a sponge."

"Do you remember the cop's name?"

"Mr. Shackelford. I seen him at the Honky-Tonk earlier tonight."

"What about the snapshot in the box?"

"Two guys out in the boonies, gotta be Veetnam. Sojers in the background. Benny's wearin' fatigues and his big old army helmet he's decorated with this peace symbol. You know the one. Looks kind of like a wishbone with a thing stickin' out the end. Benny's got this shit-eatin' grin and he's flung his arm around the other fellow, who's bare to the waist. Other fellow has a cigarette hangin' off his lip. Looks like the dog tags he's wearin' are the same as the ones in the box."

"What's he look like?"

"You know, young, unshaved, with these big old dark brows and a black mustache: dirty-looking, like a grunt. Hardly any chest hair. Kind of pussyfied in that regard."

"Any names or dates on the back of the photograph?"

"No, but it's Benny clear as day. Had to be 1965, between August tenth when he shipped out and November seventeenth, which is when he got hit. Benny was at Ia Drang with the two/seven when a sniper got him in the head. He shoulda been mede-vacked out, but the choppers couldn't land because of all the ground fire. By time he got out, he said the dead and wounded was piled on each other like sticks of firewood."

"What was Mickey's theory?"

"He didn't tell me nothin'. Said he'd look into it is all I heard."

"Where's the lockbox now? I'd like to see the contents."

"Said he had a place. I learnt not to mess with him. He's the one in charge."

"Let's go back to Duncan Oaks. How does he fit in?"

"Beats me. I figure he's someone in Benny's unit."

"That's what Mickey was looking into. I know he placed a call to a high school in Louisville—"

"Manual, I bet. Benny went to Manual, played football and everything."

"Not Manual," I said. "It was Louisville Male High. He talked to the school librarian about Duncan Oaks. The next day, he hopped on a plane and flew east. Did you talk to him later, after he got back?"

"Never had a chance. I called a couple times. He never picked up his phone so I finally went down. I's madder than shit. I figured he's shining me on."

"You didn't know he'd been shot?"

"Uh-uh. Not then. Some guy down there told me. Fellow lived next door. I forget his name now, something queer."

"Wary Beason?"

"That's him. I busted out his winda, which is how we got acquainted." Duffy had the good grace to look sheepish about the window. He still didn't seem to realize I'd been on the premises that night.

I found myself staring at the dirt floor, trying to figure out what the hell was going on. How did the fragments connect? Tim Littenberg and Scott Shackelford were both in Vietnam, but the timing was off. Benny Quintero was there early in the war and then only briefly. Tim and Scottie went later, in the early seventies. Then there was Eric Hightower, whose second tour was cut short when he stepped on a mine and had his legs blown off. Again, that was long after Benny'd been shipped home. And why was any of it relevant to Mickey's being shot? I knew Mickey well enough to know he was on to *something*, but what?

"You with me or gone?"

I looked up to find Duffy staring at me with concern. I set aside my beer. "I think I'll butt out for now. I need time to absorb this. At the moment, I don't have a clue how any of it fits . . . or if it does," I said. "I may talk to you later when I've had a chance to think. You'll be around?"

"Here or the Tonk. You want me to walk you out?"

I said, "Please. It's dark as pitch out there."

TWENTY-TWO

I let myself into my apartment at eleven-fifteen, surprised to realize my entire conversation with Duffy had
only taken an hour. I set up a pot of coffee and flipped
the switch, letting it brew while I stretched some of the
kinks out of my neck. I felt a faint headache perched
between my eyes like a frown. I was longing for bed,
but there was work to do yet. While the information
was fresh, I opened my desk drawer and pulled out a
new pack of lined index cards. Then I retrieved, from
their hiding place, the various items I'd snitched from
Mickey's.

I sat in my swivel chair, jotting down everything I
could remember from the evening. Activities at the
Honky-Tonk were turning out to be less sinister than
I'd imagined. Maybe, as Tim had said, Mickey simply
went there to drink and hustle Thea. I had to admit
philandering would have been in character for him.

When the coffee was done, I got up from my chair
and poured myself a mug, adding milk that seemed
only mildly sour. I returned to my desk, where I
remained on my feet, idly pushing at the index cards.
There were still countless minor matters that didn't fit

the frame: Mickey's being shot with my gun, the long hissing message on my answering machine. That had originated from his apartment the afternoon of March 27. Who'd called me and why? If Mickey, why not leave a message? Why let the tape simply run to the end? If it wasn't Mickey, then what was the purpose? To imply contact between us? It had certainly made me look bad in the eyes of the police.

I sat down at my desk and began to play with the cards. I had to assume Mickey was on the track of Benny Quintero's killer. That question would nag at him as long as he lived. Benny's death had never been officially ruled a homicide, but Mickey knew he'd been blamed, despite the fact that charges had never been filed. In light of his checkered history with the department, his involvement in the matter had called his credibility into question and further damaged his already tainted reputation. As he saw it, his only choice was to abandon the profession he'd loved. His life after that had never amounted to much: booze, women, a shabby apartment. He couldn't even hold on to the sorry job he'd found: Pacific Coast Security with its faux-cop uniform and dime-store badge. He must have dreamed of escape, creating a way out with his caches of money and his phony IDs. I turned over a few cards, making a column, sorting facts in no particular order.

Idly, I set two index cards on edge, using the weight of each to support the other. I added a third, leaving the right side of my brain in neutral while I constructed a maze. Building card houses was another way I'd amused myself as a kid. The first floor was easy, requiring patience and dexterity but not much else. To

307

add a second story to the first, you had to append a flat layer of cards, deftly floating a "ceiling" on the substructure until the whole of it was covered. Then began the real work: starting again from square one. First balance two cards atop the structure below, using the pair for their mutual support. Then add a third at an angle to the first two. Then add a fourth, then a fifth. At any point in the process, as the overall dimensions increased, there was always the danger that the whole of it would collapse, tumbling in on itself like — well, a house of cards. Sometimes, perversely, I'd even done this myself, snapping a corner with my finger, watching as the cards deconstructed in slow motion like a demolition project.

I glanced at the card in my hand, reading the note on it before I added it to the pile. Carefully, I added another card to the maze. I paused to remove it, reading the datum again. I experienced a jolt of insight and felt myself blink. I'd seen a connection, two index cards suddenly appearing in conjunction. What a dummy I was that I hadn't seen it before! A name showed up twice and I could feel my perception shift. It was like the sharp dislocation of a tembler, coming out of nowhere, fading away soon after. What I spotted was the name Del Amburgey, the man to whom Shack had introduced me at the Tonk. Delbert Amburgey was also the name on one of Mickey's packets of fake IDs: California driver's license, credit cards, social security card.

I set the index cards aside, pulling out the documents with Mickey's face laminated on top of what were probably Delbert's vital statistics. I swiveled in my swivel chair and studied the effect. Did these documents belong to Delbert or had his identity been lifted? Was the date of birth real or bogus, borrowed or invented, and how had it been done? I knew credit card scammers often got into "Dumpster diving," coming up with charge slips or carbons, even credit card statements discarded once the monthly bills had been paid. The information on the statements could be used to generate additional credit. The scammer would apply for cards based on lines of credit previously established by the individual in question. Any number of new accounts might be opened in this way. With a name, address, and social security number, ATM cards could be obtained, along with blank checks or proceeds from insurance policies. The scammer would supply the credit company with a substitute address, so the owner of the card remained unaware that goods and services were being charged to his or her legitimate account. The cards could also be milked through a series of cash withdrawals. Once the credit limit was exceeded, the scammer could either make the minimum payment or move on, fencing items or selling them at a discount and pocketing the profits. Actually, counterfeit documents like those in Mickey's possession were worth money on the open market, where felons, illegal aliens, and the chronically bankrupt could buy a brand-new start in life with thousands of dollars of fresh credit at their disposal.

I went back to Mickey's financial statements. I studied his savings passbook, beginning to understand the regular withdrawals of $600 on dates that corresponded with his trips to the Tonk. I thought about

Tim and the conversation we'd had about the second floor, where he was claiming he might add tables. In retrospect, I marveled at how carefully I'd been duped. He'd offered me the bait—the unlocked door—and the subsequent glimpse of what had appeared to be undeveloped floor space. I'd seen the bouncer scan the drivers' licenses of those granted admission to the bar. Since the bar retained a copy of each credit card transaction, the numbers would have been easy enough to match to the drivers' license data. I couldn't guess at the whole of it, but there were people who'd know.

I looked at my watch again. It was 1:55. I said, "Oh, shit." I'd told Thea I'd meet her as soon as she got off work at two. I leapt up, shoved all the cards in my desk drawer and locked it, put Mickey's phony IDs back in their hiding place. I grabbed my jacket and car keys. Within minutes, I was on 101, driving north again toward Colgate, restraining the temptation to put the gas pedal to the floor. Traffic was light, the freeway virtually deserted, but I knew this was the hour when the CHP would be out. I didn't need a traffic stop or a speeding ticket. I found myself talking out loud, encouraging the VW's performance, praying Thea would wait for me at the coffee shop until I arrived. The restaurant shared a parking lot with the bowling alley next door. Every slot was filled and I groaned as I circled, looking for a place. Finally, I left my car in a moderately legal spot. I cut the lights and the engine as I opened the car door and emerged. It was 2:13. I locked the car and then did a run/walk to the restaurant, pausing for breath as I hauled the door open and started looking for her.

Thea sat at a back booth, smoking a cigarette. The harsh fluorescent lighting washed all the lines from her face, leaving her expression as blank as kabuki makeup.

I slid into the seat across the table from her. "Thanks for waiting," I said. "I was caught up in paperwork and lost track of the time."

"Doesn't matter," she said. "My life's rapidly turning to shit anyway. What's one more thing?"

She seemed curiously withdrawn. My guess was she'd had too much time to reconsider. At the Honky-Tonk earlier, I could have sworn she'd confide. People with problems are generally relieved at the chance to unburden themselves. Catch them at the right moment and they'll tell you anything you ask. I was kicking myself I hadn't had the opportunity to take her aside then.

I said, "Look, I know you're pissed off because I didn't own up to who I was—"

"Among other things," she said acidly. "I mean, give me a break. You're a private detective, plus you're Mickey's ex-*wife*?"

"But Thea, get serious. If I'd said that up front, would I have learned anything?"

"Probably not," she conceded. "But you didn't have to lie."

"Of course I did. That was the only means I had of getting at the truth."

"What's wrong with being straight? Or is that beyond you?"

"Me, straight! What about you? You're the one screwing Mickey behind Scott's back."

311

"You were screwing him too!"

"Nope. Sorry. Wasn't me."

She looked at me blankly. "But you said—"

"Uh-uh. You might have leapt to that conclusion, but I never said as much."

"You didn't?"

I shook my head.

She started blinking, nonplused. "Then whose diaphragm was it?"

"Good question. I just got the answer to that myself. It looks like dear Mickey was screwing someone else."

"Who?"

"I think I'd better keep mum, at this point."

"I don't believe you."

"Which part? You know he was seeing someone. You saw the evidence yourself. Of course, if you weren't systematically betraying Scottie, you wouldn't have to worry about these things."

Her gaze hung on mine.

I said, "You don't have to look quite so glum. He did the same thing to me. That's just how he is."

"It's not that. I just realized I didn't mind so much when I thought it was you. At least you'd been married to him, so it didn't feel so bad. Is he in love with this other woman?"

"If he is, it didn't stop him from picking up on you."

"Actually, *I* pursued *him*."

"Oh, boy. I hate to say this, but are you nuts? The man's a barfly. He's unemployed, and he's older by— what, fifteen years?"

"He seemed . . . I don't know . . . sexy and protective. He's mature. Scottie's temperamental, and he's *so* self-involved. With Mickey, I felt safe. He loves women."

"Oh, sure. That's why he betrays us every chance he gets. He loves each one of us better than the last, often at the same time but never for long. That's how mature *he* is."

"You think he's going to be okay? I've been worried to death, but I can't get the hospital to say a word."

"I hope so, but really I have no idea."

"But you're hooked in, aren't you?"

"I guess. What feels strange is I'd put him out of my mind. Honest, I hadn't thought of him in years. Now that he's down, he seems to be everywhere."

"I feel the same. I keep looking for him. The door at the Tonk opens and I think he'll walk in."

"Why'd he keep coming back? Was it you or was something else going on?"

"Don't ask. I can't help you. I mean, I care about Mickey, but not enough to put my life on the line."

"Isn't it possible Scottie knows?"

"About Mickey and me?"

"That's what we're discussing," I said patiently.

"What makes you say that?"

"How do you know it wasn't Scott who shot Mickey?"

"He wouldn't do that. Anyway, his dad told us Mickey was gunned down two blocks from his apartment. Scottie doesn't even know where Mickey lives."

"Well, that's weak. I mean, think about it, Thea. Where was Scottie a week ago last Wednesday?"

"How should I know?"

"Was he with you?"

"I don't think so," she said. She stared at the table, going over it in her mind. "Tuesday, I was off. I wasn't feeling good."

"Did you talk to Scott on the phone?"

"No. I called and he was gone, so I left a message and he called me back the next day."

"In other words, he wasn't with you that Tuesday night or early Wednesday morning. We're talking May fourteenth."

Thea shook her head.

"What about the next day? Did you see him then?"

She stubbed out her cigarette. "I don't remember every single *day*."

"Start with what you do remember. When did you see Scottie last?"

Grudgingly, she said, "Monday. He and Tim had a meeting on Sunday. He drove up for the night and then left for L.A. the next day. I didn't see him again until the weekend. That was Saturday a week ago. He drove up here yesterday and goes back to L.A. tomorrow."

"What about you? Were you with Mickey at all on the night he was shot?"

She hesitated. "I went down to his apartment, but he was gone."

"Couldn't Scottie have followed you? He could have hung out in town. Once you got in your car, all he had to do was tail you to Mickey's."

She stared at me. "He wouldn't have done that. I know you don't like him, but that doesn't make him bad."

314

"Really. You told me he'd kill you if he ever found out."

"When I said he'd kill me it was . . . what do you call it—"

"Figurative."

"Figurative," she repeated. "Scottie wouldn't actually *shoot* anyone."

"Maybe his motive was something more serious."

"Like what?"

"A scam."

Thea's face underwent a shift. "I don't want to talk about this."

"Then let's change the subject. The first time I came in, Thursday of this week, Tim was pissed off at you. What was that about?"

"That's none of your business."

"Are Tim and Scottie partners?"

"You'd have to ask them."

"What kind of business?"

"I don't have a comment."

"Why? Are you involved in it too?"

"I gotta go," she said abruptly. I watched as she gathered up her jacket and her purse. She studiously avoided looking at me as she slid out of the booth.

It was 2:45 when I finally crawled into bed. I woke at 6 A.M. from long habit, nearly rolling out for my jog until I remembered it was Sunday. I lay for a moment, looking up at the skylight. The sun must have been close to rising because the sky was growing lighter as though a dimmer were being turned up. I felt oddly hungover for someone who'd drunk so little. It had to be the smoky bar, the conversation with Duffy, and tension between me and Thea, not to mention the late-night theorizing and driving around at all hours. I got up and brushed my teeth, took two aspirin with a big glass of water, and then returned to bed. In less than a minute, I was sleeping again. My bladder woke me at ten. I did an inner-body survey, checking for symptoms of headache, nausea, and weariness. Nothing seemed to be amiss and I decided I could face life, but only with the promise of a nap later on.

I went through my usual morning routine: showered, donned my sweats, and made a pot of coffee. I read most of the Sunday paper, then wrapped myself in a quilt and settled on the couch with my book. Turned out to be nap time at 1 P.M. and I slept until five. I climbed up the spiral stairs and checked myself in the bathroom mirror. My hair, as I suspected, was mashed flat on one side and sticking up in clumps on the other like dried palm fronds. I stuck my head under running water and emerged moments later with a more refined arrangement. I stripped off my sweats and pulled on a turtleneck and jeans, gym socks, my Sauconys, and Mickey's jacket. I picked up my shoulder bag, locked the door behind me, and crossed the patio to Henry's, where I tapped on his back door. There was no immediate response, but I realized the bathroom window was open a few inches, and I could hear sounds of a shower. Steam wafted out scented with soap and shampoo. I knocked on the window a familiar rat-a-tat-tat.

From inside, Henry yelled, "Yo!"

"Hey, Henry. It's me. I'm on my way to Rosie's for supper. Want to come?"

"I'll be there in a jiffy. Soon as I'm done in here."

I walked the half block to Rosie's, arriving at five-thirty, just as she was opening for business. We exchanged pleasantries, which in her case consisted of abrasive comments about my weight, my hair, and my marital status. I suppose Rosie's a mother figure, but only if you favor the sort that appear in Grimm's fairy tales. It was her avowed intention to fatten me up, get me a decent haircut, and a spouse. She knows perfectly well I've never met with success in that department, but she says *eventually* (meaning when I'm old and dotty, demented, and infirm) I'll need someone to look after me. I suggested a visiting nurse, but she didn't think that was funny. Then again, why should she? I was serious.

I sat down in my usual booth with a glass of puckery white wine. It's hellish to learn the difference between good wine and bad. Henry wandered in soon after, and we let Rosie browbeat us into a Sunday night supper that consisted of *savanyu marhahus* (hot pickled beef to you, pal) and *kirantott karfiol tejfolos martassal*, which is deep-fried cauliflower smothered in sour cream. While we mopped up our plates with some of Henry's homemade bread, I filled him in on the events of the past few days. I must say, the situation didn't seem any clearer when I'd laid it out to him.

"If Mickey and Mrs. Hightower are having an affair, her husband had as much reason to shoot him as Thea's boyfriend," he pointed out.

"Maybe so," I replied, "but I got the impression Eric had made his peace with her. I keep thinking there's more, something I haven't thought of yet."

"Can I do anything to help?"

"Not that I know, but thanks." I glanced up as the door opened and the waiter from the Hightowers' party came in with a hardback book under one arm. He wore a tweed sport coat over a black turtleneck, dark trousers, and loafers polished to a fare-thee-well. Having seen him in his white jacket serving drinks the night before, it took a moment to come up with his name.

I turned to Henry as I rose. "Can you excuse me for a minute? There's someone I need to talk to."

"Not a problem. I've been itching to finish this," he said. He brought out a neatly folded copy of the Sunday *New York Times* crossword puzzle and a ball-point pen. I could see he was half done, completing the answers in a spiral pattern, starting at the edges and working toward the center. Sometimes he wrote in the answers leaving out every other letter because he liked the way it looked.

Stewart was passing the booth when he caught sight of me. "Well, hello. How are you? I wondered if you'd be here."

"Can I talk to you?"

"Be my guest," he said, gesturing toward the booth where he traditionally sat. I gave Henry's arm a squeeze, which he barely noticed, given his level of concentration. Stewart waited till I was seated and then sat down across from me, the book on the seat beside him.

"What's the book?" I asked.

He picked it up, holding the spine toward me so I could read the title, *The Conjure-Man Dies* by Rudolph Fisher. "I usually read biography, but I thought I'd try something new. Detective novel written in the early thirties. Black protagonist."

"Is it good?"

"Haven't decided yet. I'm just getting into it. It's interesting."

Rosie appeared. She stood by the table, her eyes fixed on the far wall, avoiding the sight of us. I noticed she was wearing slippers with her bright blue cotton muumuu.

Stewart reached for the menu and said, "Good evening, Rosie. How're you doing? Any specials I should hear about?"

"You tell him is good, the pickled beef," she said. Rosie can speak in perfect order the English when it suits her purposes. Tonight, for some reason, she was behaving like someone recently admitted to this country on a temporary visa. She seldom addresses men directly unless she's flirting with them. A similar inhibition applies to strangers and women, children, the hired help, and people who pop in and ask directions of her. She might answer your question, but she won't look.

I said, "The pickled beef is great. Fabulous. And the deep-fried cauliflower is not to be believed."

"I think I'll have that," Stewart said, setting aside the menu.

"What to drink?" she asked.

"Try the white wine. It's piquant. The perfect complement to pickled beef," I said.

319

"Sounds good. I'll try it."

Rosie nodded and departed while Stewart shook his head. "I wish I had the nerve to order something else. That Hungarian stuff is for the birds. I come here because it's quiet, especially on Sundays. I go home with indigestion keeps me up half the night. Now what can I do for you?"

"I need to ask you about the Hightowers."

"What about them?" he asked, with a caution that didn't bode well for me.

I took a deep breath. "Here's the deal," I said. "My ex-husband was shot in Los Angeles. This was in the early morning hours, May fourteenth. He's currently in a coma, with no clear indication he'll pull out of it. For various reasons too complicated to go into, I'm trying to figure out what happened. Obviously, the cops are too." I was watching his eyes: intelligent, attentive, giving nothing away. I went on. "Both the Hightowers know Mickey, and I'm trying to determine if there's a link."

"What's your question for me? Because some things I'll tell you and some I won't."

"I understand. Fair enough. What's your job?"

"My job?"

"Yeah, what do you actually do for them?"

"Chauffeur, handyman. I wait table sometimes."

"How long have you been there?"

"It'll be two years in June. Same as Clifton. He tends bar at parties like the one they had last night. Otherwise, he manages the house and handles general maintenance. All the major repairs are hired out, but it seems like there's always something broken or in need of adjustment."

"What about Stephanie? Does she work for both of them or just Dixie?"

"She's Mrs. H's personal assistant. She comes in Mondays and Thursdays, noon to five or five-thirty. Mr. H takes care of his business on his own. Phone calls and letters, personal appointments. He keeps it all up here," he said, tapping his head.

"I take it there's a cook, as well?"

"Cook and cleaning crew. There's two women do the laundry and another one does flowers. Plus the gardeners, the pool guy. I wash the cars and Mr. H's van. Clifton and the cook—her name's Ima—both live on the property. The rest of us live out and come in as needed."

"Which is when?"

"It varies. I'm usually not there during the week. Fridays and Saturdays I'm always on call, especially if the two of them are going out. Other times Mr. H prefers to drive himself. Mrs. H likes the car. They have a six-passenger limo she enjoys."

"Did you drive either one of them to Los Angeles last week?"

"I didn't, but that doesn't mean they didn't go down on their own."

"You know Mickey Magruder? Good-looking guy, in his fifties, an ex-cop?"

"Doesn't sound familiar. What's his connection?"

"We go way back, the four of us. More than fifteen years. Mickey and Dixie were having an affair back then. I have reason to believe they've rekindled the flame. I'm wondering if Eric knew."

Stewart thought briefly; then he shook his head. "I don't carry tales."

"I can appreciate that. Is there *anything* you can tell me?"

"I think you'd do better asking one of them," he said.

"What about the marriage? Do they get along okay?"

Again, Stewart paused, and I could see the conflict between his knowledge and his reticence. "Not of late," he said.

TWENTY-THREE

That was as much as I was able to get from him. I must say I admired his loyalty, though it was frustrating. The evening wasn't completely unproductive. Henry's point was well taken. If jealousy was the motive for the shooting, the number of suspects had just increased. Eric Hightower was in the mix and Thea was another candidate, though not a particularly strong one. She'd risked a lot for Mickey, and while she professed her care and concern, that might have been laid on for my benefit. Dixie was another possibility. What would she have done if she'd discovered Mickey's affair with Thea?

The problem was, it all seemed so melodramatic. These people were grown-ups. I found it hard to picture any of them lurking in the shadows, plugging away at Mickey with my gun. It's not like you don't read about such things in the daily paper, but the scenario left too many things unexplained. For instance, who was Duncan Oaks? How was he related to events? Was Mickey on the trail of the person or persons responsible for Benny's fatal beating?

We left Rosie's at eight, Henry and I, walking home

in the dark without saying much. Once back in my apartment, I sat down at my desk yet again and reviewed my notes. Within minutes, I realized my heart wasn't in it. I made a pile of cards and shuffled, dealing myself a tarot reading of the data I'd collected. No insights emerged, and I finally packed it in. Maybe tomorrow I'd be smarter. There was always the outside chance.

Six A.M. Monday morning, I rolled out of bed, pulled on sweats, brushed my teeth, and went for a three-mile jog. The predawn light was gorgeous: the ocean luminous blue, the sky above it orange, fading to a thin layer of yellow, then a clear blue sky beyond. Along the horizon, the oil rigs sparkled like an irregular line of diamond scatter pins. The absence of cloud cover eliminated any special effects when the sun finally rose, but the day promised to be sunny and that was sufficient for me. When I finished the run, I headed over to the gym, where I variously stretched, curled, extended, crunched, hyper-extended, pressed, pecked, pushed, shrugged, raised, pulled down, and pulled up weights. At the end of it, I felt keen.

I went home and showered, emerging from the apartment at nine in my jeans, ready to face the day. I drove my car north on 101, taking the off-ramp that put me in range of the county offices adjacent to the VA. I parked and went into the Architectural Archives, where I gave the Honky-Tonk's address and asked to see whatever drawings and blueprints they had on hand. I was given a set of progress prints showing the vicinity plan, site plan, demolition plan, foundation and framing plans, elevations, and electrical legend. It didn't take me long to find what I was looking for. I returned the prints and headed for the parking lot where I'd seen a pay phone.

I dialed directory assistance and asked for the number of the Secret Service in L.A., the offices of which were actually listed as part of the U.S. Treasury Department. In addition to the L.A. number, I was given a telephone number for the agency in Perdido. I charged the call to my credit card, punching in the Perdido number. The phone rang once.

"Secret Service," a woman said.

How covert could it be if she was willing to blurt it out that way?

I asked to speak to an agent and she put me on hold. I stared out across the parking lot, listening to the sibilant ebb and flow of traffic on the highway. The morning was clear, the temperature in the 50s. I imagined by afternoon that would warm to the usual 70s. The line was picked up moments later, and a flat-voiced gentleman introduced himself. "This is Wallace Burkhoff."

I said, "I wonder if you can help me. I'm calling because I suspect there's a credit card scam being operated from a bar in Colgate."

"What kind of scam?"

"I'm not sure. A friend of mine—actually, my ex-husband—bought some phony documents from a fellow up here. I think the owner of the bar might be running a regular manufacturing plant." I told him about the Honky-Tonk: the scanning device for drivers' licenses and my guess about the matching of credit card charge slips to names on licenses. On the surface, it sounded thin, but he listened politely as I talked on. "A couple of days ago I saw a truck on the premises. Ten cartons had been unloaded and stacked in the corridor. The boxes were marked Plas-Stock, which the owner told me was plastic glassware and cutlery."

"Not quite." Burkhoff laughed. "Plas-Stock specializes in commercial equipment for manufacturing plastic cards and blank card stock for medical ID cards and health club memberships."

"Really? My ex has three sets of fake IDs in his possession, including drivers' licenses, social security cards, and a fistful of credit cards. I'm reasonably certain some of the data came from a regular bar patron, because I was introduced to the guy, and the name and approximate date of birth are the same."

"What's his interest in acquiring phony IDs?"

"He's a former vice detective, and I think he picked up on the operation three or four months back. I mean, I can't swear this is true, but I have the receipts he kept from a series of visits to the place and I also have the phony documents with his picture plastered all over them."

"Would he be willing to talk to us?"

"He's currently out of commission." I told Agent Burkhoff about Mickey's condition.

"What about yourself?"

"Hey, I've already told you as much as I know. This is outside my area of expertise. I'm just making the call. You can do with it as you please."

"Where's their base of operation?"

"I think it's somewhere in the building. Yesterday, the owner set it up so I had a chance to see the second floor. It was empty, of course, but I did spot a number of electrical outlets. I don't know what kind of equipment would be in use—"

"I can tell you that," he said. "Optical scanners, encoding machines, shredders, embossers, tippers—that's what puts the gold on the newly embossed numbers—laminators, hologram punch devices. You see anything like that?"

"No, but I suspect they were operating in the space until a couple of days ago. I checked with the local architectural archives and took a look at the plans submitted when the owner applied for building permits. The structure's one of the few in town with a basement and my guess is they moved the operation down there."

"Give me the particulars and we'll check it out," he said.

I gave him the name and address of the Honky-Tonk and Tim's name and home address. I added Scottie's name to the mix, along with the dates Mickey'd been there and the names on the assortment of phony documents he had. "You need anything else?"

"Your name, address, and phone."

"I'd prefer not," I said. "But I'll make copies of the IDs and put those in the mail to you."

"We'd appreciate that."

I hung up, hauled out the telephone book, found my

travel agent's number, and put a couple of coins in the slot. I told her I needed plane tickets for Louisville and gave her my budget limitations.

"*How* much?"

I said, "Five hundred dollars?"

She said, "You're joking."

I assured her I wasn't. She tapped the information into her computer. After much silence, many sighs, and some additional clicks, she told me the best she could do was an airline that had been in business for less than two years and was offering a no-frills flight to Louisville out of LAX with only two connections, Santa Fe and Tulsa. There was no advance seat assignment, no movie, and no meal service. She assured me the company hadn't filed for bankruptcy (yet) and hadn't reported any major flaming crashes to date. The point was I could get there for $577.

I had her book me on an early morning flight, leaving the return ticket open since I really had no idea how long my inquiry would take. Basically, I'd make it up as I went along. In addition to the plane fare, I reserved a rental car at the airport in Louisville. I'd find a motel when I got there, preferably something cheap. At the end of this, if nothing else, my debt of guilt with regard to Mickey would be paid in full. I went home, packed a duffel, and chatted briefly with Henry, letting him know I'd be gone for some indeterminate period. I also put a call through to Cordia Hatfield, telling her of my arrival later in the afternoon.

I stopped by the travel agent's and picked up my ticket, then drove over to the office, where I spent the balance of the morning getting life in order in case I didn't make it back. The drive to Culver City was uneventful, and I parked in the alley behind Mickey's building at 4:55. I left the duffel in the car, not wanting to seem presumptuous about staying overnight. Cordia had extended an invitation, but she hadn't seemed that thrilled.

I knocked on the Hatfields' door, wondering if they'd hear me over the blare of the TV set. I waited a moment and then knocked again. The sound was cut and Cordia opened the door.

I'd last seen the two sisters on Thursday, only four days before, but something in her manner seemed different. She stepped back, allowing me to enter. The apartment, as before, was uncomfortably warm, the temperature close to 80, windows fogged over with condensation. Steam curled from a pot simmering on the stove. The bubbling liquid was cloudy, and a collar of scum had collected on the surface. The air smelled of singed pork and something else, unfamiliar but faintly dunglike. The TV had been muted, but the picture remained: the late afternoon news with its steady diet of calamities. Belmira seemed transfixed. She sat at the kitchen table, tarot deck in hand, while under her chair, Dorothy chewed on a bony bundle of something crunchy and dead.

"Is this a bad time?" I asked.

"As good as any," Cordia said.

"Because I can come back later if it's more convenient."

"This is fine." She wore a long-sleeved cotton house-dress in shades of mauve and gray with a smocklike apron over it, trailing almost to the floor. She turned

329

to the stove, reaching for a slotted spoon that she used to adjust ingredients in the boiling water. Something floated to the surface: heart-shaped skull, short body, not a lot of meat on it. I could have sworn it was a squirrel.

"How have you two been?" I said, hoping for an answer that would clue me in.

"Good. We're fine. What can we do for you?"

Abrupt, to the point, not entirely friendly, I thought. "I'm on my way out of town, and I need to check Mickey's for something someone left with him."

Her tone was aggrieved. "Again? You were just up there last night. We saw lights on till close to midnight."

"At Mickey's? Not me. I was in Santa Teresa all weekend. I haven't been here since Thursday morning."

She looked at me.

"Cordia, I swear. If I'd wanted to get in, I'd have asked for the key. I wouldn't go in without permission."

"You did the first time."

"But that was before we met. You've been very helpful to me. I wouldn't do that behind your back."

"Suit yourself. I won't argue. I can't prove it."

"But why would I be here now if I'd already been in last night? That doesn't make sense."

She reached into her pocket and took out the key. "Return it when you're done and let's hope this is the last of it."

I took the key, aware that her manner was still stony and unyielding. I felt terrible.

Belmira said, "Oh, my dear!" She'd turned over four

cards. The first was the Page of Swords, which I knew now was me. The remaining three cards were the Devil, the Moon, and Death. Well, that was cheering. Bel looked up at me, distressed.

Cordia moved quickly to the table and snatched up the cards. She crossed to the sink, opened the cabinet under it, and tossed the deck in the trash. "I asked you to quit reading. She doesn't believe in tarot. She told you that last week."

I said, "Cordia, really—"

"Go on up to the apartment and be done with it," she snapped.

Belmira's misery was palpable, but she didn't dare defy Cordia. Nor did I, for that matter. I tucked the key in my pocket and let myself out. Before the door closed behind me, I could hear Bel protesting her loss.

I unlocked Mickey's front door and let myself in. His drapes were still closed, blocking the light except for a narrow gap between panels where the late afternoon sun cut like a laser, warming the interior. The air was dense with dust motes and carried the moldy scent of unoccupied space. I stood for a moment, taking in the scene. With no one to clean the place, many surfaces were still smudged with fingerprint powder. If someone had been in the apartment the night before, there were no obvious signs. I skipped the rubber gloves this time and did a quick walk-through. On the surface, it was just as I'd seen it last. I paused in the bedroom door. A small gauzy piece of cloth trailed out from under the bed. I got down on my hands and knees, lifted the bottom of the spread, and peeked under the bed. Someone had systematically removed the fabric covering the bottom of the box spring, and it lay on the carpet like a skin shed by a snake. I knelt by the bed and lifted one corner of the mattress. I could see a line where the fabric had been scored by something sharp. I lifted the bulk of the mattress, turning it over with the sheets still in place. The underside had been gutted, slit the entire length at ten-inch intervals. Stuffing boiled out, cotton tufts protruding where the thickness had been searched. There was something both sly and savage in the evisceration. I did what I could to restore the bed to a state of tidiness.

I checked the closet. Mickey's clothing had been slit in a similar fashion: seams and pockets slashed, linings ripped open, though the garments had been left hanging, apparently undisturbed. To the casual observer, nothing would appear amiss. The damage probably wouldn't have been discovered until Mickey returned or his belongings were moved to storage. I went back to the living room, noticing for the first time that the cushions on the couch appeared to be out of alignment. I turned them over and saw they'd been sliced open as well. Along the back of the couch, the fabric had been picked open at the seam. The damage would be apparent the first time the couch was moved, but, again, the vandalism wasn't evident on cursory inspection.

I checked both of the heavy upholstered chairs, getting down on the floor so I could squint at the underside. I lifted the chairs one at a time, tilting each forward to inspect the frames. On the bottom of the second chair, there was a rectangular cut in the padding. I removed the wedge of foam rubber. In the hole there was a gray metal box, six inches by twelve, like the one Duffy'd described. The lock had been badly damaged and yielded easily to pressure. Gingerly, I opened the lid. Empty. I sat back on my heels and said, "Mickey, you ass."

What a dumb hiding place! Given his ingenuity and paranoia, he could have done better than this. Of course, I'd searched the place twice and hadn't found the damn thing on either occasion, but *somebody* had. I was sick with disappointment, though there was clearly no remedy. I hadn't even heard about the lockbox until Saturday night. At the time, it hadn't occurred to me to drop everything and hit the road right then. Maybe if I had, I might have beat "somebody" to the punch.

Ah, well. It couldn't be helped. I'd simply have to do without. I could find a picture of Duncan Oaks in his high school yearbook, but I would have liked the dog tags and the press pass Duffy'd mentioned to me. There was something about an authentic document that served as a talisman, a totem object imbued with the power of the original owner. Probably superstition on my part, but I regretted the loss.

I returned the box to its niche, tilted the chair back into its upright position, and let myself out the front door, locking it behind me. I went down the steps and knocked on Cordia's door. She opened it a crack and I gave her the key. She took it without comment and closed the door again. Clearly, I wasn't being encouraged to spend the night with them.

I crept out to the alley, got in my car, and drove to

333

the airport. I found a nearby motel, offering shuttle service every hour on the hour. I ate an unremarkable dinner in the nondescript restaurant attached to one end of the building. I was in bed by nine and slept until five-forty-five, when I rose, showered, threw on the same clothes, left my VW in the motel parking lot, and took the shuttle to LAX, where I caught my 7 A.M. plane. The minute the non-smoking sign was turned off, all the passengers in the rear set their cigarettes on fire.

It was in the Tulsa airport, while I was waiting between planes, that I made a discovery that cheered me up no end. I had an hour to kill so I'd stretched out in a chair, my legs extended into the aisle in front of me. The position, while awkward, at least permitted a catnap, though later I'd probably require hundreds of dollars' worth of chiropractic adjustment. In the meantime, I was using Mickey's leather jacket as a pillow, trying to ease the strain on my neck. I turned over on my side, not easy to do while sitting upright. As I did so, I felt something lumpy against my face—metal zipper tab, button?—I didn't know what it was, except that it added an unacceptable level of discomfort. I sat up and checked the portion of the jacket that was under my cheek. There was nothing I could see, but by pinching the leather I could feel an object in the lining. I flattened the jacket on my lap, squinting at the seam where I could see an alteration in the stitching. I opened my shoulder bag and took out my nail scissors (the same ones I utilize for the occasional emergency haircut). I picked a few stitches loose and then used my fingers to widen the opening. Out slid Duncan Oaks's

334

dog tags, the black-and-white snapshot, and the press card. Actually, the hiding place made perfect sense. Mickey'd probably worn this very jacket when he made the trip himself.

The dog tags bore Duncan Oaks's name and date of birth. Even all these years later, the chain was crusty with rust or blood. The snapshot was exactly as Duffy had described it. I set those items aside and studied the press card issued by the Department of Defense. The printing around the border said: LOSS OF THIS CARD MUST BE REPORTED AT ONCE. PROPERTY OF U.S. GOVERNMENT. Under the line that read *non-combatant's certificate of identity* was Duncan Oaks's name, and on the left was his picture. Dark-haired, unsmiling, he looked very young, which of course he was. The date of issue was 10 Sept. '65. Four years out of high school, he was no more than twenty-three years old. I studied his face. Somehow he seemed familiar, though I couldn't think why. I flipped the card over. On the back, he'd pasted a strip on which he'd written, *In case of emergency, please notify Porter Yount, managing editor, Louisville Tribune.*

TWENTY-FOUR

My plane arrived in Louisville, Kentucky, at 5:20 P.M., at a gate so remote it appeared to be abandoned or under quarantine. I'd been in Louisville once before, about six months back, when a cross-country romp had ended in a cemetery, with my being the recipient of an undeserved crack on the head. In that case, as with this, I was out a substantial chunk of change, with little hope of recouping my financial losses.

As I passed through the terminal, I paused at a public phone booth and checked the local directory on the off chance I'd find Porter Yount listed. I figured the name was unusual and there couldn't be that many in the greater Louisville area. The high school librarian had told me the *Tribune* had been swallowed up by a syndicate some twenty years before. I imagined Yount old and retired, if he were alive at all. For once my luck held and I spotted the address and phone number of a Porter Yount, who I assumed was the man I was looking for. According to the phone book, he lived in the 1500 block of Third Street. I made a note of the address and continued to the baggage-claim level, where I forked over my credit card and picked up the keys to the rental car. The woman at Frugal gave me a sheet map and traced out my route: taking the Watterson Expressway east, then picking up I-65 north into the downtown area.

I found my car in the designated slot and took a moment to get my bearings. The parking lot was shiny with puddles from a recent shower. Given the low probability of rain any given day in California, I drank in the scent. Even the air felt different: balmy and humid with the late afternoon temperatures in the low 70s. Despite Santa Teresa's proximity to the Pacific Ocean, the climate is desertlike. Here, a moist spring breeze touched at newly unfurled leaves, and I could see pink and white azaleas bordering the grass. I shrugged out of Mickey's jacket and locked it in the trunk along with my duffel.

I decided to leave the issue of a motel until after I'd talked to Yount. It was close to the dinner hour, and chances were good that I'd find him at home. Following instructions, I took one of the downtown off-ramps, cutting over to Third, where I took a right and crossed Broadway. I drove slowly along Third, scanning house numbers. I finally spotted my destination and pulled in at a bare stretch of curb a few doors away. The tree-lined street, with its three-story houses of dark red brick, must have been lovely in the early days of the century. Now, some of the structures were run-down, and encroaching businesses had begun to mar the nature of the area. The general population was doubtless abandoning the once-stately downtown for the featureless suburbs.

Yount's residence was two and a half stories of red

brick faced with pale fieldstone. A wide porch ran along the front of the building. Three wide bay windows were stacked one to a floor. An air conditioner extended from an attic window. The street was lined with similar houses, built close to one another, yards and alleyways behind. In front, between the sidewalk and the street, a border of grass was planted with maples and oaks that must have been there for eighty to a hundred years.

I climbed three steps, proceeded along a short cracked walkway, and climbed an additional six steps to the glass door with its tiny foyer visible within. Yount's residence had apparently once been a single-family dwelling, now broken into five units, judging from the names posted on the mailboxes. Each apartment had a bell, connected to the intercom located near the entrance. I rang Yount's apartment, waiting two minutes before I rang again. When it became clear he wasn't answering, I tried a neighbor's bell instead. After a moment, the intercom crackled to life and an old woman clicked in, saying, "Yes?"

I said, "I wonder if you can help me. I'm looking for Porter Yount."

"Speak up."

"Porter Yount in apartment three."

"What's the time?"

I glanced at my watch. "Six-fifteen."

"He'll be down yonder on the corner. The Buttercup Tavern."

"Thanks."

I returned to the sidewalk, where I peered up and down the street. Though I didn't see a sign, I spotted what looked like a corner tavern half a block down. I left my car where it was and walked the short distance through the mild spring air.

The Buttercup was dark, cloudy with cigarette smoke, and smelling of bourbon. The local news was being broadcast at low volume on a color TV set mounted in one corner of the room. The dark was further punctuated by neon signs in a series of advertisements for Rolling Rock, Fehr's, and Stroh's Beer. The tavern was paneled in highly varnished wood with red leather stools along the length of the bar. Most of the occupants at that hour seemed to be isolated individuals, all men, all smoking, separated from each other by as many empty stools as space allowed. Without exception, each turned to stare at me as I came in.

I paused just inside the door and said, "I'm looking for Porter Yount."

A fellow at the far end of the bar raised his hand.

Judging from the swiveling heads, my arrival was the most interesting event since the Ohio River flooded in 1937. When I reached Yount, I held my hand out, saying, "I'm Kinsey Millhone."

"Nice meeting you," he said.

We shook hands and I perched on the stool next to his.

I said, "How are you?"

"Not bad. Thanks for asking." Porter Yount was heavyset, raspy-voiced, a man in his eighties. He was almost entirely bald, but his brows were still dark, an unruly tangle above eyes that were a startling green. At the moment, he was bleary-eyed with bourbon and his

339

breath smelled like fruitcake. I could see the bartender
drift in our direction. He paused in front of us.

Yount lit a fresh cigarette and glanced in my direction. He was having trouble with his focus. His mouth
seemed to work, but his eyeballs were rolling like two
green olives in an empty relish dish. "What'll you
have?"

"How about a Fehr's?"

"You don't want Fehr's," he said. And to the bartender, "Lady wants a shot of Early Times with a
water back."

"The beer's fine," I corrected.

The bartender reached into a cooler for the beer,
which he opened and placed on the bar in front of me.

Yount said peevishly, "Give the lady a glass.
Where's your manners?"

The bartender set a glass on the bar and Yount
spoke to him again. "Who's cooking tonight?"

"Patsy. Want to see a menu?"

"Did I say that? This lady and I could use some
privacy."

"Oh, sure." The bartender moved to the other end
of the bar, accustomed to Yount's manner.

Yount shook his head with exasperation and his
gaze slid in my direction. His head was round as a ball,
sitting on the heft of his shoulders with scarcely any
neck between. His shirt was a dark polyester, probably
selected for stain concealment and ease of laundering.
A pair of dark suspenders kept his pants hiked high
above his waist. He wore dark socks and sandals, with
an inch of shinbone showing. "Outfit okay? If I'd

knowed you was coming, I'd've wore my Sunday best," he said, deliberately fracturing his grammar.

I had to laugh. "Sorry. I tend to look carefully at just about everything."

"You a journalist?"

I shook my head. "A private investigator. I'm trying to get a line on Duncan Oaks. You remember him?"

"Of course. You're the second detective to come in here asking after him this month."

"You talked to Mickey Magruder?"

"That's the one," he said.

"I thought as much."

"Why'd he send you? He didn't take me at my word?"

"We didn't talk. He was shot last week and he's been in a coma ever since."

"Sorry to hear that. I liked him. He's smart. First fella I met who could match me drink for drink."

"He's talented that way. At any rate, I'm doing what I can to follow up his investigation. It's tough, since I don't really know what he'd accomplished. I hope this won't turn out to be a waste of your time."

"Drinking's a waste of time, not talking to pretty ladies. What's the sudden interest in Oaks?"

"His name's cropped up in connection with another matter . . . something in California, which is where I'm from. I know he once worked for the *Tribune*. Your name was on his press pass, so I thought I'd talk to you."

"Fool's errand if I ever heard one. He's been dead twenty years."

"So I heard. I'm sorry for the repetition, but if you tell me what you told Mickey, maybe we can figure out if he's relevant."

Yount took a swallow of whiskey and tapped the ash off his cigarette. "He's a 'war correspondent'—pretty fancy title for a paper like the *Trib*. I don't think even the *Courier-Journal* had a correspondent back then. This was in the early sixties."

"Did you hire him yourself?"

"Oh, sure. He's a local boy, a blueblood, high society: good looks, ambition, an ego big as your head. More charisma than character." His elbow slid off the bar, and he caught himself with a jerk that we both ignored. Mentally, he seemed sharp. It was his body that tended to slip out of gear.

"Meaning what?"

"Not to speak ill of the dead, but I suspect he'd peaked out. You must know people like that yourself. High school's the glory days; after that, nothing much. It's not like he did poorly, but he never did as well. He's a fellow cut corners, never really earned his stripes, so to speak."

"Where'd he go to college?"

"He didn't. Duncan wasn't school-smart. He's a bright kid, made good grades, but he never cared much for academics. He had drive and aspirations. He figured he'd learn more in the real world so he nixed the idea."

"Was he right about that?"

"Hard to say. Kid loved to hustle. Talked me into paying him seventy-five dollars a week—which, frankly, we didn't have. Even in those days, his salary was a pittance, but he didn't care."

"Because he came from money?"

"That's right. Revel Oaks, his daddy, made a fortune in the sin trades, whiskey and tobacco. That and real estate speculation. Duncan grew up in an atmosphere of privilege. Hell, his daddy would've given him anything he wanted: travel, the best schools, place in the family business. Duncan had other fish to fry."

"For instance?"

He waved his cigarette in the air. "Like I said, he wangled his way into a job with the *Trib*, mostly on the basis of his daddy's influence."

"And what did he want?"

"Adventure, recognition. Duncan was addicted to living on the edge. Craved the limelight, craved risk. He wanted to go to Vietnam and report on the war. Nothing would do until he got his way."

"But why not enlist? If you're craving life on the edge, why not the infantry? That's about as close to the edge as you can get."

"Military wouldn't touch him. Had a heart murmur sounded like water pouring through a sluice. That's when he came to us. Wasn't any way the *Trib* could afford his ticket to Saigon. Didn't matter to him. He paid his own way. As long as he had access, he's happy as a clam. In those days, we're talking Neil Sheehan, David Halberstam, Mal Browne, Homer Bigart. Duncan pictured his byline in papers all across the country. He did a series of local interviews with newlyweds, army wives left behind when their husbands went off to war. The idea was to follow up, talk to the husbands, and see the fighting from their perspective."

"Not a bad idea."

"We thought it had promise, especially with so many of his classmates getting drafted. Any rate, he got his press credentials and his passport. He flew from Hong Kong to Saigon and from there to Pleiku. For a while, he was fine, hitching rides on military transports, any place they'd take him. To give him credit, I think he might have turned into a hell of a journalist. He had a way with words, but he lacked experience."

"How long was he there?"

"Couple months is all. He heard about some action in a place called Ia Drang. I guess he pulled strings — maybe his old man again or just his personal charm. It was a hell of a battle, some say the worst of the war. After that came LZ Albany: something like three hundred fellas killed in the space of four days. Must have found himself caught in the thick of it with no way out. We heard later he was hit, but we never got a sense of how serious it was."

"And then what?"

Yount paused to extinguish his cigarette. He missed the ashtray altogether and stubbed out the burning ember on the bar. "That's as much as I know. He's supposed to be medevacked out, but he never made it back. Chopper took off with a bellyful of body bags and a handful of casualties. Landed forty minutes later with no Duncan aboard. His daddy raised hell, got some high Pentagon official to launch an investigation, but it never came to much."

"And that's it?"

"I'm afraid so. You hungry? Ask me, it's time to eat."

"Fine with me," I said.

Porter gestured to the bartender, who ambled back in our direction. "Tell Patsy to put together couple of Hot Browns."

"Good enough," the man said. He set his towel aside, came out from behind the bar, and headed for a door I assumed led to Patsy in the kitchen.

Yount said, "Bet you never ate one."

"What's a Hot Brown?"

"Invented at the Brown Hotel. Wait and see. Now, where was I?"

"Trying to figure out the fate of Duncan Oaks," I said.

"He's dead."

"How do you know?"

"He's never been heard from since."

"Isn't it possible he panicked and took off on foot?"

"Absence of a body, anything's possible, I guess."

"But not likely?"

"I'd say not. The way we heard it later, the NVA were everywhere, scourin' the area for wounded, killing them for sport. Duncan had no training. He probably couldn't get a hundred yards on his own."

"I wonder if you'd look at something." I hauled up my bag from its place near my feet. I removed the snapshot, the press pass, and the dog tags embossed with Duncan's name.

Yount tucked his cigarette in the corner of his

mouth, examining the items through a plume of smoke. "Same things Magruder showed me. How'd he come by them?"

"A guy named Benny Quintero had them. You know him?"

"Name doesn't sound familiar."

"That's him in the picture. I'm assuming this is Duncan."

"That's him. When's this taken?"

"Quintero's brother thinks Ia Drang. Benny was wounded November seventeenth."

"Same as Duncan," he said. "This'd have to be one of the last pictures of Duncan ever taken."

"I hadn't thought of that, but probably so."

Yount returned the snapshot, which I tucked in my bag.

"Benny's another Louisville boy. He died in Santa Teresa in 1972: probably a homicide, though there was never an arrest." I took a few minutes to detail the story of Benny's death. "Mickey didn't mention this?"

"Never said a word. How's Quintero tie in?"

"I can give you the superficial answer. His brother says he went to Manual; I'm guessing, at the same time Duncan went to Male. It seems curious he'd end up with Duncan's personal possessions."

Porter shook his head. "Wonder why he kept them?"

"Not a clue," I said. "They were in a lockbox in his room. His brother came across them maybe six months back. He brought them to California." I thought about it for a moment, and then I said, "What's Duncan doing with a set of dog tags if he was never in the service?"

"He had them made up himself. Appealed to his sense of theater. One more example of how he liked to operate: looking like a soldier was as good as being one. I'm surprised he didn't hang out in uniform, but I guess that'd be pushing it. Don't get me wrong. I liked Duncan, but he's a fella with shabby standards."

A woman, probably Patsy, appeared from the kitchen with a steaming ramekin in each of her oven-mitted hands. She put a dish in front of each of us and handed us two sets of flatware rolled in paper napkins. Yount murmured "thanks" and she said, "You're entirely welcome."

I stared at the dish, which looked like a lake of piping-hot yellow sludge, with a dusting of paprika and something lumpy underneath. "What *is* this?"

"Eat and find out."

I picked up my fork and tried a tiny bite. A Hot Brown turned out to be an open-faced sliced turkey sandwich, complete with bacon and tomatoes, baked with the most divine cheese sauce I ever set to my lips. I mewed like a kitten.

"Told you so," he said, with satisfaction.

When I was finished, I wiped my mouth and took a sip of beer. "What about Duncan's parents? Does he still have family in the area?"

Yount shook his head. "Revel died of a heart attack a few years back: 1974, if memory serves. His mother died three years later of a stroke."

"Siblings, cousins?"

347

"Not a one," he said. "Duncan was an only child, and his daddy was too. I doubt you'd find anyone left on his mother's side of the family either. Her people were from Pike County, over on the West Virginia border. Dirt poor. Once she married Revel, she cut all ties with them."

He glanced at his watch. It was close to 8 P.M. "Time for me get home. My program's coming on in two minutes."

"I appreciate your time. Can I buy your dinner?"

Yount gave me a look. "Obvious you haven't spent any time in the South. Lady doesn't buy dinner for a gent. That's his prerogative." He reached in his pocket, pulled out a wad of bills, and tossed several on the bar.

At his suggestion, I spent the night at the Leisure Inn on Broadway. I might have tried the Brown Hotel, but it looked way too fancy for the likes of me. The Leisure Inn was plain, a sensible establishment of Formica, nylon carpet, foam rubber pillows, and a layer of crackling plastic laid under the bottom sheet in case I wet the bed. I put a call through to the airline and discussed the options for my return. The first (and only) seat available was on a 3 P.M. flight the next day. I snagged it, wondering what I was going to do with myself until then. I considered a side visit to Louisville Male High, where Duncan had graduated with the class of 1961. Secretly, I doubted there was much to learn. Porter Yount had painted an unappealing portrait of the young Duncan Oaks. To me, he sounded shallow, spoiled, and manipulative. On the other hand, he was just a kid when he died: twenty-two, twenty-three years old at the outside. I suspect most of us are completely self-involved at that age. At twenty-two, I'd already been married and divorced. By twenty-three, I was not only married to Daniel but I'd left the police department and was totally adrift. I'd *thought* I was mature, but I was foolish and unenlightened. My judgment was faulty and my perception was flawed. So who was I to judge Duncan? He might have become a good man if he'd lived long enough. Thinking about it, I felt a curious secondhand sorrow for all the chances he'd missed, the lessons he never learned, the dreams he'd had to forfeit with his early death. Whoever he was and whatever he'd been, I could at least pay my respects.

At ten the next morning, I parked my rental car on a side street not far from Louisville Male High School, at the corner of Brook Street and Breckinridge. The building was three stories tall, constructed of dark red brick with white concrete trim. The surrounding neighborhood consisted of narrow red-brick houses with narrow walkways between. Many looked as if the interiors would smell peculiar. I went up the concrete stairs. Above the entrance, two gnomelike scholars were nestled in matching niches, reading plaques of some kind. The dates 1914 and 1915 were chiseled in stone, indicating, I supposed, the year the building had gone up. I pushed through the front door and went in.

The interior was defined by gray marble wainscoting, with gray-painted walls above. The foyer floor was speckled gray marble with inexplicable cracks here and there. In the auditorium, dead ahead, I could see descending banks of curved wooden seats and tiers of wooden flooring, faintly buckled with age. Classes must have been in session, because the corridors were empty and there was little traffic on the stairs. I went into the school office. The windows were tall. Long planks of fluorescent lighting hung from ceilings covered with acoustical tile. I asked for the school library and was directed to the third floor.

The school librarian, Mrs. Calloway, was a sturdy-looking soul in a calf-length denim skirt and a pair of indestructible walking shoes. Her iron-gray hair was chopped off in a fuss-free style she'd probably worn for years. Close to retirement, she looked like a woman who'd favor muesli, yoga, liniments, SAVE THE WHALES bumper stickers, polar-bear swims, and lengthy bicycle tours of foreign countries. When I asked to see a copy of the '61 yearbook, she gave me a look but refrained from comment. She handed me the *Bulldog* and I took a seat at an empty table. She returned to her desk and busied herself, though I could tell she intended to keep an eye on me.

I spent a few minutes leafing through the *Bulldog*, looking at the black-and-white portraits of the senior class. I didn't check for Duncan's name. I simply absorbed the whole, trying to get a feel for the era, which predated mine by six years. The school had originally been all male, but it had turned coed somewhere along the way. Senior pictures showed the boys wearing coats and ties, their hair in brush cuts that emphasized their big ears and oddly shaped heads.

Many wore glasses with heavy black frames. The girls tended toward short hair and dark gray or black crew-neck sweaters. Each wore a simple strand of pearls, probably a necklace provided by the photographer for uniformity. By 1967, the year I graduated, the hairstyles were bouffant, as stiffly lacquered as wigs, with flipped ends sticking out. The boys had all turned into Elvis Presley clones. Here, in candid class photos, most students wore penny loafers and white crew socks, and the girls were decked out in straight or pleated skirts that hit them at the knee.

I breezed by the Good News Club, the Speech Club, the Art Club, the Pep Club, and the Chess Club. In views of classes devoted to industrial arts, home ec, and world science, students were clumped together pointing at wall maps or gathered around the teacher's desk, smiling and pretending to look interested. The teachers all appeared to be fifty-five and as dull as dust.

At Thanksgiving of that year, the fall of 1960, the annual Male–Manual game was played. Male High was victorious by a score of 20–6. "MALE BEATS MANUAL 20 TO 6, CLINCHES CITY & AAA CROWNS," the article said. "A neat, well-deserved licking of the duPont Manual Rams." Co-captains were Walter Morris and Joe Blankenship. The rivalry between the two high schools had been long and fierce, beginning in 1893 and doubtless continuing to the present. At that time, the record showed 39 wins for Male, 19 for Manual, and 5 games tied. At the bottom of the page, in the accompanying photograph of the Manual offense, I found a halfback named Quintero, weighing 162.

I went back to the first page and started through again. Duncan Oaks showed up in a number of photographs, dark-haired and handsome. He'd been elected vice president, prom king, and class photographer. His name and face seemed to crop up in many guises: the senior play, Quill and Scroll, Glee Club. He was a Youth Speaks delegate, office aide, and library assistant.

He hadn't garnered academic honors, but he had played football. I found a picture of him on the Male High team, a 160-pound halfback. Now that was interesting: Duncan Oaks and Benny Quintero had played the same position on opposing teams. They must have known each other, by reputation if nothing else. I thought about Porter Yount's comment that these were Duncan's glory years, that his life after this never approached the same heights. That might have been true for Quintero as well. In retrospect, it seemed touching that their paths had crossed again in Vietnam.

I turned to the front of the book and studied the picture of Duncan as prom king. He was wearing a tuxedo: shorn, clean-shaven, with a white boutonniere tucked into his lapel. I turned the page and studied the prom queen, wondering if they were boyfriend/girlfriend or simply elected separately and honored on the same occasion. Darlene LaDestro. Well, this was a type I'd known well. Long blond hair pulled up in a swirl on top, a strong nose, patrician air. She looked classy, familiar, like girls in my high school who came from big-time money. Though not conventionally pretty, Darlene was the kind of girl who'd age with style. She'd come back to class reunions having married her social equal, still thin as a rail, hair streaked tastefully with gray. Darlene LaDestro, what a name. You'd think she'd have dumped it the first chance she got, called herself Dodie or Dessie or—

A chill swept through me, and I made an involuntary bark of astonishment. Mrs. Calloway looked up, and I shook my head to indicate that I was fine . . . though I wasn't. No wonder Darlene looked familiar. She was currently Laddie Bethel, alive and well and living in Santa Teresa.

TWENTY-FIVE

I postponed my return, moving the reservation from Wednesday afternoon to a morning flight on Thursday to give myself time to compile some information. I'd combed copies of the 1958, 1959, 1960, 1961, and 1962 yearbooks for reference to Mark Bethel but had found no mention of him. If Laddie'd known him in those days, it wasn't because he'd attended Louisville Male High. I made copious copies of the yearbook pages where Laddie and Duncan were featured, both together and separately, going all the way back to their freshman year. In many candid class pictures, the two were standing side by side.

I placed the stack of yearbooks on Mrs. Calloway's desk. I left the high school, driving through the area until I found a drugstore, where I bought a pack of index cards and a city map to supplement the simple sheet map I'd acquired from Frugal Rents. In the rental car again, I circled back to the public library, which was not far away. I inquired at the desk and was directed to the reference department. Then I got down to work. By cross-checking past city directories with past telephone books, I found one LaDestro and made a note of the address. The 1959, 1960, and 1961 business directories indicated that Laddie's father, Harold LaDestro, had owned a machine shop on Market and listed his occupation as precision machinist and inventor. Because of Laddie's poise, her elegance, and her aristocratic airs, I'd assumed she came from money, but perhaps I was wrong. In those years, her father was a tradesman, and there was no hint whatever that his business interests extended beyond the obvious. From the yearbook, I knew she'd graduated with honors, but the list of her achievements made no mention of college plans. She might have enrolled at the University of Louisville, which was probably not expensive for local residents. It was also possible she'd attended a nearby business college, taking a secretarial course so she could work for her dad. That was the sort of thing a conscientious daughter might have done in those days.

But where had she met Mark? On a whim, I pulled out the 1961 phone book, where I found listings for twenty-one families with the last name of Bethel and four with the last name Oaks. There was only one Revel Oaks, and I made a note of that address. As for Bethels, I had another idea how to pin down Mark's family. I ran off copies of the phone book listings and pages from the relevant city directories, adding them to the copies I'd made of the yearbook information. I wasn't sure where I was going, but why not follow my nose? I'd already spent the money for the plane fare to get here. I was stuck until flight time the next morning. What else was there to do?

I fired up the rental car and did a quick driving tour,

starting with the Oaks family home on Fourth Street, still in the downtown area. The house was impressive: an immense three-story structure of stucco and stone, probably built in the late 1800s. The style fell midway between Renaissance and baroque, with cornices, fluted columns, curved buttresses, a balustrade, and arched windows. The exterior color was uncommon: a dusky pink, washed with brown, as if the façade had been glazed by age to this mournful shade. From the sign on the lawn, the building was now occupied by two law firms, a court reporting firm, and a CPA. The property was large, the surrounding stone wall still visible, as well as the original gateposts. Two majestic oak trees shaded the formal gardens in the rear, and I could see a carriage house at the end of a cobbled driveway.

The LaDestros' address was less than two miles away, within a block of the university on a narrow side street. I checked for the number, but the house was gone, evidently razed to make way for expanding campus facilities. The remaining houses on the street tended to be elongated one-story boxes sheathed in dark red asphalt siding. Depressing. I couldn't imagine how Laddie'd been catapulted from these grim beginnings to her current wealth. Had she been married before? In those days, a rich husband was the obvious means by which a woman could elevate her social standing and improve her prospects. She certainly must have been eager to bail herself out of *this*.

While I was still in range of the central city, I located the Jefferson County clerk's office in the courthouse between Fifth and Sixth streets on West Jefferson. The fellow at the desk couldn't have been more helpful when I told him what I needed: the marriage certificate for Darlene LaDestro and Mark Bethel, who I believed had been married in the summer of 1965. I couldn't give him the exact date, but I was remembering the line I'd picked up from Mark's secretary, Judy, who told me he'd enlisted in the army right after his college graduation. What would have been more natural than to marry Laddie that summer, before he went overseas? I was also operating on the theory that Laddie (aka Darlene LaDestro) was an obvious choice for one of Duncan's interviews. She was young, she was lovely, she was local. She would have been easy to approach, since they lived in the same town and he'd known her for years. Duncan's press credentials were dated September 10, 1965. If he'd talked to Laddie at all, it was probably sometime between her marriage, Mark's departure, and his own flight to Vietnam soon afterward.

Fifteen minutes later, I experienced one of those exhilarating moments of satisfaction when, sure enough, the clerk found the marriage record.

"Oh, wow. This is great. Isn't this *amazing*?" I said.

The clerk's look was jaded. "I'm completely stunned."

I laughed. "Well, I like being right, especially when I'm flying by the seat of my pants."

He leaned on the counter, his chin on his hand, looking on while I took out my cards and jotted down the information embedded in the form. The license was issued on June 3, 1965. Assuming it was good for thirty days, the wedding must have taken place within the month. Darlene LaDestro, age twenty-two and working as a bookkeeper, was the daughter of Harold and Millicent LaDestro and resided at the address listed in the 1961 telephone book. Mark Charles Bethel, age twenty-three, occupation U.S. Army, was the son of Vernon and Shirley Bethel with an address on Trevillian Way. Neither the bride nor the groom had been previously married.

Idly, the clerk said, "You know who he is, don't you?"

I looked up at him with interest. "Who, Mark Bethel?"

"No, LaDestro."

"I don't know a thing about him. What's the story?"

"He was awarded the patent for some kind of widget used on the Mercury space flights."

"And that's how he made his money?"

"Sure. He's still famous around here. Self-taught, eccentric. He didn't even have connections to the aerospace industry. He just worked on his own. I saw a picture of him once, and he looked like a pointy-headed geek. He'd been tinkering all his life without making a dime. In hock up to here, living in a dump. Everybody wrote him off as a nut, and then he comes along and aces out McDonnell-Douglas for the rights to the thing. He died a rich man. I mean *very, very* rich."

"Well, I'll be darned," I said. "What was it, the thing he patented?"

"Some doodad. Who knows? I heard it's in use to this day. The world is full of guys who design gizmos they never get credit for. LaDestro hired a patent attorney and took the big boys down."

"Incredible."

"His daughter sure lucked out. I hear she lives in California now on some fancy estate," he said. He pointed to the license. "You want a copy of that?"

"How much?"

"Two dollars for regular, five for certified."

"Regular's fine," I said.

I drove from Jefferson to Third, then hung a left on Broadway, driving east until it angled into Bardstown Road. I followed Bardstown Road through an area of town known as the Highlands. Once on Trevillian, I found the house where the Bethels had lived. The white frame house looked comfortable, not large but well maintained in a solid middle-class neighborhood, certainly superior to the one where Laddie'd grown up. I parked in front of the house, traversed the long sloping walk, and climbed the stairs to the porch. No one was home, but a simple check of the mailbox revealed that a family named Poynter now occupied the house. This was Donna Reed country: green shutters on the windows, pansies in the flower boxes, a tricycle on the sidewalk, and a dog bone lying in the yard. All the windowpanes sparkled, and the shrubs were crisply trimmed. As I looked on, a lean gray cat picked her way carefully across the newly cut lawn.

I returned to the car, where I sat and studied my map. Gauging the proximity of schools in the area, I decided Mark probably attended Highland Junior High and then Atherton or St. Xavier, the Catholic high school on Broadway. He might have gone to private school—I wasn't sure about that—but he struck me as the sort who'd take pride in his public school roots. Now what?

I leafed through the pages I'd assembled, letting my mind wander. I'd added a number of dots, but I still couldn't see all the lines connecting them. Duncan Oaks seemed pivotal. I sensed his presence like the hub of an enormous wheel. I could trace the hometown relationship between him and Benny Quintero. Contemporaries, two high school athletes who had played the same positions on opposing football teams, their paths had crossed years later on the bloody soil of Ia Drang. After that, Duncan Oaks had vanished but Quintero had survived, keeping Duncan's dog tags, his press credentials, and a snapshot. I could also tie Duncan Oaks to Laddie Bethel, born Darlene LaDestro, who'd attended high school with him. And here's where the machinations became more intricate. Laddie was now married to the attorney who'd represented my ex-husband, a suspect in Benny Quintero's beating death seven years later. If Duncan Oaks was the hub, maybe Mark Bethel was the axle driving subsequent events.

I started the car and headed back to my motel. Even without the links, a picture was forming, crude and unfocused, but one that Mickey must have seen as well. The problem was I had no proof a crime had been committed all those years ago, let alone that it had sparked consequences in the here-and-now. It simply stood to reason. *Some* combination of events had resulted in the killing of Benny Quintero and the shooting of Mickey Magruder. I had to fashion a story that encompassed all the players and made sense of their fates. If life is a play, then there's a logical explanation, an underlying tale that pulls the whole of it together, however clouded it first appears.

Before my plane the next morning, I put in a call to Porter Yount, asking if he could lay his hands on the columns Duncan Oaks had written before he went to Vietnam. Much hemming and hawing, but he said he'd see what he could do. I gave him my address and a great big telephone kiss, telling him to take care, I'd be in touch with him.

The flight home was uneventful, though it took up most of the day: Louisville to Tulsa, Tulsa to Santa Fe, Santa Fe to Los Angeles, where I shuttled to the motel, picked up my VW, and drove the ninety minutes home. Between the actual hours in the air, the wait between planes, and the commute at the end, I arrived in Santa Teresa at 4:30 P.M. I was feeling irritable: tired, hungry, flat-haired, oily-faced. I was also dehydrated from all the nuts I'd eaten in lieu of meals that day. I had to slap myself around some to keep from whining out loud.

The minute I got home, I sat down at my desk and removed Mark Bethel's curriculum vitae from the bottom drawer where I'd tucked it Saturday. On the front page, he'd listed his date and place of birth as Dayton, Ohio, August 1, 1942. He'd graduated with a BA from the University of Kentucky in 1965. Under military experience, he listed U.S. Army, modestly omitting mention of his Purple Heart. I'd call Judy in the morning, my palate smeared with peanut butter, pretending to be a journalist so I could pin that down. If Mark had been at Ia Drang, I'd be one step closer to completing the picture, which was almost done.

I stripped, showered, and shampooed my hair. I brushed my teeth, got dressed again, and trotted down the spiral stairs.

My first thought was to have a conversation with Carlin Duffy, conveying a condensed version of what I'd learned in Louisville, though at this point I still didn't know quite what to make of it. I'd restrict myself to the facts, leaving out the speculations and suppositions I was still playing with. The contact was largely a courtesy on my part. He hadn't hired me. He wasn't paying me and I didn't feel I owed him an explanation. I was hoping, however, that he'd have something to contribute, some piece of the puzzle he hadn't thought to share. More to the point, I remembered Duffy's rage and frustration the night he'd shown up at Mickey's. I didn't relish a repeat performance and this was my way of protecting myself. Duffy's brother had died, and he had his stake in the matter.

I headed out to the nursery, where I found a parking slot in front of the gardening center. I prayed Duffy was on the premises instead of at the Honky-Tonk. The bar was open at this hour, but I didn't dare go back. I thought I'd better keep my distance in case Tim and Scottie realized I was the one who'd blown the whistle on them. It was close to five-thirty, still light out, and I made my way easily along the tree-lined paths. I could see the roofline of the shed at the rear of the lot, and I mentally marked my route. There was no direct passageway, and I angled back and forth between the crated trees.

When I reached the shed, I saw a compact yellow forklift parked in the entrance. Several large bags of mulch were stacked on the forks in front. Tall and boxy, the vehicle was an overblown version of the Tonka toys I'd played with when I was six. The phase had been short-lived, tucked somewhere between Lego and the demise of the baby doll I'd flattened with my trike. I moved into the shed, pushing aside the blanket Duffy'd hung to eliminate drafts. He'd passed out, lying shoeless on his cot. His mouth hung open and his snores filled the enclosure with bourbon fumes. He cradled an empty pint of Early Times against his chest. One sock was pulled half off, and his bare heel was exposed. He looked absurdly young for a fellow who'd spent half his life in jail. I thought, Shit. I found a blanket and tossed it over him and then placed the dog tags, the press pass, the snapshot, and a note on the crate where he'd see it when he woke. The note said I'd be in touch the next day and fill him in on the trip. I backed out of the shed, leaving him to sleep off his drunken state.

I walked back to the car, thinking how often I identified with guys like him. As crude as he was with his racist comments, his tortured grammar, and his attitude toward crime, I understood his yearning. How liberating it was when you defied authority, flaunted convention, ignoring ordinary standards of moral decency. I knew my own ambivalence. On the one hand, I was a true law-and-order type, prissy in my judgment, outraged at those who violated the doctrines of honesty and fair play. On the other hand, I'd been known to lie through my teeth, eavesdrop, pick locks, or simply break into people's houses, where I snooped through their possessions and took what suited me. It wasn't nice, but I savored every single minute of my bad girl behavior. Later, I'd feel guilty, but still I couldn't resist. I was split down the middle, my good angel sitting on one shoulder, Lucifer perched on the other. Duffy's struggle was the same, and while he leaned in one direction, I usually leaned in the other, searching for justice in the heart of anarchy. This was the bottom line as far as I was concerned: If the bad guys don't play by the rules, why should the good guys have to?

I drove back into town. It was now 5:50 and I was starving, of course, so I made a quick detour. I pulled up to the drive-in window at McDonald's and asked for a QP with cheese, a large order of fries, and a Coke to go. I was fairly humming with excitement as I waited for my bag of goodies. I'd go back to my apartment, change into my jammies, and curl up on my couch, where I'd watch junk TV while I ate my junk food. While I drove home, the car smelled divine, like a mobile microwave oven. I found a great parking place, locked the car, and let myself in through the squeaking gate. I rounded the corner, all a-twitter at the notion of the pleasures to come. I stopped dead.

Detectives Claas and Aldo were standing on my

front porch. This was a replay of our earlier encounter: same guys in their late thirties, the one dark, the other fair, same sport coats. Claas carried the briefcase, just as he had before. Gian Aldo chewed gum. He'd had his dark hair trimmed short, but his eyebrows still met like a hedge across the bridge of his nose. I longed to fall on him with a pair of tweezers and pluck him bald.

I said, "What do you want?"

Detective Claas seemed amused. Now *that* was different. "Be nice. We drove all the way up here to have a chat with you."

I walked past him with my keys and unlocked the door. Detective Claas wore a hair product that smelled like a high school chemistry experiment. The two followed me in. I dropped my shoulder bag on the floor near my desk, taking a moment to check my answering machine. No messages.

I held up my McDonald's bag, the contents getting colder by the minute, as were my hopes. "I gotta eat first. I'm half dead."

"Have at it."

I crossed to the kitchen, moving around the counter to the refrigerator. I took out a chilled bottle of Chardonnay and sorted through the junk drawer until I found the opener. "You want wine? I'm having some. You might as well join me."

The two exchanged a look. It was probably against regulations, but they must have thought I'd be easier to get along with if I were all likkered up.

"We'd appreciate that. Thanks," Claas said.

I handed him the wine bottle and the opener, and he got to work while I set out three glasses and a paper plate. I dumped the fries out of the carton and fetched the ketchup bottle from the cabinet. "Help yourself," I said.

Detective Claas poured the wine and we stood there, eating lukewarm french fries with our fingers. They were completely limp by now, and we dropped them in our beaks like a trio of birdies eating albino worms. Ever gracious, I cut the QP into three equal parts and we gulped those down, too. After supper, we walked the six steps into the living room. This time I took the couch and let them settle into my director's chairs. I noticed Detective Claas kept his briefcase close at hand as he had before. I knew he had a tape recorder in there, and it made me want to lean down and address all my comments into the opening.

"So now what?" I said, crossing my arms against my chest.

Detective Aldo smiled. "We have some news we thought you might want to hear firsthand. We picked up a partial print on the Smith and Wesson and matched it to some prints that showed up in Magruder's place."

Claas said, "You remember a gray metal box concealed in the bottom of a chair?"

I could feel my mouth go dry. "Sure." No sound. I cleared my throat and tried again. "Sure."

"We got a real nice set on the inner rim of the lid, like someone pulled it open with their fingertips."

I was going to call his attention to the matter of subject–pronoun agreement, but I held my tongue. Instead, I said, "Who?" Was that an owl I heard?

Aldo spoke up again, clearly enjoying himself. "Mark Bethel."

I stared at him, blinking. "You're kidding. You gotta be *kidding*."

"He went in there Sunday night and left prints everywhere."

"That's great. I love it. Good for him," I said.

"We're not sure what he was looking for—"

I held a hand up. "I can tell you that," I said. I gave them a hasty summary of the work I'd done, including the discovery of Duncan Oaks's credentials in Mickey's jacket lining. "I can't believe he was dumb enough to leave his fingerprints. Has the man lost his mind?"

"He's getting desperate," Claas said. "He probably saw the print dust on all the surfaces and figured we were done."

"You dusted again?"

"Tuesday morning," Aldo said.

"But why? What possessed you?"

"We got a call from Cordia Hatfield. She'd seen lights on Sunday night. You swore it wasn't you, so she suspected it was him," Claas said.

"But how'd he get in?"

"With the key she'd given him. He'd stopped by last week and introduced himself as Magruder's attorney. He said he'd be paying Mickey's bills till he was on his feet, and he was hoping to pick up insurance policies and bank deposit slips. She gave him a key. Of course, he returned it later, but probably not before he'd had a copy made for himself," Claas said.

Detective Aldo spoke up. "I don't think the computer would have caught the match without the fresh set he left. Of course, we wasted a *lot* of time eliminating yours."

367

I could feel my cheeks heat. "Sorry about that."

Aldo wagged his finger, but he didn't seem all that mad.

Claas said, "We can also place Bethel in the area at the time of the shooting."

"You guys have been busy. How'd you do *that*?"

Claas was clearly pleased with himself. "On the thirteenth, Bethel was in Los Angeles for a TV appearance. The taping finished at ten. He checked into the Four Seasons on a late arrival and then went out again, returning in the early hours of the fourteenth. He might have slipped in unnoticed, but as it happened the valet car park was a supporter and recognized his face."

"Tell you what else," Detective Aldo said. "We got somebody saw them together that night."

"No."

"Oh, yes. We went through a bunch of matchbooks Magruder kept in a fishbowl. We found seven from a dive on Pic'o near the Pacific Coast Security offices. A gal at the bar remembered seeing them." Detective Aldo sat back, the wood and canvas chair creaking perilously under his weight. "What about you? What'd you pick up back east? Your landlord told us you made a trip to Louisville."

"That's right. I just got back today."

"Learn anything?"

"Actually, I did. I'm just piecing this together so I can't be sure, but here's what I know. Laddie Bethel went to high school in Louisville with a guy named Duncan Oaks. They were the prom king and queen in '61, the year they graduated. At some point, Laddie met Mark. They married in the summer of 1965, after he graduated from the University of Kentucky. Mark enlisted in the army right around the time Duncan Oaks was doing a series for the *Louisville Tribune*. I suspect Mark served in Vietnam, but I haven't pinned that down—"

"We can help on that. We haven't been exactly idle." Claas reached into his briefcase and removed a manila folder, which he opened, leafing through the contents. "Alpha Company, First Battalion, Fifth Cavalry."

"Well, great," I said. "I don't have a clue how it ties in, but maybe we'll figure that out. At any rate, Duncan had an idea for a series and began interviewing the soldiers' wives. His intention was to talk about the war from their differing perspectives, one off in Vietnam, the other stuck on the home front. I think Duncan and Laddie had a brief affair. Pure conjecture on my part. Within weeks, Duncan Oaks went to Vietnam. He and Mark must have crossed paths. In fact, Duncan probably sought him out for the second half of the interview."

"And?"

"That's as far as I can go."

Aldo said, "Maybe Mark fragged him. That's what it sounds like to me."

"Fragged?"

"You know, offed. Eliminated. Kilt him deader than a doornail. I mean, how hard could it be with bullets flying? It's not like the medics run ballistics tests."

I thought about it for a moment. "That's probably not a bad guess. Especially if Mark found out about the relationship between Duncan and his wife. . . ."

"Assuming there was one," Claas said.

"Well, yeah."

"Anyway, go on. Sorry for the interruption."

"I start faltering here and have to resort to waving my hands. I mean, I can put some of this together, but I don't have proof. Benny Quintero was another Louisville boy. I know Duncan and Benny were at Ia Drang together because I saw a picture of the two. According to my information, Duncan Oaks was wounded—by Mark, friendly fire, the NVA—we're never going to know, so we might as well skip that. In any event, he was loaded on a chopper filled with the wounded and the dead. By the time the chopper landed, he'd disappeared without a trace."

Aldo spoke up. "Maybe Mark's on the chopper and shoves him out the door. The guy falls—what? Six to twelve hundred feet, landing in the jungle? Trust me, in two weeks there's nothing left but bones. From what you say, Oaks wasn't even in the army, so it's perfect. Who gives a shit about a fucking journalist?"

I said, "Right. The point is, I think Benny knew and that's why he held on to Duncan's ID. Again, I don't have proof, but it does make sense. Maybe he thought of a way to turn a profit on the deal."

Claas said, "What happened to Benny?"

"He was wounded by sniper fire and ended up with a metal plate in his head. In 1971, he came out to California; that much we know. Mickey and Benny got in a shoving match. A day later, someone beat Benny senseless and he ended up dead." I went on to detail Mickey's history of misbehavior and why he'd looked good for the beating when Internal Affairs stepped in.

Claas said, "I don't see the relevance."

"Mark was Mickey's attorney. He's the one who advised him to leave the department to avoid questioning."

"Got it."

Aldo leaned forward. "Speaking of which, how'd Bethel end up with your Smith and Wesson? That seems like a trick."

"I think Mickey sold it to him. I have a record of a deposit in March for two hundred dollars. Mark told me Mickey called and asked for money. I know Mickey better than that. I know he'd hoarded a stash of gold coins and bills, but that was probably not something he would have dipped into. He sold his car about then and he was probably off-loading his other possessions, trying to make ends meet. The minute Mark bought the gun, he must have seen his way clear, because it was on that same trip he made the phone call from Mickey's apartment to my machine. All he had to do was distract Mickey's attention, dial the number, and let the tape run on when my machine picked up."

"What if you'd been there?"

"Sorry wrong number, and he tries the call later. He knew Mickey and Duffy were as thick as thieves by then. Whatever his faults, Mickey's always been a hell of a detective. Mark must have known it was only a matter of time. He had a gun registered to me. He'd established a connection to me on Mickey's telephone bill. I'd be implicated anyway as soon as the gun registration came to light."

Aldo snorted. "Fuckin' devious."

Claas rubbed his hands together, then stretched his

371

arms out in front of him, his fingers laced with the palms turned outward until I heard his knuckles crack. "Well, boys and girls, I've enjoyed the bedtime stories. Too bad none of this'll fly in court."

"Oh, yeah. Which brings us to the next step," Aldo said, chiming in on cue. "Shall I tell her the plan?"

I said, "I don't like this. It sounds rehearsed."

"Exactly," Claas said. "So here's what we thought. Forget Vietnam. We're never going to get him for whacking Duncan Oaks. No weapons, no witnesses, so we're out of luck on that score."

Aldo said, "Quintero's another one. I mean, even if you prove it, the best you can hope for is a manslaughter bust, which is strictly bullshit."

I said, "Which brings us to Mickey."

"And to you," Claas said. He reached in his briefcase and pulled out the tape recorder. He held it so I could see.

I said, "I knew that was in there."

"But did you know how well it works?" He pressed REWIND and then PLAY, producing a clear, unobstructed recording of the conversation we'd just had. "We figure you can put this in your handbag, trot yourself off to Bethel's, and maybe help us out."

"You have an eavesdropping warrant?"

"No, we don't."

"Isn't that illegal? I thought you needed a court order. Whatever happened to the Fourth Amendment?" This from Kinsey Millhone, upholder of the Constitution.

"What you'd be doing is called a consent recording. It's done all the time by informants and undercover cops. As long as you're only taping comments someone makes to you, the court doesn't have a problem. Worst-case scenario—assuming what you get is juicy— you use the tape to refresh your own memory when you testify in court."

"Now I'm testifying?"

"If Mickey dies, you do. Right?"

I could feel my attention shift from Aldo to Claas, who said, "Look at it this way. We're building a case. We gotta have something concrete for the DA."

Aldo leaned forward. "That's what we're in business to do, get this cocksucker nailed, if you'll excuse my Greek."

"And Mark won't guess what I'm up to? He's not a fool," I said.

"He's Mickey's *attorney*. You're back from Kentucky with a shitload of information and you're filling him in. How can he resist? He wants to know what *you* know so he can measure the depth of the hole he's in. Of course, if he figures you're on to him, he'll want to pop you next."

"Thanks. That helps. Now I'm really feeling good about all this."

"Come on. It's no sweat. He's not going to do it in his own living room."

Aldo moved to the phone, holding the receiver out. "Give him a call."

"Now?"

"Why not? Tell him you have some stuff you want to talk to him about."

"Yeah," I said cautiously. "And then what?"

"We haven't made that part up yet."

373

TWENTY-SIX

The Bethels' estate was on the outer edges of Montebello, perched on a bluff overlooking the Pacific Ocean. I'd spoken to Laddie on the phone and she'd given me directions to the house on Savanna Lane. Mark was out, but she said he'd be returning shortly. It worried me she hadn't voiced greater surprise or curiosity about the reason for my call. I'd mentioned the trip to Louisville, that I had something to discuss, preferably with the two of them, though I'd certainly value the opportunity to talk to her alone first. If she was alarmed about such a conversation, she gave no indication.

At seven on the dot, I pulled in at the gate. Detectives Claas and Aldo had followed me in their car, and they were parked in a grove of eucalyptus trees about a hundred yards off. I had the tape recorder in my bag, but I wasn't wired for sound so there was no way they could monitor the conversation once I was inside the house. No one (meaning them) seemed to think this would present a problem since I'd be in the Bethels' home with other people (meaning servants) on the premises. Our plan—if that's what you want to call it—was for them to hover on the sidelines, falling in behind me when I left the estate. Then we'd go back to my place, listen to the tape, and see if what we'd picked up constituted probable cause. If so, we'd find a judge who could sign a warrant for Mark's arrest on charges of assault with a deadly weapon and attempted murder in the shooting of Mickey Magruder. If not, we'd move to Plan B, on which we'd never quite agreed. On reflection, even Plan A seemed a bit half-assed, but I was there at the gate and I'd already pressed the button.

I expected to hear someone on the intercom asking for my name. Instead, there was silence. The gates simply swung open, allowing me entrance. I waved to the "boys" and put the car in gear. The driveway was long, curving off to the left. The land on either side was barren except for the grasses bending under the offshore winds. Occasionally, a tree broke the line of the horizon, a stark silhouette against the milder dark of the sky. I could see the lighted windows of the house, dazzling yellow and white, set in a bulky block of dark stone. I parked out in front on an enormous apron of gravel. I shut off the engine and sat taking in the sight of the house through the driver's side window.

The structure was curiously reminiscent of Duncan Oaks's house in Louisville. Despite the appearance of age, I knew construction had been completed only five years before, which might explain the absence of mature trees. The exterior was stone and stucco. Landscape lights washed the façade with its glaze of dusky pink underlaid with brown. In theory, the style was Mediterranean or Italianate, one of those bastard forms that Californians favor, but the arches above the windows seemed remarkably similar to their Kentucky counterpart. The front door was recessed, sheltered in a portico flanked by fluted columns. Even the balustrade was kindred in design. Was Laddie conscious of what she'd done or had she mimicked Duncan's house inadvertently? What is it that prompts us to reenact our unresolved issues? We revisit our wounds, constructing the past in hopes that this time we can make the ending turn out right.

The carriage lights on either side of the door came on. Reluctantly, I reached for my bag. I'd left the zippered compartment open, the tape recorder in easy range of my hand. I emerged from the car, crunched my way across the parking pad, and climbed the low front steps. Laddie opened the door before I had time to ring the bell. "Hello, Kinsey. How nice of you to drive all the way out here. I take it you had no trouble finding the place."

"Not at all. It's beautiful."

"We like it," she said mildly. "Can I take your jacket?"

"This is fine for now. It's cold."

She closed the door behind me. "Come on into the living room. I've got a nice fire burning. Will you have a drink? I'm having wine," she said. She was already walking toward the living room, her heels clicking smartly against the highly polished marble floors.

I followed her, saying, "I better not, but thanks. I had wine with dinner and that's my limit."

We stepped down into the living room, with its twelve-foot coffered ceiling. One entire wall of French doors looked on to a patio. The room was surprisingly light, done in shades of cream: the twenty- by twenty-four-foot rug, the walls, the three plump matching love seats arranged in a U in front of the fireplace. There were touches of black in the throw pillows and lampshades, Boston ferns providing spots of green here and there. Maybe I could snitch some ideas for my spacious abode. The coffee table was a square of three-quarter-inch glass resting on three enormous polished brass spheres. A second wineglass sat near a bottle of Chardonnay in an insulated cooler. Laddie'd made quite a dent for someone drinking alone. I flicked on the tape recorder during the momentary lull as she picked up her wineglass and settled on one of the sofas that flanked the fireplace. The hearth was a glossy black granite that reflected the blaze. Really, I was taking notes—I had to have one of those.

I sat down opposite her, wondering how to begin. These transitions can be awkward, especially when you're trying to shift the discussion from niceties to the subject of murder.

She said, "What were you doing in Louisville? We used to go for the Derby, but it's been ages."

A maid came to the door. "I left Mr. Bethel's plate in the warming oven. Will there be anything else?"

"No, dear. That's fine. We'll see you in the morning."

"Yes, ma'am," the woman said, and then withdrew.

I said, "Actually, I went to Louisville on a research trip. Do you remember Benny Quintero, the fellow who was killed here a few years ago?"

"Of course. Mark represented Mickey."

377

"Well, as it happens, Benny was from Louisville. He went to Manual the same time you were at Louisville Male High."

Her lips parted in expectation. "What kind of research *was* this? I can't imagine."

"I keep thinking there's a connection between Benny Quintero's death and Mickey's being shot last week."

Laddie's frown was delicate. "That's quite a leap."

"Not really," I said, "though it does seem odd. Here the four of you come from the same hometown—"

"Four?"

"Sure. You, Mark, Benny, and Duncan Oaks. You remember Duncan," I said.

"Of course, but he's been gone for years."

"My point exactly," I said. Gee, this was going better than I'd thought. "During his stint in Vietnam, Mark was at Ia Drang, right?"

"You'd have to verify that with him, but I believe so."

"Turns out Benny was there too."

Laddie blinked. "I'm not following. What does any of this have to do with me?"

"Let me back up a step. Didn't Duncan Oaks interview you for the *Louisville Tribune*?"

She said, "Kinsey, what *is* this? I don't mean to be rude, but you're skipping back and forth and I'm confused. I really don't see the relevance."

"Just hear me out," I said. "Duncan was doing a series for the local paper. He interviewed army wives, like you, who'd been left behind—you know, talking about the war from their perspective. His idea was to tell the same story through the eyes of the husbands off fighting in Vietnam."

Laddie shook her head, shrugging. "I guess I'll have to take your word for it."

"At any rate, he did talk to you."

She took a sip of wine. "It's possible. I don't remember."

"Don't worry about the date. I've asked his editor to send a copy of the article. We can pin it down from that. Anyway, Duncan's editor says he flew to Vietnam in September of '65. He ran into Mark and Benny at Ia Drang, which was where Duncan disappeared." I was doling out pure theory, but I noticed she'd stopped offering much in the way of objections. "Seven years later Benny shows up in Santa Teresa with Duncan Oaks's ID. The next thing you know, Benny's been murdered. You see the link?"

"Benny wasn't *murdered*. You're overstating the situation. As I remember, Benny had a subdural hematoma, and his death was the result of an arterial bleed. Given the nature of his injury, it could have happened any time. Even the coroner's report said that."

"Really? You're probably right. You have quite a memory for the details," I said.

"Mark and I discussed it at the time. I suppose it stuck in my mind."

"Mickey's another link. He went off to Louisville on Thursday, May eighth. He came back on Monday, and in the wee hours of Wednesday morning he was shot, as you know."

Laddie's smile was thin. "Not to sound superior,

but you're committing what's called a post hoc fallacy. Just because one event follows another doesn't mean there's a cause-and-effect relationship."

"I see. In other words, just because Benny knew something doesn't mean he died for it."

"Is this what you wanted to discuss with Mark?"

"In part."

"Then let's leave that. I'm sure it's more appropriate to wait till he comes in."

I said, "Fine. Could we talk about your relationship with Duncan?"

"I'd hardly call it a relationship. I knew him, of course. We went all through school together."

"Were you pals, confidants, boyfriend/girlfriend?"

"We were friends, that's all. There was never anything between us, if that's what you're getting at."

"Actually, it is," I said. "I thought since you were the king and queen of the senior prom, you might have been sweet on each other."

Laddie smiled, her composure restored. This was something she'd thought about; her version of the story was preassembled and prepackaged. "Duncan wasn't interested in me romantically, nor I in him."

"Too bad. He looked cute."

"He was cute. He was also extremely narcissistic, which I found obnoxious. There's nothing worse than a seventeen-year-old kid who thinks he's hot stuff."

"You don't think he was charismatic?"

"*He* thought he was," she said. "I thought he was conceited—nice, funny, but such a snob."

"What about your father?"

She looked at me askance. "My father? What's he have to do with this?"

"This is peripheral and probably none of my business—"

"None of this is your business," she said, bridling.

I smiled to show I hadn't taken offense. "I was told he was awarded a patent that earned him a lot of money. I gather, before that, he was considered a bit eccentric."

"If he was, so what? Make your point."

"I'm just thinking his fortune must have changed people's perception of you. Duncan's, in particular."

She was silent.

"Yes? No?"

"I suppose," she said.

"You went from being one down to one up where he was concerned. He sounds like the type who enjoyed a conquest—to prove he could do it, if nothing else."

"Are you trying to build a case for something?"

"I'm just trying to get a feel for what kind of guy he was."

"A dead one."

"Before that. You never had a fling with him?"

"Oh, please. Don't be silly. We never had an *affair*."

"Hey, an affair is six weeks or more. A fling can be anything from one night to half a dozen."

"I never had a fling with him, either."

"When did Mark leave for Vietnam? I know you married him in June. His orders came through. . . ."

"July twenty-sixth," she said, biting off the words.

"The way I read the situation, Duncan was in

381

Louisville after Mark shipped out. There you were, a young newlywed with a husband off at war. I'm sure you were lonely . . . needy. . . ."

"This is offensive. You're being extremely insulting, not only to me but to Mark."

"Insulting about what?" Mark said from the corridor. He shrugged out of his overcoat and tossed it over the back of a chair. He must have come in through the kitchen. His high forehead and receding hairline gave him an air of innocence, the same look babies have before they learn to bite and talk back. Laddie got up to greet him. I watched the two of them as he bussed her cheek.

He said, "Hang on a minute while I make a quick call." He crossed to the phone and dialed 9-1-1.

Laddie said, "What's going on?"

Mark raised a finger to indicate the dispatcher had picked up. "Hi, this is Mark Bethel. I'm at Four-forty-eight Savanna Lane. I've got a couple of guys parked in a car near the entrance to my gate. Could you have a patrol car cruise by? I really don't like the looks of them. . . . Thanks. I'd appreciate that." He replaced the handset and turned to Laddie and me with a shake of his head. "Probably harmless, a lovers' tryst, but just on the off chance they're casing the place. . . ." He rubbed his palms together. "I could use a glass of wine."

I tried to picture Detectives Claas and Aldo busted by the local cops on a morals charge.

Laddie poured Chardonnay in a glass, holding it by the stem so as not to smudge the bowl. The trembling of her hand caused the wine to wobble in the glass.

Mark didn't seem to notice. He took the glass and sat down, giving me his full attention. "I hope I didn't interrupt."

"We were talking about Benny Quintero," Laddie said. "She's just back from Louisville, where she did some research."

"Benny. Poor guy."

I said, "I didn't realize you were all from the same town."

"Well, that's not strictly true. I was born in Dayton. My family moved to Louisville when I was six. I lived there till I went off to U of K."

"And you knew Benny then?"

"I knew *of* him, just as he must have known about me from football games."

"I didn't realize you played football."

"More or less," he said ruefully. "I went to Atherton, which was all girls for years. School didn't go coed until 1954. Even then, we seldom won a game against Manual or Male. Mostly, the players knew each other by reputation. I remember there was a guy named Byck Snell at Eastern. . . ."

"So Benny came to California and looked you up," I said.

"Right. He must have heard I was a lawyer and somehow got it in his head I could help him with his VA benefits. I mean, it's like I told him: Just because I'm an attorney doesn't make me an expert. In those days, I knew next to nothing about the Veterans Administration. Now, of course, I'm educating myself on the issues because I can see what a difference I can make—"

I said, "Sounds like a campaign speech."

Mark smiled. "Sorry. At any rate, I couldn't seem to convince Benny of my ignorance. The whole thing was ludicrous, but I couldn't get him off it. The guy started stalking me, appeared at the office, appeared at the house. The phone started ringing at all hours of the night. Laddie was getting nervous, and I couldn't blame her. That's when I asked Mickey to step in and see what he could do."

"Meaning what?"

I could see him hesitate. "Well, you know, Mickey was a tough guy. I thought he could put the fear of God in him. I'm not saying Mickey meant to hurt him, but he did make threats."

"When?"

"During the incident in the Honky-Tonk parking lot."

"You talked to Benny after that?"

"Sure. He called me and he was furious. I said I'd talk to Mickey. I made a few calls but never managed to track him down, as you well know."

"Because he and Dixie were together," I said, helping him along.

"So they claimed. Frankly, I've always wondered. It seemed pretty damn convenient under the circumstances."

"So you're saying Mickey went back to Benny and beat the shit out of him."

"I'm saying it's possible. Mickey always had a temper. He hated it when some punk got the best of him."

"I hardly think Benny got the best of him. Shack says it was a shoving match with no blows exchanged."

"Well, that's true. Actually, I heard the same report from the other witnesses. The point is, Mickey came off looking bad, and for a guy like him that's worse."

"You know, this is the second time you've implicated Mickey."

"Hey, I'm sorry, but you asked."

"Why didn't you ever mention you knew Benny back in high school?"

"When did I have the chance? In those days, you barely spoke to me. And since then, believe me, I've been acutely aware you're not a fan of mine. We run into each other in public, you practically duck and hide, you're so anxious to avoid contact. Anyway, that aside, you weren't speaking to Mickey either, or he'd have told you the same thing."

I felt myself color at his accuracy. And here I thought I was so subtle. "Can I ask one more thing?"

"What's that?" Mark took a sip of his drink.

"After you joined the army, you were sent to Vietnam. Is that correct?"

"Absolutely. I'm proud of my service record."

"I'm sure you are," I said. "Benny Quintero was there and so was Duncan Oaks." I went on, giving him a hasty summation of what I'd learned from Porter Yount.

Mark's face took on the look of a man who's trying to pay attention while his mind is somewhere else. I could tell he was thinking hard, composing his response before I'd finished what I was saying. His resulting smile held an element of puzzlement. "You have to understand there were hundreds of guys who fought at Ia Drang. The one/five, the one/seven, the two/seven, the Second Battalion Nineteenth Artillery, the Two-twenty-seventh Assault Helicopter Battalion, the Eighth Engineer Battalion—"

"Got it," I said. "There were lots of guys. I got that, but Duncan was a journalist and he went out there specifically to talk to you because of the series he was writing. He must have told you he talked to Laddie. My guess is you'd felt threatened by him for years. He and Laddie were tight. She was poor in those days and never good enough for him, but I'll bet her classmates would tell me she'd had a crush on him, that she'd have given her eyeteeth for his attention—"

"That's absurd. That's ridiculous," Laddie interjected.

Mark made a motion with his hand that told her to hush, the sort of command you teach a dog in obedience training. She closed her mouth, but the significance of the gesture wasn't lost on her. Mark was clearly annoyed. "Let's get to the bottom line. What are you suggesting?"

"I'm suggesting the three of you connected up. You and Benny and Duncan Oaks."

Mark was shaking his head. "No. Wrong."

I said, "Yes. Right. I have a snapshot of the two of them, and you're visible in the background."

Laddie said, "So what?"

"I'll take care of this," he said to her. And then to me, "Go on. This is fascinating. Clearly, you've cooked up some theory and you're trying to make the pieces fit."

"I know how they fit. Duncan interviewed Laddie for the paper after you shipped out. By then, her daddy had money and Duncan couldn't resist. After all, a conquest is a conquest, however late it comes. The two had a fling and you found out about it. Either she 'fessed up or he told you himself—"

Laddie said, "I don't want to talk about this. It's over and done. I made a mistake, but it was years ago."

"Yeah, and I know who paid," I said caustically.

"Laddie, for God's sake, would you shut your mouth!" He turned back to me again, his face dark. "And?"

"And you killed him. Benny Quintero saw it and that's why he was hounding you. You set Mickey up. You killed Benny and made sure Mickey took the rap for it."

Mark's tone was light, but it wasn't sincere. "And you're saying what, that I shot Mickey too?"

"Yes."

He held his hands out, baffled. "Why would I do that?"

"Because he'd put it together the same way I have."

"Wait a minute, Kinsey. Duncan's body was never found, so for all you know he's alive and well. You think you can make a charge like this without evidence?"

"I have the snapshot. That helps."

"Oh, that's right. The snapshot. What crap. I think I better call your bluff. You have it with you?"

"I left it with a friend."

Mark snapped his fingers. "I forgot about Benny's brother. What's his name again? Duffy. Carlin Duffy. Now, there's a bright guy."

387

I said nothing.

He went on. "My sources tell me he's living in a shack at Himes Nursery. With his criminal history, it should be easy enough to put the screws to him."

"I thought you weren't worried."

"Call it cleanup," he said.

"Really. Now that you're running for public office, you have to bury your misdeeds, make sure the past won't rise up and bite you in the butt when you're least expecting it."

He pointed at me. "Bingo."

"Did you hate him that much?"

"Duncan? I'll tell you what pissed me off about that guy. Not so much that he screwed Laddie the minute my back was turned, but he showed up at Ia Drang, trying to pass himself off as a grunt. I had buddies— good friends, young guys—who died with valor, brave men who believed in what we were doing. I saw them die in agony, maimed and mutilated, limbs gone, gut- shot. Duncan Oaks was a sleaze. He had money and pretensions but not an ounce of decency. He deserved to die, and I was happy to help him out. Speaking of which, I'd like to have his personal effects."

"Effects?"

"Press pass, dog tags."

"I can't help you there. You'd have to talk to Duffy about those things."

From the depths of my shoulder bag, there was a small but distinct click as the tape ran out and the recorder shut itself off. Mark's gaze flicked down and then flicked up to my face. His smile faded, and I heard

Laddie's sharp intake of breath. He held his hand out. "You want to give me that?"

"Hey, Dad?"

The three of us turned in unison. The Bethels' son, Malcolm, was standing in the door to the dining room.

"What is it?" Mark said, trying not to sound impatient with the kid.

"Can I take your Mercedes? I've got a date."

"Of course."

Malcolm continued to stand there. "I need the keys."

"Well, get a move on. We're in the middle of a conversation here," Mark said, waving him into the room.

Malcolm shot me a look of embarrassment as he entered the room. Impatiently, Mark removed his keys from his pocket, twisting the key from the ring as he separated it from the others. Meanwhile, I was staring at the kid. No wonder the photographs of Duncan Oaks had seemed familiar. I'd seen him . . . or his incarnation . . . in Laddie's son. The same youth, the same dark, distinctly handsome looks. Malcolm, at twenty, was the perfect blend of Duncan at seventeen and Duncan at twenty-three. I turned to Laddie, who must have known the final piece of the puzzle had fallen into place.

She said, "Mark." He glanced at her, and the two exchanged a quick piece of nonverbal communication.

"Where're you off to, Malcolm?" I said, ever the chipper one.

"I'm taking my girlfriend to a kegger out on campus."

389

"Great. I'm just leaving. I think I'll follow you out. I got lost coming in. Could you steer me in the right direction?"

"Sure, no problem. I'll be happy to," he said.

I kept a careful eye on the rear of Mark Bethel's black Mercedes as Malcolm drove slowly down the driveway ahead of me. In my rearview mirror, I saw another set of headlights come into view. Mark had apparently made a scramble for Laddie's BMW, a sporty red model perfect for a hit-and-run fatality or a high-speed chase. In front of me, Malcolm had just reached the gates, triggering the automatic mechanism buried in the drive. Slowly, the gates swung open. Out on the road, I spotted two Santa Teresa Sheriff's Department cars pulled onto the berm, lights flashing. Four deputies were in conversation with Detectives Claas and Aldo, who were just in the process of identifying themselves. Malcolm turned left onto Savanna and I followed in his wake. Detective Aldo caught my eye, but there was no way he could help until the deputies had finished with them. So much for Plan A.

I checked the rearview mirror. Mark was so close on my tail, I could see the smirk on his face. I hugged the back end of the Mercedes, figuring Mark wouldn't ram me or shoot as long as Malcolm was close by. Maybe I'd accompany Malcolm and his girlfriend to the kegger out on campus, have a beer, shoot the shit, anything to avoid Mark. We passed a cemetery on the left and slowed at the intersection by the bird refuge. Malcolm tapped his horn and gave a final wave, turning left on Cabana while I turned right and headed for the freeway.

I took the 101 north, keeping my speed at a steady 60 mph. I could see Mark keeping pace. Traffic was light. Not a cop on the road. I groped through my bag, fumbling among the contents with one hand while I steered with the other. I popped the used tape out, leaned over and opened the glove compartment, tossed the tape in, and closed it. I pulled a fresh cassette from the packet on the passenger seat and inserted it in the tape recorder. I didn't have my gun. I'm a private investigator, not a vigilante. Most of my work takes place in the public library or the hall of records. Generally speaking, these places aren't dangerous, and I seldom need a semiautomatic to protect myself.

Now what? I had, of course, invented the bit about Mark's being in the snapshot, visible as a backdrop to Duncan and Benny's reunion. If such a picture existed, it certainly wasn't in my hands . . . or Duffy's, for that matter. I winced. The very notion had put Mark on a tear, thinking we had evidence of their association. Big damn deal. Even if we had such a picture, what would that prove? I should have kept my mouth shut. Poor Duffy didn't have a clue as to what misery was bearing down on him. The last time I'd seen him he was drunk as a coot, passed out on his cot.

I took the Peterson off-ramp and turned left at the light. I didn't bother to speed up or make any tricky moves. Mark didn't seem to be in any hurry either. He knew where I was going, and if I went somewhere else, he'd go to Himes anyway. I think he liked the idea of this slow-paced pursuit, catching up at his leisure while

I was frantically casting about for help. I turned right onto the side street and right again into the nursery parking lot. Mine was the only car. The garden center was closed. The building's interior was dim except for a light here and there to discourage the odd burglar with a green thumb or an urge for potted plants. The rest of the acreage was blanketed in darkness.

I parked, locked the car, and headed off on foot. I confess I ran, having given up all pretense of being casual about these things. Glancing back, I could see the headlights of the Beamer as it eased into the lot. I was waiting for the sound of the car door slamming, but Mark had bumped his way across the low concrete barrier and was driving down the wide lanes between the crated trees. I cut back and forth, holding my shoulder bag against me to keep it from jostling as I increased my pace. Idly, I realized the maze of boxed trees had shifted. Lanes I remembered from earlier were gone or rotated on an axis, now shooting off on parallel routes. I wasn't sure if trees had been added, subtracted, or simply rearranged. Maybe Himes had a landscape project that required a half-grown arbor.

I yelled Duffy's name, hoping to alert him in advance of my arrival, but the sound seemed to be absorbed by the portable forest that surrounded me.

Mark was still barreling along behind me, but at least the narrow twists and turns were slowing him down. I felt like I was stoned, everything moving at half speed—including me. I reached the maintenance shed, heart thumping, breath ragged. The yellow forklift was now blocking the lane, parked beside the shed with a crated fifteen-foot tree hoisted on the forks. The shed door was open and a pale light spilled out on the path like water.

"Duffy?" I called.

The lights were on in his makeshift tent, but there was no sign of him. His shoes were missing and the blanket I'd laid over him was now crumpled on the floor. A cheap saucepan sat on the hot plate filled with a beige sludge that looked like refried beans. A plastic packet of flour tortillas sat, unopened, on the unused burner. The pan still felt warm so maybe he'd stepped out to take a leak. I heard the BMW skid to a halt.

"Duffy!"

I checked the top of the orange crate. Duncan Oaks's press pass, his dog tags, and the snapshot were still lying where I'd left them. Outside, I heard the car door slam, the sound of someone thumping in my direction. I gathered Duncan's things in haste, looking for a place to hide them before Bethel appeared. Quickly, I considered and discarded the idea of hiding the items in Duffy's clothes. The shed itself was crude, with little in the way of furniture and no nooks or crannies. In the absence of insulation, I was looking at bare studs, not so much as a toolbox where I could stash the stuff. I shoved the items in my back pocket just as Mark appeared in the doorway, a gun in his hand.

"Oh, shit," I said.

"I'd appreciate your handing me the tape recorder and the tape."

"No problem," I said. I reached in my shoulder bag, took out the tape recorder, and held it out to him. While I watched, he tucked the tape recorder up against his body, pressed the EJECT button with his free hand, and extracted the cassette. He dropped the tape recorder on the dirt floor and crushed it with his foot. Behind him, I caught a flicker of movement. Duffy appeared in the doorway and then eased back out of sight.

"I don't get it," I said. I focused on Mark, making sure I didn't telegraph Duffy's presence with my eyes.

"Get what?" Mark was distracted. He tried to keep his eyes pinned on me while he held the gun and cassette in one hand and unraveled the tape with the other, pulling off the reel. Loops of thin, shiny ribbon were tangled in his fingers, trailing to the floor in places.

"I don't understand what you're so worried about. There's nothing on there that would incriminate you."

"I can't be sure what Laddie said before I showed."

"She was the soul of discretion," I said dryly.

Mark smiled in spite of himself. "What a champ."

"Why'd you kill Benny?"

"To get him off my back. What'd you think?"

"Because he knew you killed Duncan?"

"Because he saw me do it."

"Just like that?"

"Just like that. Call it a flash of inspiration. Six of us were loaded with the body bags. Duncan was pissing and moaning, but I could tell he wasn't hurt bad. Fuckin' baby. Before we could lift off, the medic was killed by machine-gun fire. Benny seemed to be out of it. I'd been shot in the leg, and I'd taken a load of shrapnel in my back and side. Up we went. I remember the chopper shuddering, and I didn't think we'd make it under all the small arms fire. The minute we were airborne, I crawled over to Duncan, stripped him of his ID, ripped the tags off his neck, and tossed 'em aside. All the time the chopper lurched and vibrated like a crazy man was shaking it back and forth. Duncan lay there looking at me, but I don't think he fully understood what I was doing until I hoisted him out. Benny saw me, the shit. He pretended he'd passed out, but he saw the whole deal. By then, I was light-headed and rolled over on my side, sick with sweat. That's when Benny took the tags and hid 'em. . . ."

"I take it he pressed you too hard."

"Hey, I did what I could for him. In the end, I killed him as much for being dumb as trying to screw me over when he should have left well enough alone."

"And Mickey?"

"Let's cut the chitchat and get on with this." He snapped his fingers, pointing to the bag.

"I don't have a gun."

"It's Duncan's tags I want."

"I left the stuff sitting on the orange crate. Duffy must have taken it."

Mark snapped his fingers, gesturing for me to hand him the bag.

"I lied about the snapshot."

"GIVE ME THE FUCKIN' BAG!"

I passed him my shoulder bag and watched while he searched. His holding the gun necessitated working with the bag clamped against his chest. This made it tricky to inspect the interior while he kept an eye on me. Impatiently, he tipped the bag upside down, dumping out the contents. Somewhere nearby, I heard the low rumble of heavy equipment and I found myself praying, *Please, please, please.*

Mark heard it too. He tossed the bag to one side and motioned with the gun, indicating I should leave before him. I was suddenly afraid. While we talked, while we stood face-to-face, I didn't believe he'd kill me because I didn't think he'd have the nerve. My own fate had seemed curiously out of my hands. What mattered at that point was knowing the truth, finding out what had happened to Duncan and Benny and Mick. Now the act of turning my back was almost more than I could bear.

I moved toward the door. I could hear the deep growl of a diesel motor, some piece of machinery picking up speed as it advanced. My skin felt radiant. Anxiety snaked through my gut like summer lightning. I yearned to see what Mark was doing. I wondered if the gun was pointed at my back, wondered if he was, even then, in the process of releasing the safety, tightening his index finger on the trigger, speeding me to my death. Most of all, I wondered if the bullet would hit me before I heard the sound of the shot.

I heard the crack of sudden impact and glanced back, watching with astonishment as the shed wall blew in, boards splintering on contact as the tractor plowed through. Duffy's cot was crushed under the rolling track, which seemed to have the weight and destructive power of a moving tank. The front-mounted bucket banged into the space heater and sent it flying in my direction. I ducked my head, but the heater caught me in the back with an impetus that knocked me to my knees. As I scrambled to my feet, I looked over my shoulder. The entire rear wall of the shed had been demolished.

Duffy threw the tractor in reverse and backed out of the flattened structure, doing a three-point turn. I ran, emerging from the shed in time to see Mark jump into the BMW and jam the key in the ignition. The engine ground ineffectually, but never coughed to life. Duffy, in the tractor, bore down on the vehicle. From the grin on his face, I had to guess he'd disabled the engine. Mark took aim and fired at Duffy, perched high in the tractor cab. I was caught between the two men, and I paused, mesmerized by the violence unfolding. My heart burned in my chest and the urge to run was almost overpowering. I could see that Mark was corralled in the cul-de-sac formed by the wreckage of the shed, a row of crated trees, and the tractor, which was picking up speed again as Duffy accelerated. I was blocking his only avenue of escape.

Mark started running in my direction, apparently hoping to blow by me in his bid for freedom. He fired at Duffy again and the bullet zinged off the cab with a musical note. Duffy worked the lever that controlled the lift arm as the tractor bore down on him. I started running at Mark. He veered off at the last minute, reversing himself. He jumped up on one of the crates, hoping to crash through the trees to the aisle just behind. I caught him midair and shoved him. He bungled the leap, toppled backward, and fell on me. We went down in a heap. As he scuttled to his feet, I reached out and snagged his ankle, holding on for dear life. He staggered, half-dragging me into Duffy's path. Duffy stomped on the accelerator. I released Mark and rolled sideways. The tractor lurched forward, diesel engine rumbling, the bucket lever screeching as Duffy maneuvered it. Mark pivoted, trying to launch himself in the opposite direction, but Duffy bore down on him, the bucket extended like a cradle. Mark turned to face the tractor, gauging its momentum in hopes of dodging its mass. He fired another round, but it clanged harmlessly off the bucket. He'd badly misjudged Duffy's skill. The metal lip banged into Mark's chest with an impact that nearly lifted him off his feet, driving him back against the side wall of the shed. For a moment, he hung there, pinned between the bucket and the wall. He struggled, his weight pulling him down until the lip of the bucket rested squarely against his throat. Duffy looked over at me, and I could see his expression soften. He propelled the tractor forward, and Mark's neatly severed head thumped into the bucket like a cantaloupe.

It wasn't *quite* Plan B, but it would have to do.

EPILOGUE

The bust at the Honky-Tonk didn't come down for another six months. A federal grand jury returned a fifteen-count indictment against Tim Littenberg and a twelve-count indictment against Scott Shackelford for manufacturing counterfeit credit cards, which carries a minimum five-year prison term and a $250,000 fine for each conviction. Both are currently free on bail. Carlin Duffy was arrested and charged with voluntary manslaughter and he's awaiting trial in the Santa Teresa County jail, with its volleyball, indoor tawlits, and color television sets.

Mickey died on June 1. Later, I sold his handguns, pooling the proceeds with the cash and gold coins I'd lifted from his apartment. Mickey'd never bothered to change his will and since I was named sole beneficiary, his estate (including some pension monies he'd tucked in a separate account, plus fifty thousand dollars in life insurance) came to me. Probably out of guilt, Pete Shackelford made good on the ten grand Tim Littenberg owed Mickey so that, in the end, there was quite a substantial sum that I turned over to the Santa Teresa Police Department to use as they saw fit. If he'd survived, I suspect Mickey would have been one of those miserly eccentrics who live like paupers and leave millions to charity.

As it happened, I sat with him, my gaze fixed on the monitor above his bed. I watched the staggered line of his beating heart, strong and steady, though his color began to fade and his breathing became more labored as the days went by. I touched his face, feeling the cool flesh that would never be warm again. After the rapture of love comes the wreckage, at least in my experience. I thought of all the things he'd taught me, the things we'd been to one another during that brief marriage. My life was the richer for his having been part of it. Whatever his flaws, whatever his failings, his redemption was something he'd earned in the end. I laid my cheek against his hand and breathed with him until the last breath. "You done good, kid," I whispered, when he was still at last.

Respectfully submitted,
Kinsey Millhone

P is for Peril

The author wishes to acknowledge the invaluable assistance of the following people: Steven Humphrey; Captain Ed Aasted (ret.), and Sergeant Brian Abbott, Santa Barbara Police Department; Melinda Johnson; Jamie Raney, attorney-at-law; Sam Eaton, attorney-at-law; Lynn McLaren, private investigator; E. Robert Jones, D.D.S.; Hildy Hoffman, Santa Barbara's Mayor's Office; Robert Failing, M.D., forensic pathologist (ret.); Judy Crippen; Tracy Brown; Norm Arnold; Sheila Harker, Lynn Lazaro, R.N., and Joyce Tevenan, R.N.; Leslie Minschke, RHIA; Ron Shenkman of Ron Shenkman & Associates; Lorna Backus, Santa Barbara County Department of Vital Statistics; John Hunt, Compu Vision; Jamie Clark; and Neville Blakemore.

With a special thank you to Alan Cates, Chief, Medi-Cal Fraud Prevention Bureau, State of California.

ONE

The house on Old Reservoir Road appeared to be in the final phases of construction. I spotted the site as I rounded the curve, recognizing the unfinished structure from Fiona Purcell's description. To my right, I could see a portion of the reservoir for which the road was named. Brunswick Lake fills the bottom of a geological bowl, a spring-fed body that supplied the town with drinking water for many years. In 1953 a second, larger catch basin was established, and now Brunswick is little more than an irregular blue splotchlet on maps of the area. Swimming and boating are forbidden, but seasonally the migrating water birds rest on the placid surface as they make their way south. The surrounding hills are austere, gentle swells rising to the mountains that mark the northernmost boundary of the Santa Teresa city limits.

I parked my VW on the gravel berm and crossed the two-lane road. The steeply pitched lot was still bare of landscaping and consisted entirely of raw dirt and boulders with a dusting of weeds taking hold. At street level, a big commercial Dumpster was piled high with debris. A small grove of signs planted in the yard announced the names of the building contractor, the painting contractor, and the architect, though Mrs. Purcell had been quick to assure me by phone that she'd drawn up the plans herself. The design—if that's what you want to call it—would have been approved by the Department of Defense: an implacable series of concrete boxes, staunch and unadorned, stacked up against the hillside under a pale November sun. The facade was as blank as a bunker, a radical contrast to the sprawling Spanish-style homes on adjacent proper-ties. Somewhere to the rear of the house, there must have been a driveway leading to garages and a parking pad, but I opted for the stairs built into the barren hillside. At six A.M., I'd done a three-mile jog, but I'd skipped my Friday-morning weight lifting to keep this early appointment. It was just now eight o'clock and I could feel my butt dragging as I mounted the steps.

Behind me, I could hear a dog bark. Its deep-throated yaps echoed through the canyon, conveying a message of excitement. A woman was calling, "Trudy! *Truuddy!*" while the dog barked on. She emitted a piercing whistle, and a young German shepherd came bounding over the hill, heading in my direction at full speed. I waited, bracing myself for the force of muddy feet, but at the last possible second, the whistle came again and the dog sprinted off. I continued climbing Fiona's wide concrete steps, tacking twice before I reached the upper terrace with its plain limestone portico that shaded the front entrance. By then, my thighs were burning, I was huffing and puffing, and my heart was *rat-a-tat-tatting* like machine-gun fire. I could have sworn there was less oxygen in the air up here, but I'd actually only climbed the equivalent of two stories and I knew it was probably no more than three- to four-hundred feet above sea level. I turned, pretending to admire the view while I recovered my breath.

From this aerie, I could see the broad, shimmering band of the Pacific Ocean stitched to the shoreline some five miles away. Before me, the day was so clear, I could almost count the mountain ridges on the islands twenty-six miles out. Behind me, the clouds were peering over the mountaintops, a fast-moving blanket of dark gray in advance of a storm. San Francisco, four hundred miles to the north of us, was already feeling its lash.

By the time I rang the bell, my breathing had slowed and I'd done a quick mental review of the subject I was here to discuss. Fiona Purcell's ex-husband, Dr. Dowan Purcell, had been missing for nine weeks. She'd had a messenger deliver a manila envelope filled with newspaper clippings that recapped events surrounding his disappearance. I'd sat in my office, tilted back in my swivel chair, my Sauconys propped on the edge of my desk while I studied the articles she'd sent. She'd arranged them chronologically but had otherwise presented them without editorial comment. I'd been following the story in the local papers, but I'd never anticipated my involvement in the case. I found it helpful to have the sequence laid out again in this truncated form.

I noticed that over the course of nine weeks, the character of the coverage had shifted from the first seventy-two hours of puzzlement, through days of feverish speculation, and into the holding pattern that represented the current state of the investigation. Nothing new had come to light—not that there was ever much to report. In the absence of fresh revelations, the public's fascination had begun to dwindle and the media's attention to the matter had become as chilly and abbreviated as the brief November days. It is a truth of human nature that we can ponder life's mysteries for only so long before we lose interest and move on to something else. Dr. Purcell had been gone since Friday, September 12, and the lengthy column inches initially devoted to his disappearance were now reduced to an occasional mention nearly ritual in its tone. The details were recounted, but the curiosity had shifted to more compelling events.

Dr. Purcell, sixty-nine years old, had practiced family medicine in Santa Teresa since 1944, specializing in geriatrics for the last fifteen years. He'd retired in 1981. Six months later, he'd been licensed as the administrator of a nursing care facility called Pacific Meadows, which was owned by two businessmen. On the Friday night in question, he'd worked late, remaining in his office to review paperwork related to the operation of the nursing home. According to witnesses, it was close to nine o'clock when he stopped at the front desk and said good-night to the nurses on duty. At that hour, the occupants had settled down for the night. The corridors were empty and the residents' doors were closed against the already dimmed hall lights. Dr. Purcell had paused to chat with an elderly woman sitting in the lobby in her wheelchair. After a cursory conversation, less than a minute by her report, the doctor passed through the front door and into the night. He retrieved his car from his reserved space at the north side of the complex, pulled out of the lot, and drove off into the Inky Void from which he'd never emerged. The Santa Teresa Police and the Santa Teresa County Sheriff's Departments had devoted endless hours to the case, and I couldn't think what avenues remained that hadn't already been explored by local law enforcement.

I rang the bell again. Fiona Purcell had told me she was on her way out of town, a five-day trip to San

Francisco to purchase furniture and antiques for a client of her interior design firm. According to the papers, Fiona and the doctor had been divorced for years. Idly, I was wondering why she'd been the one who called me instead of his current wife, Crystal.

I saw a face appear in one of the two glass panels that flanked the entrance. When she opened the door, I saw that she was already dressed for travel in a double-breasted pin-striped suit with wide lapels. She held a hand out. "Ms. Millhone? Fiona Purcell. Sorry to make you wait. I was at the back of the house. Please come in."

"Thanks. You can call me Kinsey if you like. Nice meeting you," I said.

We shook hands and I moved into the entrance hall. Her handshake was limp, always startling in someone who, otherwise, seems brisk and businesslike. I placed her in her late sixties, close to Dr. Purcell's age. Her hair was dyed a dark brown, parted on one side, with puffy bangs and clusters of artificially constructed curls pulled away from her face and secured by rhinestone combs, a style affected by glamour-girl movie stars of the 1940s. I half-expected an appearance by John Agar or Fred MacMurray, some poor, feckless male who'd fallen prey to this vixen with her fierce shoulder pads. She was saying, "We can talk in the living room. You'll have to pardon the mess."

Scaffolding had been erected in the foyer, reaching to the lofty ceiling. Drop cloths lined the stairs and the wide corridor leading to the rear of the house. To one side of the stairs, there was a console table and a streamlined chrome lamp. Currently, we seemed to be the only two on the premises.

"Your flight's at ten?" I asked.

"Don't worry about it. I'm eight minutes from the airport. We have at least an hour. May I offer you coffee? I'm having mine in here."

"No, thanks. I've had two cups this morning and that's my limit most days."

Fiona moved to the right and I followed in her wake, crossing a broad expanse of bare cement. I said, "When do the floors go in?"

"These *are* the floors."

I said, "Ah," and made a mental note to quit asking about matters far beyond my ken.

The interior of the house had the cool, faintly damp smell of plaster and fresh paint. All the walls in range were a dazzling white, the windows tall and stark, unadorned by any curtains or drapes. A sly glance behind me revealed what was probably the dining room on the far side of the entryway, empty of furniture, subdivided by rhomboids of clear morning light. The echo of our footsteps sounded like a small parade.

In the living room, Fiona gestured toward one of

two matching armchairs, chunky and oversized, up-holstered in a neutral-toned fabric that blended with the gray cement floor. A large area rug showed a densely woven grid of black lines on gray. I sat when she did, watching as she surveyed the space with the practiced eye of an aesthete. The furnishings were striking: light wood, tubular steel, stark geometric shapes. An enormous round mirror, resting in a crescent of chrome, hung above the fireplace. A tall silver and ivory coffeepot, with a matching creamer and sugar bowl, sat on a silver tray on the beveled-glass coffee table. She paused to refill her cup. "Are you a fan of art deco?"

"I don't know much about it."

"I've been collecting for years. The rug's a Da Silva Bruhns. This is Wolfgang Tumpel's work, if you're familiar with the name," she said, nodding at the coffee service.

"Beautiful," I murmured, clueless.

"Most of these pieces are one of a kind, created by craftsmen who were masters in their day. I'd go on rattling the names off, but I doubt they'd mean much if you're not acquainted with the period. I built this as a showcase for my collection, but as soon as the house is finished, I'll probably sell it and move on. I'm impatient by nature and far too restless to stay here long." She had strong features: thinly arched brows and dark, smudged eyes, with pronounced streaks of weariness descending from the inner corners. She took a sip of coffee and then paused to extract a cigarette from a pack sitting on the table. The lighter she used was one of those small gold items and made very little sound when she flipped the cover back and thumbed the striker wheel. She held the lighter in her palm and drew deeply on her cigarette, clearly savoring the relief. She tilted her head toward the ceiling and blew the smoke out in a stream. I figured I could always drop my blazer at the cleaners on the way home.

She said, "I don't think I mentioned this when we chatted the other day, but Dana Glazer suggested I get in touch with you. I believe she was Dana Jaffe when you were acquainted with her."

"Really. How do you know her?"

"I'm helping her redecorate her home. She's now married to one of Dow's associates, Joel Glazer, whose first wife died. Do you know Joel? He's a partner in a company called Century Comprehensive that owns a chain of nursing homes among other things."

"I know the name Glazer from the papers. I've never met him," I said. Her call was beginning to make sense, though I still wasn't sure how I could be of service. Dana Jaffe's first husband, Wendell, had disappeared in 1979, though the circumstances—on the surface—were very different from the current case. Wendell Jaffe was a self-made real estate tycoon who'd faked his own death, showing up in Mexico shortly after his "widow" had collected half a million dollars in life insurance benefits. Wendell was facing jail time after a Ponzi scheme he'd cooked up threatened to unravel, exposing his chicanery. The "pseudocide" was his attempt to avoid the inevitable felony conviction. He might have pulled it off, but he'd been spotted in Mexico by a former acquaintance, and I'd been dispatched by the insurance company, who wanted their money back. I wondered if Fiona suspected her ex-husband had pulled a fast one as well.

She set her coffee cup aside. "You received the articles?"

"A messenger dropped them off at the office yesterday. I read them last night and then again this morning. The police have been thorough. . . ."

"Or so they'd like us to think."

"You're not happy with their progress?"

"Progress! What progress? Dowan is still missing. I'll tell you what they've accomplished: Zilch. I grant you, they're going through the motions—making public pronouncements, trumpeting their concerns—but it's all sound and fury, signifying nothing."

I objected to her attitude but decided not to protest just yet. I think the cops are terrific, but why argue the point? She wanted to hire me and I was here to determine what, if anything, I could contribute. "What's the latest?" I asked.

"No one's heard a peep from him—at least as far as I've been told." She took another drag on her cigarette and then tapped the ash into a heavy crystal ashtray. Her lipstick was dark and bled into the fine hairline crevices along her upper lip. She'd left a distinct half-moon on the coffee cup and a full ring around the filter of her cigarette. Her jewelry was clunky: big clip-on silver earrings and a matching bracelet. The effect was stylish, but everything about her suggested estate sales and vintage clothing shops. I fancied if I'd bent close, I'd have picked up the whiff of moth balls and cedar closets, mingled with scents from the '40s: Shalimar and Old Golds. In moments, her looks were striking, harsh flickers of beauty she seemed at pains to accentuate. She lowered her eyes. "Of course, you realize we're divorced."

"There was reference to that in one of the articles you sent. What about his current wife?"

"I've only spoken to Crystal once throughout this whole ordeal. She's gone to great lengths to keep me out of the loop. I receive up-dates through my daughters, who've made it a point to stay in close touch with her. Without them, I'd have even less information than I do, which God knows, isn't much."

11

"You have two girls?"

"Correct. My youngest, Blanche, and her husband are only four blocks away. Melanie, the older one, lives in San Francisco. I'll be staying with her 'til Tuesday afternoon of next week."

"Any grandchildren?"

"Mel's never been married. Blanche is expecting her fifth in about three weeks."

I said, "Wow."

Fiona's smile was sour. "Motherhood's just her way of avoiding a real job."

"A 'real' job sounds easier. I couldn't do what she does."

"She barely manages herself. Fortunately, the children have a nanny who's extremely competent."

"How do your daughters get along with Crystal?"

"Fine, I suppose. Then again, what choice do they have? If they don't dance to her tune, she'll make sure they never see their father or their half-brother again. You know Dow and Crystal have a son? His name is Griffith. He just turned two."

"I remember mention of the boy. May I call you Fiona?"

She took another drag of her cigarette and placed it on the lip of the ashtray in front of her. "I'd prefer Mrs. Purcell, if it's all the same to you." Smoke trailed from her mouth as she spoke and she seemed to study it, bemused.

"Yes, well. I'm wondering if you have a theory about your ex-husband's disappearance."

"You're one of the few who's even bothered to ask. Apparently, my opinion is of no concern. I suspect he's in Europe or South America, biding his time until he's ready to come home. Crystal thinks he's dead—or so I've heard."

"It's not so far-fetched. According to the papers, there's been no activity on his credit cards. There's been no sign of his car and no sign of him."

"Well, that's not quite true. There've been a number of reports. People claim to have spotted him as far away as New Orleans and Seattle. He was seen getting on a plane at JFK and again south of San Diego, heading for Mexico."

"There are still sightings of Elvis. That doesn't mean he's alive and well."

"True. On the other hand, someone fitting Dow's description tried to cross into Canada but walked away when the immigration officer asked to see his passport, which is missing, by the way."

"Really. That's interesting. The papers didn't mention it. I take it the police have followed up?"

"One can only hope," she remarked. There was

something hollow in her tone. If she could only persuade *me*, then perhaps what she said would turn out to be true.

"You're convinced he's alive?"

"I can't imagine otherwise. The man has no enemies and I can't conceive his being the victim of 'foul play,'" she said, forming the quote marks with her fingers. "The idea's absurd."

"Because?"

"Dow's perfectly capable of taking care of himself—physically, at any rate. What he's not capable of doing is facing the problems in life. He's passive. Instead of fight or flight, he lies down and plays dead—in a manner of speaking. He'd rather do anything than deal with conflict, especially involving women. This goes back to his mother, but that's another story altogether."

"Has he done anything like this before?"

"As a matter of fact, he has. I tried to explain this to the police detective. In vain, I might add. Dowan's done this twice. The first time, Melanie and Blanche were—what?—probably only six and three. Dowan disappeared for three weeks. He left without warning and returned much the same way."

"Where'd he go?"

"I have no idea. The second time was similar. This was years later, before we separated for good. One day he was here; the next, he was gone. He came back a few weeks later without a murmur of explanation or apology. Naturally, I've assumed this recent disappearance was a repeat performance."

"What prompted his departure on those earlier occasions?"

Her gesture was vague, smoke trailing from the tip of her cigarette. "I suppose we were having problems. We usually were. At any rate, Dow kept saying he needed time to clear his head—whatever that means. One day soon after that he simply didn't come home. He'd canceled his appointments, including social engagements, all without a word to me or to anyone else. The first I became aware was when he failed to arrive for dinner. The second time was the same except I didn't go out of my mind with worry."

"So in both of those instances, he behaved much as he did this time?"

"Exactly. The first time, it took *hours* before I realized he was gone. The man's a doctor and, naturally, he was often delayed. By midnight, I was wild— close to hysterical. I thought I'd go mad."

"You called the police?"

"I called everyone I could think of. Then first thing the next morning, a note arrived in the mail. He said he'd come home eventually, which is exactly what he did. I was furious, of course, but he seemed totally unconcerned. Fool that I am, I forgave him and we

15

went on as before. The marriage was good, or good enough from my perspective. I thought he was happy—until this business with Crystal. For all I know, he'd been fooling around with her for years."

"What made you stay?"

"I thought he was a good husband. That's how innocent I was. He tended to be distant, but I didn't fault him—at least, on a conscious level. I might have harbored resentments, but I wasn't aware of them. Looking back, I realize there are many ways a man can disappear."

"Such as?"

She shrugged, stubbing out her cigarette. "Television, sleep, alcohol, books, uppers, downers. I'm speaking in general terms, but you get my drift."

"And in his case?"

"Dow buried himself in his work. Went in early, stayed at the office until all hours of the night. What you have to understand about him is, he's someone who avoids disagreements. That's why he loves the elderly—because they make no real demands on him. Being a physician gives him status, which has always been better, in his mind, than having to be accountable like any ordinary mortal."

"How long were you married?"

"Close to forty years. We met at Syracuse. I was majoring in art history and he was pre-med. We married shortly after graduation. Dow went on to medical school at Penn State and did his internship and residency out here. By then, we had the girls. I stayed home with them until they were both in school and then I went back and got my master's in interior design. I designed the house we built soon afterward in Horton Ravine. Of course, we hired an architect to handle all the nuts and bolts."

"He still owns that house?"

"Yes, though Crystal doesn't care for it from what I've heard."

"You didn't ask for the house in the settlement?"

"I couldn't afford the mortgage and upkeep. To hear him tell it, he was fleeced. Strictly his point of view. Believe me, he got the better deal. He probably paid someone off—the judge, my lawyer. You know how men stick together when it comes to the almighty buck."

I noticed she was busy shading my perception, scoring points for her team. Divorced folk always seem to angle for your sympathy, casting themselves in the best possible light. It seemed odd, in this case, when the reason for my visit was to see if I could be of help in the search for him. Was she still in love with the man? "It must have been difficult when the marriage broke up," I murmured.

"Humiliating. Devastating. It was such a cliché.

17

Doctor goes through a midlife crisis, leaves his middle-aged wife to take up with some whore."

The papers had had a field day with the fact that Crystal had been a stripper. Still, I questioned Fiona's use of the word "whore." Stripping, as a way of earning money, doesn't necessarily translate into hookerdom. For all we knew, Crystal might have earned *her* master's in psychiatric social work. "How did he meet her?"

"You'd have to ask her that. The truth is, Dow developed an appetite for . . . mmm . . . unusual sexual practices. His hormones were off or his anxiety levels began to climb as he aged. Possibly his problems harked back to his mother. Everything else connects to his relationship with her. Whatever the reason, once Dowan turned sixty, he began to falter. He couldn't . . . let's say . . . 'perform' without stimulus. Pornography, marital aids . . ."

"Which didn't appeal to you."

"I thought it was *revolting*. I can't even tell you the practices he wanted to pursue—unspeakable acts that I refused even to discuss with him. He finally stopped pressing."

"Because he'd taken up with her?"

"Evidently. He's never admitted it, but I'm sure he went looking. It did cross my mind he'd go out and find someone willing to submit to his perverse requests.

18

I certainly wouldn't do it and I knew I'd made myself entirely clear on that point."

I was secretly panting for an example, but I thought it was wiser (for once) to keep my big mouth shut. Sometimes you don't want to know what people do—or refuse to do—in private. If I had occasion to meet the doctor one day, I didn't want to be distracted by an image of him cavorting in the nude with an organic carrot up his butt. "Did you ask for the divorce or did he?"

"He did. I was completely taken off-guard. I presumed he'd get his needs met outside the marriage and keep his family intact. I never thought he'd stoop to divorce at this late stage in his life. I should have known. Dowan's weak. Not that any of us relish owning up to our mistakes, but Dow always abhorred even the *appearance* of failure."

"Meaning what?"

"Well," she said, lowering her eyes. I watched her gaze dance across the floor. "I suspect his relationship with Crystal is not the union of souls he'd like others to believe. Some months ago, he'd heard she was screwing around on him. Better to disappear than admit he'd been cuckolded."

"Did he have any idea who it was?"

"No, but he was looking into it. After he disap-

19

peared, my friend Dana finally confided that she'd known the whole time. The fellow is Crystal's personal trainer. His name is Clint Augustine."

I heard a little *ding-dong* going off in my head. I was sure I'd heard the name before, possibly in the gym where I work out.

"You believe he left because of that?"

"Yes. We had a conversation—a long talk—on September 10. This was two days before he vanished. He was dreadfully unhappy."

"He said that?"

Her hesitation was distinct as she debated with herself. "Not in so many words, but you don't go through forty years of marriage without learning to read between the lines."

"What occasioned the conversation?"

"He came over to the house."

"You were seeing him," I stated.

"Well, yes. At his request," she said, her tone faintly defensive. "Dow adores this place, just as he adores the house in Horton Ravine. He was always interested in my design work, even before our relationship underwent the shift. Lately, he'd been stopping by in the evenings to have a drink with me. That night, he was exhausted. His face was *gray* with worry, and when I asked what was wrong, he said the pressures at the office were driving him insane. And Crystal was no

20

help. She's extremely narcissistic, as you'll discover when you meet her, which I assume you will."

"Were you surprised he'd confide in you after everything he'd put you through?"

"Who else does he have? Anyway, he didn't really talk about her, but I could see the tension in his eyes. He'd aged a good ten years in a matter of months."

"You're saying he had problems at home as well as problems at work?"

"That's right. He didn't talk specifics, but he mentioned in passing that he needed to get away. That's the first thing I thought of when I heard he was gone."

"Couldn't that have been wishful thinking?"

"I suppose it could," she said. "I mean, he didn't pull out airline tickets, but he did seem desperate."

"Do you remember a reference to any place in particular?"

She tilted her head. "I've racked my brain, but I really can't remember. It was an offhand remark and I didn't think much about it until this came up."

"I assume you told the police."

Again, she hesitated. "Not at first. I thought his absence was voluntary and he'd come home when he was ready. I didn't want him to be embarrassed. Leave it to Crystal to turn this ordeal into a media circus."

I could feel myself bristle. "Mrs. Purcell, he's a prominent physician, well known and loved in this community. His disappearance is bound to attract media attention. If you thought he'd gone AWOL, why didn't you speak up?"

"I felt he was entitled to his privacy," she said, her cheeks coloring slightly.

"What about all the time and money being spent on the investigation? Weren't you at all concerned about that?"

"Of course. That's why I spoke to the police," she said. "After six weeks, I began to worry. I guess I was expecting a call or a note, *some* indication he was all right, wherever he was. Now that nine weeks have passed, I thought it was time to take matters into my own hands."

"What made you think he'd be in touch with you instead of her?"

"Because Crystal's the one he's been trying to escape."

"And now you're worried something's happened to him."

"I suppose so. That's why I decided to meet with the detective last week. Odessa was polite. He took notes. But I got the impression he didn't take me seriously. He said he'd get back to me, but that's the last I've heard. The police must be working *dozens* of other cases, which means they don't have the time or resources to devote to Dow. I said as much to Dana and she agrees. That's why she recommended you."

"I don't know what to say. Even if we come to some agreement, I can't spend twenty-four hours a day on this any more than the police can. I have other clients, too."

"I didn't say you'd have to be exclusive."

"Even so, I'm just one person. You'd be better off with a big Los Angeles agency, one with lots of operatives who can fan out across the country and do this properly. You might end up having to search for him overseas."

She cut me off with a wave of her hand. "I don't want a big L.A. agency. I want someone local who's willing to report directly to me."

"But all I'd be doing is repeating what the police have already done."

"You might have ideas they haven't thought of yet. After all, you tracked down Wendell Jaffe *years* after everyone assumed he was dead."

"I did track him down, but I didn't start from scratch. Someone spotted him in Mexico and that's why the case finally broke."

Her expression became withdrawn. "You won't help."

"I'm not saying that. I'm talking about reality, which doesn't look that good."

"But what if there's an angle the police have over-looked?"

"What if there's not?"

"Then at least I'd be satisfied with the job they've done."

I was silent for a beat, staring at the floor. Inside, a little voice was yelling "*No, no, no!*" while my mouth said, "I'll do what I can, but I make no promises."

"Good. That's wonderful. We'll talk on Tuesday. Just keep track of the time you put in and you can give me an invoice as soon as I get back." She glanced at her watch and then rose to her feet.

I stood when she did. "I'll need a retainer."

"A 'retainer'?" She made a show of startlement, but I wondered if she was repeating the words for effect. Surely she didn't do business without a written agreement and earnest money changing hands. "How much did you have in mind?"

"I charge fifty an hour or a flat four hundred a day, plus expenses, so fifteen hundred dollars should cover it for now. If you give me Melanie's address, I'll overnight you a contract for your signature." In truth, I could have brought one with me, but I hadn't been sure we'd end up coming to an agreement.

She blinked as though baffled. "I'm sorry. I didn't picture anything so *formal*. Is this standard procedure in your line of work?"

"Actually, it is," I said. I noticed she didn't call it a "profession," which meant she probably lumped me in with retail clerks, short-order cooks, and Roto-Rooter men.

"What if you fail to find him?"

"That's exactly the point. If I come up empty-handed, you might decide I wasn't worth the hourly wage. Once I take a case, I persevere. I'll follow the trail right out to the bitter end."

"I should hope so," she said. She thought about it briefly, and then she crossed to an ebony-inlaid console. She removed her checkbook, returned to her chair, and sat down. "And I'm to make the check out to . . .?"

"Millhone Investigations."

I watched while she dashed off a check and tore it out of the book, scarcely bothering to disguise her irritation as she handed it to me. I noticed we were bank mates, sharing the same branch of the Santa Teresa City Bank. I said, "You're upset."

"I operate on trust. Apparently, you don't."

"I've learned the hard way. It's nothing personal."

"I see."

I held out the check. "I can return this right now if you'd prefer."

"Just find him. I'll expect a full report the minute I get home."

TWO

Before I left Fiona's, she gave me Melanie's home address in San Francisco, along with her home and office numbers. I couldn't imagine the need to call Fiona up there. She also gave me Crystal's Horton Ravine address and phone number. I'd never met Detective Odessa, whom Fiona'd mentioned in passing, but a conversation with him was the first item on my list. Driving back into town, I noticed my stomach had begun to churn with anxiety. I tried to pinpoint my doubts, laying them out one by one, though not necessarily in the order of importance.

1. I didn't particularly like—or trust—Fiona. She hadn't been candid with the cops and I didn't think she was being entirely candid with me. Under the circumstances, I probably should have declined to take the job. Already I was regretting the haste with which I'd agreed.

2. I wasn't sure I could be effective. I'm often uneasy at the outset of an investigation, especially one like this. Nine weeks had passed since Dr. Purcell was last seen. Whatever the circumstances surrounding a disappearance, the passage of time seldom works in your favor. Witnesses embellish. They invent. The memory grows foggy. The truth tends to blur with repetition, and details are altered to suit various personal interpretations. People want to be helpful, which means they embroider their stories, coloring events according to their biases as the situation drags on. Entering the game this late, the likelihood of my making any critical discovery was almost out of the question. Fiona did have a point in that sometimes a fresh perspective can shift the focus of an investigation. All well and good, but intuition was telling me that any break in the case was going to be the result of serendipity, a term synonymous with unadulterated dumb luck.

3. I didn't like the bullshit about the retainer.

I stopped off at McDonald's and ordered coffee and a couple of Egg McMuffins. I needed the comfort of junk food as well as the nourishment, if that's what you want to call it. I munched while I drove, eating with such eagerness I bit my own index finger.

I might as well take a moment here to identify myself. My name is Kinsey Millhone. I'm a licensed private investigator in Santa Teresa, California, which is ninety-five miles north of Los Angeles. I'm female, thirty-six, twice divorced, childless, and otherwise unencumbered. Aside from my car, I don't own much in the way of material possessions. My business, Millhone Investigations, consists entirely of me. I was a cop for two years early in my twenties, and through personal machinations too tedious to explain, I realized law enforcement didn't suit me. I was way too crabby and unco-operative to adjust to department regulations, with all the ethics clauses thrown in: I have been known to bend the rules. Plus, the shoes were clunky and the uniform and the belt made my ass look too wide.

Having left gainful city employment, I apprenticed myself to a two-man office of private investigators, where I put in the hours necessary to apply for my license. I've been on my own now for a good ten years, licensed, bonded, and heavily insured. A good portion of the last decade, I spent pursuing arson and wrongful death claims for California Fidelity Insurance, first as a bona fide employee, later as an independent contractor.

We came to a parting of the ways three years ago in October 1983. Since then, I've rented space from the law firm of Kingman and Ives, an arrangement that I'd begun to suspect was on the verge of change.

For the past year, Lonnie Kingman had been complaining about the shortage of space. He'd already expanded once, taking over the entire third floor of a building he owns free and clear. He'd now purchased a second building, this one on lower State Street, where he intended to relocate as soon as escrow closed. He'd found a tenant for our current digs, and the only question that remained was whether I'd go with him or find an office of my own. I'm a loner at heart, and while I'm fond of Lonnie, the whole idea of working in close contact with other people had begun to get on my nerves. I found myself going into the office nights and weekends, spending half my days working from home— anything to create the sense of space and solitude. I'd talked to a real estate broker about month-to-month rentals, and I'd responded to several classified ads. So far I hadn't seen anything that really struck my fancy. My requirements were modest: room for my desk, swivel chair, file cabinets, and a few fake plants. In addition, I pictured a small but tasteful executive potty. The problem was that everything I liked was too large or too expensive, and anything that fit my budget was too cramped, too shabby, or too far from downtown—

I spend a lot of time at the Hall of Records and I like to be within walking distance of the court house, the police station, and the public library. Lonnie's office was a haven, and he doubles as my attorney if the shit hits the fan—which it very often does. The choice was tough and I still wasn't sure what I wanted to do.

As soon as I reached the two-hundred block of east Capillo, where Lonnie's office was located, I began the usual search-and-seizure mission, hunting for a parking place. One drawback to the current building was the tiny lot attached, which only held twelve cars. Lonnie and his partner were each assigned a slot, as were their two secretaries, Ida Ruth Kenner and Jill Stahl. The remaining eight spots went to the building's other tenants, so the rest of us were forced to ferret out parking where we could. Today I nosed my way into a short length of curb between two commercial driveways, a spot I could have sworn was almost legal. It was only later I discovered I'd been wrong.

I walked the five blocks to the office, climbed the requisite two flights of stairs, and let myself into the suite through an unmarked side door. I crossed the interior hallway to my office, unlocked the door, and stepped in, carefully avoiding Ida Ruth and Jill, who were deep in conversation a short distance away. I knew the subject matter would be the same one they'd been debating for the past two months. Lonnie's partner,

John Ives, had urged the firm to hire his niece as the receptionist when the position became open. Jeniffer was eighteen years old and a recent high school graduate. This was her first job and despite being given a lengthy written job description, she seemed thoroughly perplexed about what was expected of her. She showed up for work in T-shirts and miniskirts, her long blond hair hanging down to her waist, legs bare, feet shoved into wood-soled clogs. Her phone voice was chirpy, her spelling was atrocious, and she couldn't seem to get the hang of coming in on time. She also took frequent two-to four-day vacations whenever her unemployed friends headed off to play. Ida Ruth and Jill were constantly exasperated at having to pick up the slack. Both belly-ached to me, apparently reluctant to complain to Lonnie or John. Petty office politics have never held much appeal, which was yet another reason I was leaning toward a change in venue. Where I'd once been attracted to the sense of family I felt at the firm, now all I saw were attendant psychodramas. Jeniffer was Cinderella with a diminutive IQ. Ida Ruth and Jill, like the spiteful stepsisters, were simperingly nice to her in person but talked about her behind her back every chance they could. I'm not sure what part I played, but I did my best to avoid participation by hiding in my room. Clearly, I was no more adept at resolving conflicts than anyone else.

SUE GRAFTON

In the interests of escape, I put a call through to the Santa Teresa Police Department and asked to speak to Detective Odessa. He was in a meeting, but the woman who took my call said he'd be free in a bit. I made an appointment for 10:30. I filled in a boiler plate contract and slipped it in an Express Mail envelope that I addressed to Fiona in care of Melanie's home in San Francisco. I tucked the whole of it in my handbag and then sat at my desk, making deeply symbolic doodles on my blotter between rounds of solitaire. It's not as though I didn't have a ton of other work to do, but I found myself distracted by the information circulating through my brain. I finally pulled out a manila folder and a yellow legal pad and started taking notes.

At 10:20 I locked my door and walked over to the post office, then continued to the police station, which was four blocks away. The morning air was chilly and the earlier pale sunlight had faded as the sky clouded over with the first hint of rain. The Santa Teresa "rainy" season is unpredictable. Intermittent periods of precipitation once began in mid-January and extended willy-nilly into early March. Of late, weather extremes in other parts of the world have resulted in capricious deviations. From late May until October, rain levels can still be measured in fractions of an inch, but the winter months now vary, and this one was shaping up to be one of the wettest in years. A cold front was moving down from Alaska, pushing a raw wind ahead of it. The tree branches moved restlessly, bending and creaking, while dried palm fronds broke loose and swept along the sidewalks like brooms.

The lobby at the police station seemed cozy by comparison. On my left, a small boy sat waiting on the wooden bench while his father talked to the civilian clerk about copies of an accident report. I moved to the L-shaped counter, where a uniformed officer monitored the walk-in trade. I told him of my appointment and he relayed the information to Detective Odessa's desk by phone. "He'll be right out."

I waited where I was, glancing idly into Records across the counter to my right. My friend Emerald had taken early retirement, leaving me with no buddy to slip me information. She'd never actually violated department policy, but she'd come close a few times.

Detective Odessa opened the door and stuck his head around the frame. "Ms. Millhone?"

"That's me."

"Vince Odessa," he said, and we shook hands. "Come on back."

I said, "Thanks." He handed me a visitor's badge that I clipped to my lapel.

He wore a blue dress shirt, a dark tie, chinos, dark socks, and shiny black shoes. His hair was dark and the back of his head was flat, as though he'd slept on his back for his entire infancy. He was taller than I, probably five foot nine to my five foot six. He held the door, allowing me to pass into the corridor in front of him. I paused and he took the lead. He walked ahead of me and turned left, passing through a door marked INVESTIGATIONS. I followed him through a warren of small offices. Over his shoulder, he said, "Shelly mentioned this was in regard to Dr. Purcell."

"That's right. His ex-wife hired me to look into his disappearance."

Odessa kept his tone neutral. "I had a feeling that was coming. She was in here last week."

"What'd you make of her?"

"I'll have to take the Fifth. You on the clock?"

"I haven't deposited her check. I thought it'd be smart to talk to you first."

His "office" was tucked into a standard cubicle: shoulder-high gray walls carpeted in a tight synthetic loop. He took a seat at his desk, offering me the only other chair in the compact space. Framed photos of his family were arranged in front of him: wife, three daughters, and a son. A small metal bookcase behind him was neatly lined with department manuals, texts, and assorted law books. He was clean shaven except for a line of whiskers he'd missed when his razor jumped over the cleft in his chin. His dark brows were fierce over dark blue eyes. "So what can I help you with?"

"I'm not sure. I'd love to hear what you have, if you're willing to share."

"I got no problem with that," he said. He leaned forward, checking through a stack of thick files on one side of his desk. He pulled a three-ring binder from the bottom of the pile and set it in front of him. "Place is a mess. They tell us we're switching over to computers in the next six, eight months. Paperless office. You believe that stuff?"

"It'd be nice, but I doubt it."

"So do I," he said. He leafed through numerous pages to the initial incident report. "I just got this promotion. I'm junior man on the team so this is a training exercise as far as they're concerned. Let's see what we got." His gaze zigzagged along the page. "Crystal Purcell filed a missing persons Tuesday morning, 16 September, seventy-two hours after the doctor failed to arrive home as scheduled. Records took the information. We'd had some residential burglaries that same weekend so I didn't pick up the report until noon Thursday, 18 September. As far as we could determine, Purcell wasn't *at risk*, and there was nothing suspicious about the circumstances of his disappearance." He paused to look at me. "Tell you the truth, we figured he'd gone off on his own. You know how it is. Half the time the guy shows up later with his tail between his legs. Turns out he's got a girlfriend or he's been off on a bender with the boys somewhere. Might be half a dozen explanations, all of them harmless. It's aggravating to the wife, but nothing sinister."

He leaned back in his chair. "Half a million to a million people run away each year. It's tough on family and friends. You've probably seen it yourself. At first, they get into denial. Can't believe someone'd do such a rotten thing to them. Later, they get mad. Anyway, I called the current Mrs. Purcell and made an appointment for Friday afternoon. This was September 19. Frankly, I stalled, assuming she'd hear from him."

"Which she didn't?"

"Not then and not since. From what she says, he wasn't suffering any physical condition that raised a flag on that score—no heart problems, diabetes, no history of mental illness. She said she'd called and talked to him at the office—this was 12 September, shortly after lunch. Purcell told her he'd be late, but there was no mention of his not coming home at all. By Saturday morning, she was frantic, calling everyone she knew—friends, relatives, his colleagues. Hospitals, CHP, the morgue—you name it. There was no sign of him.

"I sat with her for an hour, this was at the house in Horton Ravine. She's got another place at the beach she stays most weekends. I went through the drill. Asked about habits, hobbies, job, country club memberships; had a look at his bedroom; went through his chest of drawers, phone bills, credit card receipts. I checked his credit card accounts for any recent activity, address book, calendar—covering all those bases."

"Nothing surfaced?"

He held up a finger. "I'll get to that in a minute. Over the next couple weeks, we went through the mail at his home and at the clinic, arranged a mail cover, talked to his associates, entered him in the DOJ missing persons system, and put a stop on his license plate. Meantime, you have to understand, we're not talking about a crime here, so this is strictly a public service. We're doing what we can, but there's no evidence to suggest we got a problem on our hands."

"Fiona tells me his passport's missing."

Odessa smiled ruefully. "So's mine for that matter. Just because his wife can't lay hands on it, doesn't mean it's gone. We did come across a recent statement for a savings account at Mid-City Bank. And this is what caught our attention. It looks like he made a series of cash withdrawals—thirty thousand dollars' worth—over the past two years. Balance drops from thirteen grand to three in the past ten months alone. The last activity on the account was August 29. His wife doesn't seem to know anything about it."

"You think he was prepping for departure?"

"Well, it sure looks that way. Granted, thirty thou

won't get you far in this day and age, but it's a start. He might've milked other accounts we haven't come up with yet. It's always possible the guy's a gambler and this is his stake. She says he's not, but she might've been kept in the dark."

"Could we go back to the passport? If Purcell left the country, wouldn't Customs have a record of it?"

"You'd think so. Assuming his was the passport he used. He might have traded in his personal ID—driver's license, birth certificate, and passport—for a set of phony papers, which means he could have flown to Europe or South America under someone else's name. Or he might have driven into Canada, booked a flight, and left from there."

"Or he might be lying low," I said.

"Right."

"Wouldn't someone have spotted his car?"

"No guarantee of that. He could've run it off a cliff, or driven into Mexico and sold it to a chop shop. Park a car like that in South Central and see how fast it disappears."

"What kind of car?"

"Four-door Mercedes sedan. Silver. Vanity plate reads DOCTOR P."

I said, "You haven't mentioned foul play."

"No reason to. Or if there is, I don't see it. It's not

38

like, we found blood stains in the parking lot outside the nursing home. No signs of a struggle, no evidence of assault, and no reason to believe he was forcibly removed. We canvassed the neighborhood, hitting every house within range. Nobody saw or heard a thing that night."

"Fiona thinks he might have left on his own. What's your take on it?"

"Personally, I don't like the feel of it. Nine weeks with zip. You almost have to assume there's something else going on. We're beginning to backtrack, looking for anything we might have missed the first go-round."

"Did Fiona's story affect the investigation?"

"In what regard?"

"All this talk of his past disappearances," I said.

Odessa waved that aside. "Air and sunshine. She says he's gone off before. Maybe so, maybe not. I'm not entirely clear about her motive."

"According to her, she wants results."

"Sure, but who doesn't? We're cops, not magicians. We don't perform miracles."

"Did you believe the story she told?"

"I believe he left *her*. Whether he was having problems with the current Mrs. P. is anybody's guess." He paused. "Have you met Crystal yet?"

I shook my head.

Odessa lifted his brows and shook his hand as though he'd burned it. "She's a beautiful woman. Hard to picture anyone walking out on her."

"You have a theory?"

"Not me. From our perspective—so far—this is not a criminal matter. You got no crime, then there's no Miranda and no need for search warrants, which makes our job a hell of a lot easier. We're just a bunch of good guys trying to do the family a favor. Personally, I think things look bad, but I ain't gonna say that to anyone else, including you," he said.

I indicated the file. "Mind if I take a look?"

"Wish I could, but this is Paglia's case and he's hell on confidentiality. He doesn't mind us passing on the gist of it when it seems appropriate. The point is to find the guy, which means we cooperate when we can."

"He won't care if I go back and talk to some of these people?"

"You're free to do anything you want."

When he walked me out to the front, he said, "If you find him, let us know. He can stay gone if he wants, but I'd hate to keep putting in the hours if he's off in Las Vegas with a snootful of coke."

"You don't believe that."

"No, I don't. Nor do you."

On the way back to the office, I did a two-block detour and made a stop at the bank. I filled out a deposit slip, endorsed Fiona's check, and waited my turn in line. When I reached the window, I pointed to the account number printed on the face. "Could you verify the balance in this account? I want to be sure the check's good before I make the deposit." Another lesson learned the hard way. I don't start work until a check has cleared.

The teller, Barbara, was one I'd been dealing with for years. I watched while she typed in the account number on her computer keyboard and then studied the screen. She hit the Enter key once. *Tap*. Again. *Tap*. I watched as her eyes traced the lines of print.

She looked back at my deposit slip and made a face. "This is covered, but it's close. Want the cash instead?"

"The deposit's fine, but let's do it before another check comes in and leaves her short."

THREE

I returned to the office to find that Jill and Ida Ruth had left a note on my door. "Kinsey—Below is an itemized record of Jeniffer's tardy days, screwups, and unexplained absences. Please add any other incidents you know of, sign this, and leave it on my desk. We think it's best if we present a unified front. We mean business! Ida Ruth."

I dropped the list in my trash and put a call through to Crystal Purcell at the house in Horton Ravine. The housekeeper informed me she'd left for the beach house, where she'd be spending the weekend. She gave me the number, which I dialed as soon as we'd hung up. I hoped the woman who answered would be Crystal, but when I asked for her by name, I was put on hold until a second woman picked up. "This is Crystal," she said.

I identified myself by name and occupation, hoping she wouldn't be annoyed by the idea of yet another detective. According to the newspapers, she'd already talked to investigators from the Santa Teresa Police Department. I told her I'd met with Fiona that morning and that she'd asked me to look into Dr. Purcell's disappearance. "I know you've gone over the subject repeatedly, but I'd appreciate hearing the story from you, if you can bear telling it again."

There was a momentary pause wherein I could have sworn she was practicing her Zen deep breathing. "This is very hard."

"I'm aware of that and I'm sorry."

"How soon?"

"That's entirely up to you. The sooner the better."

There was another pause. "How much are you charging?"

"Fiona? Fifty an hour, which is on the low end of the scale. A big-city private eye is paid twice that." Briefly I wondered why I sounded so apologetic. Maybe she'd prefer to chat with someone whose services were worth more.

"Stop by at five. I'm on Paloma Lane." She gave me the number. "Do you know where that is?"

"I can find it. I'll try not to take too much of your time."

"Take all you want. Fiona's the one paying."

*

I left the office at four o'clock, stopping by my apartment on my way to Crystal's beach house. The accumulating cloud cover had generated an artificial twilight, and the smell of gathering rain had infused the air. I'd left windows open in the loft and I wanted to get the place buttoned down properly against the coming storm. I parked the car out in front and pushed through the gate with its reassuring whine and squeak. I followed the narrow concrete walk around the side of the building to the backyard.

My apartment was formerly a single-car garage converted into living quarters. My studio consists of a small living room, with a sofa bed for guests tucked into a bay window, a built-in desk, a kitchenette, a stacking washer-dryer combination, and a bathroom downstairs. Above, accessible by a tiny spiral staircase, I have a sleeping loft with a platform bed and a second bathroom. The interior resembles a sturdy little seagoing vessel, complete with a porthole in the front door, teak-paneled walls, and sufficient nooks and crannies, cubby-holes, and niches to accommodate my small store of possessions. The best part of all is the good soul who makes this possible, my landlord, Henry Pitts. He's eighty-six years old, handsome, thrifty, energetic, and competent. He worked as a commercial baker for most of his professional life and even in retirement, can't quite give up his addiction to breads, pies, and cakes.

He not only produces a steady stream of baked goods, but he caters luncheons and high teas for all the old ladies in the neighborhood. In addition, he trades his fresh breads and dinner rolls for meals at the corner tavern, where he eats three to four nights a week.

At the head of the driveway, I could see Henry's garage door standing open, though both vehicles were in place. As I turned left onto the patio, I spotted him on a ladder outside his bedroom, putting up the last of his storm windows. He wore shorts and a tank top, his long legs looking knotty, his tan all but faded now that "winter" was here. The Santa Teresa temperatures never drop much below fifty, but he's originally from Michigan, and despite the fact he's been in southern California more than forty years, his lingering attachment to the seasons dictates the installation of window screens in late spring and storm windows in late fall. The weather itself is immaterial to him.

The patio was still littered with cleaning supplies: the garden hose, wads of crumpled newspaper, a wire brush, a bucket of water mixed with vinegar, and numerous sponges gray with soot. Henry waved from his perch and then eased carefully down the ladder, whistling tunelessly to himself. I paused to help him clean up, tossing dingy water in the bushes while he rewound the hose into a terra-cotta pot. "You're home early," he remarked.

"I thought I better close my windows before the rain, assuming we'll actually have some," I said. Henry'd often complained that the rain in California lacked the bluster and theatrics of a good Midwestern storm. Many times the promised rain failed to materialize at all or arrived in a form barely sufficient to wet the pavement. We're seldom treated to the displays of thunder and lightning he remembers with such enthusiasm from his Michigan youth.

Henry said, "Why didn't you call? I could have saved you a trip. Stick the brush in that bucket. I'll take it in with me when I go."

"This was right on my way. I have an appointment at five o'clock down on Paloma Lane so I was heading in this direction. Any excuse to avoid the office. Too much nonsense for my taste."

"How's the search for new space?"

I waggled my hand back and forth, indicating not so good. "Something will come up. Meanwhile, I have a new client. At least I'm ninety-nine percent sure."

"Why the hesitation?"

"Might be the aggravation at the office, spilling over into this. I am interested in the case, but I'm not convinced I can be effective. This is the doctor who's been missing."

"I remember reading about that. Still no sign of him?"

"Nope. His ex-wife thinks the cops aren't showing the proper initiative. Frankly, she strikes me as the type who likes to make people jump through hoops."

"You'll do fine." With that, he returned to the ladder, which he collapsed and carried back across the patio to the garage. I watched him ease around his 1932 Chevy coup and hang the ladder on the wall. His garage is lined with pegboard, with the location for each item neatly silhouetted in paint. "You have time for some tea?" he asked, coming back across the yard.

I glanced at my watch. "Better not. I'll see you later up at Rosie's."

"I'll be there closer to seven than to six. She's actually on her way over so I better get washed up. She's asked me for help, but she won't say with what."

I said, "Uh-oh."

He waved dismissively. "It's probably something simple. I don't mind a bit. If she shows while I'm gone, tell her I'll be back in a flash, as soon as I've cleaned up."

Henry crossed to his backdoor and went into the kitchen, where I could see him through the window, scrubbing up at the sink. He smiled when he caught my eye and started whistling to himself again.

I turned when I heard the gate squeak. Rosie appeared moments later, toting a brown paper bag. She owns the Hungarian tavern where Henry's older brother, William, now functions as the manager. William and Rosie were married Thanksgiving day the year before, and they live in an apartment above her restaurant, which is half a block away. William is eighty-seven years old, and where Rosie once swore she was in her sixties, she now admits to being in her seventies, though she won't specify where. She's short and top-heavy with a coquettish cap of red hair dyed the color of Florida oranges. As usual, she was wearing a muu-muu, this one a gaudy jungle of orange and gold, the skirt lifting, sail-like, against the rising wind. She brightened when she saw me. "Kinsey, is good. Here's for Henry," she said, opening the bag for me.

I peered at the contents, half-expecting to see kittens. "What *is* that? Is that trash?"

Rosie shifted her weight from one foot to the other, refusing to make eye contact, a strategy she employs when she's guilty, ill at ease, or maneuvering like crazy. "Is my sister Klotilde's medical bills for hospital and after she died. Henry's going to explain. I can't make into heads or tails with this." Rosie's perfectly capable of speaking grammatically. She only butchers vocabulary and syntax when she's trying to seem helpless, thus conning you into doing her some outrageous favor. This is especially true when she's dealing with her state and federal taxes, which Henry's done without a murmur for the past six years. Now slyly, she said, "You gonna help I hope. He shouldn't do by himself. Is not fair."

"Why can't William pitch in?"

"Klotilde preferred Henry."

"But she's *deceased*," I said.

"Before she deceased herself, she preferred," she said, smiling coyly, as though that cinched it.

I dropped the argument. It was really up to Henry, though it irritated me intensely that she'd take advantage of him. The Klotilde in question was Rosie's cranky older sister. I'd never been able to pronounce her Hungarian surname, which abounded in consonants and strange punctuation marks. She'd suffered for years from an unspecified degenerative disease. She'd used a wheelchair since she was in her fifties, plagued by a variety of other ailments that necessitated copious medications and numerous hospital stays. Finally, in her seventies, she'd been advised to undergo hip-replacement surgery. This was in April, some seven months back. Though the surgery had been successful, Klotilde had been outraged by the rigors of convalescence. She'd resisted all attempts to get her on her feet, balked at nourishment, refused to use a bedpan, pulled out catheters and feeding tubes, flung her pills at the nurses, and sabotaged her physical therapy. After the customary five days in the hospital, she was moved to a nursing home where, over the course of the next several weeks, she began to decline. She'd finally succumbed to pneumonia, dysphagia, malnutrition, and kidney failure. Rosie had not been exactly stricken when she "passed." "She should have pessed a long time ago," said she. "She's a pain in the patooty. That's what happens when you don't behave. She should have done what doctor say. She shouldn't never resist help when he know best. Now I got this and I don't know what to do with. Here you take."

Judging from the weight and heft of the bag, she'd gotten into some resistance of her own, letting all the paperwork pile up. It'd take Henry weeks to get everything sorted out. He emerged from the back door and crossed the patio to us. He'd changed out of his tank top and shorts into a flannel shirt and long pants.

"I gotta scoot," I said, and set the bag on the ground. Henry peered in. "Is this trash?"

By the time I let myself into my apartment, he was already hauling the bag toward his kitchen door, nodding sympathetically while Rosie lurched through a tortured explanation of her plight.

I dropped my shoulder bag on a kitchen stool while I circled the apartment, closing windows and locking them. I turned on lamps as I went so the place would look cheerful when I got home. Upstairs, I pulled on a clean white turtleneck, which I wore with my jeans. I shrugged back into my gray tweed blazer, traded my

Sauconys for black boots, and studied myself in the bathroom mirror. The effect was just what you'd expect: a tweed blazer with jeans. *Works for me*, I thought.

Paloma Lane is a shady two-lane road that runs between Highway 101 and the Pacific Ocean, sharing the irregular strip of land with the Southern Pacific Railroad. Despite the proximity to the freight and passenger trains thundering past twice daily, many houses along Paloma sell in the millions, depending on the number of linear feet of beachfront a property claims. The houses vary in style from Pseudo-Cape Cod to Mock Tudor to Faux Mediterranean to Contemporary. All are situated as far away from the railroad tracks as possible and as close to the sand as county setbacks permit. Crystal Purcell's lot was one of the few without electronic gates. The house next door, to the left of hers, bore a discreet For Sale sign with a PRICE REDUCED banner across the center.

Crystal's house filled the narrow lot. The glass-and-cedar structure was probably forty feet wide and three stories high, each floor angled strategically to keep the neighboring houses out of sight. To the left, an open carport sheltered a silver Audi convertible and a new white Volvo, with a vanity license plate that read

CRYSTAL. The end slot was free; probably where Dow Purcell had parked his Mercedes. To the right, there was room for an additional three cars on the gravel stretch where I parked my slightly dinged 1974 VW.

The rear facade of the house was austere, a windowless wall of weathering wood. On either side of the door, a row of thirty-foot fan palms had been planted in enormous black jars. I trudged across the gravel to the entrance and rang the bell. The woman who answered the door carried a wide martini glass by the rim. She said, "You must be Kinsey. I'm Anica Blackburn. 'Nica"s the name most people use. Why don't you come in? Crystal's just finished her run. She'll be down in a bit. I told her I'd let you in before I headed home." Her dark auburn hair was slicked back, strands looking wet as though she was fresh from the shower. A faint damp heat seemed to rise from her skin, which smelled of French milled soap. Her body was slim and straight. She wore a black silk shirt, crisply pressed jeans, and no shoes. Her bare feet were long and elegant.

I stepped into the foyer. The lower level widened from the entry, expanding into a great room that utilized the entire width of the house. Tall windows looked out onto a weathered wooden deck with worn canvas chairs bleached to a hue somewhere between putty and dun. The floors were a pale wood, covered with pale sisal carpeting, probably selected for its ability to disguise sand tracked in from the beach. Everything else within view, from the walls to woodwork to the plump upholstered furniture dressed in wrinkled linen slipcovers, was as white as whole milk.

Beyond the deck, there was an apron of scruffy grass about ten yards wide. Beyond the grass, the ocean looked cold and unforgiving in the late afternoon light. The sea was a pearly gray, dark at the horizon where the water and cloud cover met and melded into one somber mass. The surf tumbled monotonously against the shoreline. Waves relaxed and fanned out, reached, hesitated, and then withdrew again. Inside, somewhere above, I could hear voices raised in heat.

"SHUT UP! That's bullshit. You are such a bitch. I HATE you! . . ."

The reply was low and firm, but apparently ineffective.

A shrieking invective was hurled in response. A door slammed once and then slammed again so hard it made the windows shake.

I glanced at Nica, who had her face upturned, regarding the ceiling with an air of bemusement. "Leila's home for the weekend—Crystal's only daughter, age fourteen. That's skirmish number one. Trust me, the fights will escalate as the hours wear on. By Sunday, it's all-out war, but then it's back to school for

53

her. Next weekend they start in again, and so it goes." She gestured for me to follow and then moved into the great room and took a seat on the couch.

"She's in boarding school?" I asked.

"Fitch Academy. Malibu. I'm the school guidance counselor and I provide personal transportation to and from. Not part of my duties. As it happens, I rent a house two doors down." She had strong, arched brows over dark eyes, high cheek bones with a smattering of freckles, and a pale wide mouth, showing perfect white teeth. "This particular Donnybrook is about whether Leila's going to spend the night with her dad. Four months ago she was fanatical about him. If she couldn't spend the weekend with him, she'd regale everyone in ear range with loud, shrieking fits. Now they're on the outs and she refuses to go. Up to this point, she was winning the battle. Once she slams the door, it's over. She loses big points for that, giving Crystal a tactical advantage."

"I'd find it difficult."

"Who doesn't? Girls her age are melodramatic by nature and Leila's high strung. She's one of the brightest kids we have, but she's a handful. They all are except for a few Goody Two-shoes. You never know where you stand with them. Personally, I prefer this, though it does get tedious."

"Fitch is all girls?"

"Thank God. I'd hate to imagine having to deal with boys that age, too. Can I fix you a drink?"

"I better not, but thanks."

She finished the last of her martini and then leaned forward and set her empty glass with a click on the pale wood coffee table. "I understand you're here about Dowan."

"Yes, and I'm sorry to intrude. I'm sure she's been through a lot since this ordeal began."

"It can't be helped."

"How's she doing?"

"I'd say fair. Of course, the strain's been enormous. The days drag on and on, some worse than others. She keeps waiting for the phone to ring, looking for his car. The rumors keep flying, but that's about all. No real sign of him yet."

"I'm sure it's hard."

"Impossible. It really gets to her. If it weren't for Griff, I don't know how she'd manage to keep sane."

"Where was she that night, this house or the other one, in Horton Ravine?"

Nica pointed at the floor. "They're usually here on weekends. Crystal's a Pisces—a water baby. This is more her style than that pretentious pile of shit Fiona built in town. Have you been there?"

"Not yet."

"No offense," she added mildly. "I know she's your client." *You poor thing* went unsaid.

"What about you? When did you hear Dow was missing?"

"Well, I knew something was going on that first night. I'd driven Leila up from Malibu as usual—we arrived about five o'clock—and she went off to her dad's. He's her stepfather, really, but he's helped raise her from infancy. At any rate, Crystal had already talked to Dow when we pulled in from school. He knew he wasn't going to be free in time for supper, so it was just Crystal and Rand and me."

"Rand?"

"Griff's nanny. He's great. He's been with the baby ever since Griff was born. You'll meet both in a bit. Rand'll bring Griff in for his good-night kiss right after his bath. By then he's had his supper and he's ready for bed. On the twelfth, we put together a cold picnic and ate it out on the deck. It was gorgeous—quite clear and very balmy for that time of year; warm enough to linger without sweaters, which is unusual out here. We chatted about nothing in particular while we worked our way through a couple bottles of red wine. At seven forty-five, Rand took Griff and went over to the other house. He's got a couple of TV shows he likes and he wanted to be there in time to settle in for those."

"Rand and the baby stay at the house in Horton Ravine?"

"Ordinarily, no. I think Crystal and Dow were looking forward to some time alone. I was probably here until ten o'clock. It wasn't late, but I was bushed, finally winding down for the week."

"What time did she expect Dow?"

"Any time after nine. That was usually his pattern when he had to work late. I guess if you're married to a doctor, you don't pay much attention to the clock. Crystal fell asleep on the couch. She called me at three in the morning after she woke and saw that he wasn't here. She thought he might've come in late and gone into the guest room to avoid disturbing her. She checked and when she realized he wasn't there, she came back down and flicked on the outside lights. His car wasn't there. She put a call through to the clinic and they said he'd been gone for *hours*. That's when she called me and I told her to call the cops. She couldn't file a report until at least seventy-two hours had passed."

"What was she thinking? Do you remember what she said?"

"The usual. Car accident, heart attack. She thought he might've been picked up by the cops."

"What for?"

"Driving under the influence."

"He drinks?"

"Some. Dow always has a couple glasses of whiskey at the clinic when he works late. It's his reward for putting in the hours above and beyond the call of duty. She's warned him about driving home afterwards, but he always swears he's fine. She was worried he might've run off the road."

"Was he on medication?"

"Hey, at his age, who isn't? He's sixty-nine years old."

"What went through your mind?"

A brief smile flickered. "Odd you should ask. I thought about Fiona. I'd almost forgotten, but it's really what popped into my mind the moment I heard."

"What about Fiona?"

"That she'd finally won. That's all she's angled for since the day he left, maneuvering to get him back, using any means she could." I thought Nica might say more, but she reached for her glass and tilted it to her lips, realizing belatedly she'd finished her drink. She sat forward on the couch. "I should be on my way. Tell Crystal I'll be at my place whenever she's done with this."

She got up and padded as far as the wide French doors.

I watched her cross the deck and disappear, striding down the path and into the sand. From the rear of the house, I could hear the sound of bathwater running, a man murmuring, and then a squeal of childish laughter rebounding against tile walls: two-year-old Griffith with his nanny, Rand.

FOUR

During the time I was alone, I took advantage of the lack of supervision to do a quick assessment of the place. Ordinarily, if left to my own devices, I'd have opened a few drawers, sorted through the mail, perhaps even scanned a letter or a credit card statement. There's ever so much information embedded in our correspondence, which is why those pesky federal mail-tampering penalties are so severe. Hunt as I might, however, I couldn't find anything of interest and I was reduced to gazing at home furnishings, trying to calculate the value—not a specialty of mine. In one corner, there was a round table draped with a floor-length cloth, surrounded by four chairs wearing those little matching dresses with the bows tied in back. I pulled up one skirt and discovered a common metal folding chair. The table itself was constructed of a round of raw plywood bolted to a cheap set of legs. This was a workaday metaphor for much that I observe during the course of my work: what looks good on the surface usually turns out to be crap underneath.

To my left, the far walls were floor-to-ceiling bookcases, a sliding ladder affixed to a railing midway up. Closer inspection revealed shelves lined with romance novels by women writers with made-up sounding names. A free-standing Swedish fireplace provided warmth on chilly nights without obstructing the ocean view. A long angled counter separated the high-tech kitchen from an eating area that looked out at the beach. To the right, there was a staircase that I surveyed with longing. The second and third floors probably contained the bedrooms, perhaps a study or home office where all the yummy paperwork was kept. Of course, it was likely her mail was sent to the main residence in Horton Ravine, which might explain the absence of letters sitting out in plain view.

I heard someone cross the room just above me, the muffled thump of bare feet on bare hardwood floors. I glanced up without thinking, following the sound. Belatedly, I realized there was a "window" in the ceiling, clear glass or Lucite maybe thirty-six inches square with a view into the bedroom directly above. Startled, I watched Crystal Purcell parade naked across my line of view. Thirty seconds later, she padded down the stairs, still barefoot, wearing wash-faded jeans cut so low her belly button showed. Her short-cropped

T-shirt was gray, the neck of it pulled out of shape by years of wear. By my reckoning, she hadn't had enough time to pull on any underwear.

Her hair was an upscale-salon blond, a little longer than shoulder length, framing her face in a tangle of soft curls. A few strands along her neck were still damp from the shower. Holding out her hand, she said, "Hello, Kinsey. I'm sorry to keep you waiting. I just came back from a run and wanted to get rid of all the sweat and sand." Her grip was strong, her voice mild, her manner pleasant but subdued. "Where's Anica? Did she leave? I asked her to keep you company until I came down."

"She just left. She asked if you'd call her as soon as you're free."

Crystal moved into the kitchen, sailing her comments in my direction while she crossed to the stainless steel refrigerator and removed a bottle of wine. "She's been a godsend, especially with Leila coming home on week-ends. It's been hard enough without worrying about her on top of everything else. Anica's the counselor at Leila's private school."

"That's what she said. Must be nice having her so close."

"She's a good friend. One of the few, I might add. Dow's Horton Ravine pals view me as beneath contempt."

I couldn't think how to respond so I kept my mouth shut. I moved as far as the counter, keeping her in view. I could see evidence of Griff's dinner. The tray on his chrome-and-plastic high chair still bore a three-sectioned Beatrix Potter plate, with drying curds of scrambled egg, toast crusts, and a smear of applesauce. A bib had been laid over the back of the chair.

"How long have you known her?"

"Really, not that long. Sometime early last spring. I saw her out on the beach and then later at Fitch at one of those dreadful parent teacher conferences. Did she offer you a drink?"

"She did. I thought I'd better not have anything just yet."

"Really. How come?" She took a corkscrew from the kitchen drawer, and began opening the bottle as she moved to the kitchen cabinet and fetched herself a glass.

"I don't know. It doesn't seem professional, given that I'm here on business."

Bemused, she took out a second glass and held it up. "You sure? It won't count against you. We can sit out on the deck and sip wine while we watch the sun go down."

"Oh, all right. Why not? You talked me into it."

"Great. I hate to drink by myself." She held out the glasses and the bottle. "If you'll take these, I'll make us

up a plate of nibbles. That way we won't get looped
. . . or any more looped than we choose."

I took the glasses in one hand, the stems forming an
X, and tucked the bottle of white wine in the crook of
my arm. I crossed the great room and pushed open one
of the French doors with my elbow. Once on the deck,
I set the items on a weathered wooden table between
two wood-and-canvas sling chairs. The wind gusting in
from the ocean was damp and smelled pungent, like an
oyster liqueur. I took a deep breath, picking up the
faint taste of salt at the back of my throat.

Two palms near the house made tiny scratching
noises as the fronds swept back and forth against the
graying exterior. I moved to the edge of the deck, my
gaze sweeping along the surf. The beach was deserted,
while out on the ocean, white lights were showing on
the oil rigs like diamonds on dark velvet. The weather
bore the edgy feel of danger. I sat down, crossing my
arms as I huddled against the chill. It was nearly
twilight; a gradual, indiscriminate darkening, with no
color visible through the heavy clouds. Far out on the
horizon, I could see patches of silver where rays from
the late sun pierced the marine layer. I heard the distant
whine of a commuter plane approaching along the
coast. Through the French doors, the living room
looked clean and cozy. I was grateful for the protection
afforded by the long-sleeved turtle neck under my

blazer. Idly, I glanced at the Chardonnay bottle with its classy black-and-silver label. I leaned closer. The price tag, $65.00, was more than I'd paid for my telephone and electric bills combined that month.

Two ornamental lamps came on, and Crystal, still barefoot, emerged from the house, carrying a tray of cheese and crackers, arranged with grapes and apple wedges. She'd pulled on a heavy navy sweater that hung, fetchingly, almost as far as her knees. She left the door open behind her, glancing over at me. "You look cold. I'm used to the ocean, but you must be freezing. Why don't I fire up the outside heaters? It'll just take a sec. You can pour the wine, if you would."

I did as she suggested and then watched as she hunkered next to a fat propane cannister with a heater element affixed. Her fingernails and toenails were both done in a French manicure, white defining the half-moon at the base of the nail and under the rim. The look was clean, though—like her hair—the effect probably cost her dearly and had to be redone every other week. It wasn't hard to imagine her doing a bump-and-grind routine. She turned a valve, using an electric match to ignite the hissing gas as it escaped. Soon after, the reddening coils glowed nearly white. She lit the second of the two heaters, turning them to face us so that warmth poured out across the space between us. "Is that better?"

"Much."

"Good. If you need something warmer, don't hesitate to say so. I have a huge supply of sweaters in the downstairs closet."

We sipped wine in silence while I tried to decide how and where to begin. "I appreciate your taking the time to talk to me."

She smiled faintly. "I considered hiring a detective myself half a dozen times, but I didn't want to undermine the police. I have every confidence in the job they're doing. Apparently, Fiona doesn't."

"She likes the idea of someone devoted solely to the family's interests. The police have other cases requiring their more immediate attention." I paused. "I just want to be clear that any comments you care to make will be safe with me. If you have relevant information, I'll report it to her, but nothing else gets passed on. You can be as candid as you like."

"Thank you. I was wondering about that."

"I'm assuming there's no love lost."

"Hardly. Fiona's done everything in her power to make my life hell on earth." Her face was angular, mouth wide. Her eyes were gray, her brows pale, her lashes thick and black. Aside from mascara, she seemed to wear little or no makeup. I could tell she'd had her eyes done and probably her nose as well. In fact, just about everything I was looking at had been augmented or improved by some merry band of surgeons working on her, piece by piece. Crystal's smile was brief. "Look. I know she's busy painting a picture of herself as the victim in all of this, betrayed and put-upon. The truth is, she never gave Dow a thing. It was all take, take, take. Dow reached a point where he had nothing left. Poor guy. When I think of the hours he worked, all the sacrifices he made for them, and in exchange for what? For years, the three of them have stood around with their hands out. Fiona in particular. She was always coming up with some new harebrained scheme, her current business venture being one. Interior design? Who's she trying to kid? She's a Horton Ravine matron spending someone else's money and suddenly, she's talking about her talent and her 'eye' for design. She only has one client—some friend of hers named Dana . . ."

"She's married to one of Dow's business associates?"

"Joel Glazer, that's right. How do you know him?"

"I don't. I know her, or I did back when she was married to someone else."

"She couldn't be too bright. Fiona's milking her for everything she's worth."

"What about Dow's daughters? What's your relationship to them?"

Crystal shrugged that one off. "They're all right. They don't know the half of what goes on. They

67

probably hate me, but at least they're too polite to say so. They're usually busy sucking up to their dad. I'm sure they're worried he'll die and leave all his money to Griffith and me, which I can understand. I'd worry about the same thing if I were in their shoes."

She picked up a butter knife and cut into a wedge of Brie. She spread the soft cheese on a cracker, which she held out to me. I took it, watching while she made a second for herself, popped it in her mouth, and chewed. "Anyway, with Dow gone, it doesn't seem important. Whatever quarrel I have with Fiona is immaterial."

"You have any idea where he is?"

"I wish. That's all I've really thought about for the past nine weeks."

"Do you believe he's alive?"

"No, not really, but I can't be sure. If I knew he was dead, at least I could make my peace with it and get on with life."

"The police detective mentioned money missing. He says close to thirty thousand dollars had been pulled from his savings over a period of the past two years."

"So I heard. I didn't know anything about that until they brought it to my attention. I know he kept a large sum of money somewhere, but he never said anything else about it. Apparently, the statements for that account were being forwarded to a post office box that I used to keep. Dowan asked about it a couple of months ago and I told him it'd been canceled. Now it looks like he was paying to keep it open all this time."

"I wonder why he asked you when he already had the answer."

Crystal shrugged. "Maybe he was wondering how much I knew."

"Why would he need that kind of cash?"

"I have no idea. He used credit cards for everything."

"Could it be extortion?"

"For what?"

"That's what I'm asking. Any ideas about that?"

"You think he's being blackmailed? That's ridiculous. How so?"

"Isn't it possible?"

She stared at me briefly and then shook her head, apparently drawing a blank. "You'd think a black-mailer would be interested in a lump sum, not a piddling three bills a week."

"Maybe it seemed more acceptable that way. It's one thing to demand a large sum of cash. It's something else again if someone asks for help making ends meet."

"I'm sure he'd have told me if someone were extorting money. Dow told me everything."

"As far as you know."

She blinked. "Well, yes."

"Besides, it might have involved you."

"In what way?"

"He might have paid the hush money in your behalf, as protection."

"I don't think so." I could have sworn her cheeks tinted, but in the fading light it was difficult to tell. Her hand certainly didn't tremble as she raised the glass to her lips. She set her wineglass on the deck and pressed her flattened hands between her knees as though to warm them.

I changed tactics, not wanting her to disconnect from the conversation. "Would you be willing to go back and talk about what it's been like for you the past nine weeks?"

She let out a breath. "It's been awful. Horrendous. At this point I'm numb, but the first two or three days, I was running on pure adrenaline and it really wore me down. The house was teeming with people—my friends, Dow's daughters, his friends and colleagues. I didn't want to see anyone, but I couldn't refuse. I didn't have enough energy to resist, so they swarmed right over me. I was barely holding on. All I wanted to do was sit and stare at the phone, pace to the door and back, scream, or get drunk. For days I'd get in the car and drive between the clinic and home, checking every possible route. I'd find myself on the road and then I'd realize how dumb it was. Dow could be anywhere and the chances of my spotting him were astronomically low."

"Was there anything unusual about the day he disappeared? Any behavior—anything he said—that seems different in retrospect?"

Crystal shook her head. "It was like any other Friday. He was looking forward to the weekend. Saturday, he was playing in a tennis tournament at the country club. Nothing special, but he enjoyed it. Saturday we were going out to dinner with friends—this was a couple who'd recently moved here from Colorado, where they owned some restaurants."

"Can you give me those names?"

"Sure. I'll give you a list before you leave."

"No one else reported anything unusual?"

"Not as far as I know. You can talk to his colleagues and the nursing home staff. I've spoken to most of them myself and asked the same question. The police have done informal interviews as well. People have tried to be helpful, but no one seems to know anything or if they do, they haven't said."

"Was he having problems at work?"

"There are always problems at work. Dow takes his job very seriously. He's involved with patients and staff, management issues. He also handles all the hiring and firing and the annual salary reviews. There's always something going on. It's just the nature of the beast. Recently, he's spent a lot of time going over the books. The fiscal year at the clinic ends November 30 and Dow likes to be on top of it."

"I take it most of his time is devoted to the clinic?"

"That's right. He retired from private practice about five years ago. Aside from a few charities still dear to his heart, he spends his time at Pacific Meadows, keeping that up and running."

"Were—are—his responsibilities medical or administrative?"

"I guess I'd say both. He's very involved with the residents—not treating them, of course, they have their own personal physicians for their medical needs, but Dow's there every day keeping an eye on things. I have to tell you, it's not always easy. When your specialty's geriatrics, you're going to lose the very people you've grown most attached to."

"Anyone in particular?"

"Well, no. I wasn't speaking of anyone specific," she said, "and I'm not saying he couldn't cope. Of course he could. He's been working with the elderly for many years. I'm just saying it took a toll on him emotionally."

"Is it possible he walked off?"

"No."

"You're sure of that?"

"Absolutely. And you want to know why? Because of Griff. That boy is the light of Dowan's eyes. If Dow got home late, he went to Griff's room first. He'd lie down on the bed with him and just watch him breathe.

Sometimes I'd find him fast asleep in there. He'd never leave Griffith voluntarily."

"I understand," I said.

"There's something else as well. Dow's writing a book. This is a project he's been wanting to do for years. He's seen so many changes in medicine. He really has wonderful stories to tell. He wouldn't abandon that."

"What about the two of you? Are you doing okay?"

"We're very close. In fact, we've been talking about another baby now that Griffith is two."

"So you're convinced something's wrong."

"Very wrong. I just can't think what. If he'd been injured or abducted, surely we'd have heard by now."

"What about his employers? What can you tell me about them?"

"I really don't know much. I've only met Joel Glazer twice and one of those occasions was the groundbreaking for the new Pacific Meadows annex, and we didn't have time to chat. As I understand it, Joel and Harvey Broadus made a fortune in construction, developing retirement communities in the Southwest. They also own a chain of board-and-care homes, plus a number of nursing facilities across the state. We used to see Harvey occasionally at social events, but he's apparently in the middle of a nasty divorce so he's keeping a low profile. He's a bit phony for my taste, but maybe that's just me. Anyway, after Dow retired in 1981, he found himself at loose ends. Everyone knows how highly regarded he is in the medical community. They approached him with regard to Pacific Meadows and asked him to take over the administrative work."

"And they all get along?"

"As far as I know. I mean, they hardly ever see each other. Joel and Harvey seem to be happy with Dow, so they tend to go their way and let him go his. An operating company does the billing. I know at first he was worried they'd interfere with the running of the place, but it hasn't turned out that way."

"How long have they owned the place?"

"I believe they bought it in 1980. It's over on Dave Levine Street right there at the corner of Nedra Lane. You've probably passed it a hundred times. Looks like Tara without the acreage—big white columns across the front."

"Oh, that. I see it on the right side any time I drive in from that end of town. There must be five or six nursing homes along that stretch."

"The staff people all refer to it as Formaldehyde Alley, no disrespect intended. Dow hates when I repeat that."

"How did you two meet?"

"Mom . . ."

Crystal glanced into the great room through the open door. "We're out here." She must have caught sight of Leila because she turned back with an expression of annoyance and disbelief. "Oh, for heaven's sake."

I followed her gaze.

Leila was clumping down the stairs in a pair of black satin pumps with heels so high she could hardly stand erect. Now and then her ankles wobbled as though she were setting off across the ice for the first time on skates. Under her black leather jacket, her top was a see-through confection of chiffon and lace, worn with a long, narrow wool skirt. At fourteen, she was still in that coltish stage of development: no bust to speak of, narrow hips, and long bony legs. The length of her skirt couldn't have been less flattering. She looked like the cardboard cylinder in a spent roll of paper towels. She'd also done something strange to her hair, which was cut short, dyed a white blond, sticking out in all directions. Some strands had been dreadlocked while the rest remained as wispy as cotton candy. She came to the open door and stood there staring at us.

Crystal snorted. "What's that getup supposed to be?"

"It's not a 'getup.' What's wrong with it?"

"You look ridiculous. That's what."

"You do, too. You look like a bag lady. That sweater's down to your knees."

"Fortunately, I'm not going out in public. Now please go upstairs and find something decent to wear."

"God, you are always so *worried* what other people think."

"Knock it off. I'm really tired of fighting with you."

"Then why don't you leave me alone? I can dress any way I want. It's no reflection on you."

"Leila, you're not leaving the house dressed like that."

"Great. I won't go then. Thanks a lot and fuck you."

"Where's your suitcase?" Crystal said patiently, declining Leila's invitation to escalate.

"I don't have one. I told you I'm not going. I'd rather stay here."

"You didn't see him last time and I swore you'd be there."

"I don't have to go if I don't want to. It's my decision."

"No, it's not, it's mine, so quit arguing."

"Why?"

"Leila, I'm irritated at all the lip you've been giving me. What's the matter with you?"

"I just don't want to go. It's boring. All we do is sit around and watch videos."

"That's what you do *here*!"

"You promised I could see Paulie."

"I never said any such thing. And don't change the subject. Paulie's got nothing to do with it. Lloyd's your father."

"He is *not*! We're not even related. He's one of your stupid old ex-husbands."

"One ex-husband. I've only been married once before," she said. "Why are you being so hostile and obnoxious? Lloyd adores you."

"So what?"

"Leila, I'm warning you."

"If he's so full of adoration why does he force me to spend time with him against my will?"

"He's not forcing you. *I* am and that's final. Now get ready."

"I will if I can see Paulie."

"Absolutely not."

"God, you're so mean. You don't give a shit about me."

"That's right. I'm just here to abuse and mistreat you. Call Children's Protective Services."

"You think Lloyd's so great, why don't you go see him yourself?"

Crystal closed her eyes, trying to control her temper. "We're not going to do this in front of company. He's got joint custody, okay? He's picking you up at seven, which means he's already on his way over. I'll come get you Sunday morning at ten. Now go back up and change. And you better pack a bag or I'll do it myself and you'll hate what I choose."

Leila's face shut down and I could see a patch of red form around her nose and mouth where she held back tears. "You are so unfair," she said, and clomped back up the stairs again. She slammed the door behind her after entering her room, then screamed the word "bitch" again from the far side of the door.

Crystal returned to our conversation, making no reference to Leila beyond a shake of her head and a rolling of her eyes. "Dow and I met in Vegas at the home of mutual friends. The first time I saw him, I knew I'd marry him one day."

"Wasn't he married?"

"Well, yes. I mean, technically speaking, but not *happily*," she said, as though Dow's marital angst justified her poaching on Fiona's turf. "You've met Fiona. She's only six months younger than him, but she looks like she's a hundred. She drinks. She smokes two packs a day. She's also hooked on Valium, which I doubt she mentioned when she was hiring you. Dow was sixty-nine last spring, but you'd never guess by looking. Have you seen a picture of him?"

"There was one in the paper."

"Oh, that was terrible. I have a better one. Hang on."

She left the deck and moved into the great room, returning moments later with a framed color photo. She sat down on her chair again and passed the photograph to me. I studied Dow Purcell's face. The picture, taken on the golf course, had been cropped so that the others in his foursome were scarcely visible. His hair was white, trimmed close, and his face was lean. He looked tanned and fit, wearing a white golf shirt, pale chinos, and a leather golf glove on his right hand. I couldn't see the head of the club he was holding up right in front of him. "Where was this taken?"

"Las Vegas. The same trip. That was in the fall of 1982. We were married a year later when his final divorce papers came through."

I handed the photo back. "Does he gamble?"

She held the framed photograph and studied it herself. "Not him. He was speaking at a symposium on geriatric medicine. He loved Vegas for the golf, which he played all year long. He was a five handicap, really very good."

I wondered at the sudden use of the past tense, but decided not to call attention to the shift. "Do you play?"

"Some, but I'm terrible. I play to keep him company when he's got no one else. It's nice when we travel because it gives us something to do." She leaned forward and set the picture on the table, studying it briefly before she turned back to me. "What happens now?"

"I'll talk to anyone who seems relevant and try to figure out what's going on."

"There's your mommy," a man said. He stood just inside the door, holding Griffith, who was dressed for bed in flannel jammies with enclosed rubber-soled feet and a diaper tailgate in back. His face was a perfect oval, his cheeks fat, his mouth a small pink bud. His fair hair was still damp, sharply parted on one side, and combed away from his face. Blond curls were already forming where a few strands had dried. Mutely, he held his arms out and Crystal reached for him. She fit him along her hip, looking at him closely while she spoke in a high-pitched voice, "Griffie, this is Kinsey. Can you say 'Hi'?"

This elicited no response from the child.

She took one of his hands and waved it in my direction, saying, "Hewwoh. I weady to doh feepy. I dotta doh beddy-bye now. Nightie-night."

"Night-night, Griffith," I said, voice high, trying to get into the spirit of the thing. This was worse than talking to a dog because at least there you really didn't anticipate a high-pitched voice in response. I wondered if we were going to conduct the rest of the conversation talking like Elmer Fudd.

I glanced at Rand. "Hi. You're Rand? Kinsey Millhone."

"Oh, I'm sorry. I should have introduced you."

Rand said, "Nice to meet you." He appeared to be in his early forties, dark-haired, very thin, jeans, white T-shirt. I could still see damp splotches on his front from the toddler's bath. Like Crystal, he was barefoot, apparently impervious to cold.

I said, "I better go and let you get the little one to bed."

Rand took Griffith from his mother and retreated, chatting to the child as he went. I waited while she jotted down the names and phone numbers of her husband's business associates and his best friend, Jacob Trigg. We exchanged parting remarks of no particular consequence, and I left with her assurance I could call if I needed to.

On the way out, I passed Leila's stepfather Lloyd, who'd just arrived. He drove an old white Chevy convertible with a shredded sun-faded top and patches of primer where various dents and dings were being prepped for repainting. His brush cut was boyish and he wore glasses with oversized lenses and tortoise-shell frames. He had the body of a runner or a cyclist, long, lean legs and no visible body fat. Even with a nip in the air, all he wore was a black tank top, shorts, and clunky running shoes without socks. I placed him in his late thirties, though it was hard to determine since I glanced at him only briefly as he passed. He nodded, murmuring a brief hello as he approached the front door. As I started my car, the first fat drops of rain were beginning to fall.

FIVE

Aside from Henry, Rosie's tavern was empty when I arrived shortly after seven o'clock. I closed my umbrella and leaned it up against the wall near the door. The Happy Hour crowd had apparently been there and gone and the neighborhood drinkers hadn't yet wandered in for their nightly quota. The cavernous room smelled of beef and wet wool. Several sections of newspaper formed a sodden door mat inside the entrance, and I could see where people had trampled their wet feet across the linoleum, tracking dirt and lines of newsprint. At one end of the bar the television set was on, but the sound had been muted. An old black-and-white movie flickered silently across the screen: a night scene, lashing rain. A 1940s coupe sped along a winding road. The woman's hands were tense on the wheel. A long shot through the windshield revealed a hitchhiker waiting around the next curve, which didn't bode well.

Henry was sitting alone at a chrome-and-Formica

table to the left of the door, his raincoat draped over the chair directly across from him, his umbrella forming a puddle of rain water where it leaned against the table leg. He'd brought the brown paper bag in which Rosie had presented her sister's medical bills. He had a glass of Jack Daniel's at his elbow and a pair of half-rimmed glasses sitting low on his nose. An oversized accordion file rested on the chair next to him, the sections divided and labeled by the month. I watched him open a bill, check the date and heading, and then tuck it in the proper pocket before he went onto the next. I pulled up a chair. "You need help?"

"Sure. Some of these go back two years if not more."

"Paid or unpaid?"

"Haven't figured that out yet. A little bit of both, I suspect. It's a mess."

"I can't believe you agreed to do this."

"It's not so bad."

I shook my head at him, smiling slightly. He's a dear and I knew he'd do the same for me if I needed help. We sat in companionable silence, opening and filing bills. I said, "Where's Rosie all this time?"

"In the kitchen making a calf's liver pudding with anchovy sauce."

"Sounds interesting."

Henry shot me a look.

"Well, it *might* be," I said. Rosie's cooking was

madcap Hungarian, the dishes impossible to pronounce and sometimes too peculiar to eat, her fowl soup with white raisins being a case in point. Given her overbearing nature, we usually order what she tells us and try to be cheerful about it.

The kitchen door swung open and William emerged, dressed in a natty three-piece pin-striped suit, a copy of the evening paper tucked under his arm. Like Henry, he's tall and long-limbed, with the same blazing blue eyes and a full head of white hair. The two looked enough alike to be identical twins on whom the years had made a few minor modifications. Henry's face was narrower; William's chin and forehead, more pronounced. When William reached the table, he asked permission to join us, and Henry gestured him into the remaining chair.

"Evening, Kinsey. Hard at work, I see. Rosie'll be out momentarily to take your supper order. You're having calf's liver pudding and kohlrabi."

"You're really scaring me," I said.

William opened his paper, selected the second section, and flapped the first page over to the obituaries. Though his lifelong hypochondria had been mitigated by marriage, William still harbored a fascination for those people whose infirmities had ushered them out of the world. It annoyed him when an article gave no clue about the nature of the final illness. In moments of depression or insecurity, he reverted to his old ways, attending the funeral services of total strangers, inquiring discreetly of the other mourners as to cause of death. Key to his query was identifying early indications of the fatal illness—blurred vision, vertigo, shortness of breath—the very symptoms he was destined to experience within the coming week. He was never at ease until he'd solicited the true story. "Gastric disturbances," he'd report to us later with a significant stare. "If the fellow'd only consulted medical authorities at the first hint of trouble, he might be with us today. His brother said so."

"We all have to die of something," Henry invariably said.

William would turn peevish. "Well, you don't have to be such a pessimist. Vigilance is my point. Listening to the body's messages—"

"Mine says, *You are going to die one day regardless so wise up, you old fart.*"

Tonight, Henry glanced at William's paper politely. "Anyone we know?"

William shook his head. "Couple of kids in their seventies; only one with a photo. Couldn't have been taken much later than 1952." He squinted at the page. "I hope we didn't look that smarmy when we were young."

"You certainly did," Henry said. He took a sip of whiskey. "If you go first, I know exactly the picture I'm going to give the paper for your obit. You in those knickers the summer we toured Atlantic City. Your hair's parted down the center and it looks like you're wearing lipstick."

William leaned closer. "He's still jealous because I took Alice Vandermeer away from him. She could jitterbug like the dickens and had money to burn."

Henry said, "She had a wen on her cheek the size and color of a small Concord grape. I never knew where to look so I palmed her off on him."

William turned several pages to the classified ads, where he compared descriptions of "found" dogs and cats with those reported missing, often spotting a match. While Henry and I continued to open and file Klotilde's medical bills, William entertained us with all the livestock currently being offered for sale. He glanced up at me. "Well, here's something. Still need office space? You should check this one out. Five hundred square feet, newly renovated, downtown. Two fifty a month, available immediately."

I stopped what I was doing and tilted my head in his direction. "You're kidding. Let me see that."

William handed me the section, pointing to the item, which read:

For lease: 500 sq ft in newly renovated Victorian, heart of down-town near courthouse; private bath and separate entrance w/private deck. $250/mon. Call Richard after 6:00pm.

The phone number was listed.

I read the lines twice but they didn't seem to change. "I'll bet it's a dump. They always embellish in these ads."

"It won't hurt to call."

"You really think so?"

"Of course."

"What if it's rented?"

"You won't be out anything. Maybe the guy has others." He reached into his watch pocket and removed a coin, which he placed on the table right in front of me. "Go on."

I took the coin and the paper and crossed the room. The pay phone was in the vestibule, the area dimly illuminated by a neon Budweiser sign. I dialed the number and read the ad again while I listened to four rings. Finally, the line was picked up on the other end and I asked to speak to Richard.

"This is he."

I placed him in his thirties, though phone voices can be deceptive. "I'm calling with regard to the office space listed in tonight's paper. Is the place still available?" I noticed a tinge of plaintiveness had crept into my voice.

"Sure, but we're asking for a year's lease, first and last month's rent, plus a cleaning deposit."

"Can I ask what street it's on?"

"Floresta. Across from the police station and about six doors down."

"And the price quoted is correct? The ad says two hundred and fifty bucks a month."

"It's only one room. It's got a closet and bathroom, but it's not large."

I pictured a phone booth. "Would it be possible to see it tonight?"

"As it happens, my brother's in there laying carpet and I'm on my way over. You want to take a look, I can meet you there in fifteen minutes."

My watch said 7:30. "Great. I can do that. What's the address?"

He gave me the information. "You can pull on down the driveway to the parking lot in back. You'll see lights on, first floor rear. My brother's name is Tommy. The last name's Hevener."

"I'm Kinsey Millhone. Thanks so much. I'll see you in fifteen minutes."

*

The building had clearly once been a single-family residence: a one-story white-frame cottage with gables in the roofline and a lot of gingerbread trim. At 7:42 I eased my VW down the driveway, my headlights cutting through the shadows. I slowed and peered out the driver's side window. The white paint looked fresh and there were flower beds along the side. How had I missed this? The location was ideal—one block away from the office I was now in—and the price couldn't have been better. I counted ten parking spaces laid out along the narrow backyard, which was paved with asphalt and fenced on two sides. A black pickup truck was parked in one spot, but the rest were empty at this hour. There was a big trash bin just at the exit to the alleyway in back. Looking up, I could see Lonnie's office windows and the back wall that framed the tiny lot behind his building. I parked and got out, trying to curb the sudden surge of hope. For all I knew, the property was on the market, or the lot was the site of a former gas station, the soil still contaminated by benzene and other carcinogens.

A wide redwood deck had been constructed across the back of the building, complete with a long wooden ramp installed for easy wheelchair access. A market umbrella with a big pale canvas shade stood open above a glass-topped table surrounded by four chairs. Several large terra-cotta pots had been planted with herbs. I was about to hyperventilate. First floor lights were ablaze. I entered a small foyer. A door stood open to my immediate right. The scent of fresh paint was strong, overlaid by the staunch, secondary odor of brand-new carpeting. I closed my eyes while I offered up a quick prayer, repudiating my wickedness and promising to mend my evil ways. I opened my eyes and stepped through the doorway, absorbing the room at a glance.

The room was twelve by twelve, with new hand-crank windows on two walls. There were two tiers of white-painted shutters in place of conventional drapes. On the far wall, two doors stood open, one leading to a small bathroom, the other into what was clearly a spacious walk-in closet. A red-headed fellow in jeans, an olive green T-shirt, and heavy work boots was sitting on the floor kicking a carpet stretcher, forcing the carpet taut along the baseboard. A phone line had been installed and the phone was currently resting on the surface of an empty cardboard box.

The carpet itself was an industrial-grade nylon, a pattern of beige flecks against a charcoal gray background. I could see his carpet knife with its fat, curved blade, and the mallet he used to pound the carpet backing onto tack strips. Carpet scraps were piled up in the center of the room. An insulated plastic cooler was positioned near the wall beside a wastebasket that was filled to the brim with more carpet trimmings. The room seemed stuffy from the glaring two-hundred-watt bulb overhead.

I said, "Hi, I'm Kinsey. Your brother said he'd meet me here at seven forty-five. Are you Tommy?"

"That's me. Richard's always late. Written guarantee. I'm the good boy, the one who shows up when I'm expected. Hang on a minute. I'm almost done here." He glanced over, flashing me a smile, all green eyes and white teeth. Deep creases formed a bracket around his mouth. With his red hair and his ruddy complexion, the effect was electric, like a black-and-white film with a wholly unexpected sequence in Technicolor. I felt myself averting my gaze with a little frisson that danced its way along my spine. I hoped I hadn't inadvertently whimpered aloud.

I watched him kick, pound, and cut, the muscles in his back and shoulders bunching as he worked. His arms were knotted with veins and matted with a fine red hair. A trickle of sweat angled down along his cheek. He shrugged, blotting the side of his face with the sleeve of his T-shirt. He tossed his mallet aside and sprung to his feet, wiping his palms on the back of his pants. He held a hand out, saying, "What's your name again?"

"It's Kinsey. The last name's Millhone with two L's."

The sun had taken its toll on his fair complexion, leaving a series of lines in his forehead, additional lines at the outer corners of his eyes. I pegged him in his late twenties, five foot ten, a hundred and sixty pounds. Having been a cop, I still view men as suspects I might be called upon later to identify in a lineup. "Mind if I look around?"

He shrugged. "Help yourself. There's not much to see," he said. "What kind of business you in?"

I walked into the bathroom, my voice echoing against the tile. "I'm a private detective."

Toilet, pedestal sink with a built-in medicine cabinet above it. The shower stall was fiberglass with an aluminum-framed glass door. The floor was done in a white ceramic tile that ran halfway up the wall. Above, there was a floral-print vinyl paper in beige, white, and charcoal gray. The effect was both fresh and old-fashioned. Also, easy to keep clean.

I moved back into the main room and crossed to the closet, peering into the four-by-six space, which was fully carpeted, empty, and painted a pristine white. Sufficient room for filing cabinets and office supplies. Even had a hook where I could hang my jacket. I turned back to the main room and let my gaze travel the perimeter. If I placed my desk facing the window, I could look out at the deck. The shutters were perfect. If a client dropped in, I could close the lower set for

93

privacy and leave the upper set folded back for light. I tried a window crank, which turned smoothly, without so much as a whine or a creak. I leaned against the windowsill. "No termites, no leaky roof?"

"No ma'am. I can guarantee that because I did the work myself. This is real quiet back here. You ought to see it by day. Lot of light coming through these windows. Trouble walks in, you got cops right across the street." His accent was faintly Southern.

"Fortunately, my job's not that dangerous."

He tucked his hands into his front pockets. His face was dappled with sun damage like a fine patina of freckles. I couldn't think what to say next and the silence stretched. Tommy launched in again without a lot of help from yours truly. "Place was in pretty bad shape when we took possession. We upgraded plumbing and electrical, put on a new roof and aluminum siding. Stuff like that." His voice was so soft I found myself straining to hear.

"It looks nice. How long have you owned it?"

"About a year. We're new out here. We lost our parents a few years ago—both passed away. Richard hates talking about that almost more'n me. It's still a sore subject. So, now it's just the two of us, my brother and me." He crossed to the cooler and opened the lid, glancing over at me. "Offer you a beer?"

"Oh, no thanks. I was just about to have supper

when someone showed me your ad. After I talk to Richard, I'll head on back and eat there."

"Don't like to drink and drive," he remarked, smiling ruefully.

"That's part of it," I said.

He rooted through the crushed ice, pulled out a Diet Pepsi, and popped the tab. I held up a hand, but not quick enough to stop him. "Seriously, I'm fine."

His frown was softened by a tone of mock disapproval. "No beer, no soda pop. Can's open now. Might as well have a sip. You don't want the whole thing to go to waste," he said. Again, he proffered the Pepsi, waggling the can coaxingly in my direction. I took it to avoid a fuss.

He reached into the cooler and extracted a bottle of Bass Ale. He flipped the cap off and held it by the neck while he seated himself on the floor. He leaned his back against the wall, his legs extended in front of him. His work boots looked enormous. He gestured at the empty expanse of carpet. "Pull up a seat. Might as well be comfortable."

"Thanks." I picked a spot across from him and sat down on the floor, taking a polite sip of Pepsi before I set the can aside.

Tommy took a long draw of beer. He looked like a guy accustomed to smoking while he worked. "I used to smoke," he said, as though reading my mind.

"Tough to give up, but I think I got it licked. You smoke?"

"Once upon a time."

"Been six months for me. Now and then, I still get the itch, but I take in a couple of breaths just like this. . . ." He paused to demonstrate, his chest expanding as he sucked air audibly through his nose. He let out his breath. "Pretty soon the craving goes away. Where you from?"

"I'm local. Went to Santa Teresa High."

"Me and my brother come from Texas. Little town called Hatcher. Ever hear of it?"

I shook my head.

"Right outside Houston. Pop was in oil. Luckily he sold the company before the bottom dropped out. Poured all his money into real estate. Developed shopping malls, office buildings, all kinds of commercial properties. California's weird. People don't seem all that friendly like they do where we come from. Especially the women. Lot of them seem stuck-up."

The silence settled again.

He took another pull of beer and wiped his mouth on his palm. "Private detective. That's a new one on me. You carry a gun?"

"Occasionally. Not often." I dislike being "drawn out," though he was probably only being polite until his brother appeared.

He smiled lazily as if picking up on my innate crankiness. "So which do you prefer? Guys way too young for you or guys way too old."

"I never thought about it like that."

He wagged a finger. "Guys way too old."

I felt my cheeks grow warm. Dietz really wasn't that old.

"Me, I like women your age," he said, showing flash of white teeth. "You got a boyfriend?"

"That's none of your business."

Tommy laughed. "Oh, come on. You seeing someone steady?"

"More or less," I said. I didn't want to piss this guy off when I was hoping against hope I'd end up renting the place.

" 'More or less.' I like that. So which is it?"

" 'More,' I guess."

"Can't be much of a romance if you have to guess." He narrowed his eyes as though consulting his intuition. "So here's what I think. I bet you're real schizy. Bet you blow hot and cold about other human beings, especially men. Am I right?"

"Not necessarily. I wouldn't say that."

"But you must've seen a lot of bad guys, the business you're in."

"I've seen some bad women, too."

"That's another thing I like. Bad girls, bad women,

renegades, rebels . . ." He lifted his head, checking his watch as he did. "Here he comes. Fifteen minutes late. You can just about bank on it."

I glanced at the window as a pair of headlights swept across the parking area. I rose to my feet. Tommy finished his beer and set the bottle aside. A car door slammed and shortly afterward Richard Hevener walked in, tapping a clipboard restlessly against the side of his leg. He wore jeans and a black T-shirt, over which he wore a supple-looking black leather sportscoat. He was taller than Tommy and a lot stockier, his hair dark. He was the somber brother and seemed to take himself very seriously. This was going to be a chore.

"Richard Hevener," he said as he offered me his hand. We shook hands and then he turned to Tommy. "Looks good."

"Thanks. Finish picking up and I'm out of here. You need anything else?"

I tuned out briefly while the two conferred. I gathered there was another property undergoing renovations and Tommy was starting work on that the following week. His manner had shifted in his brother's presence, his flirtatiousness gone. Their discussion finished, Tommy picked up the wastebasket full of carpet scraps and carried them outside, heading for the trash bin at the rear of the lot.

"So what do you think of the place?" Richard said,

turning to me. "You want to fill out an application?" His accent and his manner of speaking were much less "Texas" than Tommy's. Consequently, he seemed older and more businesslike.

"Sure, I could do that," I said, trying not to sound like I was sucking up.

He passed me the clipboard and a pen. "We pay water and trash. You pay your own electric and phone. Heating's prorated and it varies, depending on the season. There's only one other tenant and he's a CPA."

"I can't believe the space hasn't been snapped up."

"Ad just went in. We've already had a lot of calls. Three, right after yours: I'm meeting another guy tonight."

I could feel anxiety begin to mount. I leaned on a windowsill and began to fill in the information. Applications are tedious, requiring tidbits of information that are actually nobody's business. I filled in my Social Security number and my California driver's license number, circled DIVORCED in the section that asked if I were single, married, or divorced. Previous addresses, how long, and reasons for leaving. Personal references I listed, along with the bank where I had my checking account. I made a few things up. I drew a dotted line where it asked for credit card numbers and the balance on those accounts. By the time I finished, Tommy had left. I heard his truck in the driveway and then it was gone. I handed Richard the clipboard, watching while he scanned the information.

"If you want a deposit, I can give you one tonight."

"No need. I'll call your references and run a credit check. We have a couple more people coming by on Monday."

"Do you have any idea how soon you'll be making a decision?"

"Middle of the week. Make sure we have a way to reach you in case I have a question."

I pointed to the application. "That's my home phone and my work phone. I've got a message machine on both."

"This your current business address?"

"That's right. I'm renting space from an attorney named Lonnie Kingman. He and my landlord will both tell you I pay on time."

"Sounds good. Something comes up, I'll call. Otherwise, I'll be in touch once I've processed all the applications."

"Fine. That sounds great. If you like, I can pay the first six months in advance." I was starting to sound ridiculous, fawning and insecure.

Richard said, "Really." He studied me, his eyes a dark, brooding brown. "Fifteen hundred dollars, plus the additional one seventy five for the cleaning deposit," he said, making sure I knew the full extent of my folly.

I thought about Fiona's check for fifteen hundred bucks. "Sure, no problem. I could give you that right now."

"I'll take that into consideration," he said.

SIX

Saturday, I opened my eyes automatically at 5:59 A.M. I stared up at the skylight, which was beaded with rain, the entire Plexiglass dome scattered with tiny pearls of light. The breeze coming in the bedroom window smelled of leaf mold, wet sidewalks, and the dripping eucalyptus trees that lined the street beyond. Actually, the scent of eucalyptus is almost indistinguishable from the odor of cat spray, but I didn't want to think about that. I bunched the pillow under my head, secure in the knowledge that I didn't have to crawl out of bed for my run. As dutiful as I am about exercise, there's still nothing more delicious than the opportunity to sleep in. I burrowed under the covers, ignoring the world until 8:30, when I finally came up for air.

Once I'd showered and dressed, I made myself a pot of coffee and downed a bowl of cereal while I read the morning paper. I changed my sheets, started a load of laundry, and generally picked up around the place. When I was a child, my aunt Gin insisted I clean my room on Saturdays before I went out to play. Since we lived in a trailer, the task didn't amount to much, but the habit remains. I dusted, vacuumed, scrubbed toilet bowls—mindless activities that left me free to ruminate. I alternated fantasies, mentally rearranging furniture in my new office space and thinking about who to query next in my search for Purcell. With Fiona's fifteen-hundred-dollar retainer now safely in my account, I felt obligated to work through the weekend. I resisted the temptation to theorize after only one day's work, but if I'd been forced to place bets, I would have plunked down my money on the notion that Purcell was dead. From what I'd learned of him, I couldn't see him taking off without a word to his wife and small son. That didn't explain the missing passport and the missing thirty grand, but both might surface in due course. At this point, there was no reason to believe they were germane.

At eleven o'clock, I hauled out the phone book and turned to the yellow pages, checking out the section that listed nursing homes. There were close to twenty by my count. Many boasted large boxed ads detailing the amenities:

COMPREHENSIVE RECUPERATIVE & LONG-TERM CARE ...
SPACIOUS ROOMS IN A TRANQUIL SETTING ... ELEGANT
DESIGN OF BUILDING AND INTERIOR ... BEAUTIFUL NEW
FACILITY WITH SECURE GARDEN COURTYARD.

Some included cartoon maps with arrows pointing out their superior locales, as though it was preferable to decline in one of Santa Teresa's better neighborhoods. Most facilities had names suggesting that the occupants pictured themselves any place but where they were: Cedar Creek Estates, Green Briar Villa, Horizon View, Rolling Hills, The Gardens. Surely, no one envisioned being frail and fearful, abandoned, incapacitated, lonely, ill, and incontinent in such poetic-sounding accommodations.

Pacific Meadows, the nursing home that Dow Purcell managed, touted twenty-four-hour RN care and on-site chapel and pastoral services, which were bound to come in handy. It was also certified by Medicare and Medicaid, giving it a decided advantage over some of its private-pay competitors. I decided to make a visit to see the place myself. The regular staff probably wouldn't be there on weekends, which might prove advantageous. Maybe all the prissy, officious sorts were home doing laundry just like I was.

I tucked a fresh pack of index cards in my handbag,

pulled on my boots, and found my yellow slicker and umbrella. I locked the door behind me and scurried through the puddles to my car parked at the curb. I slid in on the driver's side, shivering involuntarily at the chill in the air. The rain had picked up from the early morning lull and now pounded on my car roof with the staccato rattle of falling nails. I fired up the engine and then hunched over the steering wheel, driving in slow motion while the windshield wipers gave the royal wave.

When I pulled into the parking lot at Pacific Meadows, the sky was dark with clouds and the lights in the windows made the place look cozy and warm. I chose a spot near the entrance, assigned to an employee whose name had been painted out; black on black and impossible to read. I shut down the engine and waited until the squall had passed before I emerged. Even then, I had to pick my way across the half-flooded tarmac to the relative dryness of the sheltered front entrance. I shook off my umbrella and gave my slicker a quick brush before I stepped through the door. Dripping raincoats and wide-brimmed water-repellent hats were hung on a row of pegs. I added my slicker to the mix and propped my umbrella in the corner while I took my bearings.

Along the wide hallway ahead, I could see a row of six elderly people in wheelchairs arranged against the wall like drooping houseplants. Some were sound asleep and some simply stared at the floor in a sensory-deprivation daze. Two were strapped in, their posture eroded by osteoporosis, bones melting from within. One woman, very thin, with long, white limbs, swung a bony leg fretfully over the arm of the wheelchair, moving with agitation as though prompted by pain. I felt myself recoil as if I were at the scene of a four-car pileup.

At the far end of the corridor, two women in green uniforms piled sheets on a laundry cart already heaped with soiled linens. The air smelled odd—not *bad*, but somehow alien—a blend of disassociated odors: canned green beans, adhesive tape, hot metal, rubbing alcohol, laundry soap. There was nothing offensive in any single element, but the combination seemed off, life's perfume gone sour.

To my right, aluminum walkers were bunched together like grocery carts outside a supermarket. The day's menu was posted on the wall, behind glass, like a painting on exhibit. Saturday lunch consisted of a ground chicken patty, creamed corn, lettuce, tomato, fruit cup, and an oatmeal cookie. In my world, the lettuce and tomato might appear as a restaurant garnish, a decorative element to be ignored by the diner, left behind on the plate to be thrown in the trash. Here, the lettuce and tomato were given equal billing, as though part of a lavish nutritional feast. I thought about fries and a QP with Cheese and nearly fled the premises.

French doors opened into the dining room, where I could see the residents at lunch. Even at a glance, I noted three times more women than men in evidence. Some wore street clothes, but the majority were still dressed in their robes and slippers, not bedridden, but confined by their convalescent status. Many turned to stare at me, not rudely, but with a touching air of expectation. Had I come for a visit? Was I there to take them home? Was I someone's long-overdue daughter or niece proposing an outing in the clean, fresh air? I found myself glancing away, embarrassed I was offering nothing in the way of personal contact. Sheepishly, I looked back, raised my hand, and waved. A tentative chorus of hands rose in response as my greeting was returned. Their smiles were so sweet and forgiving I felt pricked with gratitude.

I backed away from the dining room and crossed the hall. A second set of doors stood open, revealing a day room, currently empty, furnished with mismatched couches, upholstered chairs, a piano, two television sets, and a cluster of game tables. The floors were done in a glossy beige linoleum, the walls painted a restful shade of robin's egg blue. The ready-made drapes were a blend of yellow, blue, and green in a vaguely floral pattern. Countless throw pillows had been needle-pointed, cross-stitched, quilted, and crocheted. Perhaps a clutch of church ladies had been afflicted by a fit of stitchery. One pillow had a saying embroidered across the face—YOU'RE ONLY AS OLD AS YOU FEEL—a disheartening thought, given some of the residents I'd seen. Metal folding chairs were stacked against the near wall for quick assembling. Everything was clean, but the "decorating" was generic, budget-driven, falling somehow short of good taste.

I walked past the front desk, which was located in a small alcove, and cruised down the corridor, guided by signs indicating the services of a dietary supervisor, a nursing supervisor, and a clutch of occupational, speech, and physical therapists. All three doors were open, but the offices were empty and the lights had been doused. Across the hallway I saw a sign for Admissions. That door was closed and a casual try of the knob told me it was locked. Next door was Medical Records, which apparently shared space with Administration. I thought I'd start there.

The overhead lights were on and I moved through the door. There was no one in evidence. I waited at the counter, idly staring at the wire basket filled with incoming mail. Casually, I surveyed my surroundings. Two desks back-to-back, one with a computer, the other with an electric typewriter humming faintly.

There were numerous rolling file carts, a copy machine, and metal file cabinets on the far wall. There was also a big clock with a clicking second hand I could hear from fifteen feet away. Still no one. I rested my elbow on the counter, dangling my fingers near the basket full of mail. By fanning the corners and tilting my head, I could read most of the return addresses. Bills, the usual gas and electric, a lawn and gardening service, two manila envelopes from Santa Teresa Hospital, better known as St. Terry's.

"Can I help you?"

Startled, I straightened up and said, "Hi. How're you?"

The young woman had emerged from the door connecting Administration to Medical Records. She wore glasses with red plastic frames. Her complexion was clear, but she looked like she'd suffer a contagion of zits at the least provocation. Her hair was a medium brown in several irregular lengths; a layered cut grown out now and badly in need of a trim. Under her green smock, she wore brown polyester pants. The name MERRY, and PACIFIC MEADOWS were machine-embroidered on the breast pocket above her heart.

She crossed to the counter, passing through a hinged door, and took her place on the far side. At first glance, I'd thought she was in her early thirties, but I quickly revised that downward by a good ten years. She wore metal braces on her teeth and whatever she'd eaten for lunch was still embedded in the wires. Her breath smelled of tension and discontent. Her expression remained quizzical, but her tone had an edge. "Can I ask what you were doing?"

I blinked one eye in her direction. "I lost my contact lens. It might have popped out in the car. I only noticed it just now. I thought it might have fallen in the basket, but there's no sign of it."

"Want me to help you look?"

"Don't worry about it. I have a whole box of 'em at home."

"Are you here to see someone?"

"I'm here on business," I said. I removed my wallet from my shoulder bag and flipped it open. I pointed at my P.I. license. "I've been hired to look into Dr. Purcell's disappearance."

Merry squinted at my license, holding up the postage stamp-sized photo for comparison with my face-sized face.

I said, "Are you the office manager?"

She shook her head. "I'm temping here on weekends while the other girl's out on maternity leave. Monday through Fridays, I'm Mrs. Stegler's assistant."

"Really. That's great. And what does that entail?"

"You know, typing, filing. I answer phones and

distribute mail to all the residents, whatever needs doing."

"Is Mrs. Stegler the one I should be talking to?"

"I guess. She's acting associate administrator. Unfortunately, she won't be back until Monday. Can you stop by then?"

"What about Mr. Glazer or Mr. Broadus?"

"They have an office downtown."

"Gee, that's too bad. I was driving through the neighborhood and took a chance. Well. I guess it can't be helped."

I saw her gaze stray to her computer. "Could you excuse me a minute?"

"Go right ahead."

She moved around to her twelve-inch monitor with its amber print on black. She was probably using office hours to do her personal correspondence. She pressed keys until she'd backed out of the document. She returned to the counter, smiling self-consciously. "You have a business card? I can have Mrs. Stegler call you as soon as she gets in."

"That'd be great." I took my time fumbling through my handbag to find a business card. "How long have you been here?"

"Three months December 1. I'm still on probation."

I put my card on the counter. "You like the work?"

"Sort of, but not really. You know, it's boring, but okay. Mrs. S. has been here forever and she started out just like me. Not that I'll stick around as long as she has. I'm two semesters short of my college degree."

"What field?"

"Elementary ed. My dad says you shouldn't job hop because it looks really bad on your résumé. Like you're shiftless or something, which I've never been."

"Well yeah, but on the other hand, if you're interested in teaching, there's no point hanging on to a job that doesn't suit."

"That's what I said. Besides, Mrs. S. is real moody and gets on my nerves. One day she's sweet, like butter wouldn't melt in her mouth, and then she turns around and acts all crabby. I mean, what is her *problem*?"

"What's your guess?"

"Beats me. They're still looking for someone to fill the position, which gritches her but good. She thinks she should be promoted instead of just being used is how she put it."

"If she did get promoted, who would she replace?"

"Mrs. Delacorte. She's the one who got canned."

I kept my expression neutral. Not only was she bored, but she hadn't learned the basic rules, the most compelling of which is never, never, never confide company secrets in the likes of me. I said, "Golly, that's too bad. Why was she fired, has anybody said?" My lies and fake behavior are usually heralded by "Gollys" and "Gees."

"She wasn't fired exactly. It's more like she was laid off."

"Oh, right. And when was that?"

"The same time as Mrs. Bart. She's the bookkeeper since way back when. They were interviewing for her position the same time I applied for this one."

"How come?"

"How come what?"

"I wonder how the bookkeeper and the administrator got laid off at the same time. Was that coincidence?"

"Not at all," she said. "Mrs. Bart was let go and Mrs. Delacorte got upset and raised a stink. Mr. Harrington suggested she might be happier finding work somewhere else, so that's what she did. This is all stuff I heard." She stopped what she was saying and her eyes seemed to widen behind the red plastic frames. "You're not taking notes. I'm not supposed to gossip. Mrs. S. is hell on that."

I held up my hands. "I'm just making conversation 'til the rain lets up."

She patted her chest. "Whew! For a minute, I got nervous. I wouldn't want you to get the wrong impression. I mean, it's like I told her, I'd never blab anybody's private business. It's not in my nature."

"You and me both," I said. "So who's Mr. Harrington? I never heard of him."

"He works for the billing company in Santa Maria."

"And he's the one who hired you?"

"Kind of. He interviewed me by phone, but only after Mrs. S. had already approved my application. That's the way it works around here. Make the guys think they're in charge when we're really the ones who do everything."

"I thought Dr. Purcell did all the hiring and firing."

"I don't know anything about that. I was here less than two weeks when he, you know, ran off or whatever. I think that's why Mr. Harrington was forced to step in."

"Where's Mrs. Delacorte work now? Has anybody said?"

"She's over at St. Terry's. I know because last week she stopped by to visit with Mrs. S. Turns out she found a great job so it's worked out fine. Getting laid off can be a blessing, though it didn't seem like it at the time is what she says."

"What about Mrs. Bart?"

"I don't know where she went."

"Did you know Dr. Purcell?"

"I knew who he was, but that's about it. That's his office in there. He just like, you know, vanished. It really gives me the creeps."

114

"Weird. I wonder what went on."

"No telling. The whole staff's upset. All the residents adored him. He made sure everybody got a card on their birthday and stuff like that. He paid out of his own pocket just so all these pitiful old people would feel special."

"Has anyone made a guess about what happened to him?"

"It's all they talked about at first. I mean, not me so much because I hardly knew him."

"What kind of thing . . ."

I could see Merry wrestle with her conscience, deliberating a good seven seconds before She-Who-Never-Blabs leaned toward me. "Promise you won't repeat this. . . ."

"I won't even say it *once*."

She lowered her voice. "Mrs. S. thinks he left the country."

I lowered my voice, too. "Because of . . ."

"Medicare."

"Oh, that's right. Someone mentioned that before, but I didn't have a chance to ask. Meaning what?"

She said, "*F-R-A-U-D*. Last winter, the OIG—"

"OIG?"

"Oh, that's the Office of Inspector General. They're part of the Department of Health and Human Services. Anyway, OIG faxed us this list of charts and billing

115

records they wanted to see. Mrs. S. said at first Dr. Purcell didn't think anything of it. They do that sometimes just to keep you on your toes. But then they came back and he figured out how serious it was. He kept going over the information to see how it'd look to them. Not good. Up to his lower lip in poop, to coin her phrase."

"Is that why he'd been working late the last couple of months?"

"Well, yeah."

"So the place is under investigation?"

"Big time. It started as a desk audit. They wanted a bunch of stuff covering the past two years. That's when Dr. P. came in as the medical director. I mean, he's that and administrator with a hyphen in between. The way Mrs. S. tells it, if Pacific Meadows loses its funding, the place'll be shut down. Not to mention all the penalties—you know, fines and restitution. She says maybe even jail time, plus the public embarrassment. The Purcells are like this big-time la-di-dah social couple so you can imagine the disgrace. Dr. P. was the one lined up to take the brunt of it. Like his butt's in a sling. Those are her words, not mine."

"What about his employers?"

"Oh, the other two don't have anything to do with the hands-on stuff. They're all over the state, taking care of other business."

"Well, that sounds scary for Dr. Purcell," I said.

"I'd've died if it'd been me."

"I'll bet," I said. "When did this first come up?"

"I think last January, way before my time. Then in March, these two guys from MFCU swooped in unannounced—that's the Medicaid Fraud Control Unit. They came loaded with questions and a list of all the charts they wanted pulled. Everybody scrambled around practically wetting their pants. Dr. P. was notified of this big list of violations and a lot of questionable claims, meaning p-h-o-n-y. We're talking *thousands* of dollars. Half a million at least and that's just scratching the surface. He could turn out to be a major big-time crook."

"I'm surprised it didn't hit the papers."

"Mrs. S. says they'll keep a lid on it 'til they see what they've got. Meantime, they're breathing down his neck and they mean business."

"So she thinks he bolted to avoid punishment?"

"Well, I sure would if I was in his place."

"How do you know it was him? Other people must've had access to billing records. Maybe that's why the bookkeeper was laid off," I said.

She leaned forward and lowered her gaze. "You won't mention this, you swear? Cross your heart."

I crossed my heart and held up my hand.

"Mrs. Dorner—she's director of Staff Development?

She thinks Dr. P. could've been kidnapped. Snatched in the parking lot to keep him quiet."

I said, "Wow," and made a skeptical face. "Unfortunately, the cops say there's no real evidence of that."

"It wouldn't take much. Slap tape on his mouth, throw him in the trunk, and take off," she said. "They could have used his own car, which is why it hasn't been found."

I saw Merry's look as she began to busy herself, fussing with the mail. "That's a very good point."

I glanced over my shoulder. A nurse in a white uniform was standing in the doorway. She had fixed us with a look that was both shrewd and intimidating. I cleared my throat and said, "Well, Merry. I better scoot and let you get back to work. I'll stop back on Monday and chat with Mrs. Stegler."

"I'll tell her you were here."

The nurse turned and looked at me as I passed through the doorway within inches of her. I repressed the urge to shudder once my back was turned, wondering exactly how much she'd heard.

At the entrance, I retrieved my slicker and took a moment to reassemble myself in rain garb. When I emerged from the nursing home, the rain had slowed to a drizzle and a mist seemed to float on the tarmac like smoke. The eaves still dripped water at irregular intervals. I bypassed a puddle and crossed the parking lot to the slot I'd taken. I could see now, with fresh eyes, that the name newly painted out at the foot of the parking space was P. DELACORTE.

Once in my car, I opened the pack of index cards and started taking notes—one fact per card—until I'd emptied my brain.

SEVEN

After I left Pacific Meadows, I stopped by Kingman and Ives and let myself in the side door. I went into my office and peeled off my slicker, which I hung on my coat tree. Happily for me, the place felt deserted despite the fact there were lights on in most of the offices. The Saturday-morning cleaning crew had come and gone. Wastebaskets had been emptied. The air was scented with Pledge and I could see rows of fresh vacuum cleaner tracks on the burnt-orange carpeting. The quiet was divine. Briefly, I conjured up an image of the new one-person office on Floresta Street. I was already feeling competitive with the other prospective tenants.

I pulled out my portable Smith-Corona and placed it on my desk. I sat down in my swivel chair and took out the file I'd opened. I sorted through the notes I'd assembled, adding the information on the index cards. Looming large in my mind was Fiona's return on Tuesday. I could already see her, arms crossed, one foot tapping with impatience while I brought her up to date. She'd have dollar signs dancing like sugar plums above her head, thinking, *Fifty bucks an hour for this?* My strategy was to outfox the woman by presenting a beautifully constructed, typewritten report that would make it look like I'd done a lot more than drive around chatting with folks. What I labored under was the burdensome sense of Fiona's disapproval, knowing she begrudged me every nickel I spent. Even if her original display of irritation had been pure manipulation, I could feel the sting of her whip on my neck. I tried not to dwell on the notion that I should have declined the job when I had the chance.

I focused my attention on the business at hand. It took me an hour to sketch out a rough draft. I typed it and did some editing, revising it twice. I kept my language neutral, being careful to avoid drawing conclusions from what I'd learned so far. I also omitted much of what Crystal had said. I was being paid to find Dow, not to tattle to Fiona on his second wife. When I was satisfied the document was as polished as I could make it, I typed the new draft. Then I got out my calculator and added up my hours. How long had I spent with Detective Odessa? I tapped with my pencil on my front teeth. Really it was twenty minutes max, which I rounded out to half an hour. Didn't want Fiona thinking I'd short-changed her with the cops. Let's see.

I'd spent almost two hours with Crystal and I added another hour to cover my morning visit to Pacific Meadows. I eyeballed the numbers. So far, I'd only earned $175 out of the $1,500 she'd paid me up front, which meant I still owed her $1,325 worth of my life. At this rate, I'd never be out from under. Oh well. I typed the invoice and attached it to the original of my report, then placed the copies in the folder.

I stood up and stretched, working the kinks out of my neck with a head roll or two. Feeling restless, I wandered down the inner corridor, peering into offices along the way. As I passed Lonnie's office, I was startled to catch sight of him. He sat tilted back in his swivel chair, his feet propped up on the edge of his desk, a transcript in his lap, apparently catching up on work while the office was quiet and the phones were silent. In lieu of the usual dress shirt and suit, he wore a plaid flannel shirt and a pair of stone-washed jeans. His concentration was complete, a focus that caused his whole body to become still. I watched him reach for his pencil and underline a phrase, soft scratching in the quiet.

Lonnie looks like a boxer, his body dense and muscular, his nose thickened by scars. His hair is dark and unruly, growing in all directions. I've seen newborns like that, with a head of hair so thick and unexpected it seems comical. He's a man of high energy, generally souped up on vitamins, coffee, nutritional supplements, and competitive drive. This was probably as relaxed as I'd ever seen him.

"Lonnie?"

He glanced up and smiled, tossing his pencil aside. "Kinsey. Come on in. I've been wondering what you were up to. I haven't seen you for weeks."

"Not much. I didn't even know you were here. The place has been so quiet, I thought I was alone. Catching up on work?"

"Sure, but it's just an excuse. Marie's out of town. Some convention of butt-kickers down in San Diego. Tell you the truth, I'd rather be here than stuck by myself at home. Have a seat," he said. "What about you? What brings you in on a Saturday afternoon?"

"I was typing up some notes while things were fresh on my mind. Oh hey, before I forget. A guy named Richard Hevener may be calling to check my references."

"What's the deal?"

"I think I found office space, but I'm waiting to see." I filled him in on the situation, describing the newly renovated cottage with its redwood deck. "It's great. Small and quiet and the location's perfect."

"If he calls, I promise I'll sing your praises. I won't say a word about the tiny bit of time you spent incarcerated. Meantime, the door's always open if it doesn't work out."

"I appreciate that. Cross your fingers for me."

"Not a problem," he said. "Ida Ruth tells me you're working on Dr. Purcell's disappearance."

"How'd she hear *that*? I only took the job yesterday."

Lonnie waved a hand in the air. "Ida Ruth knows everything. She makes a point of it. Actually, she has a friend who used to work for him. Current speculation has it he's run away from home. Days when I think about doing that myself."

"Oh, please. Marie would come after you and hunt you down like a dog." His wife was a martial arts instructor, an expert in ways to cripple people with her size-five bare feet.

"There is that. Of course, the problem with disappearing is you can't do it on impulse. Not if you're serious. Takes long-term planning if you want to stay gone."

"So you'd think. Personally, I suspect he's dead, but his passport and thirty thousand dollars disappeared at about the same time."

"Thirty thousand dollars would be gone in six weeks. Purcell's accustomed to living well. He's not going to pinch pennies. At his age? He'd have to be nuts."

"That was my reaction. On the other hand, if he settled in a Third World country, he could live pretty well on it, and if he ran short of funds, he could probably set up a small practice with no questions asked."

"Why not just stay where he is?"

"Ah. I forgot to tell you the wrinkle I came across today." I filled him in on my visit to Pacific Meadows and the chat I'd had with Merry, the Patron Saint of Loose Lips. "According to her, the federal fraud busters are hot on his trail. Half a million dollars in bogus claims. Guilty or innocent, he might have taken off once he realized they were closing in."

Lonnie winced with impatience. "Get serious. No way. The feds aren't gonna put a guy like him in jail. The prosecutor has to prove criminal intent and how's he going to do that? Believe me, Medicare regulations would drive any honest man insane. So you weasel the deal; claim coding errors and incompetent clerical help. They might fine him and wag a finger, but any good attorney could get him off. Hell, I could do it myself and I don't know beans about that stuff. First thing you do is bore the hell out of the jury. Put up a bunch of charts and graphs, citing statistics 'til nine out of the twelve start nodding off. Suggest the old doc's gone senile or he's a poor businessman." He paused with a snort of amusement. "You hear about that case? Some

125

guy up in Fresno got acquitted because a jury decided he was too dumb to be guilty of embezzlement. His own attorney painted him as such a buffoon, the jury took pity and cut the poor dunce loose. Purcell's in no danger."

"Yeah, but did he know that? And what about the public disgrace?"

"Nobody cares about those things in this day and age." Lonnie picked up his pencil and drew a box on his legal pad. "One thing you're forgetting. If the guy's smart . . . say he's ripped off the system to the tune of half a million bucks, which is probably conservative. All they know about so far. Call it two million dollars just to make it worth the risk. A smart guy makes two, maybe three trips abroad. Picks a country where he knows he can count on extradition laws if the feds track him down. He sets up a bank account and feeds money in, transferring funds until he has what he needs. Then he can go on merrily cheating 'til someone's onto him. Situation heats up, he's on the first plane out. In that case, the thirty thousand dollars is just his travel fund."

I thought about Fiona's story of Dowan's vanishing twice without explanation. "Good point." I was also thinking about the bookkeeper, who got fired, and the assistant administrator, who quit her job in protest. Maybe that was Dow's attempt to point a finger elsewhere. The phone rang and Lonnie picked up the handset. From the nature of his comments, it was Marie checking in. I waved at him and eased out of his office, leaving him to finish his conversation in private.

I returned to my office and reread my report. It seemed okay, but I thought I'd let it sit for a day. I'd be adding interviews once I figured out who I'd be talking to next. I drew up a list from the possibilities I'd gleaned. Purcell's business associates were among the top five names, along with Dow's best friend. I made sure I had the necessary phone numbers and then decided I'd done enough and it was time to go home.

At two o'clock, I made myself some milk of tomato soup and a gooey grilled cheese sandwich that I dipped in my bowl and lifted dripping to my lips. The liquid red of the soup against the crunchy golden surface of the bread was a culinary portrait of early childhood consolation. Aunt Gin first served me this confection when I was five years old, mourning my parents who'd been killed in a car wreck the previous May. The ooze of melted Velveeta will always prompt the curious sensation of sorrow and satisfaction comingling on the surface of my tongue. This sandwich, I confess, was the highlight of my weekend, which is what life boils down to when you're celibate.

Afterward, I did what any other trained professional

investigator would do: I walked the six steps into the living room, flipped off my shoes, and settled on the sofa, where I covered myself in a big puffy comforter and started reading a book. Within minutes, I'd been sucked through a wormhole into a fictional world, traveling faster than the speed of words into a realm without sound and without gravity.

The phone rang, the sound annoyingly shrill. I'd sunk like a stone into a river of dreams and I was disoriented by the need to surface. I reached back, fumbling for the phone, which was resting on the end table above my head. I hadn't even realized I'd fallen asleep, except for the drooling, which I don't ordinarily do when awake.

"Ms. Millhone?"

"Yes." If this was someone selling something I was going to say a very bad word.

"This is Blanche McKee."

Three seconds passed. The name meant nothing. I rubbed my face and said, "Who?"

"Fiona Purcell's daughter. I understand Mother's hired you. I just wanted you to know how relieved we all are. We've been urging her to do this ever since Daddy disappeared."

"Oh, right. Sorry. I couldn't place the name. How're you?" Groggily, I sat up, pulling the quilt around me like a tribal robe.

"Fine, thanks. I hope I'm not calling at a bad time. I didn't wake you, did I?"

"Not at all," I said. The truth is, everyone knows you've been sleeping regardless of how earnestly you might lie to them.

Blanche must have decided to take me at my word. "I'm not sure how much Mother's told you—quite a lot, I'm sure—but if there's anything I can do, I'll be happy to help. Did she mention my friend Nancy?"

"I don't believe so. The name doesn't sound familiar."

"I was afraid of that. Mother tends to be a cynic, which you might have guessed. Nancy's recently moved to Chico, but she's available for consultation any time by phone."

"Nancy. Good news. I'm making a note." Whoever Nancy was.

"I'm assuming you'll want my personal impressions as well."

"Sure. I mean, eventually. That'd be great."

"I'm so happy you said that because I was thinking— if you have a minute this afternoon, you might want us to get together so I can share my concerns."

I hesitated. "Ah. Well. You know, at the moment, I'm more interested in facts than impressions and concerns. No offense."

"None taken. I didn't mean to imply that I don't have facts."

"Uh-hun." I hadn't forgotten Fiona's barely disguised contempt for her younger daughter, mother of four, soon to be mother of five. On the other hand, maybe Fiona'd told Blanche about me in order to test my perseverance, since I'd made such a point of it during our meeting.

Blanche said, "What time would suit?"

I went ahead and mouthed the bad word, adding another choice expletive from my extensive collection. "Hang on a second. I'll check my schedule." I held the receiver to my chest while I looked at my watch. 4:06. I allowed time to pass while I pretended to scan my day planner with its numerous Saturday-afternoon appointments. I had no particular desire to meet Blanche, especially at the cost of a first-class nap. I hated the idea of abandoning my lair and I certainly didn't want to traipse all over town on such a cold, damp day. My living room windows were already gray with the premature November twilight and I could see the drizzle slant against the bare branches that were tapping at the panes. I glanced at my watch again. 4:07.

I could hear Blanche breathing and when she spoke, her tone was sharp. "Kinsey, are you there?"

"I'm here. Gee, it looks like I'm booked up today.

130

Tomorrow might be possible. I could be there by ten o'clock."

"That won't work for me and Monday's out of the question. Isn't there *any* way you could stop by? I feel it's terribly important."

What I personally felt was a surge of irritation. I could just see Fiona returning from San Francisco, carping because I hadn't taken time to interview Blanche. *Fifteen hundred dollars and you couldn't even bother to see my daughter?* I said, "I could be there by five-thirty, but only for half an hour. That's the best I can do."

"Perfect. That's fine. We're up on Edenside at the corner of Monterey Terrace. The number's 1236. It's a two-story Spanish. You'll see a dark blue station wagon parked in the drive."

Edenside Road was part of a small housing development cunningly tucked into the foothills; five winding streets, each of which ended in a wide cul-de-sac. The builder had followed the terrain, taking the path of least resistance, the five streets built into the contours of the hill like rivulets of asphalt flowing from the highest point. My progress was halting, an exasperating ten miles an hour, as I slowed for a speed bump every

131

fifteen yards or so. The neighborhood was ideal for children, whose presence was announced by the number of strollers, play-houses, swing sets, bicycles, tricycles, Big Wheels, and skateboards littering the yards. It looked like a Toys "R" Us had exploded close by.

The house at the corner of Edenside and Monterey Terrace was indeed a two-story Spanish hacienda with a courtyard in front. Even in the gathering dark, I couldn't miss the three-car garage that jutted forward aggressively like a pugnacious jaw. As I watched, the low-voltage landscape lights came on, illuminating the front of the house. The exterior stucco was tinted a gaudy pink and the roof tiles, while clay, were a series of interlocking orange S's, clearly mass produced. The original clay tiles still gracing many older structures in town are now a dark faded red, mottled with lichen and shaped like a C where the worker once laid the soft clay across his thigh in forming it.

As promised, there was a dark blue station wagon parked in the drive. I pulled in at the curb, got out, locked my car, and approached the house along a crushed granite walk. The surrounding landscape was drought-proofed; all gravel and concrete, scattered with assorted cacti and oversized succulents. I let myself in through a small iron gate and crossed the tile-paved courtyard. A mock Spanish fountain splashed water by way of a circulating pump.

I rang the bell. I could hear shrieks, barking dogs, and the clattering of small feet as a pack of short folk battled for the honor of playing butler to me. As the door opened, a girl of perhaps five turned to sock the four-year-old boy-child behind her. Within seconds, fists were flailing, the children red-faced and tearful as they struggled for possession of the knob between shoves and kicks with brown hard-soled shoes. Meanwhile, two hyperactive Jack Russell terriers leaped up and down as though spring-loaded. The toddler bringing up the rear got knocked on his diaper and set up a howl. Another girl, her back turned, was walking down the hallway toward the rear of the house, bellowing, "Mom!! Mooommy! Heather's socking Josh and the dogs just knocked Quentin on his bee-hind."

"Amanda, what did I tell you about whining? Josh can take care of himself. Now please mind your own business and quit tattling or you will drive me insane."

Sway-backed, Blanche lumbered into sight, the sphere of her belly so large it looked a rogue moon, held in orbit by unseen gravitational forces. Her maternity outfit was a pale gray washable silk, palazzo pants, a long tunic, with tricky buttons and flaps. I was guessing that when the babe came, she'd be able to plop a boob out and feed the little tyke. She had long blond hair, the strands fine and glossy, reaching almost to her waist. Her porcelain complexion was tinted a pale

133

peach. Blue eyes, high forehead, finely arched brows. She looked like a storyland princess from a book of Grimm's fairy tales except, great with child.

She swooped down and gathered up the howling baby, whom she settled on her hip. She grabbed Heather by the arm, hauling her away from her brother and then giving her a push along the corridor. "You kids go out in the backyard. Amanda's going to make you some peanut butter crackers. You can have a snack out there. Just don't eat too many. We're having supper in a bit. Now scoot. I mean it. Everybody go on outside."

"Mo-om, it's *dark*."

"Well, turn the porch light on."

"But we want to watch cartoons!"

"Too bad. You do what I say. And no running," Blanche warned. Heather and Josh were already pounding down the hall, but they slowed to a power walk, knocking and bumping each other. The dogs followed, barking, while Amanda veered off into the kitchen to make peanut butter crackers without an audible complaint. Amanda, who couldn't have been much more than seven years old, was already being cast in the role of secondary mom.

While Blanche was issuing orders, she'd managed to jiggle the crying baby and his howls had subsided. She turned and labored toward the family room with me tagging along behind her as well as I could. There were toys everywhere. In order to avoid crushing plastic underfoot, I had to shuffle, making a path through the Legos strewn on the floor in front of me. A wooden gate had been secured across the stairs to the second floor and what I assumed was the basement door had a hook-and-eye closure to prevent kidlets from tumbling headlong into the yawning abyss. Ever the optimist, I said, "Your mother mentioned a nanny."

"She isn't here on weekends and Andrew's currently out of town."

"What sort of work does he do?"

"He's an attorney. Mergers and acquisitions. He's in Chicago until Wednesday."

"When's the new baby due?"

"Technically, not for three weeks yet, but he'll probably come early. All the other ones have."

In the family room, a toy chest stood open, its contents flung in every direction: dolls, teddy bears, a bright yellow school bus filled with brightly painted spool kids with round painted heads. There was a wooden bench and mallet for pounding wooden pegs, crayons, picture books, Tinkertoys, small metal cars, a wooden train. A playpen had been erected in the center of the room. I spotted a mechanical swing, a circular walker with surrounding rubber bumpers, a high chair, an infant seat, and a portable crib. Every wall socket in view had been blanked out by plastic inserts. There was nothing on any surface below see-level, every breakable object removed to a high shelf as though in preparation for a coming flood.

From outside, I could hear a piercing shriek go up, this at a higher decibel level than the earlier shrieking in the hall. Amanda started screaming, "Mommy! Mom!! Heather pushed Josh off the jungle gym and he has blood coming out of his nose. . . ."

Blanche said, "Oh, lord. Here, take him."

Without pausing, she handed off the baby like a forward pass and waddled into the kitchen. Quentin was surprisingly heavy, his bones dense as stone. He watched his mother depart and then his eyes moved to mine. Though Quentin was as yet incapable of speech, I could see the concept "Monster" forming in his underdeveloped brain. The enormity of his plight began to dawn on him, and he pursed his small mouth in advance of a round of howls.

I called, "Can I put him in his playpen?"

"No. He hates that," she yelled as she went out the backdoor. The screaming in the yard was taken up by a second child apparently vying for equal time. As if in response, Quentin's mouth came open in a cry so deep-seated he made no sound at first. He curled his body inward while he gathered his strength. Without warning, he flung himself outward like a diver in the midst of a back flip. He might have torn himself entirely out of my grasp if I hadn't grabbed him and swung him up from the floor. I said, "Whee!" as though the two of us were really having fun. The look on his face suggested otherwise.

I tried jiggling him as she had, but that only made matters worse. Now I was not only a monster, but a Monster Baby Jiggler, intent on shaking him to death. I walked around in a circle, saying, "There, there, there." The child was not soothed. Finally, in desperation, I lowered him into the playpen, forcing his stiff legs to bend until he was fully seated. I handed him two alphabet blocks and part of a half-eaten soda cracker. The howling ceased at once. He put the cracker in his mouth and banged the letter *P* against the plastic padding under him. I stood up, patting myself on the chest while I moved into the kitchen to see what was happening.

Blanche was just banging through the backdoor with four-year-old Josh on her hip, his legs hanging way past her knees. I could see a lump on his forehead the size of an egg and copious blood on his upper lip. One-handed, she dampened a kitchen towel, opened the freezer, and took out some ice cubes, which she wrapped in the towel and pressed against his head. She carried him into the family room and sank into a chair. The minute she sat down, he worked his way through a flap in her tunic and began to nurse. Taken aback, I averted my eyes. I thought kids his age had been twelve-stepped out of that. She indicated a nearby chair, paying him not the slightest attention as he suckled her right breast.

I glanced down at the chair and removed a half-consumed peanut-butter-and-jelly sandwich before I settled on the edge. Josh's medical emergency apparently entitled all of the children to escape the chill and dark outside. The next thing I knew, a cartoon show blasted from the TV set. Heather and Amanda sat cross-legged on the floor, and Josh joined them moments later holding the towel-wrapped ice cubes to his head.

I tried to concentrate on what Blanche was saying, but all I could think about was that even at my age, a tubal ligation probably wasn't out of the question.

EIGHT

I glanced at my watch, a gesture that wasn't lost on her.

"I know you're in a hurry so I'll get to the point. Has Mother filled you in on Crystal's past?"

"I know she was a stripper before she married your dad."

"I'm not talking about that. Did she mention Crystal's fourteen-year-old daughter was born out of wedlock?"

I waited, wondering at the relevance. I leaned forward, not from avid interest, but because the whistles, bangs, and manic music from the television set were loud enough to cause permanent hearing loss. I watched Blanche's lips move, putting the sentences together belatedly like the subtitles on a foreign movie.

"I'm not even sure Crystal knows who the father is. Then she married Lloyd *somebody* and had another child by him. That boy died when he was eighteen months old, an accidental drowning—this was four or five years ago."

I squinted. "And you think this is somehow connected to your father's disappearance?"

She seemed startled. "Well, no, but you said you wanted all the facts. I wanted to fill in the picture so you could see what you're up against."

"Meaning what?" A commercial came on, the sound ratcheted up a notch so the little children who lived across the street wouldn't miss the pitch for a vitamin-rich cereal that was supposed to look and taste like licorice.

Blanche was saying, "Doesn't Crystal's behavior strike you as odd?"

I was largely lip reading by now and her comment had gone completely over my head. "Blanche, could we turn down the sound on the television set?"

"Sorry." She reached for the remote control and muted the sound. The silence was heaven. The children continued to sit on the floor, arranged in front of the set as though gathered around a campfire. Frantic images danced across the screen in colors so vivid they left an afterimage if I glanced away.

Blanche returned to her commentary. "I don't know about you, but Crystal doesn't seem at all distraught about what's happened. She's cool as can be, which seems inappropriate to me."

"It *has* been nine weeks. I don't think anyone can be distraught for that long. Defenses kick in. You manage to adjust or you go insane."

"I just think it's interesting that Crystal's never made a public appeal for information about Daddy. She's never offered a reward. She's never sent out any flyers. No psychics have been consulted. . . ."

That caught me up short. "You think a psychic would help?"

"It wouldn't *hurt*," she said. "My friend Nancy's uncanny. She has this amazing, quite incredible gift."

"She's a psychic? Is that why she's offering to consult with me on the phone?"

"Of course. When I lost my diamond ring, she was able to pinpoint the exact location."

"How'd she do that? I'm really curious."

"It's hard to describe. She said she smelled something sweet. She saw glimpses of white, maybe something nautical. She did two separate . . . readings, for lack of a better word . . . and the images were the same. Then I realized the last time I remembered seeing the ring, I'd taken it off to wash my hands at the bathroom sink. I'd already searched that area half a dozen times. As it turned out, I'd set the ring in the soap dish and it was embedded on the underside of the soap, which is exactly what she smelled."

I said, "What was the white part? Was that the bathroom sink?"

"Not in that bathroom. The sink is hunter green in there, but the soap was white."

"Got it. What was the nautical part?"

Blanche's tone was defensive. "Not everything's literal. Some of the images she sees are metaphorical . . . you know, associative."

"Nautical . . . faucet water," I suggested gamely.

"The point is, Nancy's offered to consult with Crystal, but she refuses to cooperate."

"Maybe she doesn't believe in psychics."

"But Nancy's fabulous. I swear."

"How much does she charge?"

"Oh, she doesn't want money. Ordinarily, she does, but this is strictly out of friendship with me."

"Why does Crystal have to be involved? Can't Nancy do a reading and simply tell you what she sees?"

"She has to have access to the house so she can pick up on Daddy's vibes, his psychic energy. I took her over to his office and let her sit in his chair. She keeps getting this picture of him approaching a house and going through the front door. Then nothing. This has to be Crystal's beach property because she visualizes sand."

"Could be the desert."

Blanche blinked. "Well, I suppose it could."

"Anyway, go on. Sorry to interrupt."

"But that's it. She sees a door and then blank. Without Crystal's help, she can only go so far. We think he left the office and drove out to the beach house as usual, only something went terribly wrong. Of course, Crystal denies this. She claims he never arrived, but we only have her word for it."

"So you think she knows where he is and she's covering?"

"Well, yes," she said, as though surprised I'd ask. "Nancy can feel his presence. She gets the strong impression he's been hurt. He's definitely surrounded by darkness. She says he's trying to reach us, but something's holding him back."

"He's alive?"

"She's sure he's alive. She's very clear about that. However, she says there are some very negative forces at work. She says he's distressed because he doesn't know where he is. He's encompassed by this oppressive spiritual consciousness. She can feel his confusion, but that's as much as she gets. Nancy says Crystal's very connected to Daddy's plight. In fact, she probably caused it."

"How?"

"Well, she could have knocked him out and driven him away somewhere."

143

"And done what with his car? I don't mean to argue. I'm genuinely puzzled."

"There could have been two of 'em. She could have hired someone. How do I know? I'm just telling you . . . nothing would suit her better than to have him out of the way."

"Why? I mean, just for the sake of argument, let's say she had him kidnapped and he's being held against his will. What's her motive? Can't be money. There hasn't been a ransom note and no contact from anyone offering to make a deal."

Blanche leaned forward. "Listen. Before she married my father, she signed a prenuptial agreement, according to which she gets absolutely nothing if they divorce."

"Wait a minute. Back up. You still haven't told me how she intends to profit if she had him snatched."

"I didn't say she had him kidnapped. I said she knows where he is."

"What's that have to do with a pre-nup?"

"She's been having an affair."

"Your mother mentioned that as well. This is Clint Augustine?"

"Exactly. Now she wants her freedom, but she wants the money, too. If she tries to divorce him, she'll end up with nothing. The only way she benefits is if Daddy dies."

"Which, according to Nancy, he hasn't done yet."

"That's right."

"Why would she risk anything as blatant as an affair with her personal trainer? Wouldn't word get out?"

"He was her personal trainer; he's not now. Once she started screwing him, I guess they decided to discontinue the public aspects of their relationship. The rumors started flying in any event."

"How did you find out?"

"From Mother's friend, Dana Glazer. She and her husband have a house in Horton Ravine. Joel's one of Daddy's—"

"Employers. Yes, I heard about that."

"The Glazer property backs right up to Daddy's with just a little fence in between. They have a guest cottage back there, and Crystal asked if they'd consider renting it temporarily to a friend of hers. She claimed he'd bought a house he had to renovate and the work wouldn't be finished until early fall. This was back in January. Anyway, the Glazers don't use the cottage, so they decided, hey, why not? They asked eight hundred dollars a month, and the guy never batted an eye. Of course, once Dana realized what was going on, she was horrified. She found it thoroughly repulsive, which is why she hated having to tell my mom."

"Why'd she tell you?"

"She didn't. I heard it from another friend. Dana confirmed the story, but only because I pressed. Believe me, I don't gossip."

"A lot of people don't. It doesn't seem to stop them from passing stuff on. Why didn't Dana evict him if she found the situation so repellent?"

"Because he signed a six-month lease. He's gone now and good riddance. You're welcome to talk to her if you don't believe me. I mean, Dana ought to know. It happened right under her nose. Poor mother. She still thinks Daddy's coming back to her. Bad enough he left her for such a . . . *tart*, but the fact that Crystal's still *doing* it makes Daddy look like a fool."

"Which leads us to what conclusion?"

"Crystal wants him dead. She wants him out of the way," she said with the first flash of feeling I'd seen in her. Her mouth trembled and she began to blink rapidly. She looked off toward the hallway, taking a moment to compose herself. Under her maternity tunic, I saw a knot move across her lap, probably the baby's foot. I could see why people reached out impulsively to lay a hand on such a belly. Blanche directed her comments to the far side of the room. "Believe me, she married Daddy for his money. The pre-nup was just a ploy. She might have meant it at the time, but then she ran into Clint and got involved with him. Like I said, if Daddy dies, she inherits the bulk of his estate and then she's home free. If she divorces him, she gets nothing. It's as simple as that."

"Blanche, you don't know for a fact your father's dead. None of us know that. Even your friend Nancy claims he's still alive."

Blanche's gaze swung back to mine, her blue eyes ablaze. "Don't say 'even Nancy' like she's a charlatan. I resent that."

"Not my intention. I withdraw the word. The point is, she has an image of him helpless, but alive, at least from what you say."

"But for how long? The man's nearly seventy years old. What if he's tied up, what if he's gagged and can't breathe?"

"All right, all right. Let me see what I can do to check it out. So far, this is pure theory, but I can appreciate the worry."

The minute I got home, I went to my desk and began taking notes, writing down the list of possibilities for Dowan Purcell's fate. I'd dismissed the notion that he'd been kidnapped, but maybe I was wrong. He might have been forcibly removed and carted off somewhere, in which case, he was either dead (sorry, Nance) or being held against his will. I detailed the other options, writing them down as quickly as they occurred to me.

He could have left voluntarily, departing of his own accord, on the run or hiding out. He could have met with an accident while driving under the influence. If he were lying at the bottom of a canyon, it would certainly explain the fact his Mercedes hadn't been spotted yet. He could have been subject to any one of a number of fatal incidents: aneurysm, heart attack, stroke. If so, it was puzzling that no one had stumbled across the body, but it sometimes happens that way.

Or what? He could have established a secret life, having slipped from one persona into the next. What else? Fearing disgrace, he could have killed himself. Or, as Blanche suggested, someone could have killed him for gain, or to cover something worse. I couldn't think of any other permutations. Well, two. Amnesia, though that felt like an old '30s movie plot. Or he might have been assaulted by a mugger who overplayed his hand and then disposed of the body. The only other possibility was his having been arrested and jailed, but according to Detective Odessa, Purcell hadn't shown up in any law enforcement computer system. From this, I surmised that he hadn't been identified as the perpetrator of his own crimes or the victim of anyone else's.

I studied the list. There were certain variations I had no way to pursue. For instance, if Dow had been taken ill, if he'd been injured or killed in a fatal accident, I had no way to know unless someone stepped forward with information. The cops had already canvassed hospitals in the area. This was one of those times when being a small-town private investigator (and a lone operator on top of that) made the job difficult. I had no access to airline, immigration, or customs records, so I couldn't determine if Purcell had boarded a plane (or a train or a boat) in his name or someone else's (using a fake driver's license and a fake passport). If he were still in this country, he might well evade notice as long as he didn't use his credit cards, didn't rent or buy property, didn't apply for a telephone or utilities, didn't drive with expired tags, or in any other way attract attention to himself or his vehicle. He couldn't vote, couldn't do work that required his true Social Security number, couldn't open a bank account. He certainly couldn't practice medicine, which is how he'd earned a living for the past forty years.

Of course, if he'd cooked up a false identity, he could do as he pleased as long as his story was plausible and his bona fides checked out. If this were the case, finding him would be next to impossible after only nine weeks. There simply hadn't been enough time for his name to surface in the records. My only hope was to plod my way systematically from friend to friend, colleague to associate, current wife to ex, daughter to daughter, in hopes of a lead. All I needed was one tiny snag in the fabric of his life, one loop or tear that I might use to unravel his current whereabouts. I decided to focus on the areas over which I had control.

Sunday went by in a blur. I gave myself the day off and spent the time puttering around my apartment, taking care of minor chores.

Monday morning, I got up as usual, pulled on my sweats and my Sauconys, and did a three-mile jog. The cloud cover was dense and the surf was a muddy brown. The rain had eased, but the sidewalks were still wet, and I splashed through shallow puddles as I ran the mile and a half to the bathhouse where I did the turnaround. The earthworms had emerged and lay strewn across the sidewalk like lengths of gray string from an old floor mop. The path was also littered with snails traversing the walk with all the optimism of the innocent. I had to watch where I stepped to keep from crushing them.

Back at my place, I picked up my gym bag and headed over to the gym. I parked my car in the only space available, tucked between a pickup truck and a late-model van. Even from the parking lot, I could hear the clank of machines, the grunts of a power lifter straining with a dead lift. Inside, the rock-and-roll music coming in through the speakers competed with a morning news show airing on the ceiling-mounted TV set. Two women on the stair machines climbed patiently while a third woman and two men trotted smartly on treadmills set at double speed. All five sets of eyes were focused on the screen.

I signed in, idly asking Keith, at the desk, if he knew Clint Augustine. Keith's in his twenties, with a busy brown mustache and a gleaming shaven head.

He said, "Sure, I know Clint. You've probably seen him in here. Big guy, white-blond hair. He usually works out at five o'clock when the place first opens up. Sometimes he comes in later with his clients, mostly married chicks. They're a specialty of his." Keith's intermittent use of steroids caused him to swell and shrink according to his consumption. He was currently in shrunken form, which I personally preferred. He was one of those guys with a great chest and biceps, but very little in the way of lower body development. Maybe he figured because he stood behind a counter, he didn't need to buff out anything below his waist.

"I heard he's been working with Crystal Purcell."

"He did for a while. They'd come in late afternoon, Mondays, Wednesdays, and Fridays. Isn't she the wife of the guy who disappeared a while back? Man, that's a tough one. Something skanky going on there."

"Could be," I said. "Anyway, I gotta get a move on. Thanks for the info."

"Sure thing."

151

I pulled on my workout gloves and found a quiet spot. I stretched out on a gray mat and started with my ab routine, two sets of fifty sit-ups, hands behind my head, my bent legs resting on a free-weight bench. I could smell glue fumes wafting through the asphalt-gray carpeting. The Nautilus and Universal machines looked like elaborate constructions built from a full-size Erector set: metal verticals, bolts, pulleys, angled joints. Once I finished my sit-ups, I started with leg curls, the exercise I most despise. While I counted fifteen reps, I pictured my hamstrings popping loose and rolling up like window shades. I moved on to leg extensions, which burned like hell, but at least didn't threaten any crippling side effects. Back, chest, and shoulders. I finished my workout with preacher curls and dumbbell curls. I saved the best machine for last: triceps extensions, always a favorite of mine. I left the gym damp with perspiration.

Home again, I showered, pulled on a turtleneck, jeans, and my boots, grabbed a bite of breakfast, and packed myself a brown-bag lunch. I reached the office at nine o'clock and put a call through to the police department, where Detective Odessa assured me he'd do yet another computer check to see if there was any sign of Dow Purcell. He'd already sorted through numerous bulletins describing the unidentified dead throughout the state. There were no Caucasian males in Purcell's age range. Local police, sheriff's department, and CHP officers were being briefed weekly on the importance of keeping an eye out for him. Odessa had increased his coverage, papering most of the medical facilities in the surrounding counties in case Purcell showed up incoherent or comatose.

I briefed him on the people I'd spoken to so far. When I told him about the issue of Medicare fraud, he said, "Yeah, we know that."

"Well, why didn't you tell me?"

"Because it's Paglia's call and we're under orders from him."

By the end of the conversation, it was clear we were both still in the dark although he did seem to appreciate my bringing him up to date. He was even moderately charitable about Blanche's consulting a psychic, which surprised me somehow. I forget that police detectives, in addition to being hard-assed, are also capable of entertaining doubts about such things.

I pulled out the phone number for Jacob Trigg, whose name Crystal had given me, saying he was Dow's best friend. I dialed and spoke briefly to him, explaining who I was, and we set up an appointment for ten o'clock Tuesday morning at his place. I made a note on my calendar and then called Joel Glazer at the office number Crystal had given me. His secretary told me he was working from home and gave me the phone number there so I could reach him. I called the number, briefly identified myself and the fact that Fiona'd hired me. He seemed pleasant and cooperative to the extent that he gave me his address and set up a meeting for one o'clock that afternoon. I then called Santa Teresa Hospital and learned that Penelope Delacorte was now Director of Nursing Services, in her office from nine to five weekdays. I made a note of the title and decided to try her later in the day, after my meeting with Glazer. Lastly, on my own behalf, I made a call to Richard Hevener, whose machine picked up. I left a message inquiring about the status of my rental application. I tried to sound especially winsome on the phone in hopes that might tip the odds in my favor.

At lunchtime, I sat at my desk and ate the peanut-butter-and-pickle sandwich I'd brought from home. At twelve-thirty, I left the building and started walking around the block, hoping I'd remember where I parked my car. I found the VW, unmolested, at the corner of Capillo and Olivio, much closer than I'd thought and in the opposite direction. For the fifth day straight, the sky was overcast, a brooding gray, roiling at the edges where a thick mass of clouds threatened rain.

Santa Teresa is constrained on the north by the mountains and on the south by the Pacific Ocean, limiting geographic growth. The westernmost neighborhoods feather out as far as Colgate; the easternmost sweeping into Montebello where the prices jump. Horton Ravine, where I was headed, is a moneyed enclave, carved out by land grant and deed, whereby successive California governors rewarded military leaders for killing people really, really well. The resulting three thousand plus acres were passed from rich man to richer, until the last in line, a sheep rancher named Tobias Horton, had the good sense to subdivide the land into saleable lots, thus making a killing of another kind.

I took the 101 as far as the La Cuesta off-ramp, turned left, and followed the road around to the right, heading for the main entrance which consisted of two massive stone pillars with HORTON RAVINE spelled out in curlicue wrought iron arching between them. The Ravine was lush, the trunks of sycamores and live oaks stained dark from the recent rains. Most of the roads are called "Via *something*"; *via* being the Spanish word for "way" or "road." I drove past the Horton Ravine Riding Club, continued a mile, and finally took a right turn and went up a hill.

The Glazers lived on Vía Bueno ("Road Good" . . . if I remember rightly from my brief matriculation in night-school Spanish.) The house was 1960s modern, a dazzling white cluster of abstract forms superimposed on one another in what amounted to an architectural pig pile. Three soaring stories were variously angled and cantilevered with a steeply pitched tower driving straight up out of the center of the mass. There were wide decks on all sides and large expanses of glass, into which birds probably regularly propelled themselves and died. When I'd first met Dana Jaffe, she was living in a small housing tract in the town of Perdido, thirty miles to the south. I wondered if she was as conscious as I of how far she'd come.

I parked in a circular motor court and crossed to the low sweeping stairs that led up to the front door. A few minutes passed and then she answered the bell. I could have sworn she was wearing the same outfit I'd seen her in the first time we'd met—tight, faded jeans and a plain white T-shirt. Her hair was still the color of honey, with silver, as fine as silk threads, now appearing in the mix. She'd had it cut and layered, every strand falling into place as she moved her head. Her eyes were khaki or hazel, sometimes reflecting green, sometimes brown under softly feathered brows. Her most arresting feature was her mouth. Her teeth were slightly occluded and the overbite made her lips appear plump and pouty.

She said, "Hello, Kinsey. Joel said you'd be stopping by. Please come in. Let me take that."

"This is beautiful," I said as I stepped inside, slipping off my slicker, which I handed to her. While she hung it in the closet, I had time to gape. The interior was cathedral-like, a vast space crowned by a vaulted ceiling thirty feet above. Bridges and catwalks connected the irregular levels of the house and shafts of sunlight formed geometric patterns on the smooth stone floor.

Dana joined me, saying, "Fiona probably told you we're redoing the place."

"She mentioned that," I said. "She also said you suggested me for this job, which I appreciate."

"You're entirely welcome. I confess I didn't like you back then, but you did seem honest and persistent, a regular little terrier when it came to finding Wendell. Your friend, Mac Voorhies, at California Fidelity, gives you the credit for the fact I got to keep the money."

"I've wondered about that. Last I heard they were still debating the issue. I'm glad it worked out. How well did you know Dow?"

"I ran into him occasionally because of Joel, but we weren't friends. I met Fiona after they divorced, so I tend to side with her. I'm polite when I run into him, but that's about it. Joel's on the phone at the moment, but I'll take you up to the office as soon as he's done. Would you like a look around?"

"That'd be great."

"We're doing this piecemeal. Not my preference. Fiona and I wanted to do it all at once . . . a full

157

installation, which is so much more dramatic and lots more fun, but Joel put his foot down, so we're doing the job in stages. This is the living room, obviously . . ."

She rattled off the rooms as I followed along behind. "Sun room, den, formal dining room. The kitchen's in there. Joel's office is in what we call the 'crow's nest' upstairs."

The rooms were clearly in transition. The floors were covered with palace-sized Oriental carpets, probably quite old to judge by the softness of the colors and intricate designs. The furniture, which I assumed was chosen by the deceased Mrs. Glazer, appeared to be almost entirely antique, with massive armoires and occasional pieces in polished mahogany. The few upholstered pieces were done in white linen, the lines clean and clear. A variety of fabric swatches had been draped across the chairs and two-inch samples of paint colors had been taped in various places on the wall. Some of the upholstery fabrics I hadn't seen since my youth, when my aunt Gin would take me to visit her friends. Jungle prints, fakey-looking leopard skin, banana palms, bamboo, zig-zags, and chevrons in shades of orange and yellow. The wall paint under consideration was that noxious shade of green that marked most 1930s bathrooms when they hadn't been done in an oh-so-modern mix of pink and black.

"She's found us a sharkskin-top Ruhlmann desk for

this wall, with an André Groult mirror. We're thrilled about that."

"I can imagine," I murmured. I could see where Fiona's art deco taste wouldn't be completely out of place, but I couldn't for the life of me picture these cool, elegant rooms redone in black lacquer, plastic, leather, enamel, curly maple, and chrome.

Dana was saying, "Joel was widowed four years ago. He lived here with his wife for the past twenty-two years. The truth is, I'd love to level it, but he can't see the point."

Good for him, I thought. "How's Michael?" I was afraid to ask about her younger son, Brian, because the last time I'd seen him he was on his way back to jail.

"He and Brendon are fine. Juliet left. I guess she got tired of marriage and motherhood."

"Too bad."

"Well," she said, briskly, "let me check and see if Joel's off the phone."

I realized she was just as eager as I to avoid talk of Brian. She moved to an intercom in the dining room, pressing a button that apparently rang through to Joel's office. "Sweetie, are you free?" I heard his muffled reply.

She turned with a smile. "He says to come right on up. I'll walk you to the elevator. Maybe we can chat when you've finished your talk with him."

"I'd like that."

159

NINE

Joel Glazer's office was located on the third floor, a spacious, airy tower room with windows on all four sides. There were no curtains or drapes, but I could see narrow blinds pulled up to the tops of the panes to permit maximum light. His views were spectacular: the ocean, the coastline, the mountains, and the western edges of Horton Ravine. The thickened cloud cover spread gloom across the landscape, at the same time making the deep blue of the mountains and the dark green of the vegetation seem more intense.

In place of a desk, he used a heavy refectory table. All the other pieces of furniture were antiques, except for the seven-foot sofa, done in a tailored rust-colored velvet with white piping along the seams. As in the rooms below, the area rug was an oversized Oriental carpet, probably seventeen feet by twenty-three. Because of the extended use of windows, there was no art work to speak of. Bookcases and file drawers were built along the walls from the windowsills down. The office was not only immaculate, but orderly—everything arranged just so. The edges of the papers and documents on his desk were squared, pencils and pens lined up parallel to the blotter.

Joel Glazer rose to greet me and the two of us shook hands. His looks surprised me. I was so enamored of Dana Jaffe's beauty that I'd imagined a mate for her equally good-looking. My reaction to Joel was much like mine when I first saw the photographs of Jackie Kennedy and Aristotle Onassis—the princess and the frog. Joel was in his sixties, with a high balding forehead, his once fair hair turning a tawny shade of gray along his temples. Behind frameless glasses, his eyes were brown, with heavy creases near the outer corners. His mouth was bracketed with deep lines. When he stood up to greet me, I realized he was shorter than I, probably only five feet four. He was portly and his shoulders were hunched in a way that made me want to monitor my calcium intake. His smile revealed a gap between his two front teeth, which were discolored and slightly askew. He wore a fresh white dress shirt, with a pair of flashy cuff links, his suit jacket arranged neatly over the back of his chair. I picked up the faint citrus of his aftershave. "Nice to meet you, Miss Millhone. Have a seat. I understand you and my wife have a prior acquaintance."

161

I settled into a brown leather wing chair that blended perfectly with the cream, beige, rust, and brown of the carpeting. "Seems like a long time ago," I said. I wasn't sure how much Dana'd told him about her prior life and most of that story seemed too complicated to summarize in conversation.

He settled back in his chair, his right hand resting on the desk in front of him. He had a signet ring on the middle finger that glinted in the light. "No matter. You're actually here with regard to Dow. Fiona tells us she's hired you to track him down. I'll tell you what I can, but I'm not sure that's going to be much help."

"I understand," I said. "Could we start with Pacific Meadows? I gather there's been a problem with the Medicare billing."

"My fault entirely. I blame myself for that. I should have kept an unofficial eye on the day-to-day operations. Harvey Broadus and I—don't know if you've met him—my partner . . ."

I shook my head in the negative, allowing him to continue.

"We've had a host of projects in the works this past six months We've been partners for years. My background's business and finance where his is real estate and construction—a match made in heaven. We met on the golf course fifteen years ago and decided to go into partnership building retirement communities, nursing homes, and board-and-care facilities. Both of us had parents who were deceased by then, but the need for attractive housing and skilled nursing care for the elderly was something we'd both struggled to find and not always with success. Anyway, long story short, we've now put together an impressive chain of residential health care and intermediate-care facilities. Pacific Meadows, we acquired in 1980. At the time, it was shabby and poorly run. We could see the potential, but the place was losing money hand over fist. We poured close to a million dollars into the renovation and improvements, which included the new annex. Soon after that, we made the lease arrangement with Genesis Financial Management Services. Somebody—I forget now who—suggested Dow's name to Genesis as a possible administrator. I'd known him socially and could certainly vouch for his reputation in the medical community. He'd just retired from private practice and was looking for a way to occupy his time. Seemed like a worthwhile arrangement for all the parties concerned."

"What happened?"

"I wish I knew. Harvey and I are often out of town, crisscrossing the state. We've probably taken on more than we should, but Harvey's like me—the two of us thrive on pressure." The phone on his desk began to ring. He glanced at it briefly.

"You need to get that?"

"Dana will pick up. I should go back and fill you in, at least superficially, on how this business works. What you have essentially are three separate entities. Harvey and I own the property through Century Comprehensive, which is a company we formed back in 1971. By property, I'm talking now about the land and the building occupied by Pacific Meadows. The nursing home is actually operated by Genesis, as I've mentioned before. They lease the physical plant from us. They also handle all the billing: accounts payable and receivable, Medicare and Medicaid billing, DME purchases—that's durable medical equipment, in case you're wondering. Genesis falls under the larger umbrella of a company called Millennium Health Care. Millennium is publicly held, and as such, they're required by law to submit financial information to Social Security, and by that, I mean lists of assets, liabilities, and the return on equity capital. A certified public accountant has to verify those figures. Ten, fifteen years ago, an owner and operator were often one and the same, but times have changed. By law, those functions now have to be separate and distinct. It's like a system of checks and balances, keeps everybody on the up and up."

"Where did Dr. Purcell fit in?"

"I'm just getting to him. Under the management company, you have Dow, or his equivalent. He's the medical administrator of the facility, responsible for the day-in, day-out nuts-and-bolts decisions, which is where he may have gotten into trouble."

"The three of you are partners?"

"Not really. That's how Dow refers to us, but it's not technically true. For the layperson, it's the easiest explanation of our relationship. We couldn't be in partnership with Dow or the management company that runs the business. Believe me, the government gets very testy about any agreement that isn't the result of an arm's-length negotiation: in other words, two unrelated parties not in collusion with one another. Dow could hardly make unbiased decisions about billing practices if he stood to profit. What you're probably referring to is the fact he bought stock in Millennium Health Care, which is a chain we also own stock in. I guess that makes us partners of a sort. We're all in the same business, which is service to the elderly in our community. Of course we had no real say in the matter, but Harvey and I both thought Pacific Meadows would be the perfect venue for a man with Dow's experience and reputation. I see now he may not have had quite the head for business I'd been led to believe. The first we heard about this Medicare business was last May. I thought then, and I'm still convinced, any discrepancies would turn out to be simple clerical mistakes, a compilation of coding errors as opposed to

165

actual inflation of the figures with any intent to defraud. Dow Purcell is just too fine a man to stoop to cheating in that way. My guess is, he either didn't have a thorough understanding of how Medicare works or he got impatient with all the nit-picking nonsense the bureaucrats put you through. I can't fault him for that. As a physician, his first thought is always going to be for the well-being of the patient. He might have bridled at seeing all the ridiculous amounts of paperwork get in the way of first-class care, or worse still, he may have felt the government had no right to dictate to him."

"So you think he might have bent the rules a bit?"

"I prefer that explanation to the one the fraud control investigator seems to be taking. A better guess is he was careless, penciling approval on charges he should have examined more closely. The notion of Dowan actively debunking the government is incomprehensible."

"Suppose he did, though. I don't understand how he benefits. If Medicare or Medicaid are overbilled, aren't those monies paid to the operating company? Seems like it's really their responsibility, isn't it?"

"Absolutely. But outside providers, such as ambulance companies and medical supply businesses, can collect thousands of dollars for services never rendered, or goods not delivered, or goods billed out at inflated prices. If someone in Dow's position were in league with them, the contracts could mean thousands of dollars to the companies involved. For this, he'd receive remuneration—a kickback—perhaps under the heading of a professional discount or a referral fee. Now that HCFA excuse all these acronyms, that's the Health Care Financing Administration, which regulates Medicare and Medicaid programs—"

"Gets complicated," I remarked.

"Very. At any rate, now that HCFA has stepped in, they're insisting on documentation for every such transaction, including the lease agreement, which is where we come in."

"But you don't think he's really guilty."

"I don't. At the same time, it isn't looking good for him."

"You think he left to avoid disgrace?"

"Possibly," he said. "If he felt unable or unwilling to face the charges. I'm not sure how he'll deal with the humiliation if they decide to prosecute. I'm not sure how any of us would deal with that. He's a man in big trouble. I don't like to think of him as a coward as well."

"When did you see him last? Do you remember the occasion?"

"Of course. September 12, the day he disappeared. I took him out to lunch."

"I didn't realize that. Was this at his request or yours?"

"His. He called and asked to see me. Of course, I said yes. By then, I knew about his difficulties. I had some other business in that part of town so we met at a little place in walking distance of Pacific Meadows. Just a hole in the wall called Dickens, a mock English pub. It's quiet and affords a measure of privacy, which I knew he'd appreciate."

"Did he talk about the problems with Medicare?"

"Not directly. He did ramble on a bit about the ongoing investigation. He was clearly upset. He seemed to want reassurances that Harvey and I would come to his defense. I did what I could to put his mind at rest, but I told him I couldn't condone anything underhanded. I don't mean to sound pompous, but in truth, if the charges turn out to be provable, then Dow's actions are not just unethical, they're illegal. As much as I like and admire the man, there's no way I'd be willing to cover for him, even if I could."

"But why would he risk it? Especially at his age and station in life. He couldn't need the money."

"I'm not so sure about that. Dow always did well for himself financially, but Crystal is high maintenance. She costs him a bundle. He has two houses to maintain—you know he bought Crystal that beach house at her insistence. Nothing would do, but she had to have that place. Plus he has Fiona's alimony, which is burdensome to say the least. Crystal likes to travel and she does it in style, including first-class airfare and accommodations for Griffith's nanny along with everyone else. She's the kind of gal who insists on being gifted — birthdays, anniversaries, Christmas, Valentine's Day — she expects to receive jewelry and nothing cheap. She makes sure of that. Dana's theory is she's busy accruing personal assets in case the bottom drops out."

The phone rang again. This time his eyes didn't even flicker, so I went right on. "You think she married him for his money?"

He considered the question briefly and then shook his head. "I wouldn't say that. I think she genuinely loves the guy, but she's been poor all her life. She wants to make sure she's safe just in case something happens to him."

"What about the rumors of an extramarital affair on her part?"

"You'd have to ask Dana. She's the one who spotted that piece of shenanigans. I prefer to steer clear."

"Did Dr. Purcell say anything to suggest he might flee?"

Joel shook his head. "I don't remember anything of the kind. Is that the direction the police are leaning in?"

"Well, they can't rule it out. Apparently, his passport and a substantial sum of money are missing."

Joel stared at me as though trying to take that in. "If he ran, he'd have to continue running for the rest of his life."

"Maybe that's not as bad as the alternative. From what you say, he was feeling desperate."

"Exactly. He was horrified at the prospect of facing criminal penalties."

"I talked to an attorney who thinks it wouldn't be that bad. He might have to pay restitution, but he wouldn't go to jail."

"That wasn't his perception. He was deeply depressed. The government's getting tough. He knew they might well decide to make an example of him. More than anything we're talking about the loss of face, something I'm not sure he could handle." He paused, moving four pencils from one side of his table to the other.

I saw his gaze shift. "What's going through your mind?"

He shook his head. "Something I haven't dared say to anyone else. It crossed my mind—after seeing him that day—he might have been thinking of doing himself in. He was trying to cover his distress, but it might've been too much. He wasn't sure Crystal would stick with him once the scandal came to light. You have to ask yourself just how despondent he was and how far he'd go to get relief. I should have asked how he felt.

I should have done what I could to reassure him, but I didn't."

"Joel?"

We both turned to find Dana standing in the doorway.

"Harvey's on line two. This is the second time he's called."

"Sorry. I better get this."

"Sure, go ahead. I appreciate your time. It's possible I'll want to talk to you again at a later date."

"Any time," he said. He stood up when I did and the two of us shook hands across his desk. By the time I reached the door, he'd picked up the phone.

Dana walked me to the elevator with its two-person capacity, the interior about the size of the average telephone booth. I could have run down the stairs in the time it took. During its slow, whirring descent, I said, "What's the story on Clint Augustine?"

"Simple. For the six months Augustine rented from us, Dow would go off to work and the next thing you know, Crystal would come sneaking out her backdoor, through the trees, and into the cottage. She'd be there an hour or so and then slip back home. Meanwhile, Rand minded the baby, taking him for endless walks around Horton Ravine. It got to be the talk of the neighborhood." We reached the first-floor foyer.

"Couldn't there be another explanation?"

171

Dana's smile was jaded. "Maybe they were having tea."

Santa Teresa Hospital—St. Terry's—is located on the upper west side, a neighborhood once devoted to open farmland, working vineyards, dairies, and stables, all with sweeping views to the mountains on the northern edge of town. Early black-and-white photographs of the area show wide, dusty roads, shanties flanked by groves of citrus and walnut trees, all leveled long ago. It's a world that appears curiously bald and flat: rural expanses planted with pampas grass and star pines that look like mere sprigs. A few unpretentious structures from that era remain, tucked like vintage treasures among modern-day buildings. The rest—churches, the original county courthouse, the wooden boarding houses, the dry goods establishment, the early mission, the trolley car barn, and numerous snazzy three-story hotels—were razed by intermittent earthquakes and fires, Nature's demolition crews.

It was not quite two o'clock when I parked on a side street and walked a block and a half to St. Terry's front entrance. The wind had picked up and the trees seemed restless, stirring uneasily. Occasionally a miniature rain shower would shake loose from the upper branches. The very air seemed gray and I was happy to pass into the hospital lobby through the sliding glass doors that parted at my approach. On my left, the coffee shop was sparsely occupied by hospital employees and visitors. I inquired at the information desk and was given directions to the office of the Director of Nursing Services. I passed a ladies' restroom and made a brief detour before I continued my quest.

I found Penelope Delacorte in a small private office with a window looking out onto the street. Overhead fluorescent lights contrasted sharply with the gloom outside. She was seated at her desk, using her pencil point to trace the lines of print on a photocopied memorandum. When I knocked on the door frame, she peered at me above a pair of half-glasses with tortoise-shell frames. She was in her early fifties, at that stage where she hadn't quite decided whether to dye her graying hair. I pictured her in arguments with her hairdresser, unsure of herself when it came to permanent versus temporary rinses. They likely also argued about the cut; Penelope clinging to the shoulder-length page boy she'd probably been wearing for years. Her bangs were too short and I wondered if she chopped them off herself between appointments. She removed her glasses and set them aside. "Yes?"

"You're Ms. Delacorte?"

"Yes." Her attitude was cautious, as though I might be on the verge of serving her with papers.

"Kinsey Millhone," I said. "I'm a private investigator here in town and I've been hired to look into Dr. Purcell's disappearance. May I have a few minutes?"

Without much in the way of encouragement, I'd entered her office, slipped off my rain garb, and eased myself into the chair near her desk. My shoulder bag and the slicker I left in a pile at my feet.

Penelope Delacorte got up and closed her office door. She didn't seem happy with my presence. She was close to six feet tall, slim, conservatively dressed—a navy blue coat dress with small brass buttons up the front. Her low-heeled navy blue pumps were plain and looked vaguely orthotic, as though prescribed for fallen arches or excessive pronation.

She sat down and put her hands in her lap. "I'm not sure what I can tell you. I was gone by the time he . . . went missing."

"How long did you work for Pacific Meadows?"

"I was the administrator there for the past eight years, until August 23. I worked with Dr. Purcell for the last forty-seven months of that." Her voice, like her manner, was carefully modulated, as though she'd set her internal dial to "Pleasant."

"I thought he was the administrator."

"His title was Medical Director slash Administrator. I was the Associate Administrator, so I suppose you're correct."

174

"Can you tell me why you left?"

"Genesis, the management company that oversees the operation of Pacific Meadows, received notification that Medicare was conducting a rigorous audit of our records."

I raised my hand. "What prompted them to do that? Do you have any idea?"

"Probably a complaint."

"From?"

"One of the patients, a guardian, a disgruntled employee. I'm not sure what it was, but they seemed to know what they were doing. Apparently, the clinic was suspected of any number of violations, from overpaying our suppliers to submitting false or inflated claims for services. Dr. Purcell was in a panic and blamed the bookkeeper, Tina Bart, which was absurd and unfair. Ms. Bart was working for Pacific Meadows before I arrived and she was faultless in her performance. I went to bat for her. I wasn't going to let them push it all off on her. She didn't make the decisions. She didn't even pay the bills; Genesis did that. She processed purchase orders and prepared the room-and-board bills for each resident, including central supply, therapy, anything other than medication. This was Medicare, Medicaid, HMOs, private insurance, and private pay. The same information crossed my desk as well. She didn't *generate* the paperwork. She forwarded what she was given."

"Why isn't Genesis considered responsible for the problem if they pay the bills?"

"We supply them the information. As a rule, they don't stop to verify the data, nor did Ms. Bart."

"But she was fired, anyway."

"Yes, she was, and I turned in my notice the very same day. I was determined to file a complaint with the Labor Relations Board."

"What was their response?"

"I never got that far. I had second thoughts and decided not to go through with it. Tina Bart didn't want to make a fuss. She was as reluctant as I was to call attention to Dr. Purcell's situation."

"His situation?"

"Well, yes. We're all fond of him. He's a darling human being and a wonderful doctor. If he didn't have a head for business, that wasn't an actionable offense as far as we were concerned. I'm being candid in this. He just had no clue when it came to the Medicare rules and regulations—which items were billable and which would automatically be disallowed, co-payments, deductibles, claims for fee-based services. I grant you, it's enormously complicated. Make one mistake—god forbid you put a code in the wrong place or leave even one window blank—and the form comes right back at you, usually without a hint about where you've erred."

"But Dr. Purcell didn't do the billing."

"Of course not, but it was his job to review the TARs—"

"The TARs?"

"The Treatment Authorization Requests. He was also responsible for reviewing CPT codes and approving the cost of any ancillary services or DMEs. I have to emphasize, he was always genuinely concerned and very innovative when it came to patient care and well-being—"

"You don't have to work so hard to defend the man," I said. "I'll take your word for it. What I hear you saying is when it came to the day-to-day management, he was incompetent."

"I suppose, though it seems too strong a word."

"Didn't Glazer and Broadus realize what was going on?"

"It wasn't their place. They purchased the property from the previous owner, did extensive improvements, financed and built the annex. The rest was up to Genesis and Dr. Purcell. Please understand, this is just my personal opinion, but I've worked with a number of doctors over the course of my career. It almost seems that the better a man is at the practice of medicine, the worse he is at business. Most of the doctors I know have a hard time admitting this about themselves. They're used to being gods. Their judgment is seldom questioned. They have no awareness of the

limits they face, so they're easily duped. They may
have medical knowledge, but often not an ounce of
common sense when it comes to money management.
At any rate, I didn't mean to digress. I'm just trying to
explain how Dr. Purcell could have gotten himself into
such a mess."

"Didn't you explain it to him?"

"On numerous occasions. He seemed to listen and
agree, but the errors continued to accrue."

"But if you suspected he was screwing up, couldn't
you have gone to the operating company yourself?"

"Over his head? Not if I wanted to keep my job."

"Which you lost, anyway."

Mrs. Delacorte pressed her lips together, color warming her cheeks. "I felt compelled to resign when Ms.
Bart was fired."

I said, "Do you think Dr. Purcell was intentionally
cheating the government?"

"I doubt it. I can't see how he'd benefit unless he
had some covert arrangement with Genesis or the various providers. The point is, Dr. Purcell was on the
premises. Genesis wasn't, and neither were Mr. Glazer
or Mr. Broadus. It was his responsibility and ultimately,
he's the one who'll be held to answer."

"What do you think happened to him?"

"I can't answer that. I was gone by then."

"I'm still not clear why you didn't file a complaint.

If Tina Bart was unlawfully terminated, wouldn't that constitute a legitimate grievance?"

She was silent and I could see her struggle with her reply. "I suppose we were both reluctant to get into a public battle."

"With whom?"

"With anyone," she said. "Employment opportunities are limited in Santa Teresa. Talk travels fast, especially in medical circles. Despite the number of doctors, there are only three hospitals. Jobs at my level aren't easy to find. My roots here go deep. I've been in town close to thirty years. I can't afford to be labeled a troublemaker or a malcontent. You might consider that fainthearted, but I'm a widow with an aging mother to support. Now I think I've given you all the information at my disposal so if you'll excuse me . . ." She began to fuss with papers on her desk, lifting a stack and tamping the edges to even them up. Red patches, like moral hives, had begun to appear on her neck.

"Just one more thing. Where did Tina Bart end up?"

"You're the detective. You figure it out."

TEN

When I got back to the office, picked up a message slip on which Jeniffer had written, "Richard Heaven called. Pleas return his call." I could actually feel my heart begin to thump as I moved down the corridor to my office and unlocked the door. I hadn't expected to hear from him until Wednesday at the earliest. I dumped my shoulder bag on the desk and snatched up the telephone. I got a wrong number twice before I realized that Jeniffer had inverted the last two digits in the number she'd so laboriously copied. I reached Richard on the third try, saying, "Richard. Kinsey Millhone returning your call."

"Oh sure. Thanks for calling me back. How're you?"

"Fine. What can I do for you?"

"Uh, well, listen, I've been through the rest of these applicants and none of them panned out. Bunch of bums out there. The place is yours if you want it."

"Really? That's great. I'm really happy about that. When can I take possession."

"I'm heading over there now. If you have a few minutes, maybe you could give me a check. That's $1,675 with the cleaning deposit, made out to Hevener Properties."

"Sure, I could do that. I'm just across the alley. The building I'm in now looks right down on yours."

"I didn't realize that. Why don't you join me in a bit and as soon as the lease is signed, I'll give you the key." Like many people, he seemed to be uncomfortable discussing money, and I wondered how much experience he had in landlord-tenant relationships.

"What time?"

"Ten, fifteen minutes?"

"I'll see you shortly. And thanks."

As soon as I hung up I did a little dance of joy, my attention already darting forward to the practicalities of moving. Fortunately, I'd never completely unpacked in the three years since I'd landed at Kingman and Ives, so that would save time. Desk, chair, daybed, phony ficus plant. This was going to be a snap. I could park in my own spot a mere fifteen steps from my office door. I could eat lunches at the table on the redwood deck . . .

I opened my closet door and hauled out the top two boxes, looking for my tape measure, which I found at the bottom of the second box. The tape was one of those heavy-duty metal suckers with a reel-back so fast it would slice off your little finger if you didn't watch yourself. I tucked it in my shoulder bag, grabbed a yellow legal pad and pencil, made sure my message machine was on, then shrugged into my slicker and walked to my brand-new digs. I felt like skipping and then I wondered if kids ever did that these days.

I was already feeling extraordinarily possessive as I trotted along the driveway from the rear of the lot. While I could see the bungalow from Lonnie's office, I had to go halfway around the block and cut down the alleyway to reach the place. There were lights on throughout the bungalow and by hopping up just once, I caught a glimpse of the CPA who occupied the front office. I'd have to take a moment to introduce myself when time allowed. I rounded the corner, noting a sedate-looking dark blue sedan that I assumed belonged to the CPA. Tommy's black pickup was parked two slots down.

Once inside the backdoor, I was careful to wipe my feet on the shaggy cotton door mat provided for that purpose. The door to the back office was standing open and I could smell fresh paint. I peered in and found Tommy on his hands and knees, touching up the base-boards with a brush and a can of white latex paint. He flashed me a quick smile and continued with his work. He was wearing a khaki green coverall, and I was struck again by the vibrancy of the picture he presented. By day, his red hair carried glints of copper and a sheen of pale freckles seemed to make his skin ruddy.

I said, "Hi. How are you?"

"Doing good. Thought I'd get this finished while I had the chance. I hear you're the new tenant."

"Well, it looks that way. Richard said he'd meet me over here to do the paperwork." There was something nice about the fact that his attention was fixed on the job in front of him. It allowed me to study his shoulders and the soft reddish hair on his forearms where his sleeves were rolled up. I could see the lines in his knuckles where a fine bleed of white paint still clung to his skin. The hair along the back of his neck was in need of cutting and curled haphazardly.

He glanced over his shoulder at me. "Thought maybe you left, you're so quiet back there."

"I'm here." I moved over to the window just to have something to do. "The deck's great." Really, I was wondering if he had a girlfriend.

"I built that myself. I was thinking to add some trellising, but it seemed like overkill."

"Looks nice as it is. Is that redwood?"

"Yes ma'am. Clear heart. I don't like cheap materials. Richard bitches about that, but I figure in the

183

end it'll save us money. Anything cheap, you end up doing twice."

I couldn't think of anything to add to that. I cranked the window open and cranked it shut again. Idly, I lifted the telephone handset. I could hear a dial tone.

"You got a call to make?"

"I just wondered if it worked. I guess I'll have to talk to the phone company and have the service switched."

"How's the boyfriend?"

"He's fine."

Another pause while Tommy dipped the brush in the can. "Hope he's treating you good."

"Actually, he's out of town." I winced when I said it because it sounded like a come-on.

"What's he do for a living? He some fancy-pants attorney?"

"He's a P.I. like me. Semiretired. He was laid up for a while with a knee replacement." Mentally, I crossed my eyes. The way I was describing Dietz made him sound like some old geezer who could barely walk. In truth, Dietz had been gone so long that my claiming him as a boyfriend was patently ridiculous.

"Sounds old."

"He's not. He's only fifty-three."

Tommy smiled to himself. "Now see? I knew you'd be the type to go for somebody old. What are you, thirty-five?"

"Thirty-six."

"I'm twenty-eight myself, which I figure is prime for a guy," he remarked. He lifted his head slightly. "Here comes Richard."

"How do you do that? I didn't hear him pull in."

"Radar," he said. He got to his feet and stood there for a moment, running a critical eye along the baseboard. "I miss any spots?"

"Not as far as I can see."

Tommy found the lid for the can of paint and tapped along the edges to effect a seal.

Richard appeared in the doorway wearing a long black raincoat with the ends of the belt tied together in the back. He wasn't nearly as appealing as his brother and certainly not as friendly, meeting my gaze with only an occasional flicker of his eyes. "I thought you had something else to do today," he said to Tommy.

"Yeah, well I wanted to finish this. I don't like leaving a job until I know it's done right." Tommy delivered his lines without looking at his brother.

There was something edgy going on between them, but I couldn't figure out what it was. They seemed chilly with each other, as though their current conversation were part of an ongoing argument. Tommy went into the bathroom where I could hear him running water to clean his paint brush. He came out moments later and began to gather up his tools. It felt like a

185

replay of the night I'd first seen the place, except that neither of them spoke.

"Let me write you that check," I said, trying to inject a warmer note. I reached for my bag and took out the checkbook and a pen, leaning against the wall while I filled in the date. "Hevener Properties, Inc.?"

"That's right." Richard stood with his hands in his raincoat pockets, watching me idly as I wrote in the amount. Meanwhile, as Tommy headed for the door, I saw the two exchange a glance. His gaze moved to mine and he smiled at me fleetingly before he disappeared through the door.

I ripped the check from the book and handed it to Richard, who removed the lease from the inner pocket of his raincoat. He'd already filled in the relevant blanks. I began to read through the lines of minuscule print while Richard studied me.

"I hope he's not bothering you."

"Who, Tommy? Not at all. We were chatting about the deck. I stopped by to take some measurements. I'd like to put in some shelves."

"Of course. Everything look okay to you?"

"Fine. He did a great job."

"When are you moving?"

"I'm hoping the early part of next week."

"Good. Here's my card. I'm the one you should call if you need anything."

I turned my attention to the lease agreement, reading it line by line. Seemed like standard fare, no tricks, no hidden clauses, no unusual restrictions.

Richard was watching me read. "What kind of cases do you handle?"

"Just about anything. It varies. Right now, I'm looking into the disappearance of a doctor who's been gone for nearly ten weeks. January, I did a search for a missing heir."

"Mostly local?"

"For the most part, yes. Occasionally I go out of state, but it's usually cheaper for a client to hire a P.I. in their own geographic area. That way they don't have to pay travel, which can really add up." I scribbled my name at the bottom of the lease, handed him one copy, and kept the other for my files. "I'm always saying this, but the job's a lot duller than it sounds. Background checks and paper searches at the Hall of Records. I used to be associated with an insurance company, handling arson and wrongful death claims, but I prefer being out on my own." I didn't want to appear shiftless so I omitted the fact that CF had fired my sorry butt. I hoped he wouldn't press the point because I didn't want to lie to him this early in the game.

He said, "Well. I better give you a key." He dug in his raincoat pocket and pulled out a ring, sorting through ten to fifteen keys until he found the one he wanted. He freed it and dropped it in the palm of my hand. "You might want to get a second one made in case you lose this."

"I'll do that. Thanks." I took out my key ring and added it to my modest collection.

After he departed, I pulled out my tape measure and began to lay out the dimensions of the room: the spaces between windows, depth of the closet, distance to the door. I made a crude drawing on my legal pad and then I sat in the middle of the carpet, tapping on my lip with my pencil while I studied the room. Between the smell of new carpet and the scent of fresh paint, the office seemed as clean and as slick as a brand-new car. Outside the window, the day was dreary, but inside, where I was, there was a sense of new beginnings.

I was just about to pack up when the phone rang. I must have jumped a foot and then I stared at the instrument. Someone looking for Richard or Tommy; couldn't be for me. I picked up on the fifth ring, feeling hesitant. "Hello?"

The drawl again. "Hey, it's me. My brother still there?"

"He just left."

"I thought maybe the two of us might go out for a drink." His voice on the phone was low and flirtatious. I could tell he was smiling, holding the handset close to his lips.

"Why?"

"Why?" His laugh bubbled up. "Why do you think?"

"Is there a problem between you and Richard?"

"Such as what?"

"I don't know. I got the feeling he didn't like the fact that you were talking to me. So, you know, you ask me out for a drink and I'm not sure it's wise."

"You're a tenant. He's strict. That still doesn't make it any of his damn business."

"I don't want to get you in trouble."

He laughed. "Don't worry about it. I can take care of myself."

"I didn't mean it that way. I don't want to cause problems."

"I told you. It's not a problem. Quit trying to duck the question and let me buy you a glass of wine."

"It's only four o'clock."

"So?"

"I have work to do yet."

"When will you finish?"

"Probably closer to six."

"Good. We'll make it dinner instead."

"Not dinner. A drink. And only one," I said.

"You're callin' the shots. Name the place and I'll be there."

I thought for a moment, tempted by the idea of

Rosie's, which was off the beaten path. This all felt faintly sneaky, like it wouldn't be good for Richard to see us together. Still, I couldn't see the harm in having one drink. "There's a place near the beach," I said, and gave him Rosie's address. "You know where that is?"

"I'll find it."

"I may be late."

"I'll wait."

After I hung up, I wondered if I'd made a mistake. It's not a smart move to mix the professional with the personal. He was my landlord now and if anything went wrong, I'd be looking for new digs. On the other hand, I was friendly with Lonnie Kingman and that hadn't presented any problems. It did cheer me up, the notion of seeing him again. With luck, he'd turn out to be a jerk and I'd politely decline any further contact.

In the meantime, I knew I had to get down to the business of Dow Purcell. I'd go back to square one, starting at Pacific Meadows and the night he vanished from the face of the earth.

This time the parking lot at Pacific Meadows was full. I tucked my VW in the very last slot on the left, squeezing up against the hedge. I locked my car and slopped through shallow puddles to the front door. The wind was blowing at my back and my leather boots were water-stained by the time I reached shelter. I leaned my umbrella against the wall and hung my slicker on a peg. Today the air smelled of tomato sauce, carnations, damp wool socks, potting soil, baby powder. I checked the dinner menu posted on the wall near the double dining room doors. Barbecued riblet, baked beans, broccoli-and-cauliflower medley (now there was a winner) and for dessert, gelatin with fruit cocktail. I hoped it was cherry, clearly the superior flavor for any age group. As this was a weekday, there seemed to be more residents moving about in the hall.

The dayroom was nearly full. The drapes had been closed and the room felt cozier. One group watched a television news show, while another group watched a black-and-white movie with Ida Lupino and George Raft. In the far corner, a middle-aged woman was leading six elderly female residents in an exercise program, which consisted of lifting their arms and marching their feet while they remained seated in folding chairs. The human body was meant for motion, and this small group of women was still doing what they could to keep fit. Hooray for them.

I nodded at the woman at the front desk, behaving as though I were an old hand at this. Unchallenged, I proceeded to Administration, where I found Merry laying out a hand of solitaire. She looked up with guilt, pulled the cards together, and quickly slid them into her pencil drawer. She said, "Hi. How are you?" I could tell she'd recognized my face but was drawing a blank on the name.

"Kinsey Millhone," I said. "I thought I'd stop by and see if Mrs. Stegler was here. I hope she hasn't left for the day."

Merry pointed to her right just as a woman emerged from the inner office with a pair of gardening clippers and a cluster of bald and brownish ivy vines. She was saying, "That looks much better. Dr. P. would never allow me to tend to his plants when he was here." She was slightly disconcerted to see me, but she continued on to the wastebasket, where she deposited her prunings.

Her hair was bushy on top and cut quite short around the ears. She wore an oversized brown blazer, a shirt, a tie, and a pair of mannish pants. She had a gold silk cravat bunched in the breast pocket of her jacket. The toes of her brown oxfords peered from beneath her shapeless trouser legs. She could have used another two inches in the length.

"Mrs. Stegler? My name's Kinsey Millhone. I'm hoping you can give me some information about Dr. Purcell."

She plucked a tissue from the box on Merry's desk and wiped her hands carefully before she finally offered to shake hands. "Merry said you stopped by on Saturday. I'm not certain I can be of help. I make it a policy not to discuss my employer without his express permission."

"I understand that," I said. "I'm not asking you to violate a confidence. You know Fiona Purcell?"

"Of course. Dr. Purcell's first wife."

"She hired me in hopes I could get a line on him. I'm actually here at her suggestion. She felt a conversation with you was the logical place to begin."

Mrs. Stegler shook her head. "I'm sorry, but I was gone by the time the doctor left the building that night," she said, almost stubbornly. I could tell she was happy she had nothing to contribute on the subject.

"Did you talk to him that day?"

Mrs. Stegler gave me a significant look and signaled with her eyes that Merry was listening to every word we said. "Perhaps you'd like to step into his office. We can talk in there."

She held open the hinged section of the counter and I passed inside. Her eyes were as small and as round as a parakeet's, a pale watery blue with a ring of black around the iris. As we entered the inner office, she turned to Merry. "Please see that we're not disturbed."

Merry said, "Yes ma'am," rolling her eyes at no one in particular.

For my part, I was intrigued by the opportunity to see Dr. Purcell's office, which was small and neat. Desk, swivel chair, two upholstered guest chairs, and a

193

bookcase filled with medical textbooks and assorted health care manuals. On the edge of his desk sat the newly shorn ivy, looking like a cocker spaniel with a summer clip. I'd have given a lot for the chance to go through his desk drawers, but the chances of that looked dim.

It was clear Mrs. Stegler thought it inappropriate to sit at his desk. She perched on one of his guest chairs and I took the other, which put us nearly knee to knee. She scooted her chair back and crossed her legs, exposing a band of narrow, white hairless shin above the rim of her wool sock.

I said, "I hope this doesn't seem out of line, but I have to tell you I can't stand gossip. Even in my line of work, I never encourage anyone to talk out of turn or breach a trust, especially in a matter like this."

She looked at me with a hint of suspicion, perhaps sensing the bullshit, perhaps not. "We're in accord on that."

"I'd appreciate your telling me about his last day at work."

"I explained all that to the police. More than once, I might add."

"I'm hoping you'll explain it again to me. Detective Odessa told me you were very helpful."

She peered uneasily at my shoulder bag resting on the floor by my chair. "You're not recording this."

I leaned over, grabbed the bag, and held it open so she could inspect the contents. The only thing that looked even vaguely like a recorder was my government-issue, secret, plastic tampon container with its high-powered directional mike.

"And you won't quote me out of context?"

"I won't quote you at all."

She was silent, staring down at her lap. Finally, she said, "I've been divorced for years."

She was silent again and I allowed the subject to sit there between us without comment on my part or elucidation on hers. I could see that she was struggling to speak. Her face twisted suddenly, her lips pulling together as though controlled by invisible strings. She spoke, but her voice was so tight and so raspy I could hardly understand what she said. "Dr. Purcell . . . was the closest . . . thing to a . . . friend I had. I can't believe he's gone. I came into work the following Monday morning and by then everyone was whispering that he was . . . missing. I was shocked. He was . . . such a sweet man . . . I so adored him . . . If I'd known that was the last time I was going to see him, I would have expressed . . . my heartfelt thanks . . . for all his many, many . . . kindnesses to me." She took another deep breath, humming with the kind of sorrow that didn't lend itself to words. After half a minute, she seemed to regain her composure, though her grip was clearly fragile. She removed the cravat from her breast pocket and blew her nose noisily. The silk didn't seem absorbent. She folded her hands together in her lap, the wadded cloth between her fingers where she twisted it. I could see a tear plop into her lap and then a second, like a slow drip from a shower handle that hasn't been properly turned off.

I realized she was the first person, aside from Blanche, who'd shown any real emotional reaction to his vanishing. I leaned forward and clutched her cold hands. "I know this is hard. Take your time."

She took a deep breath. "Forgive me. I'm sorry. I shouldn't burden you this way. I just hope he's safe. I don't care what he's done." She paused, pressing the cravat against her lips. She took another deep breath. "I'm fine now. I'm fine. I don't know what came over me. My apologies."

"I understand. From everything I've heard, he was a wonderful man. My only purpose here is to help. You have to trust me on that. I'm not here to make trouble."

"What do you want?"

"Just tell me what you know."

She hesitated, her no-gossip policy too deeply ingrained to give up all at once. She must have decided to trust me because she took a deep breath and opened up. "That last day, he seemed preoccupied. I think he was worried . . . I mean, why wouldn't he be? Mrs.

Purcell . . . excuse me, the first one, Fiona . . . stopped by to see him, but he'd gone out to lunch. She waited for a while, thinking he might return, and then she left him a note. When he came back, he worked in his office for the rest of the day. I remember he had a glass of whiskey sitting at his desk. This was late in the day."

"Did he go out for dinner?"

"I don't believe so. He usually ate quite late or skipped supper altogether. Many evenings, he had a little something at his desk . . . crackers or fruit . . . this was if his wife was going out and wouldn't be cooking. When I tapped on his door to say good-night, he was just sitting there."

"Did he have papers in front of him? Files or charts?"

"He must have. I didn't pay attention. It wasn't in his nature to be idle. I do know that."

"You had a conversation?"

"The usual pleasantries. Nothing significant."

"Any phone calls or visitors that you know of?"

She shook her head. "Not that I remember. When I came in the following Monday, his office was empty, highly unusual for him. He was always here at seven o'clock, before anyone else. By then, the rumors were beginning to circulate. Someone . . . I forget who . . . said he'd never gone home at all on Friday night. At first we didn't attach much to it. Then, people got worried he'd been in an accident or taken ill. When the police came, we were frightened, but we still expected him to be found within a day or two. I've thought and thought about this, but there's absolutely nothing else."

"Didn't I read in the paper he had a brief chat that night with an elderly woman sitting in the lobby?"

"That would be Mrs. Curtsinger. Ruby. She's been a resident here since 1975. I'll have Merry take you over to her room. I don't want you upsetting her."

"I promise I won't."

ELEVEN

Merry walked me down the hall. I could see the meal carts being rolled out, the vertical shelves stacked with dinner trays for those who preferred eating in their rooms. It was not even five o'clock and I suspected the early supper hour was designed to condense all three of the day's meals to one long shift.

Merry was saying, "'Member the nurse who was standing there when you left on Saturday? Her name's Pepper Gray. Anyway, she started asking all these questions about you. I never let on a thing, just said you'd be back to talk to Mrs. S. today. She read me out good, saying I shouldn't be talking to anyone about the clinic. I was so P.O.d. She doesn't have any right to talk to me that way. She doesn't even work in my department."

"What do you think she heard?"

"Doesn't matter. It's none of her business. I just thought you should be aware of it in case we run into her."

We took a left, passing the staff lounge, central supply, and then a series of residential rooms. Many doors were closed, the exteriors decorated with greeting cards or wreaths of dried flowers. Sometimes the names of the occupants were spelled out in foil letters hanging jauntily from a miniclothesline of ribbon or string. Through the doors that remained open, I caught glimpses of twin-sized beds with floral spreads, photographs of family members lined up on the chests of drawers. Each room had a different color scheme and each looked out onto a narrow garden where flowering shrubs trembled with the first drops of a pattering rain. We passed an old woman, stumping down the hall with her walker. Her pace was rapid and when she reached the corner, she turned with such vigor she threatened to topple sideways. Merry reached out a hand and steadied her. The woman banked, swerving wide, and then tottered on.

Ruby Curtsinger was sitting in an upholstered chair beside a set of sliding glass doors, one of which was pushed back to admit a breath of damp, fresh air. Her feet were propped on a stool. Just outside, a bird feeder was suspended from the eaves. Small brown birds were perched on the feeder's edge. A line of birds, like clothespins, extended from the hanging support. Ruby was a tiny, shrunken woman with a small bony face and arms as thin as sticks. Her white hair was sparse, but it looked as if she'd recently had it washed and set. She turned a pair of bright blue eyes toward us and smiled, showing the many gaps in her lower teeth. Merry introduced us and explained what I wanted before she withdrew.

Ruby said, "You should talk to Charles. He saw Dr. Purcell after I said good-night to him."

"I don't think I've heard of Charles."

"He's an orderly on the night staff. He's probably here somewhere. He likes to come into work early so he can visit with Mrs. Thornton and some of the other girls. They play gin rummy for pennies and you should hear them hoot. When I have trouble sleeping, I ring for him and he'll put me in my chair and push me up and down the halls. Sometimes I sit in the staff lounge and play euchre with him. The man does love to play cards. I take my meals here in my room. There are folks in the dining room I don't much care for. One woman chews with her mouth open. I don't want to look at that when I'm eating. It's disgusting.

"The night you're asking about—when I last saw the doctor—I took my usual pills, but nothing seemed to help. I rang for Charles, and he said he'd take me on Toad's Wild Ride. That's what he calls it. In truth, he wanted to smoke so he parked me in the lobby and went outside. That's why I was sitting there, so Charles could sneak a cigarette. He's trying to quit and I guess he thinks if no one knows what he's doing, it won't count. Dr. Purcell doesn't allow anyone to smoke in here. He says too many people have problems breathing as it is. That's one thing we talked about that night."

"What time was this?"

"Five minutes to nine or so. We didn't chat long."

"Can you remember anything else?"

"He told me I was beautiful. He always says that to me, though I sometimes think he's fibbing just a tiny bit. I asked about his boy. I forget what his name is."

"Griffith."

"That's it. Doctor used to have his wife bring the little boy in to see us every week or so. Of course, she hasn't brought him even once since his daddy disappeared. I notice the child's feet scarcely ever touched the floor. They carried him every place and anything he wanted, he pointed to and grunted. I told the doctor, 'He's never going to learn to talk as long as you treat him that way,' and he heartily agreed. And then we talked about the weather. It was a lovely night outside. Felt just like spring and I believe the moon was almost full. He went through the door and that's the last I saw of him."

"Could you tell what kind of mood he was in? Mad? Sad?"

She put an index finger against her cheek and gave that some thought. Arthritis had bent the thumb on

that hand until it formed a painful-looking angle per-
pendicular to her hand. "Absentminded, I'd say. I had
to ask him twice if he could arrange an outing for us.
The food here is good. I don't mean to complain, but
eating out is fun and gives us all a lift. Any little change
makes such a difference."

A Hispanic woman in scrubs appeared at the door.
"I have your dinner tray, Miss Curtsinger. You want to
eat in front of the TV so you can watch your show? It's
coming on in five minutes and you don't want to miss
the opening. That's the best part you said." She crossed
to Ruby's chair and set the dinner tray on a small
rolling table that she pulled in close. She removed the
aluminum lid, revealing the barbecued riblet laid out
with all its accompaniments. The Jell-O was green with
a smattering of fruit cocktail submerged in its glowing
depths.

"Thank you," Ruby said, and then she smiled at me.
"Will you come back and see me, dear? I like talking to
you."

"I'll do what I can. Tell you what—next time, I'll
bring you a Quarter Pounder with Cheese."

"And a Big Mac. I see those ads on television and
they always look so good."

"Believe me, they are. I'll bring you one of those,
too."

I walked down the hall as far as the staff lounge,

203

where I stuck my head in and said, "I'm looking for Charles."

The man I saw sitting at the table with the evening paper was in his fifties and was dressed in scrubs, like the woman bringing out the trays. He was a mild, nut brown, and narrow through the shoulders, his arms hairless and scrawny. He set his paper aside and got to his feet politely to identify himself. "Charles Biedler," he said. "How may I help you, Miss?"

I explained who I was and what I wanted, repeating the gist of what Ruby Curtsinger had told me. "I know you've answered these questions before, but it would really be a help if you'd tell me what you remember."

"I could show you where he was parked and where I stood that night."

"I'd love that," I said. He picked up a folded section of the paper and carried it with him as we moved toward the entrance. I paused to retrieve my umbrella and my slicker, which I held over my head like a yellow plastic tent. Charles used his newspaper as a rain hat and we hurried outside, hunched against the rain, which was blowing against us in gusts. Charles paused at the end of the walkway, pointing toward the cars. "See where that little blue VW's parked? Doctor's space was right there. I saw him crossing the lot and then he got in his car and pulled out right around to here."

"You didn't see anyone else?"

"No, but now that corner of the parking lot was darker at nine o'clock than it is right now. Warm that night. I was in my shirt sleeves like this only without the gooseflesh. I spoke to him like always, you know, calling out a word and he said something back, kind of bantering like."

"There was nothing unusual?"

"Not as I recall."

"I'm trying to see this as you did. Ruby says he had his suit jacket over his arm. Did he carry anything else?"

"I don't think so. I can't picture it if he did."

"What about his car keys?"

"I guess he must have had those in his hand. I don't remember him reaching in his pocket."

"So he unlocked the car door and then what?"

"I don't remember nothing about that."

"Did the interior light go on?"

"Might have. After he got in, he sat a while and then he started up the engine and swung around this way so he could drive out the front."

"Was that his pattern?"

Charles blinked, shaking his head. "Most times."

His newspaper was getting soaked and I knew it was time to retreat to the overhang.

"Let's get out of this rain," I said.

We headed back to the entrance, pausing again just outside the front door.

I said, "Was there anything else? Anything at all, even if it seems trivial."

"He didn't call out good-night like he usually did when he drove past. Last thing he'd do, he used to wave and shake a finger, kind of teasing me like, because I told him I quit smoking."

"Was the car window down?"

"I couldn't say for sure."

"You didn't see anyone in the car with him?"

Charles shook his head.

".Are you sure?"

"Pretty sure. And truthfully, that's as much as I know."

"Well, I appreciate your time. If you should think of anything else, would you give me a call?" I took a business card from my bag and handed it to him. "I can be reached at this number. There's a machine if I'm gone."

As I left the porch and started out across the parking lot, I turned and waved. Charles was still there, staring after me.

I sat in my car for a while, thinking about the fact that I was parked right where Dow Purcell had been on the night of September 12. I did a 180 survey, turning my head. What had happened to him? The rain kept tapping on my car roof like the restless drumming of fingers on a tabletop. He hadn't been assaulted. He'd gotten in his car and he'd sat there a while . . . doing what? I started the car and backed out of the space, heading, as Purcell had, toward Dave Levine Street. I glanced back at the building. Charles was gone by then. The walk was empty and the rain slanting against the light made the entrance seem bleak.

I turned right, scanning the street on either side of me. The area was residential. St. Terry's Hospital was only four blocks away. There were medical buildings in the surrounding area, apartment buildings, and a few private homes, but not much else. No bars or restaurants along this stretch where he might have stopped for a drink. Once I reached the next intersection, it was impossible to guess which way he might have gone.

I circled back to the office, and by 5:30, I was typing up a rough draft of the next installment of my report. It helped to be forced to lay it all out again in narrative form. I'd done an additional four hours of work, which I deducted from the balance of the retainer, leaving me $1125 of indentured servitude. I could feel anxiety whispering through my bones. I was no wiser now than I'd been when I first started and probably no closer to finding Dr. Purcell. I didn't even have a *scheme*, no clever strategy about how to proceed. What more could I do? Fiona wanted results. I was moving, but getting nowhere. I checked my watch. 6:02. I leaped to my feet. I was already late for Rosie's, but it couldn't be helped. I shoved the report in my handbag, thinking I could work on it later if I needed to.

Traffic was heavy on the rain-slick streets. While stuck at a stop-light, I turned the rearview mirror to check my appearance. I seldom wear makeup so I looked much the same; sallow by the light of street-lamps, my hair a dense thatch of brown. I felt less than glamorous in my jeans and turtleneck, but it couldn't be helped. I didn't have time to go home and change. Into what? I don't have anything else. This is what I wear.

I parked my car in front of my apartment and dog-trotted the half block to Rosie's. I pushed open the door, dumped my umbrella, and left my slicker on a peg. Where Friday night the place had been emptied by the weather, tonight it was jammed. Both the jukebox and the television were going full-blast, *Monday Night Football* having captured a rowdy cluster of sports enthusiasts at the bar. The cigarette smoke was dense and all the tables were taken. I saw William emerge from the kitchen with a tray at shoulder height while Rosie was uncapping beer bottles as fast as she could. I searched the crowd, wondering if I'd managed to arrive before Tommy Hevener. I felt a plucking at my sleeve and looked down to find him looking up at me from the first booth on the right.

Oh, my.

He was freshly shaved and he'd changed into a white dress shirt with a sky blue wool crew neck pulled over it. He said something I missed. I leaned closer to him, taking in the scent of Aqua Velva. When he repeated himself, his voice in my ear set up a tickling chill that went down to my feet. "Let's get out of here," he said. He got up and grabbed his raincoat off the seat across from him.

I nodded and began to inch my way toward the door again. I could feel him following, one hand against my back. The gesture assumed a familiarity I should have objected to, but didn't. We paused at the entrance while I collected my slicker and my umbrella. He shrugged into his raincoat and turned the collar up. "Where to?" he asked.

"There's a place one block over. Emile's-at-the-Beach. We can walk."

His umbrella was the larger so he raised it and held it over my head as we emerged into the pelting rain. I kept my hand on the stem a fraction of an inch from his and we moved forward with the odd gait one assumes when walking in tandem. The rain was coming down so hard, the water was propelled through the umbrella fabric like a mist. A car passed, throwing up a plume that landed in front of us with a splat.

Tommy stopped. "This is nuts. I've got a car right here." He took his keys out and unlocked the passenger-side door on a new Porsche, painted candy apple red with a license plate that read HEVNER 2. I stepped from the curb to the interior, not a dainty maneuver given the low-slung chassis and the torrents of rainwater coursing through the gutter. He closed me in on my side and then circled in front of the car to his. The interior was done in caramel-colored leather, the whole of it smelling as earthy and rich as a tack room.

"Where's your pickup?" I said.

"That's business. This is play. You look great. I've missed you."

We chatted about nothing in particular on the short drive over to Emile's. Tommy let me off at the door. I went inside and staked out a claim for us while he found a place to park. We were seated at a table for two, next to the window in the narrow side room. The air smelled of sautéed garlic and onion, roasting chicken, and marinara sauce. The atmosphere was intimate with only half the tables occupied because of the rain. There was a quiet buzz of conversation and the occasional clatter of silverware. Votive candles provided circles of light in the darkened space. The waiter brought us two menus, and after a quick consultation, Tommy ordered a bottle of California Chardonnay. While we waited for that, he sat and played with a fork, making plow lines along the edges of a paper napkin. His watch was white gold and he wore a gold ID bracelet, heavy links glimmering against his ruddy skin. "I went back and read your rental application. You're divorced."

I held up two fingers.

He said, "I've never been married. Too much of a rolling stone."

"I tend to appeal to guys on the move," I said.

"Maybe I'll surprise you. Where's your family?"

"My parents died in a car accident when I was five years old. I was raised by my mother's sister, my aunt Gin. She's dead now, too."

"No siblings?"

I shook my head.

"What about the husbands? Who were they?"

"The first was a cop . . . I met him when I was a rookie . . ."

"You were a cop?"

"For two years."

"And the second?"

"He was a musician. Very talented. Not so good at being faithful, but he was nice in other ways. He cooked and played piano."

"Skills I admire. And where is he now?"

"I haven't any idea. You said your parents were gone?"

"It's weird being an adult orphan, though not as bad as you'd think. What'd your father do for a living?"

"Mail carrier. My folks were married fifteen years before I came along."

"So you only had five years together as a family."

"I guess that's right. I hadn't thought of it that way."

"Poor babe."

"Poor everyone. Such is life," I said.

The waiter returned with our Chardonnay and we watched him politely as he went through the ritual of extracting the cork, presenting a sample of wine, and then pouring two glasses. We hadn't even looked at the menus so we were accorded a few minutes to decide what we wanted. I ended up ordering the roast chicken and Tommy ordered the pasta puttanesca. We shared a salad upfront. Once the entrées arrived, Tommy said, "Tell me about the boyfriend. What's the deal on him?"

I lowered my fork, feeling defensive on Dietz's behalf. "Why should I talk to you about him?"

"Don't be so prickly. I'd like to know what's going on here. Between us."

"Nothing's going on. We're having dinner."

"I think there's more to it than that."

"Really. As in what?"

"I have no idea. That's why I'm asking you."

"What are we doing here, defining our relationship? I've known you an hour."

His smile was slow. He seemed unaffected by my churlishness, which I couldn't seem to control. "Actually, I think it's closer to two hours than one. I saw you at the rental property twice before and now this." He finished the wine in his glass and poured himself more, adding wine to my glass first. His eyes were really the most extraordinary shade of green.

I said, "Well, I haven't known you long enough. Besides, you're too young."

He lifted his brows and I found myself blushing.

I said, "How'd you decide to move to Santa Teresa?"

"You're changing the subject."

"I don't like to be pushed," I said.

"Let's talk about sex. Tell me what you like in bed in case it ever comes up."

I laughed. "Let's talk about grade school. I hated mine. How'd you feel about yours?"

"Good. It was fun. I was Captain of the Safety Council two years in a row. I went to four different colleges, but didn't graduate. I may try it again some day. I'd like to finish my degree."

"I did two semesters of junior college and didn't like it at all. I took Spanish in adult education, but I've forgotten everything except 'ola' and 'buenos dios.'"

213

"You cook?"

"No, but I'm a tidy little thing."

"Me, too. My brother's a pig. You'd never guess it by looking. He dresses okay, but his car's a mess."

"I carry cans of motor oil in my backseat."

"Part of your work," he said, forgivingly.

We chattered on in this fashion and I found myself liking his face. Also, I was not exactly unaware of his body, lean and muscular. I wondered where Dietz was tonight. Not anywhere in range, so what difference did it make? Few men appeal to me, not so much because I'm picky about *them*. I'm protective of myself, which means I disqualify all but the most—what . . . ? I couldn't think what it was that allowed some men to get through my defenses. Chemistry, I guess. I focused on cutting my chicken, trying a sample of mashed potatoes, which rank right up there with peanut butter, in my opinion.

Tommy touched my hand. "Where'd you disappear to?"

I looked up to find him staring at me. I moved my fingers away from his. "Is this a date?"

"Yes."

"Because I don't date."

"I can tell."

"I'm serious," I said. "I'm not good at this boy-girl stuff."

"You must be. You were married twice and now you have this other boyfriend on the string."

"I've had guys in between. That doesn't mean I handle it well."

"You do fine. I like you. You don't have to be a jerk. Lighten up."

Humbled, I said, "Okay."

When we left the restaurant at nine o'clock, the streets were still glistening with the rain, which had passed. I saw his Porsche parked across the street. The children's playground was dark and the boats in the marina beyond were bobbing dots of light. I waited while he unlocked the car and let me in. Once he fired up the engine, he said, "Something I want to show you. It's early yet. Okay?"

He pulled away from the curb and did a U-turn on Cabana Boulevard. We drove west, passing the yacht harbor on our left and Santa Teresa City College on our right. Up the hill on Sea Shore. Left at the next big intersection. Without being told, I knew we were on our way to Horton Ravine. He smiled over at me. "I want to show you the house."

"What about Richard? Won't he object?"

"He drove down to Bell Garden to play poker tonight."

"What if he loses and comes home?"

215

"He won't come back until morning whatever happens."

We drove through the stone pillars that marked the rear entrance to Horton Ravine. The road was wide and dark. Many properties on either side were unfenced and had the look of rural countryside; pastures and stables, house lights twinkling through the trees. The route he took was circuitous, and I suspected his intention was to demonstrate the power and handling of the Porsche. At length, he turned right and up a short driveway to a half-moon motorcourt. I caught a sweeping glimpse of the house: stucco walls, massive lines, red-tile roof. All the arches and balconies were washed with dramatic exterior lights. He reached for the remote garage-door opener, pressed a button, and then swung into the open bay of a four-car garage. The cavernous space was pristine; new white drywall that smelled of the plaster overcoating. Three spaces were empty. I imagined Richard driving a sports car as new and as flashy as Tommy's. I opened the car door on my side and let myself out while Tommy got out and fished for his house key. There were no shelves, no tools, and no junk piled up; no lawn chairs, no cardboard boxes marked XMAS ETC. He let us into the utility area off the kitchen. The indicator on the alarm panel by the door was dark. There was a half bath and maid's quarters to the left, a laundry room on the right. There were stacks

of junk mail on the kitchen counters, catalogs and
flyers. In a separate pile there were instruction manuals
for the answering machine, the microwave oven, and
the Cuisinart, which had clearly never been used. The
floors were done in dull red Mexican pavers, sealed and
polished to a high gloss. Tommy tossed his keys on the
glossy white-tile counter. "So what do you think?"

"No alarm system? That seems odd in a house this
size."

"Spoken like a cop. There's actually one installed,
but it isn't hooked up. When we first moved in Richard
set it off so often, the company started charging us fifty
bucks a pop and the cops refused to show. We figured,
what's the point?"

"Let's hope the burglars haven't heard."

"We're insured. Come on and I'll give you the ten-
cent tour."

He walked me through the house, pausing to fill me
in on their decorating plans. On the first level, wide-
plank oak floors stretched through the living room,
dining room, family room, paneled den, and two guest
rooms. The upstairs was fully carpeted in cream-colored
wool; two master suites, a workout room, and enough
closet space for ten. The place had the feel of a model
home in a brand-new subdivision, minus all the furniture and foo-foo. Many rooms were empty, and those
that had furniture seemed empty, nonetheless. I realized

Tommy traveled light, like me no kids, no pets, and no houseplants. In the family room, there was a fully stocked wet bar, too much black leather, and a big-screen television for sporting events. I didn't see any art or books, but maybe those were still packed away.

In the bedrooms, it was clear they'd purchased entire suites of furniture off the showroom floor. All the pieces matched; light wood in Tommy's room—the style, "Moderne." In Richard's bedroom, the headboard, chest of drawers, armoire, and two bed tables were heavy and dark, the design faintly Spanish with wrought-iron pulls. Everything was spotlessly clean, which probably meant a crew of three coming in once a week.

We made the complete circuit and ended up back in the kitchen. Both of us were conscious of the passage of time. Despite his earlier nonchalance, he seemed as aware as I was that Richard might roll in at any moment. He wasn't due for hours, but I could feel his presence like a ghost in every room. Tommy had made no further comment about his brother's chilly attitude and I didn't want to ask. For all I knew, the tension between them had nothing to do with me.

Finally, in a show of bravado, Tommy said, "Would you like a drink?"

"I think not, but thanks. I have work to do. I appreciate the tour. This is really great."

"It needs work yet, but we like it. You'll have to see it by day. The landscaping's beautiful." He checked his watch. "I better get you home."

I picked up my shoulder bag and followed him, waiting in the car while he locked the house again. In the confines of the Porsche, I was conscious of the charge in the air between us. We chatted on the drive, but it was make-work in the face of my attraction to him. He found a parking space near Rosie's, half a block from my place. He parallel parked and then came around the car again to let me out. He offered me his hand in support and I extracted myself with as much grace as I could manage. Sports cars should come equipped with quick-ejection seats.

The crowd noise from Rosie's was muffled, but I was aware of the contrast between the raucous din in there and the quiet where we were. Residual rain dripped from the nearby trees and water gurgled along the gutters like an urban brook. We stood there for a moment, neither of us sure how to say good-night. He reached over idly and adjusted the metal clasp on the front of my slicker. "Don't want you wet. Can I walk you home?"

"I'm just down there. You can almost see the place from here."

He smiled. "I know. I got the address from your application and checked it out earlier. Looks nice."

"You're nosy."

"Where you're concerned," he said.

He smiled again and I found myself glancing away. We both said "Well" at the same time and laughed. I walked backward a few steps, watching while he opened the door and folded himself under the steering wheel. He slammed the car door and moments later the engine rumbled to life. The headlights flicked on and he took off with a roar. I turned, proceeding to the corner while the sound of his car faded at the end of the block. I confess my underwear felt warm and ever so faintly damp.

TWELVE

Tuesday morning dawned in a haze of damp and fog. I went through my usual morning routine, including a jog so vigorous it left me rosy-cheeked and sweating. After breakfast, I spent some time working at home, finishing revisions on my report for Fiona. Maybe all these neatly typed pages would pass for progress in her eyes. This was one of the few times in my life when I could see that I might fail, and I was scared. I anticipated her return with the same enthusiasm I felt as a kid waiting for my annual typhoid shot.

I left my apartment at 9:35. With the temporary break in the storm, large bands of blue sky had appeared between the clouds. The grass had turned emerald green and the leaves on all the trees were looking glossy and fresh. My appointment with Dow Purcell's best friend, Jacob Trigg, was scheduled for 10:00. I'd studied a city map, pinpointing his street address in the heart of Horton Ravine. I drove east along Cabana Boulevard and ascended the hill as it swept up from the beach. I turned left on Promontory Drive and followed the road along the bluffs that paralleled the beach. I turned left again and drove through the back entrance to Horton Ravine. Tommy crossed my mind and I smiled in a goofy glow I found embarrassing.

A mile down the road, I saw the street I was looking for. I turned right through a warren of winding lanes and drove up the hill. Water rushed in a torrent along the berm and what looked like entire gravel driveways had washed out into the road. A tree with shallow roots had toppled backward, pulling up a half-moon of soil. Despite the numerous houses in the area, Mother Nature was busy reclaiming her own.

I peered to my right, checking mailboxes as I crept along. I finally spotted the house number Jacob Trigg had given me. Enormous black wrought-iron gates stood open and I drove up a long curving lane between low stone walls. At the top of the slow rise, the parcel became flat and I could see gently undulating acreage sweeping out in all directions. The two-story house was Italianate in feel, elegant and plain with a symmetrical window placement and a small porch in front with a circular balustrade.

I parked and got out. All the ground-floor windows were disconcertingly dark. There was no doorbell and no one answered my repeated knocks. I circled the house, checking for lights or other signs of the inhabitants. The air was still except for the occasional water dripping from the eaves. Had Trigg stood me up? I took a moment to check my bearings. Formal gardens stretched out on either side of the house, but there was not a gardener in sight. Probably too wet to do much work.

I started down the sloping lawn, hoping to come across someone who'd tell me if Trigg was home. For the next five minutes, I wandered across the property, grass squishing underfoot where underground springs had suddenly resurfaced. At the end of a row of ornamental pears, I spotted a greenhouse with a small potting shed attached. An electric golf cart was parked nearby. I picked my way forward, mindful of the mud sucking at the soles of my boots.

I could see a man working at a high bench just inside the shed. Despite the cold, he wore khaki shorts and muddy running shoes. There were braces on both legs, secured by what looked like screws driven in on either side of his knees. I could see signs of atrophy in the muscles of his calves. Propped up against the counter beside him was a pair of forearm crutches. The billed cap he wore covered a thatch of gray hair. On the redwood surface in front of him, there were five or six ratty-looking potted plants in various stages of decline.

I paused in the doorway, waiting for acknowledgment before I went in. Beyond the far doorway, the greenhouse opened up, but the angled glass ceiling wasn't visible from where I stood. Most of the side panes were an opaque white, but in places the glass was clear, admitting brighter squares of light. The air was warm and smelled of loam and peat moss. "Hi. Sorry to interrupt, but are you Mr. Trigg?"

He scarcely looked up. "That's me. What can I do for you?"

"I'm Kinsey Millhone."

He turned and looked at me blankly, a knot forming between his eyes. His mustache was iron gray and his brows were an untidy mix of black and gray hairs. I guessed he was in his early sixties; red-nosed, jowly, and heavy through his chest, which sloped forward and down into a sizeable belly.

"I was hoping you could answer some questions about Dr. Purcell," I prompted.

His confusion seemed to clear. "Oh, sorry. I forgot you were coming or I'd have waited at the house."

"I should have called to remind you. I appreciate your taking the time to talk to me."

"Hope I can be of help," he said. "Folks call me 'Trigg' so you can skip all the 'mister' stuff. Doesn't seem to fit." He leaned against the crude redwood counter and stirred a quick squirt of detergent into one of two buckets of water sitting side-by-side. He reached for a twig of miniature rose bush festooned with cobwebs. He placed his hand on the soil at the base of the plant, turned it upside down, and dunked it in the water. "I'm surprised you found me. My daughter lives with me, but she's out this morning."

"Well, I did wander quite a bit. I'm glad you don't have a roving pack of attack-trained dogs."

"That bunch is put away for the moment," he said without pause.

I really hoped this was a sample of his dry wit. Hard to tell as his tone of voice and his facial expression didn't change.

"In case you're wondering what I'm up to, I'm not a horticulturist by trade. My daughter has a business taking care of houseplants for folks here in Horton Ravine. She does a bit of hotel work, too—the Edgewater, Montebello Inn, places like that. All live plants; no fresh flowers. I guess they hire someone else to do the big fancy arrangements. She brings me the sickly kids and I nurse 'em back to health." He righted the dripping rose bush and then swished it in the bucket of clear water. He pulled it out, shook it off, and studied the effect. "This little guy's suffering from an infestation of spider mites. Suckers are only a fiftieth of an inch long and look at the damage. Used to have healthy foliage and now it's no more than a twig. I'll keep it in quarantine. We see a lot of root rot, too. People over-water, trying to be helpful between Susan's visits. You a plant person?"

"Not much. Used to have an air fern, but I finally threw it out."

"Smell like feet," he said, with a shake of his head. He set the rose bush aside and reached for a corn plant in a terra-cotta pot. I watched while he sponged a dark gray powdery coating from the leaves. "Sooty mold," he said, as though I'd inquired. "Plain old soapy water's good for a lot of these things. I'm not opposed to a systemic poison, but something like aphids, I prefer to try a contact pesticide first. Malathion or nicotine sulfate, which is basically your Black Flag-40. I'm conservative, I guess. Susan sometimes disagrees, but she can't argue with my success."

I said, "I take it you're an old friend of Dr. Purcell?"

"A good twenty years. I was a patient of his. He testified in my behalf in the lawsuit following my auto accident."

"This was before he got into geriatrics?"

"I certainly hope so," he said.

I smiled. "What kind of work did you do?"

"I was a detail man; drug sales. I covered the tri-counties, calling on doctors in private practice. I met Dow when he still had his office over near St. Terry's."

"You must have done well. This property's impressive."

"So was the settlement. Not that it's any compensation. I used to jog and play tennis. Take your body for granted until it goes out on you. Hell of a thing, but I'm luckier than some." He paused, peering over at me. "I take it you talked to Crystal. She called to say you'd probably be getting in touch. How's it going so far?"

"It's frustrating. I've met with a lot of people, but all I've picked up are theories when what I need are facts."

His tangled eyebrows met in the middle, forming a crimp. "I suspect I'm only going to add to the general confusion. I've been thinking about him, going back over things in my mind. Police talked to me the first week he was gone and I was as baffled as anyone."

"How often did you see him?"

"Once or twice a week. He'd stop by for coffee in the mornings on his way to Pacific Meadows. I know you gals think men don't talk about personal matters . . . more like sports, cars, and politics is your sense of it. Dow and I, we were different, maybe because he'd seen me go through so much pain and suffering. Without complaint, I might add. He was a man tended to keep his own counsel and I think he valued that in others. He was only eight years my senior, but I looked on him as a father. I felt comfortable telling him just about anything. We built us a lot of trust and in time, he confided in me as well."

"People admire him."

"As well they should. He's a good man . . . or was. I'm not at all sure how we should speak of him. Present tense, I hope, but that remains to be seen. Crystal tells me Fiona hired you."

"That's right. She's in San Francisco on business, but she's coming back this afternoon. I'm scrambling around, talking to as many people as I can, hoping to persuade her the money's well spent."

"I wouldn't be concerned. Fiona's hard to please," he said. "Who's on your list aside from me?"

"Well, I've talked to one of his two business associates . . ."

"Which one?"

"Joel Glazer. I haven't talked to Harvey Broadus. I talked to people at the clinic, and his daughter Blanche, but not Melanie."

His eyebrows went up at the mention of her name, but he made no comment. "What about Lloyd Muscoe, Crystal's ex-husband? Have you spoken to him?"

"I hadn't thought to; but I could. I saw him at Crystal's on Friday afternoon when he came to get Leila. How does he fit in?"

"He might or might not. About four months back,

Dow mentioned that he went to see Lloyd. I assumed it had something to do with Leila, but maybe not. You know, Leila lived with Lloyd briefly. She'd been busy telling everyone she was old enough to decide. Crystal got tired of fighting her, so Leila went to Lloyd's. She started eighth grade in the public schools up here. Wasn't here two months and she was out of control. Grades fell, she was truant, into alcohol and drugs. Dow put his foot down and that's when they stepped in and enrolled her in Fitch. Now she's strictly regulated and she blames Dow for that. Sees him as a tyrant a tyrant being anyone who won't let her have her way."

"I think she's mad at Lloyd, too. When I was over there, she was refusing to see him, but Crystal insisted."

"I don't doubt she's mad at him. She thinks it's his job to get her out of there. Doesn't want to look at her own behavior. Her age, you always think it's someone else's fault."

"What happened when Dow went to see Lloyd? Did they quarrel?"

"Not that I know, but if Lloyd intended to do Dow harm, he'd be way too wily to tip his hand with any public display."

I reached in my bag and found a stray envelope so I could make a note. "Can you give me his address?"

"I don't remember offhand. I can tell you where it

is, though. Big house, yellow shingles, pitch roof. Right there at the corner of Missile and Olivio. Lloyd rents the little studio in back."

"I think I know the place," I said. "I gather he and Crystal get along okay."

"More or less. She still tends to lick his boots. Crystal was always under Lloyd's thumb."

"How so?"

"He lived off her earnings when she worked as a stripper in Las Vegas. They had one of those hotheaded relationships full of drinking and fights. One or the other would end up calling the police, screaming bloody murder. Crystal would have Lloyd arrested and then next thing you know she'd change her mind and refuse to press charges. He'd accuse her of assault and battery, then they'd kiss and make up. Oldest story in the book. After she met Dow, she dropped everything and moved to Santa Teresa with the girl. I guess she saw Dow as her ticket out, which in a way he was. Problem was, Lloyd followed her and he was furious— couldn't believe she'd leave him after all they'd been through. Couldn't believe he'd lost control is more like it."

"How do you know all this?"

"I heard it from Dow," he said. "I think he was worried Lloyd would find a way to reassert his dominance. Crystal looks strong, but where Lloyd's concerned she's motivated by guilt. He claims she owes him big time for turning his life upside down."

"Doesn't he work?"

"Not so's you'd notice. He did construction for a while, but then he claimed he'd injured his back. He'll live on worker's comp until the money runs out. That's how his mind works. Why put out the effort if he can get what he wants by manipulating someone else?"

"But surely Crystal's out from under him."

"A woman like her is never out from under a man."

I tucked the envelope away, trying to think what other ground I might cover. "What about the book Dow was writing? That's one reason Crystal's convinced something's happened to him. She says he wouldn't just walk out: first of all because of Griffith and, secondly, because of the book he was working on."

A pained expression seemed to cross Trigg's face. "Started out, he was excited about the project, but the task turned out to be a lot harder than he thought. I'd say he was more discouraged than enthusiastic. He was also upset about Fiona. She kept pressing him for money. He knew she was convinced he was going back to her and that distressed him no end. That's why he was on his way up there."

"What do you mean 'up there'?"

"He was going to see Fiona to clarify the situation."

231

"The night he disappeared?"

"That's what he told me. We had breakfast together that Friday morning and he said she'd insisted on a meeting. She was always insisting on something. She's a pain in the ass, if you'll forgive my being blunt. I told Dow then what I'd been saying all along: she was always going to demand a pound of flesh from him. She couldn't stop him leaving her, but she could surely make him pay."

"What in the world made her think he'd leave Crystal and go back to her?"

"Oh, she had it all worked out, according to him. Said she was the only one understood him, for better or worse. I guess she was big on 'worse.'"

"Fiona tells me Dow disappeared on two previous occasions. Any idea where?"

"Rehab. He told me he went to a 'dry out' farm."

"Alcohol?"

"That's right. He didn't want it known, felt his patients would lose confidence if they knew his drinking was out of control."

"I've heard from a couple of different sources he was drinking again."

"Probably Fiona's influence. She'd drive any man to drink."

"Couldn't he have checked into another rehab facility?"

"I hope so. I surely do, but then again, you'd think he'd have let someone know by now."

"Fiona says he didn't say a word to anyone before."

"That's not quite true. He told me."

"What do you know about the business at Pacific Meadows?"

Trigg shook his head. "Not much. I know it wasn't looking good. I told him to hire an attorney, but he said he didn't want to do that yet. He had his suspicions about what was going on, but he wanted to check it out himself before he did anything else."

"Someone told me he was worried Crystal would jump ship if the uproar became public."

Trigg tossed his sponge in a bucket. "Maybe that's what Fiona was counting on," he said.

I walked into the office at 11:25 to find Jeniffer, bending over a file drawer, in a skirt so short the two crescent-shaped bulges of her hiney were hanging out the back. Her legs were long and bare, tanned from all the days she took off to go to the beach with her pals. I said, "Jeniffer, you're really going to have to wear longer skirts. Don't you remember 'I see London, I see France, I see someone's underpants'?"

She jerked upright and tugged self-consciously at the hem of her skirt. At least she had the good grace to look embarrassed. She clopped back to her desk in her wooden-soled clogs. She sat down, exposing so much bare thigh I felt compelled to avert my eyes.

"Any messages?" I asked.

"Just one. Mrs. Purcell said she's back and she's expecting you at two o'clock."

"When? Today or tomorrow?"

"Oh."

"Don't worry about it. I can figure it out. Anything else?"

"This came," she said, and handed me an Express Mail envelope. I opened the flap. Inside was the contract Fiona'd signed and returned. Shit. I already hated feeling bound to her.

"Also, someone's here to see you. I showed her into your office and took her a cup of coffee."

That got my attention. "You left her in my office by her*self*?"

"I have work to do. I couldn't *stay*."

"How do you know she's not back there going through my desk?" I said, knowing that's what I'd be doing if I were in her place.

"I don't think she'd do that. She seems nice."

I could feel my heat gauge rising into the red zone. "I seem nice, too. That doesn't count for much. How long's she been there?" To be fair, I was probably displacing my feelings about Fiona onto her, but I was pissed, anyway.

Jeniffer made a face to show she was thinking real hard. "Not long. Twenty minutes. Maybe a little more."

"Is she at least someone I know?"

"I *think* so," she said, faintly. "Her name's Mariah *something*. I just figured she'd be more comfortable back there than if she waited for you out here."

"Jeniffer, in that length of time, she could have ripped me off for everything I own."

" You said that. I'm sorry."

"Forget about 'sorry.' Don't ever do it again." I headed down the inner corridor. I looked back at her. "And get some pantyhose," I snapped. As I passed Ida Ruth's desk, she was studiously avoiding my gaze, no doubt thrilled I was being subjected to a sample of Jeniffer's continuing ineptitude.

My office door was closed: I barged in to find a woman sitting in the guest chair. She'd placed her empty coffee mug on the edge of the desk in front of her. Scanning the surface, I could've sworn my files were ever so slightly disarranged. I looked at her quizzically and she returned my gaze with eyes as blank and blue as a Siamese cat's.

She couldn't have been more than twenty-six, but

her hair was a startling silver-gray, as polished as pewter. She wore very little makeup, but her skin tones looked warm against the frosty hair, which was combed back and anchored behind her ears. She had a finely sculpted jaw, a strong nose and chin, lightly feathered brows. The skirt of her gray wool business suit was cut short and sheer black hose emphasized her shapely knees, one of which carried the vestiges of an old scar. There was a black briefcase resting near the left side of her chair. She looked like an expensive lawyer with a high-powered firm. Maybe I was being sued.

Warily, I moved around my desk and sat down. She shed her jacket with ease and arranged it across the back of the chair to avoid wrinkling it. From the shape of her shoulders and upper arms, I knew she worked out a lot harder than I did.

"I'm Mariah Talbot," she said. The black silk tank top rustled faintly as she reached across the desk to shake hands. She had long oval nails painted a neutral shade. The effect was sophisticated; nothing gaudy about this one. The most riveting feature was a gnarly white scar, probably a burn, on the outer aspect of her right forearm.

"Do we have an appointment?" I asked, unable to keep the testiness out of my voice.

"We don't, but I'm here on a matter I think will interest you," she said, unruffled. Whatever my disposition, it wasn't going to bother *her*. The image she projected was one of composure, competence, efficiency, and determination. Her smile, when it appeared, scarcely softened her face.

"What's the deal?"

She leaned forward, placing her business card on the desk in front of me. The face of it read, MARIAH TALBOT, SPECIAL INVESTIGATIONS UNIT, GUARDIAN CASUALTY INSURANCE, with an address and phone number I scarcely stopped to read. The logo was a four-leaf clover with *Home*, *Auto*, *Life*, and *Health* written in each of the four loops. "We need to have a chat about your landlord."

"Henry?"

"Richard Hevener."

I don't know what I expected, but it wasn't that. "What about him?"

"You may not be aware of this, but Richard and Tommy are fraternal twins."

"Really?" I said, thinking, *Who gives a shit?*

"Here's something else you may not be aware of. Richard and Tommy murdered their parents back in Texas in 1983."

I could feel my lips parting slightly, as though in preparation for the punch line to a joke.

The combination of the blue eyes and the silver hair was arresting, and I could hardly keep from staring.

She went on, her manner completely matter-of-fact: "They hired someone to break into the house. As nearly as we can tell, the plan was for the burglar to drill the safe and walk off with a substantial amount of cash, plus jewelry valued at close to a million dollars. The boys' mother, Brenda, was the older of two girls who came from an incredibly wealthy Texas family named Atcheson. Brenda inherited a stunning jewelry collection that she left, by will, to her only sister, Karen. These are pieces that have been passed down through the family for years."

She reached into her briefcase and pulled out a fat brown accordion file. She removed a manila folder and passed it over to me. "These are the newspaper clippings. Plus, one copy each of the two wills."

I opened the file and glanced at the first few clippings, dated January 15, 22, and 29 of 1983. In all three articles, Richard and Tommy were pictured, looking solemn and withdrawn, flanked by their attorney in a three-piece business suit. Headlines indicated the two were being questioned in the ongoing investigation of the homicides of Jared and Brenda Hevener. Additional articles covered the investigation over the balance of the year. I didn't stop to read the wills.

Mariah Talbot went on. "You'll notice their aunt Karen's name cropping up in some of the articles. The burglar was a punk named Casey Stonehart, who'd already been jailed six times for a variety of crimes ranging from petty theft to arson, a minor specialty of his. We believe he opened the safe using the combination they'd given him. Then he dismantled the smoke detectors and set a blaze meant to cover up the crime. Apparently—and this is only a guess—the deal was he'd take the bulk of the jewelry, which he was in a position to fence. The boys would take the cash and maybe a few choice pieces, then submit a claim to the insurance company for the house, its contents, the jewelry, and anything else they could get away with. Oh yes, the cars. Two Mercedes-Benz were destroyed in the blaze. Mr. and Mrs. Hevener were found bound and gagged in the master bedroom closet. They died of smoke inhalation, which is not as bad as being burned alive— lucky them. Neither boy was anywhere in the area. In fact, both by some miracle were out of town and had iron-clad alibis," she said. "Stonehart, the kid who did the dirty work, disappeared soon afterward; probably dead and buried somewhere, though we have no proof. He's been missing ever since so it's a safe bet they got rid of him. An accomplice is always the weak link in these things."

"Couldn't he be in hiding?"

"If he were, he'd have been in touch with his family. They're all deadbeats and bums, but loyal to a fault. They wouldn't care what he'd done."

"How do you know their loyalty doesn't include keeping mum about where he is?"

"The sheriff's department put a mail check in place and there's a trace on the phone. Believe me, the silence has been absolute. This is a kid with big dependency issues. If he were alive, he couldn't tolerate the separation."

I cleared my throat. "When was this again?" I knew she'd told me, but I could hardly take it in.

"1983. Hatchet, Texas. It didn't take long for suspicion to fall on the two boys, but they'd been extremely clever. There was little to suggest the part they'd played . . . beyond the obvious, of course. Financially, they cleaned up. For them, it must have been better than the lottery. To all appearances, there was no bad blood between them and their parents, no public disagreements, no recent increases in insurance coverage. There was also very little linking them to Casey Stonehart. No phone records showing calls between the brothers and him. Bank accounts showed no unusual withdrawals to suggest a down payment on Casey's services. The kid was such a lowlife he didn't even have a bank account. He kept his money in his mattress; the Sealy Posturepedic Savings and Loan. The three of them did attend the same high school. Casey was a year behind the Heveners, but there was no overt connection. It's not like they bowled in the same league or hung out together."

Anything I'd felt for Tommy had evaporated. "What about the parents' wills? Anything of interest there?"

Mariah shook her head. "No changes in the terms since the document was drawn up when the boys were born. The attorney was a bit lax in that regard. The twins had reached their majority and adjustments should have been made. Their aunt Karen was still listed as their guardian if something happened to the parents."

"What made the cops fix on them?"

"For one thing, neither of them can act. They put on a good show, but the feelings were all phony, strictly crocodile tears. At the time, both were still living at home. Tommy was one of those perpetual college students; his way of refusing to grow up and go out on his own. Richard fancied himself an 'entrepreneur,' which meant he borrowed and squandered money as fast as it came into his hands. Jared was thoroughly disgusted with them. He considered them moochers and he was sick of it. Brenda, too. This we heard about later from close friends of theirs."

"I'm assuming the brothers were charged?"

Mariah shook her head. "Police investigators couldn't cobble together sufficient evidence to satisfy

241

the D.A. Of course, the insurance company balked at paying, but the boys filed suit and forced them to perform. Since they hadn't been arrested, charged with, or convicted of any crime, Guardian Casualty had no choice but to pay up."

"How much?"

"Two hundred and fifty thousand each in life insurance. The homeowner's and auto claims came to a little over three quarters of a million dollars. This is Texas, don't forget. Not like real estate values you're used to dealing with out here. Also, despite his business acumen, Jared never managed to amass much in the way of wealth. Lot of what he did was probably under the table, which is neither here nor there. Anyway, along with the insurance, you add the cash in the safe which probably amounted to another hundred grand—and the jewelry on top of that, and you can see they did well. Guardian Casualty and Karen Atcheson, the boys' aunt, are preparing to file a civil suit to recover their losses. We're convinced the boys still have the jewelry if we can find a way to prevail. I've been assigned to handle the preliminary investigation."

"Why now when the murders were three years ago? I know proof in a civil case is easier, but you still have to have all your ducks in a row."

"Someone's come forward . . . an informant . . . very hush-hush. This is the arsonist, a professional, who talked to Casey twice—once before the fire and then again right afterward. It was his expertise Casey was relying on, because the job was much bigger than anything he'd done in his piddling career."

"What was the arsonist getting in return?"

"A piece of Casey's action. Once the arsonist found out about the killings, he wasn't willing to 'fess up to any part in it. He was nervous about a felony murder charge, or worse—that the brothers would kill him. Now he's decided to do what's right and that's why we think we have a shot at this."

"Why doesn't he go to the cops and let them handle it?"

"He will if Guardian Casualty comes up with the evidence."

I pushed the file aside. "And you're here to do what?"

Mariah smiled to herself as though privately amused. "I've been nosing around. It looks like funds are low and the boys are getting on each other's nerves. We're counting on the fact they're having cashflow problems. That's why Richard agreed to lease the place to you, if you haven't figured that out. You offered him six months' rent in advance and he needed the bucks."

"How'd you find out about that?"

"We gimmicked up another applicant, a writer looking for an office away from his home. The cash is the explanation Richard gave when he turned him down. At any rate, the friction between the brothers could really work for us. I'm always hoping one will break down and rat the other one out. We've been after them for three years and this is as close as we've come."

"What's this got to do with me?"

"We'd like to hire you to do some work for us."

"Such as?"

"We want you to pass along the name of a fence in Los Angeles. He's a jeweler by trade. The business looks legitimate on the surface, but he's actually a fence. He deals in stolen property when the quality or quantity is sufficient to make it worth the risk. With money getting scarce, the boys might be tempted to dip into the stash, which we don't think they've touched."

"But they can't get anywhere close to true value through a fence."

"What choice do they have?"

"Wouldn't they be better off trying to auction some of the pieces through Christie's or Sotheby's?"

"Christie's or Sotheby's would insist on a provenance . . . proof the jewelry was theirs . . . which they can't provide. They may try selling to a private party, which is yet another reason we're stepping up the pace."

"So I pass along the information about the jeweler and then what?"

"We wait to see if they take the bait and then we nail them. The Houston D.A.'s already talked to the D.A.'s office here and they're ready to roll. Once we know the jewelry's in the house, we'll ask for a warrant and go in."

"Based on what?"

"We'll have the fence and the fence will have at least a portion of the jewelry. The boys are going to have a hell of a time explaining that."

"What if they don't make contact with him?"

"We have another scheme in mind that I'd rather not go into. In the meantime, you might want to see the jewelry." Again, she reached into her briefcase, this time removing a manila folder with what looked like appraisals and a series of Polaroids. She sorted through the stack, laying picture after picture on the rim of my desk, rattling off the contents. "Diamond rivière necklace valued at $120,000. An art deco diamond-and-sapphire bracelet—that one's $24,000. Diamond ring with a stone weighing in at 7.63 carats, worth $64,000. And check this one: a necklace with 86 graduated diamonds. That's somewhere between $43- and $51,000. Sorry about the pics. These are preliminary Polaroids. All the good appraisal photos are being circulated through Southern California." She finished dealing out the pictures, reciting prices like a pitchman for a company selling door to door.

"What makes you so sure they still have them?"

"An educated guess," she said. "We know they bought a safe from a local locksmith. We figure they installed it at the house so each of them could keep an eye on the other. The problem is, we have no legitimate means of getting in."

"Funny you should say that. I was there last night."

"How'd you manage that?"

"Richard was gone. Tommy took me over and showed me around."

"I don't suppose you spotted the safe."

"I'm afraid not. There's barely any furniture and no wall art. I can tell you this—the entire alarm system's down. Tommy told me Richard set it off so many times they finally discontinued service. Now it's strictly window dressing."

"Interesting. I'll have to think about that. When will you see him again?"

"I'm not going to see him again! After what you've told me?"

"Too bad. We could really use your help. He's taken an interest in a woman more than once and Richard always puts a stop to it. He doesn't trust his little brother's tendency to blab. I don't think Richard realizes what a threat you are."

"*I'm* a threat?"

"Of course. Tommy's hustling you and that gives

you power—not a lot, but enough. You have access, for one thing."

"I'm not going to go sneaking around in there. I'd have no reason whatever to tour the house again. Besides, even if I found the safe, I wouldn't have the faintest idea how to open it."

"We wouldn't want you to do that. All we need is the location, which couldn't be that hard. Once we have the warrant, we don't want the boys disposing of the evidence."

I thought about it briefly. "I won't do anything illegal."

Mariah smiled. "Oh, come now. From what we've heard, you're willing to cut corners when it suits you."

I stared at her. "You ran a background on me?"

"We had to know who we were dealing with. All we're asking you to do is pass along the information about the fence."

"I don't like it. It's too risky."

"Without risk, where's the fun? Isn't that the point?"

"Maybe for you."

"I told you, we intend to pay you for your time."

"It's not about money. I don't want to be pimped."

"Meaning what?"

"I won't peddle my ass so you can nail these guys. I'm a big fan of justice, but I'm not going to offer up my body to get the goods on them."

"We're not asking you to go to bed with him. What you do in private is strictly your concern." She closed her mouth, a move I've often employed myself, giving the other person the opportunity to work it out.

I picked up a pencil and tapped it on the desk, letting my fingers slide the length as I flipped it end over end. "I'll think about it some and let you know."

"Don't take too long." She placed a slip of paper on the desk with a name and address written across the face of it. "This is the name of the jeweler. I'll leave it up to you how you play out the information. You can bill us for your time and gas mileage. If you decide you can't help, then so be it. Either way, we'll trust you to keep your mouth shut."

I took the paper and looked at the name. "You have a number where I can reach you?"

"I've been moving around. In an emergency, you can use the number on my card, but I think it'd be better if I called you. I'll touch base in a day or so and see how things stand. Meanwhile, I don't want the boys to know I'm here. I've been dogging them for years and with this gray hair, I'm not exactly inconspicuous. If they find out we've spoken, you're in the soup, so take care."

THIRTEEN

By 1:45, having confirmed my appointment with Fiona, I found myself driving once more along Old Reservoir Road. The sky was a steel gray, the earlier patches of blue covered over with thick clouds again. I flicked a look to my right, taking in the sight of Brunswick Lake. Gusts of wind skipped like stones along the surface of the water, and trees at the shoreline tossed their shaggy heads. I parked, as I had before, on the side of the two-lane road. I reached for my shoulder bag and the brown manila envelope containing my report. I looked up at the house, which was dug into the hillside as though meant to withstand attack. Four days had passed, but with the surfeit of rain, fresh weeds were sprouting across the property.

I wasn't looking forward to the meeting, but it was better than having to think about Richard and Tommy Hevener. That problem was stuck in my throat like a bone. My first impulse was to bail on the new office space, thus severing all ties, but (cheap as I am) I hated to say bye-bye to more than sixteen hundred dollars. The conflict was thorny. Morality aside, it *can't* be socially correct to consort with a couple of stone-cold killers. But how could I get out of my deal with them? Even in California, the etiquette was baffling. Was one polite? Did one confess the reasons for refusing to do business? I thought about the soft light in Tommy's eyes, then pictured him patiently tying up his mother's hands before the house was set on fire. If he called me again, should I *mention* his parents' murders or simply make some excuse? I wanted to act swiftly. Then again, by breaking off all contact, I was, in effect, refusing to help Mariah Talbot. I seldom shy away from risk and—as she had so rudely observed—I was willing to cut corners when it suited me.

As I locked my car door, I saw Trudy, the German shepherd I'd encountered on my last visit. She came racing up the road, a spirited pup, probably less than a year old and thrilled to be out in the chill November air. The dog squatted to take a whiz, then placed her nose to the ground, tracing the erratic trail of a critter that had passed that way earlier—rabbit or possum, possibly a waddling raccoon. The dog's owner, coming up behind, was keeping an eye on her progress in case she stumbled across something much bigger than she.

By the time I'd clambered up the stairs to Fiona's front entrance, the woman and the dog were already out of sight. Henry and Rosie were always after me to get a mutt of my own, but I couldn't see the point. Why take responsibility for a creature who can't even use a flush toilet?

Fiona must have been waiting because I'd barely touched the bell before she opened the door. Her latest outfit consisted of a long-sleeved crepe blouse modeled on a postwar Eisenhower jacket belted at the waist. Her black wool skirt was tubular and ended mid shin, thus exposing the least attractive portion of any woman's leg. Her high heels were chunky, with multiple ankle straps. Perched on her dyed brown curls was a version of the U.S. Women's Army Corps cap done in sequined velvet. I could smell cigarettes and Shalimar and I was suddenly reminded of my aunt's jar of Mum cream deodorant which she'd rub into her armpits with the tips of her fingers.

"You could have parked out back in the driveway instead of climbing all those stairs," Fiona remarked. The content was harmless, but her tone was resentful, as if she'd like nothing better than to pick a fight with me.

"I need the exercise," I said, refusing to take the bait. As she stepped away from the door, she adjusted her

251

watch, glancing down surreptitiously to see if I were late. As usual, I was bang on time and I thought *Ha-ha-on-you* as I followed her in.

In the foyer, the painter's scaffolding was still in place, drop cloths blanketing the floor like a thin canvas snow. Nothing had been touched since our meeting on Friday, and I assumed she didn't trust the workmen to continue without her. Or maybe it was they who knew better than to go on laboring in her absence. She was the type who'd make them redo all the work as soon as she walked in the door. I could see that the wall still bore patches of three different shades of white.

When I held out the brown manila envelope, you'd have thought I was offering her a bug on a tray.

"What's this?" she asked, suspiciously.

"You said you wanted a report."

She opened the envelope and peered at the pages. "Well, thank you. I appreciate that," she said, dismissing my labors with a glance. "I hope you won't object to talking in the bedroom. I'd like to unpack."

"Fine with me." In truth I was curious to see the rest of the place.

"The flight home was murder, one of those thirty-seat orange crates blowing all over the place. I didn't mind the up-and-down so much as the side-to-side. I thought I'd never get home."

"Probably wind from the storm."

252

"I'll never fly on one of those small planes again. I'd rather go by rail even if it takes half a day."

She picked up a makeup case she'd stashed in the hall. She barely glanced at the larger suitcase. "Grab that for me."

I picked up the hard-sided suitcase, feeling like a pack mule as I followed her up the stairs. That sucker was heavy. I watched her legs flashing in front of me as she mounted the steps. She wore stockings with seams. With her affinity for the '40s, I was surprised she didn't draw a line down the back of each bare leg the way women did during World War II rationing. We turned right at the landing and went into a white-on-white master suite, which featured a large wall of glass over-looking the road. I set her suitcase on the floor. While Fiona moved into the bathroom with her makeup case, I crossed to the windows to absorb the view.

The coastline was completely enveloped in fog, thun-der heads rising like ominous mountains in the distance. The hills were saturated with green, plant life respond-ing to the rain with a sudden burst of new growth. In the overcast, Brunswick Lake had turned silver, its surface as flat and as mottled as an antique mirror. I turned. Fiona's four-poster bed was situated so that she saw much of this: sun rising to her left, going down on her right. I tried to imagine what it would be like to sleep in a room this big. At one end of the room, double

253

doors stood open to reveal a large walk-in closet the size of my loft. At the opposite end, there was a fireplace with easy chairs and a low glass coffee table arranged in front of it. I pictured Fiona and Dow having drinks up here on the nights when he stopped by. I wondered if they'd ever gone to bed together just for old time's sake.

Fiona emerged from the bathroom and moved to the bed, where a second hard-sided suitcase was already laid open on the pristine spread. She began to remove the articles of clothing she'd packed with such care. "Why don't you start from the beginning and fill me in."

I opened my verbal recital with an improvisational medley of interviews, going back over my report in a series of beautifully articulated summations of events. I began with Detective Odessa, segued into my visit with Crystal Purcell, and then moved on to Pacific Meadows, at which point I delineated the nature of the difficulties Dow Purcell was facing. I wasn't even fully warmed up when I hit a sour note that undercut my confidence. Fiona had been moving back and forth from the bed to the walk-in closet, carrying blouses and skirts, which she hung on matching white satin-padded hangers. She said, "You might as well follow me. Otherwise, I won't hear you and you'll have to repeat. My ears are still stopped up; just one more reason for taking the train."

I moved to the closet and stood in the doorway to continue the program. "At any rate, Saturday afternoon I went up to Blanche's shortly after she phoned . . ."

Fiona turned to me. "You went over to see Blanche? Why in the world did you do that?"

"She called me at home. I got the impression you'd already spoken to her."

"I did no such thing and I can't believe you'd take such a step without consulting me. No one's to be brought into this unless I say so. I'm paying for your time. If I'd wanted you to see Blanche, I'd have given you her number."

"I thought you did."

"I gave you Melanie's, not hers. How much did you tell her?"

"I really don't remember. Honestly, I'm sorry, but she acted as if she knew all about me, so I assumed she'd talked to you or to Melanie. She said the two of them were so relieved because they'd been urging you to hire someone ever since their father disappeared."

"That's immaterial. I'll pass on information to the girls if it seems relevant, but I think it's inappropriate coming from you. Is that clear?"

"Of course," I said, stung. Having paid Richard Hevener the entire $1,500 Fiona'd given me, I no longer had the means to refund her original retainer. Deducting $50 for the time I'd spent with Trigg, I now owed her $1,075 worth of services and realized if I quit, there was no way to pay her back, short of pulling the money from my savings account.

"Please go on," she murmured, resuming her chores.

My temper emerged hard on the heels of injury and I had to bite my tongue bloody to keep from telling her where to stick it. This resolution lasted until I opened my mouth. "You know what? Fun as this is, I'm already tired of taking crap from you. I've worked my butt off this weekend and if my methods don't suit you, I'm out of here."

For the second time within minutes, I'd managed to surprise and amaze. She seemed genuinely flustered, backing down as fast as she could manage it. "That's not what I meant. I apologize if I offended you. That wasn't my intent."

There's nothing more effective than an apology for knocking me off my high horse. I backed down as fast as she had and we spent the next few minutes smoothing one another's ruffled feathers before moving on.

Then Fiona asked me about the game plan. Like I had one.

"How do you intend to go about finding him?"

"Ah," said I. "Well. I have some other people I want to talk to first and then we'll see where we stand." In truth, I was at a loss.

Her eyes glittered briefly and I thought she might challenge me, but she seemed to think better of it.

"Couple of questions," I said. "Someone thought Dow might have gone into an alcohol rehab facility on the two occasions when he disappeared in the past. Any chance he might have left the country instead?"

She hesitated. "What difference would that make?"

"Lonnie Kingman questioned it. He's the attorney I rent space from. He suggested Dowan might have been moving currency into foreign bank accounts in preparation for flight."

"It never occurred to me."

"It didn't occur to me, either, but the first time we met, you did seem to think he might be in Europe or South America."

"Well, yes, but I can't believe he'd plan such a thing all those years in advance."

"Did you ever look at his passport?"

"Of course not. What reason would I have?"

"Just an idea," I said. "Maybe that's why the passport's missing—he took it so no one could go back and see where he'd been on those earlier trips."

"You mentioned two questions."

I waited until she made eye contact with me. "Why didn't you tell me he was on his way over here that night?"

Casually, she placed a hand against her throat. The

gesture was self-protective, as though she were warding off a slash at her carotid artery. "He never arrived. I thought it was a miscommunication. I tried calling his office the next day, but he was already gone by then."

"Why was he coming?"

"I don't see why it matters since he never showed."

"Was anyone else in the house with you that night?" I asked.

"To support my story?"

"That'd be nice, don't you think?"

"I'm afraid I can't help. This is a small town. Tongues wag. I wouldn't even let him leave his car on the parking pad. I had him pull into the empty garage. No one knew about his visits."

"At least no one you told." I felt badly as soon as I said it because the look in her eyes was one of betrayal.

"He swore he wouldn't tell Crystal. He said it would only hurt her and neither of us wanted that."

"I didn't say he told Crystal. This was someone else."

"Trigg."

I said, "Yes." After all, it was her money. She was entitled to the information. My scruples, though few, are somewhat spotty as well. "What about Lloyd Muscoe? Did Dow ever talk to you about him?"

"A bit. They disliked each other and avoided contact whenever possible. At first, it was territorial—they were like rival apes—which Crystal must have enjoyed. Later, the friction between them was more about Leila's relationship with Lloyd."

"I heard that Dow considered Lloyd a bad influence on the girl."

"I don't really know Lloyd so I'm reluctant to discuss the subject."

"Oh, give it a try. I'm sure you can manage something."

"He's common, for one thing."

"Happily, that isn't a crime in this state or I'd be under arrest myself."

"You know perfectly well what I'm talking about. They're paying a great deal of money to send her to that private school. I don't see the point when she spends half her weekends with someone like him."

"But Lloyd's the only father she's known. Crystal must feel it's important for Leila to maintain a relationship with him."

"*If* that's her motive. Perhaps she prefers to have the time to herself. Leila's behavior goes way beyond the norm for her age. It's obvious the girl is seriously disturbed. I'm sure Lloyd resented Dow's interference. Instead of taking time with Blanche, you should have been talking to him."

*

Trigg had told me Lloyd lived in the little studio behind the big yellow shingle house at the corner of Missile and Olivio. I parked out in front and made my way down the narrow driveway on foot. Shaggy hedges encroached on either side, forming walls of wet foliage that showered drops as I passed. There was a 1952 Chevrolet parked on the grass at the end of the drive. The occasional wet leaf was plastered to the hood, but aside from that it seemed clean and well cared for. The backyard was overgrown and the small wood-frame studio might have been a gardener's shed at one time. I went up two shallow wooden porch steps and rapped on the frame of the screen door.

No one answered my knock. I took a few minutes to circle the studio, moving from window to window, peering in at the place. I could see four small rooms— living room, kitchen, two tiny bedrooms, with a bath between—all empty. I went back to the front door and opened the screen. I tried the knob. The door swung open at my touch. I turned and stared at the main residence, but no one seemed to be staring back at me. I entered the studio, my footsteps echoing against bare plaster walls.

The rooms smelled of mildew. The floors were covered in scuffed linoleum, the pattern worn. In the first bedroom, there were coat hangers strewn about. Nothing in the closet. In the second bedroom, there was a bare twin-sized mattress on the floor, and when I opened the closet door, I spotted two bedrolls tucked out of sight to the right. The window in that bedroom had been left open a crack, a detail I hadn't noticed when I circled the place. Maybe Lloyd crept in here to sleep now and then. Anyone could ease in along the hedges to the rear of the place, gaining access to the cottage without being seen. There was nothing in the bathroom, with its claw-footed bathtub and its toilet stained with rust. In the kitchen, cabinets stood open. On the counter, I could see a take-out cup holding the dregs of some drink. Smelled like bourbon and coke, or something equally gross. I opened all the kitchen drawers. Optimist that I am, I'm always hoping for a clue, preferably a torn scrap of paper with a forwarding address.

I did another quick tour, which turned out to be as unenlightening as the first. I pulled the door shut behind me and struck out across the yard to the wide rear porch. The backdoor was half glass and I could see an old woman in a house dress fussing with a coven of cats. There were seven by my count: two calicoes, a black, two gray tabbies, an orange tabby, and a white long-haired Persian the size of a pug. I tapped on the window. The old woman looked up, giving me a scowl to indicate she was aware of my presence.

She was tall and gaunt, her white hair arranged in

261

thin braids wrapped around her head. She was apparently in the process of feeding her brood because they circled her attentively, rubbing against her legs, their mouths opening in cries I couldn't hear through the glass. I could see her talking back, probably some long-winded comment about how spoiled they were. She put their bowls on the floor. All of the cats set to work, seven heads bowing as though in prayer. The woman crossed to the back door and opened it. The odor of cat litter wafted out through the gap.

"Not for rent," she said, loudly. "I saw you go through the place, but it's not available. Next time you might ask first before you intrude." Her dentures were loose and she settled them in place with a kind of chewing motion between sentences.

"I'm sorry. I didn't realize anyone was here."

"That's clear enough," she said. "Past sixteen years I rented it out for two hundred dollars a month. Nothing but riffraff moved in. Turnover was constant and some of 'em was no better than bums. It was Paulie pointed out that's all I'd get at those prices. Now I'm asking eight fifty and the place stays empty. Big improvement."

"I'm looking for Lloyd Muscoe. Wasn't he living out there?"

"Did at one time. Twice he was late on his rent and once he didn't pay at all, so I kicked him out."

"Good for you." Where had I heard the name *Paulie*

before? Crystal's battle with Leila at the beach house the first time we met. "Paul's your grandson?"

"Granddaughter and the name's *Pauline*. I raised her since the day her drunken mother dropped her on my doorstep when she was six years old."

"Isn't she a friend of Leila's?"

"Who?"

"Lloyd's daughter, Leila."

"Not anymore. Leila's mother put a stop to it. Said Paulie was too wild. Ask me, that Lloyd's the wild one. Thought he'd get around me because I'm old and deaf, but I surprised him. Evicted him proper and had a marshall show up, make sure he went without a fuss. Fellow like that might decide to trash the place if he doesn't get his way."

"Any idea where he went?"

"No, and I don't care. You a bill collector?"

"I'm a private detective."

"What kind of trouble is he in?"

"None as far as I know. I need to talk to him."

"Can't help. I think he's somewhere in town, but that's as much as I know. Can't even forward his bills, so I have to throw 'em in the trash. Nice-looking man, but shiftless as they come."

"So I've heard. Thanks, anyway."

"You're entirely welcome," she said, and closed the door.

I sat in the car and considered my options. The simplest course of action would be to ask Crystal where Lloyd had gone. Since the two shared custody, I assumed she'd know. I fired up the engine and headed for Horton Ravine again.

Dr. Purcell's house was built on a lush, wooded knoll with a narrow view of the ocean if you raised up on tiptoe. The residence itself wasn't impressive, despite Fiona's boasting about her talent for design. In typical fashion, she'd piled box on box in tiers up to a flat concrete roof. A reflecting pool extended from the front, providing a mirror image of the house in case you happened to miss it the first time around. The style, though futuristic, was oddly dated, imitative of architects more talented than she. It was clearly not Crystal's taste and I could see where she'd chafe at having to live there. Given her love of the glass-and-frame Cape Cod beach house, this must have felt like a prison. The white Volvo and the Audi convertible were parked in the drive, along with a snappy little black Jaguar I hadn't seen before.

When I rang the bell, I heard nothing, but within a minute, Crystal appeared at the door. She was wearing boots, black wool slacks, and a heavy black wool sweater. Her hair was feathered away from her face, the layered blond strands carelessly disarranged. "Good. Thank God. Maybe you can help. Nica, it's Kinsey! Come on in," she said to me, harried.

I stepped through the door. "What's going on?"

"Anica's just driven up from Fitch," she said. "Leila left campus without permission and we're trying to track her down before she blows it. She'll be kicked out of school as soon as they realize she's gone. Don't worry about me. I'm only going out of my mind. Rand took Griff to the zoo."

Anica appeared from the kitchen, wearing navy blue slacks and a red blazer with a gold-stitched Fitch Academy patch on the breast pocket. Her shirt was tailored, crisp white, and she wore a pair of low-heeled navy blue pumps. Her manner was straightforward, and she managed a wide smile despite Crystal's distress. "Always walking into uproar. Hello, Kinsey. Nice to see you again. How are you?" She reached forward and we shook hands.

"Fine. I'm sorry about Leila. You think she's heading this way?"

"Let's hope," Crystal said. She passed us on her way into the kitchen, talking over her shoulder. "I'm making coffee while we try to decide what to do. She knows she's not allowed to hitchhike. I've expressly forbidden it. . . ."

"That's probably why she's done it," Anica said.

265

"I'd be sick with worry if I wasn't so mad at her. How do you take yours, Kinsey?"

"Black's fine with me."

While Anica and I followed her into the kitchen, I made a quick eyeball assessment of the living room to my right. The interior of the house was curious: stone floors, stark white walls, no window covering, all angles and cold light—clearly Fiona's imprint. Over it Crystal had asserted her own taste: assorted shabby Oriental carpets laid togther like pieces of a puzzle, sagging upholstered furniture slip-covered with faded chintz. The wood tables and padded chairs were an antique white with green-and-white checkered seats. Some of the stray pieces were made of bentwood; big rounded chairs that had been woven from twigs. There was a white-painted wrought-iron daybed piled with over-sized pillows in mismatched fabrics. Books were stacked on the coffee table and there were vases of flowers carelessly arranged. The effect was comfortable and slouchy, a place where kids could roam without ruining much since everything looked ruined to begin with.

The kitchen showed the same sort of changes. I could see Fiona's bare-bones approach: cold, streamlined surfaces and the rounded art deco corners. Crystal had introduced glass-fronted cabinets and a hutch where her collection of assorted china plates was displayed. The room looked old-fashioned, a place grandma would have loved for putting up peaches and tomatoes. The appliances were obviously up to date. The stove was a six-burner Viking. I spotted two dishwashers, four ovens, and an island topped with speckled gray granite. Dried herbs hung from the rafters along with a rack for copper pots and pans. At the far end of the room, there was a red-brick fireplace that looked like it was added after Fiona's departure. Too folksy for her taste.

Nica perched on one of the stools lined up in a row along the length of the island while Crystal took cups and saucers from the nearest cabinet, saying, "She's going to get her butt kicked. I swear she's going to be grounded for months. What time did she take off?"

"Had to be nine-fifteen," Nica said. "She reported to PE at nine o'clock, but she claimed she had cramps and was going to the nurse's office. She had an appointment with me at ten. When she didn't show for that, I tracked down her roommate, Amy, who told me she'd seen Leila leaving campus with her backpack."

Crystal looked at her watch. "Where the hell could she be?"

"I just hope Amy has the good grace to keep quiet to the school authorities," Nica said, exempting herself.

"Mind if I look in Leila's room? Maybe I can pick up some clue about where she might be."

Crystal said, "Go right ahead. It's the second door to the right at the head of the stairs."

I went up. Leila's door was closed but unlocked, so I let myself in. I stood for a moment, surveying the space. The room was done in frilly pastels. Talk about wishful thinking. She was at that stage of maturity (or lack of it) where the half-nudie rock star posters ran neck and neck with the stuffed animals of her youth. Every surface was covered with knickknacks. Most looked like the sorts of items teenaged girls give each other: mugs with cute sayings, figurines, jewelry, bottles of cologne. Her bulletin board was a collage of ticket stubs, concert programs, and color snapshots: kids at pep rallies, girls acting goofy, guys engaged in drinking beer, smoking pot and other wholesome pursuits. For someone who claimed to have no friends, she had an amazing collection of memorabilia. The floor was carpeted in discarded clothes, which were also draped over chairs, garments hanging on the closet door, the window seat, and two small upholstered chairs.

I did a quick but thorough search of her drawers. Most of her underwear was already out on the floor, which made my job simple. I went through her closet— jammed full of old board games, sporting equipment, and items from her summer wardrobe. I got down on my hands and knees and made a circuit of the room, checking under chairs, under the bed, under the chest of drawers. The only discovery of interest was the narrow metal lockbox hidden between the mattress and box spring. I shook it but heard only the softest of sounds in response. Probably her dope stash. I didn't have time enough to pick the lock. I returned the box to its hiding place. I felt better for having searched, though the foraging netted me nothing.

Returning to the kitchen, I paused at the planning center to study the family calendar for November, which sat open on the desk. The calendar showed one full month for each page, which was also illustrated with a series of photographs of dogs dressed in children's clothing. November was a cocker spaniel in a navy blue sailor suit. The dog had big brown eyes and appeared to be embarrassed half to death.

Each day was given its own block, an inch and a half square. I could see that three different people had added notes about social events and other activities. Judging from handwriting and the nature of the events posted, I was guessing that Leila's was the oversized printing— angled *T*'s, puffy *I*'s. Crystal's was the elegant cursive in red ink. And Rand's was the scrawl written with a blue ballpoint pen. The personal reminders ranged from meetings to tennis lessons, dental and doctor appointments, to a weekly play group for Griff. The Audi was serviced early in the month. Various telephone numbers had been written in the margins. Notes on alternate weekends indicated Leila's return from school. She apparently wasn't scheduled for this weekend, perhaps because she'd been with Crystal the previous one.

Behind me, Crystal and Nica were busy berating Leila in absentia. I leafed back three months to July and August, noting a fourth handwriting: bold block letters in black. This (I surmised) was Dr. Purcell, whose presence was visible up until Monday, September 8, four days before he vanished. He'd jotted in notes about two board meetings, a medical symposium at UCLA, and a golf date at the country club. None of the entries seemed significant and I assumed the police had followed up.

"I've had it with her," Crystal was saying. "I don't know why I even bother to get upset. That's exactly what she wants."

Nica said, "She's probably on her way to Lloyd's. It'd be like her to make a beeline straight for him."

"Great. Let him deal with her. I'm sick of it. If she doesn't show up soon, I'm calling the cops. All I have to do is declare her an out-of-control minor and she's screwed for sure."

"What good is that going to do?" Anica said. "I know you're mad, but you turn her over to the courts and you'll regret it."

"*She's* the one who'll have regrets. This is about Paulie. I'll bet you dollars to doughnuts."

Anica said, "Quit with the Paulie stuff. It's point-less."

I picked up the calendar and moved over to the island where I claimed my coffee cup. "Mind if I ask about this?"

Crystal glanced over at me, distracted. "What do you need?"

I placed the calendar on the counter and tapped at the page. "I gather Leila doesn't come home every weekend."

"For the most part, she does. Lloyd and I usually alternate visits, but things do come up."

"Like what?"

Crystal glanced at the page, pointing to the second weekend in July. "This was the weekend she had an invitation to go home with her friend, Sherry, in Malibu Colony. Her father's in the movie business and he takes the girls to all the big premieres."

I pointed to the weekend of September 12, when Dow Purcell disappeared. "And this?"

"Same thing, different friend. Emily's family owns horses. They have a ranch at Point Dume. Leila loves to ride. Actually that weekend was canceled—I think Emily got sick—and Leila ended up over at Lloyd's. Why do you ask?"

I shrugged, checking back through the months. Leila's schedule seemed to vary, but it looked like she

271

went off with her school friends on an average of once a month. "I'm thinking she might have left campus with one of her classmates from Fitch."

"I guess it's possible, but I doubt it. Most of her friends are college prep. They'd never risk expulsion." She turned to Nica. "What do you think?"

"It wouldn't hurt to check. It crossed my mind as well, so I brought along the school roster in case we needed to phone any of the other parents." She reached down into the large navy bag near her feet and removed a spiral-bound directory with the school logo on the front. "You want me to go through these and see what I come up with?"

Crystal said, "Hold on a second and let me try Lloyd again." She crossed to the planning center and picked up the phone. She punched in seven numbers and listened for a moment, and then replaced the handset. "He's still not answering. Leila's stepfather," she added by way of explanation.

"I know. I saw him at the beach house the day I met you."

"I've been calling him since Nica arrived. He's there, if I know him. He's always got collection agencies on his case so he refuses to pick up. I've left six messages so he knows this is serious. You'd think he could manage to call back."

I said, "Look, I need an excuse to talk to him,

anyway. Why don't you let me go over to his place and see if Leila's there? If she's not, I can start scouring the roads."

"That's not a bad idea. Nica and I can stay here in case she decides to make an appearance." Crystal reached for a pen and scribbled down some numbers on a scratch pad, tearing off the sheet. "These are my numbers and Lloyd's address and phone."

"You have two lines?"

"That's right. This one's personal. The other's business."

I pointed to the first. "Why don't you leave this one free? You can use the other to check with some of Leila's friends."

"If you find Lloyd, you can tell him I'm tired of doing this alone. It's time he took his fair share of the load."

Walking out to my car, I had to wonder how kids of divorced parents survive all the bickering.

FOURTEEN

Lloyd lived on a street called Gramercy Lane, which looped along the foothills, one of those roads that proceeded by fits and starts. I checked my street map of Santa Teresa, looking up the coordinates. I'd have to intercept Gramercy at some point and then check house numbers to see where I was in relation to Lloyd's address. I left the map open on the passenger seat while I turned the key in the ignition. The rain was picking up again, oversized drops that popped on my hood like gravel being flung up from a roadbed. I flipped on my windshield wipers and glanced at my watch. It was currently 3:15. Between the short November days and the gloom of the rain, twilight seemed to start gathering by 4:00 in the afternoon. At the moment, I felt more like heading for home than cruising the town in search of a runaway teen.

I sailed through the stone gate that marked the front entrance to Horton Ravine and followed the road as it curved around to the right. At the first red light, I glanced at the map again, tilting my head. Gramercy Lane, or parts of it at any rate, were within a two-mile radius of the Purcell house in the Ravine. If Leila had thumbed a ride from Malibu traveling north on the 101, she'd probably have asked to be let off at Little Pony Road, which was one off-ramp south. The light changed and I eased into the stream of southbound traffic, hugging the outside lane. Little Pony Road was less than a mile away.

The notion of Leila thumbing a ride made my stomach churn. Odds were some decent citizen would offer her a lift, but there was also that freakish chance that she'd miscalculate. Not every soul on the road had her best interests at heart. At fourteen, she still felt invincible. For her, assault, rape, mayhem, and murder were events she read about in the papers, if she read them at all. *Perversion* and *deviance* were words on a high school vocabulary list, not vicious behaviors with any relevance to her. I hoped her guardian angels were hovering.

I took the Little Pony off-ramp. At the top, I turned left and headed toward the mountains, scanning both sides of the four-lane road. My windshield wipers were thunking merrily, smearing a swipe of dirt back and forth across the glass. I passed a couple huddled under an umbrella. They were walking on my side of the road with their backs to me. I was looking for Leila on her own so I dismissed them at first. I could tell the two were young. It wasn't until I passed them, catching a second glimpse in my sideview mirror, that I identified Leila's cottony white-blond hair and her long, coltish legs. The boy at her side was tall and lean, toting a backpack with the straps arranged awkwardly across the shoulders of his black leather jacket. Both of them wore tight jeans and hiking boots, and their heads were bowed against the rain. I could have sworn the two were sharing a joint. I slowed and pulled in at the curb just ahead of them. In the sideview mirror, I saw Leila hesitate, then drop something on the ground and step on it. As they walked by my car, I leaned over and rolled down the window on the passenger side.

"Can I give you a ride?"

Leila leaned forward, looking across her companion. When she saw me, her expression registered a look of confusion that signaled recognition without context. She knew she knew me, but she didn't remember how. The kid with her levered a gaze at me filled with hostility and disdain. I took in the smooth complexion, the rain-bedraggled lank brown hair, the plain white T-shirt visible under the open leather jacket. I was startled by the boobs, since I'd assumed the kid was a male. This had to be Paulie. I could see she was destined to be beautiful even though, at the moment, she was unkempt and had defiance written into every inch of her slender frame. She wasn't conventionally pretty, but she had a fierce, worldly air: big dark eyes, cheekbones sharpened by poor nutrition. A photographer with the right instincts could make a fortune from the image of belligerent sexuality she projected.

I focused on Leila. "Hi. I'm Kinsey Millhone. We met last Friday at the beach house. I just came from your mom's. She's worried about you. You should have let her know you were leaving school."

"I'm fine, but tell her thanks for her concern." Leila's tone was sarcastic. Her flippancy was intended to impress her friend, but the insolence was hard to sustain with rainwater dripping down her face. Two strands of hair were plastered to her cheek and the mascara on her lashes had turned to a watery ink.

"I think you should tell her yourself. She needs to know you're okay."

Leila and Paulie exchanged a look. Paulie said something to Leila under her breath; co-conspirators, trying to make the best of the fact they'd been caught. Paulie eased the backpack from her shoulders and passed it to Leila. After a few murmured words, Paulie took off toward the highway at a pace meant to convey nonchalance.

Leila leaned closer to the half-opened window. Her eyes were heavily lined, the lids shadowed with turquoise blue. Her lipstick was dark brown, too harsh a shade for her fragile blond coloring. "You can't make me go home."

"I'm not here to *make* you do anything," I said. "You might consider getting out of the rain."

"I will if you promise not to tell Mom who was with me."

"I'm assuming that's Paulie."

Leila said nothing, which I took as assent.

"Come on. Get in. I'll drop you off at your dad's."

She thought about it briefly, then opened the car door and slid into the passenger seat, shoving her backpack into the cramped space at her feet. Her hair had been bleached so many times it looked synthetic, still arranged in the odd mix of dreadlocks and tufts that must have made the boarding school authorities wring their hands in dismay. Or maybe Fitch was progressive, a school where students were allowed to "express themselves" through outlandish appearances and oddball behaviors. In the body-heated confines of the car, I could smell eau-de-marijuana and the feminine musk of undergarments worn several days too long.

I glanced over my shoulder, checking the flow of traffic behind me, and pulled onto the road once the passing cars had cleared. In my rearview mirror, I could see Paulie's departing figure, reduced by now to the size of a toy soldier. "How old is Paulie?"

"Sixteen."

"I take it your mom's not that fond of her. What's the problem?"

"Mom doesn't like anything I do."

"Why'd you leave school without permission?"

"How'd you know where I was going?" she asked, bypassing the issue of truancy.

"Your mother figured it out. When we get to a phone, I want you to call and tell her where you are. She's been worried sick." I didn't mention royally pissed off as well.

"Why don't you do it? You'll turn around and talk to her, anyway."

"Of course I will. You're a minor. I'm not going to contribute to your bad behavior." We drove for a block in silence. Then I said, "I don't get what's bugging you."

"I hate Fitch. That's what's bugging me, if it's any of your business."

"I thought you got sent to Fitch because you screwed up in public school."

"I hated it up there, too. Bunch of goof-offs and retards. Everybody was so dumb—I was bored to death. Classes were a joke. I've got better things to do."

We crossed State at the intersection and headed into a residential area called South Rockingham. "What's wrong with Fitch?"

279

"The girls are such *snobs*. All they care about is how much money their fat-ass daddies make."

"I thought you had friends."

"Well, I don't."

"What about Sherry?"

Leila stole a look at me. "What about her?"

"I'm just wondering how you enjoyed yourself in Malibu."

"Fine. It was fun."

"What about Emily?"

"Why are you asking me all these questions?"

"Your mom said you liked riding horses at her place."

"Emily's okay. She's not as bad as some."

"What else did you do?"

"Nothing. We made grilled cheese sandwiches."

The arrow on my bullshit meter zinged up into the red zone. I was much better at lying when I was Leila's age. "Here's my best guess. I'll bet you skipped both those visits and spent the weekend with Paulie."

She said, "Ha ha ha."

"Come on. 'Fess up. What difference does it make?"

"I don't have to respond if I don't want to."

"Leila, you asked me to keep my mouth shut. The least you could do is tell me the truth."

"So what if I saw Paulie? What's the big deal about that?"

280

"What about all the other weekends you were sup-posed to be off visiting classmates?"

Another sullen silence. I tried another tack. "How'd you two meet?"

"In Juvie."

"You were in Juvenile Hall? When was this?"

"A year ago July. Bunch of us got picked up."

"Doing what?"

"The cops said loitering and trespass, which is crap. We weren't doing anything, just hanging around."

"Where was this?"

"I don't know," she said, crossly. "Just some boarded-up old house."

"What time of day?"

"What are you, a district attorney? It was late, like two o'clock in the morning. Half the kids ran. Cops were all bent out of shape and took the rest of us in. Mom and Dow came and picked me up and they were pissed."

"What about Paulie? Was she in trouble with the law?"

Leila said, "You just missed my dad's street."

I slowed and pulled into the next driveway, then backed out. I retraced the half block to Gramercy and turned left. This section was only a block and a half long, a jumble of cheap cottages that might have once served as housing for itinerant pickers in the nearby

281

avocado groves. The road here was unpaved and there were no sidewalks. I spotted one streetlight along the entire block. Leila pointed at a weathered A-frame sitting on a small dirt rise. It was the only structure of its kind—a funky wooden chalet among shacks. I pulled into the driveway and killed the engine. "You want to see if he's there? I'd like to talk to him."

"What about?"

"Dr. Purcell, if it's all the same to you," I said.

Leila snatched open the door and reached for her backpack, which I snagged with one hand. "Leave that with me. I'll be happy to bring it in if he's home."

"Why can't I have it?"

"Insurance. I don't want to see you taking off on me. You're in enough trouble as it is."

She sighed, exasperated, but did as she was told. I decided to ignore the vigor with which she slammed the car door. I watched her hurry to the house along a gravel path. Rainwater streamed down the hillside, flattening the long strands of uncut grass. She reached the porch, which was protected by no more than a narrow inverted V of wood. She knocked on the door and then huddled with folded arms, staring back at me while she waited for him to respond. The place looked dark to me. She knocked again. She moved over to a front window, cupped her hands, and peered in. She knocked one more time and then splashed her way back to the car and let herself in. "He's probably coming right back. I know where he keeps the key so I can wait for him here."

"Good. I'll wait with you. The two of us can visit here in the car until he gets home."

The suggestion didn't seem to fill the child with joy. She kicked at the backpack with her muddy hiking boots. "I want to go in. I have to pee."

"Good suggestion. Me, too."

We got out of the car. I locked the car doors and followed her along the path. Once we reached the house, Leila shifted a pot of dead geraniums and removed the house key from its terribly original hiding place. I waited while she unlocked the door and let us in.

"Does he rent this?"

"Nuhn-uhn. He's house-sitting for a friend. Some guy went off to Florida, but he's coming back next week."

The interior was basically one big room. The ceiling soared to a peak. To the right, a narrow staircase led to a sleeping loft. In the living area below, the wood furniture was clumsily constructed, covered with imitation Indian rugs. The wood floors were bare. I could hear grit popping under the soles of my shoes. There was an old black pot-bellied stove exuding the scent of cold ash. At the rear, a counter separated the kitchen, which looked dirty even at this distance.

I spotted the phone sitting on a small side table. "You want to call your mom or should I?"

"You do it. I'm going to the bathroom and don't worry—I'm not going to run away."

While she availed herself of the facilities, I put in the requisite call to Crystal. Temporarily honor-bound, I omitted any mention of Paulie. "I'm going to stay here until Lloyd gets home. If it gets too late, I'll try to talk Leila into coming back to your place."

"Honestly, I'm so mad at her I really don't want to see her. I'll be better in a bit, as soon as I have a drink. Anica's calling the school. I have no idea what she'll tell them. It would serve Leila right if she were suspended or expelled."

"I hear you," I said. "I'll keep you posted on our progress. Wish me luck."

I heard the toilet flush and Leila emerged from the tiny bathroom located under the stairs.

"What'd she say?"

"Nothing much. She's not real happy with you."

Leila moved over to the lumpy sofa. Ignoring me, she opened her backpack and removed a zippered pouch filled with her makeup. She took out a compact and opened it so she could study her face. She cleaned up the smeared mascara and then peered closer at herself. "Crap. A fuckin' zit," she said. She put the compact away. She picked up the remote control and turned on the television set, muting the sound with a glance at me.

I said, "I used to be just like you when I was your age."

"Great. Can I smoke?"

"No."

"Why? They're only clove cigarettes."

"Don't push me, Leila. The place smells bad enough without throwing in clove smoke. Tell me about Dow. And don't get all huffy. I'm bored with that shit."

"Like what do you want to know?"

"When did you see him last?"

"I don't remember stuff like that."

"Here, I'll help. September 12 was a Friday. Emily was sick and she cancelled so you must have been home. Were you at the beach house?"

"Nuhn-uhn. I was here."

"Do you remember what you did that night?"

"Probably watched a video. That's what I usually do. Why?"

"I'm wondering when you last talked to Dow."

"How should I know? I try not to talk to him at all if I can help it."

"You must talk occasionally. After all, he's your stepdad."

"I know who he is," she said. "I thought you weren't allowed to question a kid without a parent present."

"That's only true if you're detained by the police."

"What are you?"

"A private eye. Phillip Marlowe in drag." From her expression, I could tell she thought Phillip Marlowe was a rock band, but she was smart enough not to commit herself on that score. I said, "How old were you when Dow and your mom got married?"

"Eleven."

"You like him?"

"He's all right."

"You two get along?"

"About as well as you'd expect. He's old. He wears dentures. His breath smells all moldy and he has a bunch of really stupid rules: 'I want you home and in bed by ten. I don't want you sleeping late. Help your mother with your brother,'" she said, mimicking him. "I told him, 'Hey, that's what Rand's for. I'm not her fucking maid.' My grades have to be perfect or I'm grounded for weeks. He won't even let me have my own phone."

"The bastard," I said. "Where do you think he is?"

"In Canada."

"Interesting. What makes you say that?"

She stared at the television screen, flipping from channel to channel.

"Leila?"

"What!"

"I asked why you thought he was in Canada?"

"Because he's a shit," she said. "All he ever cared about was looking good. I heard him talking to some woman on the phone. I guess six months ago these people came into the clinic and picked up financial records and a lot of patient files. He was shitting bricks. Whatever it was, I guess he could have gone to jail for it, so I think he skipped."

"Who was he talking to?"

"I don't know. He never said her name and I didn't recognize her voice. Just about then, he figured out I was on the line so he waited 'til I got off before he said anything else."

"You were listening in?"

"I was up in my room. I wanted to make a phone call. How was I supposed to know he was on the line?"

"When was this?"

"Couple weeks before he went."

"Did you tell the police?"

"Nobody asked and besides, it's just a guess. Can I watch this now?"

"Sure."

She hit the mute button again and the sound came blasting back. MTV.

I went into the bathroom, which wasn't as tacky as I thought it'd be. I closed the door. It looked like Lloyd had made a modest effort to keep the sink and the bathtub clean. The toilet water was rendered a permanent blue from a pungent smelling cake of something hung in the tank. Once I peed and flushed, I checked the medicine cabinet and sorted through his dirty clothes basket.

When I got back to the main room, Leila had sunk into that hypnotic state television generates. The A-frame was getting dark. I turned on some lights. Since she was paying absolutely no attention, I took advantage of the moment to search the desktop and the contents of the drawers. Most seemed to be filled with the other fellow's junk. I wasn't looking for anything in particular. I simply couldn't resist the urge to stick my nose in where it didn't belong. I sifted through a handful of Lloyd's bills, all overdue. Restlessly, I moved into the kitchen. The refrigerator didn't yield much, but the pantry turned out to be better stocked than mine. Dried pasta, jars of sauce, canned soups, condiments, peanut butter, the strange orange macaroni and cheese in a box that only kids and dogs will eat. I was bored and getting hungry.

I moved across the great room and climbed the stairs to the loft, peering over the rail. Below I could see Leila, still engrossed in the flickering images on the screen. I couldn't believe she was leaving me to snoop at will. Lloyd's bed was unmade. On the bed table there was a framed eight-by-ten photograph of Lloyd and Leila. I picked it up and studied it. The picture must have been taken at a birthday celebration. The two were sitting at a kitchen table, a wobbly-looking chocolate cake festooned with candles in front of them. Lloyd and Leila had leaned their heads close together, grinning and clowning for the photographer. Lloyd's right ear was pierced. A newly opened package was visible and Lloyd was holding one of a pair of earrings to his ear—a tiny dangling gold skull and crossbones—apparently a gift from her. Hard to tell how long ago this was; sometime within the past year, judging from her hair.

A check of the dresser drawers revealed nothing except a wide array of flashy-looking boxer shorts. I turned and surveyed the area. There was a telescope on a tripod standing by the window and that interested me. I crossed and studied the view with my naked eye at first, orienting myself to my surroundings. This was not a neighborhood I knew and I had no idea what Lloyd could see from here. Startled, I realized his current digs were located just across the reservoir from Fiona Purcell. Through the haze of mist and rain, I could see the barren outline of her house, jutting out from the far hill like a fortress. Lloyd's view was toward the mountains while Fiona's view stretched in the opposite direction taking in the ocean and the islands twenty-six miles out. I bent to the eyepiece on the telescope and squinted through the lens. Everything was black. I removed the lens cap, which improved the visibility, though at first, all I saw was the surface of my own eye. The landscape was reduced to a big yawning blur: objects distorted by the magnification.

I lifted my face and found the focus mechanism, then peered through the lens again and adjusted the knob. Abruptly, the far shore came into sharp relief. I could see the scarring on a boulder standing out in such sharp contrast it looked as if it rested just a foot away from me. The water in the reservoir was ragged where the raindrops hit. The sky was reflected in hammered silver on its surface. I caught movement to the right and shifted my view a hair.

There was Trudy, the German shepherd, barking at a stick—one of those brainless behaviors dogs seem to thrive on. I could see her mouth open and shut like a doggie hand puppet. The enthusiasm of her barking caused her whole body to shake, but the sound was reduced by the window glass to the faintest report. Her legs and feet were muddy and I could clearly see the raindrops beading on her coat. Behind her, a wide path through the undergrowth had been flattened and I could see white where a line of saplings had been snapped off at ground level. Maybe a boat trailer had been backed down close to the water's edge to launch an outboard. Faintly, I heard Trudy's owner whistle and then her barely audible call. "Trudy! *Truuudy!*"

Trudy looked over her shoulder with regret, torn between her current obsession and her need to obey. Obedience won out. She went bounding up the hillside and disappeared over the crest. I lifted my sights to Fiona's house, where the lights were winking on in sequence, probably on timers. I zoomed in on her bedroom window, but there was no sign of movement. Odd that she appeared to be living so close that I nearly reached a hand out to touch a windowpane. Traveling by car, her place was actually a mile and a half away, the long way around. Her side of the reservoir was peppered with expensive homes, where this side was shabby: board and batten rentals without much market value. I wondered if Lloyd realized whose house he had in his sights. I wondered if he stared in her bedroom window, watching her undress at night.

I shifted my view again, feeling like a bird skimming across the surface of the lake. I let my gaze come to rest on the narrow end of the reservoir where the vegetation grew densely all the way to the point at which the water met the hill. A sign was posted on a fence post and I could read the larger of the lines. Swimming and boating were forbidden. The light was fading rapidly and I could feel myself strain. I lifted my eyes and stared at the gathering dark. What had I seen?

I closed my eyes and when I opened them again, I felt my perception shift. The alteration was abrupt, like the test to determine which eye is dominant. Cover your left eye with your palm and stare at your right index finger, held out at arm's length. Then remove your palm from your left eye and cover your right eye instead. Looking through the dominant eye, the alignment of your finger against the background remains constant. Using the nondominant eye, the finger will appear to jump to one side. In reality, nothing changes. The finger remains where it is, but the brain registers a difference. I felt a spurt of anxiety and my heart began to thump.

I turned and trotted down the stairs. Leila emerged from her trance long enough to look up at me. She was stretched out full-length, her sock feet resting on the arm of the sofa, her hiking boots on the floor.

I said, "I have to go out for a few minutes. Will you be all right by yourself?"

"I'm here alone all the time," she said, insulted.

"Great. I shouldn't be long, but I'd appreciate your staying put until I get back. Okay?"

"Yeah." She turned her attention to the set again and switched through several channels, finally settling on an old *Tom and Jerry* cartoon.

I closed the front door behind me and picked my way down the muddy path to my car. The light was draining from the sky and the air temperature was dropping. The rain wasn't falling hard, but it was annoying, nonetheless. I unlocked my car and slid under the wheel. I reached over and popped open the glove compartment. I took out my flashlight and I pushed the button, gratified to see that the battery was still strong. I turned off the flashlight, laid it on the passenger seat while I started the car, and backed out of Lloyd's short drive. I swung around and headed back to the main road. At the intersection, I turned right, drove half a mile, turned right again on Old Reservoir Road, and began the winding ascent. The curves were familiar and I drove with a thumping heart, wishing I had stopped to pee again before I left. Fear is a powerful diuretic.

Ahead, Fiona's house came into view and I pulled over on the berm. I grabbed my flashlight, got out, and set off on foot. Out here, there was still enough ambient light that I could see my way. I climbed the wet grassy hill, my feet slipping out from under me when I least expected it. I paused at the crest of the hill, looking out across the reservoir to the A-frame where Lloyd was living. The lights glowing in the house made it look like a chapel perched on the opposite hill. I hoped Leila wouldn't disappear while I was scrambling through the dark.

Traversing the downside of the hill was even trickier, and I found myself losing purchase, half-slipping, half-sliding as I maneuvered my way along. At the bottom, I turned on my flashlight. The area was cold and silent and the air smelled dank. The water was black near the shoreline and showed no evidence of a current. In places, I could see Trudy's paw prints. I shone the beam of my flashlight along the hill behind me, locating the boulder I'd seen and the path of broken saplings. I stood where I was, following the line of the hill to the top. From where I stood the road wasn't visible. I turned my beam on the silty water, tracing the shallows. The lake bottom apparently dropped off abruptly, but I could see the curve of a chrome bumper glowing dully, like buried treasure. I couldn't read the name on the vanity plate, but I knew I was looking at the trunk of Dow Purcell's silver Mercedes submerged in the depths.

FIFTEEN

An accident scene at night is as bleak and gaudy as a carnival. It was now fully dark, close to eight P.M. The coroner's car, the mobile crime lab, and a Ford sedan were parked on the berm, along with two patrol cars with red-and-blue bar lights flashing, radios squawking insistently between spurts of static. Two uniformed officers stood together talking while the police dispatcher, like a barker, issued a monotonous, nonstop account of crimes and misdemeanors in progress: complaints about noise, a call reporting a domestic disturbance in another part of town, a prowler, a drunk urinating on a public street. Santa Teresa is a town of eighty-five thousand with more crimes against property than crimes against persons.

Five minutes after I'd spotted the submerged Mercedes, I'd scrambled up the hill and down the other side to the road. I'd crossed and climbed Fiona's stairs two at a time, not pausing for breath until I reached the top.

I pounded on her front door and rang the bell simultaneously, willing her to respond. I'd been reluctant to leave the scene unattended, but I had to notify the cops. I rang the bell again. Having observed Fiona's house from Lloyd's loft across the lake, it didn't take much to persuade me she was still out somewhere. I trotted around the side of the house to the rear where the driveway entered the property from the roadway above. There were no cars on her parking pad and all three of her garage doors were down and locked.

Fiona's nearest neighbor was just across the road. I knew knocking on doors at random would be a pain in the ass. Though it wasn't late, it was dark out. Everyone had heard stories about intruders using a ruse to gain entrance to the victim's house. What choice did I have, short of hopping in my car and driving until I found a public phone? I rang the bell, talking to myself the whole time: *Come on, come on, be here, help me out here.* I peered through the glass side panels, which afforded me an abbreviated view of the foyer. I could see someone moving around in the kitchen, probably preparing supper. She appeared in the hall and approached the front door. I waved, trying to look like a law-abiding citizen instead of a cunning and devious crazed killer. She was middle-aged, in a sweater and slacks, with an apron tied around her waist. If she was apprehensive at the sudden summons, she gave no indication. She turned on the porch light and studied me with caution.

I spoke loudly, hoping she could hear me through the glass. "I'm a friend of Fiona's. She's out and I need to use your phone."

I saw her eyes stray toward Fiona's house while she assimilated the request. She made sure the burglar chain was secure, and then she opened the door a crack. I don't remember now how I explained the situation, but I must have been persuasive because she let me in without argument and showed me to the phone.

Seven minutes later, the first black-and-white patrol car had come careening up the road.

Nearly two hours had passed and neighbors from many of the surrounding houses had straggled out to the road. They stood in clusters under the meager shelter of their umbrellas, conversing in subdued and fragmentary bursts while the rain pattered on. Word had apparently spread that the doctor's car had been found. Under ordinary circumstances, they probably didn't have much occasion to meet. None of the houses up here were built close together and with many residents holding day jobs, my guess was their paths seldom crossed. A rag-tag crew, they looked like they'd pulled on their coats and their rain boots in haste. They waited with patience, their vigil ritualistic, a community of the concerned conferring at this unprecedented gathering.

A temporary fence of plastic pylons and tape prevented their approach. Not that there was much to see from where they stood. Looking toward the city, the roadway itself was cloaked in darkness, no streetlights within range. In the opposite direction, the asphalt petered out. Beyond the last cul-de-sac, there were only black and looming foothills, raw land knit together with sage and chaparral.

I sat in my car, feeling tense with the cold. At intervals, I fired up the engine so I could keep the heater running and the windshield wipers on, though the steady *thunk-thunk-thunk-thunk* nearly put me to sleep. To my right, the hill rose at a thirty-degree angle for a hundred yards or so before it crested and curved down to the lake. From the water's edge, the floodlights glowed eerily, silhouetting the few scrub trees stretched out along the crest. At intervals, the light was broken by shadows as the police went about their business. I'd spoken briefly with Odessa when he'd first reached the scene. He'd asked me to stay and said they were putting a diver in the water to check the car's interior before they hauled it out of the lake. He'd set off up the long slope and I settled in for the wait.

At some point, Leila had appeared, accompanied by her stepfather, Lloyd, who'd come home while I was in the process of discovering Dow's car. They stood to one side under a black umbrella, maintaining a distance from the neighbors. I was guessing the two had been attracted by the lights and had hopped in Lloyd's car. For once, Leila seemed to be experiencing an emotion other than boredom or contempt. With her thick black mascara and heavily shadowed lids, she looked like a waif, big-eyed and solemn, shivering uncontrollably. I knew I should go over and introduce myself to Lloyd, but I couldn't bring myself to do it. Down the road, I spotted two mini-cam crews, one from KWST-TV, the other from KEST-TV. The blond reporter from KEST was already picking up film clips and interviews for the eleven o'clock news. She stood under a big black umbrella, talking to one of the neighbors. I didn't see any other reporters, but they were doubtless around somewhere.

I adjusted my rearview mirror and watched as a pair of headlights swept into view around the curve in the road. I was hoping to see Fiona, but the vehicle turned out to be Crystal's white Volvo. She slowed as she approached. She waited while a smattering of people ambled out of the roadway and passed in front of her, and then pulled in and parked on the berm just ahead of me.

I grabbed my slicker from the backseat and held it over my head as I left the comfort of my VW and moved gingerly along the road to her car. She turned and caught sight of me and rolled down her window. Her face was drawn, her hair pulled back in an untidy knot at the nape of her neck. Gone were the black slacks and sweater she'd worn earlier, She looked like she'd dressed in haste, pulling on jeans and a gray utilitarian sweatshirt bearing the name of our gym. She said, "I was already in my robe and slippers when the officer came to the door. He wanted to bring me over in his patrol car, but I wanted my own wheels. What's happening?"

"Nothing much. This is worse than a movie set, with all the people standing around. Where's Anica?"

"She had to get back to school. Hop in."

I said, "Thanks." I opened the door and slid into the front seat. Behind me, Griffith's car seat was buckled into place, the surrounding area decorated with an assortment of cookie crumbs and broken pretzels. A plastic baby bottle filled with apple juice had left a sticky residue in the spot where I rested my hand. There was a pink plush squirrel on the floor by my feet. I pictured him flinging his binky, his bottle, his snacks, and stuffed animals, a hurricane of objects announcing his presence. The interior air smelled of flowers and spice, Crystal's cologne.

I said, "How are you?"

"Numb."

I said, apropos of nothing, "The car might have been abandoned."

"Let's hope that's all it is." She angled the rearview

mirror in her direction and ran a knuckle under her lower lashes where her eye liner had smeared. She pushed the mirror back and slouched down on her spine. She leaned her head back on the seat and closed her eyes. In profile, I could see the irregularities of her features. Her nose was too sharp, her lower jaw too narrow for the width of her brow. Properly done up, she seemed more intimidating than she was in the moment. "When did you get here?" she asked, as though talking in her sleep.

"Hours ago. At six."

"They said not to hurry. I was watching TV when the officer arrived at the door."

"You're lucky. I'm starving. I missed dinner. I'm about to eat my arm."

Crystal reached over to the glove compartment and flipped the door down. "Try this." She removed a battered Hershey's bar and passed it over to me. "How'd they find the car?"

"I was the one who spotted it and called 911. The cops are over there now doing God knows what." I removed the outer wrapper and opened the white inner paper liner. The scent of chocolate rose like a vapor. I broke the candy bar into perfect sections and placed one on my tongue. I could almost read the engraved letter *H* as I pressed one softening chocolate square against the roof of my mouth.

"How'd you know the car was his?"

"The vanity license plate."

We were silent. Crystal turned on the radio and then thought better of it and turned it off again. The rain on the roof was a soft percussion, a drummer's brushes on cymbals. The atmosphere was oddly intimate. We were both out of our natural habitats, constrained by the unfamiliar setting, bound by the wait. "I take it they haven't pulled the car out of the water yet," she said at length.

"They're waiting for the tow truck. Odessa said he'd let us know as soon as there's something to report." I ate an *E* and stuck the rest of the Hershey's in my shoulder bag. I crossed my arms in a vain attempt to get warm.

Crystal made a sound that was half sigh and half something else: tension, impatience, simple weariness. "I knew he was dead. That's the only explanation that made any sense. I told you he wouldn't walk off and leave Griff."

"Crystal, they haven't even brought the car up. We don't know he's in there."

"He's there. Leila's going to freak."

"How so? She doesn't like him."

"Of course not. She treated him like dirt. How's she going to make her peace with that?"

I hesitated, wanting to press. She was more vulnerable than I'd seen her. This might be my only opportunity. "What's her anger about?"

"It's too complicated to go into."

"Nothing's too complicated if he's dead."

Crystal roused herself and turned. "Why should I tell you? You're not working for me."

"I'm not working against you, either. What's her problem?"

"Why is that any concern of yours?"

"It isn't, if you put it that way, but it's going to get worse."

"I don't doubt that," she said. And after a long pause, "There's been a certain amount of trauma in Leila's life. She needs help sorting it out."

"She's seeing a shrink?"

"She's been seeing one for years. At first, three times a week. Now it's down to twice a month on weekends when she's up from school."

"He has appointments on weekends?"

"It's a she."

"Sorry. I didn't think psychiatrists were that obliging."

"This one is. She's truly fabulous with kids. This is the fifth shrink Leila's seen and I was at my wit's end."

"How'd you find her?"

"We were lucky for once. Charlotte Friedman's a woman Anica went to school with. Her husband retired and they moved here from Boston."

"What sort of trauma? I'm still not getting it."

Crystal seemed to debate with herself. She stared straight ahead and when she spoke her tone was as flat and distant as an old phonograph record. "I had a little boy who drowned. Of course, it affected us all. That was the beginning of the end where Lloyd and I were concerned. Some things you never recover from. A child's death is one."

"What happened?"

"That was Jordie. My sweet one. He was eighteen months old. I was working one night and left him with the woman next door. She was talking on the phone when Jordie toddled out the screen door and fell in the pool. By the time she found him and called the paramedics, he couldn't be revived."

"I'm sorry."

"I thought I'd die, but it was worse for Leila. Children aren't prepared for loss. They don't understand and it's hard to explain death in terms that they comprehend. I've never been religious. I didn't want to sell her a fairy tale, especially one I wasn't buying myself. Dr. Friedman says when faced with the death of a sibling, some children disconnect. They act like nothing's happened. Others, like Leila, start acting out.

She's difficult. You've seen it yourself. Rebellious. Emotional. I've talked to Charlotte with Leila's permission of course. Charlotte feels Leila's behavior is her way of distancing herself, creating a barrier between herself and a world that she finds treacherous. If she doesn't care about anyone, she can't be hurt. At any rate, I know I'm protective. I'm not even sure how I'm going to tell her about all this."

"She's here. Didn't you see her back there with Lloyd?"

Crystal sat up abruptly. "I had no idea. Where?"

"Far side of the road, about three cars back. At least they were a while ago."

"I better see how she's doing." Crystal reached around the seat for a big black umbrella that was stashed on the floor. She opened the car door a crack and stuck the umbrella out, popping the automatic latch that caused it to *thwop* into full sail.

"Thanks for the Hershey's. You saved my life."

"You're welcome."

The tow truck appeared, its headlights illuminating the roadway as far as the next curve. I opened the door on my side, tented my slicker over my head, and got out, closing the door behind me. I turned, watching as the tow truck driver's assistant hopped out of the cab. Crystal passed him, trekking back along the road while the driver did a three-point turn and started backing up

305

the slope. The heavy tires slipped, chewing two channels in the grass. The driver craned a look over his shoulder, one hand on the wheel. His assistant whistled sharply and gave rolling-arm instructions about the angle of ascent. The blond reporter caught sight of Crystal and moved to intercept her. Crystal shook her head, waving her off.

I retreated to my car and turned the key in the ignition. The rain was reduced by now to an icy mist, soaking the unwary onlookers by slow degrees. The interior temperature had dropped while I was gone and the tepid breeze generated by the heater wasn't even as effective as my own breath. I watched the tow truck slip sideways and then lumber backward up the hill to the top. I couldn't imagine how they'd manage to haul the Mercedes out of the water and up the sodden hill.

I turned, looking over the backseat to check Crystal's progress. She'd reached Leila, who was standing by the side of the road with Lloyd. Lloyd had his arm around her, but the minute Leila saw Crystal she fled to her mother's embrace. Crystal held her and rocked her where they stood, resting her face in Leila's hair. After a moment, the three conferred; Leila looking miserable, Lloyd withdrawn. Whatever the debate, it was evident that Crystal prevailed. Mother and daughter passed my car in their return to the station wagon. Crystal was talking earnestly while Leila wept without sound. I watched as she settled her daughter in the front seat and then went around the rear of the car and slid in under the wheel.

I adjusted my rearview mirror, keeping a watchful eye on Lloyd, who'd started toward his car, his head bent, hands in his jacket pockets. Maybe the two were in competition, playing good parent. Leila was the prize and Lloyd had been forced to forfeit this round. In mirror-reverse, I saw him light up a cigarette and belatedly I smelled smoke drifting through the damp night air. Idly, I wondered how far out into dark I'd have to go so I could pee without being arrested for indecent exposure.

Detective Odessa, in a hooded water-repellent jacket, appeared at the crest of the hill and began his descent, his footing as tenuous as mine had been. He spotted my VW and began to tack in my direction. I leaned over and cranked down the window a couple of inches. He reached the car and peered in. Drizzle had collected on the shiny surface of his jacket and the water slid in runners along the stitching in the seams. His nose was slightly too prominent and something in the shape of it left him just short of handsome. He gestured toward the work lights on the far side of the hill. "I want you to meet Detective Paglia."

I said, "Sure." I rolled up the window and killed the engine. I got out, taking a moment to shrug into my slicker before I followed him up the hill. The two of us struggled together, Odessa holding on to my arm as much for stability as for support.

I said, "How's it going?"

"It's a bitch," he said. "I see Crystal's here. I sent an officer to the house. I thought she should know what was happening."

"What about Fiona? Anybody heard from her?"

"Nope. We notified the daughter, but she can't make it over here until the nanny gets back from dinner."

"Does she know where her mother is?"

"Not offhand. She says she'll put in a few calls and see if she can track her down. Otherwise we wait and hope she comes home."

We scrambled the last few yards to the top of the hill and stood there together staring down at the lake. The light from the flood lamps had washed the color from the scene. Steam rose like smoke where the rain came in contact with the hot metal flanges. An assortment of people stood in clusters, apparently waiting for additional technicians or equipment. I could see an eerie green glow moving under the surface of the water as a search went on in the depths. With the angle of the floodlights, the butt end of the Mercedes glimmered incongruously. "Is he in there?"

"Don't know yet. We've got a diver in the water. The shelf drops off sharply to a depth of twenty feet

. . . this is five or six yards out. Car got hung up against a boulder or it'd be down on the bottom and we'd be out of luck."

The diver surfaced in a dark blue wet suit and hood, a compressed-air cylinder strapped to his back. He removed his mouthpiece and let it dangle as he waded ashore, algae clinging to his fins. He lifted off his face mask and left it resting on the top of his head like a hat. Once on shore, he was intercepted by the coroner and another man, both in raincoats, who listened while he reported, complete with gestures.

Meanwhile, the tow truck had backed down within range of the shore. Two men in hip boots and yellow slickers had entered the water in preparation for the salvage operation. One was already attaching a chain to the Mercedes's axle. As I looked on, one of the two men miscalculated and slipped into deeper water, his slicker billowing out around him like a deflated life raft. He flailed, cursing, while his partner snorted with suppressed laughter and pushed forward through the water to lend him a hand.

Odessa nodded in the diver's direction. "That's Paglia with the coroner."

"I gathered as much."

As if on cue, the other detective turned and caught sight of Odessa and me. He excused himself and headed in our direction across soft ground already trampled with footprints. Days of rain had obliterated any trace of tread marks, but the projected path of the car had been secured and searched. Evidence was doubtless in very short supply after so much time had passed. When he reached us, Detective Paglia held out his hand. "Ms. Millhone. Jim Paglia. Con Dolan's spoken to me about you." His voice was deep and uninflected. I placed him in his fifties. His head was shaved, his freckled forehead etched with a trellis of vertical and horizontal lines.

We shook hands and said hi-how-are-you-type things. Lieutenant Dolan had been in charge of the homicide unit until a heart attack dictated his early retirement. "How's Dolan doing these days?"

"So so. Good, but not great. He misses the job." Paglia's eyebrows were black twists that tipped up at the outer corners like a pair of wings. He wore small oval glasses with thin metal frames. If the raindrops falling on the lenses annoyed him, he gave no sign of it. He'd been smoking a cigarillo with a white plastic tip, dead by the look of it, extinguished by the rain. He removed it from his mouth and glanced at the tip. "We owe you a big one. How'd you happen to come down?"

Odessa touched my sleeve. "You two go ahead. I'll be right back."

I watched him cross to the diver, whom he engaged in conversation out of earshot of those nearby. I turned my attention to Detective Paglia, whose gaze had settled unrelentingly on mine. I pegged him as ex-military, a man who'd seen death and dying at close range, possibly administering a fair amount of it himself. His manner suggested friendliness without the irksome encumbrance of any underlying warmth. If he was personable, it was a trait he'd acquired by meticulous application of the 'personable behavior' rules he'd observed in the world around him. If he was pleasant, it was because pleasantries usually got him what he wanted, which in this case was aid, information, cooperation, and respect. If I were a career criminal, I'd be wary of this man. As it was—given my past tendencies toward lying, breaking and entering, and petty theft—I made certain to frame my explanation with care. While I didn't imagine he suspected me of anything, I wanted to appear honest and artless—not difficult since (in this one rare instance) what I had to offer was the truth. "I'm not sure how to describe the process. I was up at Lloyd's. He's Crystal's ex-husband."

"Leila's stepdad."

"Right. This morning, she left boarding school without permission and Crystal figured she was headed for his place. I told Crystal I'd see if I could track her down, so I began cruising the area there at Little Pony Road and the 101. She must have hitchhiked because I spotted her walking on the berm. I talked her into letting me drive her up to Lloyd's. He was gone when we got there, so she let us into the house. His is that A-frame," I said, and pointed to the far side of the lake. Under the weight of Paglia's gaze, my tone sounded false and I found myself adding a few extraneous details. "Well, it's actually not his. He's house-sitting for a friend who went to Florida. Anyway, I was just messing around while we waited for him to show. Leila was watching TV and I went up to the loft. I saw the telescope and thought it'd be interesting to take a peek. I was surprised to see where I was. I hadn't realized that section of Gramercy put him directly across the reservoir from Fiona."

"You think there's a connection?"

"Between Lloyd and Fiona? I don't know, but I doubt it. I've never heard anything to that effect."

He took out an Altoids box. He opened the lid and deposited the dead butt. I could see he'd filled the bottom of the tin with ash, his way of avoiding contamination at the scene. He returned the box to his raincoat pocket and his gray eyes met mine.

I said, "Do you consider this a crime scene?"

"Suicide's a crime," he said. "Go on with your story." His lower teeth were buckled together in the center and rimmed with stains. It was the only thing about him that seemed out of control.

"When I looked through the telescope I saw the

dog—this is a German shepherd named Trudy. I'd seen her up here on my two visits to Fiona's house and she was always over in this area, barking her head off."

Paglia said, "Dogs can smell a body even under water." This was the first piece of information he'd offered me.

"Really. I didn't know that. I could see she was excited, but I had no idea why. Aside from Trudy, I could see some scarring on that boulder halfway up the slope." Again, I pointed like a fifth-grader giving an oral report. "There was also damage to the vegetation, saplings snapped off. At first I figured somebody must have backed a trailer down to launch a boat, but then I caught sight of the posted warning and I remembered that swimming and boating were forbidden."

He seemed to study me, his expression one of calculated kindness. "I still don't understand how you made the connection."

"The idea just suddenly made sense. Dr. Purcell was last seen at the clinic. I'd heard he was on his way up here to see Fiona so I—"

"Who told you that?"

"A friend of Purcell's, a fellow named Jacob Trigg. Dow told him he had a meeting scheduled with her that night."

"You talk to her about this?"

"Well, I *asked* her. Why not? I was pissed. I work for her. She should have given me the information the moment I hired on."

"What'd she say?"

"She claims he didn't show, called it a 'miscommunication.' I assumed he stood her up and she was too embarrassed to admit it."

"Too bad she didn't mention it to us. We could have canvassed-up here. Somebody might've heard the car. Nine plus weeks later, who's going to remember?"

Behind him, I heard the high whine of the gear, the rumble as the cable was wound around the drum, dragging the Mercedes from the lake. Water gushed from the open windows, from the underside, from the wheel mounts. Nearby, the coroner's van was parked in the grass, its rear doors open. The coroner's assistant and a uniformed officer were removing a long metal trunk, which I recognized as the stainless steel tank in which a floater could be sealed.

Paglia said, "Kinsey."

I turned my gaze back to his. I felt cold.

"The diver says there's someone in the front seat."

The Mercedes was now suspended in a forward tilt, front end down, three of the four windows opened. Lake water poured from every crack and crevice, draining through the floorboards, splashing onto ground already soaked by days of rain. I watched, my responses suspended as the vehicle was hauled partway up the slope, gushing like a tank that had sprung a sudden leak. The window on the driver's side had been shattered, the bottom half still a maze of crazed glass, the upper portion gone. In the front seat, I caught a glimpse of a vaguely human shape, amorphous, all bloat and slime, face turned toward the window gap as if peeking at the view. After weeks in the water, the once living flesh was bloodless, bleached a pearly white. He still wore his suit coat, but that was all I could see of him from where I stood. I turned my head abruptly and made an involuntary sound. The glue holding his bones together had loosened and given way so that he seemed flaccid, indifferent, his eye sockets swimming with a pale gelatin. His mouth was open, his jaw relaxed. His lips had widened in a final expression of joy or surprise—a howl of rage perhaps.

"I'll be in the car," I said.

Paglia didn't hear me. He was heading for the Mercedes. The morgue crew stood back. Peripherally, I saw flashes as the police photographer began to document her work. I couldn't watch any longer. I couldn't be in that place. These people were schooled in the sight of death, tutored by its odors, by its poses, by the peculiar posture of bodies caught in their final bow to life. Ordinarily at such a scene, after the first jolt of revulsion, I can become detached. Here, I couldn't manage it, couldn't shake off the feeling that I was in the presence of something evil. Purcell—assuming the body was his—had either killed himself or been killed. There was no way he could have driven up that hill and down into the lake by accident.

SIXTEEN

By the time I returned to my apartment, it was after ten o'clock. The crime scene technicians were still busy at the reservoir, though I couldn't imagine what remained to be done. I'd hung around for a while and then decided to head home. I'd never eaten dinner. In fact, as nearly as I remembered, I hadn't eaten lunch. Hunger had asserted itself and then faded at least twice during the evening, and now had dissipated altogether, leaving a nagging headache in its wake. I was both wired and exhausted, a curious mix.

Mercifully, the rain had moved on and the temperature had warmed. The streets seemed to smoke, vapor rising in drifts. The sidewalks were still wet, water dripping from the tree limbs as silently as snow. The gutters gurgled merrily, miniature rivers diverted by debris as the runoff traveled downstream into sewers to the sea. A fog began to accumulate, making the world seem hushed and dense. My neighborhood looked unfamiliar, a landscape made alien by mist. Depths were flattened to two dimensions, bare branches no more than ink lines bleeding onto a page. My apartment was dark. I'd left home at ten A.M., nearly twelve hours earlier, and it hadn't occurred to me to leave lights on for myself. I paused in the process of unlocking my door. Henry's kitchen window was aglow, a small square of yellow in the hovering mist. I tucked the keys in my pocket and crossed the flagstone patio.

I peered into the upper portion of his backdoor. He was seated at the table, which was littered with paperwork: stacks of medical statements, canceled checks, and receipts, all sorted into piles. He was wearing his bathrobe, a ratty blue-flannel number with blue-and-white striped pajamas visible under it, cuffs drooping over his battered leather slippers. On the floor near his feet, he'd placed a wastebasket and the brown accordion file he was using to organize Klotilde's bills. The grocery bag of bills Rosie'd given him was sitting on a chair and still appeared to be half-full. As I looked on, he ran a hand through his hair, leaving strands sticking out in three directions. He reached for his glass of Jack Daniel's and took a swallow, then frowned when he realized the ice had long since melted. He got up and moved to the sink, where he tossed the watery contents.

I called, "Henry," and then tapped on the glass. He

looked over, unperturbed by the interruption, and gestured for me to enter. I tried the knob and pointed. "Door's locked."

Henry let me in. While I doffed my slicker and hung it over the back of the chair, he opened the freezer door and removed a handful of ice cubes, which he plunked in his glass, pouring a fresh round of whiskey over them. I picked up the scent of his afternoon baking— something with cinnamon, almond extract, butter, and yeast.

The litter on the table looked even worse at close range. "This is cute. How's it coming? I'm almost afraid to ask."

"Terrible. Just awful. The codes are gibberish. I can't figure out who owes what or which of these is paid. I had 'em sorted by date, but that turned out to be pointless. Now I'm filing them by doctor, hospital, and procedure, and I seem to be getting somewhere. I don't know how people ever make sense of these things. It's ridiculous."

"I told you not to do it."

"I know, but I said I'd help and I hate to go back on my word."

"Oh, quit being such a wuss and give the damn things back to her."

"What's she going to do with them?"

"She'll figure it out or she can have William do it. Klotilde was *his* sister-in-law. Why should you get stuck?"

"I feel sorry for her. Klotilde was her only sister and it's bound to be tough."

"She didn't even *like* Klotilde. They barely spoke to each other and when they did, they fought."

"Don't be so hard on her. Rosie has a good heart," he said. Having bitched, he now felt guilty for complaining behind her back. I could see that arguing with the man was only going to make things worse.

Mentally, I rolled my eyes. "I'll let you off the hook temporarily, but I won't give up."

Henry took a seat at the table. "So what's up with you? You look beat."

"I am." I lifted a stack of medical statements from the seat of the chair and stood there, puzzled about what to do with them.

Henry jumped up. "Here, let me take care of those." He handed me his drink while he shoved the papers to one side and cleared a space at the table. He scooped up the grocery bag and the accordion file and put both on the floor, then took the papers from my hand and put them on the floor as well.

I said, "Thanks" and took a swallow of Jack Daniel's, which flamed through my system like a sudden case of heartburn. I could feel my tension ease and

320

realized, belatedly, how very tired I was. My head had begun to pound in a rhythm with my pulse. *Ka-thong, ka-thong*. I passed the glass back to him and sank into the chair he'd just cleared.

"What's going on?"

"We found Dr. Purcell's car and his body—assuming it's him. I can't really talk about it yet. Give me a few minutes to collect myself."

"Can I fix you a drink?"

"Don't think so, but if you have any Tylenol, I could use about forty, preferably extra-strength."

"I have something better. You just stay where you are."

"No problem. I'm incapable of moving. I'll fill you in momentarily unless I pass out first."

I crossed my arms on the table in front of me and laid my head down, feeling my body go limp. This was the pre-nap posture we adopted in "kinneygarden" and it still represents the ultimate in personal relief. At the age of five, I learned to drop into a deep sleep the minute my head hit my arms. I'd wake ten minutes later, the nerve endings in my fingers all sparkly for lack of circulation, my cheek hot with dreams.

I heard Henry cross to the refrigerator and transfer containers to the counter. I listened to the restful clink of jars and cutlery. It was like being in a sickbed, hearing homely sounds emanating from a nearby room.

I must have dozed for a moment, the same fleeting lapse of awareness that'll send you careening off the highway when it happens at the wheel. Sound faded and returned, a brief slip into unconsciousness. "What are you doing?" I murmured, without lifting my head.

"Making you a sandwich." His voice seemed to come from very far away. "Roast beef with red onion that I've sliced paper thin."

I propped my head on one fist and watched him place two thick slices of homemade bread side-by-side. He spread them liberally with mayonnaise, spicy brown mustard, and horseradish. "This is virulent, but you need something fierce. Pep you up." He cut the sandwich in half and laid it on a plate with a sprig of parsley; pickles, olives, and pepperoncini clustered to one side.

He set the plate in front of me and returned to the refrigerator, where he opened the freezer and removed a beer mug so cold that a white frost formed instantly on the glass when it hit the air. He opened a bottle of beer and poured it gently down the side of the mug to avoid the foam. He picked up his whiskey glass and sat down across from me.

I took a bite of the sandwich. The horseradish was so ferocious it brought tears to my eyes. Pungent fumes licked through my sinuses making my nose run as well. "Mph. This is great. I can't believe how good it is.

You're a genius." I paused, using my paper napkin as a nostril mop. The roast beef was succulent, its chill tenderness the perfect foil to the heat, salt, and sour of the condiments. Now and then I'd suck down a mouthful of cold beer, all tingle and bubbles tasting of hops. Life was reduced to its four basic elements: air, food, drink, and a good friend. I shoved in the last bite of sandwich, licked the mustard from my fingers, and moaned in gratitude. I took a long, slow breath, noting the fact that my headache was gone. "Better."

"I thought that might help. Now tell me about the doctor."

I gave Henry a summary of events leading up to my discovery. He knows how my mind works so I didn't have to fill in all the nitty-gritty details. Most intuition is the sudden leap the mind makes when two elements fuse. Sometimes the connection is made through trial and error; sometimes the underlying question butts up against observation and the answer pops into view. "I didn't spot the car so much as I spotted the traces it left in its journey down the hill."

"So that is the end of that job."

"I'm assuming as much, though I haven't spoken with Fiona."

"What now?"

"The usual. Dr. Yee will do the autopsy in the morning. Don't know how much they'll learn, given the shape the body's in. The vehicle's probably been sub-merged since the night he dropped from view. As soon as the post is done, I'm guessing they'll cremate the remains."

"I'm sorry to hear this. It's too bad."

"It has to be worse when the questions are unresol-ved. At least now his family knows and they can get on with life."

We chatted on in this vein, exploring our reactions and speculations until the subject petered out. Henry picked up my plate and took it to the sink.

"I can do that," I said.

"Stay where you are." He ran hot water in the sink and picked up a dish sponge with liquid detergent in the handle. He soaped the plate, rinsed it, and set it in the rack. "By the way, I saw a friend of yours tonight."

"Really. Who?"

He put the cutting board in the sink and began to put the condiments away. "Tommy Hevener came into Rosie's. He was looking for you, of course, but we ended up having quite a chat. He seems like a nice fellow and he's clearly smitten. He asked a lot of questions about you."

"I have a lot of questions about him, too. That's the part of my day I haven't told you about yet."

He paused with his hand on the refrigerator door. "I don't like the tone of this."

"You won't like the rest of it, either." I waited until he returned to the table and took a seat.

He said, "What?" with apprehension, like he really didn't want to hear.

"Turns out Tommy Hevener and his brother hired a punk down in Texas to break into the family home and steal the valuables, including close to a million in jewels. The burglar did as instructed and then set fire to the house to cover his tracks. What the boys failed to mention to him was that Mom and Dad were stashed in the closet, bound and gagged. They died of smoke inhalation while the place burned down around them."

Henry blinked. "No."

"Yes."

"But that can't be true."

"It is," I said. "The insurance investigator—this is a woman named Mariah Talbot—came to the office this morning and showed me the clippings from the *Hatchet Daily News Gazette* or whatever the hell it's called. I left the file at the office or you could see for yourself."

"But if that's the case, why aren't they in jail?"

"There was never enough evidence, and since the 'boys' were never charged, they managed to collect on the fire loss, life insurance, and the inheritance. All told, they walked off with a couple million bucks. Their aunt and the insurance company are preparing a civil suit, hoping to recover whatever assets remain."

"But how do they know the burglar wasn't the one responsible? He might have surprised the parents, thinking they were gone when he broke into the house. Maybe he was the one who tied them up and gagged them."

"Unfortunately, the burglar hasn't been heard from since. Speculation has it they killed him, too."

"But they can't be sure," he said.

"That's why they've reopened the investigation. Recently, an informant stepped forward and Guardian Casualty is prepared to go forward on the basis of this new information."

"I can't believe it."

"I had the same reaction until I saw the articles. I mean, here's what gets me. The first time I met Tommy? He *told* me his parents died in an accident. He didn't want me to mention it to Richard because he said his brother was still 'touchy' about the subject. I thought, well, those poor dear fellows. Here I am, thinking about my parents and feeling *sorry* for these guys. It really galls me to think how easily I got sucked in. Such bullshit. According to the paper, they even offered a big reward—a hundred thousand dollars—for 'information leading to the arrest and conviction of the killer or killers of Jared and Brenda Hevener.' Why not offer millions? They're in no danger of paying unless one rats the other out."

"How can you do business with them?"

"That's what I'm getting to. I signed a year's lease and paid six months in advance, plus a cleaning deposit. We don't want to forget that little item. Now I can't figure how to get out of it. I'm willing to forfeit the money, but it pisses me off."

"Let Lonnie handle it. He'll know what to do."

"Good thought," I said. "Not that it ends there."

"Why not?"

"Mariah thinks the jewelry's still somewhere in that big fancy house of theirs. She's hoping I can locate the safe so the cops can get a search warrant. She says the Heveners' funds are just about depleted. They've been traveling in the fast lane and now they're close to broke. She's hoping they'll try to sell at least a portion of the jewelry. Since they filed a claim for the loss and since they've steadfastly denied any knowledge of the stash, it's not going to look good. If she can get them to tip their hand, the cops will step in with a warrant for their arrest."

"Why would they risk selling? They're not dumb."

"Not so far, but they're getting desperate."

"How's she going to persuade them? I can't imagine such a thing."

"Ah. She's not. She wants me to do it." I fished the piece of paper from my handbag. "She gave me the name of a fence in Los Angeles and asked me to pass the information on to them."

Henry took the scrap of paper on which she'd written the jeweler's name. "Cyril Lambrou's a pawn broker?"

"A jeweler. She says he runs a legitimate business, as far as it goes. He also deals in stolen property when the goods warrant it. In this case, no sweat. She showed me the Polaroids—rings, bracelets, necklaces. Gorgeous. Really beautiful."

"Why can't *she* give them the information?"

"Because they know who she is and they'd never fall for it."

"But why you?"

Henry's tone was becoming belligerent and I could feel my face heat. "Because Tommy's interested in me."

"So what?"

"Mariah's shrewd. She ran a background on me and she knows I'm not above bending the rules."

"Aren't you talking about entrapment?"

"Why would it be entrapment? I mention a guy who buys jewelry. If they're not guilty, they won't have anything to sell. Entrapment's where the cops entice someone to break the law. I'm not encouraging them to steal. They've already done that."

"But they're going to smell a rat. You mention a jeweler. They pawn the stuff and shortly afterwards they're arrested and thrown in jail? You can't be serious."

"By then it's too late. They're already behind bars."

"Suppose they post bail? The minute they hit the street, they're going to come looking for you."

"Come on, Henry. Give me credit here. I won't come right out and say, 'Gee, anybody have any stolen jewels to lay off on this guy?' I'll think of a story to tell, something plausible."

"Such as what?"

"I don't know. I haven't made that part up yet."

Exasperated, Henry leaned back in his chair and stared at me. "How many times have we had a conversation like this? You come up with some stupid scheme. I urge you not to do it, but you go right ahead and do it. You always find some way to rationalize your behavior."

"So does everyone else."

"More's the pity," he said. "I'll tell you this once and then I swear I won't mention it again. Don't do this. Don't get involved. It's none of your business."

"I didn't say I would."

"How're you going to find the safe? You'll have to get into the house."

"Tommy's taken me up there once. All I have to do is talk him into taking me again."

"Which he'd do in hopes of getting in your pants."

"I can handle that."

"But why take the risk? I don't think you should be alone with either one of them."

"Not to make light of it, but I've done a lot worse with a lot less justification."

"*I'll* say."

"Henry, I promise you I won't act in haste. I haven't even figured out what I'll say ... you know, assuming I decide to take the job."

"Why do this to yourself? Surely, you don't need the money."

"Money isn't the issue here. I just don't think people should get away with murder."

"It isn't up to you. If the police had had sufficient evidence, the Heveners would've been arrested and convicted back then. There wasn't any proof. That's the way the law works. You stay out of it. Please."

"You know what? I'm tempted to do this for exactly the same reason you're tempted to help Rosie. Because you can't resist. So here's the deal. You want me to butt out of this? You butt out of Rosie's business and we'll call it a wash."

"It's not illegal or dangerous to help a little old lady pay her sister's medical bills."

He had a point, but I refused to acknowledge it.

"Skip it. Enough. Let's quit arguing. You take care of your life and I'll take care of mine."

"You're right. It's not my concern. Do anything you want."

"Don't play injured. It's not that. I think you worry too much."

"And you don't worry enough!"

It was 11:03 when I left Henry's place and headed to my apartment. We'd made a superficial effort to patch up our differences, but nothing had been resolved. I was feeling anxious and out of sorts and so, I suspect, was he. I let myself in and set my bag aside. I turned on the television set and turned to KEST. I'd missed the lead-in to the story but caught the report in progress: ". . . the silver Mercedes-Benz recovered this evening from Brunswick Lake has been positively identified as the vehicle belonging to prominent local physician Dowan Purcell, missing since September 12. Detective Paglia of the Santa Teresa Police Department would not confirm . . ." Over her commentary there was a series of clips: a shot of the hillside near the reservoir, a shot of Crystal arriving by car, a photograph insert of Dr. Purcell, followed by a shot of the family home in Horton Ravine. The anchor moved on to a story about a cat stuck in a length of pipe. Nine and a half weeks of agony reduced to less than a minute. Folks would probably have more sympathy for the cat.

There was a tap at my door. I figured it was Henry coming over to apologize. Instead, I found Tommy Hevener standing on my porch. "Hey. Where you been? I called you earlier, but your machine was on. I thought I'd see you at Rosie's."

"Henry told me he saw you."

"Yeah, we had a nice chat. He's a great old guy."

"Look. I've had a hard day. Something's come up on a case I've been working."

"You want to talk about it? I'm a good listener."

"I don't think so. I appreciate the offer, but I'm bushed and I think I better go to bed."

"I hear you. No problem. Call me tomorrow. I want to see you again."

"Okay, I'll do that."

"You take care."

"Yeah, you, too," I said. As soon as I closed the door, my heart began knocking rapidly in my throat. I threw the deadbolt home and leaned against the wall to wait until I heard his departing steps. Outside, a car started up and I listened as the sound of the engine diminished down the street.

I don't know how I managed to get to sleep that night. I had no emotional attachment to Dow Purcell, but the sight of that body in the front seat of the car had left me unsettled. I'd seen death many times, but I couldn't seem to block the image of that four-wheeled silver coffin and its hoary contents. I replayed the moment . . . floodlights hissing in the rain, the sound of water gushing from the underbelly of the car, the smell of mud and crushed grass, followed by the quick flash of the body in its formless repose, eyes turned toward the window, mouth open with amazement. I didn't think it would take long to identify the body . . . half a day at best. It would take longer to examine the car and come up with a theory about how it had ended up in the lake. There was also the question of whether Purcell was dead or alive when he went into the water. Again, I flashed on that face, the wide grin, the sightless eyes . . .

I made a conscious effort to divert my attention, fixing on the problem of Tommy and Richard Hevener. Despite my obstinate and disputatious stance, I *had* seen Henry's point, which I knew was correct. I'm forever sticking my nose in where it doesn't belong, often with consequences more serious (and potentially deadly) than I care to admit. I was under no obligation to assist Mariah Talbot or Guardian Casualty Insurance, so why put myself in the line of fire? The "boys" were not my problem. Mariah had even hinted she had an alternative if I decided not to help. I still had to find a way to break the lease and recover my deposit, but maybe Lonnie could write the brothers such a blistering letter they'd be begging to get me out. As for the murder of their parents, I had to believe the law would catch up with them eventually. As much as it grieved me to admit it, retribution wasn't mine. Oh, darn.

SEVENTEEN

Much of Wednesday I was occupied tidying up odds and ends. At 6:00 that morning, I'd managed to squeeze in a three-mile jog between cloud bursts, after which I'd gone to the gym. I'd come home, cleaned up, eaten breakfast, and arrived at the office at 9:15. I spent the bulk of the day catching up on paperwork, including my personal bills, which I paid with the usual sense of triumph. I love keeping all the wolves at bay.

Twice, I sat down at the typewriter to frame my final report to Fiona, thinking I might as well go ahead and drop it in the mail to her. However, having delivered both a report and an invoice just the day before, I was a tiny bit short on bullshit and a tiny bit short on cash. I thought it could be bad form to charge for the time I'd spent waiting for the cops to pull Dow out of the lake. Since I'd forked over her $1,500 to the infamous Hevener brothers, the $1,075 I owed her would have to come out of my checking account, which currently showed a balance of $422. I had plenty of money in savings, but I didn't much feel like dipping into it. Besides, I was still entertaining the fantasy that Fiona would write off the balance out of appreciation for the speed and efficiency with which I'd concluded her business. She'd hired me to find Dow and I'd found him sooner than either one of us expected, though not in quite the condition one would have wished. I couldn't help but hope for a $1,075 pat on the back. *Ha, ha, ha,* she thought.

I considered calling Crystal to offer my condolences but couldn't bring myself to do it. I wasn't a family friend, and I was afraid my motivation would be interpreted as ghoulish curiosity, which of course it was.

Just after lunch, I went back to the file Mariah Talbot had left. I glanced at both wills, picking my way through sufficient legalese to confirm that the Atcheson jewelry had been left to Brenda's sister, Karen. I then went back and reread the news clips. Hatchet, Texas, was located roughly sixty miles from Houston and had a population of twenty-eight hundred souls. There'd only been one other murder in the town's entire history, and that was back in 1906 when a woman took a piece of fire wood to her husband's skull while he was sleeping. She'd killed him with six blows after he got drunk once too often, knocked her teeth out, blackened her eyes, and broke her nose. Satisfied he was dead, she'd tossed the log on the fire and brewed herself a pot of tea.

The death of Jared and Brenda Hevener made headlines as far away as Amarillo, where Brenda had been born and raised. According to the paper, the bodies were discovered in the rubble the day after the fire. The blaze had been fierce and fast, fueled by accelerants, fanned by dry winds. The volunteer fire department was called at 1:06 A.M., arriving on the scene within seventeen minutes. By then the house was completely engulfed in flames and their efforts were largely focused on preventing the fire's spread to adjacent properties. Neighbors quickly realized the Heveners were unaccounted for. At first, the fear was expressed that all four family members had been taken unawares and had perished in the conflagration. As it turned out, Tommy Hevener had been visiting friends in San Antonio. He managed to track down his brother, Richard, who was traveling in the south of France.

The initial newspaper accounts were filled with shock at the deaths and sympathy for the sons whose loss everyone assumed must be devastating. There were long biographical pieces about Brenda and Jared: her community service, his rise in the business world. The turnout for the funeral was impressive. Newspaper photos showed the cortege stretching out for blocks. Pictures at the cemetery showed the two coffins surrounded by flowers, Richard with his head bowed, while Tommy stared bleakly at the grave site with an expression of despair. Mariah hadn't been impressed with their acting skills, but I could see how easily their grief could have been interpreted as heartfelt.

Within days, the time-delay device and accelerants were identified and traced to Casey Stonehart, twenty-three years old and clearly not that bright, as he'd purchased the materials in a town only sixteen miles away. With his troubled criminal history and his questionable IQ, it wasn't hard to conclude he was acting in concert with somebody else. He clearly wasn't smart enough to plan and execute the job by himself. Over the next six months, the tone of the story changed as public skepticism grew and the ongoing investigation shifted to the possibility that the two sons had been involved. On their part, there were many outraged denials and vigorous protestations of their innocence. Law enforcement authorities and the fire marshal responded with a number of carefully worded statements, hoping to avoid a lawsuit if their suspicions turned out to be groundless. The story played for weeks and then died away. There were periodic updates, but most of the later coverage seemed to be an endless rehash of the original account. Casey Stonehart warranted very little in the way of column space beyond the occasional query as to his whereabouts.

Reading between the lines, I could see the bureaucratic tensions begin to accumulate. The D.A. was
accused of bungling. Pressure was brought to bear and
he was forced to resign. Despite the launching of a
second, even more extensive investigation, no new evidence came to light. Formal charges were filed against
Casey Stonehart in absentia, but Richard and Tommy
Hevener managed to evade official blame. A year later,
two short clippings referred to the law suit they'd filed
against Guardian Casualty, trying to collect various
insurance benefits. Six months after that, there was a
brief mention of the close of probate and the settling of
the estate. What a depressing chain of events. I shuffled
through the articles again just to make sure I hadn't
missed anything.

The story made me restless. I could feel the Masked
Avenger aspect of my personality girding her loins,
prepared to seek justice and to right old wrongs. At the
same time, Henry's accusations had hit perilously close
to home. I'll admit I'm (occasionally) foolhardy and
impetuous, impatient with the system, vexed by the
necessity for playing by the rules. It's not that I don't
applaud law and order, because I do. I'm simply indignant that the bad guys are accorded so many rights
when their victims have so few. Pursuing scoundrels
through the courts not only costs a fortune, but it offers
no guarantee of legal remedy. Even assuming success,

a hard-won conviction doesn't bring the dead back to life. In this matter, though I hated to be practical, I'd come around to Henry's point of view. I intended to mind my own business for once.

I left the office just before three o'clock and walked over to the bank. Fortunately for me, the check I'd written to Hevener Properties hadn't yet cleared. Maybe he accumulated rent checks and made a deposit on a regular basis instead of one by one. I put a stop payment on it, returned to the office, and wrote Richard a brief, apologetic note, indicating that circumstances had changed and I wouldn't be renting space from him after all. Given my signature on the lease, he might well take me to small claims court. I didn't think he'd do it. Surely, in his position, he'd prefer to avoid legal wrangles. At five-thirty I locked up. On my way home, I drove by the main post office and dropped the letter in the outside box. I reached my apartment twelve minutes later, feeling lighter than I had all day.

Before I unlocked my front door, I crossed the patio to Henry's place. I wanted to tell him I'd heeded his words. In declining involvement, I'd offer him full credit for motivating this rare evidence of common sense on my part. His kitchen light was on. I tapped on the glass, expecting to see him come into the kitchen from the hall. No sign of him, no sound of his piano, no hint of activity. I picked up the tantalizing scent of one of his oven baked stews so I didn't think he'd gone far.

I returned to my apartment and let myself in. I turned on the desk lamp and set my shoulder bag on a kitchen stool. I gathered up the mail that had been pushed through the slot and was splayed out across the floor. All of it was junk and I tossed it in the trash. The message light on the answering machine was blinking merrily. I pushed the play button.

Tommy Hevener.

"Hey. It's me. I've been thinking about you. Maybe I'll catch you later. Give me a call when you get in."

I pressed Erase, wishing I could do the same with him.

I went into the kitchen. Saturday's can of tomato soup was the last I had so I already knew there was nothing in the house to eat. Dutifully, I checked my cupboards and my refrigerator shelves. I've never actually seen a recipe that calls for two plastic packets of soy sauce, half a cup of olive oil, Cheerios, anchovy paste, maple syrup, and six rubber carrots asprout with something that looks like hair. A clever home economist could have whipped up a nourishing dish out of just such ingredients, but I confess I was stumped. I picked up my bag again and headed out the door. Dinner at Rosie's—what a pleasant change of pace.

341

The night air was misty and smelled of basements. It had been raining, off and on now for six full days. The novelty had worn off and those who'd rejoiced in its arrival were now cursing the rain's persistence. The ground was saturated and the creek-beds ran high, a noisy rush of water pushing debris in its path. Unless we had a few dry days, the torrents would jump the banks and flood the low-lying areas. There were already county roads awash with mud and stones, covered with creeping sheets of water that made driving perilous.

Given the ebb and flow of business at Rosie's, the bar area was teeming. The Happy Hour crowd would be gone by seven P.M. as soon as the drink prices went up. The noise level had risen to a harsh, edgy pitch that seemed to reflect the mounting irritability levels. People were tired of raincoats, wet shoes, and mold spores that made their allergies flare up in a rush of sneezes and clogged sinuses.

I left my umbrella propped against the wall by the front door, shed my slicker, and shook off some of the accumulated water before I hung it up. I made a useless display of wiping my feet just to be polite. As I stepped through the inner door, I spotted Tommy Hevener sitting by himself at a table near the front. I felt a flash of irritation, feeling cornered. How was I going to get him out of my life? He was drinking a martini, the wide-rimmed glass at his lips when he caught sight of me. I halted in my tracks—a split second of indecision—because the second person I saw was Mariah Talbot sitting in a booth at the rear. Adrenaline blew through my system like a hit of speed. Her telltale silver hair had been concealed beneath a dark, shag-cut wig, her blue eyes masked by glasses with plastic and rhinestone frames. The raincoat she wore made her body appear bulky. Unless you saw past the facade to the elegant bones of her face, she appeared frumpy and drab, not someone you'd notice in a crowd of this size. Tommy couldn't be expecting to see her, but he might make the same leap of recognition if he glanced in her direction. Looks as classic as hers are nearly impossible to hide. The minute Mariah and I made eye contact, she rose from the booth and slipped into the seat on the opposite side of the table with her back to us. I hoped the shock of discovery hadn't registered on my face, but I wasn't sure how I'd manage to hide my astonishment. My gaze flicked to Tommy's. His expression was quizzical, as though he'd sensed my surprise. He turned in his chair and scanned the rear of the bar. Abruptly, I crossed and sat down at his table. I touched his hand. "I'm sorry I was such a bitch last night."

His gaze returned to mine and he smiled. "Don't worry about it. The fault was mine." The mild Texas accent I'd found so attractive a day or two before now seemed to be an affectation. He was wearing a cashmere

343

sweater, a soft downy gray that played up his florid hair color and the green of his eyes. He was making intense eye contact, enclosing my hand in his. He lifted my fingers and placed a kiss in my right palm. I wanted to shiver—not from arousal, but from dread. What had once seemed seductive was only cheap display. He knew he was handsome and he affected the shy country boy to enhance his appeal. I knew too much about him, and the force of his sexuality struck me as pure manipulation. In a quick recap, I realized that from the moment we'd met, he'd worked to dominate, beginning with my declining to drink a beer with him. He'd proposed a Diet Pepsi instead, popping it open before I could refuse. I'd taken the path of least resistance and he'd established his control. After that the transitions were smooth and well rehearsed. He'd enlisted my sympathies by rolling out the reference to his parents' death and then he'd offered up his comment about California women being so stuck up. Immediately, I'd worked to prove him wrong. His final move was adroit. "*Which do you prefer? Guys way too young for you or guys way too old?*" I couldn't believe I'd been so easily taken in.

Peripherally, I saw Mariah leave the booth and head for the ladies' restroom. I rested my chin on my hand. "Are you free for dinner? We could go back to Emile's or try somewhere else."

"Buy me a drink first and we can talk about that."

I pointed to his glass. "What are you having?"

"Vodka martini." He lifted his glass and tumbled the green olive onto his waiting tongue.

I took his glass and got up. "I'll be right back." As I moved by him, he reached out an arm to halt my passage. I stared down at his face, which he'd tilted up to mine. I could smell his aftershave. I could feel his hot, proprietary hand on my ass. I shifted out of his grasp and leaned closer, keeping my tone light. "Don't be a bad boy."

His voice was low and laced with confidence. "I am a bad boy. I thought you liked that about me."

"I wouldn't count on it," I said.

I crossed to the bar where William was at work, pulling beers and mixing drinks. I ordered two vodka martinis and we exchanged inane remarks while I watched him pour a stream of vodka into a silver shaker and add a stingy dash of vermouth. William set two chilled martini glasses on the bar.

"Could you do me a favor? When you're done, will you take those over to that guy in the gray sweater? Tell him I'm in the loo and I'll be there in a second. He can go ahead if he wants. I'll have mine when I get back."

"Happy to be of help," William said. He put two doilies on a tray, set a martini on each, and came out from behind the bar.

I proceeded to the ladies' room and pushed through the door. The room smelled of bleach and had only one stall. I knew from sad experience the wooden toilet seat was cracked and pinched when you sat. Mariah was standing at the basin making an adjustment to her wig. Aside from the sink, there was only a big plastic-lined waste bin and a grille-covered window that opened onto a narrow backyard. Up close, I could see that under the raincoat, she'd pulled on a bulky knit sweater and a pair of flabby blue print slacks with some form of waist-thickening padding underneath. The Birkenstocks and white socks were a nice touch. Very chic.

She said, "What do you think?"

"That disguise is lame. I've seen you once in my life and spotted you straight off the minute I walked in."

She took a hair fork from her purse and lifted the top layers to increase the height. "Shit. This cost me a fortune and it's not even real hair."

"What are you *doing* here? Do you know how close you've come to blowing it?"

"Tell me about it. Me and my big ideas," she said. "I tried to call, but all I got was your answering machine. I didn't want to leave a message. It's not cool. You never know who's going to be there when those things are played back. I didn't want to take the chance Tommy'd hear my voice. I figured it'd be easier to find you here. I walk in, thinking I'm safe, and there he sits. I nearly had heart failure."

"You and me both. How'd he miss seeing you?"

"Don't even ask. It was dumb luck, I guess. He was fussing with his raincoat so I pretended to spot a friend and headed for a back booth. I sat there for fifteen minutes, planning an exit through the kitchen. Then I happened to look up and saw you come in. "What are the chances you can get him out of here?"

"I'm doing what I can, but I don't like it. Last night he stopped by my apartment. I managed to avoid a visit, but he's persistent. I'm trying to turn him off and now I have to turn around and suck up to him to cover for you."

"Life's tough." She rearranged a few strands of artificial hair and then smiled to herself. "Here's a piece of good news. All their credit cards are maxed out. Six to eight cards each, eighteen percent interest on the unpaid balance. They're making minimum payments, just trying to keep afloat. Fancy watches, fancy cars. The mortgage is fifteen grand a month on that monstrosity they call home. They've got their nuts in a vise and they're feeling the squeeze."

"They're completely broke?"

"They will be if they don't act fast." Her eyes met mine in the mirror. The combination of the wig and the outfit made her seem coarse, not the cool professional she'd been in my office when she'd laid out her credentials. Maybe she was more of a chameleon than I'd given her credit for. "I don't suppose you've had time to tell Tommy about the fence?"

"I'm not going to do that. I really can't help you there. I'm sorry."

"Don't sweat it." She tucked the hair fork away and then turned and leaned against the sink so she could study me. "I'll get the fuckers with or without your help."

"How'd this become so personal?"

"Murder's always personal. I take offense when I see guys like them getting off scot free. Aside from that, Guardian's promised me a big fat bonus if I can bring this one in." Behind the glasses, her eyes were a clear blue and very cold. She nodded at the door. "You better get out there. Prince Charming awaits."

I left the restroom and stepped into the blast of noise unleashed by all the alcohol. Smoke was adrift in the cavernous room. I felt as though I'd been gone an hour, but a glance at my watch showed less than ten minutes had passed. I pushed my way through the crowd, returning to the table where Tommy waited. Henry had joined him and he was sipping his usual glass of Black Jack over ice. His elbows rested on the surface of a manila envelope and I wondered if he was planning to do some work later on. I experienced a momentary surge of hope. His presence would at least spare me any intimacies.

I sat down. "Hi, Henry. I knocked on your door earlier, but I couldn't seem to rouse you." I was sounding way too perky, but I couldn't help myself.

"I popped over to the market. I needed some fresh parsley to finish off my stew."

"Henry's stews are legendary," I said in Tommy's direction, though I couldn't meet his eyes. I lifted the martini glass and took a sip, then steadied the wobbling glass as I set it down again. I licked at my hand where the vodka had slopped over the rim.

Henry glanced over at me and we exchanged a brief look. I knew what he was up to. He was feeling protective. He had no intention of letting me consort with the enemy unchaperoned. His gaze settled thoughtfully on his drink. He said, "By the way, I looked into that business you were asking me about."

I said, "Ah." Thinking, *Business? What business?*

"The guy you want to try is Cyril Lambrou in the Klinger Building, off Spring Street in downtown Los Angeles. The woman I talked to sold him an assortment of her mother's antique jewelry. This was stuff she hardly ever wore and she was tired of paying the exorbitant insurance premiums."

I felt myself separating from my body. I couldn't

SUE GRAFTON

believe he was doing it. I'd backed away from Mariah's scheme and here he was laying out the bait. Henry had launched himself on his maiden lie, which he'd offered in my behalf. I knew why he was doing it. If the jeweler's name came from him, how could I be blamed for it later when the deal went sour? Henry and Tommy had spent the previous evening together. Tommy would trust him. Everybody trusted Henry because he told the truth and he was straight as an arrow.

I said, "I can sympathize. I pay a fortune for insurance and I could use the cash." My voice sounded hollow. I moved my hand out from under Tommy's with the intention of lifting my glass for another sip of my martini, but I realized I was shaking too much to get the glass to my lips. I tucked my fingers under my thigh. I could feel how cold they were even through my jeans.

Meanwhile, Henry went on as smoothly as a con artist with an easy mark. "I called the fellow myself and described the diamond to him. He wouldn't make a commitment on the phone, but he seemed interested. I know you don't want to *give* the ring away, but you're going to have to be realistic. You'll never recoup the actual value, but he sounds a lot more generous than some. I think this would be for his personal collection, so it might be worth a shot."

I tried to reconstruct from his comments the phony tale he must have had in mind. The implication was that I had my mother's pricey diamond ring and was in the market for some cash. Apparently, I'd consulted him about selling it and he'd asked around. So far so good, but the trick with a good lie is not to push. I thought we might go another round or two, but then we'd have to move on. String a lie out for too long and it can trip you up.

My mouth was dry. *How much?* I cleared my throat and tried it again. "How much? Did he give you any idea?"

"Between eight and ten thousand. He says it depends on the stone and whether he thinks there's any secondary market, but he swore he'd be fair."

"The ring's worth five times that," I said, indignantly. I knew the ring was imaginary, but it still had sentimental value. Under the circumstance, eight to ten thousand sounded like chickenshit to me.

Henry shrugged. "Check around if you want. There are other jewelers in the building, but as he says, better the devil you know."

"Maybe. We'll see about that."

Tommy's expression hadn't changed. He seemed to listen politely, no more and no less interested than any ordinary guy would be.

351

I felt a trickle of sweat inch down my spine to the small of my back. I pointed and said, "What's in the envelope?"

"Oh. I'm glad you reminded me. I have a present for you." He passed me the envelope, watching expectantly as I undid the clasp and folded back the flap. Inside, neatly secured with a paper clip, was a handful of bills, presumably Klotilde's.

"Okay, I'll bite. What *is* this?"

"See for yourself. Go on and open one."

I slid off the paper clip and picked up the first bill, which appeared to be a lengthy itemized list of charges, most of them for medical supplies:

Brush, hair	$1.00
Steri-strips, 3m ¼ × 3	$1.22
Steri-strips, 3m ¼ × 3	$1.22
underpads, polymer 23 × 36	$3.35
syringe, monoject ins	$0.14
syringe, monoject ins	$0.14
syringe, monoject ins	$0.14
catheter, all-purp Davol	$1.59
baby lotion	$1.62
tray, bard irrigation	$2.69
cups, denture	$0.14

There were roughly thirty items in all. The total was $99.10. None of the charges seemed out of line to me.

I glanced at the next statement, a record of therapeutic exercises and physical therapy sessions, totaling 130 minutes over the last few days of July. The box for each day bore the initials *pg*, the therapist who rendered the treatment.

I looked at Henry with puzzlement.

He said, "That whole batch is hers. I came across them this morning and thought you'd be interested. Take another look."

I picked up the next invoice. This was a claim for portable X-ray equipment, the transport for the portable X-ray, and two X-ray exams, one of the wrist and one of the hand. The total was $108.50. I glanced at the top of the form and then shuffled back through the first two. All three were generated by Pacific Meadows. "I didn't realize she'd been a patient at Pacific Meadows."

"Neither did I. I showed them to Rosie and she said Klotilde was admitted last spring. Pacific Meadows was one of several facilities where she'd been a patient in the last few years. I don't know if you ever paid much attention, but she'd be hospitalized for something—a fall, pneumonia, that staph infection she picked up. With Medicare, she was only allowed X number of days—I think, a hundred per illness. She was so cranky and disagreeable, a couple of places refused to take her. They just claimed there wasn't room. Are you following this?"

353

"So far."

"Check the date services were rendered."

"July and August."

Henry leaned closer. "She passed away in April. She'd been gone for months by then."

For a moment, I let the information sink in. This was the first tangible evidence of financial shenanigans that I'd seen. But how had they managed it? Klotilde must have died at just about the same time the paper audit was being conducted at Pacific Meadows. According to Merry, a substantial number of charts had been ordered for review. Maybe hers wasn't one. I tried to recall the sequence of events whereby deaths were reported to Social Security. As nearly as I remembered, the mortuary filled out the death certificate and sent it to the local office of vital statistics, which in turn forwarded the original to the county recorder's office. The death certificate was then sent to Sacramento, where it was archived and the information sent on to Social Security.

"Henry, this is great. I wonder if there's any way to check it out?" I was of course pondering the notion of persuading Merry to do some snooping for me. I'd have to wait until the coming weekend, which was when she filled in. I didn't think it'd be politic to approach her during regular weekday hours with Mrs. Stegler standing by. Plan B was maybe doing a little search of my own if I could figure out what to look for. I glanced up to find both Tommy and Henry watching me. "Sorry. I was trying to figure out what to do with this."

Tommy must have decided he'd been polite long enough. His hand settled over mine. His grip was firm and prevented my pulling free without being conspicuous about it. "Hey, Henry. I hate to butt in here, but this lady's promised to buy me dinner. We're just having a quick drink before we walk over to Emile's."

Henry said, "Well, I better get back to my stew before it starts sticking to the pan." He flicked a look at me as he rose to his feet. I knew he didn't want to leave me, but he didn't dare persist. At the prospect of his departure, I felt the same desperation I'd felt when I was five and my aunt walked me over for my first day of elementary school. I'd been fine while she lingered, chatting with the other parents, but the minute she left I had a panic attack. Now, I could feel the same roar of anxiety that dulled everything, but my longing for her. Henry and Tommy exchanged chit chat and next thing I knew, Henry was gone. I had to get out of there. I tried to withdraw my hand, but Tommy tightened his grip.

I tapped the manila envelope. "You know what? I really need to look into these. I'll have to take a rain check on dinner. I hope you don't mind."

Tommy minded. I watched his smile fade. "You're reneging on a promise."

"Maybe tomorrow night. I've got work to do." I knew it wasn't smart to go up against this man, but the notion of an evening alone with him was intolerable. Mariah had to be gone by now and if not, that was her problem.

He began to rub my fingers, the contact slightly rougher than was strictly necessary. The friction became uncomfortable, but he seemed unaware. "Why the sudden change of heart?"

"Please let go of my hand."

He was staring at me. "Has someone told you something about me?"

I could feel my jaw set. "What's there to tell, Tommy? You have something to hide?"

"No. Of course not, but people make things up."

"Well, I don't. If I say I've got work to do, you can take my word for it."

He gave my fingers a squeeze and then released my hand. "I guess I better let you go, then. Why don't I call you tomorrow? Or better yet, you call me."

"Right."

We stood at the same time. I waited while Tommy shrugged into his raincoat, picked up his umbrella, and adjusted the clasp. When we reached the entrance, I retrieved my slicker and umbrella. Tommy held the door. I made short work of the fare-thee-wells, trying to control my desire to flee. I turned toward my apartment while he walked off in the opposite direction on his way to his car. I forced myself to stroll though my impulse was to scurry, putting as much distance as possible between him and me.

EIGHTEEN

I went back to my apartment and locked myself in. Tommy gave me the creeps. I went from window to window, closing the latches, pulling the shutters across the panes so that no one could look in. I didn't relax until every possible bolt and bar had been secured. I sat down at my desk and found Mariah Talbot's business card, which I'd tucked in my bag. I was nervous about my association with her. Tommy'd been uncanny in his suspicions about me. I pictured him rummaging in my purse the minute my back was turned, coming across her card. People like him, obsessed with control, need the constant reassurance that no small detail has eluded them. I committed the number to memory and cut the card into small pieces. I was uncomfortably aware that he still held my rental application, which spelled out more about me than I really wanted known. He'd never fully believe I was focused on matters related to Dow Purcell. In his mind, whatever I was up to must have something to do with him. Narcissism and paranoia are flip sides of the same distorted sense of self-importance. In the eerie way of all psychopaths, he'd picked up on my newly minted fear of him. He must be wondering who or what had caused my attitude to shift.

I sat down at my desk and dialed Mariah's Texas area code and the number on the card. I knew I wouldn't reach her, but at least I could leave her a message to get in touch with me. I thought about how deftly Henry had stepped in with the name of the fence. He'd lied as well as I did and with the same finesse. The question now was whether Tommy would act on the information.

Mariah's answering machine clicked in. "Hello, this is Mariah Talbot. You've reached the offices of Guardian Casualty Insurance in Houston, Texas. My usual work hours are eight-thirty to five-thirty, Monday through Friday. If you're calling at any other time, please leave a message giving me your name, the time, and a number where I can reach you. I check my machine frequently and I'll get back to you as soon as possible. Thank you."

I said, "Hi, Mariah. It's Kinsey. We need to talk. Please call me at my office number. If I'm unavailable, leave me ten seconds of silence. After that, just keep checking your messages. I'll call and suggest a time and a place to meet. Thanks." As I spoke, I found myself hunched over the phone, my hand cupping the mouth-piece. What did I imagine? Tommy Hevener pressed against the outside wall with a hand-held listening device? Well, yeah, sort of. Talk about paranoid.

Having placed the call to Mariah, I turned my attention to the bills Henry'd given me, sinking into the comfort and safety of the job before me. The first in the pile bore the heading "Medicare Summary Notice" and further down the page, a line that read "This is a summary of claims processed on 8/29/86." If I could lay my hands on her medical chart, I could find out what the doctors had been treating her for. I knew about some of her illnesses, but I wanted to see what medications and supplies had been ordered for her. I could then compare the actual orders to the items for which Medicare had been billed. Shuffling through, I found an Explanation of Medical Benefits form; account statements with codes, boxes for co-pays and deductibles; invoices; plus several records of daily treat-ment—physical therapy by my guess. No diagnosis was ever mentioned, but in the first half of August, the charges for medication alone totaled $410.95. Hun-dreds of additional items, many of them minor, had been billed to Medicare in the months since her death. Of course, this *could* be an error, a mixup in accounts with goods and services being charged inadvertently to the wrong patient billing number. On the other hand,

Klotilde's surname, with its odd, impossible Hungarian spelling, appeared throughout, so this was hardly a matter of someone misidentifying a "Smith" or "Jones," or switching one "Johnson" for another with the same first initial. Most helpful to me was the fact that while the claim number changed, Klotilde's Medicare number followed her from form to form. I made a note of the information on a scrap of paper, folded it, and slid it into my jeans pocket. I wondered whether her records were still available at Pacific Meadows. Almost had to be, I thought. She'd died in April and I assumed the facility would keep her records in their active files for at least a year before retiring them to storage.

I waited until 9:30, filling my time with various household chores. Cleaning out a toilet bowl can be wonderfully soothing when anxiety levels climb. I scrubbed the sink and the tub, and then crawled around on my bathroom floor, using the same damp sponge to wipe down the tiles. I vacuumed, dusted, and started a load of laundry. From time to time, I looked at my watch, calculating the hour at which the residents of Pacific Meadows would be bedded down for the night. Finally, I exchanged my Sauconys for black tennis shoes and then slipped into a black windbreaker, which was better for night work than my gaudy yellow rain gear. I separated the house key and the VW key from the larger collection on my key ring, transferred my driver's license and some cash from my wallet to my jeans, and then added a small leather case that contained my key picks. This particular kit had been designed by a felonious friend who'd spent his spare moments in prison fashioning an assortment of picks that looked like a manicure set. In between breaking-and-entering gigs, I could nip my cuticles and file my nails. The only other item I took with me was a flat flashlight the size of a playing card that fit neatly in my bra. On my way to the nursing home, I made a detour by the drive-through window at McDonald's, where I picked up a sack of burgers, two Cokes, and two large orders of french fries.

When I arrived at Pacific Meadows, the parking lot was close to empty. The day personnel had departed and the night shift operated with a considerably reduced staff. I parked my car in a darkened area, picked up the sack of fast food, and locked the door behind me. The rain had been held in abeyance, stalled over the mountain range just north of us. Meanwhile, we'd enjoyed a sufficient break between showers that the pavement was dry in patches. Crossing the tarmac, I reviewed the layout of the building, calculating the location of Ruby Curtsinger's room. I knew a bird feeder hung outside her sliding door, and I was hoping I could use that as a reference point. I had just reached the corner of the building when a car turned into the lot behind me.

In stealth mode, I stepped into the protective shadow of a juniper while the driver backed the vehicle into a slot midway down the row. The car was a classic, long and snub-nosed, fenders softly rounded, its make and model one I wasn't able to identify on sight. The body looked like something from the '40s: the paint color, cream; the front bumper, a chunky affair of highly polished chrome. Four doors, no running board, a set of dazzling whitewall tires, no hood ornament. The man who emerged was as smart looking as the car. He tossed a lighted cigarette aside and I watched it wink briefly on the asphalt before the damp extinguished it. He wore a pale raincoat over a dark three-piece suit, black wingtip shoes with heels that tapped sharply as he walked. As he approached the lighted entrance, I could see his thick mustache and a substantial head of silver hair. He disappeared from view. When I was certain he was gone, I continued around to the rear of the building on the walkway that paralleled the narrow gardens.

Most of the residents' rooms were dark, the drapes drawn securely across the sliding glass doors. I closed my eyes, trying to picture Ruby's room in relation to her neighbors; difficult to do since I'd only visited her once. I searched for the bird feeder that had graced her eaves, hoping the nursing home hadn't provided one per resident. Ahead of me, one of the sliding glass doors was partially opened and I could see the flickering gray light of a television set. Outside, an empty bird feeder was visible, hanging like a little lantern from a thin strand of wire. I leaned close to the screen. "Ruby? Is that you in there?"

Her wheelchair was parked no more than two feet away. She leaned forward and peered through the screen door at me. It seemed to take her a moment to figure out who I was. "You're Merry's friend. I'm sorry, I don't remember your name."

"Kinsey," I said, holding up the bag. "I brought you something."

She unlatched the screen door and motioned me in, her bony face brightening. I slid open the screen and stepped into her room. She pointed to the bag. "What's in there?"

I held it open to her and she peered in while I identified the contents. "Two Big Macs, two QP's with Cheese, two Cokes, two fries, and numerous packets of ketchup and salt. I figured you'd need that." I passed her the sack. "The stuff's probably cold and I apologize for that."

"I have a microwave."

"You do? Good job. I hope you're hungry."

"You bet." She set the bag in her lap and wheeled

herself over to the low chest of drawers. On top, she had an electric tea kettle and a microwave oven the size of a bread box. She put the bag in and set the timer. Over her shoulder, she said, "Make sure the coast is clear."

I crossed to the hall door, which had been closed for the night. I turned the knob, opened the door a crack. The corridor was dim. At the far end, I could see the nurses' station in a hot oasis of light. Standing with his back to me was the gentleman I'd seen entering only moments before. Maybe a relative making an after-hours visit. The door across from Ruby's opened abruptly and a nurse came out wearing a snappy white uniform, with a starched white cap, white hose, and crepe-soled white shoes meant to stave off varicose veins. I didn't think nurses even dressed like that these days. The few I'd seen wore street clothes or nursey-looking pantsuits made of machine-washable synthetics. It was Pepper Gray, the bitchy nurse who'd eaves-dropped on the conversation between Merry and me during my initial visit. She had a stethoscope hung around her neck and her expression was preoccupied as she checked her watch. She turned toward the nurses' station and padded briskly down the hall.

Behind me, Ruby's microwave oven pinged. I jumped and swiftly pushed the hall door shut. There wasn't a lock and I hoped the cheap, heady fumes of junk food wouldn't bring attendants running. Ruby retrieved the bag from the microwave and wheeled herself back to her place by the sliding glass doors. She pulled the rolling tray between us and pointed to a chair. I wasn't sure about sharing her food, but I'd really brought more than she could eat and I was starving to death. She seemed tickled at the company and wolfed down her Quarter Pounder almost as fast as I did. Both of us made little snuffling sounds as we moved on to the Big Macs and the cartons of fries.

"I hope your heart doesn't seize up," I said, taking a sip of my Coke.

"Who cares? I've got a no-code on my chart and I'd rest in peace." She held up her Big Mac, delighted at the sight of juices dripping out the bottom. She licked a dab of special sauce from the corner of her mouth. "Not as big as the ones on TV, but it's good."

"I'm a sucker for these things. So how've you been?"

She tilted her head, so-so. "I heard they found the doctor's car so I thought you might stop by. I was looking for you all day."

"Took me a while to get myself together. How are people dealing with the news?"

"Some are upset, but I don't think many of us are surprised. Was the body his?"

"Don't know yet. I'm assuming it was. The autopsy was done today." I filled her in on the story, adding a few of the grimmer details, which she appeared to enjoy. I said, "Tell me about the night staff. They do much prowling around at night?"

"Not often, no. When I'm wheeling myself up and down the hall, I see them sitting at the desk chatting or doing paperwork. Some have coffee or watch TV in the staff lounge. Most nights it's quiet unless someone dies."

"How many total?"

Ruby did a head count. "Seven, if you include the orderlies, the nurses, and the nurse's aides."

"Do they make regular rounds checking on the residents?"

"Half the time they don't even check on us if we ring for them. Why? Are you casing the joint?"

"Absolutely." I paused to wipe my mouth and wad up the paper napkin and the wrappers in my lap. "Actually, I need to check some files. Think they keep the records locked up?"

Ruby shook her head, tucking a bite of burger in her cheek so she could answer. "Hardly anybody wants to steal geriatric charts."

"How'd you like to be a lookout? I could use some help."

She hesitated, suddenly a lot less cocky. "Oh, dear. I don't know if I could do that. I'm not good at sneaking. Even as a child, I could never manage it well."

"Ruby, it takes practice. You can't expect to be good unless you're willing to apply yourself."

Her already diminutive body seemed to shrink. "I'll try, but I don't think I'll do a very good job of it."

"I'm sure you'll do fine."

Moments later, I watched through her partially opened door as she wheeled herself down the hall toward the nurses' station around the corner. Her single responsibility—aside from chatting with the staff—was to park her chair so she could keep an eye out, making sure no one headed for the office while I was mucking around in there. The layout of the corridor was such that I could get in without being seen, but I was worried one of the nurses would come looking for a chart that wasn't out on the floor. Seemed unlikely, but I'd have no way to explain myself if someone happened to barge in.

I allowed time enough for Ruby to reach the nurses' station, and then I slipped out of her room, pulled the door shut behind me, and turned right, walking down the hall as though I had legitimate business there. I passed the dayroom, the entrance, and the dining room The doors to both the dayroom and the dining room stood open, but all the lights were out. I paused, leaning against the wall. Like an animal on the hunt, I closed my eyes, taking in the scents, deciphering the secrets that lingered in the air. This was the world of the elderly: cinnamon rolls, pine scent, freshly ironed cotton, and gardenias.

When I reached the administrative offices, I took a deep breath and tried the knob. Locked. I considered using my key picks, but I was uneasy at the prospect of loitering for fifteen minutes while I manipulated the tumblers with assorted snap picks, torquing tools, and bent wire. Surely, there was a better way to go about this. I retraced my steps, returning to the front desk, which was abandoned at this hour in the dimly lighted alcove. I slipped behind the counter and searched through drawer after drawer. I kept my ears tuned, alert to any warning sounds that might signal someone's approach. In the bottom drawer, I saw a metal file box that opened at a touch. Inside was a small compartmentalized tray with various keys, all neatly tagged and labeled. Yea for my team. This was really more exciting than a scavenger hunt. To be on the safe side, I took three; one for Administration, one for Admissions, and one for Medical Records. I closed the lid on the box, slid the drawer shut, and scurried down the hall again.

I started with Administration. My hands trembled slightly, 1.2 on the Richter scale, but otherwise I did all right. Once inside, I didn't dare risk a light, though the door itself was solid. My chief concern was that someone pulling into the side parking lot would wonder why the windows were alight at this hour. I reached down my shirt and removed the flat pinch flashlight from its hiding place in my bra. When I squeezed it, the plastic felt warm and the beam emitted was wee, but sufficient for my purposes. I took a moment to reorient myself. I'd seen this office previously by day and I had a fair sense of how the space was organized.

On the far side of the counter was Merry's desk, which was arranged back-to-back with an identical desk. In addition, there were several rolling file carts, the copy machine, and a row of metal file cabinets along the far wall. Merry's computer screen was dark, but a small dot of amber pulsed steadily like a heart. In the darkness, I couldn't see the big wall clock, but I was aware of its relentless *click, click, click* as the second hand measured the circumference of the face. To my right was the door to Dr. Purcell's office where I'd had my chat with Mrs. Stegler. To the left was the door that connected this office with Medical Records. I flashed the light on my watch. It was 10:22.

Cautiously, I tried the door to the Medical Records department, which I discovered was unlocked. Oh, happy day. I swept my light across the space, yawning and dark, with four desks, a work table, assorted chairs, and a copy machine. File cabinets were built along the periphery of the room with an additional double bank down the middle. On the far wall, I saw a second door.

I crossed and tried that knob and was delighted to find that it was unlocked as well. I poked my head in. From a quick survey of the space beyond, I realized I'd gained access to Admissions; all three offices were connected by a series of interior doors. I was sure the medical records personnel, the secretaries, and front office clerks appreciated the ease with which they could move from one department to the next without resorting to the public corridor. I was getting happier by the minute.

I went back into the Medical Records department. I focused on the job at hand, that being to find Klotilde's chart in this warehouse of densely packed medical records. I toured with my tiny hand-held beam, scanning the drawer fronts for a clue about the game plan here. I'd hoped for an organizing principle as basic as A, B, C. No such luck. I opened the first drawer and stared at the endless march of paperwork. The charts seemed to be arranged according to a number system— a row of six digits. I selected fifteen charts, which I chose randomly, looking for the underlying principle that linked that particular run of charts. None of the fifteen patients shared age, sex, diagnosis, or attending physician. I stood there and stared. I flipped pages back and forth. I couldn't see the pattern. I opened the next drawer down. Still, not a patient name in sight. I moved to the bottom drawer and tried ten more charts. I couldn't spot the defining shared characteristics. The patient identification numbers bounced all over the place: 698727 ... 363427 ... 134627. I tried a file drawer two cabinets over. How could I hope to find Klotilde's chart when there had to be thousands more in these drawers? I looked for a common denominator: 500773 ... 509673 ... 604073. I'm embarrassed to say how long it took me to spot the element that linked each particular series of charts, but it did finally dawn on me that they were grouped according to the last two digits in the numerical sequence.

I pulled out the scrap of paper on which I'd jotted down her Medicare number. It seemed to bear no relationship to the numbers on the charts, which were apparently assigned to each patient on admission. I could feel my frustration mount. I really hate it when my illegal efforts turn out to be fruitless as well. Somewhere in this room there had to be a list of patients in alphabetical order. Nobody could keep track of all these charts otherwise. I closed the file drawers and made a circuit of the room. The beam from my flashlight had taken on that worrisome yellow tint that suggests the battery is about to peter out and die.

I checked the windows. No sign of movement in the parking lot. I crossed to the light switch and turned the damn thing on. I did a slow visual assessment, turning in a circle so that I could take in every aspect of the room. Near the door, I spotted an eleven-by-fourteen-inch book with a heavy cover, containing what looked like computer-generated pages to a height of three to four inches. I moved over to the book and opened the front cover. Oh, glory. This was the Master Patient Index, laid out, most blessedly, in alphabetical order. I found Klotilde's impossible last name, picked up her patient ID number, and went back to work. I left the lights on, thinking, *To hell with it*. I renewed my search, this time tracking her chart according to the last two digits in her patient ID number. I found her within minutes, removed her chart from the drawer, and stuffed it down the front of my underpants.

I flipped the lights out and moved back into Administration. I was just about to let myself out into the corridor when I had the following thought: *If anyone was ever going to succeed in uncovering the truth, the fraud investigators would need to find Klotilde's files on the premises. "Down my underpants" was not going to be admissible in a court of law. Once I removed the records from this facility, the evidence would be tainted and the proof of Dow's innocence or guilt would be irreparably compromised.*

Well, shit.

I flew back into the Medical Records department, where I laid the chart open on the nearest desk. The pages were filed in reverse chronology: the most recent entries first, going back page by page to the last in the chart, which was her admissions form. I lifted the prongs and removed the metal clasp. Heart pounding with panic and impatience, I lifted the cover of the copy machine and laid the first sheet facedown. I pressed the button. With a whirring, the copier began to warm up. At an agonizing pace, the bar of light traced its way across the data and then back. The finished copy slowly appeared in the tray to my left. I lifted the cover and replaced the first sheet with the second. At least there was plenty of light to see by. Many of the doctors' notes were cursory, and I could see where the cheaters might take advantage of the gaps. Aside from the items of a medical nature, who could possibly track back and determine if the patient received Steri-strips or a bottle of baby lotion? As each page emerged, the bar of light glowed brightly just long enough for me to insert the next page. What would I do if someone happened to walk in? In between worrying about that, I worried I was being permanently sterilized.

Sixteen minutes later, I'd completed the run. I straightened the stack of copies and slid those, still warm, back in my underpants. I reassembled the pages of the chart, put the prongs back in place, slid the clasp onto the prongs, folded them over, and secured them. Now what? I couldn't take the chart with me and I couldn't be sure someone wouldn't come along later and destroy the information. I went back to the drawer where I'd uncovered her medical chart. The last two digits in her six-digit patient ID number were 464. I moved over one bank of drawers and slid her chart among the ID numbers ending in 54, instead. That way I'd know where she was, and any medical records clerk would simply discover that her chart was gone. It was always possible someone would stumble across the chart in its new location, but I'd have to take that chance.

I left Medical Records, closed the door behind me, and returned to the main office, where the pulsing dot on Merry's screen provided surprising illumination. By now I was accustomed to the dark and I could see the clock face. 11:34. Time to scram. I pushed through the hinged gate in the counter and I'd just reached the hall door when I heard approaching footsteps. I froze, trying not to panic. The tapping sound of hard-soled shoes was soft but distinct. News must have traveled about the overhead light in the records room because someone was definitely heading in my direction to investigate. I didn't want to believe anyone would actually walk into the office, but in the interest of caution, I made a beeline through the hinged gate. I scanned the area for the easiest hiding place. I crossed to Merry's work station, pulled out her rolling chair, and crawled into the knee-hole space under her desk. I found myself sitting on a tangle of fat power cords, my head angled unnaturally to keep it from banging into the underside of Merry's pencil drawer. The corners of Klotilde's chart cut into my stomach and chest and made a strange crackling sound as I drew my feet up and hugged my knees.

The office door opened.

I expected the light to be turned on, but the room remained dark. I had no idea if any portion of my person was still visible, but I had to trust in providence that whoever had come in would soon go out again. A moment later, the door opened a second time and a second someone entered. I could hear a whispered consultation, a minor argument, and then the sound of the gate as first one and then the other pushed through into the area where I was (I hoped) concealed. Who were these two? Maybe we were on the verge of a burglar's jamboree, all three of us stealing files for differing but nefarious purposes. They had to be up to no good or why not turn the lights on?

Much shuffling of feet and suddenly the two of them were standing in front of Merry's desk. The dull glow of her computer screen shone softly. I closed my eyes like a kid. Maybe if I couldn't see them, the two of them couldn't see me. I heard rustling as someone removed a coat, settled it across the back of Merry's chair, and pushed it out of the way. When I opened my eyes again, I could make out a pair of men's trouser legs and the back of his heels. I could have sworn it was the fellow with the silver hair I'd spied in the parking lot. He now stood toe-to-toe with a woman whose ghostly white hosiery and sensible thick-soled shoes I'd seen earlier. Pepper Gray.

I heard a flurry of indistinct susurrations, a guttural moan, protests on his part, and intimate urgings on hers. I picked up the quiet but unmistakable rip of a zipper being lowered on its track. I nearly shrieked in alarm. They were about to play doctor and I was going to be stuck in the examining room! He leaned back against the desk—I could see his fingers grip the edge for support. Meanwhile, she dropped to her knees and started to work on him. His protests began to die down as his breathing increased. He clearly had a letch for nursie types, and she was probably turned on by the possibility of getting caught.

I did my best to distract myself. I tried to think worthy thoughts, elevating myself to a Zen-like plane. After all, I had only myself to blame for the predicament I was in. I decided to stop breaking and entering. I made up my mind that I'd repent my sins. Not that I wasn't already paying a stiff price, in a manner of speaking. For someone who gets as little sex as I do, this surely constituted punishment of a most cruel and unusual kind. Pepper was only three feet away from me, happily occupied with the guy's throbbing manhood, as it's euphemistically referred to in novels that abound in such scenes. I have to tell you, other people's sex lives are not that fascinating. For one thing, a guy moaning, "Pepper, oh Pep" didn't seem that romantic from my perspective. Besides, he was taking forever and I worried her jaw would unhinge like a snake's. She began to make little encouraging noises in her throat. I was tempted to chime in. From under the desk, even the surge protector made a small enthusiastic peep, which seemed to spur him on. His vocalizing was muffled, but the sounds accelerated and began to rise in pitch. Finally, he grunted as though his finger had been slammed in a door and he was trying not to scream.

All three of us fell back exhausted and I prayed we wouldn't have to pause for a postcoital smoke. Ten more minutes passed before they pulled themselves together. After a whispered discussion, it was decided that she would leave first and he would then follow at a suitable interval. By the time I crawled out of my hiding place, I was cranky and sore and had a crimp in my neck. This was the last time I'd ask Ruby to man the lookout post.

NINETEEN

It was 12:30 when I let myself into my apartment for the second time that night. I'd returned the keys to the front desk and walked straight out the front door, the stolen chart pages pressed against me like a paper truss. When I reached the parking lot, the vintage automobile was gone. I continued across the asphalt to the shadowy corner where I'd left my VW. Before I slid behind the wheel, I removed the stolen file copies and shoved them under the front seat. The pages looked battered, dog-eared by careless association with my thighs and ribs. I started the engine and put the car in reverse.

Once back in my apartment, I made a thorough tour of the place, assuring myself that all the doors and windows were locked as I'd left them. Tommy Hevener was never far from my thoughts. I was itching to work my way through Klotilde's medical chart, but for the moment I refrained. Instead, I sat at my desk and consigned a few new nuggets of information to my index cards. It was odd reviewing the assumptions about Purcell now that I knew the end of his sad tale. There wasn't any doubt in my mind that the body in the vehicle was his. In theory, I could imagine him substituting someone else's body. In reality, this was not so easily accomplished, especially in a drowning, where critical features remain. It wouldn't take long for the forensic pathologist to compare his dental records and his fingerprints and make a positive ID.

I laid the cards out in a line, arranging them first in chronological order, then in the sequence in which I'd actually done the interviews. I wasn't being paid for this, but then again, I hadn't been officially fired. Idly, I shuffled the cards together just to witness the effect. The story always came out the same. Whether by his own hand or another's, Dow Purcell was dead and the life he'd left behind was a mess. Three questions nagged. Where was his passport and where had the thirty thousand dollars gone? There was also the minor but troubling matter of the post office box. If Dow had paid to keep it open for his personal use, why ask Crystal if she was still renting it?

At nine A.M., I put a call through to Fiona. Naturally, I didn't reach her. In the message I left, I told her I was hoping to track down the missing thirty thousand dollars and I implied, perhaps truthfully, that someone in Crystal's household might be responsible for the theft. I proposed putting in a couple more hours' work if she'd approve the expense. I was hoping she'd take advantage of the possibility of incriminating Crystal or someone dear to her. If not, I'd probably pursue it anyway just to satisfy myself. Not everything in this business is about the bucks.

It was not quite noon by the time I cleared my office calendar and dealt with phone messages from the day before. Joniffer had called in sick, which meant she and her pals were off to Los Angeles to hear their favorite band in concert. She'd told Jill she'd dropped the outgoing mail at the post office on her way home from work the day before. It's not that I doubted her. I was simply curious as I settled in her chair and began to go through her desk. I found what looked like a week's worth of letters piled together in the bottom drawer, among them my newly paid bills, all stamped and ready to go. I promptly ratted her out to Ida Ruth, who swore up and down she'd tell Lonnie and John and get her booted out the door.

Meanwhile, I put the batch of mail in a box and dumped it off at the post office myself. I wondered how soon Richard Hevener would get my letter and what he'd do when he figured out he couldn't cash my check. Too bad for him. He should have made the deposit the day I gave it to him. I walked from the post office to the police station hoping to catch Detective Odessa before he went out to lunch. Apparently, he and another detective had left on foot five or ten minutes before I arrived. I asked the desk officer if he had any idea where they'd gone. "Probably the Del Mar. They've been doing that a lot. If not, try the take-out window at the Arcade. Sometimes they bring back sandwiches and eat at their desks."

I put a business card on the desk. "Thanks. If I miss him, would you have him call me?"

"Sure thing."

I zipped up my windbreaker and trotted down the outside steps to the street. When I'd checked the weather report in the morning paper, the satellite photo showed a thick, white whirly-gig where yet another storm system spiraled toward the coast. The forecast was for morning low clouds and fog, with a 40 percent chance of rain in the afternoon. Temperatures were hovering in the mid-50s. Soon the local citizens would turn all cranky and mean-spirited, depressed by the bitter cold and the partly cloudy skies.

There was no sign of Odessa in the Del Mar so I hoofed it the half block to the Arcade, a sandwich shop with a pint-sized interior consisting of a counter, three marble-topped tables, and assorted bentwire chairs. The take-out window was located around the side of the building, where two picnic tables and four wooden benches had been added in the shelter of a black-and-white striped awning. Detective Odessa was hunched over a red plastic basket that contained a massive paper-wrapped burger and a load of fries. The detective sitting across the table from him was Jonah Robb. This was better than I'd hoped.

I'd met Jonah initially about four years before when he was working Missing Persons and I was looking for one. He'd since been transferred to Homicide, promoted to lieutenant, and made unit supervisor—Paglia's boss, in effect. At the time we became acquainted, Jonah's on-again, off-again marriage was in one of its off-again phases, and we'd dallied for a season on my Wonder Woman sheets. Subsequently, his wife, Camilla, returned with their two girls in tow. The next time I ran into him, he told me she'd taken a job as a court clerk, a career move cut short when she left him again. This time, she'd returned pregnant with someone else's child. The purported father took off, leaving poor Camilla to fend for herself. Of course, Jonah'd taken her in and the last I heard he was busy parenting his patched-together brood. From the onset of our relationship, there'd been entirely too much melodrama to suit me. I'd finally bowed out, but I hadn't yet reached the point where I could see him without feeling a flicker of embarrassment.

Vince Odessa spotted me and waved.

I said, "Hi, guys."

Jonah turned on the bench and we both made a point of greeting each other with a pleasant distance in our voices, eyes not quite meeting. We shook hands as you would with the pastor of your church. He said, "How are you?"

"Fine. How's the baby?" I said. "He must be what, four months old by now?"

"He's great. He was born July 4, right on schedule; weighed in at eleven pounds eight ounces. What a brute."

"Wow. What'd you call him?"

"Banner."

"Ah. As in 'star-spangled.'"

Jonah hesitated. "How'd you know? Camilla came up with the name, but you're the first to get it."

"Just a raggedy-ass guess."

Odessa gestured. "Sit down. Are you having lunch?"

Jonah promptly held out his plastic basket. "Here. You can have half of mine. Camilla's bugging me to diet. I bet I picked up fifteen pounds in the last few months of her pregnancy. Hers came right off, but I can't seem to get rid of mine." The hunk of flesh he pinched on his side formed a considerable sausage between his thumb and index finger.

I was standing closest to him and thought it'd be too

conspicuous if I circled the table and settled beside Odessa, so I sat down on the bench beside him. I checked Jonah's sandwich, which was cut on the diagonal: bacon, lettuce, and tomato, with a gruel of guacamole in between the layers of mayonnaise. I added a snow flurry of salt to the mix. I hate to pass up a chance to give my kidneys a thrill.

"What are you up to?" Odessa asked. He'd caught me with a mouthful of sandwich, and while I struggled to clear my palette, he went back to their conversation. "We were just talking about Purcell. Jonah attended the post."

"Such as it was. Condition of the body, Dr. Yee says he can't run biochemical or biophysical tests. From the gross, it looks like he died from a single contact shot to the head. We found the gun on the front seat. A Colt Python .357 Mag with one shot fired. The cartridge casing was still in the cylinder. Yee says there's a 99.9 percent probability he was dead when he went into the water."

"The gun was his?" I asked.

Jonah wiped his mouth and then crumpled the paper napkin in his hand. "He bought it before he and Fiona split. Crystal wouldn't let him keep it in the house on account of the kid. She thinks he either kept it in his desk drawer at work or in the glove compartment of his car."

Odessa said, "We're trying to figure out how he got up to the reservoir in the first place."

I raised my hand. "He was supposed to go see Fiona. She says he never showed, but she could be lying."

Odessa nodded happily, his mouth full. "Don't think it's escaped our attention that the guy turns up dead practically in her front yard."

"And catch this. She's the sole beneficiary on a life insurance policy. Part of the divorce settlement. We checked it out," Jonah said.

"How much?"

"A million."

"That would do it for me," Odessa said.

"Risky to kill the guy so close to home," I remarked.

"Maybe that's the beauty of it," Jonah said. "Could have been someone else. Lure him up there on some pretext and put a bullet in his head."

Odessa made a face. "How're you going to get him up there?"

Jonah said, "Ride in the same car. You call and arrange a meeting, say you want to go some place quiet and talk about a situation, but you need a lift."

"What's the pretext?"

I said, "Who needs a pretext? You hide in the backseat and pull the gun on him."

"Then what? How do you get back down the road in the dark?"

386

Jonah said, "You hike. It's not that far."

I said, "What if you're seen? Now you've got some-one who can place you at the scene."

Odessa said, "Could have been two of them. One meets him up there and does the job while the other one waits in a car parked somewhere down the road."

"But doesn't adding a co-conspirator increase the risk?"

"Depends on who it is."

Jonah sipped his Coke. He offered me the cup and I took a sip as well. We were silent for a moment, con-templating the images before us.

I said, "On the other hand, Purcell was in trouble with the feds and facing social disgrace. He must have considered suicide. Wouldn't you in his shoes?"

Jonah said, "I guess." He sounded glum at the prospect. "The guys are still working on the Mercedes. He had this mohair blanket over his lap, empty whiskey bottle on the floor of the passenger side. Headlights off. Key in the ignition, which was turned to the On position. Radio's off. ID, his wallet, all of that was on the body, including his watch, which is still running by the way. Damn thing didn't lose a second after all those weeks."

Odessa perked up at that. "What make? Hell of an endorsement. We should get in touch with the com-pany."

"Breitling, watertight down to four hundred feet."

Odessa said, "Remember that ad with the fountain pen?"

"That was a ballpoint."

"It was? I'm talking about the one that writes underwater. What was it called?"

"Who the hell cares?"

Odessa smiled sheepishly and said, "Sorry. What else?"

"Not much. The tempered glass in the driver's side window was crazed—some glass missing, but most of it intact—where the bullet exited. I sent two guys back over there with a metal detector, hoping they can pick it up. The passenger-side window and the two in the backseat were opened, ostensibly to speed the water pouring in."

Odessa wadded up his paper napkin and made an overhead shot, aiming at the waste bin where it bounced on the rim and tumbled out. "I'm not sold on suicide. It makes no sense."

Jonah said, "I'm eighty-twenty against based on a couple of things."

"Like what?" I asked.

Jonah crossed his arms. "Let's assume he shot himself, just for the sake of argument. How did he manage to sink the car? But why even bother?"

"Maybe he was embarrassed," Odessa said.

"Ashamed to kill himself so he hopes he can disappear."

"To spare his family the mess," Jonah said.

"Sure, why not?"

"Maybe the insurance policy has a suicide exclusion," Odessa said.

"So what? Fiona can't collect anyway until the body's been found. The minute that happens, the cause of death is going to be obvious. Bullet to the head and the gun's sitting there on the seat?"

"Might have a point there. Nobody's going to believe the guy shot himself in the temple by accident."

Jonah made a face. "Sorry to burst your bubble, but there isn't any suicide clause in the policy. I checked."

"Let's get back to the window on the driver's side. Why leave that up when all the others are open?"

"To muffle the sound of the shot," I said.

"Yeah, but why does he care? I mean, what's it to him if someone hears the gun go off? He's knows he's a dead man, so what difference does it make?"

"Wouldn't muffle much anyway if the other three windows were wide open," Odessa pointed out.

Jonah said, "Exactly. Something about it doesn't sit right. I don't like the redundancy. Shoot yourself before you drown? Seems like a bit much."

Odessa said, "Most suicides don't go in for drowning. It's too tough. Even if you want to die, your overwhelming impulse is to come up for air. Too hard to control."

"Virginia Woolf did it that way," I said. "She put stones in her pockets and walked into the water."

"But why double up the effort? That's what bugs me."

Odessa said, "People do it all the time. Take an overdose of pills and put your head in a plastic bag. Mix vodka and Valium before you slit your wrists. One doesn't work, you have the other to fall back on."

Jonah shook his head. "I'm just trying to picture it. What's the order of business here? He opens three windows, puts a blanket over his lap, takes out his gun, puts it to his temple, and pulls the trigger. Meanwhile, the engine's running, he's got the car in gear, and his foot on the brake. Blam. Foot slides off the brake pedal, car rolls down the hill and into the lake. It's too elaborate. Seems like overkill."

"As it were," Odessa said.

"Another thing. I don't like the whiskey bottle. It's melodramatic. Guy wants to off himself, why's he need to take a drink?"

"To calm his nerves?" I suggested.

"Nah, you don't need an excuse to drink," Odessa said. "You drink because you love it and what better occasion? Toast yourself before you go. Bon voyage and all that."

"Yeah, but everything I heard about him, he's a straight-ahead kind of guy. Doesn't seem like his style, this whole complicated setup."

I said, "He did drink. A friend of his told me when he disappeared before, he was off at rehab getting dried out. I guess he fell off the wagon the last six months or so."

Odessa said, "I'd been him, I'd have put together a nice little cocktail of really fine drugs. He must've had access to anything he wanted. Vicodin, Codein, Percocet, Halcion . . ."

"I'd be worried about constipation," I said to no one in particular.

Jonah was still feeling argumentative. "Drugs take too long. He knows enough about human anatomy to do the job right. Path the bullet took, I'm telling you that was the end of that."

"Pretty messy, though, for a guy that conservative," I said. "The quick glimpse I got, he died in his suit, wearing a dress shirt and tie."

"And his seat belt," Jonah added.

"Nothing conservative about his marriage. A Las Vegas show tart? That's a walk on the wild side," Odessa said.

"Maybe that's not as much of a stretch as you think. Fiona claims he was having problems with impotency, getting into sex toys and pornography, that sort of thing. She thought it was disgusting. She says she refused to have anything to do with him and that's when he went out and found Crystal." I popped the rest of the sandwich in my mouth and reached for one of Odessa's fries.

Jonah said, "It bugs me there's no note. The guy might've been desperate, but he's not mean-spirited. Suppose the car's never found. Why leave everyone hanging? Guy wants to kill himself, all he has to say, 'Sorry, folks, but that's it. I can't take any more and I'm out of here.' And why put the car at the bottom of the lake? What's the point of that move?"

"Right," Jonah said. "What if we take the opposite tack. Let's say somebody did it for him. You shoot him with the windows up to muffle the sound. Then you open three of 'em to make sure the car sinks fast. You don't want an air bubble caught against the roof because the whole thing might float. The deal wouldn't be that hard to pull off. You do the guy, get out, release the emergency brake, give the car a quick shove, and send it on its merry way."

Odessa said, "Which brings us right back around to where we started. Look at it as murder, then the sinking of the car makes a lot more sense."

"The killer assumes the car's twenty feet down and won't be found," I said.

"Exactly. Now the scenario heats up. You find the

car, and now he's forced to cope with something he never counted on."

I said, "If you're looking for a motive. I heard a rumor that Crystal was having an affair."

"Who with?"

"A personal trainer of hers. Some guy she worked with eight or ten months ago."

Odessa glanced at his watch. "Hey, I gotta get a move on. I promised Sherry I'd run an errand." He stood and picked up his plastic basket, picking up Jonah's as well. Jonah offered to help, but he was already at the take-out window. He left the baskets on the counter. "I'll see you back at the place."

"I better be going myself. You walking in that direction?"

I said, "Sure, if you don't mind." I picked up my shoulder bag and we walked for a beat in silence. "So how are things really?"

"Better than you'd think," he said.

"Good. I'm glad to hear it. I hope it works out for you."

"Something I never said. That time we spent together, I appreciate what you did. You helped me keep my head on straight or I'd have never made it through."

"I didn't see you as a charity," I said.

"That's how I feel, though; fucking grateful."

"Well, I am, too." I took his arm for a moment and then thought better of it. I moved my hand, pretending to adjust my bag higher on my shoulder. "You know, I'm still on Fiona's payroll and I owe her some hours."

"Meaning what?"

"I was going to clear this with Odessa, but it's probably better if I talk to you. I went through my notes last night and I'm curious about Dow's passport and the missing thirty thousand bucks. If I can get Fiona to underwrite it, do you care if I pursue that?"

"Depends. What are you proposing?"

"I'm not sure. For starters, Crystal mentioned a post office box. It was hers at one time, but she claims she let the rental on it lapse. She assumed Dow kept it so he could divert bank statements, but I'm wondering if that's true."

He studied me for a moment. "I can't stop you."

"I know, but I don't want to step on any toes."

"Then don't fuck it up. You find out anything, I want you coming straight to me. And no tampering with evidence."

"I wouldn't tamper with evidence," I said, offended.

"Uh-huh. You wouldn't lie about it, either."

"Well, I wouldn't lie to you."

We paused at the corner, waiting for the light to change. I stole a glance at his face, which was looking weary in repose. "You really believe he was murdered?"

"I think we'll operate on that assumption until we hear otherwise."

I went back to the office. Fiona had left me a message, authorizing two hours, but no more. I sat in my swivel chair, feet on the desk, and swiveled for a bit while I stared at the phone. I was reluctant to call Crystal in the midst of the current crisis, but I had no alternative. If Crystal was upset about Dow, I'd just have to muddle through. I picked up the handset before I lost my nerve. I tried the number at the beach house, picturing her retreating to the place she loved best. Anica answered after two rings.

"Anica, it's Kinsey. I thought you went back to Fitch."

"I did, but then Detective Paglia called this morning to tell Crystal the body'd been identified as Dow's. She called me and I turned around and drove right up. I told them I'd take vacation days through the end of next week. This takes priority. We'll be here until Sunday and then we're going to the other house so we can sort through Dow's things."

"How's she doing?" I could hear murmuring in the background and I got the impression Crystal might have been nearby.

Anica lowered her voice. "She's a mess. I think it's

the finality that's getting to her. Rand says she just lost it the minute she heard. She always swore something happened to him, but the whole time she must have been praying she was wrong."

"What about Leila? How's she taking it?"

"Oh, you know her. She was up in her room listening to music at top volume, driving everyone nuts. She and Crystal got into it, so I finally called Lloyd and asked him to pick her up and take her for the day. The quiet is heavenly."

"What about the funeral? Is she planning to have a service?"

"She's talking about Saturday if she can pull it together. She'll have to get the notice in the paper and an officiant lined up. Dow wasn't religious, so this is really more in the way of a memorial to him. I just called the mortuary and they said they'd make arrangements to pick him up. She's having him cremated . . . not that she has a lot of choice in the matter."

"I guess not."

"What happened? Detective Paglia never said, but I'm assuming he drowned."

I could feel my heart lurch. "Ah. I don't know. I haven't heard anything definitive. They're probably still working to determine that. In the meantime, is there anything I can do to help?" The question seemed false even to my lie-corrupted ear, but I had to get her off the subject.

"Not at the moment, but thanks, anyway. I should probably get back, but I'll tell Crystal you called."

"While I have you on the line, I wondered if I could get some information. Crystal mentioned a post office box she used to keep here in town. I need the number and location."

"Hang on for a second." Anica placed a palm across the mouthpiece and I heard her muffled conversation with someone in the background. It reminded me of days spent at the public pool as a kid. I'd emerge from the water to find my hearing blocked, with much the same effect. It sometimes took hours before the tiny trickle of hot water cleared my ear canal.

Anica removed her hand. "P.O. Box 505. She says it's the Mail & More over in Laguna Plaza. Be sure and let her know what you find."

"I'll do that."

I'd no more put the phone down than it rang.

Mariah Talbot said, "Hi. Are you free to talk or do you want to meet somewhere?"

"This is fine. The phone's secure. All this cloak-and-dagger stuff feels dumb, but I can't help myself. Thanks for returning my call." I picked up a pen and began to doodle on a scratch pad . . . a dagger with blood dripping off the tip and a hangman's noose, one of my specialties. Sometimes, focusing on a doodle helps me articulate my thoughts.

"What's up?"

"Well, here's the situation." I went on to describe the conversation at Rosie's the previous night when Henry had laid out the bait about the jeweler in L.A.

"You think Tommy bought it?"

"I have no idea. I thought I'd report it because the last time we spoke I told you I wasn't going to help. Now the deed's been done, but only because Henry stepped in and did it."

"What a cool move on his part. If it's coming from him, it'll never occur to Tommy he's being conned."

"It's still a long shot."

"Not so. They're hard up for cash and their property is mortgaged to the hilt. The jewelry's their only asset. They have to sell to survive," she said. "By the way, where did you and Prince Charming end up? Not in the bedroom, I hope."

"Absolutely not," I said. "I canceled our dinner plans, which he didn't like. He pretended it was okay, but he was pissed. I wish I knew how to dump the guy without setting him off."

"Oh, good luck. He's never going to let you get away with that. Tommy's an egomaniac. He dumps you. You don't dump him."

"He's like a spider. He lurks. Every time I go somewhere, he crawls out. He's really getting on my nerves."

"Well, what do you expect? These boys are both wacko. You ever want to see Richard lose it, ask him about Buddy and the bike."

"Why? What's that about?"

"This is a story I heard when I did the background work. This guy, Buddy, swears by the time those kids were ten, they were already competitive little shits, always at each other's throats. Jared thought it was time they learned to share, so he gave 'em a bike and said they had to take turns. Richard wasn't into taking turns so he stashed it somewhere and told his dad the bike got stolen. For weeks, he kept it hidden so he could ride it anytime he wanted."

"Didn't their father figure it out?"

"No, but Tommy did. They had a mutual friend—Buddy—who'd seen Richard do it. Buddy says Richard was always pounding on him, broke his nose once, so Buddy tattled to Tommy just to get even. Tommy waited until Richard was off somewhere. He stole the bike back and pushed it off the side of a bridge."

"He got away with that?"

"Richard guessed right away, but what could he do? It still pisses him off. The thing about those two is both would rather forfeit everything than see the other enjoy his half. Happened with a girl once and she ended up dead."

"You're really cheering me up here." I wrote "THE END" on the scratch pad and gave the letters a look of three-dimensions in the manner of gang graffiti. "Happily, I'm hanging up my spurs. I called to fill you in in case one of 'em makes a move."

"Come on. You can't leave me now with the job half done. What about the safe? You have to hang in until you locate that."

"Find it yourself. I'm bowing out of this."

"Just think how good it'll feel when we finally nail those guys."

"What's this 'we' shit? The problem isn't mine. It belongs to you."

Mariah laughed. "I know, but I keep hoping I can talk you into it."

"No, thanks. Nice doing business with you. It was fun," I said, and hung up. I lifted my eyes from my drawing to find Richard Hevener standing at my door, wearing a black raincoat and black cowboy boots.

I felt the icy-hot sensation of a bad sunburn, a stinging heat on my skin that chilled me to the bone. I had no idea how long he'd been there and I couldn't remember for the life of me if I'd mentioned his name or Tommy's in the final moments of my conversation. I didn't think I'd used hers.

I said, "Hello," trying to sound unconcerned.

"What's this?" He pulled an envelope from his pocket and tossed it toward the desk. My letter whicked through the air and landed in front of me.

I could feel my heart begin to thump. "I feel bad about that. I probably should have called, but it seemed so awkward somehow."

"What's going on?"

"Nothing. It's just not going to work."

" 'It's not going to work.' Just like that."

"I don't know what else to say. I don't want the space. I thought I did, but now I don't."

"You signed a lease."

"I know and I apologize for the inconvenience—"

"It's not a matter of inconvenience. We have an agreement." His tone was light, but unrelenting.

"What do you want from me?"

"I want you to honor the terms of the lease you signed."

"You know what? Why don't you talk to my attorney about that. His name is Lonnie Kingman. He's right down the hall."

Ida Ruth appeared in the hall behind him. "Everything okay?"

Richard flicked a look at her and then looked back at me. He said, "Everything's fine. I'm sure we'll find the perfect solution to the little problem we have."

He backed out of the room. I watched him turn in her direction, careful not to touch her as he passed. He moved out of my line of sight, but Ida Ruth continued to stare. "What's with him? Is he nuts or what? He seems off."

"You don't know the half of it. If he shows up again, call the cops."

I locked my office door and placed a call to Mariah's Texas number, leaving another message on her answering machine. I wasn't sure how soon she'd check back, but I really didn't like the direction this was starting to take.

TWENTY

I headed north on the 101 to the off-ramp at Little Pony Road, a distance of three to four miles in light traffic. I found myself reviewing that phone conversation with Mariah, the easy banter between us at the Hevener boys' expense. I was almost positive I hadn't tipped my hand. In the meantime, I had no idea what Richard had in mind for me, but I figured his "perfect solution" lay somewhere on a continuum between small claims court and death. I kept an eye on the rearview mirror, flicking a quick look at any car that pulled up even with mine.

Laguna Plaza is an aging L-shaped strip mall, much classier than some, but a far cry from the massive retail stadiums being built these days. No glass-enclosed atrium planted with full-sized trees, no food court, no second and third tiers with escalators running in between. I pulled my VW into a slot directly in front of Mail & More, a franchise that boasted private mailbox rentals, mail receiving and forwarding, copy machines, a notary public, custom business cards, rubber stamps, and twenty-four hour access, seven days a week.

The interior was divided into two large areas, each with an entrance, and separated from each other by a glass wall and lockable glass door. The space on the right contained a counter, the copiers, office supplies, and a clerk to assist with the packaging and mailing services. Through a doorway in the rear wall, I could see banks of flat cardboard boxes in assorted sizes, continuous rolls of bubble wrap, wrapping paper, and bins of Styrofoam packing fill.

The clerk was gone, but she'd left a note on the counter: CLOSED FOR PERSONAL EMERGENCY. SORRY FOR THE INCONVENIENCE. BACK MONDAY. TIFFANY. If she was anything like Jeniffer, the personal emergency consisted of a tanning session and a pedicure. I said, "Yoo hoo" and "Hello" type things to cover my ass while I took the liberty of walking around the counter to inspect the back room. Not a soul in sight. I returned to the front and stood for a moment, feeling thoroughly annoyed. Anyone could waltz in and steal the office supplies. What if I had a package to ship or a critical need for a notary public?

I crossed to the glass wall and peered into adjoining space: a veritable cell block of mailboxes, numbered and glass-fronted, floor to head height, with a slot on the far wall for the mailing of letters and small packages. This was the section open twenty-four hours a day. I pushed through the glass door. I followed the numbers in sequence and found box 505—fifth tier over, five down from the top. I leaned over and looked through the tiny beveled glass window. No mail in evidence, but I was treated to a truncated view of the room beyond where I could see a guy moving down the line, distributing letters from a stack in his hand. When he reached my row, I knocked on the window of 505.

The fellow leaned down so his face was even with mine.

I said, "Can I talk to you? I need some help out here."

He pointed to my right. "Go down to the slot."

We both moved in that direction, he on his side of the boxes, me on mine. The slot was at chest height. This time, I leaned close, catching a glimpse of mail piled in the bin beneath. The guy was much taller than I and the difference in our heights forced him not only to bend, but to tilt his head at an unnatural angle. He said, "What's the problem?"

I took out a business card and stuck it through the slot so he could see who I was. "I need information about the party renting box 505."

He took my card and studied it. "What for?"

"It's a murder investigation."

"You have a subpoena?"

"No, I don't have a subpoena. If I did, I wouldn't need to ask."

He pushed the card back at me. "Check with Tiffany. That's her department."

Her *department*? There were two of them. What was he talking about? "She's gone and the note says she won't be back until Monday."

"You'll have to come back then."

"Can't. I have a court appearance. It won't take half a second," I said. "Please, please, please?"

He seemed vexed. "What do you want?"

"I just need a peek at the rental form to see who's renting it."

"Why?"

"Because the man's widow thinks he might have been receiving pornographic material at this address and I don't think it's true. All I want to know is who filled out the form."

"I'm not supposed to do that."

"Couldn't you make an exception? It could make a really big difference. Think of all the grief she'd be spared."

I could see him staring at the floor. He appeared to be forty, way too old for this line of work. I could well imagine his debate. On one hand, the rules were the rules, though I personally doubted there was any kind of policy to cover my request. He wasn't a federal employee and his job didn't require a security clearance. Executive mail-sorter. He'd be lucky to earn fifty cents an hour over the minimum wage.

I said, "I just talked to the police and told them I'd be doing this and they said it was fine."

No response.

"I'll give you twenty bucks."

"Wait right there."

He disappeared for what felt like an interminable length of time. I pulled the twenty from my wallet, folded it lengthwise, bent it, and balanced it on the lip of the slot, thinking he might be morally dainty, shying away from a direct hand-to-hand bribe. While I waited, I kept my back to the wall, my attention fixed on the entrance. I entertained a brief fantasy of Richard Hevener crashing his sports car through the plate glass window, squashing me up against the wall like a dead person. In movies, people were always diving out of the path of runaway trains as they plowed into stations, flinging themselves sideways as jumbo jets smashed into airline terminals, or buses went berserk and jumped the curb. How, in real life, did one prepare for such a leap?

"Lady?"

I looked back. The guy had reappeared and the twenty I'd left in the slot was gone. He had the rental form with him, but he held it behind his back, apparently uneasy about letting go of it. I waited until his face was in a plane with mine and tried asking him some easy questions, just to get him in the mood. This is called private eye foreplay. "How's this done? Someone comes in and pays the fee for the coming year?"

"Something like that. It can also be done by mail. We put a notice in the box when the annual fee comes up."

"They pay in cash?"

"Or personal check. Either way."

"So you might never actually see the person renting the box?"

"Most of them we don't see. We don't care who they are as long as they pay the money when it's due. I notice some renters have fancy stationery done up, acting like this is their corporate office with individual suites. It's a laugh, but it's really all the same to us."

"I'll bet. Can you push the form through the slot so I can see it better? This is a legitimate investigation. I'm really serious about that."

"Nope. I don't want you touching it. You can look for thirty seconds, but that's the best I can do."

"Great." What kind of world is this—you bribe a guy with twenty bucks and he still has *scruples*?

He held the card up on his side, angled so I could see it. He was checking his watch, counting off the seconds. Big deal. Little did this fellow know that as a kid my prime talent was the game played at birthday parties wherein the mother of the birthday girl put a number of articles on a tray, which she then covered with a towel. All the little party goers clustered around. Mrs. Mom would lift the towel for thirty seconds, during which we were allowed to look, committing all the items to memory. I always won this game, primarily because it was always the same old stuff. A bobby pin, a spoon, a Q-tip, a cotton ball. I would use my thirty seconds to make note of any new or unexpected object. The only sad part of this contest was the prize itself, usually a plastic jar full of bubble syrup with the blower inside.

The rental form was a no-brainer and I assimilated the information in the first two seconds. The signature on the bottom line appeared to be Dow's, but he hadn't written in the data on the lines above. The printing was Leila's, complete with the angled *t*'s and puffy *i*'s. Well, well, well.

I said, "One more tiny thing. Would you spit on your finger and run it across the signature?"

"Why?"

This guy was worse than a four-year-old. "Because I'm wondering if it was done with a pen or a copier."

Frowning, he licked his index finger and rubbed the signature. No ink smear. He said, "Hnh."

"What's your name?"

409

"Ed."

"Well, Ed. I appreciate your help. Thanks so much."

I returned to my car and sat for a minute, considering the implications. Working backward, I had to conclude that Leila'd intercepted the rental renewal notice when it arrived with its request for the annual fee. Crystal had told me the Mid-City Bank statements were routed to the P.O. box. Very likely Leila had notified the bank, perhaps typing the request on a sheet of Pacific Meadows letterhead, forging Purcell's signature or affixing a photocopy, and asking that the statements for that account be mailed to 505. I let my gaze stray across the store front, thinking how easily she could have stopped by the Mail & More when she was up from school.

I started my car, backed out of the parking place, and headed for the exit. When I reached the street, I realized the Laguna Plaza branch of the Mid-City Bank was located on the opposite corner. Even from this distance, I could see the ATM she'd used to drain the account. All she really needed was the bank card and pin number for the account, which Dow probably left in his desk at home.

True to my word, when I got back to the office, I put a call through to Jonah.

"Lieutenant Robb."

"This is Kinsey. If you don't scrutinize my methods,

I'll tell you what I found out. I swear I didn't mess with anything. I left it all in place."

"I'll bite."

I explained my trip to the Mail & More, leaning heavily on Leila's behavior while glossing over mine.

Jonah didn't say much, but I could tell he was taking notes. "You better give me the location of the P.O. box."

"The Mail & More at Laguna Plaza. The number's 505."

"I'll check it out," he said. "Devious."

I said, "Very," on the assumption he was talking about her.

"Any idea where she is now?"

"I heard she was up at Lloyd's, but maybe I should check it out. Leila's got a friend named Paulie, some gal she met in Juvie . . . this was a year ago July, I think. Paulie's been in trouble before. It crossed my mind the two of them might be planning to take off. It might be interesting to track Paulie's history and see what she's done."

He told me he'd check into it, and I hung up. I was already feeling guilty. The last thing Crystal needed was to have her only daughter brought up on charges of grand theft.

I went out to my car again and made the trip up to Lloyd's. I had questions to ask him, anyway, and this would give me an excuse. If Leila decided to take off, there wasn't much I could do, but it wouldn't hurt to keep an eye on her.

Approaching his A-frame, I could see that lights were on. I pulled up to the driveway, parked the car, and got out. Lloyd was working in the small unattached garage. He'd raised the hood on his convertible and his hands were dark with grease. He looked over at me without reaction, as though my arrival at his doorstep was an everyday occurrence. I had no idea what he was doing to the guts of the engine—something manly no doubt. He wore cutoffs and a well-worn sweatshirt. Flip-flops on his feet. I could see a smudge on one lens of his glasses. He no longer wore the earring with the skull and crossbones.

"You're Millhone," he remarked as much to himself as to me.

"And you're Lloyd Muscoe."

"Glad we got that straight."

"I was in the neighborhood and thought I'd drop in. I hope you don't mind. Is Leila here?"

He smiled slightly to himself. "Depends on what you want."

I studied the exposed engine, which looked like it

was made entirely of parts that would explode. I'd learned to pump my own gas. It was my big automotive triumph. "What's wrong with the car?"

"Nothing that I know of except that it's old and tired. I'm changing the oil, putting in new spark plugs, stuff like that."

"A tune-up."

"Of sorts. I'm taking off in a couple days." He reached in and removed a little knotty thing and wiped it clean with a rag before he put it back. He adjusted something down among the major organs.

"Where to?"

"Vegas. I thought I'd ask Crystal if I could take Leila with me. What d'you think?" He wasn't actually consulting me, just making conversation while he went about his business.

"I can't believe she'd say yes."

"Never know with her. She's tired of Leila's problems."

"That doesn't mean she'd kick her out," I said. I waited for a beat and when he said nothing, I went on. "You think it'd be good for Leila, moving her again?"

"At least over in Vegas she behaved herself. She hates that school she's in. Bunch of spoiled, rich debutantes. What a fuckin' waste."

"She seems to hate everything."

He shook his head. "She needs handling, that's all. Someone like me who won't let her get away with all the shit she pulls."

"Limits and boundaries."

"That's what I said."

"She gets that at Fitch and so far, it hasn't helped."

"Too much carrot. Not enough stick."

"How does Leila feel about it?"

He looked at me sharply. "Feeling doesn't have anything to do with it. She's headstrong and lazy. Leave it up to her and all she'd do is lie around watching TV. Crystal's too busy trying to be her best friend. Doesn't work that way. Kid needs a parent, not a pal."

I kept my mouth shut. Crystal wasn't going to let her go, but I wasn't there to argue with him.

His tone of voice turned wry. "You ever going to get around to telling me why you came?"

"Sure. I could do that," I said. "I understand Purcell came up here to talk to you about four months ago. I was wondering why."

"He'd heard a rumor Crystal was having an affair. He assumed it was me. Too bad I couldn't up and confess. I'd have taken a certain satisfaction shoving that in his face."

"It wasn't you."

"I'm afraid not."

"How long were you married to her?"

"Six years."

"Bad years? Good?"

"I thought they were good, but like they say, the husband's the last to know."

"I've heard your relationship was volatile."

He paused and leaned on the fender while he wiped his hands. "We had chemistry. Stone and flint. We'd come together and the sparks would fly. What's wrong with that?"

"She didn't have sparks with Purcell?"

"Are you kidding? The way I heard it, he liked the kinky stuff. That must have been the shock of her life. Here she marries the guy thinking he's the answer to her prayers. Turns out he drinks like a fish and can't get it up unless she wears high-heeled boots and beats his ass with a whip. It doesn't surprise me she'd cheat. I might have slapped her around, but I never did that stuff."

"Was she faithful to you?"

"Far as I know. I don't put up with any shit on that score."

"How'd you get along with Purcell?"

"Considering he walked off with my wife, we did fine."

"You remember where you were?"

He smiled, shaking his head. "The night he took a dive? I already went through that. The cops were here yesterday."

"What'd you tell them?"

"Same thing I'm telling you. I was working that Friday, the night of the twelfth. I had a gig driving cabs—it's on the company books. Leila was here with her friend Paulie, watching videos. Crystal picked her up Sunday morning as usual. You can ask her yourself if you don't believe me."

I watched him for a moment. "What happened to the earring?"

"Took it out for an interview I had a few months back. Didn't want the guy to think I was a fruit."

"You get the job?"

"No."

"Is that why you're going back to Vegas, to change your luck?"

"Here's my theory. Things get bad? Think about the last place you were happy and go there."

In a fit of guilt, I devoted all of Friday to other clients. Nothing exciting went down, but at least it paid the bills.

*

The memorial service for Dr. Dowan Purcell took place at 2:00 o'clock Saturday afternoon in the Presbyterian Chapel on West Glen Road in Montebello. I donned my black all-purpose dress and black flats and presented myself at 1:45. The sanctuary was narrow, with high stone walls, a beamed ceiling, and fifty pews divided into two sections of twenty-five. Outside, the day was damp and gray and the six stained-glass windows, done in tints of deep scarlet and indigo, reduced most of the available light to a somber gloom. I don't know much about the Presbyterian faith, but the atmosphere alone was enough to put me off predestination.

Despite the fact the mourners were assembled by invitation only, the crowd was sizeable and filled the chapel to capacity. Crystal's friends sat on one side, Fiona's on the other. For some, the decision seemed easy. Dana and Joel, for instance, took their seats without hesitation, studiously avoiding Dow's second wife out of loyalty to his first. Those I judged to be mutual acquaintances seemed torn, consulting one another surreptitiously before they slid into a pew. While the stragglers were being seated, an unseen organist worked her (or his) way through a selection of dolorous tunes, the funereal equivalent of Top Forty Dirges. I used the time to contemplate the brevity of life, wondering if Richard Hevener intended to shorten mine. Mariah, when she'd called back, didn't seem that

417

SUE GRAFTON

alarmed. Her theory was the Hevener boys would never risk another murder so soon after the first. This was not a comfort.

Crystal had arranged things in haste and it felt about like that. I guess organizing a funeral is like planning any other social event. Some people have a flair for it, some people don't. What made this one odd was the absence of a casket, a crematory urn, or even floral sprays. The announcement in the paper had suggested that, in lieu of flowers, a charitable donation should be made in Dr. Purcell's name. There wasn't even a photograph of him.

In the matter of seating, I'd suffered a bit of conflict. Crystal had asked me to attend, but since I was still technically in Fiona's employ, I felt fiscally obliged to sit on her side of the church. I'd settled on the aisle in the last pew, affording myself a panoramic view. Fiona's older daughter, Melanie, had flown in from San Francisco and she walked her mother down the aisle as solemnly as a father giving away his daughter in marriage. Fiona was dressed, not surprisingly, in black; a two-piece wool suit with big rhinestone buttons on the jacket and the skirt cut midcalf. Her curls had been subdued under a black velvet cloche and she wore a veil suggestive of the Lone Ranger's mask. I saw her press a tissue to her mouth, but she might have been blotting her lipstick instead of holding back tears. Mel's hair, like her mother's, was dark, though the style was quite severe; hennaed and blunt cut with dense, unforgiving bangs. She was taller and more substantial, in an austere charcoal pant suit and black ankle boots.

Blanche followed them down the aisle in a voluminous maternity tent. She moved slowly, both hands framing her belly as though holding it in place. She walked as carefully as someone whose soup is threatening to slop out of the bowl. Her husband, Andrew, accompanied her, his pace slowed to hers. She'd left the children at home which was a mercy on us all.

Mrs. Stegler, from Pacific Meadows, sat just in front of me, brown suit, brown oxfords, and her mop of red curls. There were also numerous doctor types in dark suits and several elderly people I took to be Dr. Purcell's former geriatric patients.

On the other side of the aisle, Crystal and Leila were ushered to their seats in the first pew on the left. Crystal wore a simple black sheath, her tumble of blond hair giving her a look of elegant dishevelment. She looked tired, her face pinched, dark circles under her eyes. Leila had forsworn the outlandish in favor of the strange: a black latex tube top matched with a black sequined skirt. Her short white-blond hair stood out from her head as though charged with static electricity. Jacob Trigg, in a coat and tie, swung into the church on his forearm crutches. He eased into a seat on Fiona's side, near the rear. Anica Blackburn appeared and smiled at me briefly before she took her seat in the pew across from mine. There was the usual rustle and murmuring, an occasional cough. I checked my program, wondering how Crystal managed to get it printed up so fast. Altogether, we were looking at a scattering of hymns, a doxology, two prayers, a soloist singing Ave Maria, followed by the eulogy, and two more hymns.

A latecomer arrived, a woman with medium blond hair whom I recognized belatedly as Pepper Gray, my favorite nurse. I watched her shrug out of her coat and tiptoe halfway down the aisle, where she paused while a fellow rose to let her into the pew. She walked as if she was still wearing crepe-soled shoes.

The minister appeared in a robe like a judge, accompanied by his spiritual bailiff, who intoned the corollary of a courtroom "All rise." We stood and sang. We sat and prayed. While all heads were bowed, I occupied my thoughts by reflecting on the state of my pantyhose and my unruly soul. I don't know why pantyhose can't be designed to stay in place. As for the state of my soul, my early religious training would have to be considered spotty at best, consisting as it did of sequential expulsions from a variety of church Sunday schools. My aunt Gin had never married and had no offspring of her own. After I was so rudely thrust into her care by the death of my parents, she fell headlong into parenting without any experience, making up the rules as she went along. From the outset, she labored under the misguided notion that children should be told the truth, so I was regaled with lengthy and unvarnished replies to the simplest of questions, the one about the origin of babies being my earliest.

My most unfortunate Sunday-school experience came that first Christmas in her care when I was five and a half years old. She must have felt some obligation to expose me to religious doctrine so she dropped me off at the Baptist church down the block from our trailer park. The lesson that Sunday morning was about Mary and Joseph, of whom I instantly disapproved. As nearly as I could tell, poor baby Jesus had been born to a couple of deadbeats, with no more sense than to birth him in a shed. When my Sunday-school teacher, Mrs. Nevely, began to explain to my little classmates how Mary came to be "with child," I was apparently the only one present who knew how far off the mark she was. Up shot my hand. She called on me, pleased at my eagerness to make a contribution. I can still remember the change that came over her face as I launched into the doctrine of conception according to Aunt Gin.

By the time Aunt Gin came to fetch me, I'd been set out on the curb, a note pinned to my dress, forbidden to say a word until she arrived to take me home. Fortunately, no blame attached. She made me a "sammich" of white bread and butter, filled with halved Vienna sausages out of a can. I sat on the trailer porch step and ate my picnic lunch. While I played croquet by myself in her tiny side yard, Aunt Gin called all her friends, spoke in low tones, and laughed quite a lot. I knew I'd made her happy, but I wasn't quite sure how.

When the minister finally stepped up to the pulpit, he made the sort of generic remarks that were safe for any but the most depraved decedent. The service finally ended and people began to file out of the church. I lingered near the door, hoping to catch Fiona before she left the premises. I wanted to set up a time to chat with her so we could sort out the details of our relationship. I finally caught sight of her, leaning heavily against Mel, who walked in tandem with her. Melanie must have known who I was because she shot me a warning glance as she guided her mother down the steps and out to the parking lot.

Anica touched me on the arm. "Are you coming back to the house? Some people are stopping by."

"Are you sure it's okay? I don't want to intrude."

"It's fine. Crystal told me to ask. We're at the beach."

"I'd like that."

"Good. We'll see you there."

The parking lot emptied slowly. The crowd dispersed as though from a movie theater, people pausing to chat while departing vehicles inched by. I returned to my car and joined the thinning stream. The overcast had light-ened and a pale hint of sun seemed to filter through the clouds.

The beach house was only two miles from the church on surface roads. I must have been one of the last to arrive because the gravel berm on Paloma Lane was completely lined with expensive cars. I grabbed the first spot I saw, locked my car, and walked the rest of the way to the house. I sensed the crotch of my pantyhose had slipped to midthigh. I hoisted the suckers back into place by giving a little jump. For ten cents, I'd peel 'em off and toss 'em in a bush.

As I turned into Crystal's driveway, I saw the same vintage auto I'd seen at Pacific Meadows. Cautiously, I paused and scrutinized the area, noting that I was protected from view. The entire rear facade of Crystal's beach house was windowless and the roadway behind me was momentarily empty. I circled the vehicle, check-ing the manufacturer's emblem affixed to the right front fender. A Kaiser Manhattan. Never heard of it. All four doors were locked and a quick look into the front and backseats revealed nothing of interest.

The front door had been left ajar and the sounds spilling out were not unlike an ordinary cocktail party. Death, by its nature, reshapes the connection between family members and friends. Survivors tend to gather, using food and drink as a balm to counteract the loss.

There is usually laughter. I'm not quite sure why, but I suspect it's an integral part of the healing process, the mourner's talisman.

There were probably sixty people present, most of whom I'd seen at the church. The French doors stood open to the deck and I could hear the constant shushing of the surf beyond. A gentleman in a cropped white jacket walked by with a tray, pausing to offer me a glass of champagne. I thanked him and took one. I found a place near the stairs and sipped champagne while I searched for the man with the mustache and thick silver hair.

Jacob Trigg came up behind me, pausing as I had at the edge of the crowd. Many of the mourners were already engaged in animated conversations and the thought of breaking into any given threesome was daunting. Trigg said, "You know these people?"

"No, do you?"

"A few. I understand you were the one who found Dow."

"I did and I'm sorry he died. I was hoping he'd gone off to South America."

"Me, too." Trigg's smile was bleak.

"Did Dow ever mention money missing from his savings account?"

"I know he was aware of it. The bank manager became concerned and sent him a copy of the statement

424

with a query attached. Dow thanked him, said he knew what it was and he'd take care of it. In truth, it was the first he'd heard. Initially, he figured it had to be Crystal since the statements were being routed to her P.O. box."

"Did he ask her?"

"Not about the money, but about the post office box. She told him she'd dumped it about a year ago. He didn't want to press the issue until he'd looked into it. It almost had to be someone in the house because who else would have access to the bank card and the pin number for that account?"

"Who'd he suspect?"

"Crystal or Leila, though it could have been Rand. He'd obviously narrowed it down, but he wouldn't say a word until he knew for sure. He and Crystal clashed over Leila so many times, she'd threatened to walk out. If he'd had a problem with Leila, he'd have handled it himself. Of course, when it came to Rand, Crystal was just as fierce. Why take that on? There'd have been hell to pay there, too."

"How so?"

"He's the only one she trusted with Griff. Without Rand, where's her freedom? Dow was in a bind any which way it went."

"Why not close the account?"

"I'm sure he did."

"Did he ever figure out who it was?"

"If so, he never told me."

"Too bad. With his passport missing, the cops figured he might have left of his own accord. I wonder why Crystal didn't fill them in."

"Maybe she didn't know. He might have decided pursuing it wasn't worth the risk."

"He'd let someone walk off with thirty thousand bucks?"

"Dad?"

Both of us turned. A woman with a thick blond braid halfway down her back stood behind us. She was in her forties, no makeup, in a long cotton sweater, a peasant skirt, and sandals. She looked like the sort who never shaved her legs, but I didn't want to check. She was too smart to wear pantyhose, so I gave her points for that. Mine were sinking again. Any moment, they'd slip down as far as my knees and I'd have to start hobbling, taking little mincing steps wherever I went.

"This is my daughter, Susan."

"Nice meeting you," I said. We shook hands and the three of us stood chatting for a while before she took his arm.

"I hope you don't mind if we go. This is all a bit rich for my blood," she said.

"She thinks I'm tired, which I am," Trigg confessed. "We'll talk again soon."

"I hope so."

TWENTY-ONE

As soon as they left, I set my glass down and found the nearest bathroom. The door was shut. I tried the handle and found it locked. I waited, leaning against the wall, making sure I was first in the one-person line. I heard the toilet flush, water running in the sink. Moments later, the door opened and the man with the mustache and silver hair emerged. He smiled at me politely and went into the den.

I shut myself in the bathroom and availed myself of the facilities. Having hoisted my pantyhose up the pole like a flag, I went out and found a perch on the stairs, three steps down from the top, the perfect vantage point from which to view the gathering. Rand was making the rounds with Griffith affixed to his hip. Griff was outfitted in a sky blue sailor suit, and Rand mouthed Griff's imaginary monologue as though the child were a ventriloquist's sidekick. I hadn't seen Leila but figured she was in the house somewhere. Crystal would never tolerate her boycotting the event.

The caterers had finished setting out a cold buffet of boneless chicken breasts, three kinds of salad, marinated asparagus, deviled eggs, and baskets of fresh rolls. People loitered near the table in clusters, everyone trying to avoid going first. Ordinarily, I'd have left Crystal's long before now, but I was curious about the man with the silver hair. I saw him return to the great room, this time in the company of a gaunt brunette, who had a wineglass in one hand, the other hand hooked through his arm. She wore a black long-sleeved leotard under skin-tight black leather pants, cinched by a wide silver belt. The stiletto heels on her boots looked like five-inch toothpicks. This was an outfit more appropriate to soliciting on street corners than attending a wake. Her body wasn't *quite* slick enough to bear up under such pitiless revelations. Her liposuctionist should have slurped another pint of fat from the top of each thigh.

She seemed watchful, her gaze flitting uneasily around the room. Her smile, when it appeared, was self-conscious and never quite reached her eyes. I'm not sure I buy into talk like this, but her "aura" was dark; I could almost see the magnetic force field surrounding her. She was bristling, battle-ready. What was the deal here? The guy seemed to know quite a few people. Relaxed and at ease, he chatted first with one group and then another while she clung to his arm. In contrast to her tartlike ensemble, his suit was well cut, a conservative dark blue that he wore with a pale blue shirt and a tone-on-tone pale blue tie. I pegged him in his late fifties, one of those men who'd aged well: trim and fit-looking. He had to be a doctor. I couldn't think what else he'd have been doing at Pacific Meadows at midnight, aside from the impromptu game with Pepper Gray.

He murmured to the woman and then took his place in the supper line, picking up his plate and a napkin-wrapped bundle of silverware. Though she moved into line behind him, they didn't speak to each other. I watched him fill his plate to capacity while she helped herself to a demitasse of salad and four asparagus spears. He settled on the couch in the only remaining space. He rested his wineglass and his plate on the pale wood coffee table and began to eat. When she tried to join him, there was no seat left. She stood there for a moment, clearly hoping he'd scoot over and make room for her. He seemed intent on his meal, and she was forced to take a chair by herself at a distance. She busied herself with her plate to cover her discomfiture, though no one else present seemed to notice. The server walked by with a bottle of Chardonnay. She looked up at him sharply and held out her glass, which he filled generously.

I sensed motion behind me and glanced up to find Anica coming down the stairs. She paused for a moment to peer over the rail. She was, as usual, dressed in understated good taste: a long-sleeved white silk shirt; wide-legged, pleated black wool slacks; and black leather loafers as soft as slippers. Her auburn hair had been moussed, a pompadour in front with the sides combed back into sweeping ducktails. "Good place to sit. Have you had something to eat?"

"I will in a minute when the line goes down. I've been doing some people watching. Who's that silver-haired fellow on the couch in the dark blue suit?"

She followed my gaze. "That's Harvey Broadus. He and Joel must be dividing the honors. Joel and Dana went off to the country club where Fiona's holding court. Harvey came here. That way, they can't be accused of playing favorites."

"Who's the woman in the leather pants?"

"Celine, Harvey's wife of twenty-ump years. He walked out on her eight months ago and now he's come crawling back."

"Oh, right. Crystal mentioned he was in the middle of a nasty divorce."

" 'Was' is correct. I guess the tab got too steep. He

decided he was better off living with her than being stripped of his assets. He's a jerk, but I sometimes feel sorry for him. She drinks like a fish. Most of the year she's either checking into Betty Ford or checking herself out again. The rest of the time, she goes off to some luxury spa—La Costa or the Golden Door. Nothing but the best for our girl."

"Aren't married people ever happy?"

"Oh sure. They're just not often happy with the person they're married to." I saw her gaze shift "Uh-oh. I better go down. Talk to you later."

Anica slipped by me and headed down the stairs. I glanced over at the front door, where Pepper Gray had appeared. Anica spotted her and made her way over to the door. The two exchanged polite busses. Anica took her coat and then signaled the waiter, who veered in their direction with a tray of champagne glasses. Shorn of her white cap and white uniform, she seemed softer and prettier, less like a woman who'd perform extramarital first aid. I looked down at my silver-haired friend, wondering if he'd noticed her at the same time I had. Pepper moved into the great room. They had to be aware of each other, but neither paid the slightest attention—no nod of recognition, no greeting of any kind.

Celine looked up and her body grew still, a forkful of food poised over her plate. Anica took Pepper by the arm, guiding her through the French doors and out onto the deck. Celine's head seemed to swivel, her gaze glassy and fixed. She watched Pepper with all the caution of a rabbit when a fox is in range. Either she knew for a fact that her husband was philandering or her radar was superb, probably a little bit of both. It didn't take much to guess how the dynamic played out. He screwed around on her as compensation for the fact that she drank too much, and she drank too much to console herself for his screwing around. As I watched, she got up and left the room.

I waited on the stairs until the desserts had been arranged at one end of the table and then joined the buffet line, which had shrunk considerably. I wasn't particularly hungry, but a seat near Harvey Broadus had opened up and I wanted to take advantage. I filled my plate in haste and then crossed to the couch. He looked up as I approached. Nice blue eyes.

"Anybody sitting here?"

"No, go right ahead. I'm ready for dessert so you can save my place."

"Sure, no problem."

While he was gone, a woman in uniform came by picking up abandoned plates. I focused on the food, which turned out to be terrific. I ate with the usual animal enthusiasm, trying not to snuffle, belch, or spill down my front. Broadus returned with his dessert plate and a fresh glass of wine. "Thought you might need this," he said, setting the wineglass on the coffee table next to me.

"Thanks. I was about to go in search of the fellow with the Chardonnay."

Broadus held out his hand. "Harry Broadus."

"Kinsey Millhone," I said, shaking hands with him. I surveyed his dessert plate: a brownie, a wedge of fresh fruit tart, and a chunk of coconut sheet cake. "That looks good."

"My sweet tooth." He sat down again and balanced his plate on one knee. He chose the sheet cake first. "I caught sight of you earlier, sitting on the stairs."

"I'm not one for crowds and I don't know a soul. What about you? Are you a friend of Crystal's or Dow's?"

"Both. I was in business with Dow."

"Pacific Meadows?"

"That's right. What sort of work do you do?" He moved on to the brownie, making short work of it.

"Mostly research," I said. I took a big bite of roll so I wouldn't have to elucidate.

"Sad day," he said. "I feel terrible about Dow, though I wasn't surprised. He was unbelievably anxious and depressed in the weeks before he disappeared."

Oh good. Gossiping at a wake about the dead. How fun. I said, "The poor guy. About what?"

"I don't want to go into it . . . let's just say he left the clinic in a mess."

"Someone was telling me about that. Something to do with Medicare, wasn't it?" I took a bite of salad while he tackled the fruit tart.

"You heard about that?"

I nodded. "From a couple of different sources."

"I guess word must be out. That's too bad."

"What's the story?"

"We think it was probably an honest mistake, but we may never know."

"Doctors can sometimes be real dopes about business," I said, aping Penelope Delacourt.

"Tell me about it. We were shocked."

"I don't get what went on. I mean, as I understand it, the clinic doesn't actually do the billing. I thought there was an operating company to handle that."

He nodded. "Genesis Financial Management Services. They have offices downtown. Joel and I . . . you know Joel?"

"Met him once. I know his wife."

"Dana's great. I'm really crazy about her. Joel and I own the property through a company called Century Comprehensive, mostly real estate development, though we do other things as well. Genesis leases the physical plant from us. They also handle all the billing: accounts payable and receivable, Medicare, Medicaid—that sort of thing."

"So how'd Dow screw up?"

"That's what we're trying to figure out."

"Because I thought, you know . . . by law your company and the operating company had to be completely separate."

"True. But Genesis has to rely on the information they receive from Pacific Meadows. No one from the operating company's on site. If Dow reviewed and forwarded billing charges, Genesis took his word for it."

"So he could have told 'em anything he wanted."

"Could and did."

"How'd he get caught?"

"We're not sure. It might have been a guardian or relative of a patient who noticed the discrepancies and phoned in a complaint."

"What, to you guys?"

"To Medicare."

"A whistle-blower. Bad luck for him. So the fraud busters jumped in and followed up."

"That's our guess. At this point, we don't know what they have."

"What if it turns out it wasn't him?"

"His reputation's still ruined. A town this size, once

you've been tainted by rumor, it's almost impossible to recover your good name. People will be polite, but it's the kiss of death."

"I guess from Dow's perspective, the whole thing looked hopeless no matter what."

"More or less."

"What if it turns out he's innocent?" I said.

"Either way, we're left holding the bag." He glanced at his watch, set his plate aside, and got up. "Well. I better go find my wife. Nice talking to you, Kinsey. I hope our paths cross again in happier times."

"I hope so, too," I said. I lifted my wineglass. "Thanks for this."

"Glad to be a service."

I watched him cross the room, scouting for Celine.

What a bullshitter. Joel Glazer had been on the phone with Broadus the day I talked to him. I wasn't out of his office door before the information was passed on. What Broadus had told me about their business troubles was almost word for word the story I'd heard from Joel.

When I got back to my apartment, the phone was ringing. Two rings. Three. I let myself in and snatched up the phone before the machine kicked in. Tommy

Hevener. The moment I heard his voice, I realized I should have been screening my calls.

He said, "Hey, babe. It's me." His tone was both intimate and assured, like I'd been waiting all day in hopes of hearing from him. The sound of his voice gave me a jolt sufficient to make me salivate like a dog. I had to remind myself that while I didn't want to see him, I might need his help in getting Richard calmed down.

I ignored his seductive manner and said, "Hi. How are you?" All breezy and matter-of-fact.

"What'd you do to Richard? He's pissed as hell at you."

My stomach did a flip. "I know and I'm sorry. I feel terrible about that."

"What happened?"

"Ah. What happened. Well." *Think, think, think, think, think*. The lie lurched from my lips. "Lonnie wanted me to stay in the office, so he offered me a fifty percent discount on the rent."

"Why didn't you just say so? Richard would've understood that."

"I never had a chance. He was in such a rage I couldn't deal with him."

"Why didn't you tell me? We could have worked something out. Christ, and then on top of that he found out you went and put a stop on the check? You should

437

have seen him. He was screaming at the top of his lungs. You don't know what he's capable of once he gets like this."

I thought I knew Richard's capabilities. "Can't you talk to him for me?"

"That's what I've been trying to do. I thought if I heard your version of the story I could reason with him. You blew this one bad."

"You're right. I know that, but it's like I explained to him . . . I thought writing him a note would be less awkward than telling him in person."

"Big mistake. That's what set him off."

"I got that already. What do you think will happen next?"

"Hard to say with him. Maybe the whole thing will blow over. We can hope," he said. "Anyway, enough about him. When can we get together? I've missed you." His tone was playful, but it was all a front. I could either yield to him now or he'd go right on working on me until I did. I could feel a slow, stubborn anger begin to rise in my gut. I tried to keep my tone mild, but I knew the message wasn't one he'd accept. "Look, I don't think this relationship is going to work for me. It's time to let go."

There was dead silence. I could hear breathing on his end. I let the silence extend. Finally, he said, "This is your pattern, isn't it? Distancing yourself. You can't let anyone get close."

"Maybe so. Fair enough. I can see how you'd think that."

"I know you've been hurt and I'm sorry about that, but give me a chance. Don't shut me out. I deserve better than that."

"I agree. You do deserve better. Truly, I wish you well and I'm sorry things didn't work out."

"Can't we even talk about this?"

"I don't see the point."

"You don't see the *point*? What the hell is this?"

"I'm not going to argue. I'm sorry if I gave you the wrong impression—"

"Who the hell are you, thinking you can talk to me like this? You were the one came on to me."

"I'm hanging up now. Good-bye."

"Just a fuckin' minute. You stick it to my brother and I come to your defense and you think you can turn around and pull this kind of shit with me? You're out of your mind."

"Great. Perfect. Let's let it go at that." I set the phone down in the cradle. Belatedly, my heart began to bang like someone dribbling a basketball. I stood there waiting.

The phone rang and even though I was expecting it,

I jumped. Two. Three. Four. The machine picked up. I heard my outgoing message and then he hung up. Thirty seconds passed. The phone rang again. I lifted the handset and depressed the plunger, terminating the call. I turned off the ringer and then, for good measure, I unplugged the phone.

I sat at my desk and took a few deep breaths. I was not going to let the guy get to me. If I had to, I'd talk to Lonnie about getting a restraining order. In the meantime, I had to find a way to get him out of my head.

I took out my index cards and scribbled down numerous new notes, filling in a few blanks. Like a Tarot reading, I laid out a spread of cards for review. Joel Glazer, Harvey Broadus, and Pacific Meadows formed an arc. Attached to those cards, there were two more: Penelope Delacorte, the associate administrator, and Tina Bart, the bookkeeper, who'd been fired. Joel Glazer and Harvey Broadus had gone to great lengths to suggest that Dow was at fault in the Medicare scandal brewing under the surface. The one item that didn't fit was the note I'd made about the liaison between Broadus and the frisky charge nurse who serviced him.

I returned to the card for Tina Bart. Where had she gone? No doubt Penelope Delacorte knew, but she wasn't about to tell me. On impulse, I leaned over and opened my bottom drawer. I hauled out the phone book and turned to the *B*'s. When in doubt, says I, why not start with the obvious? Five *Barts* were listed; none of them *Tina* or *T*. There was a *C. Bart*, no address, conceivably short for *Christine* or *Christina*. Single women do this abbreviation bit to avoid all the heavy breathers out there who dial numbers at random while pinching their pants. I plugged in the phone again and tried the number for C. Bart. After two rings, a machine cut in. The voice on the other end was one of those mechanical butlers, some computer-generated robot who talked like he was living in a tin can. "Please leave a message." Use of this proto-male was another device used by single women, who like to create the illusion of a guy on the scene. I reached for the Polk Directory and looked for the telephone number listed for C. Bart. The Polk Directory, also known as 'the crisscross,' lists addresses and phone numbers in two different ways. Unlike the usual phone book, which orders its infor-mation alphabetically by name, the crisscross arranges the listings by the street address in one section and by the telephone number in the second section. If you have only a phone number without a street address, you can look up the number in the Polk and find the corre-sponding street and house number, plus the name of the person living there. Similarly, if you have only an address, you can track down the name of the occupant, along with the phone number, providing the number's published. In this case, I found C. Bart at an address on Dave Levine Street, not far from Pacific Meadows. Penelope Delacorte had told me that Tina Bart was already working at Pacific Meadows when she arrived on the scene. Time to find out how much she knew.

Before I left the apartment, I searched out my old gun and tucked it in my shoulder bag. The gun is a Davis .32 semiautomatic with a five-and-a-quarter-inch barrel, loaded with Winchester Silvertips. During the past three years, I've taken a raft of shit about my use of this firearm, which I'm told is cheap and unreliable — a judgment that hasn't altered my lingering affection for the piece. It's small and tidy, weighing a nifty twenty-two ounces, and it feels good in my hand. I didn't believe Richard or Tommy would actually come after me, but I couldn't be sure. And that, of course, was the nature of the game they played.

TWENTY-TWO

It was close to five o'clock as I traveled north on the 101. The afternoon light was already gone. Drizzle swirled through the moving traffic like a vapor and the action of the windshield wipers formed a fan-shaped smear where the mist settled on the glass and was waved away. Dave Levine is a one-way street heading toward town, so I was forced to take the Missile off-ramp and turn left onto Chapel. I swung up and around, catching the street at a higher point and following it down again. I passed Pacific Meadows on my right and began to scrutinize descending house numbers. The building I was looking for was only a block away. I found parking on the street and approached on foot, hunched against the misting rain.

The structure was a plain stucco box, four units in all, two up and two down, with an open stairwell up the middle leading to the second floor. Apartment 1 was on my right, with Apartment 2 just across from it.

SUE GRAFTON

The name Bart had been written in black marker pen and attached to the mail box for Apartment 3. I backed up ten steps and checked the second-story windows. Lights were on in several rooms on the front right-hand side. I climbed the stairs, knocked on the door, and waited. Behind me, through the open space between the halves of the building, I could see the rainfall like gauze swaddling the streetlights. A draft of air was being funneled through the gap and it was cold.

"Who is it?"

"Ms. Bart?"

I heard her secure the chain and then she opened the door a crack. "Yes?"

"Sorry to disturb you at home. I'm Kinsey Millhone. I'm a private investigator, working for Dr. Purcell's ex-wife. Could I talk to you?"

"I don't know anything. I haven't seen him in months."

"I'm assuming you heard his body was found up at Brunswick Lake?"

"I read that. What happened? The paper didn't really say."

"Would it make a difference to you?"

"Well, I don't believe he killed himself, if that's what they're trying to prove."

"I tend to agree, but we may never know. Meanwhile, I'm trying to reconstruct events that led up to his death. Can you remember when the two of you last spoke?"

She made no response, but there was information in her eyes.

A shift in the breeze blew a breath of fine rain against the side of my face. Impulsively, I said, "Could I come in? It's really getting chilly out here."

"How do I know you're who you say you are?"

I reached in my handbag and took out my wallet. I pulled my license from the windowed slot and pushed it through the crack to her. She studied it briefly and then handed it back. She closed the door long enough to undo the chain. She opened the door again.

As soon as I stepped inside, she went through the whole process in reverse. I removed my slicker and hung it on a hat rack near the door. I paused to look around. The interior was a curious mix of old charm and annoyances: arches and hardwood floors, narrow windows with yellowing wooden Venetian blinds, a clunky-looking wall heater near the bedroom door. The living room boasted a fireplace with a grate that supported a partially charred log resting on an avalanche of ash. The air in the apartment wasn't much warmer than the air outside, but at least there wasn't any breeze. Through an arch on the far wall, I caught a glimpse of the bathroom tile, a retro maroon-and-beige mix, probably installed when the place was built. Without even

445

seeing it, I knew the kitchen was bereft of modern conveniences: no dishwasher, no compactor, no garbage disposal. The stove would be original, a vintage O'Keefe and Merritt with two glass-fronted ovens and a set of matching salt and pepper shakers in a box on top. Rechromed and fully reconditioned, the stove would cost a fortune, though one oven would never work right and the hip young thing who bought it would unwittingly underbake her bread.

Tina indicated that I could take a seat in a gray upholstered chair while she returned to her place on the couch. She was younger than I'd expected, in her forties and so lacking in animation I thought she might be tranquilized. Her hair was the color of oak in old hardwood floors. She wore a sweat suit: gray drawstring pants and a matching jacket with a white T-shirt visible where the front was unzipped. She had her shoes off. The shape of her foot was outlined in dust on the soles of her white cotton crew socks. She seemed undecided what to do with her hands. She finally crossed her arms and tucked her fingers out of sight, as though protecting them from frostbite. "Why come to me?"

"Last Monday, I went over to St. Terry's and talked with Penelope Delacorte. Your name came up so I thought maybe you could fill in some blanks. May I call you Tina?" I asked, interrupting myself.

She lifted one shoulder in a careless shrug, which I

took as assent. "I know you and Ms. Delacorte left Pacific Meadows at about the same time. She said the choices here were pretty limited in the health care field. Have you found another job?" I hoped to give the impression of a long, friendly chat between Ms. Delacorte and me instead of the one we'd actually had.

"I'm still looking. I'm collecting Unemployment checks until my benefits run out." Her eyes were a pale gray, her manner flat.

"How long did you work for them?"

"Fifteen years."

"Doing what?"

"Front office. I was hired as a file clerk and worked my way up. Nights, I put myself through school and finally got my degree."

"In what?"

"Hospital Administration and Finance, which sounds more impressive than it is. I've always been more attracted to the accounting end of the business than to management, so I was happy where I was . . . more or less."

"Could I ask you some questions about Pacific Meadows?"

"Sure. I don't work there anymore and I have nothing to hide."

"Who owned the building before Glazer and Broadus?"

447

"A company called Silver Age Enterprises. I never knew the owner's name. There might have been more than one. Before that, there was another company called the Endeavor Group."

I reached into my handbag and took out a little spiral-bound notebook with a pencil tucked in the coil. I made a note of the two names "With Silver Age, was the place owned and operated by the same people or were those two functions kept separate?"

"They were separate. The Medicare and Medicaid programs were enacted in the '60s and neither had much provision for fraud prevention. The regulations about arm's-length ownership and operations probably didn't come until the late '70s, when Congress passed legislation establishing fraud control units . . . for all the good that did. You have no idea how many different agencies go after these guys: the Office of Inspector General, the civil and criminal divisions of the U.S. Attorney's Office, the FBI, HHS, HCFA, and MFCU— the Medicare Fraud Control Units. Doesn't deter the fraudsters. Cheaters love rules and regulations. Every time you put up a barrier, they figure out a way around it. One of the many challenges of the entrepreneurial spirit," she added drily. "I saw Pacific Meadows change hands three times and the price came close to doubling with each of those transactions."

I made another note, thinking about ways to check

out the dollar figures on those deals. "Did you work for Endeavor or Silver Age?"

"Actually, I think Silver Age was a subsidiary of Endeavor. The head of Endeavor was a woman named Peabody. She used to run all her personal expenses through our accounts payable. She'd renovate her house and write it off to Pacific Meadows as 'maintenance and repairs.' Or she'd put in new draperies at home and claim she'd had them installed in all the patients' rooms. Groceries, utility bills, travel and entertainment—she never missed a trick."

"Isn't that illegal?"

"Mostly. Some of it was probably legitimate, but a lot was fraudulent. I called a few items to the administrator's attention, but he told me, in effect, I'd better mind my own business. He said the company accountant routinely reviewed the books and everything was okay. I knew if I pressed the point, I'd have been out the door right then. It seemed easier to shut my mouth. When Silver Age came in, someone else handled the books for a while. Then he got fired and I took over again. There was probably some tinkering going on at that point, but I never figured out what it was."

"Why didn't you quit and find another job?"

"I loved the work."

"You could have loved the same work somewhere else, couldn't you?"

449

"True, but I got stubborn. I figured one day they'd crash and burn and I'd be there to watch, maybe throw additional fuel on the fire."

"Did anything change when Dr. Purcell arrived on the scene?"

"Not the first couple of months. Then I noticed an increase in the number of charge slips for things like ambulance service and physical therapy, portable X-ray equipment, wheelchairs. I started keeping notes and then I wrote a memo to Mr. Harrington, the head of the billing department at Genesis. That was a mistake as it turned out, but I didn't care. He never said as much, but I'm sure he didn't appreciate the effort because it put him on the spot."

"You were a regular troublemaker."

"I sincerely hope so."

"So even before the audit, they were unhappy with you."

She nodded and said, "Very. They let some time pass and then they fired me. Dr. Purcell tried to intervene, but he had no power and he was overruled. Penelope got upset and she quit in a huff, which really worked in their favor. It made it look like we were guilty of wrongdoing and Genesis was cleaning house. That still gave them Dr. Purcell as a fire wall if the MFCU investigation proceeded . . ."

"Which it did."

"Oh, yes. They're not going to give up until they nail this one down."

"As I remember it, Joel told me Genesis was part of a group called Millennium Health Care."

"It is, but my guess is that some, if not all, of those companies are shell corporations, set up to conceal the real ownership."

"As in what?"

"Company A, owned by Mr. Smith, buys a residential nursing home. Smith sets up a phony company with a slate of officers who appear to be unconnected to him. His company, A, sells the facility to this second company—also his—at a greatly inflated price, effectively converting the profits into capital gains . . ."

"Which are taxed at a lower rate," I said.

"Right. The second company can use the trumped-up value of the newly purchased facility as collateral for new loans. Meanwhile, bogus company C comes along and leases the building and grounds from the 'new' owner with a substantial boost in rents."

I held a hand up. "Hang on a minute." I ran the chronology back through my mind, trying to figure out what had caught my attention while she was laying it out to me. It wasn't anything she said; it was something I'd been wondering since I'd arrived at her door. "The night he disappeared, Dr. Purcell left Pacific Meadows at nine o'clock. Did he, by any chance, stop by to talk to you?"

She paused so long I didn't think she'd answer me. "Yes."

"About what?"

"He told me he had a meeting scheduled with the FBI. He thought he knew what was going on and who was behind it, namely Harvey and Joel."

"But those two wouldn't have been in any jeopardy, would they? I mean, from what I was told, they had nothing to do with the day-to-day running of Pacific Meadows. The real fiddle must have come from Genesis, since the Medicare checks were sent to them."

"There may be more of a connection than you think. Dr. Purcell must have gotten greedy because he began to sign off on charges he knew were fraudulent: X-ray and ambulance services among them. He probably took kickbacks for those. The FBI put the squeeze on him and that's why he agreed to help."

"But what would be the point of silencing him? There must be plenty of other people who know about the scam. You, for one."

"I never had any real authority. Now that he's gone, they can blame it all on him."

"Did he tell anyone else what he knew?"

"He never said so if he did."

"But why come to you? I gather you didn't even know him that well."

"He wanted my help. He figured I had nothing to lose."

"Do you think he told Joel and Harvey what he was up to?"

"Not if he was smart. I know he had lunch with Joel that day, but he didn't say anything else about it to me."

"I don't get it. With all these agencies at work, how come they haven't been caught?"

She shrugged. "Most of what they submit is legitimate and where the figures are false, everything else looks good. They use standard diagnoses and standard treatments. They're careful not to cross the line in any obvious way. It's like playing the float. They know how far they can push the system before the flags go up."

"But the flags did go up. Any idea why?"

"Someone must have phoned in a complaint because I talked to the fraud investigator last week and most of what I told him he already had in his files."

The phony bills for Klotilde had to be part of the scheme. "I've got some information that should be of help and I'd be happy to do a paper search early in the week if there's time."

"That'd be great. I'll be talking to him again and I can pass it on."

"Something else I'm unclear on. Why take the chance on billing items out to someone deceased?"

"Listen, you're dealing with the local, state, and federal governments. You get caught, you say 'Oops' and give the money back. You think the government would prosecute for a couple hundred dollars' worth of 'errors'?"

"Yeah, right. What's the story on Harvey Broadus and nurse what's-her-name . . . Pepper Gray?"

"He left his wife, Celine, for her and then I heard he went back."

I studied her carefully, wondering if she'd answer the question that had just come to mind. "Were you the one who phoned in the complaint to Medicare?"

"Someone else did that."

"Who?"

"I'm not sure, but I suspect she did."

"Pepper?"

"Yes."

"Pepper was the one who dimed them out?"

"Well, think about it. When Harvey broke off their relationship, she was in the perfect position to blow the whistle on them. I noticed her name or initials showed up most frequently on charges for questionable goods or services. She probably dummied up the slips from the floor. Why should she go on protecting him once he dumped her?"

"Well, they're certainly tight now."

"Really. That surprises me. Imagine the bind that puts her in if he finds out what she's done . . ." She let the thought trail, punctuated by a nearly imperceptible smile.

On my way home, I stopped by the office to pick up some index cards. I had two fresh packs in my desk drawer and I wanted to transfer the notes I'd managed to scribble in my spiral-bound notebook. I drove down Dave Levine as far as Capillo, where I made a left. Passing State Street, I could see that downtown Santa Teresa was deserted in the rain. It was after six P.M. on a Saturday and most retail stores had closed. Their windows were lighted, but the interiors were dim, sporting just enough wattage to foil the roving bands of burglars. I turned into the driveway running under Lonnie's building and parked in the narrow lot beyond.

I got out and locked my car door. Over the back wall, I could see lights coming from the cottage across the alleyway. I was unable to resist looking at the office space I'd leased one short week ago. The parking lot was empty: no sign of Tommy's pickup truck or his little red Porsche. The upper shutters along the right side of the one-story building were open, but the lowers had been closed. I saw a shadow intersect the light.

Maybe Richard was showing the office to someone new.

I turned away from the sight, knowing I was well out of it. What was done was done and there was no point entertaining regrets. I counted myself lucky Mariah Talbot had showed up when she did. Otherwise, I'd be renting from a couple of stone-cold killers. I crossed Lonnie's lot and trotted up the stairs to the third floor. I let myself into the law offices, which were lighted but empty. I went down the silent inner corridor and unlocked my office door.

I crossed to my desk, opened the bottom drawer, and picked up the two packs of blank index cards still in their cellophane wrap. I opened one and began to make notes. For the next hour, I felt safe, absorbed in my work. At 7:15 I put a rubber band around my note cards and tucked them in my handbag along with the extra pack of blank cards.

I locked the office and let myself out again, trotting down the outside stairs. At the first turn, I glanced out through the opening in the stairwell. It's not a window in any true sense of the word, just a slot, one foot wide and maybe two feet high, intended to help with ventilation. From the second floor, I had a clear view across the alleyway to the rear of the Heveners' cottage. The backdoor now stood wide open. In the office to the right (which I still thought of as mine) the shutters stood open. The light was on, but the window now had the blank look of unoccupied space. Something seemed off, but I wasn't quite sure what it was. Maybe someone had gone out for a moment, leaving the backdoor open for convenience. Whatever it was, I had no intention of going over there to snoop around.

I continued down the stairs and crossed the small parking lot to my car. I drove home by way of the supermarket, stopping long enough to pick up toilet paper, wine, milk, bread, eggs, Kleenex, and a tall stack of frozen entrées. Once in my neighborhood, I was forced to park a block and a half away, which annoyed me no end. With my bag and two loads of groceries, I had to struggle to let myself in the gate. Halfway across the patio, I caught a flash of movement to my right and someone stepped out of the dark. I jumped half a foot, barely managing to suppress a scream as I dropped one grocery bag and clutched at the other one. Tommy Hevener stood there, hands in his raincoat pockets. "Hey."

"Goddamn it! Don't do that! What are you doing here?"

"Let's talk."

"I don't want to talk. Now get out of my way." I hunkered to pick up my keys. One bag had ripped. I began to toss items back into the other bag. Half the carton of eggs were broken and the bread was mashed flat where I'd grabbed it in haste. I had no idea how I'd get into the apartment, lugging the few items that were still intact. "Oh, forget it," I said. I found my keys and crossed to my door, aware that Tommy had moved to intercept my path. He stretched out an arm, hand flat on the door, his body crowding against mine.

I turned my face to one side, trying to avoid contact. "Get away from me." I thought about my gun.

"Not until you tell me what's going on."

"If you don't get off me, I'm going to scream."

"You won't scream," he murmured.

"HENRY!"

"Shh!"

"HENRY!!"

Henry's back light went on. I saw his face appear in the door.

"HELP!"

"Bitch," Tommy said.

Henry came out the backdoor with a baseball bat. Tommy glanced at him, turned and walked away at a leisurely pace, showing his contempt, showing he wasn't intimidated. Henry came across the patio at a quick clip, bat raised, looking as angry as I've ever seen him. I could hear Tommy's heels clatter down the sidewalk, sound diminishing. "What was that about? Should I call the police?"

"Don't bother. By the time they get here, he'll be gone."

"Did he hurt you?"

"No, but he scared the shit out of me."

"I think you should file a police report. That way they'll have something on record in case he does this again."

"I'll talk to Jonah on Monday."

"Do more than talk. That guy's dangerous. You need to get a restraining order out against him."

"For all the good it will do. Really, I'm fine. Would you help me get this stuff in?"

"Of course. Open the door and we'll get this picked up in no time."

Sunday was full of hard rain and gloom. I spent the day in my sweats, stretched out on the couch under a quilt in my sock feet. I went through one paperback novel and picked up the next. I had another two for backup, so I was in good shape. At five o'clock, the phone rang. I listened to the message, waiting to hear who it was before I picked up. Fiona. I felt such relief I almost warmed to her. She said, "Sorry I didn't have a chance to speak to you after the service yesterday. Blanche had her baby late in the afternoon."

"She did? Congratulations. What'd she have?"

"A little girl. Seven pounds, eight ounces. They named her Chloe. Blanche was actually in labor at Dow's memorial. She and Andrew skipped the reception at the country club and went straight to St. Terry's. There wasn't even time to get her into the delivery room. She gave birth on a gurney in the corridor."

"Wow. That was close. How's she doing?"

"She's fine. The baby had to stay an extra day because of jaundice, but the doctor seems to think she's fine now. We'll bring her home this afternoon. I told Blanche I'd keep the children tomorrow so she can get some rest. I wish she'd have her tubes tied and put an end to this. She can't keep churning out infants. It's ridiculous."

"Well, I'm sure you're relieved everything's okay."

"Actually, I'm calling about something else. Last night when I went to the hospital to visit Blanche, I saw Crystal's white Volvo parked in the driveway of a house on Bay. You know that neighborhood. Parking's always at a premium. The hospital lot was full so I had to circle the block to find a space or I wouldn't have seen the car. Naturally, I was curious, so I went over again this morning and there it was. I'm assuming there's a way you can find out whose house it is."

"Sure, I can do that. Why don't you give me the

address?" I made a note as she recited it and then said, "What's your concern?"

"I think she's finally showing her true colors. You know the rumor about Crystal's affair with that trainer of hers, Clint Augustine. I put it out of my mind until I spotted her car and then I began to wonder. Whatever she's up to, I think it's worth pursuing, don't you?"

"Assuming it was her."

"The license plate said CRYSTAL, big as life."

"How do you know she was driving? It could have been anyone."

"I doubt that. Like who?"

"I don't know, Rand or Nica, one of the household help."

"Melanie suggested that as well, though I don't know why either one of you would stoop to defending her. I called Detective Paglia and told him you'd be looking into it. As I said to him, this is exactly the sort of thing they should have been doing from day one."

I was certain Detective Paglia appreciated her input.

After we hung up, I dialed the gym and Keith answered the phone. I could hear weights clanging in the background. The Sunday faithful. "Hi, Keith. Kinsey Millhone. When I was in there last week, I asked you about Clint Augustine. Do you happen to have an address and home phone number for him? I've been thinking a personal trainer might be fun for a change."

"Let me see what I got. Hang on." I could hear him open the desk drawer and then flip through the tattered three-hole binder I'd seen on other occasions. "I know I got it somewhere. Here we go."

I jotted down the information, noting that the address he gave me was a match for the Glazers' house in Horton Ravine. "How recent is this? Someone told me he had a place near St. Terry's on Bay."

"Don't think so. Least it's the first I've heard."

"When did you last talk to him? He might have moved."

"It's been months. Might have been February, March, back around then. He used to come in here regular, maybe eight, ten times a week, although he might have moved his clients to another gym. Let me know if he's out of business and I'll take his name off the books. I got other good trainers if he can't help."

"Great. I appreciate that."

I pulled the crisscross from my bookcase and leafed through the pages until I found Bay Street. I ran a finger down the house numbers until I came to the relevant address. I'd hoped Fiona was wrong, but the listed occupant was *J. Augustine*, though the phone number was different from the one Keith had given me. I dialed the number Keith had and got a disconnect; no surprise there. That must have been Clint's phone number while he was in the guest cottage on the Glazer property.

Clearly, Keith's information was out of date. I returned the crisscross to my shelf. I couldn't believe Crystal had gone looking for Clint the very day of Dow's memorial service. I picked up the phone and dialed the house on Bay.

The man who answered had a phone manner that bordered on the rude. "Yes?" His voice was harsh and full of impatience.

"May I speak to Clint?"

"He can't come to the phone. Who's this?"

"Never mind. I'll try later."

The house on Bay Street was an old Victorian, probably built in the late 1800s: two stories of white frame with a wide porch that stretched across the front. This was a neighborhood where many of the single-family dwellings had been converted to medical offices servicing the hospital half a block away. There was no sign of Crystal's Volvo in the drive. A white picket fence surrounded the yard, which was small and bare of grass, thickly planted with rose bushes, pruned now to clusters of thorny stems. I could imagine, in full bloom, the blossoms would smell as dense and sweet as a potpourri. The soil was darkly saturated from the rain, which was falling now in a soft haze.

I cruised past the house, did a turnaround at the

corner, and came back. I parked across the street and settled in to wait. Visiting hours at St. Terry's wouldn't begin in earnest for an hour so the streets were close to deserted. Even protected by a gauzy curtain of rain, I felt conspicuous sitting in the car by myself. This wasn't a surveillance—more like a sortie in the battle between Dow's wives. I didn't want to think about Crystal, whose history with men had been a series of disasters. She'd gotten pregnant by one guy and apparently been left to raise the child on her own. She'd had one husband who abused her and another who looked oh-so respectable on the surface, but, in fact, drank too much and had a peculiar bent in bed. Clint was in his early forties, a good-looking guy, big and well built. He didn't seem that bright, but he had enormous patience with his clients, whose struggles with fitness were both diligent and short-lived. The last time I remembered seeing him was just after New Year's when a new batch of converts arrived at the gym, whipped into a frenzy of repentance after the holiday indulgences. His clientele was literally always heaviest around that time. Crystal had way too much class to dally with the likes of him. On the other hand, she was only one marriage away from life as a stripper, and as slick as she seemed, she probably wasn't a whole lot smarter than he. In love, as in other matters, people end up seeking their own level. I adjusted my rearview mirror, ever mindful of Tommy Hevener. Just because I didn't see him didn't mean he wasn't there. I could feel my bowels squeeze down every time I thought of him.

By 6:25 I decided Crystal wasn't going to show. I'd already started my car when a white Volvo turned the corner off Missile and headed in my direction. She was at the wheel.

465

TWENTY-THREE

I killed the engine and sat, watching as she slowed and pulled into the drive. I grabbed my umbrella and got out of my car as she was getting out of hers. This was one of those occasions where asking a direct question seemed the obvious route. I wasn't going to lurk in the bushes or peep over windowsills in search of the truth. "Crystal?"

She'd already let herself through the gate and she turned to look at me. She wore a rain-repellent parka, cowboy boots, tight jeans, and a heavy white cableknit sweater. She clutched a neat stack of shirts against her body to protect them from the damp. Her makeup was light and her tousled blond hair was pulled into a knot. She stood with one hand on the latch and I could see her puzzlement.

"Can I talk to you for a minute?"

Her response time was ever so faintly slow. "About what?"

"Clint. We happen to be members of the same fitness gym."

"What do you want?"

I shook my head. "Someone saw your car here and thought you might show up again."

She closed her eyes and then opened them again. "Fiona."

I didn't cop to it outright, but I didn't see much reason to deny it, either. What was the point? She knew I'd been working for Fiona and who else, really, would be dogging her steps. "You should probably be aware she talked to Detective Paglia."

"Fuck. She just can't leave anything alone. What's she going to do, monitor my actions for the rest of my life? Have me followed around so she can point a finger at me? What I do with my time is none of her damn business."

"Hey, babe. It wasn't my idea. If you're pissed off, take it up with her."

"Oh, right." She paused while she struggled to get a grip on herself. When she spoke again, her tone was more resigned than angry. "Let's get out of the rain. It's ridiculous to stand here getting soaked."

I followed her through the gate. We went up the front steps and took shelter on the porch. I lowered my umbrella, pausing to shake off the water.

"I guess there's no point pretending you didn't see me today."

"I don't like it any more than you do."

"You know, the entire time I was married to Dow, she did everything she could to make life miserable for me. How much more shit am I supposed to take?"

"She's not the only one who heard the rumor about Clint."

"Who'd she get that from? Dana Glazer, no doubt. What an evil bitch she is."

"People talk about these things. Sooner or later, it was bound to come out."

"Oh, for pity's sake. You know what? There's no law that says I can't visit a friend, so why don't you go back and tell her to get fucked." She gestured dismissively, annoyed with herself. "Skip that," she said. "Why add fuel to the fire? Clint was my trainer. We did weights. End of sentence. There was never anything sexual between us. Ask him if you doubt me. I'll be happy to wait out here."

"What would that prove? I'm sure he's too much of a gentleman to kiss and tell."

"Don't you have any male friends? Does everything between a man and a woman have to be sexual?"

"I didn't say you were guilty of anything. I'm telling you how it looks. Tongues have been wagging. Fiona saw your car here yesterday and here you are again today."

She stared at me briefly and then seemed to make a

decision. "Why don't you come in and I'll introduce you properly."

"Why would I do that?"

"Why not? As long as you've come this far. By the way, I found Dow's passport when I was going through his clothes. It was still in the breast pocket of the overcoat he wore when we went to Europe last fall."

"Well, that's one question down. Are those his?" I said, pointing to the shirts.

"Someone might as well get some use out of them."

She unlocked the front door, using a key, I noticed, from her own key chain. She pushed open the door and stepped aside, allowing me to pass in front of her and into the house. I don't know why I should have felt embarrassed, but I did.

The front room was done up as an old-fashioned parlor with a camelback sofa, occasional tables, and assorted Queen Anne chairs. Every item of furniture sported a hand-crocheted doily designed as protection from dirt and grease stains. There was a grandfather clock and lots of knickknacks; milk glass, cranberry glass, Steuben glass, Lladro, framed photographs of family members long since deceased. Crystal scarcely gave the room a glance as she proceeded down the hallway and through the kitchen to a glassed-in porch. Clint was seated in a Lazy-Boy looking out toward the yard. She put the stack of shirts on a small wooden table next to him. Crystal gave him a brief kiss on the top of his head. "I brought you some shirts and I also brought a friend. You remember Kinsey? She's a member of your gym."

At first, I thought: not Clint, mistake, has to be someone else. But it was him. Whatever his disability, he was considerably diminished. He was suffering contractures of his hands and a muscle weakness so pronounced, he could hardly move his head. He'd lost an enormous amount of weight. His eye sockets were puffy, a reddish-purple color, as though he'd been punched out. I could see skin lesions on his forehead and his arms. I tuned the rest of it out. Through the window, I could see a burly old guy working in the yard, tying up some vines; probably Clint's father, the man who answered the phone.

Crystal was saying, "We just ran into each other and she was asking about you."

"How're you doing?" I said, feeling like a fool. Clearly, he wasn't doing well and might never do well again.

"Clint has a systemic connective tissue disease called dermatomyositis. Severe in his case. It may be an autoimmune reaction, though nobody really knows. This has been going on since, what . . . the end of January, isn't it?" She addressed her remarks to him, as though for confirmation. "The doctors were hoping he'd go into remission so it seemed advisable for him to lay low."

"Is that why he rented the Glazers' cottage?"

"That's right. I wanted him close so I could keep an eye on him. After the lease ran out, it seemed best to have him move in with his parents for a while." She leaned closer to him. "Where'd your mom go, is she out?"

Clint's response was garbled, but she seemed to understand him, probably because she'd tracked his degenerating speech patterns for the past ten months.

"Why didn't you let people know what was going on?"

"Clint asked me not to and I honored his request. As long as you're prying, will there be anything else?"

"I'll have to tell Fiona."

"Of course," she said. "That's what she pays you for. I'm surprised you'd even mention it."

"It might go a long way to getting her off your back."

Crystal smiled at Clint, who was watching her with a doglike devotion. "Cat's out of the bag," she said. "Remember Dow's ex-wife? She finally figured out we were having a torrid love affair. Kinsey's caught us in the act."

I could feel myself flush. Clint seemed to enjoy the joke and I could hardly protest. I said, "I probably ought to go."

"Good. He gets tired when we have visitors. I'll walk you to the door."

I could feel a brittle rage radiating from her as she accompanied me. I knew she resented the invasion of privacy, both his and hers. "Look, I'm sorry."

"Forget it."

"Did Dow know?"

"Someone else might have told him. I certainly didn't. People want to believe the worst. That's the hell of it," she said.

The freeway traffic was crawling, cars end to end, apparently slowed by an accident farther up the road. I drove home on surface streets to avoid the mess. All the streetlamps were on and the roads gleamed like patent leather in the falling rain. In my neighborhood, the houses glowed with light. I found parking right in front of Henry's. I was grateful for that as it saved me the half-block of splashing through puddles. I went through the squeaking gate and around the corner of my studio to the rear. Henry's kitchen lights were out. He was probably over at Rosie's where I'd catch up with him in a bit.

I unlocked my door and let myself in. As I closed the door behind me, someone slammed against it from the outside and sent me hurtling. My shoulder bag struck the floor with a *thunk* and I saw my key ring sail off and land on the rug. I went sprawling, hands flying out instinctively to catch myself. I hit the floor and rolled as Tommy Hevener grabbed me by the hair, pulled me upright, and dragged me backward. I stumbled into him and he sat down abruptly, pinning me across his knees. I'd been flipped like a turtle and I was on my back, flailing for purchase. His raincoat was in a tangle but offered enough protection that I couldn't land a blow.

He choked me with one hand while he squeezed his fingers around my face, digging into my jaw so hard it forced my mouth open. He stuck his face against mine. I could feel his breath against my mouth. "Henry gave you the name of a jeweler in L.A. Turns out there isn't any such guy, so what the fuck was that about?"

The door swung back again and banged once against the wall. I shrieked, rolling my eyes in that direction. Richard was standing in the doorway in his black raincoat. He closed the door behind him, looking on with indifference as Tommy tightened his grip.

"Answer me."

"I don't know. I never dealt with him. Someone told Henry. He was just passing it on. You were there."

473

"No." He shook my head, using my hair for leverage.

I clawed at his hand, trying to pry his fingers off. The pain was excruciating. "Let go, let go. That's it. That's all. I never called the guy. I swear."

"Tell me you didn't find the safe and help yourself."

"What safe?"

"The fuckin' safe in the office. Don't play dumb. You know exactly what I mean. You broke in. You ripped us off and we want the stuff back."

"What stuff? I don't even know what you're talking about."

Richard said, "Get her up."

Tommy didn't move. His grip on my hair was so tight, I thought he'd tear out a hunk of my scalp. I couldn't move my head. I was nearly sick with fear. What had Mariah done? Had she set me up?

Richard said, "Tommy."

Grudgingly, Tommy loosened his grip. I turned on my side and rolled away from him. I lifted myself as far as my hands and knees, shaking my head while I gasped for breath. "I don't know anything about a safe. I never saw it." I put one hand against my throat, trying to suck down air. "I'd have to be an idiot to break in. I still have a key. It's on my key ring."

I fumbled across the rug for my keys and held them up to him. "Look at this. Think about it. If I'd done it, I'd have closed the place so you wouldn't know. Why would I leave it open and call attention to the break-in?"

"How'd you know the place was left open?" Richard asked. He seemed calmer than Tommy, but no less dangerous. He took the ring of keys and sorted through them until he found the office key, which he worked out of the bunch. He tossed the remaining keys to Tommy. I directed my response to both, looking from one to the other.

"Because my office is right there. Across the alley-way." Richard was silent and I felt myself babbling on. "I'm telling you the truth. Last night I stopped at the office. I looked across the alley and saw the door standing open."

"What time?"

"Seven, I think. Sometime around then."

Tommy said, "Why didn't you call the cops?"

"I thought it was Richard and he was showing the place."

Tommy was sitting with his knees drawn up, shaking his head. "Jesus. You don't know how much trouble we're in. Christ, everything is gone. Every goddamn . . ."

"Shut up, Tommy. She doesn't need to know. Let's get her out of here before someone shows up."

"I'm sorry your valuables were stolen, but it wasn't me. I swear."

"Yeah, well we're sunk, anyway. Wiped out. It's over."

"Knock it off," Richard said, and hauled me to my feet. "You take her. I'll drive."

"*I'll* drive. It's my truck."

"Right." Richard locked his arms around me, pinning my arms against my body. He lifted me off the floor and walked me to the door, half-dragging me, half-carrying.

I grabbed the door frame long enough to get my feet down. I stiffened my knees, forcing him to halt. "Let me get my bag," I said, gesturing. I felt like a kid pleading for her teddy bear. Tommy leaned down and picked up my shoulder bag. He did a quick search, pawing through the contents. He found the Davis, checked the load, and tucked it in his pocket, tossing the bag aside. There went that hope. I glanced back, watching him turn the lights out and pull the door shut before he joined us on the patio.

His truck was parked around the corner. Richard held my left arm, his fingers digging into me so hard I knew I'd bruise. The two of them crowded against me, walking in a lockstep that forced me to trot along. What were they going to do with me, rape, maim, and kill? What would be the point of that? If they took me to the house, I could scream my bloody head off and no one would hear.

We reached the pickup truck. Richard opened the door on the passenger side. He flipped the seat forward and shoved me into the narrow space behind the seats, knocking my head against the frame in the process.

I said, "Hey!" This was pissing me off. I managed to rub my head while I squeezed into the well. Tommy got in on the driver's side. The two doors slammed in quick succession like rifle shots. Tommy jammed the key in the ignition and the engine fired to life. He pulled out with a chirp that probably left a little skid of rubber on the pavement. I clung to the seat back, trying to assess the situation.

For the moment, I was safe. Tommy was too busy driving to pay attention to me and Richard didn't have a sufficient angle to turn around and level more abuse. Rain was stinging against the windshield. Tommy flipped on the wipers.

I said, "Where'd you have the safe? The place always looked empty to me."

Tommy said, "In the closet floor, under the wall-to-wall carpeting."

"Don't play dumb." Richard was bored.

"How many people knew besides the two of you?"

Tommy said, "No one."

Richard snorted. "What's this, twenty questions? Would you give it a rest."

"Who opened it last?"

"Jesus, Tommy, this is bullshit. Are you buying this act?"

"He did. We had something we wanted to sell. He goes all the way down to Los Angeles on Friday and there isn't any such dude. He thought I pulled a fast one and he was pissed."

"When did he get back? Was it late?"

"No, it wasn't late," Richard snapped, exasperated. It's five o'clock. I go over to the office and put the piece back in the safe."

"Everything else was still there?"

"Of course it was. Now would you shut the fuck up?"

"Maybe someone saw you with the stuff and followed you back. If they saw where the safe was hidden, they could have waited until you left and ripped you off."

"I said, shut your mouth!" He raised his left arm, torqued around in the seat, and bashed me in the face with a backhanded swing. The blow didn't have much force, but it hurt like a son of a bitch. I felt tears burn my eyes. I put my hands across my nose, hoping he hadn't broken it. Didn't feel like that.

Tommy said, "Hey! Cut it out."

"Who put you in charge?"

"Just leave her alone."

"Why, because you're fucking her?"

"He is not!" Who wants to be accused of screwing some guy you can barely tolerate? There was a moment of silence. Then, I said, "Anyway, how'd they get the safe open? Was it drilled?"

"You are just not going to shut up, are you?"

I thought the question was a good one, but I shut my mouth and leaned away from the front seat, out of range. The space where I was sitting was small and cramped, scratchy with cheap carpeting. I groped around, hoping for a weapon—a wrench or a screwdriver—but found nothing. I felt along the circumference of the well and my fingers closed over a ballpoint. I didn't think it'd be effective, but then again, why not? I clutched the pen in my fist, wondering what would happen if I jammed it in Richard's ear.

The drive to the house took seven minutes at top speed on the wet-slick roads that wound through Horton Ravine. I held on for dear life, the turns throwing me first this way and then that. As Tommy wheeled up the driveway, he picked up the remote control for the two double garage doors and hit one of the buttons. The double door on the left began to roll open and a light came on. He pulled in, coasted to a stop, and set the hand brake. The adjacent bay was empty. Tommy's red Porsche sat in the next bay over and on the other side of that was a second Porsche, a shiny black one, presumably Richard's.

479

Richard opened the door and got out. He left the truck door ajar. I could see the two big garbage cans just outside the kitchen door where they tossed their trash. Above them, I could see a line of buttons on the wall. I thought he meant to hit one so the garage door would grind shut, but he peered into the truck bed. He opened the tool box and fumbled among the contents. I measured the distance, but I wasn't going to have time enough to lean forward, pull the door shut, and lock it before he got to me. I turned to Tommy. "You were at my house last night. I saw someone in the office when I stopped off on my way home. You couldn't have stolen anything and then showed up at my place so soon afterward."

He turned to look at me. "What?"

"If it wasn't you, it was him. Who else knew the combination? Just the two of you, right?"

Richard came back with a coil of rope. "Nobody asked you. Now get out."

"Tommy, think about it. Please."

Tommy sat there for a moment. He got out of the truck and moved around the front to the passenger side. "Richard, what are we doing? This is dumb. We should have left her where she was. She doesn't know anything."

Richard scarcely looked at him. "Back off. I'll take care of it."

"Who put you in charge? What the hell is that for?"

"I'm going to tie her up and kick the shit out of her until she tells us where she hid the stuff."

"You're not thinking straight."

"Who asked you?" Richard said. "I told you not to fuck with her. This is all your fault."

"Oh, really. Now it's my fault," Tommy said. His annoyance had passed and there was something new in his face. He put his hand in his coat pocket; I knew he'd put the gun in one pocket, but I couldn't remember which. "You know she's got a point. I know where I was last night and I can prove it because of her. How do I know you didn't clean out the safe yourself?"

Richard snorted. "Why would I do that? I don't have anyone to lay it off on, if you'll remember."

"You say that now. You could have taken everything to L.A. when you went on Friday. You could have sold it all and kept the money, then come back here and made it look like a burglary. There's only your word you put it back where it was. I never saw the jewelry after you came back."

"That's bullshit."

"I'll give you bullshit. The safe wasn't drilled. Somebody had the fuckin' combination. There are only two of us who knew. I know it wasn't me, so that leaves you."

"Stick it up your ass," Richard said. He put his hand

on the seat back so he could reach for me. I leaned forward and swung the pen in an arc and brought it down hard on the back of his hand. Richard bellowed with rage. He tried to grab me, but I scooted back to the driver's side of the truck. Enraged, he flipped the seat forward, prepared to haul me out. I braced myself and kicked twice at his hand. I caught him smartly with the heel of my Saucony, jamming three of his fingers.

"Fuck!" He pulled his hand back, flashing a furious look at Tommy. "Jesus, Tommy. Help me out here."

"Answer my question."

"Don't be an idiot. I didn't take anything. Now let's get her out of here."

"You and I were the only ones who knew. Fuck this burglar shit. There wasn't any burglar."

Richard slammed the passenger side door. "All right, you shit. I'm telling you the truth. I didn't do it. You get that? I wouldn't do that to you, but you'd do that to me because you've done it before. So how do I know it wasn't you?"

"I didn't open the safe. You did that, Richard. You made a point of going down to L.A. alone. The jewelry's gone now, you—"

Richard flew forward and grabbed Tommy by the front of his coat. He pulled him forward and then shoved. Tommy stumbled but regained his footing and came back at him. I saw Richard's fist fly out, catching

Tommy in the mouth. He went down, tumbling backward into the two plastic garbage cans that shot apart like bowling pins. I leaned down and reached around the side of the seat, fumbling for the lever that would release the seat back. I felt the lock give way. I opened the door on the driver's side. I slithered through the gap, crouched, and came up along the fender still in a crouch. I could hear the chilling sound of flesh on flesh, a grunt as someone took the brunt of a blow. I lifted my head. Tommy was dragging himself to his feet, trying to free the Davis from his raincoat pocket. His legs seemed to weaken under him and he went down. There was blood streaming from his nose. He moaned, looking up at his brother in a daze. Richard kicked him. He bent down and took the gun from Tommy's rubbery grip. He stepped back and levered the Davis at his brother. Almost lazily, Tommy put a hand up and said, "Oh, Richie, don't."

Richard fired. The bullet tore into Tommy's chest, though the blood was slow to come.

Richard looked blankly at his brother's body and nudged him with his foot. "Serves you right, you little shit. Don't accuse me."

He tossed the gun aside. I heard it clatter across the garage floor and skitter under the truck. He hit the button that activated the other garage door. His manner was matter-of-fact as he moved around the red Porsche to the black one and got in. He started the car and put it in reverse. Engine whining, he backed out of the garage and down the drive.

I scrambled around the front of the truck on my hands and knees. I crawled over to Tommy to check his pulse, but he was dead. I spotted the gun. I was just about to pick it up when I caught myself. My hand veered off abruptly like an airplane pilot aborting a landing. No way would I mar the fingerprints that Richard'd left on the gun. I got up and went through the back door, turning the deadbolt behind me as I headed for the phone. I was feeling cold with dread, worried Richard would turn around and come back for me.

I dialed 911 and told the dispatcher about the shooting. I explained who the shooter was, gave her his name, a description of his Porsche, and his license number, H-E-V-N-E-R-1. I recited the address in Horton Ravine, repeating everything twice. She told me to remain at the scene until the officers arrived. I said, "Sure" and hung up. After that, I dialed Lonnie.

TWENTY-FOUR

I finally crawled into bed at midnight. Detectives Paglia and Odessa arrived at the Heveners shortly after Lonnie showed up and they at least *pretended* to be sympathetic as they talked me through the events leading up to Tommy's death. They viewed me as a witness, not a suspect, which greatly affected their handling of me. Lonnie rode herd on them, nonetheless, protecting my rights any time he thought they were crossing the line in the course of the interview. The crime scene investigation seemed to take forever: fingerprints, sketches, and photographs; the endless narrative loop, in which I laid it all out again in excruciating detail. They bagged and tagged the Davis as evidence. It would probably be a year before I saw that gun again. Richard Hevener was picked up within the hour, driving south on the 101, on his way to Los Angeles. I figured it was still remotely possible he'd taken the jewelry, but I was not convinced. Lonnie was the one who drove me home.

Monday morning, I skipped the run and then I skipped the gym. I was feeling creaky and sore, my body a patchwork of bruises. Emotionally I was feeling battered as well. I drove to the office and circled the block, finally finding a parking spot about six blocks away. I hobbled the distance and took the elevator up. When I walked into the firm, Jeniffer was sitting at her desk, applying a final coat of polish to her fingernails. For once, Ida Ruth and Jill didn't seem interested in persecuting her. I found the two of them chatting in the corridor. At the sight of me, they fell silent and fixed me with compassionate looks. Jill said, "Coffee's on in back. Shall I bring you a mug?"

"I'd appreciate that."

I went into my office and dialed Fiona's number. When she answered the phone, we exchanged the obligatory chitchat. I was guessing she hadn't heard about the shooting because she never mentioned it. Or maybe she didn't care. That was always a possibility with her.

In the background, I could hear metal banging, the scraping of chairs, and assorted shrieks: Blanche's four rowdy kids spending the day at Grandma's. With Fiona's bare cement floors, it sounded like a roller rink or bumper cars. I said, "I have the answer to your question about the person living in that house on Bay. Turns out it's Clint Augustine's father and Clint's living with him . . ."

"I told you they were having an affair."

"Well, not quite."

Jill appeared and set a mug of coffee on my desk. I blew her a kiss and went on to describe Clint's medical condition, which I gave Fiona by name. I'd read about dermatomyositis in the *Merck Manual* I have sitting on my desk at home. Altogether not good, and his particular symptoms seemed severe. "I'm guessing that in the last year, he's been in no shape to engage in a sexual liaison or any other kind, for that matter." I found it a relief to be talking about something other than the night before.

Fiona's response was grudging. "Perhaps I've misjudged her."

"Hard to know," I said, not wanting to rub it in.

"What about the missing money?"

"The cops are looking into it so I'll leave that to them. I won't be charging for the time I put in."

She seemed to shake off her disappointment. "Well, I suppose that takes care of business. If you like, you can calculate what I owe you and deduct it from the balance of the retainer. No need for a final report. This call will suffice."

"Sure, I can do that. I'll put a check in the mail to you this afternoon."

There was a moment's hesitation. "I wonder if I could ask you to bring me that in cash?"

"Sure. No problem. I can have it up there this afternoon."

I was sitting at my desk, cleaning and organizing my files when Jeniffer came and handed me a note.

Kinsey,

Sorry I had to do that to you, but I didn't have a choice. Here's the difference between us: basically, you're decent and have a conscience. I don't.

Mariah

"Where'd you get this?"

"It was just sitting on my desk."

Feeling sick I finally lifted the receiver and dialed 713 ... the Houston, Texas, area code ... and then 555–1212, for Directory Assistance. When the operator came on, I asked her for the sheriff's department in the county where Hatchet was located. She gave me the number and I made a note of it. I let it sit on my desk while I took out the file Mariah Talbot had given me. I glanced through the news clippings until I spotted the name of the sheriff who'd handled the Hevener murder case. I tried Mariah's number first and got the same recorded message I'd heard before. "Hello, this is Mariah Talbot. You've reached the offices of Guardian Casualty Insurance in Houston, Texas, . . ." I depressed the plunger. Anyone can leave a recorded announcement on an answering machine. Anyone can have a stack of business cards printed.

I dialed the Texas number and asked for Sheriff Hollis Cayo. I identified myself and told him where I was calling from. "I'm wondering about two murders you investigated in 1983. This was Jared and Brenda Hevener."

"I remember them," he said. "They were both fine people and deserved better than they got. How can I help?"

"I thought I should pass along some information. Tommy Hevener died last night. His brother shot him in the heat of an argument."

There was a moment of quiet while he took that in. "I can't say I'm surprised. I hope you're not telling me Richard's headed this way."

"No, no. The cops picked him up and put him in the county jail out here. I understand he's broke so the public defenders office will probably handle the case," I said. "One thing I was wondering. Was Casey Stonehart ever caught?"

"No, ma'am. He's gone, disappeared right after the

murders, probably the work of them two boys as well. Our best guess is he's dead, but we may never know. Texas is a big state. Lot of acreage available for unmarked graves."

"I understand Brenda Hevener's sister and Guardian Casualty Insurance intend to file suit. Have you heard about that?"

"Yes, ma'am. I believe they're in the process of gathering information even as we speak. What's your interest?"

"I had an insurance investigator come into my office a week ago and I wondered if you knew her. This is a woman named Mariah Talbot."

I could hear the smile in his voice. "Yeah, we know her. 'Mariah the Pariah.' You're talking five foot nine, a hundred and forty pounds, twenty-six years old. Blue eyes and her hair's turned prematurely gray."

"Well, I'm glad to hear you say that. I was beginning to think she'd misrepresented herself. How long has she worked for Guardian Casualty?"

"I never said she did. Fact is, Talbot's the name of Casey's older brother. Got another one named Flynn. I think there's another couple brothers in there some-where, but those are the two I dealt with. The fact is, that whole family's bad. In jail and out, a bunch of sociopaths."

I could feel myself squint. "And what's her connection?"

"The woman you're talking about is Casey's sister, Mariah Stonehart. The only girl."

I said, "Ah."

After we hung up, I laid my little head down on the desk. I should have known, I guess, but there was no doubt about it, she was slick.

At 10:30 I went over to the courthouse to do a records check for Tina Bart. I figured it would be a comfort to bury myself in endless mundane paperwork, where the chances of violence and betrayal were reduced to a minimum. Besides, I was genuinely curious about Glazer's business dealings, specifically his connection to Genesis Financial Management Services. The MFCU investigator was probably tracking the three larger corporations I'd heard mentioned—Millennium Health Care, Silver Age, and the Endeavor Group. Somehow I had the feeling things were beginning to snowball for Joel Glazer and his partner, Harvey Broadus.

I started with the Assessor's Office in the County Administration building, where I looked up the property tax records for Pacific Meadows. As expected, Glazer and Broadus were listed as the owners. Under their individual names, I checked for other properties they might own and made a list of those. I left the Assessor's Office and walked over to the courthouse to the County Recorder's Office. Files there were arranged according to the Grantor and Grantee Indexes: those who sell and those who receive. I spent an hour working my way through real property sales, grant deeds, trust deeds, tax liens, quit claims, and reconveyances. Tina Bart had been right. The Pacific Meadows building and lot had changed hands three times in the past ten years, and each sale had represented a substantial jump in price. The property was sold to Maureen Peabody in 1970 for $485,000. She'd sold it, in turn, to the Endeavor Group in 1974 for a tidy $775,000. The property sold again in 1976 to Silver Age for $1,500,000, and was finally purchased by Glazer and Broadus's company, Century Comprehensive, in 1980 for a whopping $3 million. By calculating the documentary transfer tax on the grant deed, I could see that the current assessed value was $2,700,000.

I crossed the street to the public library and started working my way back through the city directories, looking for Maureen Peabody. Moving back and forth between the city directory and the crisscross, I discovered she was the widow of a man named Sanford Peabody, who'd been an officer at the Santa Teresa City Bank from 1952 until his death in the spring of 1969.

Maureen had probably used the money she inherited from his estate to buy the nursing home.

On a hunch, I returned to the courthouse and checked the marriage records for 1976 and 1977. In February of 1977, I found a record of the marriage license issued to Maureen Peabody and Fredrick Glazer, a second marriage for both. She was fifty-seven at the time and he was sixty-two. It didn't take much to figure out that Maureen was Joel Glazer's stepmother. I was betting Maureen's name would appear again among the corporate officers of both Endeavor and Silver Age. The only question remaining was who owned Genesis, the operating company for Pacific Meadows. I found the company listed among the applications for registration of a fictitious business name. The owner of record was Dana Jaffe, Doing Business As Genesis Financial Management Services. The mailing address was in Santa Maria. For her home address, she'd used the house in Perdido, where she'd lived at the time I was looking for Wendell Jaffe. Joel Glazer had probably talked her into signing the DBA application before they married. She may or may not have understood the significance. On the surface, Genesis appeared to be separate and unrelated to Pacific Meadows. In truth, Glazer controlled both, which put him in the perfect position to reap the benefits of all the bogus Medicare claims. I was glad

I wouldn't be around when Dana found out she was married to another crook. She was pissed when I helped to put her son in jail. Wait until she had to forfeit her life in Horton Ravine.

I left the courthouse, blinking at the hazy light as though emerging from a darkened theater. I glanced at my watch. It was now close to noon and I was curious what was going on with the police investigation. I deducted the two additional hours' work Fiona'd authorized. I then went by the bank and withdrew the $975 I owed her. I crossed Anaconda and walked along Floresta to the walkway where the Arcade sandwich shop was located. The take-out window was open but didn't seem to be doing much business. The picnic tables and benches were still way too wet for use. As I passed the plate glass window, I caught sight of Odessa sitting by himself at one of the small marble tables. The place was empty except for him, though the funky indoor coffee shop across the way was jammed. I waved and went in. I sat down in the bentwire chair across the table from him.

"How're you doing?" he said.

"I've been through worse. I thought you'd be doing take-out and eating at your desk today."

"Too depressing. I need light. Fluorescent bulbs make me want to kill myself." He was working on another paper-wrapped burger in a red plastic basket surrounded by fries.

"At least you're eating well."

Odessa smiled. The damp air had added a halo of frizziness to his already unruly dark hair. Any woman in his position would be despairing, trying a succession of hair sprays, gels, mousses, and anti-frizz products. Paglia had it right: he'd shaved himself bald. Odessa gestured at the fries, fully expecting me to take one.

I shook my head. "I'm fine. I've just been nosing around in the public records. It looks like Dr. Purcell's business associates have been working a Medicare scam and trying to push the blame off on him."

"You're talking about Glazer?"

"And Harvey Broadus. Purcell had figured it out and had a meeting scheduled with the FBI. Who knows how far the two of them were willing to go to keep him quiet. What's the coroner have to say?"

"He found powder tattooing on his right temple. He didn't have much to work with, but he says it looks more like near-contact than a contact wound. Means the gun was held a short distance away instead of pressed right up against the skin. Purcell could have done it himself if his shooting arm was another eight inches long. They went back to scour the area near the reservoir, but so far no bullet. I think they're going to broaden their search. Could be he was shot somewhere else and then the car was moved."

"That'd be tricky, wouldn't it? With him sitting at the wheel?"

"That bugged Jonah, too. You know him. He got to thinking about that blanket Purcell had over him. Mohair, pale green? He asked Crystal and she said it was a gift from her. A year ago she put together this emergency road kit in case he ever got stuck: snacks, flashlight, bottled water, first-aid supplies—all of which he kept in the trunk of his car. Blanket was part of that. Jonah thinks the killer could have spread it over the body and then sat on his lap to drive him up to where we found the car. The blanket was used to keep the blood off his clothes."

"Well, that's pretty cold-blooded. Wouldn't the mohair leave fibers on the killer's pants?"

"Sure. Blood traces, too, but there's been plenty of time to dispose of the evidence."

I picked up a french fry, doused it in catsup, and put it down again. "I talked to Crystal last night. She came across his passport in an overcoat pocket from the last trip they took. What about Paulie? What's the story on her?"

"Jonah had me check on that after you talked to

him. She got picked up the first time when she was thirteen. Grandmother thought somebody stole her car so she called the police. Turned out Paulie took it. She also got picked up once for loitering and once for malicious mischief. She's a kid with too much time on her hands and not enough supervision."

"She and Leila are sure trouble."

"We're still working on that. We sent someone down to the school to see if we can get a match on the dates she was off campus and the money being pulled from the ATM. Those girls go any place but home for the weekend, they have to get permission from a parent or guardian, plus an okay from the person they intend to visit. It's already looking like she managed to play both ends against the middle. Not easy to do. School officials have seen every trick in the book, but she's smart. We've subpoenaed the bank records and the records from the mailing service where he kept his post office box. The D.A. and probation are talking to the judge this afternoon. We're hoping to wrap that up."

"Here's something else. The other day I stopped over at the Horton Ravine house. Leila had left school without permission. Crystal was having fits and gave me permission to search her room. She's got a locked metal box hidden under the mattress. It's probably dope, but it might be the missing money. She and Paulie may be planning to take off. You might be smart to keep an eye on them."

"We can do that," he said.

I got back to the office at 1:15. The rain was picking up again and I was tired of it. A curious depression had descended in the wake of the shooting with the adrenaline rush that accompanied it. The subsequent crash was accelerated by my conversation with Odessa. I envied them the hunt—Jonah Robb, Odessa, and Jim Paglia. Purcell had been murdered and though they might not be any closer to finding out who killed him, the process was under way.

I sat at my desk and I stared at the leaves on my fake ficus plant. From halfway across the room, the accumulated dust resembled a light layer of talcum powder. One day soon I'd really have to wipe that down. I swivelled in my chair and picked up a pencil. I drew a box on my blotter.

I spent the rest of the afternoon catching up on all the chores that I'd been putting off for the past week. I typed up the information I'd unearthed about Genesis and made photocopies of Klotilde's bills, adding as much of her chart as I thought reasonable. I was hoping no one would ask how I acquired the medical data. While I stood there at the machine, feeding in copies, watching the light on the copier go back and forth, I pondered Fiona's request for the $975 in cash. There was probably a simple explanation. I didn't think she was seriously concerned my check would bounce, so it had to be something else. The picture that kept coming to mind was her weedy hillside property. I visualized the front hall of her house with its decor of drop cloths and permanent scaffolding.

I was also brooding about that green mohair blanket Crystal had given Dow, about someone sitting in his lap after he'd been shot to death. You wouldn't want to drive far. Certainly not out on public roads where a pedestrian or a driver in the next lane might look over at just the wrong moment and spot you in the dead man's embrace. If you were the killer, you'd think about the reservoir—how nice it would be if both the dead man and the car disappeared from view. Jonah had been assuming the killer made an unfortunate mistake, miscalculating the position of the boulder, which prevented the car from being fully submerged. What if the reverse were true? Maybe the killer *intended* to have the car found. If Dow's death was meant to look like suicide, then maybe the causal error went the other way. The killer knew the boulder was there and thought the car would still be visible when daylight came. Instead the vehicle veered slightly and sank too far down to be seen easily.

It wasn't until late afternoon that I opened my bottom drawer and hauled out the phone book, turning to the yellow pages under the section that listed painting contractors. There must have been a hundred, column after column, some of them with box ads, some with catchy sayings: DON'T PAINT YOURSELF INTO A COR-NER WHEN YOU CAN LET US DO IT. CHARLIE CORNER & SONS, PAINTING. I had a quick vision of the Corner family sitting around the kitchen table, tossing back shots, coming up with log lines to stretch the advertising budget.

I started with the *A*'s and ran my finger down the names until I found the one I remembered from Fiona's sign out front. One line of print. RALPH TRIPLET, COLGATE. No street address. I made a note of the phone number. Fiona struck me as the sort who'd pick a lone operator, somebody too hungry for business to argue with her. She'd by-passed all the splashy half-and full-page ads.

I dialed Ralph Triplet's number. I was going to cook up a ruse, but I couldn't think of one.

The phone was picked up on the first ring. "Ralph Triplet Painting."

I said, "Hi, Mr. Triplet. My name is Kinsey Millhone. I just finished doing some work for Fiona Purcell up on Old Reservoir . . ."

"I hope you got your money up front."

"That's why I'm calling. Is she a slow pay by any chance?"

"No pay is more like it. You seen that place of hers? White everywhere. You think that'd be simple enough, but we've gone through six shades so far. Everything from Frost to Alabaster, Eggshell to Oyster. Couldn't find anything to suit. I'd get half a wall up, and then she'd want something else. Too green, she'd say. Or get the pink out of it. Meantime, I haven't been paid in weeks. The architect filed a lien against the property and I'm threatening to do likewise. Meantime, I finally got around to checking her credit. Should have done that in the first place, but how was I to know. She puts on a good show, but she's busy using one credit card to pay off another. What'd you say your name was?"

"Doesn't matter," I said, and hung up.

I pulled out the rubber-banded packet of index cards. This time I didn't add anything. I shuffled back through my cards, checking the information I'd picked up in the past week, particularly the details about Dow's last day. In passing, Mrs. Stegler had confided an item that caught my attention in light of everything I'd learned since then. She said while he was out at lunch, Fiona had stopped by. She'd waited in his office and had finally departed, leaving him a note. I'd sat in that office myself and I know how easily she could have opened his desk drawer and taken his gun.

Driving up Old Reservoir Road in the gathering dark, I could feel myself in a state of suspended animation. The only sign of agitation was that I was taking the curves a little too fast for the current road conditions, which were wet, wet, wet. I had an idea, an intuition to verify before I called Jonah Robb. I turned left on the road that angled up beside her property and pulled into the parking area behind the house.

I went around to the front door and rang the bell. She took her sweet time coming to the door. I stared off at Brunswick Lake. In the waning light, the surface was as silvery as mercury. It had been eleven days since I first stood in this spot, looking out at the same sweeping views. The steep sloping lot was now a fairyland of knee-high weeds: fox tails, wild oats, and rye bending in the passing breeze. With much more rain, the now-softened hillside would slide down into the road.

The door opened behind me. Even babysitting for her grandchildren, Fiona was decked out in a black wool suit with big shoulder pads and a pinched-in waist. The lapels and jacket cuffs were done in a faux leopard print. She had her hair concealed in a matching

502

leopard print turban. Gloria Swanson had nothing on her. I held out the envelope. "I included an invoice for your records. I hope you don't mind signing for the cash."

"Of course not. Won't you come in?"

I stepped into the foyer. There was a tricycle in the hall and the floor was covered with the same sort of kiddie detritus I'd seen at Blanche's house: Tinkertoys, blocks, a sock, broken crackers, crayons. The kids had built an enormous tent with the painter's drop cloths, which were now draped over all the chairs in the living room. I could see them bumping around in there, erupting in the sort of harsh, artificial giggles that signal the prelude to a big stinking fight.

Fiona scribbled her signature on the receipt. Her fingernails were dark red. She wore the same shade on her lips. She had a smudge of lipstick on the surface of her two front teeth. The effect was odd, like a virulent attack of bleeding gums. I tore off the top copy and handed it back to her.

"How's Blanche doing?"

"She's fine. At least she's had peace and quiet for the afternoon. Andrew's picking the kids up after supper tonight . . . assuming we live that long."

"Mind if I use the bathroom?"

"There's one off the kitchen. You can help yourself."

"Be right back," I said.

Fiona returned to the living room and I could hear her issuing orders about the cleanup. The kids even seemed inclined to cooperate.

I walked through the kitchen and unlocked the door leading into the three-car garage. It was dark outside and the yawning space was gloomy. There was a BMW parked in the nearest space, but the other two were empty. She'd told me when Dow came to visit, she made him pull into the garage each time so the local tongues wouldn't wag. I flipped on the overhead light, which didn't help that much.

I took the flashlight from my shoulder bag and crossed to the far wall. I imagined myself sitting in Dow's silver Mercedes. I looked to my left and calculated the trajectory of a bullet fired from the front seat through the driver's head, through the car window, and into the wall. Right about there, I thought. I'd have bet money she never bothered to pry the bullet out of the dry wall. She'd had enough white paint on hand to cover any evidence of what she'd done. Who'd even think to look here? The cops with their metal detectors would be scanning down the hillside as far as the road.

In the light of the faulty overhead bulb, the wall appeared to be smooth. I ran a hand lightly over the finish, expecting to feel the faintly irregular patch of plaster fill. The wall was unblemished. Not a mark anywhere. I shone the light at an angle, hoping for the roughness in the surface to jump into bas-relief. There was nothing. I made a circuit of the space, but there was no indication whatsoever that Dow had been shot to death here before the car was moved. No fragments of glass, no oil patches on the floor where his car had sat. I stood there astonished. I wanted to wail with disappointment. This had to be right. I had been so sure.

The door to the kitchen opened and Fiona appeared. She stood and stared at me. "I wondered what happened to you."

I looked back at her, mouth suddenly dry, desperate for an explanation that would cover my behavior.

"Detective Paglia was up here earlier, doing exactly the same thing. He checked the walls for a buried bullet and found none."

"Fiona, I'm sorry."

"I'm sure you are." She paused a moment. "One question, please. If I'd actually killed Dowan, why in the world would I hire you?"

I could feel my cheeks grow warm, but I knew I owed her the truth. "I thought you needed to have the body found to collect on the insurance. If you hired me, you'd appear to be above reproach."

Her gaze bit into me, but she never raised her voice. "You're a very arrogant young woman. Now get out of my house."

SUE GRAFTON

She withdrew, closing the door behind her with a sharp report.

I let myself out. I got back in my car and started down the hill, reeling with shame and embarrassment. What defense did I have? I'd been wrong about her. I'd been wrong about Crystal and Clint Augustine. I'd been wrong about Mariah, who'd made a fool of me. I turned left at the intersection. I'd driven a block when I caught sight of a familiar figure walking backward along the side of the road. Paulie, with her thumb stuck out. Jeans, hiking boots, the same black leather jacket I'd seen her in before. Nice quality leather, too, and I wondered if she and Leila had paid for it with a portion of the stolen thirty grand.

I slowed and pulled over on the berm while she hurried to catch up. By the time she reached the car, I'd opened the door for her on the passenger side. "Hop in. Are you on your way to see Leila?"

"Yeah. She's staying down at the beach." She got in and slammed the door, smelling of dope and cigarettes. Her hair was brown and straight and might have been shiny if she'd kept it clean. I could see raindrops, like sequins, sprinkled among the strands. She had unconventional looks, but there was something haunting about her eyes, which were large and dark brown. "You can let me off in town. It's no problem finding a ride from there."

"I don't mind driving you. I could use the air," I said. I waited for passing traffic and then pulled onto the road. "You're lucky I came by. I'm usually not over in this area. Were you up at Lloyd's?"

"Yeah, but he was out and I couldn't find the key. I didn't want to wait for him in the cold. Aren't you sick of this fuckin' rain?"

I let that one pass. "The two of you are friends?"

"Kind of, because of Leila."

"How's she going to feel about it when he moves to Las Vegas. Think she'll miss him?"

"Big time. She was really bummed when she heard."

"Is she back at school?"

"Not until Wednesday. Her mom's driving her down."

"Well, maybe she'll get to visit Lloyd once he's settled," I said. "When's he taking off? He said a couple of days."

"Something like that. I'm trying to talk him into taking me along."

"You'd leave town?"

"Well, sure. I don't give a shit about this place."

"Don't you have family here?"

"Just Gram is all and she wouldn't care. She lets me do anything I want."

I looked over at her. "Have you ever *been* to Las Vegas?"

"Once when I was six." A smile lit her face and her expression became animated. "We stayed at the Flamingo. Me and my sister swam in the pool and ate so much shrimp cocktail she barfed in a bush. After it got dark? We went around and finished all the drinks people left on the tables. What a blast. We were acting like nuts. We couldn't even walk straight."

"I didn't know you had a sister."

"I haven't seen her or my mom since."

I was curious about that, but I'd already asked a lot of questions and I didn't want her to think I was interrogating her . . . though I was, of course.

"I'd have a hard time with the heat."

"I like it. Even in summer, I bet it wouldn't bother me a bit. I could live there easy. What a hoot."

"Seems like money would be a problem."

"Not at all. I have lots." I could hear her hesitate, pondering the slip. Clearly, she'd told me more than she intended. "I could probably get a job parking cars at one of the big casinos. Something that paid good tips. This guy I know says a parking valet can make up to a hundred a day."

"I thought you were sixteen."

"Everybody says I look older. I got a fake driver's license says I'm over eighteen. Nobody checks. As long as you show up for work, what do they care?" She thought she had street smarts, but her notions of how the world worked were wishful thinking on her part. "You think I don't know how to take care of myself?"

"I'm sure you do."

"I'm fine on my own. I'm used to it by now. I'm living on the street half the time, anyway, so better there than here. Maybe Lloyd'll get a place and I can live with him."

"You think that's appropriate?"

She gave me an indignant look. "I'm not *banging* the guy. He's just a friend."

"What will Leila do if you leave? I thought the two of you were inseparable." What I was really thinking was how easy it would be for Lloyd to tuck the girls in the car with him before he left the state. I didn't believe Paulie would go anywhere without Leila. I glanced at her and watched her struggle with her response.

"That's her problem. She'll figure it out."

We reached Crystal's beach house. I pulled into the gravel parking area and Paulie got out. I didn't think Crystal would be glad to see her, but she'd probably be polite. I figured Leila and Paulie, inseparable as they were, would end up in jail together within the next few hours. So much for Vegas and her fabulous career as a valet car park.

I left the engine running, waiting while Paulie rang the bell. I noticed the house next door had a SALE

PENDING banner now affixed to the FOR SALE sign. Crystal came to the door. If she objected to Paulie's presence, she seemed to keep it to herself. Maybe Leila was easier to get along with in Paulie's company. Crystal caught sight of my car and waved. I returned the wave and backed out of the drive, my headlights washing across the open carport where I could see the Volvo and the convertible. The slot on the extreme left was empty and I was guessing that was the space where Dow had kept his car. I felt a tiny jolt of electricity. I made the turn onto Paloma Lane, drove half a block, and then pulled the VW over to the side of the road. I got out and walked back to the house. As I moved into the drive, my footsteps crunched on the gravel like someone chomping on a mouthful of ice.

Crystal had closed the door and the area was dark. I could smell ocean. I could hear the pounding of the waves. The quiet was like nectar wafting through the still night air. The rain had left the heavy scent of seaweed, pine boughs, and solitude. I swear the very dark had an odor of its own. *Dare to be stupid*, I thought to myself. *Some people think you're stupid, anyway, so what difference does it make?*

As I had at Fiona's house, I placed myself in a spot that approximated the location of the Mercedes' front seat, picturing the car parked as it would have been had

Dow pulled in that night. Maybe Crystal had promised him sexual treats, spelling out the possibilities in such succulent detail that he'd by-passed his scheduled visit with Fiona and come home to his wife. He must have pictured her coming out to meet him in a flimsy night-gown . . . something diaphanous . . . a thin, silky fabric that the ocean breezes would lift flirtatiously, exposing her legs. Crystal knew how to use her body to good effect. She could have retrieved the .357 Magnum on an earlier occasion. She'd told the cops Dow kept it in his desk at work or in the glove compartment of his car. She had access to both, especially with Griffith's visits to the nursing home. Even if she appeared wearing sweats and running shoes, all she had to do was open the car door, lean across the seat, and kill him as sweetly as a kiss. Driving the body up to the reservoir was a nice piece of misdirection—the risk of being spotted on the highway apparently less important than this chance to put Fiona in the soup. Given the amount of money Fiona stood to gain, the police would nat-urally pursue the notion that she'd killed him herself.

I looked to my left and calculated the trajectory of a bullet speeding in that direction. After all, if a shot had been fired from a Colt Python across the space of the front seat and through the kindly doctor's head, one could only imagine the bullet traveling right on, smashing the car window, crossing ten feet of space, and plowing through the shingle siding of the house next door.

I crossed the patchy stretch of grass that lay between the carport and the structure next door. It might have once been a detached garage, joined to the house now and converted to a guest wing or family room. I took out my flashlight and turned it on. I moved the bushes aside and swept the beam across the rough-hewn shingles. The bullet hole was big, as black as a spider sitting on the side of the house.

I retraced my steps across the gravel parking pad to Crystal's front door. I rang the bell. She opened it a moment later, with an expression on her face as if I might be someone soliciting for charity or selling door-to-door. She said, "Oh. I didn't expect to see you. What's going on?"

"I'd like to use your phone."

She seemed puzzled, but stepped back and let me pass in front of her. She was barefoot, wearing sweats, her hair pulled up on the top of her head. She peered out. "Where's your car?"

"It's parked on the road. The engine cut out and I need a way to get home."

"I can do that," she said. "Hang on a minute and I'll grab my keys."

"No, no. Please. I wouldn't want to trouble you. I

have a good friend nearby and he's an experience mechanic. I'll just ask him to take a look. Maybe he can fix it right there and send me on my way."

"Well, if that doesn't work out, I can always run you home."

From upstairs, I could hear the thunder of music being played at top volume. I pictured Paulie and Leila planning their escape. I really hoped the cops would show up before they made good on their "get-away." I wasn't sure where Rand was. Maybe off in the bathroom, getting Griffith ready for bed.

She showed me into the den and then stood in the doorway while I took a seat at the desk. I smiled at her briefly and said, "This won't take a minute," hoping she would leave. I picked up the receiver and dialed Jonah's home number. If Camilla answered, I was screwed. On other occasions, she'd left the receiver on the table and walked off, refusing to tell Jonah I was on the line for him. When the call was picked up, he said, "Jonah Robb."

"Oh, hi. It's me."

"Kinsey?" He sounded puzzled, as well he should have.

"Yes, it is."

"What's up?"

"I'm at Crystal's beach house. I've got a little problem and I'd love to have you take a look."

"All right," he said, cautiously. "I'm buying this. Like what?"

"No problem. I can wait. Is that convenient for you? Because if it's not, I can always try Vince."

"Well, you know, I'm right in the middle of something. Is this important?"

"Completely. You have the address?"

"I know the place. Are you in trouble?"

"Not yet, but I could be. I'll see you shortly and thanks. I appreciate this."

I replaced the receiver and when I looked up again, Anica had joined Crystal in the doorway. The two stood close together, Crystal in front, Anica slightly behind. Anica's hand was on her arm, and I suddenly understood what I'd been looking at all along. Anica said, "Is there a problem?"

"Not really. I'm waiting for a friend of mine to come give me some help. I had some trouble with my car. He'll be here in a bit."

"Oh. Well, why don't you join us for a glass of Chardonnay while you wait."

"I guess I could do that."

I followed them out onto the deck. We sat in the dark, just the three of us, sipping wine and chatting, listening to the surf rumble on the beach until Jonah arrived.